Greezy Creek

A Novel

George R. Justice

Greezy Creek
George R. Justice

Published September 2019
Little Creek Books
Imprint of Jan-Carol Publishing, Inc.

ISBN: 978-1-950895-20-5
Library of Congress Control Number: 2019950681

You may contact the publisher:
Jan-Carol Publishing, Inc.
PO Box 701
Johnson City, TN 37605
publisher@jancarolpublishing.com
jancarolpublishing.com

To Eric, my son...and my sun.

Letter to the Reader

I was born in Pikeville, Kentucky, in 1944, in the old Methodist Hospital that sat halfway up a mountain on the backside of town...its buildings now converted into classrooms as part of Pikeville University. My mother went there just long enough to have me, then like any good mountain woman, swaddled me up and headed back to Greasy Creek as soon as she could stand. That's where we lived up until I was four, until my daddy decided that running moonshine across the Kentucky/ Virginia line carried more risk than reward. Detroit is where we ended up (where the work was anything but coalmining), and living in a one-room flat with a shared toilet down the hall. And though removed from the sights and sounds we knew as home, the inherent richness of Momma and Daddy's storytelling kept me tuned to the mountains, moreover to Greasy Creek and its hardscrabble ways.

Daddy was the oldest of twelve and Momma from a family of faith healers and Primitive Baptist preachers. Together their accounts wove a tapestry as real and rich as the earth itself. I learned early on that Greasy Creek was not merely a backdrop against which their lives evolved (and which formed the borders of their world), but one which acted upon them as well.

It's from their accounts that I know firsthand what rails within its deep green valleys: what rankles and what inspires, what causes us to seethe and what begs for our forgiveness; what shakes us to the core of our funny bone, and what shamefully fastens itself to those who would embrace it. It is this background that I bring to *Greezy Creek*, that allows me to take readers into a world only few can know intimately.

Prologue

Equal Parts Angel and Demon

On a bluff of virgin pine and in a site removed from even the remotest road was a moonshine still that Bobby Yonts took me to after I went to live with my Great Aunt Mary Olive in a place called Greezy Creek. The still belonged to Bobby's uncle, Corbin Fairchild, and a man named U. J. Slough. U. J. and his son, Donald MacNeal (Don'l Mac), did the stilling; Corbin did the selling, the bootlegging. Corn liquor's what they made, Kentucky's finest.

The site itself was as hushed in shadow as it was in thicket, as dark a place as any I'd ever known given the daylight, and one fixed with eyes that warned of things hungry and undone. Under a huge outcrop of rock, out of the reach of rain and away from the likes of snow and falling leaves, cords of hardwood, split and stacked, dried in quietude. The still sat at the far end where spring water trickled steady and cool out of the rock's face and into a huge wood barrel. As all-embracing as I'd ever seen, it sat tucked away where silhouettes against the sky were nonexistent; where saplings were laced and tied and stacked in such a way that even hunters coming close might never know it was there.

The climb getting to it was long and steep, one that U.J. and Don'l Mac made most everyday with ol' Jenks, their black-on-black mule, hauling what they needed, in and out. I was there only once, when Bobby led me through the mountains on a trek that took the better part of a day. But from the moment we stepped under that huge outcrop of rock, my mind quickened to being beyond the veil of comfort: feeling like I was all at once tied to a secret I had no business knowing.

Days later when Bobby told Corbin where we had been, Corbin didn't as much as flinch, just hesitated long enough to spit and swipe his lips with the back of his hand. After several long minutes, and with eyes black and piercing, he said, "Am I gonna have to worry 'bout it?" He was looking dead at me when he said it, searching my face to see if I understood his meaning; if I grasped the gravity of what I'd been allowed to see.

"No," I said. "Not in the nine lives of nine cats."

He said nothing for a time, trying, I imagined, to discover in me some affirmation of loyalty, something that said he had my trust. Finally, he shifted a bit, rubbed the back of his neck and hiked his foot onto the running board of his Model-A. "Awright then," he said, the look in his eyes steely, yet settling, letting me know that nothing more needed to be said.

There was something gathering about Corbin, something that vanquished fears and instilled the type of confidence that was rooted in nobility. The same something, I suspected, that lived and breathed within his ancestral lines. It was that same all-telling force that rattled around in Bobby as well, that propelled them both higher than what their stations saw fit to grant. And though they lived by a set of standards that ran amuck of the Old Regular Baptists and the parameters of what Deputy Sheriff Virgil Blair abided by, I couldn't help but feel elevated by their presence. Somehow, I saw them as knights: as absolute as they were set apart and living by what dared them. My sense was that they were equal parts angel and demon, and equally tempted by both.

Part I

One

Heard About Bobby Yonts

From my front porch, a long gentle slope of sour grass and pokeweed clustered and wound through a grove of cottonwoods clear to the road, a good hundred yards away. I sat out there most mornings when I could still get the shade and when whittling took the place of worrying.

About the time the sun worked its way to the top step I heard Burl Newsome's Jeep on the dirt road and saw the curl of dust rolling up behind it. Burl was never content to leave the mail in the box by the side of the road when it had even the slightest element of curiosity. Personal letters and anything with an official seal or a government return address were nearly enough to bring him in a straight line.

Burl was as agile as he was animated and dismounted just before his Jeep rolled to a full stop. "Hey, son." Burl called everybody *son*.

"How 'bout it, Burl Newsome?"

"Got sump'm fer ye," he said, getting right to it. "Save ye a trip down t' the box."

It was little wonder Burl was so attentive. What he handed me was a long white envelope with a return address in old English lettering from the Third Circuit Court of Appeals in Cincinnati, Ohio. It had all the trappings of official business, and Burl lingered *just-so*, his posture coaxing me toward its exposure, its revelation.

"Reckoned you'd want it right quick, being a lawman an' all. Well, ex-lawman. You know what I mean. How long's it been, anyways? Thirteen year I figure. How right am I?" Burl knew exactly how long it had been since I last pinned a badge to my shirt. He'd even been there, to Jerry's restaurant, to the "goodbye and good-luck" supper in my honor. God knows we'd talked about it often enough. I suppose it was just his way of assuring me of his allegiance to never forget, kind of an unspoken oath to our fraternity.

"Thirteen this month," I said.

"I knowd I was close," he said, a self-congratulatory grin deepening the wrinkles in his face.

I didn't say anything, just fingered the letter knowing full well who it was from. As Pike County Sheriff for nearly forty years, I'd been witness to more mystery and skullduggery than most folks could imagine in a lifetime—too much to fathom without a curiosity on the scale of Burl Newsome's. After a moment of uneasiness, I folded the letter and slipped it into my shirt pocket. Burl stood frozen with a blank-but-wounded look.

"It'll wait," I said. "Got enough to ponder as it is."

Burl pulled a wadded handkerchief from his back pocket and made an overt gesture of blowing his nose; gave several deep breaths and stretched right big, then scratched in several hard to get at places before he said, "Might be best if ye open it now." He was motioning with his head toward my breast pocket. "Looks official."

"I ain't got the nerve for official anymore, Burl. The mind either. Fact of the matter is I've got half a notion not to open it a'tall."

"Reckon it's bad news?" he asked, trying with all his might to spur my interest.

"What else could it be?" I said, taking some small pleasure in his fidgeting for the right thing to say.

"Well," he said after a noticeable suck to an eyetooth and moving some gravel about with the toe of his boot, "reckon I'll be headin' on down the road." He paused with a hang-dog look, seeing if I would take the bait. Threatening to leave was Burl's way of warning me that I was about to lose his counsel. I didn't say anything, just rose up out of my rocker long enough to spit over the edge of the porch.

"I'd say you'll have that read by tomorrow," he said, squinting up at the sun. I knew it was his way of saying he'd be back, whether he had mail for me or not.

"Maybe. Maybe not," I said. He gave me an "Uh huh" and a long, all-knowing pause before hoisting himself back into his Jeep. Without a second look, he made a big U-turn in the yard then bounced back onto the road. In a matter of seconds his big wave was swallowed up in the Jeep's rooster tail of dust.

Dear Rubin:

Just wanted to tell you that I recently became acquainted with a fellow who must surely be one of your relatives. I was called upon at an eleventh hour to serve on a three-judge panel that would be taking a plea in a murder case. All I knew at the time was the name of the defendant, Clayman Ray Cain.

When they brought Mr. Cain into the courtroom, I wondered why his left eye—actually the hole where his eye should have been—was nothing more than a murky white blob that was off center toward the side of his head. I soon found out. The man was entering guilty pleas to two counts of aggravated homicide with death penalty specifications, meaning the panel could send him to the death house. He had, in a fit of rage, shot his girlfriend and her lover, then, undone by remorse, turned the gun on himself. But as with so many things that don't go as planned, he lived. He could even talk. He told us that for some time prior to the shooting he had been doing the devil's work: dealing drugs and fencing stolen goods. "From now on, though," he said, "I'll be doing the Lord's work so's I'll be able to see my momma in heaven." A Bible had become his constant companion since being released from the hospital, and he opened it and read from Matthew 6:33—about seeking the kingdom of God.

The defense attorneys said they wanted to present some evidence of mitigating factors, and brought the defendant's sister to the witness stand. Her name was Darby Kendall, frail for the most part and right away uneasy, but determined to speak on behalf of Clayman Ray. She sat with her hands folded and eyeing the room non-stop long after council had introduced her, but finally gathered herself long enough to thank us for the opportunity to speak, because, she said, we couldn't possibly understand Clayman Ray unless we understood how he was raised. Given the heinousness of the crime, we agreed that what she might reveal could be beneficial to Clayman Ray's defense, so we allowed her free rein.

She started by saying that she and Clayman Ray, along with four other siblings, spent their early childhood in Keen Mountain, Virginia. After that, and for the next half hour, it proved to be the only thing she related that wasn't somehow framed in destitution—all brought about by their daddy, Randle. She then gave a rather insipid account of Randle's demise: his unsolved homicide, albeit forty years ago. But it was when she said her mother had grown up in Greezy Creek, Kentucky, that I nearly came out of my seat. I even asked her to repeat it while trying to disguise a look of disbelief. I felt it best not to tell her I was from Pikeville and had in all probability sat in judgment, at one time or another, of some of her kin. After doing the math, I'm thinking you had to know her ... or at least know of her. Her maiden name was Flowers. Fayella Flowers.

As for Clayman Ray, it's a fate not worth recounting. Suffice it to say, we decided against the death penalty in favor of life behind bars. However, I believe he is beyond any help our penal system can provide.

Anyway, that's about all I can tell you, Rubin, except that it's a small world ... and certainly a crazy one. We don't see enough of each other, my friend, and there is only so much that phone calls and Christmas cards can do for friendship. I'm of the thinking that old judges and retired sheriffs should make more of an effort. I'm not getting any younger and God knows there's not much time left for you. You need to know that I'm keeping track of those five dollar lunches you keep promising, and I'm hoping to get back there one of these days to settle up.

In the meantime, you ought to think about coming to Cincinnati before you forget the way. Cincinnati ain't Pikeville, but it's not as flat as you might think.

Still behind the bench up here in enemy territory,
Calvin

p.s. Heard about Bobby Yonts. I'm here if you need me.

Calvin loved to reference anyone from Greezy Creek as being one of my relatives, my *kin*. So in-bred, he thought, that we were all cousins to one degree or another. No amount of protest was ever sufficient enough to change his mind. He said there were simply too many blue eyes for it to be a coincidence. Considering that Greezy Creek was so cloistered, and with what seemed like more than its share of *tom catting,* I don't doubt that he may have been more right than I was willing to admit.

Fayella Flowers was a name I would forever remember, from the time growing up till she was sent away to what we then called the crazy house. Just fourteen, she was, right when Bobby Yonts and I went off to the war. It was twenty-two years before I saw her again, before she came back to Greezy Creek. I don't remember the color of Fayella's eyes, only the color of what was once raw and resilient in them, in each of us for that matter; colors intense and devoid of make-believe, and in keeping with the mountains we knew as home.

The name Randle Cain still comes with seamless loathing, his demise (his murder, actually) never being one that struck me as any great loss. The state police was nearly of the same opinion, neither of us particularly duty-bound toward its resolution; Randle's life being most of what the devil devised and what I'd spent a fair amount of time trying to forget. The file on Randle is officially still open, his killer still at large—forty odd years after the fact. The unofficial side is I know the name of Randle's killer—knew it the very day Randle went off to hell. As high sheriff, I knew most of what went on behind the scenes, what got kicked to the side of the road and what was best left unsaid; knew what most folks didn't and for good reason—Randle's killer being right up there with what I call *the incontestable.*

Randle's killer was not a perfect soul. Perfect was just never anything that lent itself to the deep hollows and back roads of Greezy Creek, although my Grandmaw Spicy, in my studied opinion, came as near to it as anybody could. Some say Randle's farewell was too long in the coming, that he got exactly what he deserved. I didn't disagree, but was careful never to say so. His departure simply didn't need any more attention, especially from someone suppressing evidence. There was speculation enough considering all those who wanted him dead. I wasn't particularly proud of keeping what I knew locked down, but I don't know that anybody else would have done any different given my circumstances. A posture of nonalignment, distancing myself from a situation altogether untenable—what some called *the advantaged side of politics*—suited me just fine. It was less abrasive and something that kept state police investigators and newspaper reporters out of my face. I can't say that Randle's killer was evil, only affected by the better side of good—a reason strong enough to leave me convinced it had been the right thing to do. The shortfall is having carried its stain better than half my life.

Two

Closer to Crazy Than I Ever Wanted To Be

I turned ten in the spring of 1931, six weeks after I went to live with Grandmaw Spicy—a year after Momma died of the fevers. We never knew much about the fevers or what brought it on, just that Mamma was poorly for the most part and not able to fight off things like most of the Scot/Irish hybrids up and down the Appalachian chain.

Daddy was the one who called it "the fevers." The names that brought it on (typhoid, cholera, pneumonia, croup, consumption) meant little to me beyond their sobering assertions that we were either strong enough to survive them or we weren't. They were names that just seemed to hover together in some infinite black-on-black place, as lost and set apart as night winds through a graveyard.

I don't know as anybody understood much about the fevers except that they were always there amongst us waiting to prove their mastery over our already brief and ill-famed existence. Kentucky's high mountains and long deep hollows, as sequestered as they were unforgiving, all but guaranteed it.

The fevers had crippled Momma for the better part of a week and attracted a steady stream of neighbors, in and out at all hours and talking just above a whisper. It was a blighted brand of comfort they brought, first crowding-in with too many questions, then staying well past the time it took to get on our nerves; some staying long enough to eat what little Daddy could scrape together for the table.

Like most everything else that plagued us, the fevers, in whatever form, took the weaker ones first: the babies and the elderly, then the frail—like Momma. The remedy never seemed to vary much: fetch Hollace Ballard to come *try* on us—his laying on of hands and groaning in the Holy Spirit—then send for Grandmaw Spicy to come with her herbs and powders and potions. Both were a welcomed presence, the last vestiges of hope in the absence of any real doctors. Though, oftentimes, together with our faith, they were enough.

It was a full year after Momma died—one year to the day—that Daddy gave up trying to justify the pain of her being gone. "Life can be a blessin'," he said, "if you don't weaken. An' I ain't never been all that strong to begin with." It was always a somber note when he said it, but it was the one thing he'd become accustomed to saying since she'd been gone. Somehow, I knew it was his way of preparing me for what was to come.

I was just eight when I first heard Daddy talk about the coal mines cutting back, due to something he called the depression, its reality settling on us with a boding evil.

A number of mines remained in operation long after the one Daddy worked for shut down; one up near The Breaks in Roseann, Virginia, one across Abner Mountain in a place called Wheelwright, and the one over in Wolfpit just a stone's throw from Greezy Creek, none of which could be walked to-and-fro in a day's time. They were big mines with their own boarding houses, places for miners lucky enough to hire-on. But little good it did seeing as they had more help than they could ever want—what with the glut of miners out of work and as desperate as they were destitute.

I watched the nightmare on Daddy's face grow solemn and more pronounced day after day; watched him become thin and troubled trying to hide the discredit of not working, of not having the means to feed us properly.

Depression, a word that carried the idea of deprivation, lingered on the lips of most everybody; hung on their faces and languished in their eyes even without the mentioning. I can still remember the shame of watching Daddy beg for enough credit to buy seed. For us, the depression meant that we ate what we grew, what we hunted when we had the shells, and what was given to us by neighbors and family. Many times we hired ourselves out to hoe corn, or cut and bundle fodder. A dollar a day is what we got, from sunup to sundown and without an ounce of shade, and cornbread soaked in milk brought to us at high noon. Daddy even helped some with making liquor: moonshine.

Moonshining, "*shining*," brought money to many of our neighbors, but making it was a risky proposition: from the Old Regular Baptists who thought it their Christian duty to report it (provided it wasn't some of their own making it) to the sheriffs and deputies and federal agents who stalked the hills armed and all-too-willing to maim and even kill in their single-minded effort to uphold the law. It just wasn't Daddy's temperament to risk such a deadly game, but hunger will cause a man to do most anything.

Living off the land was not something we were strangers to, but knowing it was all we had tolled on Daddy a lot worse than most. Feelings of scarcity and deficit became his hallmark, permeating him even when he smiled. In the long days of his idleness, when his mind had little else to reflect upon, his brooding took on the loss of dignity.

It was nearly a year after Daddy's mine was boarded over that Momma began to grow pale and thin and without the life to move about for more than a few minutes at a time. She stayed that way for months, right up until the fevers took her. After that, a deepening sense of uselessness carved away at Daddy like he was a piece of deadwood, drained him until he was the empty-eyed ghost that preceded him to his grave.

The depression had left us penniless and just a short jump from starvation. But with Momma's passing, Daddy finally gave in (one year to the day) to the stark and never-ending certainty that she had left him too alone too soon, and with too many memories coming much too often.

"Shot the top of his head clean off," said Garland, his tenor voice above all the rest. Garland Sawyer was High Sheriff and spoke with the annoyance of someone with a lip full of tobacco and needing to spit real bad. "Stuck 'at barrel right up 'ginst the roof of his mauth. An' let me tell ye boys, a twelve gauge can play a whole lotta music at that range." Garland was a good man, and sympathetic, but never quite able to resist an audience. The desire to elaborate, even pontificate, was bred deep and left him feeling morally and legally charged to bring clarity to whatever was at hand. It was a self-imposed obligation, and somewhat painful to those who had to listen, but Garland was duty-bound to shed light. It was his way of bringing calm and understanding to the farmers, coal-miners and dirt poor he had been elected to serve. It was his way of easing their tension and curiosity; just another thankless thing he did in the name of the law.

"Ain't never seen nuthin' like it," Garland said, shaking his head from side to side. "Reckon his Rachel bein' gone is what done it." His words were simple and few, strangely enough, but rang as true as church bells to the neighbors who had gathered to witness Daddy's final expression of love for his Rachel. It was their final glimpse at his mourning.

I was the one who found him. Crumpled up on the kitchen floor, his head slumped against the wall like he was passed out drunk. High up on the wall above him was where the top of his head had let go. A red explosion, breath robbing and surreal, the way crimson leaves explode against an autumn sky. From there, a big red trail, painted with the back of his head, followed him to where he lay.

I don't remember how long it was that I stood there fastened on the picture of his corpse, at the hole in the top of its head, at the blood clotted and shining in his hair. Don't remember how long it took me to pull away, only that I did. And I managed to run all the way to Grandmaw's before collapsing on her porch steps, my cries rending the jungle that encircled her cabin. I remember her crouching next to me ...yelling...yelling... but I don't remember her words, or my own for that matter. The one thing I do remember was feeling closer to crazy than I ever wanted to be, and the god-awful notion that *somebody* needed to do *something,* and that they needed to do it *now.*

Three

Grandmaw Spicy

From our front gate to Grandmaw Spicy's was four hundred and forty paces—*up* the road. I'd stepped it off many times on my way back and forth: forth with things from our garden like tomatoes and beans, cabbage and squash, and back with things like honey and sassafras, mustard and elderberry tea: things from her wilderness medicine chest.

I went to live with Grandmaw after Daddy was gone. There was never any question about it; just went there as natural as chickens go to roost.

"You awright, Rubin?" It was the one question Grandmaw heaped on me day and night during those first months.

"Yeah, Grandmaw, I'm awright. Why wouldn't I be?"

"Just wondrin', 'at's awl."

Grandmaw preferred quietness as a way of connecting to the world about her, seldom relying on the troublesomeness of conversation except to the few chickens she kept penned and ol' Dan, her one-eyed mule she rode sideways and without a saddle to sick beds as far away as Virgie and Ford's Branch, as far away as ol' Dan could walk in a day. What little she said was outright and most always with that same question at the end: "You awright?" I grew used to it, and after a time began asking her the same thing. What we said to one another never seemed to be enough until 'You awright?' was tacked on the end. Weeks into it, she straightened herself one afternoon and said, "You need to quit askin' me that. It's got me to thinkin' you're seein' sump'm I ain't."

"Well," I said, "then I reckon we both oughtta quit." She didn't say anything after that, just wiped at her eyes and nose and went on with the batch of burdock root and red clover blossoms she was brewing into cough syrup while pretending not to watch me from the corners of her eyes. Before long, her habit proved stronger than what we'd agreed on and once again 'You awright?' floated at me with the intonations of a love song.

Grandmaw was the closest thing to a doctor most folks in these parts ever knew. Kentucky's eastern highlands, with their endless assortment of roots and herbs, nuts and berries, mosses and barks, serving as the source of her prescriptions. Between what the mountains gave and the wisdom passed down from her grandmother, Leonne, she gave as much healing as faith would allow, and as much as many ever came to expect.

Her cabin sat far back off a narrow, pockmarked trail we called a road—about halfway up Indian Mountain. It was the very last house in the head of Pine Fork of Caney Creek and sat on a small flat alongside a stream that trickled out from under a giant bedrock cliff. There were no roads beyond it, no trails—only Flatwoods wilderness and a hermit's cabin about a days walk due south. It was a cabin so choked by vegetation that breezes and even light seemed to have trouble getting to it. From the middle of the road, the only things that could be made out were some rusty portions of tin roof and a slow steady stream of smoke from her chimney, day and night, summer and winter. So swallowed up it was in mountain laurel and morning glory, pipe vine and honeysuckle, that she long ago gave up even hacking it away from her windows. Except for a narrow path and the steps leading to her porch, it would have been hard to tell which direction it faced. The thickets surrounding it were so dense and of such lethal size and proportion—all of them so twisted and tangled and intertwined—that it almost defied approach. The yard was of the same order, so choked with periwinkle and trumpet creeper, bull thistle and ironweed, that it loomed as the epitome of grand seclusion, less disturbed than disturbing.

Except for concoctions of drying herbs—heavy, earthen fragrances so assaulting they could choke the air—Grandmaw's cabin was the perfect retreat from Kentucky's brutal summer suns. Still, despite its seclusion and sense of decay, there was life there in the thickets surrounding it. By day, finches and titmice, hummingbirds and chickadees, darted in and out of their nests, foraging and gathering. By night, bats and owls screeched and dove about in the darkness as if her cabin had been set aside and kept just for their frenzy and appetites. One could only guess what else lived there behind the mesh of underbrush and hellvine, but often there was a lizard or two on the porch steps, frozen in a still-life and warming in the sun. And there were the endless tracks—skunk and 'possum, fox and coon and rabbit—left in the dirt and dew. Oftentimes there was a twitch and a vibration in the grass, a flash of color—charred and blended—and the quiver of a tail slithering off to someplace thicker and less traveled, where copperheads and rattlers find the greatest solace.

Grandmaw's cabin was a menagerie of nature's offerings, as much her laboratory as her home. Except for the room where she slept, shelves lined each and every wall as high up as she could reach. Jars and tiny paper boxes, tins and glass dishes, lids and gourds, whittled blocks and spooned-shaped rocks—anything that could hold even the tiniest seed—were used to keep and store what she so painstakingly culled from the hills.

I grew taller than Grandmaw right after I turned eleven. In the fashion of an elf, she was, small enough that her face would almost disappear behind an upturned cup, but it was never a deterrent to her scouring the mountains for what grew precious and rare. Ageless seemed to describe her best. Unchanging. Familiar. Forever hunched under the protection of a shawl, summer and winter, and forever drawing breath through a cob pipe. Near to sixty to the best of her recollection, she was as dogged as she was capable of identifying and harvesting most everything medicinal the mountains had to offer. What time she didn't spend searching the slopes and hollows of the wilderness that surrounded her, she spent indoors rendering her collections into *medicines.*

Grandmaw knew just about everything there was to know about the mountains and the things that could leech onto us; things taught to her by her Grandmaw Leonne, her mother's mother and someone impossible to remember unless it was said at least once that she was half Cherokee. Unlike her brothers and sisters, Grandmaw had spent her childhood in the care of Leonne, collecting and gathering, drying and processing what nature gave for healing and longer life. She had taken to it early and came to know it as her calling, her gift. It was in that light, that mystery of doctoring, that she was known, that kept me hushed and wide-eyed far into many a night with names like thrush and colic, diphtheria and dysentery—names I was certain were fixed with agony, disfigurement and death.

From the time I was old enough to remember, even when Momma was upright and well, I spent what time I could with Grandmaw, learning her ways, following her into the mountains, digging and gleaning what she was so adept at spotting. Hers was a tireless pursuit, and I was always the dutiful child. Together, we cured, separated, scraped, crushed, boiled, steamed and steeped all the things predestined for mending and curing, what seemed to be ordained of a higher power.

I never knew a single thing that was outside of Grandmaw's doctoring. Be it worms or lice, warts or moles, goiters, sores or boils; be it toothaches or tremors, rickets or scurvy, shingles, pinkeye or the grippe, she was always there with elixirs and poultices, ointments and pastes. It was her arsenal of stores that entreated as much as bedazzled, concoctions without names or identities except to her. Tonics and brews from the clearest and lightest reds to the direst and blackest blacks stood ready against the likes of "the bends" and "the vapors," "the chills" and "the trots," "the crabs" and "the piles," things as onerous as they were contentious. There were roots to chew on, liniments to soak in, leaves and stems to hold beneath your tongue, treatments all born of nature. Young or old, man or woman, from jaundice (*janders*) and snakebite to the annoyance of dandruff, confusion, and nosebleeds, Grandmaw just seemed to have what most folks needed most of the time—and all of it there within arms reach and without ever a doubt to its purpose, steering us as if by the stars.

Payment *of any kind* was nigh unto ignoble for Grandmaw, even from those who could afford it. She saw her gift as a help and a blessing. Still, folks offered out of a sense of rightness. Self-respect ran deep for highlanders. Being beholden would never do, even from those as poor as they were poorly. But it wasn't money so much as goods that they offered: things they had made or gathered from their garden, but most often what they had canned ("put up"). The offering and the acceptance was an intricate game, a delicate balance of pride and humbleness. It was the caring, as much custom as habit, that took the place of obligation, that elevated what was given to the ranks of appreciation. And Grandmaw's kitchen, press, and pantry, continued to grow with every visit. From hominy to ham hocks, from sorghum to sauerkraut, folks gave in endless assortments, bounty so overflowing that we oftentimes stacked it in corners, wedged it under the beds and laid it helter-skelter in beds of straw under the porch. It was near impossible to say *No* to those who knew giving as a way of preserving dignity.

With the strictest adherence to bloodlines, Spicy was my momma's aunt and second oldest of seven sisters and two brothers. There was Mary Olive, Spicy, Bordis, Eunice, Callie, Truman, Hester, Althea, and Lorali. Except for Bordis and Hester, they were all very much alive and devoted to complaining about their varied and various stages of miseries (*rheumatitis, arther-itis, and inflatagion).* Except for Spicy, Mary Olive and Lorali, each was blessed with nearly a half-dozen of their own, and a few of those already squeezing them out like brood mares. Bordis died of something called TB just a month and a day before I was born, and my Grandmother Esther died giving birth to Rachel, my mother. From that very first day, Rachel was passed from one aunt to another, but it was Spicy who did most of the raising. She was always Momma to my mother and always Grandmaw to me.

My days with Grandmaw were filled mostly with the business of survival, combing the fields and woodlands for the leaves, roots, and stems destined for what made well. There were times when my presence was more necessary than others: when ginseng berries were red and bright and easy to identify, its dried roots promising up to five dollars a pound;

and when blackberries and raspberries, gooseberries and huckleberries needed to be picked ahead of the birds and bears. It was an on-going crusade, but Grandmaw was never lacking in the what, when and where of it all. Over time, it became somewhat familiar to me, enough to know there were times she would send me scouring for no good reason: when I knew there was nothing to bring back. I reckoned there was only so much of my being under-foot she could stand. But then I came to realize that spending time alone—'head time' Grandmaw called it—was for my sake as much as hers.

The summer after I turned twelve is when Grandmaw first put a gun in my hands. "Take this here .22 a'mine," she said, "an' hunt us a squirrel." That's all she said, but it was enough, and left me feeling about as close to being a man as I could be. The heft and feel of her .22, the blended smell of its steel and gunpowder, had the comfort of exactness, something that felt centuries-old and rooted in things born of instinct. From that time on I just seemed to grow in unity with the mountains. There was a sense of freedom to it, something that took the work out of being alone.

I knew the mountains around me: their heap and swell, their sodden-sidedness, their solitariness. I didn't know the word rhapsody or even how it might be applied to the mountains—its glens and glades and pastures, flats and peaks and hollows—or to the spirits I was certain that lived there until I was secluded among them. I never knew their power to stir and evoke wonder until I was alone with their collective heartbeats.

I never ventured far at first, just enough to be out of earshot and to know the rest that comes from the cool deep stillness of fern beds, of moss growing along mud banks and the stir of pine needles in the wind. It wasn't until I was nearly thirteen that I took to rambling, inching my way up slopes and following foot trails and logging roads until I was as familiar with the outcrops of rock as I was with the numerous stands of hardwood; until I was crossing over from one ridge to the next and not coming back till most of the sun was gone. They were long days, full of the endless discovery of seasons and color and light, newness and decay, and with sounds that rushed and fluted and drummed: sounds that came together into a continuous backdrop so muted and recurrent that they were lost to me until I was stilled by shadows and the softness of forest floors, until the hush of breezes stirred the conifers and brushed back the wood sorrel just enough to sweeten the air.

About midday in mid-July, about the time I began to feel stealthy enough to call myself Cherokee-footed, I stumbled on a small flat about two miles south of a place called Sutter's Knob. It was the fire I smelled first, then noises unlike what I was used to. That's when I realized I'd never been this far or this high up, and only partly sure I could find my way back.

Grandmaw never worried about me losing my bearings. "Just walk down the mountain," she'd say. "Keep going down and down till you come across a creek or a road. You'll light upon one 'tother soon enough. Guarantee you'll find a cabin or two adder that. They'll point ye home. No need to scare about it."

Grandmaw armed me with just the sort of confidence to take me higher and further each day, the sort of confidence that now eased me closer to the smell of smoke, despite an uneasy feeling that I was not alone. On instinct, I readied my .22 and hunkered low in a clump of jack pine. About fifty yards straight ahead and in a sizable clearing, I could see what looked like a big washtub with a fire crackling hot beneath it. Something cone shaped was sitting on top of it, and a long piece of curly-cue sticking out its side. Nearby were sacks of something-or-other, a huge pile of split hickory and any number of quart-sized Mason jars, the kind used for canning. The only thing living and breathing as far as I could make out was a mule tied to a felled log clear to the other side. None of it made sense. There was no cabin or shelter of any kind, which made me wonder why anybody would come this far and this high to can. It made no sense.

About the time I was ready to pull back, I felt something stir close to my ear. But before I could take a breath, a voice so deep it sounded like it was coming from the bowels of the earth said, "Move and I'll kill ye dead."

I can't say how long I was out, only that I was nudged awake. "Stand up and look at me, boy." They were commanding words and delivered down the barrel of a twelve gauge shotgun pointed at the space between my eyes. In my mind I wanted to stand, but my knees wouldn't allow it.

"I ain't meanin' t'morrow," the voice came again, cold and grave-digger deep. I was so dry-mouthed that it hurt to swallow and I was numb clear to my guts. After several tries, I finally stood on legs all but helpless under my own weight. It was then that I realized I'd wet myself clear through to my backside.

"What's yer name, boy?" a man's voice demanded, the end of his twelve-gauge moving to within an inch of my nose. "What in hell you doin' up here? Wherr 'bouts you from? Who you b'long to?" One question after another, and coming faster than I could answer. They were things he was crazy to know, all the while with his cheek wedged against the stock of his gun and looking straight down the barrel into my eyes. After a minute or so of my babbling and nearly crying, he told me he'd had a bead on me for some two hundred yards back, and that if he had good sense he would just go ahead and finish me off right here and now. "Ought scatter-gun ye guts 'cross the ground. Leave ye fer buzzards and bear." His message hung for a time in the stillness, then stirred restless-like in the wind. "One thang fer shore, it's what ye kin count on if ever you come back." He waited until he was sure I understood, until his words inched hard and irretrievable into my place of remembrance. "You hear what I'm sayin'?" he asked. I was never so clear about anything in my life.

We stayed that way for a very long moment, me shaking with my eyes closed and waiting for the shotgun blast from hell. But it never came, though its effect was almost the same. "Open yer eyes, boy, an' remember what ye see." Unforgettable, it was, even to this day: those two hollow cylinders of death aimed square into my face and the shadow of a man's face buried beneath a ragged, dirty-brown Fedora. It was the image he wanted me to carry long after I was gone, one that would bring straightness to my spine, even in the middle of the night if I was to ever even think about setting foot on his mountain again. "Now GET!" was the last thing he said before I broke and ran, gulping for air and trying to outrun my own legs. I don't know where I was before I stopped running, only that I was next to a trickle of a stream, shivering and as lost as I'd ever been. I followed the stream down and down till it cut into a creek, but no road. I waded the creek for what seemed like better than a mile before I spotted the first sign of a cabin. I was far from Caney Creek.

"Worried about ye, Rubin," was all Grandmaw said when I stumbled in just before dark. That, and "Where's yer gun?"

The quiet solemn look on Grandmaw's face was enough to let me know she understood there was far more to where I'd been than what I was willing to tell. But she didn't press it, just let me be, even knowing that I'd be a sight better off unburdening myself than keeping it bottled up. Spitting it out, though, meant reliving it, and for the time being more than I wanted to do.

It was late when Grandmaw came and sat next to me on my bed, when she asked me if I was *awright*. It was a kindness that spoke to my fears, and all it took to unlock what I had hidden away. She listened without saying a word, just nodding quiet-like, puffing and drawing gently on her pipe. There was deep thinking on her face, then and for a long time afterwards. "Shiners" was the only word she uttered, an utterance that left an echo long after she left the room.

I knew little if anything about moonshining. Nothing beyond what the boys at school tossed back and forth between their tough talk and swagger; nothing beyond the shame Daddy felt for having to resort to it after Momma died. But it was a reminder that it was as real as anything else the mountains held, as potent a commodity as the brews Grandmaw coaxed from her roots and berries and leaves. I just needed to never forget it.

Four

Share of Reckoning

Except for Eugene Ramsey—our closest neighbor down the road—Grandmaw and I were all but isolated in the head of Caney Creek. Eugene had been in what Grandmaw called The Great War, but then didn't do much of anything afterwards except sit on his front porch and stare at the mountain across the road till his house swallowed him up in flames, and him just sitting there letting it ... like he couldn't feel a thing ... like it didn't matter ... till the porch finally let go and sent him and the rainbow of ribbons he kept pinned to his shirt into the hellish roar of fire. We smelled the smoke about the time its light torched up the sky, but by then it was too late. The crackling and popping of timbers is what I remember most, that and the absence of any voice crying for help.

Things stayed pretty much the same after Eugene was gone except for us now being out of earshot of anyone. Not that Eugene was a help of any kind, even in times of need, but, still, his being gone was a loss of a comfort we couldn't explain. And though Eugene lived a life free from the ruin of natter, silent except for sounds that might come from batting his eyes, his being gone somehow made things seem even quieter.

I didn't mind the solitude so much—what with school and tagging along in the wake of Grandmaw's doctoring—but more and more I wondered what was beyond Caney Creek besides the endless roll of mountain ridges and the hollows that filled them. The mere mention of other places were without the slightest meaning; still, their names stirred in me a wonder to know. The farthest I'd ever been was Shelby Creek; drifted there on its river fishing with Daddy, right up to where it spilled into the Levisa River–what everybody called the Big Sandy. I even watched motorcars sputtering back and forth on the blacktop highway, smooth as a ribbon along its banks, all the way to places like Pikeville and Elk Horn City, worlds I could only imagine. And though they were places far removed from anything I knew, I'd heard enough about them to believe that they were real. Still, I never had the interest to know them firsthand until now.

I stayed with Grandmaw right up till I turned fourteen and school let out for the summer. After that I went to live with her sister, my great aunt Mary Olive, in a place called Greezy Creek. Mary Olive was having *fainting spells* about every time she turned around, and when she finally upended off the porch, Grandmaw decided it was high time she needed someone other than Lorali, youngest of the siblings, to look after her. That someone was me.

"Mary Olive's stout enough, but not steady enough," was the way Grandmaw put it. And though there were more relatives on Greezy Creek than I could begin to know, none of them could afford to pack up and go live with Mary Olive; and Mary Olive sure as hell wasn't about to go live with any of them. She was like Grandmaw: determined to live out her days surrounded by what was hers. So, with the intention of doing what was best, the family nudged us together ... as much for our sakes as theirs.

"Besides," Grandmaw said, "you need to be gettin' on. You're nearly a man now, and it's purdy soon you'll be wantin' things that can't be found on Caney Creek. Greezy Creek ain't no glory land, but it's a whole lot more'n you'll ever find here."

My fourteenth year seemed fixed with more than its share of reckoning. Grandmaw no longer went from here to there, but stayed put, leaving people to come to her, the *on and off* of ol' Dan, and the coarseness of the ride itself, did most of the deciding.

Crushing recollections of Momma and Daddy, for reasons I couldn't explain, increased until they became all I had strength for: like the way my daddy smelled after coming in from the field, and the frail, pale, gentleness of my mother and her hands as soft as rain in my hair. Their dying so close together had been beyond me, nothing I could get my mind around with any comfort. And there was all that preaching and wailing, the ghost-faced mourners and their songs, the caskets being carried and lowered, that final goodbye. All of it in someway tied to the workings of the Almighty. It left me to wonder what He might be planning to do next.

Right in with the memories of Momma and Daddy were questions I didn't even know I had in me, and feelings I couldn't understand. Too often there seemed to be two of me: one that kept my mind stirred and the other that worked without letup trying to settle it. And there were times when I felt like I couldn't breathe, and when wanting to punch a hole in the wall was all too real. Then, too, there were times when I felt like I needed to hold onto something, or for something to hold onto me; times when I felt put out and put upon, tired of the whole damned mess—when I just wanted to run from everything I knew. Grandmaw did what she could, but seemed lost for the biggest part, devoid of the right words for a fourteen-year old boy. But she did say that a grieving heart made for a troubled mind, and that it wasn't so much about Momma and Daddy letting go of me as it was about me turning loose of them. I knew she spoke the truth, but there were other things that had left me feeling plowed under. Like the on-going thoughts of the girls I knew from school and the wonder they brought to me when they weren't even around. And those ladies in the Sears and Roebuck catalog all pressed and combed, silky and smooth as wet rocks; the ones in undergarments and nothing else, without even a thread of a dress to cover them, or even the shame to want to. And the times when I'd pee off the porch, when even the faintest breeze would *stir* me, excite feelings that were not easily put down. And though I'd never had a drink of moonshine, I was well past wanting it. It was one hell of a time for me to be going to Mary Olive's.

I didn't know Mary Olive but for the rare times we rode ol' Dan to Greezy Creek to doctor her. Except for Cousin Truman and his wife Inez, I didn't know but a handful of kin. But each day, when twilight shadows stretched from one mountain to the next, I drew closer to understanding the importance of putting distance between me and the old home place. To most, Momma and Daddy's old house was a picture of repose, nesting peacefully behind the sycamores that lined the road. But to me it cried out, empty-eyed and fallow, moaned to me in the moonlight, creaked and called to me on the wind.

I felt relief when Cousin Truman finally came to get me. He came mid-morning, lumbering in an old splintery plank wagon and driving Gert, the stoutest looking dapple-gray mare I'd ever seen. Grandmaw and I said little in parting, just gave each other forlorn and far-away looks. Then after a moment of near impossible silence, we hugged and said a last goodbye. And though I didn't understand it, there was a sense of gladness and a sense of shame because of it. But as much as anything, I was all of a sudden scared clear into the pit of my stomach.

Except for the rattle of the wagon and the clop of Gert's shoes on the road, Cousin Truman and I rode in silence. The old home place loomed like an albatross as we passed. I watched it as though it might reach out and grab me, try to pull me in. But other than Gert's hoof beats against the rocks and the creak and clatter of the wagon, we rolled by without event. For a second I imagined the crash of Daddy's shotgun and the ugly hollowness that followed it. Other than Grandmaw's cabin, it was the only place I'd ever known as home, and now I watched it, weathered and sagging under an ancient tin roof, slip without a sound behind the grapevine that hung in profusion from the mountain behind it. I didn't know much about Greezy Creek, but I knew what Caney Creek had become: a place too far removed from what I was becoming.

Five

Greezy

The three hours Cousin Truman and I spent getting to Mary Olive's, rattling over dirt roads and through creek bottoms, was done mostly without talking. Gert's powerful gait, steady and melodic against the road's rocks and ruts, was the only sound either of us seemed to want, as clear and earthen as the newness that unfolded around every bend, as welcomed as the dogwoods and redbuds coming into bloom, as comforting as the rush of the creek and the promise of freshly plowed fields. It was the sound that marked my coming ... deeper and deeper into Greezy Creek.

Cabins of every shape and size, listing and leaning on stilts and propped against hillsides, lined the creeks from one patch of ground to the next. Silhouettes filled their doorways and tracked me in eerie silence. I wondered if I would ever come to know such a place as home, or even if I'd ever want to.

Greezy Creek (its true spelling being *Greasy* Creek) was a high mountain wilderness oasis carved deep into Kentucky's Appalachian bedrock and a place as closed-ranked as its timbers were dense. Greezy was all anybody ever called it; *Creek* was just understood. In total, it was twenty-odd miles of unspoiled back roads, creeks and hollows (hollers), and with an even greater web of Indian trails. Its main roads were hard-packed dirt and rocks that followed the creek down and around the base of the mountains, past yards and gardens and bottoms, and just wide enough to accommodate the few bedraggled wagons that lumbered from one mud hole to another. Higher up, there were no roads at all, just logging trails worn hard by mules and sleds, and where brush was cleared along the way to graveyards. It was as green and lush a place as God ever made, but rugged with rock cliffs and steep bluffs, and thick with the likes of horseweed, nettle, and briar. It was, in many regards, an unforgiving place, never giving all that much except what could be extracted by sheer will.

I learned early on that life on Greezy was more apt to mean *survival* than anything else, and, as a rule, something that was done more by instinct and a fearsome knowing that hard times could always get worse.

"Ain't beholdin' to nuthin' or nobody, by God" was pretty much what its people were most proud of—and what they were most willing to share about themselves. Raw-boned and fiercely independent, they were dirt farmers and coal miners, fox hunters, loggers, and moonshiners. They were a people fashioned by lives around the care and preservation of family, and fixed just far enough from the throes of society to be reliant on little beyond the fabric of their own mettle, bound by a world of time and tradition—and, as often as not, lost to it as well.

The name itself—*Greasy Creek*—came into prominence after a local slaughterhouse that specialized in skinning and butchering bear (mostly for their skins) saw fit to use the creek as a sluice for its greasy runoff; runoff that gathered along the creek's banks and clung to anything that dared get in its way. It even clung to itself. Before long, it not only rose in stench, but laid waste to everything that had once grown green and lush along its banks. Some called it Dead Creek. But as time and demand outgrew supply, the hunters and the slaughterhouse moved to more abundant territories. It was years before enough rain and the rush of spring floods could flush the creek bed of all the fat deposits left behind. Still, long after their waters flowed clear and silvery again, and its banks returned lush and green, the name Greasy Creek held fast. But it was the "flute and caw" of the high Appalachian plain's accent that always made it sound like *Greezy* Creek. It was a name that would remain for all time; eventually becoming synonymous with words like *obstinate* and *unruly*; a name for a place as dogged as the grease that had once clung to its banks.

From our speckled understanding, we knew that Greezy Creek and most of Pike County rested on the northern rim of the Cumberland Plateau. Where such a thing as the *Cumberland Plateau* began and ended, I had no idea—only that we were part of it. There were so many landmarks with the name *Cumberland* attached to it: the Cumberland Mountains, the Cumberland River, the Cumberland Gap, the Cumberland Trail, the Cumberland Falls, the Cumberland Valley, the Cumberland Plateau—that I couldn't be sure where we fit in, only that we did in some peripheral way. The name *Cumberland* itself, in whatever context, signaled that it was someplace not far from home; a point of reference I had no idea how to use, only that it helped to partially define who I was.

Nestled in the nether regions of Pike County, Greezy was as secluded and sequestered from outside influences as its treacherous slopes and twelve hundred foot ridges would allow. Four main roads defined its length and breadth, three of them intersecting right where Andrew Clemmons' apple-red general store sat big as a hotel. From there, they ambled in uneven lines, across mountains and following the creek's meander along the valley floor. Gardner Fork angled upward to the south, then southeast, all the way to the top of Wolf Pit Mountain. Dry Fork rose toward the west then fell away for a long five miles, twisting and winding, and eventually turning north until it ended at a place called Shelby. Lower Fork fell away to the north, snaking in long even turns till it reached the banks of the Big Sandy River. Main Fork intercepted Gardner Fork a half-mile or so south of Andrew Clemmons' and curled toward the southwest, all the way to the gap that led to the long stretch of valley called Rock House.

Branching off of these four main roads, like veins off of arteries, mazes of hollows cut deep into the mountains clear to their crests. Following the cut of their creeks, the hollows wound back and away from all things familiar, where cool-rock springs stood clean and unspoiled, and where the wind often carried the names of the dead and forgotten. They were dark and verdant places, fortified behind impenetrable walls of rhododendron and where Sweet William and wild columbine carpeted the slopes and bluffs with as much fragrance as color; where its herbs: ginseng and bloodroot, horsetail and goldenseal, bearberry and coneflower, garlic and wild ginger and mint, lay secreted to even the most diligent eyes. But they were also home to the poisons of ivy, oak, and sumac, the strewn varieties of briars and burrs, and all waiting with malice and no regard to anything but their own puncture and bite. They were havens for hawks and wild turkey, copperheads and rattlesnakes, groundhog and bobcat and bear, all as cunning as they were abundant, and as vengeful as they were silent; places fearsome and untamed, unsympathetic and even unfair—but mostly far from strangers.

Up and down the creek from Andrew Clemmons' General Store, Greezy's coalmine camp-houses stretched as far as the eye could see. One hundred and fifty of them, side by side and in perfect alignment along a single lane: identical two-family dwellings, white with tin roofs and black trim, and each with a common porch and a common wall. They had been built by the McKinney Steel Company right after WWI to house the influx of workers needed to mine Greezy's coal, which lay millions of tons rich beneath the shelves of mountain bedrock. We called them "The Camps."

Workers of every ilk came to work the mines and live in The Camps. Mostly they were poor and rugged, men without choices except for hard labor, and then only when they could get it.

They came from as far south as Mississippi and Alabama, and as far north as New York and Pennsylvania, as far away as Eastern Europe—Hungary and Poland and Yugoslavia—places we'd only heard about and imagined with a sense of intrigue. They came in every fashion: some in wagons, some walking, some straddling a mule, and often with little beyond the clothes they wore. There were some who had never set foot in a mine, and some speaking just enough English to make us wonder how they ever found their way. They came and left without concern to time or seasons, some coming and going even in the same day. Many were drifters, working just long enough for a paycheck and the chance to lay it down with a deck of cards, some just for the whiskey it would buy. Mary Olive said it never made much sense to try and get to know them since so many were such a short-time here, their hellos and goodbyes as easy as the Big Sandy River under a harvest moon.

Coalmining was not for everybody. Crawling around on hands and knees in killing dampness and breathing coal dust miles from the light of day had a way of weeding out the weak. Many first timers knew by the end of the day what it meant to work with their backs stooped and hunched in a mineshaft no more than three feet high, and always—all day and every day—with the threat of a mountain caving in on them. To them, it was a one-time lesson in what they never intended to do again. To some, though, it was their only reality, their only hope.

The Camps lasted until 1928, when the mines closed and most everybody moved out. The Camps had been a place with a school, a hospital, and even a theater. It was also where Angus Walker built his pool hall, and where he bootlegged moonshine for Corbin Fairchild. And though The Camps were for the most part now empty and boarded up, the pool hall remained a hub of activity: a place where whiskey drinking and poker playing was tolerated, and where strange and profane women gave patrons the pleasure of their company. Oftentimes, it carried tales of shootings and stabbings, and people being beaten and left for dead; a place that Deputy Sheriff Virgil Blair was more than willing to let govern itself, and a place he frequented only when he had to.

Mary Olive's house rested near the lower end of Gardner Fork, half a mile up the road from Andrew Clemmons' general store. It sat alongside the creek bank at the edge of a low plain. And though it rested firmly on pillars of hickory logs, it remained susceptible to things like spring thaws and heavy rains, when creek waters and the Big Sandy River were always a threat to climb over their banks.

By the time Cousin Truman pulled ol' Gert to a stop in front of Mary Olive's, my heart had all but fallen in on itself. I felt alone and estranged, constrained to a foreign land and with memories of Momma and Daddy now pouring over me in ever-widening streams. I barely spoke to Mary Olive, barely raised my head long enough to know her face. I just stood there in the midst of her welcoming, trying with all my might to feel something besides not knowing where I belonged.

I fell asleep shortly after Cousin Truman left. Just collapsed right there in the middle of the day—across the bed in the lower room—with my clothes still on and my pillow case stuffed full of belongings next to me. It wasn't until the next morning that I felt strong enough to sit up. I even managed, after a time, to utter a word of thanks to Mary Olive.

Mary Olive was patient with me, moving quietly about the house while I sorted through the strangeness of my new surroundings and how I came to be here. She was content to let me be, at least for the time, offering nothing but the gentle stirring of her presence. I guess she figured it wasn't *her* thoughts I needed as much as my own—learning to come to some sort of peace with my having been passed from one to the next. But it was the smell of side meat and fried bread that finally got me to the table. I ate until my stomach pushed tight against my belt, until I hurt through to my back and up into my ribs. Throughout, Mary Olive sat mostly in silence, never pushing me to talk. I guess she figured I'd come around to it soon enough. And I did, days and nights later when I realized she was all I had.

"Water bucket's empty." I wanted Mary Olive to know I was observant. She was rocking, gently, rhythmically, clenching down on the stem of her cob pipe and squinting in my direction.

"Water bucket's empty," I said again, the sound of my voice landing flat against the newspaper-covered walls. "Do you want me to draw some?" I asked, as if I needed to be told exactly what to do.

"Well," she said, "I 'spose *I* could go git it. Just hop up on these sixty-two-year-old legs an' run out to the well right quick while you relax." She was talking around the stem of her pipe and looking out of the tops of her eyes, over the rim of her spectacles. "Rubin, honey," she said, her voice a slow easy rhythm in perfect time with her rocking, "I'm the cook. The rest is up to you."

That was the first real conversation we had, but it was all we needed to get us started. My role was as clearly defined as the wrinkles that ran soft and threadlike through her cheeks. It was no mystery that my being there with Mary Olive was more than a charitable coincidence. Our being together was for reasons far deeper than simply easing the weight of being alone. It was more about adding life to our days, about pulling us out of our brooding places. Even with forty-eight years separating us, we came to know in short order that we were better off *with* each other than *without*. And though her *fainting spells* and *slipping in-and-out of her thinking* was something I soon came to know as her being a little too deep in Corbin Fairchild's demon rum, her diversion of choice. It taught me that patience was a virtue and a thing paramount to our wellbeing.

During our first month, Mary Olive wandered off on three separate occasions to look for Audrey—one of her cats that had been dead for more than thirty years. During that same time, she shot a hole in the wall above the kitchen door with the shotgun she kept within arms reach of where she slept. She said she thought it was that one-eyed boy of Drayton Whitehead's trying to break in. It was true enough that Drayton Whitehead had fathered a son with only one eye, but he died just six days after being born—nearly forty years ago. And it was on the order of once a month that she put me on notice that she was leaving: "*Going to sleep in the orchard*," she'd say. She called the crabapple tree next to the house *the orchard*. It was punishment, I reckoned, for some imagined offense: something I had said or done, perhaps even in one of her dreams. At first I tried to stop her, then realized it made little difference because by the time she got to the crabapple tree she forgot why she was there. In a matter of minutes she'd come wandering back as if nothing had happened. Other times she would tell me about every ancestor on both sides of the family as far back as the Mayflower, then the next minute ask me what she'd been talking about. One minute joyful with camp meeting songs, the next ponderous with trying to remember what she'd set out to do; one minute, purposeful and duty bound, the next ruminating with ghosts. In the course of a day, she was liable to be just about anybody or anywhere: sometimes a whole host of people, then no one at all. Though I never understood it exactly until I learned to recognize the whiff and tang of moonshine on her breath—what she claimed for both health and exultation. After that I simply came to accept it as the essence of who she was and even how it was so vividly expressive of the place that had become my home.

A steady flow of friends and neighbors came and went at Mary Olive's, all of whom seemed to be a cousin of one sort or another. In and out without the slightest warning, each of them with what seemed like a half-dozen young'ns in tow, and with at least as many tales about each one. The ebb and flow of faces and voices got to be one of the few constants in our lives, whether we wanted them or not. But after a time, I got to where I liked it, and, at times, even welcomed it. So long as they didn't bother to stay too long, they were all pretty much tolerated, even the ones always expecting to eat.

Most renowned was Lorali, private as she was. Of all the siblings, Lorali turned out most different: slender-boned and willowy in the way of a new fawn, and tall in the way of her daddy to where my eyes were on the level with her chin, though this was due in part to her neck: angular and with a bit of a stretch, swanish. Her hair was chestnut with the slightest threads of silver, and gathered in one forever-long braid to the center of her back. And although her heart was as fresh as a new morning, it was the silence that marked her, defined her. Lorali did not speak, had never spoken, even with lips full and with the pink of red clover—near perfect for kissing, but without ever the chance. And there was the faint-and-angelic smile, as fixed as the candle-glow in her eyes: buckeye-round and the color of autumn's last-felled leaves. It was only in moments of glee that something akin to "*eee*" would find its way up and out of her… and even then to her own surprise.

"I swan," Mary Olive said to me in a whisper, "Lorali ain't a bit twitter-witted. Got a whole head full a sense; quick to mull an' cipher. Just cain't let any of it out of her mouth."

Lorali was the solitary contrast to Mary Olive and what helped hold us to the light of what was odd and unconventional. From season to season, she went from one household to another, as often as necessities dictated, to gift us with an extra set of hands and to mend and pattern our clothes.

We never knew what to expect from her beyond selfless devotion to tasks and kindnesses alike, that willingness to do for the rest of us even when we quit on ourselves. She had no place of her own except what doors were opened to her—over and again—and staying as long as hearts and nerves would endure. But as set apart as she seemed, with only a shadowed smile and the busyness of her hands to make sense of a loud and blaring world, she was as bright as spun gold with needle and thread. From bloomers to blouses, curtains to wedding gowns, all were done with the finest detail, unmatched down to the cinch and size of stitch. Her genius was a gift as ingrained as the old maid that ran to unplumbed depths within her, even at thirty-five. She came and went like a wisp.

Grandmaw came too, but not as often—sometimes to spend the day, sometimes the night. She was spirit-like, Grandmaw was, the tiniest of angels balanced atop ol' Dan and the horsehair blanket she used for a saddle. I never understood how she kept from breaking, how her bird-like bones and paper-thin skin managed to hold her together from her place to ours. Yet she was as pliable as she was permanent beneath her shawls and the wool scarf that more-times-than-not framed her face. Her coming was never fixed with a date or time, just brought on by her notion that we were in need. It was easy to be right about such a thing seeing as how Mary Olive was most always in some need of repair. Being *down with the miseries* often served Mary Olive in an amiable way, brought her the attention she craved and what she thought she deserved. What ailed her was anybody's guess; we only knew that it was many-layered and poles apart from one day to the next, but never anything that couldn't be comforted with a little taste of corn liquor. "Just to soften my mouth," she'd say.

To Mary Olive's delight, Grandmaw always kept a pint bottle of shine in the bottom of her kit bag for things like snakebite and to hold back pain when she had to remove buckshot or set a bone. But Mary Olive was far more resourceful than having to wait for Grandmaw. She traded canned goods and the whatnots of mending, washing, and ironing, for the feel-good of clear corn liquor. Corn liquor was her all-in-all, her make well; good for whatever afflicted.

By any stretch, Mary Olive's house was not the perfect respite, or even a place that lent itself to much beyond a cool drink of water on a steamy day, but it did possess the richness of gossip; a place that blended shanty decadence with a sense of welcome. The house was simple enough: three big rooms fastened together in the shape of an 'L', and covered in materials of various kinds: weather board, tar paper, tin, most anything that would hold a nail and shed the rain. But even after decades of cleaning and airing, bracing, shimming and shoring, it had begun to go the way of all things: settling and fading, yielding to the ravages of time. And though it had a frail and crippled look, it remained a collage of texture and color, light and sound; its rooms seasoned by the mustiness of wood ash and smoke, but most often alive with the smell of cornbread and soup beans, and the labored sounds of Mary Olive's camp-meeting singing.

From up the road, the house appeared to hunker behind a chicken-wire fence tangled forever with pink, white, and purple clematis. From down the road, a single crabapple tree, along with huge vines of wisteria bent low with their own weight, greeted with a sense of somnolence. Its tar-paper roof and repeated signs of patching and repatching, along with its time-honored windows and screen door—none of them being the least bit plumb or square—gave it a crumpled look, but relaxed and resilient despite its years. On its lower side, trilliums and Jack-in-the-pulpits, wood lilies and forget-me-nots bloomed in quiet seclusion beneath the crabapple tree. On its upper side—the garden side—buttercups and daisies, poppies and black-eyed susans, lady slippers and irises sprouted in a profusion of colors from crocks and old pieces of cookery scattered throughout the yard.

From the porch to the well, frayed and faded dishrags, towels and aprons, dangled daily from the clothesline like one-of-a-kind flags. And there were bunches of green beans, onions and peppers strung and hung to dry across the porch's lower end, along with unmatched rockers, high-backed and warped into contours of comfort. And there were the fire pits lined with stones right where the garden began and where we set the big galvanized tubs on washdays. And there was ol' Jess, a mostly-sleeping blue tick hound who gratefully ate whatever scraps were thrown his way, and who begrudgingly shifted his arthritic bones throughout the day to keep aligned with the sun's relentless trek across the porch.

Out back was an old weathered hen house that hadn't seen a chicken in the thirty-odd years Mary Olive came to live there. Brittle and ready to collapse from the years of hard winds and rain, it was the embodiment of neglect—a thing that had all but given up. Off to its side was the well: a big salt box with a slanted tin roof. A chain with a battered bucket hung from a rusted pulley that made soft creaking sounds when I drew water, and in the slightest breeze when I didn't.

Even further back was the outhouse propped up on the side of the hill, looking like some ageless monster rising up out of the earth. It was covered with an array of old tin signs: Nehi Grape Soda, Pears' Soap, Beechnut Chewing Tobacco, Prince Albert in a can—anything that might block the wind from whistling through the knotholes and the gaps between its planks. The weeds surrounding it, thick and high with cockleburs and larkspur, were so dense that it looked like each one was trying to strangle the other. It was a place that blacksnakes and wasps guarded with impunity, and a place where we made a lot of noise when approaching. Despite listing painfully to one side, it stood as stalwart as a sentinel from one season to the next and as a reminder to the necessities of life.

Then there was the garden, hot and steamy, and big enough to feed us for a year with the right amount of attention and our devotion to canning. It started a ways out from the porch, and ran clear to the buckeye tree that marked our property line on the upper side. And though Mary Olive worked me like a borrowed mule most of the summer with all the planting, hoeing and weeding, it was a garden that never failed to give back with abundance: pole beans and squash, potatoes and peas, cabbage and turnips, peppers and beets, mounds of pickles, hills of onions, tomatoes and strawberries and corn, even chicory and Indian tobacco for Mary Olive's pipe. We had everything we could ever want despite our shirt-and-trouser-scarecrow-on-a-stick never living up to what he was made to do. Some mornings, the garden looked like invitations had been sent out to every crow that ever lived. The sight of them at first light was like a pestilence on the land: their strutting and shitting wherever they felt like it, and squawking at me as if I ought to go back inside and wait for them to finish. I could only imagine how many of them I kept alive by my very own sweat and effort.

That first summer was the hardest. I wasn't used to working in the garden the way Mary Olive expected, wasn't used to such care and tending—not only the planting and weeding, but the stripping, cutting, and canning as well. Nor was I used to the rest of it: chopping wood, building fires, drawing water, scrubbing clothes and floors and outhouse walls. I wasn't used to the work of a man, but it came to me soon enough.

"I ever tell you about Hollister McEuen?" Mary Olive was much more of a storyteller and historian than Grandmaw, but Cousin Truman warned me that hers was a memory given more to convenience than accuracy, though he could never be sure. The only *sure* thing I came to know was that it worked exactly the way she intended it.

"Married him, and me just sixteen year old," she said, smoke rings rising from the bowl of her pipe, in concert with the back-and-forth of her rocker. "A time when I was tryin' to get to a place that had a little hope. Filled with the want to be a woman, I was, an' doin' what I thought would get me there the quickest. But mostly, it was tryin' to figure a way outta the life I wanted to leave behind. I thought Hollister was my ticket, but it didn't take me long 'fore I knew he wanted me for all the wrong reasons. I was hopin' for a mite more love, but it never come—our time together never amountin' to more'n a hollow feelin', even on the best a days. Ugliness was what it was—what it turned into—a blight on both of us. Still, I punished with it, let it eat at me day after day till I was less than I wanted to be. *Strivin'* was about all it amounted to: a life without wonder, without gladness. Just flat and gray we was, an' without the hope of it ever bein' diff'ernt." She stopped just long enough to clear her throat and spit into the coal bucket next to the stove. "He was a hard-enough worker and purdy for a man, but empty of soul." She lingered with the thought, her rocking stilled, her pipe cradled in her hands. Then in a bright-eyed revelation said, "An' not much for makin' babies, neither." She laughed real big at this and coughed even harder. "But I learnt a right bit from it," she said, catching her breath. "Mostly it's more than the *coverin'* that's the make and matter of a man." Her words were gentle with truth. "Stayed together longer'n the Lord intended, I b'lieve, 'fore he just up and walked off. Just headed out to the mines like always, 'fore daylight. Just never come back." Her voice trailed, thoughtful and weak with the memory. "Can't say as I blame him," she said, "bein' the way we was, so lackin' an' all. Weren't no divorce. Don't reckon we knowd about such a thang, 'cept it bein' a taint an' a stain. Not the sort a thang a feller like Hollister McEuen needed to bother with. Me neither for that matter. That was fer high-minded, city types. Here on the creek, we just suffer one 'nuther. Just *take it* for better or worse. 'At's what we vow 'fore the Lord, you know: *'For better or worse'*. It works for most. For some, though, like Hollister an' me, being cobbled was the bigger part of a burden. I reckon for me it was too much expectin'. But adder while, it just never quite added up for either one of us. But I'll give him credit; it takes a lot to draw on the heart, then act on it too."

We sat for sometime in silence with nothing but the faintest breeze angling its way through some rusty screen Cousin Truman had tacked across one of the kitchen windows. "He ever come back around?" I asked.

"No," she said without the trappings of regret. "A few say they've seen him over in Harlan County working at Yellow Jacket Mine, but it don't make a diff'ernce. Gone is gone, an' I thank the Lord ever'day for it."

There were pictures, but not many, of Mary Olive as a young woman. Her hair was straight, raven, and hung clear to the small of her back. It was a breathtaking contrast to the gray bun she now kept knotted to the back of her head. Her face was round then, and full, and didn't know the many lines that now ran through it in a kind of grace.

"Rubin, honey," she would say when she saw me studying her pictures, "I b'lieve I was a pretty good-looking woman, don't you?"

"I do, sure enough, Mary Olive. I sure enough do." On that we were as clear as we were kin.

Six

Cornbread Red

Looking up the road from our porch, we could make out Olin and Gracie Yonts' big white house at the mouth of Big Will Hollow. They lived there with their nine children, the fifth being a fourteen-year-old huckster named Bobby.

During those few but precious years I spent with Grandmaw, I became accustomed to walking the mountains, being under their spell and soft invitation. They were like strongholds, protective and shielding me against what gnawed and what dared to penetrate the darker parts of my aloneness. In many ways, they were like Grandmaw, curative, there to heal and restore the emptiness left by Momma and Daddy. After a time, I came to rely on the lull that emanated from their shadows and speckles of light, from the quiet in their earth. They were things pure and simple, unlike the roads that stretched new and strange before me. Between the hills and Grandmaw, I'd been able to cover my hurt—at least some of it—but it wasn't until Bobby Yonts that I was able to look at Appalachia's highlands and even life itself with ripe fascination.

During that first week after I came to live with Mary Olive, Bobby came by every day, sometimes twice. One time he brought us a chicken. As usual, he stayed close to the base of the hill where the brush was thick and he was out of sight of his mother. Mary Olive was grateful for the chicken, but questioned him more than once if it was okay with his momma and daddy. After she'd asked about the third time, Bobby just stepped back and wrung the chicken's neck. "There," he said. "Ain't no use worrying about it now. Sumbitch is dead, and somebody ought to eat it." Mary Olive just stood there stoking on her pipe and watching that chicken flop around in the dust until it went limp. Finally, she reckoned Bobby was about as right as he ever was, and without another word cleaned it and fried it in her biggest cast iron skillet nearly an inch deep in grease. We ate our fill that evening, along with pinto beans and cornbread, finishing just in time for Bobby to run to the head of Big Will Hollow to roundup his cows.

Bobby was the fifth of Olin and Gracie Yonts' nine children, and the younger of two boys. He wasn't what I ever thought of as skinny, but more along the lines of what Mary Olive called *leanish*, as opposed to me who she called *narrowly built*. Bobby had dark red hair and even darker freckles, and walked the way he talked: fast and full of kick. We stood eyeball to eyeball, and though we were similar in build, he was possessed of a certain readiness that I lacked, a certain edge packed with spit and diceyness that made him seem older than he was. His thick neck and arms, though disproportionate to the rest of him, gave the impression, even at fourteen, that he could knock a hole through a barn door. I was always glad he was on my side, and even gladder that he was always so quick to smile, to find laugher in even the direst of things. It was one of his constants, as wry as the glint that shone in his paler-than-pale blue eyes.

Olin and Gracie's big white house sat as a reminder of how richly blessed we were to have such neighbors, how beyond price they were in both good times and bad. Below their house, a long narrow field between the road and the foot of the mountain swelled with a garden big enough to feed General Lee's army and a pasture where they penned ol' Hank, a dun colored mule fifteen hands high and about as big around as a coal car. Mary Olive said he was big enough to stand flat-footed and shit in the back of a wagon. But it took the likes of ol' Hank to pull the necessary plows through eight acres of packed earth and rock every spring (one acre for the garden, one for sugar cane, and six for corn high on the hill). Ol' Hank was a brute they treated like a baby, much like Bobby's older brother, Ben, and worth every penny it took to feed him.

The size of Olin and Gracie's garden was appropriate to feed eleven, though in actuality more like twelve, given that Ben ate the equivalent of two. It was Ben who supplied the brawn to the farm's endless everyday rhythm, who busted clods and held ol' Hank to a straight line as they plowed. But then it was Bobby who was made to look after Ben.

Bobby slipping away and coming to see us everyday got to be more habit than exception. What made it remarkable was that he never came empty handed, even if it was only to bring us a piece of gossip we always swore never to repeat. It gave him a sense of power knowing that he carried around bits of information not common to most. He was careful to dole it out little at a time, never giving us more than he thought we could handle. What with his uncle Corbin being the main moonshiner on the creek and parts beyond, and his daddy being political buddies with the deputy sheriff, magistrate, presiding judge and most everybody who was an elected official, Bobby's tales took on a life of their own—each one bigger and wilder than the one before.

Mary Olive allowed that Bobby's tales were true enough given that nobody could make up stuff that good. She went as far as saying he was possessed of a sixth sense, one that maneuvered him through life like a cottonmouth through riverweeds. Like a mystery, Bobby was, like how he'd show up, day after day, somehow knowing exactly when Mary Olive had cornbread on the stove—even when she made it at different times. Cornbread was one of the little things that made life worth living for most of us, one of our staples, our increase for having lived another day. It was the single most sought-after recompense for what we sweated out and left in the fields. We were plain in our likes, and cornbread spoke to that simplicity. It was one of the common denominators that kept us liking who we were. That and a green onion were Bobby's favorites, as much a part of him as rain was to rainbows, and what fueled his daily trek to fetch his cows. Cornbread Red was a handle Mary Olive hung on him not long after I came, a name he came to favor and one he became accustomed to carving and scratching into most everything he could wherever we went.

I wasn't long in learning that the chores Mary Olive had for me were as ceaseless as the day was long. But they were light compared to Bobby's. *Doing* meant survival. No one was exempt. Drawing water and chopping wood, making soap and churning butter, slopping hogs and clearing land was as endless as it was necessary. Digging toilets, coal and potatoes; whitewashing everything that couldn't be picked up or eaten; pitching and shoveling, building and mending; shucking corn and robbing the bees; cutting cane and making molasses, keeping a fire in the stove and making sure the hen house door was locked at night was as knotty as it was relentless, and Bobby was a major player even at fourteen, even with having to keep vigil over Ben. But, outside it all, the one chore he owned as much as it owned him was the trek he made to the head of Big Will Hollow every day, into its crags and thickets, to find the cows and herd them home; then his to milk and feed, water and bed down for the night; then, again, his to milk in the morning before turning them back to the mountains, before resuming all that would be forever undone.

It was late afternoon in late June when Bobby first took me along, when he handed me a hunk of cornbread and a green onion like it was an automatic thing. "Get you a bite," he said through a smile bigger than life. "Makes goin' tolerable. Stouten you up." With that, he bit off a loving mouthful, then another...then chewed and eyeballed me till he commenced to laugh and then choke, his funny bone wheezing for breath and a drink of water that never came. "Last one up the holler's a mule's ass," he bellowed. And with that we were off: streaks of lean meat and bare feet digging and churning upwards, the stain of cornbread and onions on our breath.

We ran till we couldn't, our imaginations spiked and feeling like we were one. We were winded and loped about listening for sounds rank and familiar, anything that might bring us closer to the Guernseys we called *milkcows*. I learned right off that there was no way of telling where cows might be or what obstacles might have to be overcome to get to them. They were a curious lot, gentle enough, even at times comical, but never the least bit predictable. Left to themselves, they could be anywhere: hunkered under a rock cliff or perched like a goat on the side of a slope, grazing in a field of clover and vetch, or stuck udder-deep in horse nettle and briar. One simply had no way of knowing. Finding them simply meant following the clank and clang of the tin bells that hung like medieval jewelry around their necks.

After several tries to rock a soaring chicken hawk, Bobby came to a dead stop. I waited, thinking he had heard something I hadn't—but after a thoughtful moment and a light in his eyes that could have sparked a fire, he led me up and over a grassy patch of bald mount and across a field thick with milkweed and teasel, then stopped short and raised his hand for quiet. We waited, motionless, until nothing could be heard except the gentlest breeze and the hypnotic repetition of meadowlarks off in the distance. When the look in his eyes finally said he was satisfied we were alone, he moved us in the direction of a giant red oak. Twenty-odd paces to the right of it, Bobby rolled away a big flat rock then brushed away a layer of dirt to get at a rusty tin lid. Under the lid, the mouth of a twenty-pound lard bucket yawned big and black.

"Looky yander," he said, his eyes the size of saucers. The bucket was packed with half-pint bottles of liquor, as clear as the runoff from a mountain spring. "Kentucky Moon," he said, "...an' plenty of it." And with that, he reached down and helped himself to one that was about half empty. "Y'ever see anything so purdy?" he said, holding it up to the sun and the filminess of a bluebonnet sky. I said nothing, just waited while he unscrewed the lid and took a big-eyed pull like it was lemonade on the fourth of July.

"Whooo-eee," he bellowed through a gaping mouth and a breath like a dragon. In the next instant, he reached the bottle to me. When I didn't take it, he said, "Don't reckon yer scairt." His smile was wily. "C'mon," he said, "it'll light a far in yer britches." I reached out with a reluctant hand, then drew it up close to my nose. At the first whiff, trouble welled in my stomach.

"Hellfire, son," he said, "yew ain't no preacher are ye?" His smile was as playful as his eyes. I shook my head then waited for some courage to run through me. After a quiet moment, he cocked his head and said, "Reckon yew outta quit whatever it is you're thinking on an' take a taste.

Hit ain't a thang that'll hurt ye."

Without a word, I closed my eyes and touched it to my lips. Carefully. Cautiously. Still, I couldn't keep from shuddering, then gagging, then coughing right big, then spitting three or four times. I don't know that any of it got much further than my back teeth, but the fire that raged on my lips was enough. I handed it back with still another shudder. Bobby howled like he was straight-up chasing the moon. "Hi-ho Silver," he said, raising the bottle in mock toast, then, with his one-of-a-kind grin, sipped in a most genteel fashion. I couldn't imagine him liking any part of it except maybe for its jolt and the wave of bravado that left him flushed and buried in a look of indulgence. For just a moment, he seemed to search my face. Then, with a sizable grin, said, "Hell, you'll get used it. Might even come to like it."

After we returned the bottle to the bucket, reset the lid and replaced the dirt and rock, it would have taken an Indian scout to detect anything out of place. Then once again we headed out to fetch the cows. But when we finally heard the clank of bells, Bobby's focus shifted yet again, and in a matter of minutes we were topping a high ridge. The cows would have to wait.

"Down there," he said, pointing. "'At's the head a' Shop Branch. Wherr Dixie lives." He stood quiet-like for a time, listening, then guided us like night thieves until we came to a big rock ledge above Dixie Wainwright's house. It was a vantage point that gave a clear view of her splintered cabin, and just far enough away so that her daddy's dogs weren't set to barking. It was a spot covered with shade and at just the right angle to see her if she were to come out the door, front or back; a spot tailor made to catch a glimpse of her before dusk, before her image turned to dreams. We hunkered there, but not for long. There were the cows, after all.

"Don't reckon there's much chance a' you takin' Dixie away from me," he said, his cockiness covered with a smile as smooth and bright as a brand new dime.

"You reckon there's any chance I'd want to?" I said.

"Would be, if you was to get a good look at her." His Cheshire cat smile was always the punctuation that said he'd gone one up. But I could never give him the benefit of the doubt until we boxed each other around a bit, danced and feinted and dodged until the comedy of it elevated our wildest notions of who we were and even the possibilities of what we might become.

Whatever it was that Bobby saw in Dixie Wainwright would remain a mystery until late August, until school commenced, until she and all the others would crowd into the big three-room schoolhouse that sat in the huge open bottom below Mary Olive's. In the meantime, the rest of summer held its own surprises, things I hadn't been ready for and things that added their own grisly light.

Seven

Saturday Night

Five-card draw was being bet heavily, drunkenly and profanely on the big flat above the schoolhouse. No more than six feet away, seven-card stud was being dealt on an old bed sheet spread tightly on the ground. It was Saturday night and Greezy was rich with coalmine paychecks and bootleg whiskey ... and poker.

Poker eyes, white and wild, ghostly and uneasy in the carbide glow. Poker hands: hard and knuckled, thick and coarse, veined and sooty, shuffled and dealt, bet and grabbed and held onto what was theirs and what they dared others to try and take. Poker talk was low and threatening, severe and without caution, stirring even the nerve fibers in the ground. But there was a rhythm to it, a cadence, ill-fated and in the face of the stars, poisonous and against the wonder of the mountains. It was part of what they were: rawboned, mule-driving mountaineers who "*didn't know no better*" and didn't give a damn when they did. They were infidels, one to another, whiskey breathed and poker bent, as inseparable from it all as they were consumed by it.

Bobby and I held carbide lamps against the night, keeping them adjusted so their flames burned a brilliant sapphire while casting a stark-white light. It was a light most were familiar with, the same kind that burned on the front of coalminer helmets and lit their way through endless seams of darkness. They gave us a nickel apiece and we took it with hungry appreciation, but would have done it for nothing. Just being there was payment enough.

The huge bottom below Mary Olive's was where Greezy Creek's big three-room schoolhouse sat high atop concrete pillars. Come Saturday night, it was a gathering place for honky-tonkers and coalminers with a week's worth of hard-earned dollars: good ol' boys out for a high ol' time. But it was behind the school, high upon a flat thick with hemlock and Virginia pine—and out of sight of Sheriff Virgil Blair—that Saturday nights and the serious side of poker came alive. It was a place where moonshine was shared and scores often settled, a place to chew and spit, swap and brag, and to see who could get the drunkest; a place of refuge for the lawful and lawless alike, and a place to beat the hell out of one another when the circumstances called for it—and do it without interference. It was neutral territory, an equal and level playing field that provided its own order for hard and unconstrained natures. But most of all it was a place of rituals that needed regular attention, where change didn't come easy, and where loyalties and a man's word dared not be broken. And though Virgil Blair knew very well what went on up there on the flat and pretty much to a man who was there, he never bothered to assert himself or his authority. Getting up there was too slippery a slope for a man with a stiff leg and a hip that had been shot clean through. And even if he had been able to steer ol' Jake, his lean, black, Tennessee Walker up its steep bank, he would have scared everybody off long before he got there. So he kept his distance, resigned to deal only with the trepidation that good ol' boys leave in their wake.

"Brang me a sip a *clear*, son." A sip of something clear was well understood. With that being said, Bobby was off into the night; and within minutes he'd be back with a pint bottle of his uncle Corbin's finest. Fifty cents on the barrelhead. Simple. The way both sides liked it.

Corbin made it clear that Bobby was to be like a ghost in the wind. "Never carry whiskey on you, but always have it close enough to make'em think you can pull it outta the air whenever you want to."

There was a formula for bootlegging whiskey. By day, Bobby took orders with only a nod, walk off until he was out of sight, to one of the many places he kept liquor hid, then move it to another place altogether.

Once done, the mention of a stump or a rock told the buyer where they could find it: a place they could get to without being seen and a place where they could leave their money. It was all very clandestine, neither side ever witnessing the actions of the other. At night, whiskey and money could be exchanged rather simply: vanish into the night then reappear sometime later with liquor. Swapping it for cash was easy in the dark. It was all very choreographed and vague enough to avoid the odd-chance of leaving a trail. It was just one of the things that drove Virgil Blair crazy.

"B'lieve we need a chaser!" It was a request that came across like an order. Seven Up was what Bobby kept hid. It was a dime, despite all the cussing. "Ain't but a damned nickel at the pool hall!"

"Then whyn't you go to the pool hall an' get it?!" It was Bobby's all-time rejoinder, his bite and taunt. It was enough to get the dime, but not enough to spare him from the rain of blasphemies that followed, the ones mingled with the vagaries of uncertainty and drunkenness.

Saturday night was often outside the rule of law, still, it tempted, induced us to risk reputations for what lay on the other side of moderation. It was especially true for Bobby, and, after a time, for me as well. Truant and unrestrained is what Corbin said of us, of our ambling. It was a less than holy depiction, but one that seemed to characterize our looseness and fascination with what went on after dark, Saturday nights in particular, random as they were.

How they began was the way they always began—with a lie: Bobby telling Olin and Gracie he was staying the night with me, and me telling Mary Olive I was staying the night with Bobby. It was the oldest ruse known to mankind, but simple enough to work if not overdone. And, so, with deception as our keystone, we rambled from Lower Fork and Helmer Bilbry's barn lot, where cock fighters assembled from as far away as Prestonsburg, to Gardner Fork and Hurley Sloan's front porch, where banjos and guitars, fiddles and mandolins rang throughout most of the night; from the flat above the schoolhouse, where poker was as refined as it was deadly, to Angus Walker's pool hall where only the barest minimums were left to the imagination; and from Homer Lawson's barn at the mouth of Joe Bonner Hollow, where anybody with a quarter could go five minutes with Homer in a winner-take-all, bare-knuckle-knockdown; to any number of houses up and down the creek where friends and kin smoked and sipped and shared the memories of loves lost and true ... and all the while with Bobby ducking in one thicket after another to magically appear minutes later with pint bottles of Corbin's corn liquor—what Bobby called *a fifty cent ride on the joy train*. It was Saturday night in the mountains, a time to escape the weightiness of life as much as to celebrate it. But either was enough.

Eight

Occupation of Choice

Shop Branch Hollow is where Dixie Wainwright lived, nearly a mile up the road from Bobby. But where Bobby lived at the mouth of Big Will Hollow, Dixie lived all the way in the head of Shop Branch, a good half mile from where it turned off of Gardner Fork. Two hollows separated by a single ridge and a high point called Ripley Knob. Except for the footpath that followed Shop Branch's creek, Dixie's cabin sat disconnected from even the most inquiring. She lived there with her younger half brother and sister, Franklin and Fayella (twins); her somewhat befuddled and bewildered mother, Emmaline, and a man named Haman Flowers whom she called her stepdaddy—though no one ever remembers Haman and Emmaline ever marrying.

So childlike was Emmaline that she was an object of pity for most. Though for a few, her being addle-pated meant that she was an object of caution, someone who might have been touched by the devil, a notion not all that far removed when considering Haman Flowers. The one twin, Fayella, was rumored to be like Emmaline, though a might more feral, even at nine years old. Haman, by all accounts, was the devil himself, an incarnate spirit of sin rolled up under the same hat. He never did gainful work of any note, nor, as far as anybody could tell, ever intended to. He kept to himself mostly: hunted, kept a garden, raised goats, made liquor and stole what he could on nights without a moon.

There were any number of men on the creek who made liquor, most for their own pleasure. It was their corn and, by God, theirs to consume anyway they saw fit. Some sold a quart or two here and there, but never enough to mount a threat to those who worked it for profit: men like Corbin Fairchild and Haman Flowers.

Corbin Fairchild was the son of a prominent Pikeville wholesaler, lean and courtly looking, always smelling of hair oil and aftershave, and with a manner similar to his talk: unhurried, as ingratiating as his handshake and as polished as the shine on his shoes. He was only half-a-head taller than Bobby and me, but with a presence that seemed to cast a much bigger shadow.

Haman Flowers, on the other hand, was someone who had been drawn to the coalfields of Greezy Creek. Not to work them, but to offer his mix of moonshine as his stock in trade. Haman knew as well as any man the vulnerabilities and characteristics of hard-working miners with paydays coming at the end of each week. With the understanding that there would always be a demand for moonshine, the only thing Haman needed were those with enough money to pay for it, whether they could afford it or not.

Starting in the early twenties, with Greezy's abundant coalfields and its mines operating round the clock, Haman could be assured of a ready clientele for years to come. With Greezy's vast mountain wilderness as a backdrop, he had about as natural a base camp as he could hope for. Deep seclusion lent itself to such men. Add to that his willingness to help settle grudges—to hire himself out to anybody with money as big as their hatred—and Greezy became a place he readily embraced as home.

If there was a commonality to be found between Haman and Corbin, it was the weakness they shared for the taste and effect of what they made. Liquor held them both in a grip as fervent as it was diabolical. Neither was apologetic for it, nor saw any reason to be. But where Corbin was compromising and favorable in countenance, seeing the world often through the eyes of a poet, Haman only knew what was black and white and what made life coon mean.

Most of Bobby's accounts of Corbin were firsthand and what was passed along by his mother, Gracie. It was no secret that Corbin was inclined toward drink even as a young man, but never enough to diminish his worthiness as a scholar. And it was only after the demise of the family business during the depression that he was forced to return home from Charlottesville and the University of Virginia. "He was purt' near a lawyer," Bobby said. "Didn't have but a year to go. But when the money run out, and him drinkin' more'n he was eatin', he just come on home."

Corbin was witness to his family's ruin, but even in the aftermath never lost sight of his raisings: that part of him that was tuned to the fabric of the mountains. "I saw it as a choice," Corbin told us. "I could either choose to waste away in regret like my daddy, turn ugly just for the grave, or get smart in the ways of lending institutions: institutions that take, under the guise of a helping hand, from them that got, and even from them that don't. Losing everything the way Daddy did was a lesson in hunger, but I soon found that hunger teaches better than anything else. I come home broke, but with a whole new take on *commerce*."

Haman Flowers never pretended book smarts, or anything remotely similar. To him, life was what a man could endure, what he could wrench from the land, and what he was willing to risk when it came to the law. Outside of that, Haman did what came naturally—which was *unnatural* for most—and never letting himself miss out on what disadvantages might befall his neighbor. It was life, after all, and none of it worth the aggravation that comes from trying to make it *fair*. What mattered was being postured to take hold of what each day might bring: things that separated the survivors from those on a slow-march to the cemetery. It was all a matter of fate to Haman, the only variable being degrees of debauchery.

From our very first meeting, I saw Corbin Fairchild as more poised than postured, his bearing more genteel than the hard-rock mountains that framed his world. And though he was as much a part of the heat and dust that menaced in endless profusion on Greezy's valley floor, he never failed to look like he'd been scrubbed clean, pressed and gathered in all the right places.

On the contrary, Haman was about as greasy as fresh killed hog—and twice as likely to stay that way. His tobacco-colored teeth and the sweat stain around the rim of his wilted brown fedora were in perfect harmony with the grit and grime that filled the wrinkles in his face. His diseased-looking shirt and trousers, and the perpetual stubble that shaded his jawbone made him look a lot like a dog with the mange.

Were it not for its inherent dangers of prosecution under federal law and the eminent threat of death, moonshining would have easily out-distanced all else as Greezy's occupation of choice. Its profits were tax exempt, its distillation and distribution void of regulations, and its market price wittingly below store-bought varieties, what everybody called *red liquor.* There was no paperwork, no financial report, nothing to trace where you had been or what you were planning to do next. It was clean: in the front, out the back. Cash and carry. Thank you and good night.

For most, making moonshine was not so much a question of morality as rightful ownership, but it was the selling that marked the divide. Just the label alone, *bootlegger,* marshaled condemnation from family and neighbors alike, and carried with it a disposition to disassociate. But Corbin Fairchild never let the stigma of what others might think deter him, never let issues of morality cloud what he clearly saw as too much government intervention in the first place. His was an uncomplicated, one-man consortium of supply and demand. Nothing more. From the sheriff to many of the Old Primitive Baptists, moonshine liquor was a thing most sought after. Always had been, always would be ... and his turning his back on it would have been tantamount to neglect, to say nothing of inept business practice. And even though bootlegging never carried the air of refinement that encircled Corbin, it did provide him with a formidable independence. Where he considered government taxation a subtle derivative of thieving, his business ethic was never painted with the same brush, his handshake functioning as his unswerving bond. "I reckon bootleggin' ain't as easy as ever'body makes it out to be," he once told me. "If it was, I'm guessin' ever'body'd be doing it. Never thought of myself as quite the *type*, but seems I was wrong. Circumstances have a way of altering even the most noble intentions."

Though it was hard to think of Corbin and Haman as being in anyway similar, they were, in the narrowest sense, akin: both willing to risk dire consequences for a high-stakes piece of the pie. But where Corbin was resolved to partnerships and the grand swell of influence, Haman was more about the here and now, and for letting the big dogs eat the little ones. Haman's stake was greed without a plan except to make it through the day and then the night by whatever means. It was simply what he knew.

Nine

Kentucky Moon

The first step to making bootleg liquor (*Moonshine, Mad Dog, White Lightening, Mountain Dew, Scat, Stump* ... its delineations inexhaustible) is finding *just the right place* to make it. The most ideal is somewhere high up in the mountains, high enough that the fumes from distillation will rise and keep on rising, circumventing any telltale traces that might be carried on the wind; a place where spring water runs cool and clear; clear enough so as not to foul the mash, and cool enough so that when it pours over the worm (the still's long corkscrew downspout) it can quick-cool the still's alcoholic vapors into liquid. And it has to be a place that can be secured, a place just out-of-bounds enough to keep sensible folk from drawing nigh, a place that can be camouflaged—and where dogs and trip wires can be positioned to warn of intruders hundreds of yards away. Location is preeminent, the first and most crucial step to any successful operation.

The principle is simple enough: boil a fermented concoction of sprouted corn, corn syrup, sugar, yeast, and water; trap its vapor and cool it to where it condenses into liquid.

The process begins by converting the starch of the grain into sugar. This is done by sprouting the corn: soaking shelled kernels in water for a couple days, then spreading them out to dry until the kernels sprout, about three days for two-inch sprouts. The sprouted corn is then ground into meal and stirred together with a measured amount of sugar and yeast and scalding water. The result is mash, though Corbin's recipe calls for adding corn malt to the mash for a more pronounced corn flavor. It's only fair to mention that there are many and varied combinations to making mash: personal *add-ins* that lend certain flavors, smoothness, and bite—most of them family recipes guarded with the utmost secrecy—that render it *unique*. The mash is then covered, kept at room temperature and left to *work* (ferment) for about four days, until it stops bubbling and gurgling, and a white cap forms over its surface. Once the white cap begins to separate, the fermentation process is complete. The mash (sometimes called *beer* or *wash*) is then poured into the still's cooker and boiled to burn off the alcohol, its rising vapors captured in the still's cap, then channeled into the arm and finally into a coiled tube called the worm. By running cool water over the worm, the vapor condenses into liquid: *moonshine*. All in all, a process simple enough, but impossible without the rudiments of a still.

Like most things hewn from the mountains, stills are simple by necessity. Though their design varies from one mountain to the next, they are, in total, distilleries with four main parts: cooker, cap, arm, and worm ... and each easy enough to forge by even middling blacksmiths.

The cooker is a copper tub, variable in size, but typically holding anywhere from fifty to a hundred gallons, and with a rounded or cone-shaped lid. The lid has about a nine-inch diameter hole in its center to allow rising vapors to escape. *The cap is* a copper pot that sits atop the lid. It has about a nine-inch diameter hole in its bottom, which aligns with the nine-inch hole in the cooker's lid; it also has a hole in its side to accommodate the arm. The cap serves to collect the rising vapor and also as a safety valve in the event of excess heat build up. *The arm* is a length of copper tube, about four or five inches in diameter on one end and tapering down to about one or two inches on the other. The large end is soldered in place over the hole in the side of the cap and serves to channel the vapors away from the cap and into the worm. *The worm* is a coiled piece of copper tube anywhere from a half inch to one inch in diameter, and usually running about ten feet long, that is soldered to the tapered end of the arm. It is in the worm that the vapors are cooled and condensed into liquid. The cooling is achieved by keeping all but the tip of the worm submerged in cold water, or by channeling cold water over it. The resulting condensation is pure, straight-up alcohol (Kentucky Moon), which trickles out the end of the worm into waiting jars.

If there is anything that gives shiners away, it's the smoke from the fire they keep under the cooker. The smell of burning wood is common in the mountains seeing as how everybody uses it to cook and heat. But smoke far from cabins has the promptings of suspicion. Hardwoods (hickory, ash, oak and birch) offer the best solution. When cured, they not only burn hotter and longer, but cleaner, with the least amount of smoke.

U.J. and Don'l Mac did the stilling for Corbin. Corbin was more about the business end, the distribution and the cash flow, which, in part, meant making sure Virgil Blair was properly taken care of—to the tune of two pints a week. It was a small price for never having to look over his shoulder.

With a finely tuned understanding of customer service, Corbin would see to it that one of his pint bottles be delivered for half a dollar, for almost anybody at any time. But it was his gallon jugs, and his hauling it to roadhouses and honkytonks up and down the Big Sandy River, even into Virginia, that paid him dividends coal miners could only dream of.

Haman Flowers, on the other hand, was the whole show. He was the factory, the warehouse, and the store; the maker, the bottler and the seller; the first, last, and only say in how it was done. The *whereabouts* of his still, however, was forever changing, meaning he was forever moving it from place to place to stay ahead of the law, and often to the very spot where revenuers, though rare, had last searched. It was a tactic that decreased his chances of being caught, but did nothing for the quality of his liquor. It was simply not of the same caliber as Corbin Fairchild's. It was whiskey made mostly from sugar, and without the crystal clarity or the bead that signals purity of distillation, without the misty-smooth bite that follows an effortless slide across the tongue. But he sold his pint jars for a dime less than Corbin, and that made him viable in the eyes of coal miners working for four dollars a day.

Most of the liquor Haman made, he sold to miners on payday, taking it to them in a gunny sack strapped across the back of his mule. He waited for them in The Camps and in out-of-the-way places up and down the creek, in the turns of the road and out of sight of women, children, and Old Regular Baptists. They were places where he could scan the landscape—before and after transactions—as if Virgil Blair or anyone else hadn't the slightest idea what he was doing.

As Deputy Sheriff, Virgil Blair knew he couldn't very well arrest Haman without doing the same to Corbin. And he couldn't very well arrest Corbin since it was Corbin who padded his paycheck and kept him supplied with pint bottles of Kentucky Moon week after week. So, like he did with so many things, Virgil just turned a blind eye. To Virgil, the idea of bringing the law to bear on Corbin and Haman was as senseless as it was useless. He knew everybody on the creek to a man, and knew that they were going to have their liquor one way or the other, whether he stood in their way or not. So he let them be. The dime difference in price, though, was something he knew to be a taut knot on the inside of Corbin, one that grew bigger by the day, and something Corbin considered a little more than friendly competition.

Other than Friday and Saturday nights, Haman showed himself so seldom that we never thought much about him except when people would send for him to come shoot their dogs, or to do some other dreaded task that tormented men's souls. I suppose there were times when we needed men like Haman Flowers, but it seemed they were so few and far between that it hardly justified the space they took up or the air they breathed. Mary Olive was of the same mind, and on more than one occasion stood on the porch and shot blindly into the dark when she believed it was Haman Flowers out there lurking in the weeds. "I know it's him," she'd say. "It's the onliest times ol' Jess won't settle. One a' these days the Lord'll do us awl a favor and let me put a hole in him!" Those were nights when I swore she never slept, just sat there rocking and pulling gently on her pipe long after the night's hush had descended and the soft rush of the creek lulled me into the nightly memories of Momma and Daddy, and my thoughts of the long and endless days ahead without them.

Ten

Interminable Intermingling

Franklin and Fayella came five years after Dixie, and by the time they were two, pretty much Dixie's to raise. Dixie also had two older brothers: Joncy, who worked the coalmines and lived in one of the camp houses some twenty miles away at a place called Henry Clay, and Augustine (Aug) who lived just a short walk over the mountain in Winston's Creek. Aug didn't have a feel for the mines so, he made do with the back-break of logging and the noise of its sawmills. Dixie also had an older sister, Hazel, who left home when she was thirteen, shortly after Haman arrived. Talk had it that she went to live with her grandmother in Virginia, somewhere in Buchanan County near the town of Grundy. Why, nobody knew for sure, but there were rumors, most of which were indictments against Haman and what a man in his lowest state would stoop to. But they were only rumors.

I came to know more than I ever wanted about Dixie's family through Mary Olive and Bobby. What one didn't know, the other did, or at least claimed as much. Their accounts of poor Emmaline and the speculations about who fathered what child, were as far reaching as they were incriminating. Mary Olive recognized it mostly as gossip, but also saw it as having a kernel of truth, and that for her was enough. She claimed that there was right cause to know about your neighbor's lineage, survival being at the core of it. She reckoned if anyone could be established as kin, then it, straightaway, established a line of loyalty. That's why it was commonplace to explore a person's genealogy upon first meetings. Bloodlines were essential to understanding a person's nature and character. Inquiring about a person's background, where they were from and who their momma and daddy were, provided a lot of answers about who one was talking to and what they stood for. Mary Olive was an endless source of who belonged to who and who didn't; who so-and-so's real daddy was, who was whose half-brother or sister and by whom; and who were first, second and third cousins, double cousins, and third cousins thrice removed. Most of it was near impossible to untangle. The overlap and backlash of interminable intermingling had left one generation after another swinging precariously on a multitude of branches from an altogether embarrassment of trees. To sort through it with an eye toward honest resolution would have taxed even the most forgiving. For us, though, it was a subject that brought us round after round of laughter despite Mary Olive's daughter, Seriann, having spawned a whole generation of like and kind.

What I didn't know about Seriann, Mary Olive was all too willing to tell. It seemed to be one of the things she did best: recount what most were willing to concede to time. They were accounts that took her from sorrowful and weepy to cackling and bending double with laughter; from angry enough to bite through the stem of her pipe to being joyful enough to keep me wide-eyed and waiting for each word and each one thereafter. And though there were lines she wouldn't cross, where her stories came to an abrupt halt, there were never any such boundries with Bobby.

By the time Seriann was old enough to be thought of as womanly, Mary Olive said the home place took on the look of a boarding house for men. "The high-hatted and high-booted, every known shape and size of gravy-eatin', coal diggin', whiskey-smellin' hillbilly that ever treaded mud," was the way she put it. Such a profusion of man-traffic coming and going out of every door and window, and at all hours of the day and night, that Mary Olive finally found relief when one of them carried Seriann off to Virgil Blair who also served as Justice of the Peace.

Within a year of Seriann marrying and leaving home, she was back with no more than what she'd taken with her—with the exception of a baby, that is. Baby Woodrow. About the time Woodrow was born, Seriann's husband decided that riding the rails was preferable to her volatility, in particular her quickness to put a butcher knife to his throat at the least altercation. So, her moving back home became as prudent as it was necessary. With no money, there was simply nowhere else to go.

Despite Woodrow, the man-traffic once again became a thing of reckoning. A woman with a baby and without a man made courting an altogether serious game, the stakes sparked by the most virulent heat. But it was almost two years before she was again carted away, and just eight months after that before she gave life to Wilma Lee. This time, though, she stayed gone a good three years before she wound her way back. Seems that over the years she'd held her husband at gunpoint about as often as the wind changed direction, and even once doused him with hot grease. But it was when she threatened to cut his head off and throw it down the well, that he finally put her out, but not before she hit him over the head with an iron skillet while he was sleeping. *Divorce* had finally come to the mountains.

According to Mary Olive, Seriann was only home about six months before some brogan-wearing, tobacco-chewing, half-wit took her and her two young'ns to live somewhere clear the other side of Wolf Pit Mountain, in a place called Marrowbone. And it was barely nine months after that that she pushed out her third: Wilson. This time, though, coming back home didn't take but a month and not much more than the effort to walk six miles of bad road with a new born in her arms and Woodrow leading Wilma Lee, her taking four steps to each one of his. By the time she wound her way back, Mary Olive said she was just about half alive, her old man having beat and choked her nearly half to death just the day before. Not to be outdone, she took his twelve-gauge and shot out all the windows in the house and blew a big hole in the front door right before she left. She said it was her way of saying goodbye to the no-working, pig-eyed, sonofabitch. The men and women of the mountains can, at times, veer wildly off course when there is no one to restrain them. Virgil Blair said as long as there wasn't anybody killed, it was just another matter of a man and his old woman getting into it. That was about it. Nothing the law should have to contend with.

Seriann stayed home close to five years this time before she gave birth to Sherman, her fourth. She gave Sherman her maiden name, determined to keep the father's identity a secret, but for whose benefit no one could figure. It was shortly after Sherman was born, that she took it on herself to move into an old log house that was partly burned but patched and gone-over enough so that it shed most of the rain and blocked a fair share of the wind.

The rent was two dollars a month. Nobody in the family knew how she was even going to buy food, much less manage two dollars a month for rent. It was rumored that certain members of the family, the few who were better off than most, were especially sympathetic to her children. There was also rumor that Wilma Lee's daddy was not above a charitable hand now and again so long as he wouldn't be held to a regular accounting. Then, too, it was said that Seriann may have been hungry enough to accept a dollar or two, here and there, from those with whom she kept company, gentlemen types. And in the light of even more rumor, *tolerable sums*—though not often enough—from Little Sherman's daddy, mystery that he was.

The move into the log house lasted about as long as anybody expected. Staying solvent and ahead of the rent was not always easy, and often meant moving before being asked to. As a result, Seriann moved so often and lived in so many out-of-the-way places, that it was hard to keep track of her from one season to the next. Considering how often she changed houses, it was amazing how she never got beyond a six-mile radius of where she was born and raised. Just as amazing was the endless assortment of hovels that attracted her. They were either strung along riverbanks or crowding the shoulders of dusty dirt roads, and either in danger of being washed away in heavy rains or being forever buried under clouds of coal dust from an endless stream of rail cars. And even though her nomadic ramblings were as emotionally trying as they were physically exhausting, the family was never without empathy, and always there with enough gumption to get her out of one place and into another—and always before the hand of the law closed in around her. But after years of helping her, to the tune of eight or nine times, and always with the same old borrowed mule, Cousin Truman became committed to getting her settled once and for all, even if it meant bearing the full burden of the cost. He needed the peace. He reckoned if he gave her enough money for some little place or other, the rest of the family could help her make it tight and warm enough for living. As it worked out, Cousin Truman knew Eulis Meeks, who was a friend of Vernon Posey, who was a neighbor of Keenis Burtran who happened to own some ramshackle shanty his daddy had deeded him in a place up the river called Millard. Keenis let it be known that his house being *for sale* was just a figure of speech since he was practically giving it away.

"It's up the river apiece," Keenis said. "It ain't much, but don't reckon Seriann needs a whole lot." Keenis fancied himself a born wheeler-dealer, though he'd never traded for a thing in his entire life except his buttermilk-and-cornbread dinner for a bone-handled pocketknife when he was twelve. "Sets just on the upper side a town, on a little flat down over the bank," Keenus said. "White-washed with a big ol porch, a good well, an' a fresh-dug toilet. It'll be there long after we're gone; you can count on that. Reckon I could let her have it fer a hunerd dollars." It had been a handshake and a done deal, but not before Truman had shamed him down to eighty-five. That was just about twelve hours before a big summer rain washed the stilts out from under it and sent it crashing into a thousand pieces under Millard's big iron bridge.

Fortunately for Truman and Seriann, there hadn't yet been an exchange of money or a deed. As it turned out, they were both spared the humiliation of being the first and only ones ever swindled by Keenis Burtran. But that just about convinced Truman, once and for all, that anything having to do with Seriann was near to snake bit and would only bring misery on anybody thinking they could make it otherwise.

But these were only bits and pieces of stories from Mary Olive and Bobby; stories I had put together from the muted whisperings of Cousin Truman, and even from those deep into the clear mountain runoff of Corbin Fairchild's corn liquor. Still, Seriann's was a story that seemed to coalesce into a mosaic of unpredictability and danger, yet one that lingered in the mysteries and uncertainties, even cruelties, of romance.

Eleven

Witches, Brews, Hexes and Spells

Canning what we pulled from the garden was a dreaded chore—even hateful—even with the added hands of Lorali, with her knack and unalterable smile. Yet, even with her help, *putting up* came with its own special drudgery: the scalding water, the briny solutions, the pungent smells, the lifting and straining, the fires and the steam and the burns. From June through October, there was the constant attention to whatever came in (became ripe). Even then, it was never any less confusing about exactly *when* to pick, or by *whom*. It was bad enough trying to figure out when to plant: sometimes by a new moon, sometimes by an old one; sometimes in the wax, sometimes in the wane; never before the first equinox (except for peas) and never after the first day of summer (except for turnips and collard greens); always in conjunction with the *signs*, the almanac and the seed catalog, and never with a lack of forgiveness in your heart. The conditions were endless, and Mary Olive knew them all, abiding by them as surely as if they were Scripture.

But just as in planting, there were omens for harvesting: never by a woman *in her time*, or by anyone with a headache or a feeling of vexation; never on the day after a rooster had crowed during the night, and never if a crow was seen perched above the outhouse door; never if a caterpillar left a trail across your porch, and never if a preacher appeared in your dreams the night before; never if you found a bird's nest robbed, and never if the wind blew open the pages of the Bible. We had to be on constant alert. There were any number of signs that could spoil a whole season's growth, and we knew it was better to satisfy the conditions of specters and spirits than to risk the consequences. There was evil in the nether world, and the best defense was knowing what to do when it came a-knocking. Because of those who had gone before us—those special few who had been allowed a glimpse into the *dark and foreboding*—we were prepared for just such mischief. Some of it could be warded off by doing such things as laying five sticks in the shape of wagon spokes inside a circle drawn on the ground; or tying a knot in the corner of an apron, then taking ten steps backwards and turning around three times while holding your breath; or by spitting on a flat rock and burying it wet-side down. There were any number of rituals to protect us, and we embraced them all as a way of warding off inevitable doom. We planted and harvested by them; courted, married and conceived by them; bought and sold, and even hunted and butchered by them. What our forbearers brought from the British Isles, along with what we inherited from the Cherokees, made us a distillation of legends and lore, discovery and adaptation, witches and brews, hexes and spells—the DNA of Kentucky's primitive frontier. And yet it lingered with the fullness of truth, and it was our *believing it* that made it so.

The mountains never failed to add to our larder. They were alive with persimmons and papaws and haws (hawthorns); apples and walnuts and grapes; watercress and mint and the boundless profusion of berries, things free for the taking provided we could get to them ahead of the neighbors, the birds, and the bears.

"I'd go a-berryin'," is pretty much how Mary Olive would start, "if I knew these old legs would hold me." From there she would lapse into quiet while she studied her feet, waiting for my sense of duty to an old woman to take hold, which never took all that long.

I went without quarrel, and with ol' Jess to help ward off snakes. Little good it did today seeing as how he struck a track—a fox?, a coon?—and peeled off on a dead run before I even came to the shoulder of the mountain. But then what did I expect after he'd lazed in the porch shade for days—and now with energy to burn?

It was about midday with a white-hot sun, an early July full of chiggers and dry to the point of prickly. My shoulders ached from holding the water bucket I'd picked nearly full, still I was leaning as far as I could into a devilish tangle of prickers, desperate to get at berries big as my thumb, when the all-too familiar and paralyzing rattle of a diamondback froze me.

Details get fuzzy when life and death conjoin, but in a single moment, in a void with as much black as white, I sent the bucket of berries in the direction of the rattle and flung myself back and away without a second's thought to the near vertical slope behind me—one steep as a mule's face and a good two hundred feet to its bottom.

It was a downward spiral. Down and down I went, pitching and plummeting, the ground bashing and thumping the breath right out of me; stumps and roots rising to meet me and flying past me in flashes of color and light; weeds and brambles and briars cutting and tearing at me until I lay crushed under my own weight, blurred and blinded in the cold hard mud at the foot of the mountain.

I lay prone, unable to move and not knowing if I was dead or if there were parts of me missing. The only thing that registered was the pain knifing through my neck and back and ribs—all the way into my arm that lay pinned beneath me. There were no sounds, only my garbled breaths, and there was no light. My temples throbbed and my jaw lay open, loose, unhinged, and there was the taste of blood. Chances were I was broken in a hundred places, and I lay there, heavy and without the wherewithal to move. Spots, vivid and crimson, moved in slow circles behind my eyes and in tune with the wakefulness that kept coming and going. I was so heavy ... and the earth so cool. A stillness enfolded me, bathed me, held me lifeless against the earth's grave-like chill.

I knew it would be late in the day before Mary Olive missed me and came looking. But given the mountains and with summer on us, I knew that chance favored a copperhead finding me first. But then consciousness trickled to nothingness.

Sometime later, something like a hot poker between my ribs brought me back to the ranks of the living. All about me things were hushed and draped in sepia-colored light. I wanted to move, but couldn't. Wanted to shout, but was without the strength. What didn't burn, throbbed. What wasn't seared in pain lay dulled. And it hurt to breathe. Only fragments of lucidity, portioned and faint, filtered like mist. But then came the sound of footsteps, halting, cautious, the parting of brush, the smell of sweat and tobacco, of being lifted and the all-prevailing cruelty of pain and the last of consciousness.

I don't know how long I was there, outstretched alongside the outhouse, before Mary Olive found me, before she went to shouting and shooting in the air, bringing what Yonts' there were in the garden on a dead run. It was Bobby who reached me first, then Ben. I was awake, but just enough to know I was alive ... and only with the function of a rag doll.

The ring of faces staring down on me and the cold wet cloths daubing at the places raw and weeping is most of what I remember—that and Grandmaw hovering above me in the glare of a coal-oil lamp, sponging and patting, plying and slathering me in the headiness of boiled elder leaves and strained suet. She was gentle, silent, and as sure as her variant combinations of herbs and all that was mumbled and muffled in prayer. It had taken what light was left in the day and the senses of Cousin Truman and ol' Gert under a quarter moon to get her to me. After that, it was her certainty that rendered all that I needed.

"I knowed when I heard a whistlin' woman," said Mary Olive, her voice weighty and tinged with the tone of haints, "that there was a *evil* comin'. Middle a' the day an' that Alifair Whitley comin' down the road a-whistlin' like a circus parade. An' you know *evil* is just one letter away from *devil*."

"Am I all right?" I asked, my head in a fog, my tongue parched and lifeless, my lips cracked and swollen.

"Don't reckon yer outside a' fixin'," Grandmaw said, "or beyond what time can do." The trail of her pipe was familiar, comforting. "Right now you need to be real still and bite down on this here piece a hide. Put it way back in your mouth like a horse bit. That's it. Now steady y'self." In the next instant, someone thick and massive (Ben?) rolled me gently onto my side then hooked and held me under the arm.

"Bite," was the last thing I heard before pain tore through my arm like I'd been kicked by a mule. For a split second I blanked out, then, with veins bulging, cried out through clenched teeth until my arm was stretched and its crookedness made right for mending, and until I was reduced to whimpering and the blessedness of sleep.

I woke to cold wet cloths pressed to my temples and my left arm harnessed between four bands of flat wood and wrapped tight with rawhide. The morning and biggest part of the day came and went without me. By evening, my hair and pillow were soaked in sweat and I was warm with fever.

The night was fitful and the morning heaped in fresh misery. My right eye was swollen shut despite the apple poultice, and the left one so scratched and full of dirt that it hurt to blink. Still, I could make out different parts of me: some wrapped in cloth, but most looking like raw bacon glistening with grease. There were places that stung with liniment, and others that stunk like fresh-killed 'possum. Some places were bruised and blue, some puffed and inflamed—and there was the arm, as rigid as the barrel staves that held it.

"You ain't the purdiest sight," said Mary Olive, "an' Lord knows yer Grandmaw's got you perfumin' like a bull's ass, but right now you're 'bout as good as good gets. But, so help me, I don't know if 'at stink's a help or a hindrance. It's a wonder you ain't wantin' to jump up an' run away from yourself." Her rambling was low-key, and for several quiet minutes she went about touching me gentle-like and holding her mouth in a manner suggestive of deep concentration. "You know," she said, "yer grandmaw can fix ever'thang from a broken heart to a hole in the sky—but I b'lieve she's about to kill us all with pong. I do know it's making my eyes smart considerable." She grinned deep, amused at her own prattle, her own brand of comfort, as curing as salt was to hog meat.

Grandmaw packed garlic and vinegar plugs up my nose, laid a decoction of pennyroyal and onion juice over most of my joints and all that was black and blue, and soaked my fingers in something boiled from hawthorn berries to draw out the wood splinters driven up under my nails. Except for Mary Olive spoon-feeding me oat gruel, the constant in-and-out of family, friends, and neighbors—and the near impossible task of using the five-pound lard bucket Mary Olive purposed for a chamber pot—I rested in knotted quietness. But it was the third day, right after Grandmaw washed me, tapped me, poked me, swabbed and daubed me, plied me with combinations of skunk oil, bear grease and renderings of pork fat, rewrapped my chest and ribs with sheets torn in two and soaked in garlic juice and baking soda, and right after her mulish stance that I rinse my mouth with yellow root tea and then swallow it, that she left the way she came: in the wagon next to Cousin Truman.

For days, the house remained pungent with counterpoisons, and Mary Olive went about hanging stinging nettle to help ward off the flies. "Lord knows we'll need it," she said, "what with all this stench. Puts me in mind a' sauerkraut left in the sun." I was too pained to pay her much mind and drifted toward sleep as often as it would have me. Grandmaw being gone was a lonely note that played over and again, one that made me realize how much I missed her. And though there was acceptance and a sacred love with Mary Olive, the memories of Grandmaw and Momma and Daddy left me knowing once again how I missed being a part of something eternal.

I stayed stove up for four long days after Grandmaw left, unable to take deep breaths and struggling to maneuver around the chamber bucket. Through it all, Mary Olive was more agreeable than not, given that there was nothing *lasting* wrong with me—and despite my not being able to help her make preserves. Bobby came throughout the day, as always, and then again each evening to spend the night till I was able to fend for myself without having to catch my breath with each twist and turn. He always brought a deck of cards. It was just Bobby's way, and how Mary Olive and I came to learn seven-card stud.

We played for matchsticks. Still, the betting was fierce and ugly, as down and dirty as if each one had been a twenty-dollar gold piece. Mary Olive didn't have the slightest sense of poker or the nuances of betting, but came to a fair grasp of it after Bobby's relentless tutoring and continued badgering. The repetition that was so necessary for her understanding tutored me all the more.

For the games, Bobby always wore an old gray fedora with the front brim pinned straight up and with matches wedged behind his ears and in the corners or his mouth. It was the look of a cheap crook in some river town honkytonk with smoke as thick as early morning fog. He liked to keep one eye closed and his mouth at about a half yawn whenever he tried to back us down. Other times, he liked to drum his fingers on the table, close his eyes to just a sliver and roll a matchstick from one side of his mouth to the other. It was high drama in the shadow of a coal-oil lamp. They were practiced antics, things he had seen over and over on the flat behind the schoolhouse. But they were wasted on Mary Olive. She could never see him as anything but half crazy, and it was never very long before she'd commence to tittering and snorting ... enough to shatter Bobby's whole persona.

"Pot's right." Bobby was a commander when he dealt, announcing what-was-what at all times. "Cards!" he said out the side of his mouth just before dealing the first two face-down. "Up to you Molly." He called Mary Olive "*Molly*" when she played cards. She grinned whenever he said it. Said it made her feel like a dance hall floozy: all blushed on the inside.

"I fold," she said.

"FOLD? You can't *fold*! The game hasn't even started yet!"

"Well, I'm folding. I ain't got a pair."

"You've only been dealt *two cards*. You ain't *supposed* to get a pair every time you get two cards."

"Well how am I supposed to win?"

"I'll be dealing five more cards. Remember?"

"OK. I don't fold."

"Well, if you're not folding, you have to check or bet."

"Checkerbet? What's checkerbet?"

"Check *or* bet. *Pass or make a wager.*"

"Well I ain't got nothing but a two and a five."

"YOU CAN'T BE TELLIN' WHATCHA GOT. *You can't win if erbody knows whatcha got.*"

"Well, give me two more then."

"Two *more?*"

"In place a what I got."

"That ain't how it works, Miss Molly. Poker's like life. You gotta play the hand yer dealt."

"But you'ns know what I got."

"I can't help it if you told us."

"Well then tell me what *you* got. Make it fair for ever'body."

"Lordy!" Bobby let out a big breath. "Let's start over."

And so it went, hand after hand, night after night, Mary Olive going all bug-eyed and daring us to bet whenever she had a good hand ... and pouting like we had purposely ganged up on her when she got a bad one. Her face was an ongoing symposium of confusion, dismay, defiance and wonder. It was impossible not to know what she had, and hard to watch her without wanting to accuse her of trying to cheat. At first, her cheating was covered over in innocence, not being familiar with the rules. Then, after a time, it was simply 'If ye ain't cheatin' ye ain't tryin'. But poker was what we did in the wake of my healing and for the sake of sanity, and arguably, a hint of love. But I saw it as more. I saw it as Bobby's very own hobbyhorse, and what made him believe he was born to ride it at full gallop. I saw it in his fourteen-year-old eyes, in the blister of his passion and the way it filled a room. But it was only a trace of all that churned within him, and only a hint of what lay at his core. I understood it only as something that rallied him. What I couldn't know is that it was a precursor of things to come.

We played every night for nearly a week, right up till Mary Olive began to take on a polished lacquer for checking and betting; till the matches, with stinging regularity, began accumulating in ever-increasing piles on her side of the table, and her poker face became as natural as her rustling up a pone a bread. Bobby and I didn't have anything to say after our last hand that last night. We just sat digging at our molars with broom straws while she counted her matches ... one by one.

Twelve

As Far As Suspicion Would Allow

None of us could figure how I, after being so busted up and plummeting so far, came to be resting against the outhouse. The sound of that rattler and then falling backwards was the bulk of what I remembered—that and clawing to grab hold of something, anything, to save myself. The rest was fogged, even my waking.

All the faces I loved and cared for were hovered together, cringed and squinted, trying to make sense of it. I tried recounting till my brain seemed to swell, but nothing more ever came. "Seems there was sump'm," I said, "but I can't be sure. Just things like a dim light through a web, an' a feelin' like I was floatin'. And there was some smell or other. Like Daddy, but sour."

"Reckon you had just enough in you to get up and get to the outhouse." Mary Olive wanted it to be simple. "Headed up adder that, I'd say. Just give out soon's you hit flat ground." All were nodding except for Bobby.

"Ain't likely," Bobby said. "He ain't walked for days as it is. He couldn't a' come outta there on his own, 'less he laid down and rolled out."

"You sayin' somebody packed me out?"

"Alls I'm saying is, if you'd a' walked out, you'd shore as hell remember it. Pain's a strong reminder."

"Don't reckon somebody'd pack me out then leave me."

"Would if they didn't want it known."

Try as I might, from one day to the next, I couldn't get beyond the void left from blacking out. How I got to the outhouse would, at least for the time, remain a mystery, but only as far as suspicion would allow.

It had been a week and still no sign of ol' Jess. Cousin Truman said it was likely he'd run himself clear into another county, and just as likely that he got hungry enough to humble himself at somebody's backdoor. "Somebody's got him put up," he said, "an' they'll keep him till we get there. Word of a found dog travels fast amongst hunters. We'll know in due time."

Cousin Truman was the most likely of the family to strike a positive note even when prospects were bleak. We held him up as a yardstick against things worth measuring and when we needed suggestions of things holy, right, and good. He lived with his wife, Inez, and their four daughters on the right-hand branch of Main Fork, near its head, where the road narrowed and gradually disappeared into wilderness. Odd as it was, he was four miles (following the angling twists of Greezy's mud roads) from Mary Olive's and four miles (as the crow flies) from Grandmaw's.

Truman used to come around every now and again when Momma and Daddy were still alive, always with a cooker of beans when times were tough, and always with a prayer even when we couldn't appreciate it. A jack-of-all-trades, Truman was, doing what most only wished they could. So handy at things, he never had to rely on the mines for a living. Outside of farming (everybody was a farmer), he prided himself as a diviner, cooper, casket maker, and wheelwright; he shoed horses, dug wells and graves, cut timber and hair, and about every third month found his way to the Old Primitive Baptist Church House. Even though he was my great uncle, he insisted on being called Cousin Truman—not only by me, but by everybody, and made it the first order of business whenever he made a new acquaintance. He saw it as his way of *connecting*, of being a part of everyone outside of family. *Cousin* rolled off everybody's tongue as if it was his first name. *Brother* Truman, he believed, was too invasive, its religious undertone more hindrance than help to kinships. Besides, *Brother* Truman was reserved for the Old Primitive Baptists, the brethren who knew him as a devout and dedicated vessel. Truman saw us all as a part of God's family. And even though the Primitive Baptists were not always tolerant of those who weren't, there was something about Cousin Truman that separated him from the common fold.

After I went to Mary Olive's, Truman came around every week, sometimes twice, with fresh eggs and milk, a generosity that never waned. Most times, he came early mornings and stayed till there was just enough light to get home. I thought he was more generous than most considering all the work Mary Olive needed done. And though he spent considerable time shaking his head and mumbling under his breath at the falling-to-pieces shape most everything was in, it was just being alongside him that I came to treasure. From his leathered hands to the smell of his sweat, the sense of him being close is what I clung to.

"You awright, son?" was always the first question he had for me after he hugged me real big. He asked it with that same tone and look Grandmaw had, the one that said he was ready to gather me up in his arms if I was anything other than fine.

"Yeah," was about all I ever said when he asked, though there were times I didn't mean it as much, and even times when I didn't mean it at all. It wasn't like lying, exactly, but something I did without thought, like yawning or waving a bee away from my face. I don't know that Truman was ever fooled by it, but he did study me considerably at times, trying to see behind the blue there in my eyes, wanting to know things beyond my simple "Yeah."

Unlike Grandmaw, though, Truman liked to go on—from one subject to another, often without taking a breath—then, without warning, pause to enjoy the hush. He was never hurried in the things he did, especially when it came to me. It was like he knew our time together held a far greater reward than the jobs we did for Mary Olive. And though I was likely to go chasing after a June bug right in the middle of us working on something, I came away from our times together knowing that *staying with it* was how things got done. There was aptness to Cousin Truman, to his lessons and labors. It was the stuff of men and he brought it to me. It was that way, off and on throughout the summer, right up until the time school started. I don't know that I was ever a help of any kind, but just being with him was its own reward. I couldn't help feeling it was the same for him.

For days on end, my mind was full of ol' Jess and how he might be trying to fight his way back; or how he might be laid open somewhere, gashed by a bear; or snake bit at the bottom of some pit; maybe even trapped on a rock cliff, thirsting and counting his breaths till I could find him. They were thoughts that claimed the biggest part of me until the morning I waded half asleep through the dew and past the crows on my way to the outhouse. It didn't register at first, just sort of blended with the mist and dew of day peep, it's black and brown in harmony with all that had yet been touched by the sun. But once I came near, it seemed to rise up out of the huckleberry like a grave marker, defiant and stone cold, and in the very place Mary Olive had found me. It was Grandmaw's .22.

Thirteen

Hard Times

Grandmaw came often in the weeks that followed to poke and prod my every part, to thump and tap, pinch and knead, and in general look me over like she would a pig at auction, till she was content that I would last another season. In between times, Cousin Truman was ever faithful with provisions assorted and otherwise. Sometimes he brought us a chicken, sometimes a slab of smoke-house meat; whatever he could spare and whatever he reckoned we needed. We never asked, nor did he. He just brought it, natural and without expecting anything for it. He also brought dresses and blouses, skirts and shirts to add to the pile Mary Olive took in for mending what time Lorali wasn't there. Bobby, though, came by everyday to draw water and chop wood, and do for Mary Olive what it took two able-bodied hands to do, the sum total of which never amounted to much more than an hour, but what he had his momma and daddy believing was the biggest part of the day.

Despite what Bobby told Olin and Gracie, we did little beyond the bare necessities. Mostly, we sat in the shade of the porch and with the warmth of July's blanket tucked in around us. It suited us just fine.

"Your momma must think I'm workin' you to death," Mary Olive said.

"Momma *thinks* a lotta things," Bobby said. "It's the *believin'* she aint real good at."

"I 'spect her believin' has a lot to do with what she gets told."

A sheepish smile thinned out across Bobby's lips. "I ain't sayin' I'm above doctorin' what gets told, but I ain't about to tell the straight-up truth when there's a chance of Momma takin' the top of my head off with a stick a stove wood."

Bobby seemed to radiate the sun, even in the shade. "You know," he said, "the truth ain't all there is to sump'm. I b'lieve it's more about interpretation: how we see somethin' an' the words we put to it, how we *give it body*. It ain't lyin' so much, but more about softenin' what we say." He thought for a minute, the light dancing in his eyes. "I mean what I have to say ain't always what people want to hear." His tone was playful, his smile almost at a laugh. "So either I say nothin' at all, which ain't never been my custom, or tease it to where it lingers like a taste a shine."

Mary Olive cackled right big and said, "I b'lieve, you'd rather tell a lie, Bobby Yonts, even when the truth would make you sound better."

Bobby laughed, tickled about the riddle he had become. "It's like a protection," he said, "against the harshness that comes from the truth. Bold-face truth can be a ruinous thang in the wrong mouth."

"Well, now," said Mary Olive, intensifying her rocking a tad, "if 'at's the case, how can we know when you *ain't* lyin'?"

"You can't," Bobby said. "And that's the truth."

We laughed at most of what Bobby said, truth or not. It was the ease with which he said it that made us want to believe it, even gravitate toward its high-flying potentials. It was the stuff of wonder and imagination that lifted us beyond all that was worn and weathered, what we embraced as life.

"What'r you plannin' on doin', little brother, after yer momma and daddy put you out?" Mary Olive enjoyed being a huckleberry to Bobby.

"Preach, I reckon."

"I'd say you and that Uncle Corbin a' your'n would make a couple good ones."

"Could be," said Bobby. "Pat'm on the back with one hand and sell'm whiskey with the other." He laughed, enjoying its near truth.

"I'd say you wouldn't be the first," said Mary Olive. "But, as long as you've brought it up, I'm b'lievin' you an' Corbin—Rubin, too, for that matter—need more a' what the Good Book has to give. It's a help in hard times, an' once you've lived as long as I have you'll know hard times ain't never that far off."

"I ain't figurin' on no hard times, Mary Olive, once I put in with Corbin."

"Ain't no getting' away from hard times, Bobby Yonts. Hard times is what these mountains is all about. They's sometimes better'n others, but it's a right livin' that keeps us in the hope of good times. That an' the Book. We're just in a wilderness without it."

"If it's anything a-tall," Bobby said, "the Book's got sump'm to say about it. Says so damned much it's hard to keep it all straight. Soon's you get one thang figured out, they's ten more to take it's place. Can't turn left 'less it's tellin' you turn right; can't sit less it calls it idle; can't give a hard thought to a purdy face 'less they's some black angel waitin' to suck out your soul. Keeps me afraid of what God put in me in the first place: things natural an' what we're all of a sudden supposed to turn away from. I ain't wantin' to turn away from none of it ... hard times or not."

"That's just the devil talkin'," Mary Olive said, a feeble breeze doing its best to stir what few tendrils of hair fell alongside her face. "But the one thing you gotta keep in mind is that he ain't never gonna leave you alone. You might as well get used to that. It's what he does; what he's here for: to keep you lookin' at what *you* are and not what *Jesus* is."

Bobby thought for a while before he said anything, his eyes seeming to search the air for what might tender a response. "Corbin says they's hope for even the lowliest sinner; that God's forgiveness reaches even beyond the grave."

Mary Olive gnawed gently at the stem of her pipe, enjoying it like she would a piece of horehound. "That Corbin's got a whole head full a sense," she said. "A knowin' man, he is. Deep minded. No question about it. An' I'm shore he's got the Book papered out just like he needs it ... just like the rest of us if truth be known. I don't know what's in store for us beyond the grave, Bobby, just that there's hard times an' sweat enough on this side of it."

The porch seemed hollow after Bobby left, its shadow lengthening toward the creek, an old brindled cat stretched out across its bottom step.

"Bobby looked quarreled," Mary Olive said. "Talk a' hard times don't set well with them bent on havin' it all. 'Course I can't blame him for wantin' it. Natural, I reckon. But then it's my learned belief that hard times is sump'm we'll never be rid of. Take 'at Haman Flowers an' all what goes on in that heart a' his. Now they's a hard time there. But, close as I can come to it, they's evil in there too. An' when they's childern to suffer, that's a evil worst of all. An' the Book tells us the Lord can't abide where evil is. Now that's the *A-Number One* hard time: bein' apart from the Lord. I ain't judgin' nobody, 'cause Lord knows I got enough to answer for, but there'll be a reckonin' if we can b'lieve what's wrote ... for each an' ever'one of us ... an' I'm b'lievin' it'll be a torment for Haman Flowers. But that's the Lord's to deal with, not mine."

The creak in Mary Olive's rocker and the snap of the green beans we broke and dropped into the big wash pan between us was all at once a comfort, in harmony with the shade and lull of the porch. She made listening easy, Mary Olive did, her manner ever-bending toward incantation, even mollifying the cat. We sat quieted by it all, the spill of the creek and the drone of honeybees adding to our thoughts of Jesus, The Bible, hard times and the devil.

"Momma used to say hard times was like a test a faith," I said, my voice amped in question.

She stopped and, just for a moment, watched the cat elongate itself, stretching to where its bones seemed to separate, its hair spiking in the way of straw. "Yer momma was a good woman," she said. "Better'n most. She knew a hard time and how it could bring you down if you let it. It's what we grew up knowing: holding tight to what little faith we had, trusting that things'd get better. Still, there were times when going hungry was enough to sweep faith right out the door. But then you don't quit on somethin when it's all you got." She paused and smacked her lips. "T'other side a' Tom Brown Rock is where we's raised: me and yer momma, yer grandmaw and Truman ... awl ten of us ... an' never knowin' a bite but what we didn't wrench from the ground, an' nothin' separatin' us from the grave 'cept will." She chuckled then knocked her pipe against the leg of her chair. "I don't mean to be tellin' it more'n what it was, but it was so thin sometimes we'd have to take an' eat us a apple for breakfast, then later that evenin' take us a big drink a water an' let that apple swell up so's we'd have sump'm for supper." She was never above laughing at what she said, even at the thought of hard times. "Whew," she said, wiping at the tears in her eyes. "But there was ten of us, which I don't know if it made it better or worse. There was more hands to do the work, but then a whole lot more work to do. Seen times when Daddy'd have six or more of us hitched up an' pullin' the plow. It was a pitiful sight, but it weren't nothin' when put next to bein' hungry. The thought a not eatin' can help a body decide real quick what it needs to do. It's more able than you think." She stopped, giving her memory time to reflect. "It's a miracle," she said, "how we all made it; how we did what we did when a whole lotta the time it meant doing without."

"You reckon that was a test of faith?"

"Reckon so," she said. "That way for most, though: hard an' hungry, The Good Book keepin' us stout, but most times so starved we'd want to boil it's cover an' eat it as to listen to what it said."

She stopped just long enough to pick a piece of tobacco off the tip of her tongue. "You needn't be puttin' thoughts a' hard times on yourself, little brother. The Book says the poor will be with us always. That means hard times'll be there too. It's just life, Rubin, and there ain't no changin' it 'cept what we do to ease one another's burden. We're headed where we come from; get what we give. It's really all that simple.

Fourteen

Always with a Fix on the Bible

Grandmaw said that whoever left the .22 by the outhouse knew it belonged to me and me to it. Its return, though, was rankled in mystery. Was it a gesture of neighborliness, returning what was rightfully mine without the trappings of a thank you or the sting of confrontation? Or was it to let me know that the mountains had eyes; that they not only knew who I was but where I slept.

Grandmaw came six weeks in a row, all of them balanced atop ol' Dan and following the wilderness ridge between Hopkins Fork and Poor Bottom. She never stayed longer than the time it took to tend me and eat what wonders we pulled from the garden. The last time, though, she stayed the night.

"Don't know why anybody'd want to come to Greezy on purpose," Mary Olive jibed.

Grandmaw said, "I'm just lookin' for a place where the livin' is easy an' the cook ain't mean."

"Well, honey," Mary Olive said, "If you ever find it, I'll give a gold tooth an' a pint jar a' pig's feet if you lead me to it."

Laughter was the all-purpose antidote for what ailed and even what didn't, as much a gift to share as it was to take the edge off things abysmal. It worked to both ends after Grandmaw finally took the staves off my arm and settled in.

"Me an' ol' Dan's about give out," Grandmaw said. "Him bein' nearly as old as I am, an' saggin' like a porch swing. Me fightin' to get on, then fightin' not to fall off. If we're gonna last, we'll be needin' help 'fore long."

"Come lately," said Mary Olive, "help's a thing in short supply 'round here, what with *old* and *one-armed* bein' the main of what we got."

"Not for long," said Grandmaw. "'Cept for bein' stiff an' sore, 'at arm a' Rubin's is 'bout as good as new. But I can't fix old. That's yours to deal with."

Mary Olive and Grandmaw stacked one on top of the other wouldn't be much taller than a gatepost and not much heavier than a bucket of beans, but when they were together and times were good, they were as tall as timber, and always with a fix on the Bible—as loose as their interpretations were want to be.

"I know the Lord ain't just about making me happy," Mary Olive said, "but I reckon He favored me with Rubin." She was eyeing me and swelling with an almost tangible gladness. "Been a blessin', him hepin' the way he does." She stopped long enough to give her pipe a pull. "He's a fine 'un, even with a broke arm. More will than most." I sat listening, not believing I'd done anything out of the ordinary, yet feeling like an apple shined.

"Don't reckon I ever stop studyin' 'bout him," she said. "Vexes me that he ain't never had much."

"Like the rest of us," mused Grandmaw.

"Honey, don't I know it. I was just hopin' life would a' been a little more generous by now."

"I'm b'lievin' it's exactly the way Lord God intended it. His perfect timin' in it all."

"Yea, Lord," said Mary Olive. "It's the foretaste of blessings, I reckon." She thought for a moment, eyes straight ahead, "I just can't give 'at boy what I want to, an' it sits contrary to what little peace I have."

"You can't give what you don't have."

"Yeah, but that don't take away the *want to*."

"You're puttin' too much on worldly treasures," Grandmaw said. "Things a' the world is the way they've always been, Mary Olive: the rich get richer and the poor get to watch. But you know the Book tells us the rich will weep and groan on that final day, that their riches will rot away."

"Still, we have needs."

"S'long's you don't let needin' turn to wantin'," Grandmaw said. "You know as well as the next that mankind is never satisfied ... always wanting more'n what he's got. Wants more even after he gets more. It's the wantin' that's the offense. The Book says it's not money that's the root of our undoin', but the *lust thereof*." Her voice rose right along with her upturned hand. It was a point that begged for praise.

"Pray me up, Sis," cackled Mary Olive.

"Same's true of drink I reckon. It hain't the drinking, but the drunkenness."

"AAAA- MEN!" said Mary Olive. And her half-pint bottle, like a silver star plucked from the sky, passed between them with the reverence given to a Sunday sermon.

"Don't reckon the Good Lord, shore an' certain, would deny us a taste a' liquor now an' again," said Mary Olive.

"No more'n what we could afford anyway," chuckled Grandmaw.

"Not a God who died for sin and sinner alike."

"Amen to that, sister!"

And again the bottle did a quick to and fro.

"You reckon there's hellfire 'tatched to takin' a drink?"

"Don't reckon," said Grandmaw. "Ain't no God in heaven nor nowhere else would burn the very childern he made for drinkin' the same wine he did. Hardly neighborly."

"Alls I know is He put the fire to'em when He got to Sodom and Gomorrah. Now that's a proof if it was ever known."

"'At's different," said Grandmaw. "'At was earthly punishment. 'Sides, 'at was afore the law. But now comes the grace a Jesus."

"AAAA-men to that, sister woman!"

"Zat sump'm yu'd drank to?"

"As God is my witness."

And the bottle was made known once again.

Their tasting was all telling: the delicate closing of the eyelids, the pursed lips and ginger-like pull from the upturned bottle, the immediate wide-eyed recognition of the fire-trail across the tongue and the "*ahhhhh-hhh*" that helped cool the hot coal sensation left in the back of the throat. Then there was the whispered "whewwww," the big-mouthed smile and a watery eye ... and always with the anticipation of the *next time*.

"You ever tell Rubin 'bout Dempsey?" Grandmaw said.

"He don't want to hear about no Dempsey."

"He might."

"Then *you* tell him."

"Ain't mine to tell. 'Sides, it's best comin' from you. Save it bein' miss-told an' you jumpin' in every other word to retell it."

Mary Olive eyed us both for a long moment, till she saw the readiness in my face. She shifted a bit, rocked and sniffed, then waited while Grandmaw relit her pipe. Then she reckoned aloud that they ought to have a little taste before she began. And the bottle was delivered up yet another time.

Mary Olive was slow to screw the cap back on, eyeing the bottle like it was something that needed ciphering. "Well," she said, settling back in her rocker, then pausing, waiting for something to register, to clear. "Remember me tellin' you 'bout Hollister McEuen?"

I nodded.

"Well, I married again," she said ... when I was near to thirty. It was to a man named Dempsey Compton." The mention of his name brought a smile to her face as broad as it was glad. "We's just together fer a year an' a half." Pain, lightning quick, dislodged the smile. "It was a shared love," she said, "uncomplicated enough to be healthy." We laughed at the irony then waited while she daubed at the corners of her eyes. "Flashy, he was, tall and purdy built. Face like an angel." Grandmaw grunted and shifted in her rocker. Mary Olive waited then said, "But he wasn't much for work ..."

"HA!" Grandmaw barked around the stem of her pipe. Mary Olive stopped while Grandmaw's eyes drifted to me then up toward the ceiling.

"You gonna let me tell this or what?" said Mary Olive.

Grandmaw wiped at her nose and said, "Go ahead on, honey. Cain't nobody tell it like you."

"But he was right smart about different thangs," Mary Olive said to me, but letting one eye take a bead on Grandmaw. "Y'might say he was more'n what most deputy sheriffs like to tolerate." I thought I heard something rattle within Grandmaw, but not enough to stall Mary Olive. "But he did awright by me. Put me in store-bought dresses an' nylon stockin's. Like he knowed what it was that pleasured. Lawd, he was a dandy. Brought me boxes a chocolates an' French step-ins the likes a' Greezy ain't never seen. Why, he even got me this here gold tooth and this here house. Bought 'em with cash money. Some say he bootlegged a might, but I never seen it, though he did brang a right smart of it home often enough. Me an' him got right fond of it adder while. Not enough to hurt us, but enough to make us forget what we couldn't otherwise." She paused and sat still for a while, her harkening of times and places resonating with a life of their own.

"Lawwww, honey," she went on, "he'd take me to Rocky Gap: wildest honkytonk on the face a' the earth, I reckon—least ways in these parts. But dangerous didn't mean nothing to Dempsey. Don't reckon I ever seed him scairt. Wasn't much for fightin', but he carried a little two-shot pistol in his pocket. Little bitty thang; fit right in the palm a' ye hand. I still got it. Show it to you sometime. Said he kept it for snakes, both kinds: the ones that crawled on their bellies and the ones that somehow learned to walk upright. I never saw him use it, but there were stories.

"That honkytonk was all anybody could handle," she said. "Sat right there at the mouth a Little Creek. We'd walk it. Only way we had to get there. Weren't but three mile, up Dry Fork to the top a' the hill, then over it and down into Stagger Fork. Just a short piece adder that. We'd wear old shoes an' carry our shiny ones. Then dance an' drank bathtub gin till daylight. 'At's what they called it: bathtub gin. Moonshine's what it was, pure Mountain Dew. Most times, we'd be the last ones to leave. Walk home watchin' the sun come up.

"The music was always loud at Rocky Gap, the smoke too thick and the drink too strong. But he loved it an' I loved him, so I'd go even when I didn't want to. It's just the way it was: we belongin' to each other the way we did, him lovin' me in a way that kept me knowin' he was all I needed. He shore was all I wanted. 'Cept for what times he was in and out of lockups over in Whitesburg an' Jackson for nothin' on earth 'cept rustlin' a few cattle, an' one time runnin' off with a church collection, he was the best young'un ever was. An' for that other time over in Frankfort when they accused him of robbin' a feed store, an' 'at one time for some little ol' shoot-out with a man over some misunderstandin' 'bout his wife, you couldn't find a better feller. Then there was all that talk about him runnin' 'round with Andrew Clemmons' daddy an' them holdin' up a freight train full of liquor." She paused long enough to shake her head as if trying to rid herself of the memories, then sighed real big and exchanged looks with Grandmaw.

"But he left me, too," she finally said, "only in a coffin. Shot square in the chest runnin' out of Pikeville's First National Bank, one hand wavin' a Colt 45, the other one clutchin' a five-pound feed sack stuffed full a' dollar bills like he was holdin' a chicken by the neck." She stopped to remember, the stillness around her as solemn as the trails of smoke above her head.

"It was Lawyer Bearsocks," she said in a voice heavy and far away, "High Sheriff and lucky enough to be in the right place at the right time. Shot him dead on the spot with a single shot and without as much as a word." After that, she sank back in her rocker without rocking, the soft entrails of her hair stirring ghostlike in a waft of air coming through the screen door. "Dempsey was my last," she said. "Me and love? ... we just never hit it off adder that."

The image of Dempsey Compton being shot to death was a raw one, but it left me knowing that it was the kind of justice most familiar with highlanders: copperhead sudden and just as final.

"We didn't have it long, but we had it good," Mary Olive said, letting the thought and its sweetness linger. After a moment she said, "But that ain't all of it. He left me somethin' I sometimes think of as a curse, other times a blessin'." She chuckled with a sliver of mockery. She raised her head to see if I was paying attention, then held me in her stare for a very still moment before she said, "Seriann." We all waited in silence before she spoke again. "He left me with Seriann growin' deep inside me. Turns out, she's more like him than if she'd been his twin. She's my one an' only claim I have 'gainst the fate of a life alone."

I waited while she gathered herself, while she smiled deep and turned to face me straight on. "It's just life, Rubin. You're here and then you're not, and everthang in between is just a story."

Grandmaw clapped her hands and rose partway out of her rocker. "YOU KNOW THAT'S RIGHT," she hollered.

"It's life, but it ain't all there is."

"TELL THE TRUTH!" Grandmaw shouted.

"This ain't our home, children. It's just a getting-ready place."

"SAY IT PROUD, SIS!"

"Truth is, 'We shall reap what we sow.'"

"The Book ain't wrong 'bout that," said Grandmaw. "'Cept when it comes to men. I lived long enough to know you can sow all the good you want to, water and hoe till you're hobbled and broke, and still have a failed crop."

"A*aaaa*-men," they chorused, leaning in to shake hands, certain they had unlocked a sacred truth. Then, without asking, Mary Olive unscrewed the lid to her bottle and bent forward to pass it to Grandmaw. Grandmaw met her halfway. The bottle finding a home with them both.

"Aaaahhhh," they sighed in agreement before Mary Olive slow-motioned the lid back in place, then slipped it cloak-and-dagger-like back into her apron pocket.

We all grew quiet after that, their rocking barely discernable, their pipes at rest in their laps, before Mary Olive said: "I believe you told what's gospel, Sis. 'Bout men, I mean."

"Gospel to me, anyway," Grandmaw said. "Truth to most, I s'pect."

"Truth's a beautiful thang," said Mary Olive. "An' The Book says it will set us free."

"Much like a taste a' liquor as I recall."

"Yeaaah, buddy," twanged Mary Olive ... and the bottle, once again, passed between them like a rare and precious stone.

The creak of their rockers were now melodic and in unison. "The truth about truth," Grandmaw said all at once, "is that it's exactly what we want it to be. The Book included. As for bein' set free, I don't reckon I know what that means, exactly, 'cept it havin' sump'm to do with believin' what we're doin' is the *right* thing whether contentment's in it or not."

"Don't know 'bout that," said Mary Olive. "Seems that doin' the right thing is what brings contentment in the first place."

"Most times," said Grandmaw. "But there's times when it brangs pain, too. To yourself *and* to others. I don't know that we can feel set free at such times ... or content either for that matter. We just have to be satisfied simply knowing it's a right thing."

"I cain't do a thang 'cept drink to that," said Mary Olive. And so they did.

The afternoon grew long and lazy, and their dialogue began to hang in the air with great pauses. "So what you're tellin' us," said Mary Olive, her head slumping then snapping back upright, then shaking itself from an almost undetectable nap, "is that truth for one may scold another."

"'At's about right," said Grandmaw, trying to bring moisture to her mouth.

"Well, hell," said Mary Olive. "How can that be when He made us all the same?"

"Well now," said Grandmaw, burping and waving at the sour vapors. "I'm here to tell you that I've lived and doctored long enough, I reckon, to know that there's not heart, mind, soul nor body-one made the same. Not meant to be. If it was, it *would be*."

"Ponder that," said Mary Olive. And the rocking stopped. And the bottle, again, went this way and that ... twice. Fire was now visibly in their eyes, and their lips lubricious and with the pinkness of newborn pigs.

"Awwright, Mary Olive," Grandmaw slurred, "give us a little tune."

"Would, but I'm just about afraid you'd dance a hole in the floor."

Gales of laughter pealed and recoiled, bounced from floor to loft.

"Law, honey, yer crazier'n a dog fight!" Grandmaw shrieked, rocking full out.

"I'll drank to that!" screeched Mary Olive.

"I figured you would," cackled Grandmaw."

And the bottle went round again.

"Let's send an' get Truman and Inez."

"I'd sooner kiss a bobcat's ass," said Mary Olive. And their ballyhooing rose and mingled with the day's eighty-five degrees and the smell of collard greens on the stove.

A confusion of cats poked curious noses at us from under the curtain leading to the upper room; their eyes, wild and worried, called out with the same umbrage that caterwauled from deep within them. They bolted just as Mary Olive drained the last of it, the empty bottle slipping through her fingers and tumbling across her rubbed-out linoleum floor.

I waited in silence, but their rocking was as still as the shadow across the porch. "You reckon the Lord knows our sufferin', Sis?" Mary Olive said under her breath. It was a question that hung in the air without ever being answered, as locked and frozen as their chins resting on their breast bones; the sunbeam through the window as stilled as the hush that enfolded them, and the veins in their eyelids as blue as the irises behind them.

Fifteen

A Nip and a Green Apple

What little corn Mary Olive and I grew we canned, pickled some and kept some sealed in a glass jar for popping. Big growers like Olin Yonts heaped most of their corn into burlap sacks and carried it off to Luck Hanner to be ground into meal. Luck's payment was a one-gallon scoop out of every bushel ground.

Olin Yonts had more corn to be ground than most, and offered me a fifty-pound sack of meal if I helped with the shelling, and then helped with its hauling to and from Luck's mill. With my arm now mended and free of splints, I agreed and spent the next three nights with their whole family hovering over a washtub in the middle of the living room shelling what corn Ben had shucked. Our being so close together had the makings of a party, but with the very real ingredient of work. We made it as enjoyable as we could: swapping ghost stories, reliving legends and tales of Indians, trading dreams and names of sweethearts, and trying to bring what laughter we could to red and callused hands. Though there was no quota, my sense of pride pushed me to keep up, to do my part, but it was near impossible when stacked against Ben.

Ben held ears of corn like a ball bat, one hand on top of the other. Then with a *wrench* (one hand twisting left, the other twisting right), back and forth—five, maybe six times—till there was nothing left but a cob. Stripped, shelled—seven seconds tops—as bare as if blackbirds had been at it all day. It was that quick and something Ben repeated three and even four times to my once—to my thumbing and nudging, each kernel its own challenge, its own reward. At least I kept up with the girls.

Ben was twenty or there abouts, and the oldest of the children. He took after his daddy's side of the family, with shoulders about as wide as ol' Hank's ass, and about as high. He was as affable as he was mountainous, docile and oddly gentle, childlike. And though limited in his ability to learn, he was altogether obedient to his role as a tireless and devoted worker. As was his girth, so was his ironic blending of hard labor and joy. And except for his appetite, the trust born of innocence was what he brought to all who knew him, men and creatures alike.

There was little, if anything, Ben couldn't do with respect to farming—and do it he did, with gladness and measures of gentle coaxing from Bobby. And though Bobby grew up with the understanding that farming was as much a test as a task for survival—doing what was demanded when it demanded it—Ben was clearly the main source of muscle, and the only person I ever knew who was talked about in terms of horsepower.

We loved Ben. Loved him unconditionally, from his sturdy bib overalls to his run-down brogans and for the sublime way he made us feel. Whether sitting at the table or holding the plow line behind ol' Hank, his enormous smile and infinitely shy and searching eyes were enough to let us know that he was set apart, cured in the mix of all that was honest and true.

But what things seemed common to most was not always the case with Ben. The fact that everybody called him Ben, only stood to reason that he should do the same. It was only logical. "Ben's hungry, now," he'd say, or "Ben thinks that's pretty," or "Bobby and Rubin rode on Ben's back." Ben never seemed to require much beyond kindness and meals proportionate to what two, and sometimes three, might eat three times a day. "Ben's hungry now."

Given that Olin Yonts was up at first light and on the road six out of seven days made him a farmer in name only. His buying and selling livestock was a chief source of income, as necessary as sunshine was to crops, but the day-to-day running of the farm was left to Gracie and the children. Each had their charges, but it was by way of Gracie's law. For

Bobby, it was a simple law: be kind to Ben. Swift judgment and stinging justice–usually in the form of a willow switch provided she could catch him–would be the antidote for anything otherwise. And since Ben was not always open to Bobby's way of doing things, Bobby often found himself in a scat, ducking and running from Gracie's switch, something that delighted Ben to no end.

As excited about life as Bobby was, he was never *excitable*. The same could not be said for Ben. The dinner bell clanging was a prime example. Another, was the time I helped him cut and stack wood. He said nothing at first, but then ran to tell Bobby that I was stealing his work. Bobby wasted no time in reassuring him that I didn't know any better. That seemed to satisfy him, but only some. He was forever watchful of me afterwards, resting in the notion that *what was his was his*, and hardened with the intention of keeping it that way. I would have to find my own work.

It was evident to all who knew him that Ben was as right for farming as rain was for flowers. Ben knew only one way: up at first light and to bed with the last of it, sit jubilantly at the table three times a day and wallow in the blessedness of toil. It was this single mindedness that allowed him to greet each day with the same uncomplicated peace of mind and make it possible for Bobby to sneak away as often as he did. To Ben, Bobby's disappearing day after day meant that there was less work he (Bobby) could steal.

When it came to shelling corn, Bobby was as close as anybody could get to being absent. He was never *at it* any more than a few minutes at a time before he was up looking for something, attending to something, pretending something ... and spending as much time in his charade as the rest of us did in the actual slog of it. By the end of the third night, and to his credit, he was the only one without the sting of blisters and the raw stiffness to his hands.

The heat of August made sissies out of most of us. It was simply not a time to overextend or move around too fast. Luck Hanner knew it as well as anybody. That's why he let us help with the grinding, and why, about every fourth sack, gave us a nip of shine and a bite out of a green apple for a chaser. Luck didn't much care that we were only fourteen.

I was still without the taste for liquor, without the disposition or the tongue for its assault. For the first time, though, I understood that Luck's offering, his passing the bottle, was the ultimate compliment—and a gesture that would have been insulting to refuse. It was, in so many words, a testament to our friendship, to my worthiness as a worker and a sign that honored me as a man. I still found it difficult to get it past my gums, and when I did, found it especially difficult to hold it down. Bobby was not so timid. His nipping with the poker players and cock fighters he aligned himself with, those who placed little significance on living by example, had seasoned him, even at fourteen. But it was not the case with me. I was forever in a fight: first, to get it down, and, then to keep it from backing up. Still, I was determined to withstand it as a show of appreciation.

My being with Luck and Bobby, I figured, was destiny, and his passing the bottle as something profound, an occurrence to help me confront my slowly emerging manhood. Bobby reasoned that we were, after all, doing the work of men, and deserved to be rewarded in like kind. It only made sense and felt only natural that I follow his lead, recognizing for the first time that moonshine carried with it a code of masculinity. And though I detested its fiery repugnance, I knew it was as integral to our social structure as the hellfire and damnation preaching that condemned it. I sipped at it despite myself, and because I saw it as something with the power to bond, to seal, to meld us into a kind of brotherhood. It wasn't until much later that I came to understand it as having quite a different power: one that divided, even ruined.

It took from early morning clear to suppertime to get all the corn ground; to go back and forth to Luck's in a flat-bed wagon behind ol' Dan; to get all thirty-six sacks of meal, one of them being mine, loaded and unloaded and into the barn; and to develop a thrill and a fear for the white-hot burn of Luck Hanner's liquor and the dense, green-tart taste of his apples.

Sixteen

Seared in a Long Good-bye

He was sweated, caked in dirt and with nothing to show but a tongue lolled to one side, his hide bloody and torn through in several places. Ol' Jess had come home. Limped and sore, and barely able to hold himself upright, he stood in the shadow of the porch, unable to mount its steps. His face was worn and wane and his tail drooped without a wag; his haunches and rib cage were thin and drawn, lacking in muscle and meat, and draped in the hungriest of skin. I stood unable to move, almost fearful, almost in tears. His eyes were pooled, watered with just enough life to beg for a leg up and a place to rest.

He was sore to the touch and I carried him ever gently to the porch. Mary Olive teared up-and-over, and sank to her knees to cradle his head in her apron. Where on earth and in God's name had he been? There were no signs of him having been fed or doctored, only the marks of a rope tied too tight around his neck. Perhaps someone had tied him up at one point, waiting for his owner to show. Perhaps. Maybe. Maybe they'd even fed him a time or two. Maybe. Maybe even thought they had themselves a new hound after so many days and no one coming to claim him. Maybe they even gave him a try at a fox. But I'm guessing it was ol' Jess who decided *what* and *how much*, and *when it was time to go*. Maybe it was a slipped noose and his yearning to be free that did it; maybe it was a moon struck night with memories stronger than the smell of game that turned him toward home. Maybe. The possibilities were endless. Where ol' Jess had been and what he'd endured would remain a mystery forever, but the one thing we could be sure of was that he'd made it back, broken and bent and with a look as worn and wounded as the adoration in his eyes.

Bruised to the core, ol' Jess was, and in several places as raw and weeping as I had been weeks earlier. Mary Olive held him and rocked him, stroked him and cooed to him till his eyes *heavied-over* and his moans carried the sound of love. I tried feeding him a biscuit, held it ginger-like to his mouth. There was thanks from the slits in his eyes, from the almost nonexistent twitch in his dust-dry nose. He licked once, just a mite, then efforted a nibble. Too sore and exhausted to chew, he lay still, cradled in Mary Olive's lap as if that was enough.

We stayed with him throughout the day, patting and cleaning and smearing him in Grandmaw's green elder ointment. I tried forcing him with water and scraps dipped with bacon grease and gravy, but he was having none of it. We kept him on the porch and in the shade, kept him cooled with rags soaked in cold water, kept him knowing we loved him as big as the sky. But it was along toward evening that his breaths became labored, shunted and stuttered, before they gave way to wheezing. Mary Olive held his head and soothed him with her mix of chant and moan, until his eyes, watered over and far away, opened just enough to say I love you and goodbye.

Ol' Jess took a final breath with both of us clutching to him as tight as heaven and earth would allow, and hoping beyond hope that we could breathe life back into him, before he left us forever, before the mountainsides railed with our sorrow.

We buried ol' Jess in a grave that Bobby dug on the hillside above the house, on a bluff sprinkled with wild mint and lily of the valley and in the shade of poplars. I tried holding back all what I was feeling as we said our final farewells, tried making sense of him being gone and the cycle we were all born to, but it was a doomed battle I was waging, little I could defend against. In many ways it felt like the ground was giving way under me, like I was tumbling down that mountain once again with nothing but its rock bottom to break my fall. Mary Olive placed dried thyme and rosemary around his face before we wrapped him in muslin; something she said would sweeten his journey and give height to his dreams. I said nothing what time Cousin Truman and Bobby lowered him and covered him up, just stood there, numb and foraging for words that never came. It was a day seared in a long goodbye.

Seventeen

Without Ever a Lock on the Door

Cousin Truman said it was okay to miss ol' Jess, that it'd be unnatural if we didn't. His hand on my shoulder helped to ease the misery. A few days later he came rumbling up in his wagon behind ol' Gert. "Been thinkin' 'bout you an' Mary Olive," he said. "Here by yeselves an' up against what all walks the mountains of a night." He paused letting his words take hold. 'At's why I'm offerin' you a friend," he said. His eyes went from me to a scraggly looking redbone hound, half asleep in the back of the wagon. In a second or two, he lumbered to his feet like it was a chore then went about sniffing the air as if he could use a bite to eat. His eyes were dark and sorrowful under heavy brows, but when I went to pet him, he melted, soft and smelly, into my arms. His hair was slick and smooth, his nose wet and cold. A look, lost and dumbfounded, blanked his face. It was love, old-fashioned and convenient, but love nonetheless.

"He don't look like much," Truman said, "but he's got heart. And the longer ye live, the more you'll know that's the main thang. He won't ever let nothin' get ahold of ye, but I'd say out runnin' it might serve ye better. No chance a him runnin' off so long's he gets a dinner plate onct a day. I've seen him work, an' he can hunt the green off a mountain ... but that's been a while I'd say. Name's Bartley."

And that was it. From that day forward, it was Bartley who warned us at night and who we stumbled over during the day; Bartley who never did much beyond mosey from one shady spot to another, a host of flies forever in tow; Bartley who lined up to eat long before it was time, then seemed to carry on niggling debates with himself over what we gave him; and Bartley who was not above a total look of innocence (one that said "Who, Me?") even when chickens came up missing at the Yonts' and him with feathers between his teeth. But to his credit, he kept the crows out of the garden. We don't know what set him to it except maybe a thought of how they might be as tasty as chicken. To our knowledge he never caught one, but it never stopped him from trying, and in the process trampled most everything in his path. "Just like Seriann. Part blessing and part curse," was the way Mary Olive put it. But, then, after a time, things just settled into a state of neutrality: the crows seeming to grow tired of being chased, and Bartley just as tired of chasing them. As far as a sidekick and for tagging along beside me, Bartley wasn't much interested, choosing instead the cool underside of the porch as a way of life. At night, though, he dragged himself up the steps to sleep on the corn-shuck pallet by the door, the same place ol' Jess slept, summer and winter.

What with Bartley now being the only thing between us and what stalked the night, he became the thing most immediate to our well-being; Mary Olive's shotgun being a close second. It was a single-shot twelve gauge she could shoot and reload in the time it took to clear her head from its recoil. She kept it propped by the head of her bed at night and next to the kitchen stove during the day—places where she could lay hold of it without the slightest thought, or without the slightest hesitation of using it. To her, it was every bit as essential as the garden. Though there were times when her storming onto the porch in the dead of night with it cocked and threatening to blow the guts out of whoever was out there, became as worrisome as when she'd take it beyond the lamplight of the kitchen window, lurking and listening for the unfamiliar. In a very short time, I understood Mary Olive's shotgun as a thing tantamount to our security, though I had trouble sharing her fondness for it in the wake of Daddy. But then I couldn't deny it providing us with the means to add squirrel to our table just about whenever we wanted it, and rabbit when we got lucky. Outside of that, it was the fitting extension of her most dreaded self, and, in light of Bartley's indifference, her *equalizer* when it came to getting us through one black night after another without ever a lock on the door.

Eighteen

Opportunities

Having lied once again to Gracie and Mary Olive, Bobby and I headed into another Saturday night—its lure too tempting and too full of things that wooed, even with a dime being all we had between us.

"What we need to do," Bobby said, "is turn this dime into a quarter real quick-like."

"What good will that do us?" I asked.

"It'll get us closer to a dollar. And that'll get us closer to the next one." Bobby's logic never seemed to be without vision or laced with the vestiges of hope. Most of all, it was the degree of certainty he brought, the single thing that helped stave off the ravages of being without, particularly on Saturday nights.

In light of all those out for a good time, Bobby figured we had a better than average chance of doubling our money by pitching nickels; and what better place than the pool hall? Angus Walker was as intense as he was profane, his pool hall brackish and ready with bootleg liquor and back-room poker—where he took a nickel out of every pot. For a dime, Angus would even bring you a bologna sandwich and a shot of whiskey. Angus's animal instinct knew it was all about the customers, about getting them drunk and keeping them that way. Bobby called them *opportunities*.

Just as we made our way around the turn at Andrew Clemmons' and headed into the Camps, there, in full view was Corbin's Model-A, and with the top down. "Well," Bobby said, "things are looking up already."

We knew Corbin was good for a quarter, even two, if we caught him at the right time, so we waited for him in the creek brush, away from the light pouring through the pool hall's single window. When he came out, he hesitated just long enough to survey the shadows and light a cigarette. Caution seemed to contain him there in the faint glow as if he were waiting for a sense of *all right* before stepping to his car. For several long minutes, he just sat there behind the wheel looking straight ahead. Then, without the slightest movement, said: "Well, you gonna stay hid awl night or you got sump'm t' say?"

We eased our way out of the brush and ambled up alongside his car. "How'd you know we was there?" Bobby asked.

"Reckon it's why I've lived this long," he said. "I knew you were there because I *have* to know." Corbin's eyes were as black as coal in the shadows. He looked up at Bobby without seeming to breathe.

"Well, okay, then," said Bobby. "Where we headed?" Corbin didn't flinch, just smiled right big, adjusted his rearview mirror and smoothed back his long black hair. "I mean me and Rubin here figured we could ride along. Help you with ... you know ... whatever you do."

"Zat right, Rubin?" Corbin said, staring straight ahead and sipping from a silver flask. "You and Bobby wanna go ridin' off in the night under awl them stars and not knowing if you'll ever see daylight again?" I said nothing, just nodded and felt the need to pee real bad. Corbin rolled his head in my direction, "You wanna help me with the ruination of mankind? Help me go against the laws of God and man and all that's sure to haunt you long after you want it to?"

"Yeah, *all* that," said Bobby. "Right, Rubin?"

I was all of a sudden feeling weak in the knees and not really wanting to be a part of Corbin's dealings, despite Bobby's coaxing. My imagination took me as deep as I cared to go. My carefully guarded apprehension was already stretched just thinking about pitching nickels with drunks in the pool hall. Up until now, what I knew of Corbin was only what he had allowed me to see. Now he had all but offered to take me behind the veil of what I could only imagine was dark and private and a target of the law and lawless alike. It made sense to be scared. I not only thought about what possessed him, but what kept him slogging up a narrow, slippery slope without ever a time or place he could know as safe. I had trouble enough keeping up with Bobby, much less Corbin Fairchild. As often was the case, I wanted only to retreat to my own private mountaintop I kept locked inside—when thoughts crowded me or cried out for clarity. There was safety there, freedom from obsession, a place where I could set aside things like regretting and the need to be right. It was a place to breathe and dream, a place without voices, only light and color and what I envisioned as being God made.

"Reckon if I's to let you go, yer momma and daddy'd skin me," Corbin said.

"Yeah, so what's the problem?" asked Bobby.

Corbin just smiled big and broad and wiped at his mouth with the back of his hand. Then, after a time, said "What the hell." It was his approval. And with it, we were off, Bobby jumping in the front seat and me in the back. I felt as if night devils had jumped in the back seat with me and were at that very minute licking their lips and staring at me with glowing green eyes. I knew I was where I shouldn't be and heading for places I didn't belong, but at least Bobby was with me. Damn him, anyway.

The night was cool, as it always was in the mountains, and by the time we got to the top of Dry Fork Hill, Corbin pulled over and put up the top, much to Bobby's protest.

"Where we headed, anyway?" asked Bobby.

"Places for your memory only," said Corbin.

Bobby smiled and nodded his approval, then eyeballed me with a big "Hell yes!" After that he was off to talking a mile a minute. His need for danger had always eluded me. He was, after all, Bobby Yonts, always needing to stretch whatever it was inside him to the breaking point. I huddled alone in the back seat, shaking almost hard enough to hear my teeth chatter and thinking how it was my first time ever in a car.

Dew begins to settle early in the mountains, right after the sun dips below the highest peak. In the time that it takes to chop and bring in enough wood for the night, draw a bucket of water and wash our feet, dew can settle thick and heavy, wet and bone cold—even in the middle of August. Dew can make staying upright near impossible on grassy slopes and riverbanks, even with the help of moonlight. It was that way when Corbin pulled to a stop on a desolate stretch of blacktop near the mouth of Fed's Creek, just before he turned off his lights and pulled onto the shoulder of the road, then into the high weeds near the river's edge.

"Whoa," said Bobby. "That bank's liable to let go."

"*Liable to* don't mean it will," said Corbin.

"Why we stoppin', anyway? Ain't nothing here."

"Just 'cause you can't see it, don't mean it's not here." Corbin spoke very little, but when he did it was a pretty good bet it was worth listening to. "C'mon," he said.

I was already halfway out by that time, ready to jump if the riverbank had notions of coming loose. Corbin was already moving like a cat through the thicket, skating through its dew without the slightest hesitation. Bobby and I followed close behind, leaving the Model-A covered nearly all the way up in switch grass and wild rye. After about a minute, Bobby and I were breathing hard, fear and anxiety working on us as much as the wet grass and the steep slope leading down to the water's edge.

We finally came to a small clearing where the river ran fast but silent at our feet and where night clouds and a canopy of leaves gave us a glimpse of the moon only now and again. We stood frozen, silent, our eyes adjusting to the blackness and trying to cover up raspy breathing. "Listen," said Corbin, his admonition to be still. He stood before us lost in shadows, as black and unmoving as the night, listening for what he called *the signal.*

"What kind a' signal?" Bobby said.

"Don't know, exactly," said Corbin. "But I'll know it when I hear it. You will too."

For several long minutes, I heard little beyond my heartbeat, monstrous and vibrating up into my neck. "You boys ever hear a song called 'Knoxville Girl?'" Corbin's voice was a husky whisper.

"No, huh uh," I said, then waited until Corbin decided it was okay to speak.

"It's 'bout this here feller who took his sweetheart down to the river one night, and—shhhhh." Corbin stopped in mid-sentence, then waited without breathing before turning his head. "Thought I heard sump'm," he said. "Anyway, this here feller takes his darlin', his pretty, down to the river under the pretense of a romantic interlude ... then drowns her. Holds her down in the water till that spirit-life dissolves right there in his hands. And awl the time he's sayin' 'Go down, go down, you Knoxville girl.'" Corbin's voice struck a low chord, like he was hearing it for the first time and couldn't quite wrap his mind around it. "I'd say that's about as chilled as a man can get. Cold as ice water on a winter's day." He left us there, dangling on a death note. I swallowed hard, wondering why he was telling us this. "I think about that song ever time I come down here," he said. "Like I can feel her ghost on these waters, like she's tellin' me to run, turn from my ways, 'less I want to be down there in the water with her." The din of bullfrogs seemed to close in around us. "Wonder what's in a man's heart to make him want to feel a body's ghost come out, draw to a close?"

Silence was never so silent and I was never so close to a burst of pleading that he not say another word, when a click, sharp and distinct, metal on metal, cracked in the darkness. "Whoo," said Corbin, a screech owl alive within him.

"I'm seein' ye," came a voice about as close to us as we were to each other. In the next instant, a man about the size of all three of us put together, pushed through the brush and stood close enough for me to smell the sweat and snuff that eked from his pores. He filled the clearing, packed it like there was six to a bed. He looked down on us, and though his face was lost in darkness, his breathing was heavy and the shotgun cradled in his arm bounced the shine of the moon. "I knowd it was you, son," he said in the direction of Corbin. "I just didn't know 'bout the rest of'em."

Corbin spoke in a low steady cadence. "These here boys is mah kin. This un's my sister's boy, and this un here's bound to be a cousin of one sort or another, if we go back far enough." Corbin knew what worked.

We stood without moving while this night giant eyed us in the pitch black. "Reckon we can go ahead, then," he said. And with that he and Corbin slipped like otters into the night.

"Wait here," was all Corbin said before he disappeared altogether.

I didn't have to worry about my voice cracking and my fear showing, because Bobby was all too willing to volunteer his take on the whole thing and to scare the hell out of what was left of me.

"You know who that big sumbitch is?" he said. "That's Hooker Hopkins. I knowed it the minute he stepped in here. Ain't but few in these parts 'at big 'cept Ben. Don't know his real name. People call him *Hooker* cause he killed a man years back in some roadhouse over in Haysi, Virginia. Killed him with one lick: a left hook. Carried the name Hooker ever since. Broke 'at man's neck is what he done. Weren't no law ever brought in on it. Peoples was afraid, I reckon. Yer lucky he didn't just pick you up with one hand and squish ye into a mud pie." I could almost see the wiliness on Bobby's face. "And ye know what else?" Bobby was a never-ending spreader of lore. "Has it that he'll kill a man for hire, then lay down an' go to sleep just like nuthin' ever happened. 'Course it's just a rumor."

Snapping in the brush caught us up short. Corbin came into the clearing just long enough to say, "Let's go." Without another word, we scrambled up the bank, grabbing onto every limb and bush we could to keep from sliding backwards. By the time Bobby and I fought our way up and out, we were soaked from the dew. Corbin was already there, standing by the car smoking a cigarette and looking like he'd just stepped off the page of a Sears and Roebuck Catalogue.

"Hell's bells," said Bobby. "What was 'at awl about?"

"Business," said Corbin. "Fair trade. A quality product for a just and impartial price ... between gentlemen."

"What product?" I asked.

Bobby looked at me and said, "You're kidding, right?"

"No, I don't mean what *product*. I meant *what* product? I didn't see you take nothing to trade with."

"Well, you see," said Corbin, "I have a number of warehouses up and down the river bottom. Their locations, however, change each and every time my friend and I meet. I take him to where I've stored my product and he gives me money. It's a time-honored tradition. One built on trust and respect, and without the cumbersomeness of taxes." Corbin sipped from his silver flask then half wittingly offered it up, but then laughed and pulled it back just when Bobby made a reach for it. After a moment he said, "Just one. Just this once for the whole night." With that Bobby took a longish pull and passed it back. Corbin offered in my direction, but I declined. He nodded and replaced its lid with a slow deliberate turn.

I was beginning to sense a very real part of Corbin, not so much as to understand him, but appreciate him: his rifeness, his wit, even what I saw as a sense of honor. "Let's saddle up," he said. "Commerce calls and we got more people to see than we got night." I had no idea where we were headed, only that my adrenalin had pushed me to a level where I no longer needed to go to my inner mountain top. For the first time, I began to sense that wild and wonderful something that lay beyond the boundaries of my otherwise uneventful life.

"Who was 'at big sumbitch, anyway?" I asked, feeling freer and more alive than ever before.

"He's somebody you need to know about," said Corbin. "Maybe even somebody you might want as a friend. If you know what I mean." The things Corbin said were not like the words of most men, but more like things we were apt to find in books or what we'd want to carve on a tombstone; things that made me feel full and even attentive to the starkness left by his long pauses. "Them that know him, call him Hooker," he said. Bobby looked at me with the widest grin. "He's a man who can hurtchee dead. Kinda like that feller in that song 'Knoxville Girl.'" That was all Corbin intended to say. The next thing I knew, we were back on the blacktop and heading in the opposite direction, toward Pikeville.

We by-passed a big steel bridge that led into Pikeville until we came to a cutoff that took us down a gentle grade and along the river to rows of shanty houses without yards and so close together they looked joined. We eased along its one narrow lane with our lights out, past an occasional window with a light filtering weak and low behind gathered curtains before coming to a stop along a chain of storefronts thirsting for paint. *Barbershop* was painted in the window of one, *Dry Goods* in another, and one that simply read *Store*. Next to them were several that sat empty and one off to itself with *Jesus, Bread of Life Cathedral* painted above its door. Connecting them was an overhang against sun and rain, and a plank sidewalk that sagged and dipped right along with the road. The word *Teddy's* in big red letters glowed from the side of the barbershop. A big red arrow next to it pointed up a long flight of stairs where boogie-woogie music and hard laughter filtered on the night air, and where a yellow and red neon light sputtered the word *Schlitz*.

Bobby was as restless as I was quiet, his eyes wide and full of the moon. "You wantin' to get us killed?" he whispered in the direction of Corbin.

Corbin rolled his head toward Bobby, "I'd say them that's afraid a' dyin' ought not of come along."

"Tellin' me you ain't afraid?" said Bobby.

Corbin laughed. "You'll discover as you edge upwards," he said rather languidly, "that the greatest peace comes with the understanding, and ultimately the grasp, of your own mortality." The smoke from his cigarette rose in soft gentle curls around his face. "Simple enough in concept, as I see it," he said, redirecting his gaze out his window, talking to the night. "We are born to life and death alike," he said, pausing to give reverence to his point. "... each of us with the breath of *here and now*, but only an expectation of what lies beyond. I envision the *beyond part* as bein' on a much grander scale than what we're used to, but, then again, maybe it's nothin' a-tall. But it's that *expectation* that adds romance to goin' beyond safe harbors."

"Whyn't you tawk like regular people?" said Bobby. "I know we ain't gonna live forever if that's what you mean, but I'm wantin' to bite off as much as I can while I can. We're just a short time here and a long time gone, and if we don't turn our asses around real quick, short's gonna get shorter and long even longer."

Corbin sat without moving, staring straight ahead. "Business first, young Bobby Yonts," he said. "It's about eatin'—an' money of course. It's the capitalist way. Besides, any life we're apt to have beyond this is surely to be less troublesome than what we already know."

"Yeah, well, that sounds real peaceful like," said Bobby, "but I'm b'lievin' dyin's a whole lot scarier'n you make it out to be. Or could be I just ain't as ready as you are—or willin'."

"You reckon that's what I want?" mused Corbin. "Down deep, I mean. To end up like 'at Knoxville girl?—floatin' face-down in the river?"

"I don't know," said Bobby, checking over his shoulder like he was expecting his flanks to come under attack, "but if it's awl the same to you, I'd appreciate you doin' yer dyin' some other time—an' if you can help it, away from me."

The lack of a breeze added to the dead calm coming off the river and the heaviness of the music drifting down from Teddy's. Except for my eyes searching this way and that, and listening for the unfamiliar, I sat without moving, waiting for Corbin to do whatever he came to do.

"What is this place, anyway?" I said in a half whisper.

Bobby and Corbin rolled their heads toward me, their faces satiny in the moonlight.

"Stringtown," said Bobby, a lilting grin riding in his voice.

"What's that?"

Corbin turned back around and eased himself out of the car without answering. He stood for a long minute letting his feet get used to the ground and filling his chest with night air. In a slow, but deliberate motion, he wiped the tops of his shoes against the back of his pant legs and ran a comb through his long black hair. He tugged just-so at the sleeves of his jacket then removed the silver flask from its breast pocket. He studied it for a time against the faint glow of neon radiating from Teddy's then reverently touched it to his lips. "Ahhh," was the only sound that followed: raw and satisfying and emanating from someplace deep within. "A thing both numbing and defying," he said before turning to where his eyes were even with Bobby's. He was a still life, Corbin was, his eyes in a search for the oneness with himself, or so it might appear. "Hold onto this for me," he said, reaching the flask to Bobby through the open window. "I'll be back in a minute."

We watched him cross the narrow lane, then climb the long flight of stairs toward the neon Schlitz sign, the boogie-woogie music and the laughter.

"Wonder what's up 'ar?" Bobby said. "I bet it ain't the Old Regular Baptists," he said without waiting for my reply. All at once, he put the flask to his lips and turned it straight up like he was going to drain the whole thing, then lowered it, his grin unmistakable, even in the darkness. "Didn't even leave me a drip," he said.

Just then, across the lane, on the plank sidewalk and from the shadow of the barbershop, two women inched their way into the pale light. They were talking in low tones, laughing and trying to see inside the car.

"Hey there," one said, her voice rich and full, and as fluid as her walk.

"Now you know where we are?" Bobby asked, eyeballing me in the faint light.

"Hey, back!" Bobby said, leaning across the seat.

They inched closer till they were next to the car, then in the next instant, leaned in through the window as if we were neighbors. For the first time in my life I was face to face with a new manner, nature, type and kind. I'd never seen such skin: as black and satiny as the night itself. Heard, but never seen, until now.

We stared, each of us with as much wonderment as the next. "Name's Maxine, and this here's Wanda." Maxine was looking at me with lips full and flushed, and smelling like a bouquet of roses.

"This here's Rex and I'm Lonny," Bobby said, smiling like he was charmed clear to his socks. "You girls just out for a walk?"

"Yeah," Maxine said, "sump'm like 'at."

"Actually," said Wanda, "we're headed up to Teddy's," motioning over her shoulder. "Yew wonna come?"

I was all at once scatty, full of awe and marvel. "Hell yeah," I said.

Right then, Bobby raised his hand in front of my face. "Uh, like to," he said, "but we got business." I was too fixated on Maxine and her big-as-almond eyes, on her slender frame and the way she brushed about, to pay much attention to Bobby. Without a second thought, I pushed past Bobby and was out the driver's door.

Right then, Maxine grabbed me by the arm like we had known each other our whole lives. She was playful and flirty, and with the smell of Juicy Fruit on her breath.

"Ah, hold on here, uh . . . uh . . . Rex," Bobby said.

"Awww now, come on, Lonny," Wanda said to Bobby, leaning even further through the window. "Me an' Maxine likes comp'ny. Don't we Max?" Wanda was soft and round, with titties as big and round as the tires on Corbin's Model-A. I watched as she angled and pushed them against the door. *Cornbread Red* began to take hold within Bobby, within the space of Wanda's magic and the lure of the trinkets that dangled from her wrists and ears. Without another word, Bobby was out the door and around the car, grinning like he'd discovered gold.

"Well, hell then," he said, "let's go!"

Right then, Corbin came down the steps, followed by a scrawny little man wearing a straw hat a size too small. Right behind them was a man about the same height, but twice as round. For the first time, it crossed my mind that Corbin, Bobby and me might be the only ones of our kind in Stringtown. I wasn't sure if that was good or bad, but it did dawn on me that it was different.

"Hey there Maxine, Wanda," Corbin said. Bobby and I looked at each other with the same wide eye. I was beginning to believe that Corbin wasn't a stranger to anybody.

"Hey, sugar," Maxine and Wanda chimed in unison. "We see yew gotcha some bodyguards." They laughed loud, their grips tightening on our arms.

"Damned right," Corbin said. "Lotta good they do me, though."

"Theys sweet as they can be."

"Well, I'm lookin' to marry 'em off, so go ahead and try 'em out. Just brang 'em back 'fore daylight."

Just then, the little fellow with the straw hat walked around to the side of the car, the wide man close behind. "Evenin' boys," he said. Then to the girls, he said, "You ladies excuse us if you will." He had a somber look and two gold teeth, and seemed to command the respect of someone with influence. Just like that, the girls let go of us and sashayed off in the direction of the barbershop, but not before blowing Bobby and me a kiss and telling us to make sure and come back when we wasn't so busy. Corbin stood there in the mixed-light of moon and neon, squinching his face and giving loud sucks to his teeth until Bobby and I climbed back in the car.

From behind us, the three of them fumbled and rattled in the trunk of the Model-A, counting and cussing and talking in hushed tones until they finally agreed on whatever it was that brought them together in the first place. Then with a tone of satisfaction, the two men walked back up the long flight of stairs, each with two gallon-jugs of what I knew to be Corbin's corn liquor.

"Where's my flask?" Corbin asked.

"Under the seat," said Bobby. "Along with all the air you left in it?"

We rode in silence until we were clear of Stringtown. "Where'd you think you were headed, anyway?" Corbin asked. "With Wanda and Maxine, I mean."

"Teddy's," said Bobby.

"Teddy's?" said Corbin. "You were goin' to Teddy's?" And with that he started to chortle, quietly at first, but quickly grew to where it was wheezy and chesty, then throaty and loud. When he started smacking the steering wheel and stomping with his free foot, we started laughing along with him, realizing we had stared a lion in the mouth without consequences. "I've always been told the Lord looks out for drunks and babies," he groaned, "but the growin' evidence here tonight is that He's no less attentive to the *less traveled*—or in your case *the don't know no betters.*"

We about laughed ourselves out by the time Corbin pulled off the road and into scrub grass and brush, ripples of sniggering giving way to the belief that everything was in its rightful place. We got out, stretched and tried making sense of the night.

"The Lord is a god of order," Corbin declared, his sudden Baptist incantation coming at us like crowd noise and with a bit of charade. "It's something I've come to understand in the light of buyin' an' sellin'. It's a quality as pragmatic as it is fiscally responsible."

"You know," Bobby said, "I might have sump'm to say about that if I knew what the hell you meant."

"There's reason for it." Corbin continued, not bothering with Bobby's complaint. "Mainly to satisfy cause. An' I'm here to tell you that tonight, cause *was* satisfied. Just as the Lord intended it." He smiled long and leaned against the Model-A while he smoked and talked in modulated tones about the heavens and the arrangement of stars. That was just before he reached under the front seat and pulled out a pint bottle of U.J.'s new-made liquor. "Ahhh, yes," he said. "The reward that's always worth the wait." He stopped to study us in the moonlight, as if contemplating whether to offer us a taste—then thought better of it, helping himself instead.

"Clear crystal runoff," he said, holding the bottle up to the moon, waiting out the fire on his breath. "Look how the moon hits it, and causes it to shine. There's nothin' quite as iridescent, but it needs the moon to make it so. Thus what we've come to know as *moonshine*," he said, the sparkle in his smile almost as shiny as the glint off the bottle. "Some say it's a word with English origins; from the 1700's that referred to occupational pursuits that necessitated working by the light of the moon. One had its roots from the effect, the other from the intent. Germane on both accounts. Don't you agree?"

"I might come to understand what you're talkin' 'bout," Bobby said, "if you was to be a little more generous with sharing a taste now and again."

"I worry about what guides you, young Bobby Yonts," Corbin said, taking us, yet again, in another direction, "...what manner of conduct influences you in the majority. Although I think I know the answer."

"Well, now; I'll just tell you," Bobby said, as if he had the answer on the tip of his tongue. "It's poetry. I b'lieve they's poetry in me."

"Poetry," Corbin said, the word flat on his tongue, going nowhere.

"Yeah, sump'm 'at dances around inside me like it's bustin' to get out: like I'm all the time swingin' on the end of a rope, about to fly; one a' them things 'at pumps me up to where hell won't have me, an' leaves me bigger'n what I was made to be. Like I'm touched, intended for things higher and faster. You know: poetry."

Corbin rested red-eyed against the front fender until he went to rubbing his forehead and pulling at his ears. "You know," he said, his funny bone a little imped, "I believe they's a right smart a' that in the family. I'm just wonderin' if we can avoid the irony?" He stopped, took in Bobby's blank look. "What I mean to say, little brother, is I believe there is a similarity to you and me, a likeness if you will, to what harkens, to what flows free and unchecked around the portals of our inner man. It has never been a question that the poet sits highest in the saddle." Bobby's smile was along the lines of a Barlow knife edging through softwood. "But," Corbin interjected, "this is about you. Not me. And what you're tellin' me is that it was poetry that put you in mind to head off in the direction of Teddy's—with Rubin here and two negresses in tow."

"That's the thing about poetry," Bobby said. "What's inside me, anyway. Leaves me ziggin' one minute and zaggin' the next. Sometimes runnin' me through the fire, and other times walkin' me around it. It's part a' the mystery—an' the most fun you can ever have if you're tough enough to hold on for the ride. I call it *Moving on. Taking the hill.*"

Corbin pressed the heels of his hands against his eyes. "Chivalrous, then."

"That sounds about right."

"So...," Corbin's tone now more intuitive, instructional, "...we have poetry that lionizes and improves one to chivalry. Not entirely unworthy, though there is often a murky line between the seeds of chivalry and what some might see as rashness. One must be on guard never to confuse the two."

Corbin took his time screwing the lid down on his bottle. "We need to be heading back," he said, the taste of *white dog* thick on his tongue. "I got me some business over in Virginia. Don't know if I'll be back ... this night or ever." He laughed, his words dire and with the suspicions of truth.

We drove with Bobby talking as if he had much to say and little time to say it, his *poetry* trying our souls. We finally rolled to a stop in front of Angus Walker's, then sat there in its watered-down light with the motor running, and with Corbin in a deep study. We stayed that way for several long minutes, Corbin's eyes leveled and tuned to the darkness beyond his headlights, before Bobby and I opened the door and stepped out. "I'm convinced," Corbin said all at once, catching us by surprise, "that the War of Northern Aggression lasted as long as it did because the Union failed to take into account one very important element about the Confederacy." He paused, stilled by his own thought. "And that was the intangibleness of *chivalry*. It was, long after hope was gone, the one remaining remnant that elevated the Confederacy beyond themselves and the moral and political ideologies that corrupted. It was, loosely speaking, their only victory. But chivalry or not, it ended the way it did because there was a power greater than any of us who opposed it." He waited, giving his thoughts time to find their way home. "We mustn't ever," he said, "let ourselves become convinced that we are more than what we are, or what we were intended for. It's the surest and quickest way to return us, chivalry and all, to battlegrounds best left to memories." He nodded, as much to himself as to us, then pulled slowly away. It was his good night.

The dew was thick and heavy as we watched Corbin's taillights disappear up Dry Fork Hill, the night's dampness chilling us to the bone.

"Whaddaya suppose he meant by all that?" Bobby asked.

"That you'd do good not to sit too high in the saddle." Bobby made several passing looks between me and the braying that came from Angus Walker's, thoughts of poetry fragile and lost in light of our predicament. For a time we stood motionless, the clack of pool balls and a honkytonk jukebox sullying what was soon to be a Sunday sunrise. Finally, a smile, Cornbread-Red wide, crept angelic-like onto his lips. "You still got that dime?" he asked.

Nineteen

The General Store

Andrew Clemmons (whom Bobby and I called Old Man Andrew behind his back) and his wife, Pearl, owned and ran the general store. They lived there as well—on the first floor, behind the long sack-cloth curtain that hung in the doorway between the dry goods and their drab little rooms in the back. Some mornings, when the wind was just right, we could hear Old Man Andrew bellowing from his back porch like a tribal warrior readying himself for battle—his way of clearing his head, or so he said. Apart from that, he was the closest thing Greezy had to a legitimate businessman. And though he was pot-gutted and walked like a barnyard goose, he was never in anything but starched shirts and suspenders, and always with spit-shined shoes and hair. Pearl was quite the opposite: pale and thin, and as shapeless as a soda fountain straw.

Pearl never thought it necessary to smile or involve herself with customers except in matters of commerce. For her, any conversation not directly related to the dispensing of goods was best left to others. Andrew, on the other hand, though business minded and rightly sober, had a spirit that could on occasion be touched and brought good-naturedly to the surface. Pearl, though, was predictably prune-faced and as dry as the goods she sold. Together they were an odd lot, not at all what comes to mind as a matched set—and never any more generous than three dollar's worth of credit.

I went to work for Andrew in the middle of August, just one week before school began.

"When I was growing up," Mary Olive said, "times could be mean. No meaner'n it is now, I reckon, but back then it just seemed like it ... me bein' just a young'un' an' all. But it was the men what made it so. Some of 'em just meant for orneriness, I reckon; always ready to throw down, even when there wouldn't be nothin' but the wind a-blowin'. Andrew Clemmons' daddy was that way. Horace was his name. Big ol' nervy type, always thinkin' what he couldn't buy, he could bully. Never wantin' but what he got. Always too free about huggin' on the girls that come around, them lucky enough with a penny to spend. Tried huggin' on me a time or two till I put a pocket knife 'tween us. Told him I'd rather have nothing an' a nickel than the likes a him. That put a stop to it, dead in it's tracks. Guess I was meaner he was, an' I guess he knew it.

"Once he built his store, he acted like he owned Greezy. A real big shot in his own mind, he was, but sinister in his ways. Had a real secret side to him. People used to talk about him: how he kept everthang locked up on the upper floor. Called it his office. Used to chuckle when he said it, then give you a little wink. Had the world right where he wanted it before he coughed up a blood ball and died face down on his desk, all alone and in the middle a' the night. His old woman didn't find him till the next mornin'—climbing a flight a' stairs to get to him and then having to peel away a ledger sheet from his face, stuck and dried there by his own blood.

"I had to laugh whenever anybody had the nerve to mention Horace Clemmons' *office*. There was more whiskey drunk an' poker played up there than anywhere else in Pike County." She stopped here to laugh, her funny bone working overtime, her mind as sharp as a two-bitted axe. "An' ye know Pike County ain't never been very tolerant of either one. 'Course 'at never meant a thang to Horace Clemmons. Men like him gonna do whatever it is they want to. Thang is, they's always wantin' the same thangs: whiskey, women and poker. An' Horace liked all three."

Mary Olive was stoked to where hell wouldn't have her, and rocking hard enough to sound like a freight train on a steep grade. She was forever meant to say what was on her mind. And once she got her pipe and rocker into high gear, there was nothing beyond sleep that could stop her. Most of all, she enjoyed talking about what she knew, didn't matter what it was or even if she liked it. If she was familiar with it, then those within earshot were going to hear it.

"An' ol' Horace liked music, too," Mary Olive said. "Banjer pickin' mostly. An' *see*gars. He liked 'em *see*gars. An he'd been known to fight: liked rollin' aroun' in the mud an' blood adder bein' drunk awl night." Mary Olive grimaced and shook her head. "He was a sight," she said. "Carried on like 'at fer all the years I knowd him—right up till he went face down. There wasn't a jot's diff'ernce 'tween the whole lot: Dewey Thacker and Carter Mayfield, and that whole bunch from Lower Fork, all a' them *good ole boys.* Good fer nothin' if truth be known. Awl of 'em so old they was bent. Seems to me they was *born* old. Grandpaw lookin' thangs. No tellin' what went on up 'ar on 'at upper floor. What used to get me was Horace's poor old woman actin' like he and them bunch a' heathens was just upstairs playin' checkers an' readin' the Bible. I guess she really didn't know no better. He always made her feel like she was lucky to have him. He said it to her so many times I guess she started b'lievin' it. If she didn't, she pretended real good.

"Then there was all that tittle-tattle about him and his bunch robbing a train. A whole boxcar full a' liquor to hear people tell it. 'Course it was just a rumor, but one of them things I couldn't ever dismiss altogether, knowin' him the way I did."

May Olive went quiet after that, her memories seeming to fall in on one another, taking her to places she didn't want to go.

It was Olin Yonts who spoke to Andrew Clemmons on my behalf, who *spoke up* for me. Andrew hired me on the spot to sweep out the store and stock the shelves each evening before he closed. It took me a good hour and was worth a shiny dime each and everyday, six days a week.

Mary Olive and I never had it so good, but that was before we went to sleeping four to a bed.

Twenty

Four to a Bed

I might never have appreciated the complexity of Seriann had Cousin Truman and Inez not showed up that second Sunday in August. The second Sunday was Greezy Creek's turn on the Old Primitive Baptist's rider circuit, which meant Cousin Truman was in line to preach, but an unexpected number of guest preachers made it near impossible. Time-honored tradition favored guest preachers, a privileged lot and always first in the order of sermons. They were nine in number that day, good for three hours of preaching and on the border of unnecessary, even unwanted. Add song and prayer and the laying on of hands, and it was lucky, even merciful, that it was held to a mere four hours. But Truman and Inez appeared no worse for the wear and came ready to unload what they'd kept penned up all morning long.

When Truman came up the steps it was with a smile and a strut, and his chest looking like it was about to break through the white shirt he kept buttoned up to his neck. It was his new car that had him so pumped up: a twelve-year-old Model-T, to be exact, that he'd half-swindled from Lamar Tibbs, a good friend and Bible salesman in Pikeville. "A purdy good bull and a half-dried-up milk-cow is what bought it," he said, certain that The Lord had favored him with a slice of life's abundance. Inez was her usual jovial self, using what little breath she could draw through the swelter of August's ninety-plus degrees to enlighten us about most everything we had absolutely no interest in. She came with her dress to her ankles, her hair winced back and tightened in a bun; with skin flushed to a hot pick and fanning herself with a lace handkerchief.

Truman was about as tall and wiry as Inez was short and broad, but they were a team fixed and unwavering in their devotion. Odd as it was, they never touched or acknowledged one another except to ask for confirmation of what the other had said: "Ain't that right, Truman?" ... "Ask Truman if that's not the truth." ... but then never waiting for a response, but then never really expecting one either. Conversation for them meant that everyone else should listen while they talked *in tandem*, and never on the same subject. It was hard enough to keep up with what *one* was saying, but with both of them blowing hot and changing subjects about every third word, it was no wonder Mary Olive kept finding excuses to go look for something in the lower room. But that never deterred or detracted either Inez or Truman. They just kept right on talking, and even raising their voices so Mary Olive wouldn't have to miss a single word ... "I swear it's the truth. Ask Truman."

They spent the day, from early afternoon to early evening, sitting around the kitchen table, yapping and eating the fried chicken Inez brought. Stories about Seriann came full throttle with little-to-no let up until Mary Olive disappeared behind her smoke rings, rocking and staring off into space and leaving me alone to feign interest. She rejoined us now and again, one minute dotting our conversation with quick asides, the next, laughing out loud at the wrong time, wrapped up only in where her mind had taken her. By the time Truman and Inez left, she had fallen asleep in her rocker, and in the comfort of a moonshine stupor. Her trips to the lower room had served her well.

My head reeled in the aftermath of Truman and Inez, in the echo of their voices and their lavish accounts of Seriann. I'd heard enough to know her a dozen times over, but wondered why she had been the topic of choice for most of the day. A day later I knew why. After walking home from Old Man Andrew's, I found her standing in the kitchen with all four children and what looked like everything they owned heaped into a mound in the middle of the floor.

We stood eyeball to eyeball, Seriann and me, her eyes reflecting the blackness of her hair, it hanging without a curl and framing the bony narrowness of her face.

"Lord, Honey, let me lookit yew," she said, her smile leaping to greet me. "Why, I b'lieve you're 'bout the purdiest thang I ever seen!" And with that she threw her arms around my neck and squeezed me hard enough for pressure to build behind my eyes. "Yew know who I am?" she asked. Instinct told me yes, but I said no. "I'm SeriANN," she said, her voice rising as if it were an obvious truth. "Mary Olive's girl, an' your first cousin once removed." She laughed as if it were a thing worthy of celebration. Next thing I knew, I was surrounded and being stared at like something they found by the side of the road. There was Woodrow, Wilma Lee, Wilson, and Little Sherman, names I'd only heard about, come to life. Before I knew it, they were rambling on about who in the family I resembled most, and trying to figure out whose fault it was that we were just now meeting for the first time. Almost at once, we gave in to the fact that we were all cousins of one sort or another, born and bound by blood. Aligning one's self on the family tree was a bonding ritual, both responsible and necessary. It not only affixed lineage, it established unwritten creeds. There were particular loyalties attached to blood.

From the looks of things (boxes and bags and pillowcases stuffed with goods from all seasons), they were here to stay. And so we went about putting things away, and being cautious about what we wanted known and what we didn't.

After a homecoming supper of cornbread, dried peas, hominy, and pickled beets, we sat on the porch, in the rockers and on the steps, and in the coolness that came off the mountains, until we talked and yawned right up to dusk. Seriann and Wilma Lee slept in the upper room with Mary Olive. The boys slept in the lower room, all four of us squished into one bed: head to toe, head to toe.

I lay awake in the blackness that first night trying to get used to feet next to my face and a room full of jagged breathing. The sounds of crickets and bullfrogs and the creek gurgling just outside the window were now only things that came between grunts and snorts and snoring. In between my breaths and theirs, we became just another part of the night's rhythm.

I can't be sure how long I was asleep before being jolted awake, back into the jet-black of night. A mountain lion—bobcat at the very least—had landed in a full-out rage on my chest, and with such force that I let out a scream. By the time Seriann stumbled to life and lit the lamp, there was another attack, triggering yet another spasm.

"It's just 'em ol' cats," Seriann said, pointing to two huge toms scurrying under the curtain into the upper room. By then, everybody was at full laughter.

"Where'd they come from?" I said.

"Up 'ar," said Wilson, pointing to the rafters above the bed. There were two more: perched and waiting their turn to fall from the sky.

"No," I said. "I mean where'd they *come* from?"

"They follered us here, I reckon" said Seriann.

"They foller us ever'where we go," said little Sherman. "They's a whole bunch of 'em. Ain't they Mommy?"

Seriann just laughed. "Go on back t' sleep," she said. "I'll put 'em out."

I watched her shoo the other two out of the rafters then listened while she herded the lot of them out the door. In a few minutes she was back, part of the shadows cast by the lamp. It was only minutes before we were again blanked in blackness and headed toward sunrise.

Twenty-One

Sour and Full of Earth

Running a batch of moonshine was a craft as exact as it was artful: an all-night ordeal and about as focused a thing as two men could do, what with all the hardwood that needed to be chopped and the water that needed to be hauled. It was tireless attention to detail that separated good whiskey from bad: tending to a fire that needed to be kept at just the right temperature and the mash percolating *just-so* in order to keep the vapors and runoff from tasting burnt—and keeping the pressure in the cooker from building up and blowing body and still alike to kingdom come.

Vapors needed to rise fast and full throughout the night to make the effort worthwhile, therefore the water: the gallons-upon-gallons that needed to be fetched and added as the mash continually boiled away. And there was the stirring and churning so the vapors would yield a consistent proof. And then there was the collecting: filling one jug after another with the run-off, replacing full ones with empty ones and emptying the full ones into quart jars and pint-sized bottles to make it marketable. From one to the other and back again ... and again ... and again ... until the mash was cooked out, devoid of alcohol.

Most men welcomed help, but not Haman Flowers. He was hardened to it, content to work it alone, the solitude suiting him just fine, even preferring it. It was a chore, to be sure, but most of life was a chore for Haman. He seemed to know it as the hand he'd been dealt, and the one he was determined to play, albeit with the same severity as a hoot owl on nights without a moon.

None of us knew much about Haman Flowers except that he didn't have any kin to speak of and that he kept to himself even when he came out of his hollow. He was tallish, rangy and gnarled in the way of a wolf cut out of the pack and left to go it alone. Except for the exaggerated facial contortion from a lifetime of tobacco (backer) plugs packed torturously into his cheeks, he was a study as black as the dirt that lay in the creases of his neck; the same that lay fermenting, deep and purple, under his fingernails. His eyes, cat-gray and forever in the shadow of an old brown fedora, leered in the same way as a black snake's when it freezes its prey. And though the right one was half-closed from a scar that started just above his brow and ran clear to the middle of his cheek, the left one was wide and wild like a treed coon. The only time I'd been close to him was when he stepped into the store one late Friday evening. He walked right up behind me without my even knowing it. All I recall was a sense of darkness coming upon me, and a smell that was sour and full of earth. I turned to find him blocking what light spilled in through the door and reaching over me for a plug of Brown Mule. I stood rooted and weak-legged, his presence as thick and daunting as any I'd ever felt. The very space around him seemed to cloud and put me in mind of the air that hovered over Momma after her last breath. He never waited for Pearl to come attend him, or for her hollow "*Thank you and come again.*" He just laid his nickel down on the counter and moved off toward the porch.

Corbin said we too often give men like Haman Flowers more credit than they deserve, allow them a posture of evil so we can somehow justify our fear of them. *Unwarranted paranoia* is what he called it, what men like Haman were good at exploiting. The clearer view was understanding them, he told me. It was only then that we could with a good deal of certainty steer clear of their predictable natures. I clung to most everything Corbin said, but there was something to Haman Flowers that teetered disturbingly toward the *un*predictable; like a dog gone mad, one as likely to go against his predictable nature as not.

I followed Haman from the corners of my eyes that day, powerless to stop myself. At the last minute, just before walking out the door, he slowed his step then halted altogether before giving his head a slow deliberate roll in my direction, his wide gray eye on me like a hard rain. The day of reckoning and the image of a rider on a white horse flooded over me. But then without as much as a flinch and through lips so thin and flat they were all but nonexistent, he sent a long trail of tobacco juice in my direction. It landed in a wet straight line on the floor between us, linking us as surely as if it were an iron chain. It was a message that said he could just as easily make it a bullet if I had trouble minding my own business.

He was cagey, Haman was, wily and without scare, things that made him all the more devoid of predictability. I watched him till he walked off, his old brown hat wilted and cocked menacingly to one side, and without ever a thought of looking over his shoulder. He left no doubt about what he intended me to know: that he was connected to a darkness that made him as dangerous as he wanted to be.

None of us ever spoke of Haman Flowers unless we called him by his full name, unless we called him Haman Flowers, like he was someone on a wanted poster down at the post office. We had little we could put to his name except rumor, and all of it unnerving as a hen's crow. He was more than just an idea of wrongdoing, he was proof of it—his very existence enough to keep honest men thinking twice about the consequences of reckless procreation.

I often wondered what made Haman Flowers the way he was, and if he ever saw himself as the runt of the litter, muscled out of this and that till he was pushed to boundaries more resigned to his brand of umbrage. I couldn't be sure if it was ignorance or isolation (or both) that lay at his core, that lay in the furthest reaches of what some might call a soul: a place I would wager no man could get to except with an ice pick and the help of the devil.

Twenty-Two

Seriann

Seriann's nose was thin and hooked slightly beyond the point of being regal; and when she laughed, it seemed to erupt into a perfectly prescribed beak. She was a full five feet two if you included the dirt baked to the soles of her feet, and a solid hundred pounds coming away from a Christmas dinner. She ate what the rest of us did, but never any more than was necessary to keep her alive. To say she was thin would be extending a kindness. *Scrawny* was much closer to the truth. She was, with all charity, mostly bones and veins—but as hard-wearing as the mountains that framed her world.

"The only thing I want out of life is my way," was her favorite thing to say, a kind of profane independence she liked to dole out whenever there was the occasion for us to be reminded. Darting black eyes and a jutting grin left little doubt to her veracity, but then there was her laughter: the head-thrown-back, uncultivated kind that said life was only worth it as long as mirth endured.

Stout independence was but a part of Seriann, but it was the biggest part. "I ain't much for knucklin' under," is the way she put it. "Wasn't never much for what I *ought* to be, what the church an' a bunch a' preachers want me to be, or what the law says I need to be. Life's a mite more knotty than that. We don't need this bunch over here and that lot over there tryin' to make us mind. It's in us to do right if we've the stomach. That's all that's ever needed. Alls *I* ever needed anyways. It's rightness, an' it comes like a still quiet voice if we'd just pay attention to it. Helped me, anyways, to rid myself of husbands not worthy of the name."

She stopped, fumbled in her apron pocket for rolling papers, then formed one into the shape of a canoe around the tip of her index finger. She poured it full of Indian tobacco from a small cotton pouch with a drawstring, then spread it evenly, packed and squeezed and rolled it all together before giving it a lick and running both ends in her mouth; before twisting and pinching the ends; before tightening the drawstring with her teeth and shoving the pouch back in her apron pocket like returning a six shooter to its holster. Then, like a magic wand, she flicked a stove match against her thigh, stirring a flame the size of a torch. It was a solemn glance at the piece of Cherokee in her.

"Best I can tell, a husband's only good for a couple things," she said into a cloud of smoke. "After that, he's just a boy in a big pair of britches and figuring just because he needs mothering is reason enough to expect it." Like Mary Olive, she was never above laughing at the things she said. "If it ain't gettin' an' fetchin' for 'em, it's turnin' a blind eye an' keepin' yer mouth shut so's he can think he's ruler of the ground you walk on. I can see how a woman can get twisted by it, but it's beyond me how they can make a habit of it. If the Lord gave anything a-tall, He gave us the mind to know. An' if we ain't got the strength to act on it, then we just a hollow thing in His sight. One day when we stand before Him ... and we will ... I want to say I stood up, did what You put in me to do. I want to say I had the strength to bring what little heaven I could to me and mine. An' that's a whole bunch more'n just 'bein' churchified."

Seriann's hair was of the purest black and trailed to where it covered her hips. Running a comb through the length of it meant she had to extend her arm as far as it could reach. If she thought we were looking, she would toss it about like it belonged on a wild mare, or tuck the ends into her dress pockets, or wrap the whole lot of it around her neck and hold it up like a noose. We were always her best audience, even into the night when her theater made our blood run cold as well water.

Theater is what filled our evenings after Seriann came, what aligned us with things most playful and mischievous. It was in the upper room where we gathered and played our parts; where we acted out whatever came to mind. It was all about who could tell the funniest story, or the scariest, or who could sing the prettiest or preach the loudest. The world was ours to do whatever we saw fit, to pull whatever we could from our imaginations. Camp meeting songs were Mary Olive's to share, trumpeting from her like Gabriel blowing his horn, and with the same frequency as Little Sherman's rendition of the old troll and The Three Billy Goats Gruff trip-trapping across his bridge.

Little Sherman always had to be first because he couldn't hold his excitement—or his pee—if he was made to wait. Each night he told the story of the old troll like we were hearing it for the first time, and beholden to react with the same horror and surprise. He was the tale's owner and crafter, and telling it moved him to grinning like a conquering hero.

Woodrow's only contribution was being the loudest, laughing and clapping and egging us on. But as good an audience as he was, he only stayed around for nine days before he up and left for the Army: just a day after he turned eighteen. He left the very day Wilson and I started back to school, our sleeping four to a bed adding even more reason for his goodbye.

Wilson was only ten, but a born troubadour, given to thumping and banging on some old flat-top guitar with a warped neck and a number two pencil for a bridge that one of Seriann's suitor's left behind years ago. He was a perfect blend of funny bone and mischievousness, and never balked at making up songs about his mother.

"Now there came a fair maiden,
From Greezy Creek it's said,
A beauty rare, a beauty bright,
Blacking eyes an' cracking heads.

"This maiden she was tender,
But with thunder in her hand,
She left her mark on lovers' heads
With a fist an' an iron pan."

On and on it went, in an errant mixture of melodies, until he had exhausted what was most sacred about Seriann and the assortment of cats that followed her from place to place.

Wilma Lee danced and sang. And though she never went beyond the fifth grade, she could pick and strum a dulcimer with amazing nimbleness. Her voice was husky, her songs grave and forlorn: lamenting ballads of false-hearted love, of jealous lovers, and crimes of passion. She had an endless repertoire of tragedy and sorrow: "*Pretty Polly*," "*Wayfaring Stranger*," and "*I Am a Man of Constant Sorrow*." Up and down the scales of the dulcimer, her voice blending with her carefully fingered runs, carrying the sadness of her tales to their tragic ends. Other times she would clog in a way she'd learned from her mother, as if stomping out fires on the side of a hill. Wilma Lee dreamed of being a movie star.

When it came my turn, I would make up stories about Old Man Andrew and Pearl, and about the people I saw and the stories I heard at the store. No one was beyond being a target of my irreverence. On occasion, I even took a turn, as did everybody else, at hellfire and damnation preaching. As long as there was laughter, there were no limits as to how far we might go.

When it came to Seriann, the mood shifted from tomfoolery to *the strange and unusual*. Even the night air would take on a restlessness and an intensity I could see as much as feel. Being true to form, she would dim the lantern to a low amber, leaving just enough light to match the low quivering tone of her voice. From there, she would proceed to enchant us with tales so gruesome that none of us ever slept without an accompanying nightmare, or without the gratitude of knowing there were others in the bed with us. There were tales of children being stolen by gypsies, of red-eyed wolves that came out only at night, of haints and saints that walked just beyond our doors, and of mothers and fathers and favorite sons waiting on the gallows to say their last good-bye. With her words sounding like warnings and her eyes flickering and darting like a cat following the flight of a bee, she never lacked the darkness to conjure a tale so grave that it would scare us out of a month's growth. Sometimes she would pause, but just long enough to let the night's stillness settle around us, and then begin again—chanting in some unknown tongue and with her eyes rolled back in her head, looking like her next breath would be her last. But then, like a cobra, rise up and point a bony finger at our wide-eyed faces before calling the cats and stirring them into choruses of agony and pain. Then, at last, when she laughed, it came with the fullness of lust and pleasure. She reminded me of sin.

Seriann's tales never ceased to send chills through our brains and bowels alike, but she knew we would settle for nothing less. We were thrilled by her, drawn to her like cats to cream. It was as if everything she said was filled with the mystery and wonder of a headless horseman, as if she had the power to freeze us and hold us captive while she summoned unthinkable demons to devour us, heads and all. And though we allowed her, night after night, to lead us deeper and deeper into worlds eerie and haunting, we never allowed it without thinking that good would somehow triumph, that the darkness she painted would eventually yield to the light of day. Except for Wilson, we were like puppies huddled together to ward off some creeping chill. Wilson never let on that he could be scared by Seriann's tales, but afterwards he would never go to the outhouse alone.

Bedtime was filled with its own mysticism. It was the time when Wilson and Little Sherman and I would look out for the girls while they made their way to and from the toilet in the light of the lamp they carried. Then Wilson and I would go, but without the lamp, stopping about halfway to pee in the weeds behind the hen house. Little Sherman always peed off the porch.

While it was still warm, we boys slept in the lower room. It was called the lower room because it was on the lower slope of the mountain, next to the creek. It was a sparse room with walls covered in layers of newspaper, each layer flour-starched to the next, and with a plank floor covered in worn and odd shaped pieces of linoleum scavenged from *throwaways* and *giveaways* up and down the creek. Off to one side, a well-preserved chifforobe and chiffonier flanked a large-but-rickety iron bed, where

Little Sherman, Wilson and I slept. In the middle of the room sat a small potbellied stove with a layer of rust blanketing it like orange colored moss. The stove was never used, even in the dead of winter, because it had never been vented—mostly because there was no stovepipe to vent it with. But it was not an item to be thrown away. There was little, if anything, ever thrown away. So it sat as a permanent fixture, worthless except for its possibilities.

The upper room was the *main* room, where we did most of our living and where we sang and danced and playacted each night. Its walls, too, were covered in newspaper and its floor with oddities of linoleum. On either side was an iron bed: one for Mary Olive, the other for Wilma Lee and Seriann. In the corner opposite the fireplace was an outsized dresser with picture postcards pinched between its mirror and frame; postcards of France and the Netherlands from kin who had been in the Great War and decided, at least once, to reach out to Mary Olive. In the middle of the floor, in front of the grate, a hodgepodge of lopsided chairs held together with bailing wire and straps of rawhide flanked a twig rocker Cousin Truman had cut and fashioned from branches of birch and willow.

What we had was tolerable, if you didn't include the beds. The beds, their springs and cotton-batting mattresses, were so collapsed in the middle that sleep was often filled with dreams of trying to crawl out of a hole or shimmy up the side of a hill. After Woodrow left, our bed never slept any less than three, which meant the person in the middle was forever being crushed and smothered by the two on the outside. In fairness, the middle position was rotated, a fate each of us needed to bear up under every third night.

The night-chill, the heavy dew and dampness brought on by the mountains, made quilts a part of every night, summer and winter. Mary Olive's quilts were dense and leaden, and made from swatches of aprons and feed sacks, plow pants and everything else that had been handed down for a final time. There was a deep mustiness to them, the result of thousands of nights in dank and unheated rooms. It was in the abyss of total darkness that their odor and heaviness became familiar and comforting realities. Along with the sound of the creek washing gently outside our window, their doughy smells were always the last thing I remembered before giving way to the cats and whatever else the night might bring.

Each night and in the dull glow of the oil lamp, Seriann assumed the role of protector and made repeated trips from one room to the other, ensuring that all was secure and that we were all accounted for. A faded muslin curtain hung in the doorway between the upper and lower rooms. Sometimes it was a backdrop to Seriann's scurrying, sometimes a screen to her silhouette. Her hair, straight and black and flowing behind her like a cape, hid her face just enough in the lamplight to turn her eyes into flat black holes and just enough to make her nose look long, sharp, and broken, and just enough to turn her smile into a sneer. Though she busied herself night after night with our safety and comfort, I never stopped imagining the broom she rode after the lamp was out.

Twenty-Three

Big Room and Little Room

By the end of August, summer wore like a hair shirt, its days melding into one another with the persistence of an oven. And while it was never certain what I was liable to encounter from one day to the next, it was a fair bet that I'd encounter at least part of it with Bobby. School was no different.

The schoolhouse was a simple structure: two large rooms fastened together (one behind the other) and set against the base of a mountain that rose majestically behind it. It rested on concrete pillars and leveled against the slope of the land. Plain weatherboard, and without insulation, made its function far less noble than its intention. It was built in the early nineteen hundreds in the aftermath of the Great War. Outside of a whitewashing about every fifth year, its weatherboard brandished the same dust and grit as its grassless schoolyard, and was most of the time never without the appearance of neglect.

Grades one through four were taught by Miss Fields, and grades five through eight by Mr. Tacket. Each room was identical in size, but designated as the little room and the big room simply by the grades that filled them. For lighting, each room had eight windows. For order more than comfort, there were six rows of desks running from front to back: three on either side of a big potbelly stove. Add to that, a blackboard and a flag, the teacher's desk and a water bucket by the door, and one had the sum total of all we ever knew as the schoolhouse.

School ran from late August to early May, letting out just in time for plowing and planting. I don't know which I considered more painful: sitting in the sweet, chalky mustiness of a room that had been closed up for a whole summer, with air so heavy and still that it caused my shirt to stick to me like an extra layer of skin, or being let out into a season of endless labor, its days intensified with heat and sun, and with nothing but a hat for shade.

Each school day started with Mr. Tacket rankling the air with a big brass bell then waiting for us to line up and calm ourselves before filing orderly past him to our seats. It never took any longer than he allowed, because when Mr. Tacket beckoned it was taken with a serious note—and rightfully so.

Mr. Tacket was only a half-a-head taller than me, but had the girth of a bore hog, thick and broad, and muscled from bow tie to shoes. His image was not so much of a schoolteacher as it was a blacksmith or a rail driver. And though he was pleasant enough and quick with a smile, he was the understated rule of authority, able to straighten our backbones with just a look.

After roll call, Mr. Tacket would pick one of the boys to go draw a fresh bucket of water. Since it required going outside to the well, it was treated as a reward and typically granted to whoever had done the best at his books. We all got a turn now and again. All of us, that is, except King Charles Bliver. Schoolwork just wasn't King Charles' long suit, and he didn't hold much stock in drawing and hauling water, even if it did mean getting to leave the building. King Charles was more than content with just being King Charles, happy just to throw spit balls, pass notes, and go to the toilet as often as he could get away with it. Mary Olive used to say King Charles Bliver was so dumb he was happy. But King Charles was a good heart, about as long and lanky as Abe Lincoln, and about as gentle as moonbeams on a porch swing. Along about the third day, King Charles amazed us all with the correct answer to an arithmetic problem. Mr. Tacket stopped right in the middle of everything and invited King Charles to go draw a fresh bucket of water. Well, this even amazed King Charles. But it wasn't until Mr. Tacket slammed a big book down on his desk to stop everybody from laughing, that King Charles stood up and made like a hero to the water bucket, grinning like a 'possum through his big brown teeth.

After some time had passed and King Charles' being gone took on the appearance of having skipped town, Mr. Tacket went looking for him. When he found him, King Charles was lying on his back in the tall grass out behind the girls' outhouse, lazing away under a blue sky and smoking a cigarette. That's when Mr. Tacket told him to go cut a switch.

Getting a whipping was bad enough, but the added insult of cutting your own switch was unique to Mr. Tacket's authority, and a guarantee that it was going to be an *example-setting* experience. But, having been in this situation before, King Charles knew right off what he needed to do. He figured that by running his knife blade around the switch about every eight inches or so would weaken it enough so that it would break apart each time he was hit. He was right. When Mr. Tacket came around on him the first time, the end of the switch snapped clean and flew clear to the back of the room. The next blow, delivered with a bullet-like force, caused even more of it to snap off, sending pieces whizzing past our heads and bouncing off the walls. With only a stub left in his hand, Mr. Tacket ordered King Charles back to his seat. Nothing more was said. But as Mr. Tacket stood there studying the stick in his hand, King Charles knew he had been found out. And he knew, as did the rest of us, that the worst was yet to come.

The next morning King Charles was standing in our kitchen with his pants down around his ankles while Bobby worked at wrapping his legs in tarpaper. Bobby figured it was sure protection from the certainty of Mr. Tacket's encore performance.

King Charles' pants being down around his ankles kept Seriann from letting Wilma Lee into the kitchen, and the sight of his pasty-white legs and knobby knees sticking out of his old rusty drawers about two sizes too big gave us over to unrefined hysteria. The tarpaper was Bobby's idea, something he'd been saving for himself if the time ever came, but figured nobody needed it more than King Charles needed it now. Bobby even wrapped his chest and back. He was taking no chances. This was a *first*, but drastic situations required drastic measures, and Bobby was just the man for the occasion.

By the time Mr. Tacket rang his big brass bell, King Charles was as cool as a cucumber. As far as he was concerned, Mr. Tacket could beat hell out of him if he wanted to. It didn't make any difference. He was ready, by God. This time around, though, Mr. Tacket had cut the switch himself. It was a willow switch, big around as a buggy whip and as long as he was high.

It was no surprise that right after roll call Mr. Tacket called King Charles to the front of the room. As King Charles strolled past us, he shot Bobby and me a glance of pure confidence. He was feeling stone-cold protected, even cocky. He even gave us a little wink just before Mr. Tacket came around on him the first time. The switch made a sinister sound as it cut across King Charles' hindquarters. Immediately, King Charles' eyes took on the look of something horribly gone wrong. He got nine more, each one sending him reeling faster and jumping higher, until he was no longer able to hold back the sounds that come from blistering pain.

At recess, the eighth-grade boys (all six of us) followed the creek bed until we were out of sight. We needed to assess the damage. When we peeled off the tarpaper, it was almost a choir song, everybody saying about the same thing at about the same time, "Gaaaahd DAMN!" "Hellllllll farrr!" It had been a disaster. Instead of dampening and absorbing the blows, the tarpaper had acted like a conductor, intensifying each stroke and leaving welts on King Charles the size of number two pencils, some blistered, some like poker burns. We threw as much cold water on them as we could and cussed Mr. Tacket enough to send him straight to outer darkness. But as far as we were concerned, King Charles had won the battle. Few of us could have taken such a whipping then sat and punished with it for the next two hours, feeling a whole lot like he was on fire. We stayed in the cool shade by the creek soothing King Charles' wounds as best we could until we heard the big brass bell. As we made our way back, somebody joked about what a genius Bobby had been.

"At least, by God, I tried," Bobby said, ready to fight. But there was no time for fighting. Mr. Tacket was beckoning. And when Mr. Tacket beckoned, it was taken with a serious note—and rightfully so.

Dixie Wainwright was small and thin with faint bronze freckles, and with mouse-colored hair that hung fine and without even the thought of a curl down to the middle of her back. Her lips were thin, but pouty, and looked as if they carried the stain of ripe raspberries, and her eyes were the size of robin's eggs and of the same pale blue. She walked mostly with her head down and her legs churning about as fast as spokes on a wagon wheel, as if she had many places to go and many things to do, and without a spare second to exchange even the simplest hello. Mary Olive said she was as pretty as a two-penny postcard, but with nary a hip one.

By every account, Dixie was small to the point of frail, and spent an unfair amount of time keeping her hand-me-down dresses from sliding off her shoulders and properly fastened. The rest of us were pretty much the same: knowing hand-me-downs as a thing most common, and our patching and mending them so they might last long after hope and good sense told us they would. We didn't know what we didn't have, and it made us resilient. The difference came in knowing what we *did* have, and that made us happy. We knew, for instance, that Dixie was an angelic sight, everything a fourteen-year-old boy could ever hope to possess. And nobody knew it more than Bobby.

Dixie's best friend was Imogene Riley, and except for a trip now and again to the toilet, neither made a move without the other. Imogene was haughty and rangy, and always ready to kick us in the shins as a way to rectify what she didn't like about us. Most of the time a scowl surrounded her dark green eyes and forever pursed lips. Her demeanor was braced, as if she was on constant alert for warfare: to counter it, or, if necessary, launch it. Her hair was copper colored and looked coarse enough to scour pots. A few times I caught her being almost feminine, her face calm, reflecting. But then I was quick to remind myself that she was inherently evil, as hard and tough as the gristle we tossed to ol' Bartley.

From the time we took up books to the time we put them away,

Imogene was forever the main victim of catcalls, the favorite target of every boy from the first grade to the eighth. But it was duly noted that they did it under the risk of a beating if she ever caught them. That was guaran-damn-teed. But the boys figured the risk of a beating was what made it all the more fun. A good beating, especially from Imogene, was just something to help them feel more like they were alive.

School broke for dinner every day from noon until Mr. Tacket rang his big brass bell. Most brought their dinners with them. Sometimes it was just a biscuit, sometimes cornbread crumpled in milk, as common to us as well water and pinto beans; sometimes a green apple or a potato; and sometimes nothing at all. Dinner pails were lard buckets, and those needing to be kept cold were placed in the water, in the shady part of the creek. Outside of springhouses, the creek and its shade was the only source of refrigeration we knew. During the winter, dinner buckets were kept inside the classroom, lined up against the back wall where the draft along the floor kept them chilled—never enough to freeze, but cold enough to hurt your teeth from first bite to last.

Dixie always ate with the twins, Franklin and Fayella, her charges, until Fayella's *detachment* and spates of violence removed her from school altogether. Now she sat only with Franklin, sharing bites of this and that, passing a spoon back and forth between them until the last morsel was scraped and licked, and their eyes settled into doe-like quiet: searching, yet knowing that it was all there was. Imogene never ate anything. She just sat lurking like a bird of prey, watching and waiting for something to kill, for somebody to step even the least bit out of line so she could beat the snot out of him.

Then there was the playground, an ever-present surge of motion, and never without its allure: the place where girls were teased and chased, and where boys wrestled each other into submission; where the big ones bullied the little ones; where everyone had to be on constant lookout for green apples and hawthorns whizzing by their heads; and where cocklebursc overtly tossed into someone's hair stood out as the torment of choice. But it was also a place for hopscotch and tag, fox and hound, crack-the-whip, and baseball played with a hickory stick and a sponge ball that Mr. Tacket kept in the bottom drawer of his desk, and gave out with the direst instructions for its return. It was a place coveted for jump rope and marbles, Annie over, olly olly oxen free, blind man's bluff, tug a' war, and every kind of foot race we could think of. It was a place where a big rope swing hung from a giant ash at the base of the hill, and where we swung two and three at a time, and dared to go higher and higher with each attempt. The playground was, all in all, a world apart, and nothing spared in the way of games short of what could be imagined. It was every mountain child's dream: a place unobstructed by trees and as flat as a checkerboard. And, too, it was the place that most accurately determined the pecking order, and where Imogene Riley ruled without the slightest uncertainty as king of the hill.

As a part of our arithmetic lesson, we were made to go to the blackboard every day to demonstrate how well we were learning. We tried to help each other as best we could: whispering back and forth, passing notes and copying off one another's papers—but when we got to the blackboard, we were wholly and utterly on our own. It was common knowledge that Mr. Tacket was not very tolerant of anyone failing to learn. He simply saw it as laziness, and on many occasions would let fly an eraser at our heads to demonstrate his disgust. But for Cobbie Parsons, his presence at the blackboard had long ceased being anything but amusing, even for Mr. Tacket.

The way Cobbie went about scribbling his numbers sent ripples of laughter throughout the room. But he was happy with himself and the role he had established. He even came to accept it with an element of good-natured innocence. Just the mere calling of his name would start everybody to giggling. And by the time he got up to the front of the room, he would be laughing himself. He knew he didn't know the first thing about adding and subtracting, and all those *numbery* things. Mr. Tacket knew it too, but he never stopped insisting that Cobbie try. I guess he kept thinking that someday he just might get one right, just might pull that arithmetic-rabbit right out of the hat. As best as I recall, though, he never did, but he never coward from trying. He simply couldn't get it, but always went back to his seat to a round of cheers and laughter, always with a huge smile and his arms held over his head in total acceptance of those who loved him for who he was rather than for what he didn't know.

There were only eight of us in the eighth grade, six boys and two girls. Clifford Potter and Preston Mullins were the biggest. They were also the oldest, having repeated several grades several times. Neither was the least bit cooperative or enthusiastic about books, and sat, for the most part, with scouring looks, and, except for Mr. Tacket, daring even the slightest glance in their direction. The rest of us were fourteen and pretty much where we belonged.

Being in school for the biggest part of the day didn't mean fewer chores. It only meant that we had to work faster to get them done. Bringing books home to study was an odd concept and something that seemed to matter little to any of us. School was the place for books. The time at home needed to be spent girding against the unpredictability of the seasons and submitting to the defenses of life. So the night continued to be ours to share, unencumbered by books and the notion that their contents could somehow free us from the bonds of our raisings.

Twenty-Four

The Fireman

Right up to the middle of October, most everybody went barefoot. It wasn't by design, but simply the way we lived, the way we made do with what we didn't have. Winter, though, presented us with a tougher version of life. Shoes, as unnatural as they were in summer, became a necessary component from November up through sometime in April, even when it meant wearing the ones that didn't fit, the ones handed down from brother to sister and even sister to brother. Most of all, they allowed us to escape the inscrutable nonsense of staying indoors during recess and trying to bear up under games like *Mother-May-I, Eye Spy* and *Button-Button-Who's-Got-The-Button.*

Wearing what was available was the general rule throughout most of our lives. But during the winter months, we went to wearing most anything and everything we could get our hands on. It was a time that made most of us look like the ragged, patched-and-tattered hillbillies that we were. But despite our outward appearance, there was a tenacity to us, something that most of us weren't even aware of, something that said we were tougher than all the elements of the world—and that our showing up everyday shivering, ruddy and willing was proof of it.

The playground never became any less inviting despite the ice and snow, as deep as it was at times. The games stayed pretty much the same, but with the ice and snow they had the added excitement of slipping and falling, and making others wet and miserable. The girls were still chased, the boys still wrestled one another into submission, and the big ones still bullied the little ones. Only now, instead of green apples and hawthorn berries whizzing by our heads, it was snowballs packed as hard as granite.

Despite our moth-eaten caps and scarves, and our layers upon layers of colors (our mix and match of checks and plaids and prints) we needed fire in the potbellied stoves, at least from November through March. Keeping fires in the stoves and keeping us from turning the palest shade of blue right where we sat, was the most important job outside of being the teacher. The fires had to be started a good hour before we took up books, even then it fell far short at holding back the bitter drafts that flowed unchecked around the windows, under the doors and across the floor. In truth, it was only those who sat within a few feet of the stove who could testify to its warmth. Those who sat beyond its radiance were not warm by any means, but were merely spared the bitterness that comes from having no heat at all. Those on the outside aisles who were continually blessed with warm saving breezes throughout the spring and early fall, were now huddled against the hoarfrost of their every breath. Complaining about it was as empty-headed as it was futile. We all lived in houses of the same order and knew that adaptation and adding more layers of whatever-kind were the only options against the endless and dreaded miseries that thrived in a backdrop robbed of heat.

Building the fires and keeping them going throughout the day was a paid job to someone unwaveringly committed to being there at daybreak, each and every morning, to get both stoves started (one in each room), stockpile enough wood and coal to keep them going throughout the day, then attending to them while keeping up with books. It was a job that required unfailing attendance and a willingness to work hard, but the dollar a week more than made up for it.

When Clifford Potter and Preston Mullins both wanted the fireman's job, it was left up to Mr. Tacket to make the final selection. At first, Clifford and Preston wanted to settle it with a fistfight. The rest of us agreed that that seemed fair given they were both about the same age and size. But Mr. Tacket said he would disqualify them both if they fought. Instead, he said it was going to be settled by having them go head-to-head in a spelling bee. "A *spelling bee?*" It's mere mention was met by everyone's riotous approval. There was more clapping, stomping, and ballyhooing than any ten cockfights might have raised.

Seeing that Preston and Clifford were both just a hair above misspelling their own names, we figured a spelling bee would be more fun than watching somebody work. Mr. Tacket's thinking was that it might motivate them to a positive end. After all, this *was* school. To our amazement, Mr. Tacket went as far as to give them a list of the words he would be asking them to spell, and a whole week to study them. It was about to become a hot time in the old schoolhouse come Friday week.

As expected, there wasn't a single absence that Friday. And right after the second recess, Clifford and Preston were called to the front of the room. While most everybody snickered and laughed, shuffled their desks and feet, and hooted out the side of their mouth, Preston and Clifford stood with their backs against the blackboard, expressionless as pallbearers. Mr. Tacket was considerably more lenient than usual, allowing for a bit of circus. The smile on his face said he was not above a little fun himself. It wasn't often that the littler ones could dish it out to the bigger ones. Preston and Clifford might as well have been in stocks, the targets of rotten fruit. Finally, Mr. Tacket brought the whole thing to order. There was, after all, a considerable prize at stake.

Before Mr. Tacket began, though, he made Clifford spit out his wedge of snuff, then gave him a severe warning for having it in the first place. After the rules were explained, Mr. Tacket then asked if there were any questions. There being none, he proceeded. There were twenty words altogether; the thinking being that it would be settled long before they ever got to twenty. We were never more mistaken. What we didn't count on was neither of them getting a single one right. By the time they had both missed number nineteen, there was so much mayhem, that Mr. Tacket was compelled to call for order—even complete silence. It was the last word, and Clifford's turn to go first. After a slight pause, Mr. Tacket, very concisely and very audibly said, "*Father.*" He paused. Then again, "*Father.* Children often refer to their parents as mother and *father.*" The word hung in the air as if it had been placed there by a demon. Clifford looked dazed, pained, his face contorted with thought. Then, after an agonizing wait, and with an assuredness that comes from being born again, he echoed the letters, "F…A…R…T."

By the time Mr. Tacket regained control of the big room, Clifford had surmised that something was wrong, but he didn't know what. But, then, neither did Preston. It wasn't until Mr. Tacket asked Preston to spell '*father*,' that Clifford realized he had misspelled it. So after thinking about it for a long, excruciating minute, Preston, never more sheepishly, uttered, "F…A…T…T…E…R."

Mr. Tacket hung his head in a gesture of total defeat just before the laughter reached a deafening crescendo. Both Preston and Clifford stood dumbfounded, neither one certain of what had happened. Finally, Mr. Tacket signaled for quiet. "I must congratulate you both," he said, panning back and forth between them, "for being such tough competitors." He waited again while a trickle of giggles subsided. "You both made a real contest out of it—and in the final analysis, you both spelled real words." Snickers and even a yelp came riding from the back of the room. "And I must hand it to you," he continued, "because it's out of this experience here today that I can understand why you originally chose to fight." There was another good round of laughter … but none from Preston or Clifford. "I don't doubt that fighting it out would have been far more satisfying for both of you." Clifford was suddenly awakened by Mr. Tacket's mere suggestion, and, on the spot, threw down a big oath at Preston. Preston straightaway commenced to unbutton his shirt, letting Clifford know he was ready. But Mr. Tacket brought them to an immediate halt and even made them shake hands. Then, in an air of openness, Mr. Tacket turned to the class and announced that since the spelling bee hadn't worked to distinguish either of the candidates, he was perplexed about what to do. The classroom grew cautious and still as he surveyed our faces. "King Charles," he said at last, "can you spell father?" King Charles was stirred to life and moved about in his seat as if struck with a sudden urge to scratch at a hard to reach place. At last, he took a deep breath, lowered his head and began recounting each letter—pausing painfully between each one—and finally finishing with a resounding 'R'. Letter perfect.

"There you have it, people," bellowed Mr. Tacket. "Your new fireman, King Charles Bliver." And that was that. The celebration was both instant and ear-shattering, the entire big room erupting in a cataclysm of laughter and cheer. Class was dismissed five minutes early with King Charles leading the way out the door, dancing with most everybody in a state of jubilation and doffing his cap to one and all. That's when I noticed the tiny scrap of paper lying on the floor next to King Charles' chair. The word 'father' was penciled on it in small black letters. Imogene followed my gaze, then froze me with the slits in her eyes. She held me that way until she was satisfied that I could feel my own pulse pounding in my neck. She then stepped nonchalantly to where the paper was laying and magically covered it with her foot, all the while holding my gaze with hers. There was never a question that King Charles would have to *work* for his twenty cents a day; neither was it a question that he'd have to give Imogene a nickel of it.

Across the aisle from Bobby, next to the outside wall and directly behind Imogene, is where I sat. Bobby sat directly behind Dixie. There was little, if anything, that took place between Dixie and Imogene that eluded us. Sitting behind Dixie was Bobby's dream come true, but as for me sitting behind Imogene ... well, there was nothing I could do about it.

Bobby was forever writing love notes to Dixie, notes she seemed obliged to always throw back at him. Bobby's persistence was a constant amusement to everybody around him ... everybody except Imogene. Bobby was a total annoyance to Imogene, and Imogene's annoyance was a constant irritation to everybody else. Everybody except Dixie. But despite the cold war between Bobby and Imogene, Dixie never took sides. And even though Dixie threw Bobby's notes back at him, none of us ever got the idea that she meant it as anything other than a challenge for him to try again. None of us except Imogene. Imogene simply saw it as an excuse to wage war: her objective for living.

Aside from her on-going rejection of Bobby's notes, Dixie was always the picture of order: an old soul, the mark of good sense and apt behavior.

Despite her size, she could run faster than anybody in the whole school; and despite the fact that she never said more than a few words at a time, she was always the one with the right answers and the highest marks. She never missed school, even when she should have, and was never late except for the times when ice and snow blanketed us all. She watched over and cared for her younger brother and sister, the twins, like she was their mother, and without benefit of reward except what might come from their company. It was simply what she did, despite the odds. For what she lacked in size, she made up for with will as ironclad as the bond she shared with Imogene.

Imogene, on the other hand, was, endowed with stature, could punch as hard as any of the boys and was every bit as mad-dog mean as she made herself out to be. To most, Imogene wasn't capable of emotion beyond wanting to inflict pain. We passed notes, but never to Imogene.

Seriann said Imogene was on the verge of womanhood, and us not treating her as such was the reason she stayed so stirred up. Whatever the reason, she stayed that way until just before Thanksgiving when she dropped a note on my desk on her way back from the water bucket. She did it right in the middle of arithmetic, right when things were the quietest. I checked to see if anybody had seen her; the last thing I needed was a rumor linking me to Imogene. To my relief, nobody had—not even Bobby. Still, I waited for a time before I read it. In big bold letters, it said, "YOU WANT TO SMOKE? I DO. I GOT CIGARETTE." The first thought that crossed my mind was that I was doomed: that her note was just a lure, her way of getting me alone somewhere to help me better understand her notions of dominance. After a while she adjusted herself in a sort of sideways posture in order to get a glimpse of me, however brief, without being too obvious. I don't remember much, just her lips fighting against the smile trying to infiltrate them ... and her eyes. For the first time I noticed her eyes. They weren't beaded like usual, but big and round and the color of jewelweed at first light.

I wrote her back and told her I didn't smoke, hoping that would be the end of it. But right after Thanksgiving, her persistence made me realize she was working toward something far greater than wanting to share a cigarette. She became almost civil during the weeks leading up to Christmas, slipping me pieces of chewing gum and writing me little messages about how she was having these bothersome dreams, and how I happened to be in them most of the time, and what did I think about Jesus, and did I know that Dixie really loved Bobby and how I wasn't supposed to tell, and was I ever going to smoke that cigarette with her. Our special friendship went on this way, in silence and in secret, right up to Christmas—neither of us daring to exchange a single word except by note. After a time, I was convinced that her intentions were harmless enough, though I suspected something self-serving behind it all. To this end, I kept a mindful watch and secretive eye on her every move. The fact that she had become noticeably less aggressive, and having found something akin to happiness—or so it seemed—made me as fearful as suspicious. The one thing, though, I feared most was that her happiness might have something to do with me. It wasn't long before my fear was confirmed. It had *everything* to do with me.

Twenty-Five

His Soul All Up in Whiskey and His Mind All Up in Books

Winter would have been a more dismal time had Corbin not come around so often. I was certain Seriann was the main reason, but there was an almost tangible aura that endeared him to the rest of us as well. His *being there* was a wellspring for what Mary Olive called *the bitters*: the long, gray, house-state of winter. And though there were times when he would disappear, long days and nights when we would hear nothing from him, his return was never any less eventful, never without the presence we knew as all abiding. It was like he belonged to us, like Bobby.

Corbin was never more charming than when Mary Olive served up her iron-skillet cornbread and cookers of string beans we'd hung and dried throughout the summer. "Ahhhh ..." he'd utter, "the heavenlies of cornbread and beans; what anchors us to our raisings."

"'At Corbin's *flowery*," said Mary Olive, "big and proper with words I ain't never heard tell of. Serpent's tongue I reckon's what's got him; his soul all up in whiskey an' his mind all up in books. Do him better to get in a church house now and again, my way a' thinkin'."

He loved to surprise, Corbin did, seldom without some token of fun or fondness whenever he came around: blow gum and penny candy for Wilson and Little Sherman; R.C. Colas and Moon Pies for Seriann and Wilma Lee; half pints of shine for Mary Olive—something he'd slip in her apron pocket when no one was watching. Then there was the dime pressed secretly into my palm before he was drawn to leave. He never forgot.

For the biggest part, Corbin was quiet and unassuming, with the gift to put others at ease while, without ever a mention, letting them know they were better off being his friend than not. Yet, while he was given to composure and fits of pondering, there never seemed to be any question that he was marked by trial. Whether from God or the devil was hard to tell, only that he was possessed of something that kept him resistant to the likes of demise and what it might bring. I guessed it was never anymore than wanting a taste of fulsomeness, and without having to sell his soul to get it, that kept him free from things like fear and self-condemnation, from the constraints imposed by the likes of customs and religion. Mostly, it was something that lived inside as a promise, something forged in determination and constructed to help those he cared for, that brought him to things otherwise out of reach, that stemmed the tide of not having what was dreamed and all that had, so many times, faded like lightening bugs in the sun ... all the while believing that it was more in God's hands than his anyway.

Twenty-Six

Christmas Time

Each grade drew names for Christmas. There was supposed to be no swapping; the name you picked was the name you got. But as it turned out, Bobby gave Preston Mullins a pack of Cloves chewing gum for Dixie's name. Preston went for it, even though it meant he'd be stuck with Clifford Potter.

King Charles Bliver drew my name, but then told me on the sly that Imogene had made him trade with her. He said he wasn't going to do it, but changed his mind after she told him not to be surprised if one of his dogs just up and died.

King Charles ended up with Bobby's name, and gave him a single-bladed Barlow pocketknife he stole from Luck Hanner. Bobby gave Dixie a horsehair bracelet no bigger 'round than a water reed, but with a teeny glass heart tied to it the color of a ruby. Bobby had gotten it from his Uncle Corbin. He said Corbin had taken it in trade for a pint of moonshine, but Seriann said he took it off some old whore down in New Orleans. Wherever it came from, it was about the prettiest thing we'd ever seen. At first, we just stood there ogling it and trying our level best not to touch it. Dixie knew full well what Bobby's intentions were, and held her pouty face until she couldn't hold it any longer. Her eyes were the first things to let go, widening, brightening, accepting that someone thought enough of her to give something so lovely and out-of-reach. Next was her smile, widening, lips thinning, stretching so far and tight into her cheeks that it seemed like it might be locked there forever. We stayed lost in her joy for a time, until she whispered thank you in Bobby's direction. It was all he needed.

When it came time for Preston to give Clifford his gift, he just said he didn't get him anything. Clifford said he was glad of it—and that even if he had gotten him something, he would have thrown it down the hole in the shithouse anyway. Clifford then told Cobbie that he'd drawn his name and that he had him something, but forgot to bring it with him. Cobbie gave King Charles a ring from a Cracker Jacks box, and I gave Preston two brand new number two pencils with erasers. King Charles paraded around the room wearing his ring like it was an heirloom, even though it only went up to the first knuckle on his baby finger. And it was only minutes later that Preston bit the erasers off his pencils and flicked them at the back of my head. Dixie finally eased her grip on her bracelet long enough to give Imogene three big blocks of fudge she'd made herself, wrapped in pressed muslin.

Exchanging gifts was the last piece of official business before the school turned out for Christmas. When Mr. Tacket was sure all the exchanging had been done, he pulled out a poke with enough blow gum so that everybody in the room got a piece. He wished us all a Merry Christmas as we headed out the door, and warned us to have our gum chewed up by the time we came back.

I pretended to pack up slowly before leaving, not moving any faster than Imogene, just in case she suddenly remembered that she had my name. After the room was nearly cleared out, she took a halting step in my direction and reached toward me with a stiff arm and a clenched fist clamped around something shiny. Her face was stoic, but not hard; her eyes steady, but not menacing. "Take it," she said. "Hit don't work, but I was hopin' you'd like it anyways." After an awkward second or two, she placed it tenderly in my hand. It was a pocket watch, wonderfully worn and smooth, and with scrolling on its back and face. "You like it?" she asked. I stood for the longest time just staring at it, marveling at its heft, its silver-gold color. I nodded, realizing that these were some of the first words she'd ever spoken to me. Her voice seemed too kind. "Thought you might be up to fixin' it," she said. I nodded again and heard myself say, "Thank You." She smiled and without another word, packed up and headed toward the door—but then stopped and back-tracked to where she'd left me standing, unfolded the cloth and broke me off a wedge of her fudge. "Oh," she said, smacking her lips around a piece she'd broken off for herself, "don't ever tell where you got it. That watch, I mean. Daddy'd kill me if he ever found out I was the one who took it." It was the last thing she said before she turned and headed toward home.

Clifford and Cobbie waited on the playground to see what Imogene gave me. I told them she had made me a butterscotch cake and was bringing it to me as quick as she could get home and get it. Clifford said that beat everything except what he got Cobbie, then disappeared over the edge of the creek bank. When he climbed back out, he was carrying a pint-sized Mason jar full to the brim, its content crystal clear and with a heavenly shine. It was all Cobbie's, but a gift Clifford was confident that Cobbie would share. In fact, it was a gift we would all share come Saturday night.

Twenty-Seven

Crazy Water

Dark had settled long before Clifford and Cobbie hobbled their way onto our porch, their arms extending well past the end of their coat sleeves and looking red and raw from the cold. They were out of breath, their bedraggled boots lopsided with mud, and their hair wet and covered with snow that was falling in great soft lumps.

"Lord, young'uns," Seriann said, "get in here by the stove. Freeze me to death just lookin' at you."

They said little, just kicked off what mud they could on the edge of the steps, then hurried past us to the stove, their hands reaching toward the warmth like they were in need of new skin. Seconds later Bobby came in behind them.

"I declare," wheezed Mary Olive, "if you'ns ain't like the three wise men, I don't know what is." Laughter was all around, Saturday night slowly becoming as welcome as hot apple pie.

We kept the kitchen stove stoked day and night since it gave off twice the heat as the grate in the upper room. It was where we stayed most of the time, and the perfect place for Mary Olive's half-bed Cousin Truman had hewed out of railroad ties that remained after Greezy's rail spur was dismantled. I can't say Mary Olive was ever really content scrunched up under all them quilts so much of the time, and with her head wrapped in an old wool scarf and tied in a big knot under her chin, but it left her arthritis a lot less cantankerous and her grumbling about it a lot less frequent. Still, the cold left her weary, stiff and achy, hacking and wheezing with what she called *the miseries.* We cared for her, each in our own way, taking turns fetching and mounting one assault after another on what the cold drafts brought under the door. Grandmaw sent an assortment of cures by Cousin Truman: red root for chewing and nursing the throat, elderberry tea to help with the breathing, and brown paper to be soaked in liniment and laid on whatever part that throbbed. Mary Olive discounted most of it most of the time in favor of Corbin's shine (her *Crazy Water*) that she sneaked at every turn, believing it had its own medicinal powers. But, by far, the biggest problem we had was with her chamber bucket. It sitting in that god-awful freezing lower room was bad enough, but then there was the on-going dispute between Wilson, Wilma Lee, Seriann, and me over whose turn it was to empty it.

"Quick," said Seriann, "tell us what you brung us for Christmas."

"Zactly what you got us," Clifford said. Laughter was infectious that night, the onset of Christmas pouring through each of us. One by one, we huddled around the upper room grate, close to one another and with our coats on, the fire crackling and popping and warming our front sides. Standing every so often to turn our backside to the grate was as necessary as it was inconvenient, chilblains working to leave us as cold as day-old gravy.

Wilson's attempts to untangle one guitar chord after another soon transformed Wilma Lee from the Hollywood image she had of herself to the ugly half-sister insisting that he "Put that damned thing down." Except for these short but twisted outbursts, she was right neighborly all the way around, but I thought there was something a mite more noticeable in her attentions toward Cobbie, much like a cat throwing off its scent.

After Mary Olive's insistence that we help her from her bed in the kitchen to her rocker by the fire, and after Seriann popped the popcorn Bobby stole from his daddy's crib, Little Sherman was primed to tell about the old troll. It was, by far, his best performance of all time and left us, to the last man, rolling in laughter. But laughter was not what he wanted. The whole point was to scare us. So we did a dead-quick turnaround and scolded him for taking years off our lives. In a matter of seconds he was peeing toward the stars in a great arch off the porch.

It was a semicircle we sat in, around the grate and with Clifford and Cobbie's feet stretched toward the fire, close enough that their cold wet boots hissed and sent tiny trails of steam to mingle with the room's chill. We sat for the longest time clutching at our coats and feeding the fire, and being aggravated by Wilson's injurious strumming. Cobbie was generous in offering up his liquor, which he insisted on calling *muleshine*, the bottle making its way from Clifford to Bobby, then back home to Cobbie. I was close to touching it to my lips on its return trip, but then thought better of it after a cold stone stare from Seriann. Cobbie was not above manners, and, time and again, offered the jar to Mary Olive. But Mary Olive was consistent with her *No thank you*, declining it with a sour and disdainful look, one that proclaimed she was above such vileness. "Lord, honey, a taste a' that stuff is like siding with the devil. Seen it kill more'n it's cured. Shore to damage a woman like me," her sober-faced conviction and a weak and wheezy cough showed just how fragile she could be.

Bobby, the single best agitator that ever lived, coaxed Wilma Lee into singing us a song. But before she could get started, Mary Olive started in with "*Amazing Grace*." After we worked our way through all four verses, Wilma Lee grabbed hold of her dulcimer and started fingering up and down its neck till she settled into a rhythm and chorus of "*Down in the Valley*." Her voice was as sweet as it was haunting, arching up then down, from the back of her throat to the roof of her mouth, sweeping and half yodeling from one note to the next. Wilma Lee was half loony half the time, but could melt the strings of a dulcimer and sing like she'd been schooled by angels. She led us in one song after another: "*Sweet Betsy From Pike*," "*Great Speckled Bird*," and "*Black is the Color of My True Love's Hair*." It was then that the Mason jar made another round. We pushed into the night with songs as tireless and wild as the fire we kept heaped with wood and coal. Woeful and sorrowful renditions of "*Am I Born to Die*," "*Down in the Willow Garden*," "*Barbara Allen*," and "*Come All You Fair and Tender Ladies*" rang in high mountain tenors, Clifford and

Seriann straining to reach the spirits beyond. But as the night lingered, there was a noticeable up-tempo. Songs like "*Coo-Coo Bird*" and "*Roving Gambler*," and even a dulcimer redition of "*Sally Goodin*"–songs for hot footin'—pinged and danged from the frayed and worn strings of Wilson's guitar. All the while, the Mason jar wound down and around between our whooping and howling, between the carnival that had laid hold of us, and until the three wise men were tolerably red eyed and far from restraint.

Without the slightest provocation, Clifford started in singing a floor-stomping rouser called "*Cripple Creek*." Wilson did his level best to keep up, but stayed about a half-note behind. But it was Wilma Lee who stole the show, her moment of truth, and we hooted and hollered when she sprang to her feet and went into a clogging frenzy. Wilson quickly found his groove and together they rent the air with what was clearly mountain thunder. On and on they went until Seriann finally jumped into the fray, kicking and skipping as high and hard and fast as a chicken running across hot coals. In the next instant, Bobby was off his chair, and in mockery, fanning their feet with his hat. It was only seconds later that Cobbie was brought to the full upright position and went to scooting across the floor like a dog hard after fleas. All at once Cobbie was everywhere, dancing like he was made out of coils and springs. His long bony legs hitched and churned, twisted and twined, jerked and stomped till I thought he was going to kick a hole in the floor. His longer-than-long arms flailed about his head like he was beating away a swarm of bees. The gargantuan smile plastered to his face told the plain and simple truth of a clodhopper and halfwit numbed painless by corn liquor. The floor was all of a sudden nothing but Cobbie and Wilma Lee, step for step, stomping and high-kicking, faster and faster, and faster still—fighting with all their might to outdo the other. All the while, Mary Olive was grinning like a 'possum in a turnip bed. We were all rolling in laughter and shouting so loud that we were helpless to react when Cobbie's drunken top-heaviness suddenly sent him reeling toward the north at the same time his feet were going south. In the time it takes to bat an eye, his own vertigo sent him sidewinding across the floor and toppling headlong through the curtained doorway into the lower room. Almost in the same breath, we heard him carom off one of the iron beds and land hard on the floor, the unmistakable sound of Mary Olive's chamber bucket crashing beside him. By the time we got to him, the room's air was already too foul to breathe, and the cats had clambered into the rafters where they sat mewling in terror and disgust.

Almost at once, Wilma Lee started crying and moaning as if Cobbie had been shot, then began gagging once the stench of the chamber bucket reached her. Seriann began running through the house trying to get at poor Wilson for not emptying the goddam thing when she'd told him to. Wilson ran out the door and disappeared somewhere in the dark, then sneaked back in and hid under Mary Olive's bed. Meanwhile, Bobby and Clifford were slipping on the linoleum, trying to lift Cobbie to his feet. Little Sherman thought the whole thing was the best show he ever saw and climbed up in the middle of the bed, and jumped as high as he could for as long as he could amid Seriann's torrent of blasphemies. I just stayed back out of the way, figuring I'd be just as damned if I did as if I didn't. By the time Bobby and Clifford got Cobbie to his feet and out the door, Seriann and Wilma Lee were already mopping and scrubbing the floor with lye.

The three wise men left in a fallen state, drunk as skunks and carrying the smell of Mary Olive's bucket, and with Cobbie having to be half-carried. Little Sherman and I stayed on the porch listening to them cackle and stumble across the creek and down the road into Greezy's eternal blackness. Cobbie's voice was loudest of all, pleading over and over for Bobby and Clifford to take him back so he could kiss Wilma Lee goodnight.

A few minutes before midnight, the lye had thinned just enough to make the air tolerable. But when we went to help Mary Olive out of her rocker and back to her bed, we found her sound asleep. When we tried to wake her, an empty half-pint bottle tumbled from under her shawl and landed with a hollow clunk on the floor beside her. We realized then that she wasn't so much asleep as she was passed out. She hadn't needed Cobbie's jar of corn. She'd had her own. And the first thing she slurred when we got her to her feet was that she needed to use her bucket.

Twenty-Eight

A Chicken Under Each Arm

We closed off the lower room after our night with the three wise men, the night we called *the big spill*, hung a quilt in the doorway and let it slag onto the floor, blocking what draft made its way down through the rafters and around the window. What time I wasn't schooling and working for Old Man Andrew, I was busy chopping up what wood I could drag down the hill and picking up what coal I could scavenge from the slag heaps around Greezy's defunct mine. McKinney Steel Company owned and operated the mine (a joint venture by Price McKinney and Jim Corrigan), but McKinney being president and leading stockholder had authorized two camps: one at Greezy and one at Wolfpit about five miles to the southeast. The Wolfpit mine was in operation just prior to WWI, and on a rail spur with several other mines in nearby Marrowbone. The Greezy Creek mine could not be constructed until the old railroad tracks originally built by the Yellow Poplar Lumber Company sometime back in the 1880's were rebuilt, a spur that ran all the way from the Big Sandy River clear into Gardner Fork. Once rebuilt, in the aftermath of WWI, building materials could then be easily transported, and the construction of Greezy's mine began in earnest. Operations began shortly thereafter: tunneling and blasting through the coal seams that ran all the way from Big Bug Hollow to the top of Wolf Pit Mountain. Price McKinney had actually built a whole community around the two camps: schools, libraries, theaters, hospitals, general stores, pool halls, houses for its workers, even bathhouses. The two mines combined employed hundreds and worked round the clock six days a week for upwards to ten years, until the death of McKinney in 1926 and Corrigan in 1928. By that time, the Greezy Creek mine had played out, and its successors left to salvage what remained of materials and equipment. What they left behind were miles and miles of shafts through what was once bed-rich seams of coal. Still, a person could scratch out a sack or two here and there if he wanted it bad enough: if he had the gumption to climb all the way up to the old mine entrances, pick through its slag heaps, chip away at what was scant and insufficient, then lug it all the way home. I know, because I did it often enough. Bobby and Wilson were with me most times, when it was the coldest and the hills lay blanketed in snow. It took the better part of a day, the sky being nearly black by the time we made it home.

What coal we gathered was done lump at a time and put in burlap sacks till they weighed forty pounds or better, whatever each of us could carry. It was Bobby's idea to tear the tin roof off an old mine shed and use it to sled our coal down the hill. It saved us the back-break of slogging it down snowy slopes in shoes with soles as slick as wet rocks. It was loutish work, but something we did out of necessity, to keep the blue off our lips and the deep freeze out of our beds. We went every week or so, depending on what rawness blew off the mountains and how much of it our newspaper-covered walls could turn away.

What few cats stayed on for the winter spent most of their time behind the stove or in front of the upper room grate, depending on which offered the greatest sense of seclusion. Outside of skulking about in perfect silence, stalking what was not there half the time, sleep and a persistence for eating was the sum total of their existence. And though the cold made for a shortage of kill, it never stopped them from their nightly ramblings, choosing the *out of doors* even on the bitterest nights to reenact their stealth and their search for the unsuspecting: those tasty morsels unfortunate enough to find complacency in the snow. And though a *kill* was never guaranteed, the cats never seemed discouraged. It was simply the *prospect* that kept them insulated, that stood them against all that had slowed down and frosted over. Come cock-crow, though, they were once again there to resume their rightful places behind the stove and in front of the grate, their fascination with the rafters replaced by the warm slow burn of coal.

Throughout the winter and into spring, we all slept in the upper room except for Mary Olive who slept on her half-bed by the kitchen stove. Our hovering together was more of a necessity than a choice, given the lower room was without any means of heat.

Wilson's job before going to bed was to draw a fresh bucket of water, which got done about half the time; mine was to bank the fire, stack as much wood on the grate as it would hold, then cover it with a thick layer of coal, enough so the grate worked like an oven, baking and fueling the embers beneath it. Still, it was a fire that needed to be tended, stoked, then stacked and banked a second time before the night was over. That second tending was Seriann's to do, and though she was mouse-quiet, I never failed to wake just long enough to know her tiny shadow and gentle attentions. Knowing that the night and its eternal dampness was being battled head-on, and that I was not alone, came with its own kind of warmth.

Seriann was also the first one up, scurrying about tending to Mary Olive, the stove, and what she could put together for breakfast: sometimes what we had for dinner the night before, sometimes fried bread and the preserves we'd put up; sometimes a bite of gravy when we had the flour; and then sometimes just a flitter and a good cold drink of well water. We never had a lot, but we always had enough.

We stayed deep under mounds of quilts during those frosty mornings until we felt our overalls land on top of us, after Seriann had warmed them by the grate. Most mornings we could see our breath; mornings when ice had to be chipped off the top of the water bucket and the wind slipped unrepentant under the door. North winds were the most unforgiving, no matter the layers we heaped on ourselves or the amount of coal we heaped in the stove and grate. We hung quilts over the windows at such times and shoved rags under the door. We looked like hobos huddled in coats and wrapped in blankets in front of the stove, our faces hovering over the steam rising from hot cups of tea steeped from sassafras root. And then there were days when the wind was only a phantom and the sun so hard at work that a simple fire in the grate was all we needed.

Two days before Christmas I went with Cousin Truman to fetch Grandmaw. She wasn't expecting us, but swanned at our invitation. The ride back was cold and Grandmaw sat huddled between us, under her many layers and wrapped tight in the sturdiness of a quilt. Aside from the Model-T's god-awful jostling, we rode in a spirit of hope, fed by Cousin Truman's Holy Ghost blessings and the promise of being together come Christmas.

When we got to Old Man Andrew's, I asked Truman to stop so I could walk the rest of the way. His and Grandmaw's protests were light, but I walked as a way of clearing my head and linking myself to Christmases past, to voices and faces I feared would somehow disappear before I was ready. I thanked all the diamonds passing themselves off as stars that they hadn't.

Bobby left early Christmas Eve before we'd told a single story, played a game, or sang a song. He said he had to get home to hang his stocking. With that, the rest of us ran from one room to the other, digging around for socks big enough to hold our notions of a dream. Supper was as good as it gets: cornbread and fresh churned butter, cooked white half runners, and fried potatoes. Afterwards, we sat drawn in tight around the grate and singing every Christmas carol we could think of, the night outside as still as breath.

Wilma Lee continued long afterwards, humming the soft melodies of carols we didn't have words for. Her renditions never failed to reach clear into my soul, each note velvety and throaty, even and easy, and as soft as corn silk. It was her magic, what joined us to this night and allowed me the memories of Momma and Daddy. I was alive to Wilma Lee's gentle moan and where it carried me: to that plane between gladness and regret.

We hadn't seen nor heard from Corbin in over a week, hadn't known of his whereabouts until he came through the door without knocking, and in a coonskin coat down to his ankles. "Lord a mercy," hollered Mary Olive. "I b'lieve a bear's gone an' swallered Corbin clear up to his neck." From there we were filled, our laughter contagious. We never knew what to expect from Corbin apart from surprise.

"Me an' mah horse'r lookin' for beds," he said. "Saw yer light an' was hopin' you might show a kindness." He was looking straight at Seriann. "Solitary out there t'night. Not a time for lost souls, such as myself, to be alone."

Seriann sat studying him with a cool eye and hunched behind the smoke drifting up from her cigarette. Deadpan. Serious. "Don't cotton much to outsiders, but don't reckon we'd turn'r backs on a stranger needin' a bite a bread an' a pillow."

"I'm obliged to you, ma'am. Can't stay but a week—maybe two—an' I ain't got but a dollar an' fourteen cents."

"You gotta name?"

"Folks just call me Hardluck, 'cause 'at's what I got most of."

"Where 'bouts you from...Hardluck?"

"Got no home to speak of...just passin' through is all. Raised by wolfs what time I was learnin' to crawl. Slipped off one night 'fore they could figure out I was sump'm to eat. Went to walkin' an' wearin' shoes adder that."

"And how is it you come upon us...Hardluck?"

"Bright star in the east showed me the way. Hangin' up 'ar like a Mason jar full a' lightnin' bugs."

"Seems like we've heard tell of such: them from yonder-off follerin' stars. The Book says we ought do fer strangers—s'long's you don't mind sleepin' four to a bed."

"Four beats five," he said.

"Well, then; welcome!"

With that, we clapped and bellowed till we were made warm by it; by the folly and the newness it brought.

Corbin said nothing of his long absence nor did we ask. His being there was joy enough. After Seriann fed him, we scrunched even closer together and listened to Mary Olive tell us about the wise men and the baby Jesus. Though at one point Seriann had to redirect, because Mary Olive had somehow included Moses in the story. We stayed huddled around the fire well into the night, a feeling of peace seeming to press in around us until our heads were as heavy as our eyes. Seriann sat with little Sherman asleep across her lap, his arms and legs in four different directions—like a cornhusk doll left too many times in the rain. Mary Olive sat lifeless, her head lolled to one side and snoring in a soft, steady drone while Wilma Lee sat like a brood mare, droopy-eyed and hoping Cobbie Parsons would come warm himself by our fire. Grandmaw had long since gone to bed and Wilson was asleep on the floor, curled in a quilt and as close to the fire as he could get without being in it. Ol' Bartley was curled up next to him (one of the few times he was allowed in the house), twitching and whimpering his way through a dream I could only imagine being a hot pursuit on the heels of a fox. Corbin sat the way he did most times, studying on things he never talked about, smoking and staring into the fire's hypnotic glow. We stayed that way for the longest time, just being at ease with Christmas, its eve and its meaning.

We woke Christmas morning to the sound of Seriann's laughter and Corbin standing in front of the stove stirring gravy. We were surprised to see him so early, and even more surprised that he had taken care of the fire and even brought in more wood and coal. "Ain't seen no Christmas stockin's," he said. "'Course I didn't look behind the stove." That was all Wilma Lee and Wilson needed. They charged at once, sending the cats scattering and causing Corbin to nearly upend the gravy.

The glee was enough to fill the room, yet we went about making sure one didn't get more than the other. It was just as it should be, each of us with the same things: the biggest and prettiest orange that God ever made, a package of Teaberry chewing gum, a candy cane as big around as a candle stick, and a brand-new pair of brown shoe laces. Wilma Lee was the only one who got something extra. It was a tortoiseshell comb, which little Sherman, Wilson, and I didn't care about anyway. For the longest time afterwards, we talked about when we were going to eat our oranges, and just as important, where we were going to hide them until we did.

Corbin surprised us with a dozen eggs and a quart jar of molasses. Then he surprised Seriann with a dress he bought in Pikeville. It was tiny and shiny and red, thin and light to the touch: full of spark, and flash, and fancy. Well, this started Seriann to crying to where she had to put her head down on the table. She said she didn't think she would ever own a dress like this as long as she lived. Well, then, that started Wilma Lee to crying because she'd never had a new dress and figured she needed one more than anybody, and certainly more than Seriann. Then that started Mary Olive to crying because of the confusion between Wilma Lee's misery and Seriann's jubilation. With all three of them crying, Corbin thought he would join in, adding a bit of mockery. It was only seconds before Wilson and little Sherman decided to do the same. That's when Wilma Lee turned it up a notch. "Y'all don't give a damn 'bout meh. S'long's yew got everthang yew want, it's just nervermind 'bout Wilma Lee. She don't need nothin' no ways." That's when Wilson started yelling for her to shut up, and when Seriann tried telling her they could *share* the dress, and when Grandma started asking the Lord to forgive Wilma Lee's ol' filthy mouth. Then Corbin chided in saying to Wilma Lee that he was sorry for trying to make Seriann happy. That's when Wilma Lee went running to the upper room and the cats came running back into the kitchen; when little Sherman ran to the porch to pee, and when Woodrow, looking like the general of the whole United States Army, came bounding through the kitchen door. There was so much shouting and commotion at the sight of Woodrow that most everything else was forgotten. Corbin burned the gravy, and quite by providence, our tears of discontent turned to joy.

Woodrow came loaded down: a duffel bag with his personals, and a burlap sack stuffed with a ten-pound sack of cornmeal, six cans of Spam, twelve cans of Vienna sausage, a five-pound slab of bacon, two pounds of coffee, and a poke full of jawbreakers. It was a long time before we could get Seriann to stop crying again.

I don't remember much after that except everybody bawl-babying and hugging—all of us talking loud and fast, and all at once. It was, for the world, like watching a short circuit of minds, but a morning full of the sights and sounds of joy, where the past and its sorrows were covered over, where touch replaced all that lay empty and fallow, and where gladness of heart became as tangible as the sound of Seriann pounding out biscuits and Wilma Lee, with the whole end of her candy cane in her mouth, slicing and frying bacon. We fried up most everything Woodrow and Corbin brought, along with the skillet of gravy Corbin insisted on remaking. The smell was intoxicating and the noisy confusion was never sweeter until Bobby came bursting through the door with a chicken under each arm. It was Christmastime at Mary Olive's.

Twenty-Nine

Hawleywood's Layrite Deluxe Pomade

Woodrow stayed for a week, then left on a Greyhound bus just before the New Year. What time he was with us, he wore his uniform day and night, and by the end of the week it was as sad looking as the rags he had on the day he signed up. His days were spent mostly in bed due to his nights so taken up with rambling. Every night was Saturday night to Woodrow, going from one honkytonk to another, the odor of whiskey and cigarettes on him as heavy as the Hawleywood's Layrite Deluxe Pomade he kept cranked into his hair. His big-time buddy, Clell Akers, was all too happy to share in Woodrow's new prosperity. For Clell, it was like having stumbled onto free whiskey. But when the prosperity ran out, so did Clell.

When it came time for Woodrow to depart, Corbin and Seriann put him in the back of the Model-A and drove him to Pikeville where they helped him, drunk as he was, onto a bus back to Fort Benning, Georgia. He left without ever a wave of thanks, and, by the kindness of Corbin, two dollars from flat broke: two dollars he swore to pay back, but which I never remembered him doing. It was a goodbye that left us confounded, not knowing if he was even a part of us anymore.

Thirty

The Natural Order

When we took up books after the New Year, snow came full and arctic-like, as did the pitying accounts of chills and croup. Half stayed home half the time, and the rest stayed huddled around the big potbellied stoves even at recess, the playground having lost all appeal to the icebox we knew as January. After nearly three long weeks of it, one of Seriann's strays had a litter right behind the kitchen stove ... all stillborn. Mary Olive went on for days about how it was a sign, cautioning that there were spiteful days a-commin'.

Near the end of the month, winter returned to a bearable state and Dixie Wainwright, for the first time I could remember, came late to class; just stole in right after the Pledge of Allegiance, her head low and her face hidden, and without as much as a glance in any direction. Mr. Tacket's eyes narrowed as she shuffled to her seat, but then he was one of constant vigil. Dixie sat without moving, her head slumped like an insurmountable weight. To say or do anything was to risk Mr. Tacket's wrath, so I sat like everybody else: still as a statue in the din of overloaded thoughts, and with the smell of coal cooking in the stove. It was like sitting in church for the most part, no one daring to look left or right. Dixie was the quietest of all, the model of stillness sitting with her head so low that her hair fell and flanked her face the way blinders flank the eyes of a plow mule. Once, though, I ventured a backward glance, a quick sweep between King Charles and Clifford, Cobbie and Preston, but all

I got in return were grim looks and headshakes that warned me off. My rubber-necking caused Mr. Tacket to stop in the middle of what he was doing to ask me if I was having a problem, and did I need to be excused. Survival instincts brought me to square myself in my seat, give him a *no-thank-you* headshake, and bury my face deep in a primer of ABC's.

Minutes later, notes drifted to me from all directions, Dixie being their focus. The note from Clifford and the one from Preston took the longest to decipher, because what they wrote weren't words so much as hieroglyphics. They couldn't actually be *read*, only *figured out*. Even *the* was spelled *thu*.

Bobby was quieter than I'd ever seen him, no help at all. He accepted no notes nor sent any, just sat there staring at the back of Dixie's head.

Mr. Tacket always started his lessons with the fifth grade on the far side of the room then worked his way up to us eighth graders on the opposite side. Until he got to us, we were fearful enough to keep quiet and look busy. It wasn't long before he made his way up our aisle, before he stood staring down on us, his stature elevating him to colossal proportions, as if he were sole proprietor of the world. Today was no exception except for his attention going directly to Dixie, her head bowed and still as night.

In a manner unlike the brawn that defined him, Mr. Tacket slipped a beefy finger under Dixie's chin and tilted her head upward. Gingerly. Gingerly. Without the slightest change in expression, he let his eyes wander over the deep purple colors swollen tight into her cheeks and lips, and around her eyes, which were close to pinching shut.

"How do you feel, child?" Mr. Tacket asked, his voice just above a whisper. Dixie said nothing, just nodded as if to say Fine, then returned her chin to her chest. Most everybody in the front rows had turned to stare. Mr. Tacket gave them a congealed glare, which sent them reaching with all diligence for papers and pencils and books. He paused for a second before giving us the same look, which sent us pretending harder than ever to look entranced by the frayed and faded pages of our readers. From the corners of my eyes I watched him rest his hand on Dixie's shoulder. Feather like. Then return to his lesson.

On occasion, it became necessary for Mr. Tacket to place a meaty hand on the head of someone who failed to understand the simple rule of minding his own business. He would, with weight and bully, twist their head back around to the front. And though he strolled up and down the aisles spouting facts and asking questions, I watched his gaze drift to Dixie time and again. Checking. Making sure.

Our workload was light that morning, Mr. Tacket's attentions being directed more toward the lower grades, keeping attention away from our side of the room. At recess and then again at noon, Mr. Tacket took Dixie to the little room, where Miss Fields stayed with her—along with Imogene, of course. I huddled with the others at the upper end of the schoolyard, listening to what they knew about Dixie and her family, and about Haman Flowers. Bobby said nothing the whole time, just stood there, alone, like a toad in a garden. We stayed right up till we heard Mr. Tacket's big brass bell.

Whippings were not uncommon for any of us. *Gettin' what's comin' to you* was something we all understood, something ingrained from the time we were old enough to know better. It was a simple concept that taught the fundamentals of consequences. Learning it early on helped us become better adapters; accepting it made us better survivors. As long as the offense didn't violate laws of the land, doling out punishment was not only the *right* thing to do, but the *duty* of those entrusted with our raising. It was a mountain tradition, time-honored and expected, as blameless as it was biblical; something as sound as learning a lesson, and oftentimes every bit as valuable as teaching one.

Nobody ever said much about a welt or two on his backside. It just meant we had stepped out of line, made a miscue, veered off course. We had all been there at one time or another, and knew full well that we were always just one wrong move from being there again. My daddy always told me that if I ever did anything that caused the teacher to give me a whipping, then he would give me another one when I got home. Respect for authority and our elders were not choices, but rather a way of life. And if we didn't believe it, then we were made to feel it. After a while, thoughtfulness and personal responsibility became the natural order.

Whippings had no particular regimen. They could be thought out or delivered on the spur of the moment. The spur-of-the-moment kind, though dodgy, called for the most dexterity, and for Mommas and Daddies being able to use the first thing they could grab and wield without actually maiming. Whippings that were thought-out were most always done in private with something recognizable, such as a switch or leather strap. Spur-of-the-moment whippings were typically done in a vein-bursting adrenaline rush, and without the slightest regard for who was watching. Swift and vivid with weaponry, they were: cattails, plow lines, hair brushes... It didn't matter what thing was snatched up—just whatever wasn't nailed down and whatever they could get their hands on first—whatever lent itself to pain. It wasn't long after I'd come to Greezy, that I saw Bobby's mother come across his back with a stick of stove wood. And there was Clifford Potter's mother who broke a broom handle over the top of his head, and the time I watched Seriann chase Wilson with a dipper from the water bucket. What mattered most, though, whether thought-out or spur-of-the-moment, was the sheer act itself: caring enough to show disapproval, and understanding that lessons oftentimes meant significant emotional experiences, to say nothing of physical pain. It was love of a different kind, but love nonetheless, and the one thing common to us all. But what of whippings undeserved?—those sheer acts of cruelty?—those done to the front side and not the back? Dixie showing up with her face the color of plums spoke volumes about how someone had clearly crossed the line, had elevated a whipping to a beating. Even for uncomplicated crime-and-punishment mountaineers, there were boundaries. And even though there was nothing written that defined such boundaries, there was a keen understanding of excess. If lessons couldn't be taught in the accepted manner, then the fabric of our existence was in jeopardy. If time-honored punishment was ignored for acts of heinousness, or traditional ways set aside in favor of violence, then we'd be no better off than the perpetrators themselves. The only alternative was the unalterable certainty of knowing that there was *a price to pay*. If the offense was one of pure wickedness, the price could be severe: even to the point of putting an end to the offender.

In the same way that everyone understood that traditional ways needed to be respected, they understood that things flying in the face of them were cancerous, needing to be cut out. When bird dogs cowered at the blast of a shotgun, they were cut out. When fox hounds quit their scent in order to chase a rabbit, they were cut out, their line halted so not to contaminate future litters with the same weakness. It was the simplest of nature's laws and something we understood with impunity.

After Mr. Tacket called Dixie's name for a second time on the second day, he scanned our blank faces as if searching for clues to her whereabouts.

"Her little brother ain't here neither," pealed through the air, breaking the silence. It was Imogene, her tenor voice attacking the silence the same way I imagined it called hogs. We wondered if she might get a scolding for speaking out without raising her hand. But after fixing himself with a strong jaw, Mr. Tacket just nodded in her direction and said, "Thank You."

Throughout the morning, Dixie's being gone sparked a new flurry of notes, all of them laced with unsettling dread, a feeling that Imogene elevated at recess with her unholy banter of what she knew to be ungodly and unforgivable. Finally, it was her pleading that Bobby and I *do something* that changed things forever.

At noon, and under the siege of Mary Olive's camphor-infused rag she kept tied to her chest throughout most of the winter, we went to see Seriann: Imogene, Bobby and me. It had been Imogene's insistence, her pleading tone and the quiver in her lip that softened us, which betrayed the demeanor that said she was all hickory knots and cuss.

We stood around the stove for the longest time, talking without uttering much of anything, not knowing how to say what we came for and listening to Mary Olive recount her miseries. After a time, Cobbie Parson's familiar voice called out from the yard, riling ol' Bartley to a frail yelp. It was only seconds later before his big grin lit the way to his entrance, opening the door without as much as a knock.

"Figured you was here," he said, inviting himself in. It was only those as harmless as Cobbie who could just walk in without anybody reaching for a gun. "Whatcha'll doin' anyway?" he said. We didn't answer, just smiled real big and made room for him at the stove. I couldn't ever imagine him not being welcome anywhere. Wilma Lee disappeared as soon as he hunched through the door, but then reappeared only minutes later looking like she was about to board a train to Hollywood. Her lavish amounts of rouge and lipstick were as painful looking as her too-small dress, stretched-to-bursting around her abundantly grown-up bosom. She seemed to know the scent she threw. Cobbie's flared nostrils said he knew it too.

"We come hopin' you might help us with sump'm, Seriann," Imogene blurted, unable to hold back for another second, despite Cobbie Parsons now as a witness. "It's about little Dixie. Dixie Wainwright. She's mah best fren' an' I'm feared on account a' what's happened to her. I'm vexed, an' mah dreams is comin' dark an' devilish of a night. We're hopin' you might know what to do. Don't seem like there's nary other soul we can turn to." Seriann just listened, Little Sherman in a soft bounce on her knee. We all waited. Even Cobbie and Wilma Lee ceased their barefaced indulgence of one another.

"Go ahead, child," Seriann said. "Tell me what you know."

Imogene wiped at her eyes almost ashamed. "Well," she said, "it's like this: I been up 'ar where she lives a time or two, an'... Well, there's a evil about it: sump'm I can feel in the shadders (shadows) that fill the lane, an' in the quiet that just seems to creep up outta the ground, like they's ghosts a-stirrin'. Ain't never been inside her cabin. Cain't make mahself. I just turn an' head on home when we draw near to it, when the rocks an' trees start in, freezin' me like they had eyes. I been studyin' on it awl night, an' I can't let go what it's tellin' me, 'bout it bein' a ugly time up 'ar in 'at holler."

It was only seconds later and in the silence that gripped us all, that we heard Mr. Tacket's big brass bell. We'd succeeded in scaring ourselves into thinking the worst before heading back to the schoolhouse, and feeling even less certain than ever. As I closed the door behind us, I heard Mary Olive's half whisper: "I knowd them dead kittens was a sign a' bad things to come."

"Been better'n a month since I dropped over into Shop Branch," Bobby said. "Ever since we penned the cows up for winter." He talked while he helped me chop wood. "I'm b'lievin' we might oughtta head on over an' get a look." I could tell he was feeling me out. He didn't say anything else, just waited until I had time to think about it—then offered me a chew from a plug of Beechnut, something we seldom indulged in except when needing to feel large and connected to things male. It felt sturdy 'twixt my cheek and gum, harsh and sweet at the same time, resting me with a feeling of brotherhood. I could sense we were about to make a pact.

Dixie's third day of being gone was when her little brother, Franklin, brought word to Mr. Tacket that she'd run off. "Never come home adder school t'other day," he said. Just walked me to the mouth a' the holler an' tole me to go on to the house, that she'd be back directly. 'At's the last we seen her. Gone to Aug's, I reckon: our brother over in Winston's Creek. Haman's fixin' to go git her. Said she's his an' he's brangin' her back if he has to drag her by her hair—an' that he'll kill Aug, if he has to. 'At's ever word the truth, Mr. Tacket."

It was late that evening before Bobby came up with how we'd go about getting Dixie out of Shop Branch if Haman found her and brought her back. I wasn't sure how I felt about a lot of things, but I was as sure as I'd ever been that it was a plan with the built-in potential for not coming out alive. As a way of covering up my want to tell him he was crazy, I suggested that we first run it by Corbin. I trusted he would listen to Corbin before anybody else. As it turned out, Seriann was all over us before we could finish our opening sentence, threatening, as only she could, to cut our heads off and throw 'em down the well if we uttered another word about it.

Seriann had wielded her ax of horror in a matter of seconds; held it high and directly over our heads, then dared us to do anything about it.

She had gone ahead of Corbin, interjecting her will when we hadn't been talking to her in the first place, but she had gotten our attention in a way we knew not to ignore. In the end, it was enough to stop us from entering into a game we knew nothing about. Corbin sat with his hands laced behind his head and his feet propped up above the grate. He stayed that way until Seriann walked out of the room then rolled his head in our direction. "Is there anything else I can help you with?" he said.

"By God, we can still go up 'ar an' look around," Bobby said after we left. I could see I was up against a beast that didn't know *No* for an answer. "Maybe we ought to tell somebody where we're going in case we don't come back as quick as we should," I said.

After aiming a half-dozen rocks in the direction of the big dipper, Bobby finally accepted my idea as being part-way redeemable provided the person we told was somebody we could trust. First off, we thought of Cobbie then realized the chances of him being able to remember anything we might tell him were too slim to chance. Even if he did remember, somehow we knew that nobody would believe him until it was too late to do us any good. Next, we thought about King Charles, but then realized how he was apt to tell everybody on the creek. The last thing we needed was Haman Flowers knowing what we were going to do before we did it. Then we thought about Clifford and Preston, but knew that neither of them would go for it unless they could go with us and do something like burn his barn down or poison his well. In the end, we were left with only one choice, the only choice that seemed to truly fit. We would tell Imogene, consummate warrior that she was.

The first thing Imogene did after we confided in her and swore her to secrecy was to tell Mr. Tacket. It was betrayal, something neither of us could easily forgive, and something we agreed to let slide until a later time—when stress levels weren't at an all-time high.

Although Mr. Tacket was sympathetic to our plan, he was reluctant. "I don't know much about Haman Flowers," he said. "Just what I've been told and what's more or less common knowledge. But that's enough to make me advise you to stay as far away from him as you can." His look was solemn. "I hope you understand what I'm saying," he said, his eyes darting back and forth between us. Sensing Bobby's resolve, he added, "If anybody needs to check on Dixie, it ought to be me."

"You mean go up 'ar by yerself?" asked Bobby.

"Why, yeah," said Mr. Tacket.

"Even after what you know?"

"What do I have to be afraid of," he asked. "I'd be going with honorable intentions, and I'd be unarmed. How could a man find fault with that?"

"Well," said Bobby, squinting, "that might work for some, but I'm guessing Haman Flowers wouldn't recognize honorable intention no more'n he would the inside of a church house."

Mr. Tacket studied Bobby for a time, then said, "I don't have to tell you the risks of sneaking around places uninvited, Bobby. I think you know 'em. So we have to be smarter'n Haman Flowers, 'cause if anything was to happen to either of you, it would make things worse for all of us—especially Dixie. You want to carry that load?" Mr. Tacket's words seemed to fall out of his mouth in big block letters. "Besides," he said, "even if Haman Flowers didn't catch you, he'd know you'd been there. I mean there's snow on the ground. He'd track you all the way home." He laughed. "And on top a' that, you told me he's got dogs. Unless you're gonna do your snooping a hundred yards away, you got no business up in that holler except to fetch your cows ... and they're penned up for the winter." He searched our faces for the longest time. "What's more," he said, "we don't know if Dixie's even there: if Haman's tracked her down and brought her back, or if she's still hiding out—which means Haman'll be looking to kill somebody over it. Either way, it's about as dangerous a situation as a man could walk into."

We left without arguing with what made perfect sense, the irony to Imogene's betrayal proving to be our salvation. Without it, we may have erred on the side of things lethal. Though she was not completely absolved, it did bring her a step closer to our forgiveness.

Friday came and still no word of Dixie. At the end of the day, Mr. Tacket informed Bobby and me that he was on his way to pay Haman Flowers a visit, though he had little doubt about its risks. He had a legitimate concern about Dixie not coming back to school, about her welfare. How he intended to address it with Haman Flowers was anybody's guess, but it was a sure bet that it would be with the better part of fortitude, raw guts, and will.

Mr. Tacket announced his coming by whistling an old Baptist hymn called "*The Sun Shines Bright*," an attempt, I imagined, to ward off the ghosts Imogene warned him about. But by the time he drew near, Haman's dogs had him all but treed. Haman met him in the lane that led to his yard. Was there waiting for him, actually, the twin barrels of his shotgun cradled in his arms.

"Howdy," said Mr. Tacket above all the baying. Haman didn't bother to answer, just stood there amidst his dogs and their howling frenzy, as if rooted in the snow. "Name's Tacket. Arlan Tacket," he said, extending his hand and sending the dogs into near meltdown.

Haman eyeballed his outstretched hand, all the while tonguing the gargantuan plug of tobacco wedged hatefully in his cheek. "Know who y'are," he drawled without moving his lips, his manner as grave as the chiseled hardness of his face, as assaulting as his grungy, brown, felt hat slanted and at such an angle that it proclaimed he was the cock of Shop Branch, by God, and the twelve-gauge he carried being all the proof he needed. Haman was without the thickness of Mr. Tacket; still, he stayed his ground almost with the hope that Mr. Tacket might have something to prove.

"Hope I didn't interrupt nothin'," said Mr. Tacket, pulling his hand back slowly. The dogs continued to circle and yelp as if waiting for a command to do something extreme. "I was just wonderin' about Dixie an' how she was gettin' along. Been out nearly a week now. SHE ALL RIGHT?" he asked, trying to make himself heard over the dogs. Haman tongued the corners of his mouth, then spit a short brown burst without looking to see where it landed. "I'm meaning no offense," added Mr. Tacket. "Just payin' respects is all, she bein' one a' mine at the schoolhouse."

Haman's eyes were riveted on Mr. Tacket, watching, it seemed, for the slightest movement that would give him cause for something more than talking. He stared for the longest time then winced, tightening his cheek and squeezing moisture from the chaw packed against his molars. "Nothin' to tell," he said. "Don't reckon it's nobody's business but mine, no how."

Mr. Tacket tried to add a smile to his tensed expression. "I reckon you're right about that," he said, his voice steady, but edging upwards. "Be right nice if she could finish out the year, though. Make her good enough to go on if she had the want."

"HUSH UP," snapped Haman at the dogs, sending them wining and cowering in confusion. "I'm the one decides the want 'round here, Mister Tacket! "An' far as I know, it ain't nuthin' I need he'p with." He wiped at his mouth with the back of his hand then waited, his message seeming to hang in the bite of winter wind.

Mr. Tacket stood unblinking, thick and solid, thinking, I was sure, about the best way to tear Haman into pieces small enough to feed him to his dogs. After a frightening stillness, he nodded, the need to press forward seeming to vanish in the very air. "Well, then," he said, pausing long enough to study what lay over Haman's shoulder—searching, maybe, for some sign of Dixie, "I reckon I'll be finding my way back." A cold, unbroken breeze came off the mountain, adding to the almost palpable uneasiness that filled the space between them.

"No need comin' back," Haman said. "Dixie's already knowin' more letters than she'll ever need. Awl your readin' an' writin'... It's taken up enough of her time, and mine to boot. 'Sides, she's not yourn to think on. I'll be the decider a' where she needs to be. Don't reckon you'll need remindin'." It was Haman's final word. Mr. Tacket turned slowly and walked off without looking back, his footsteps soft in the mud and snow. Haman watched after him long after he was out of sight, and long after the dogs had returned to the boredom of each other.

Bobby and I had watched from behind the same outcrop of rocks we hid behind most every time we fetched his cows, whenever he needed a glimpse of Dixie. It was true what Bobby said, that if we lay real still we could hear just about everything except Emmaline's hens alaying. We stayed hunkered there long after Haman had turned and walked back toward his barn. It was early night by the time we picked our way back over the ridge and into the head of Big Will Hollow.

By the time we got to the foot of the hill, Bobby had taken me through a half-dozen scenarios how he was going to *fix* Haman Flowers once and for all, for everybody's sake—skinned, scalped, and left to rot being the least of it. I stayed with him a long while listening to his rage, all the while trying to make sense of the life Dixie endured in the head of Shop Branch. But no matter how Bobby cut it, he never got beyond wanting to jump Haman some drunken Saturday night and maul ten to twenty years off his life. Bobby turned fifteen just two weeks before Christmas and declared to me that he was as much a man as anybody he knew, and, by God, was going to do what needed to be done. I never really understood what he meant exactly, only that he sounded like he meant it.

I headed home well after dark, my breath raspy and my footholds useless against what lay frozen beneath the snow, and thinking on the trouble that was now upon us. Ol' Bartley met me at the gate, the cats falling away at his coming.

I ate cold cornbread and what was left of the fried okra and stewed squash while Seriann questioned me about where I'd been. Mary Olive was already asleep, jerking and mumbling at her dreams. We talked in low tones until one lie after another worked its way in and around my eyes, until Seriann grew tired of pretending she believed me. After a time, she got up and left without as much as a look back, leaving me alone and disconnected, and with nothing but the sound of my chewing.

I wasn't good at lying and felt ashamed about it. I had been where I swore I wouldn't go, and figured there wasn't much that could be served by telling about it. Besides, I was ashamed to admit I'd spied on Mr. Tacket and put myself within the range of Haman Flowers' hate. After some time, I slinked in to sit by the fire, to join Seriann hunkered and staring trance-like at its flames.

"I'm sorry," I said just above a whisper. Seriann said nothing, just held me with her solitude, her eyes on something far away.

"I was up in Shop Bran—"

"I know where you was," she said, cutting me off. Her tone was sharp and without any intention of hiding its anger. I felt its full weight and sat resigned to taking what I had coming. Her eyes were penetrating, burrowing. "I can't be tolerant of lies, Rubin." She waited, letting her words eat at my guts. "I was hopin' we'd never be needin' a talk like this."

"I'm sorry," I said again, the only thing I could think to say.

"I'm fearful, little brother, of you ending up like just some other sorry-ass pretender; somebody who thinks he's clever enough to get away with whatever he wants, then stoops to puttin' a lyin' mouth to it. They're shameful people, Rubin. Imposters. Lowest a' the lows. Livin' deceit, then heapin' it higher by lyin' about it. An' all the time thinkin' they're foolin' ever'body. Truth is, they ain't foolin' nobody. Been around enough of 'em to know. It's a sickness: them spinnin' the truth like they're so much smarter'n everbody else, like nobody but them could ever tell the difference. I b'lieve they's a good many that can't help it; truly I do. But help it or not, there's a rankness to it...a thing without respect an' full a' contempt for ever'body who's made to listen to it. There ain't nuthin' 'bout a lie or a liar that ain't at the very bottom of a black hole."

We stared at each other for the longest time, until I couldn't look anymore. "I knowed where you was," she said, "soon as you started coverin' up. It was the only reason you had to lie.

"I know you're needin' to be goin' an' doin' what all you think it takes to be a man, an' I'm all the time prayin' no harm'll come to you, that you don't fall in with the wrong bunch. I b'lieve yer right-minded an' wouldn't never do nuthin' hurtful to nobody, not purposeful anyway. What it comes down to is what's in your heart: if it's a deceiver and a betrayer, or one fit with nerve. The heart's where it all begins. If it's right, the rest of you ain't got nuthin' to worry about. It's where the spirit lives ... where love gets added.

"Now, I 'preciate you tellin' me you're sorry. I just hope an' pray you'll never have to know a time when bein' sorry ain't enough, when you know that what you've done can't be fixed no matter what...no matter how many *I'm sorrys* you come up with. It might help ease yer pain, but it can't never take back what's done. What's done is ever'body's to live with. It's the thought and the deed in the first place that says what's really in your heart. Tellin' me you're sorry is one thang, but another is how it weighs me down with the burden of forgiveness—sump'm we all have *enough* trouble with, but then there's the forgettin' that *none* of us is all too good at. It's the forgettin' that never wants to go away, that leaves us feelin' like we been kicked in the stomach—an' laughed at on top of it.

"Bein' made a fool of ain't sump'm I'm good at, Rubin. I'm meant for better. What would I be if I didn't think so?"

We fell silent after that, gripped by the fire's gentle flames and the hiss of its coals. I understood the wrong I'd done and the potential dangers all too common for the untested, like Bobby and me, like anyone on the brink of discovery. I sat with my head low, feeling my heartbeat and listening to the steady breathing of those already asleep. Strange as it was, I felt heartened by Seriann's willingness to say what needed to be said, to love me. She had in so many ways become my mother. I knew from here on out that she would always be with me, that I'd carry her with me in a thousand different ways.

Seriann found my eyes and gave me her warmest smile, "Why don't you slip in there an' get you one a' them fried apple pies I put up for breakfast. Ain't nobody'll know an' there prob'ly still warm." I sat limp, recounting her words, embracing them for the gesture of what they were: her forgiveness. I could only hope that she'd forget in the same way.

"'At's okay," I said. "I'll wait." And with that, we leaned in closer to the fire, the front of us near-to-cooking, our backsides cold as smokehouse meat. I was long past wanting to put an end to the day when one of Wilma Lee's out-loud dreams about how pretty Cobbie Parsons was made helped send me on my way. I banked the grate with what wood and coal it would hold then broke the ice off the top of the water bucket, knowing full well I'd have to do it again come morning. Wilson and Little Sherman were already asleep by the time I shivered in beside them. It was my turn next to the wall, its icy-wetness glistening in the firelight, radiating the rawness that gripped it and turning my breaths into frosty vapors.

The night passed without much beyond the grate's soft flutter of flames and their shadows that danced like goblins against the loft. There was something avowing about the fire, something that silenced me, that connected me to the night, yet separated me from all that would devour. I slept without dreaming, with my back pressed against Wilson's and listening to the start of a drumming rain. It was the kind that would soon melt the snow and bring more than a fair share of mud off the mountains. For all our sakes, I hoped Dixie would come with it.

Thirty-One

Awl 'at Rain

Seriann and Wilma Lee set out peas the day after Groundhog Day. The almanac was clear on that despite a cold drizzle. There was still snow high up, but none on the valley floor, nothing that prevented us from moving about as freely as we liked except for the mud from three days of an on-again, off-again rain.

"Early thaw," said Mary Olive, confident in her assessment and sweeping at the ashes that lay scattered in front of the grate. Her moving about with a broom was a welcomed break from her camphored wheezing around the kitchen stove. "Awl 'at rain," she mused. "Seen it many a time. I'm a-feared of it in light a' them kittens born dead, their momma yawlin' like the devil was tearin' 'em right out of her. You can mark my words, it's a hard knock a-comin'."

The cold radiating up from the floor and through our shoes kept us coughing a good part of the time and, as always, in close proximity to the stove and grate. But there was simply no other place to go to escape the ice in the air, or the prophetic images Mary Olive saw fit to feed us: visions ominous and burdened, and full of the dread that comes from being a seer.

"Heavy melt," Mary Olive said, her words hanging in the cloud from her pipe. "A trouble comin' best I can tell."

"Grandmaw, hush," said Wilma Lee. "Your scarin' what little sense I got left."

She liked hearing herself, Mary Olive did. And it was best at such times just to let her go on. Just our occasional affirmations of "Uh-huh," or "That's right," or "Never thought I'd see the light," was sufficient enough for her contentedness—a detail we never missed aiming for. "Awl 'at rain," she said, "melt awl 'at snow in a hurry-up."

"Sho-nuff, Mary Olive."

If anything, *awl 'at rain* was the only constant for the next five days. It went from drizzle to never-let-up steady, enough to melt the last of the snow off the mountains—and with mud to boot, tons of it. From the churchyard to the schoolyard, from the path to the outhouse to the long winding arteries that tied us to the blacktop highway, all was mud.

The schoolhouse was no exception. It was full of mud, red and gray, wet and caked and dried, and everything in between despite Mr. Tacket's ranting about keeping it outside where it belonged. But no matter what we did, we were unable to stop it from following us to our seats. There was only so much we could do. Brooming it each time we came through the door became as tedious as it was futile. After awhile, we knocked off what we could and grew used to the rest.

Saturday came with more of the same. By noon, the steady patter gave way to an onslaught, and then to a cloud-bursting, torrential downpour. I could never remember so much rain at once, and with clouds so thick and dark that we had to light lamps in the middle of the day. For days, the creeks had been rising steadily, surging in a great rush and threatening to climb over its banks. It was a *wash out*, nature's way of rending the earth anew: loosening and dislodging what was dead and used-up, and sending it through the creek-troughs to the Big Sandy River.

Creek water had a way of gathering momentum as it increased in volume, allowing it to sweep away everything in its path—intended or not. It cascaded, crashed over rocks and boulders, oftentimes quicker than it could be channeled away. At the mouth of the Big Sandy River, the point where the creek gave up its spoils and mixed it's copper mud color with the thousands of streams that flowed in ahead of it, it melded without as much as a splash. From there, the Big Sandy swelled and carried it to territories we could only imagine from the lines and divides on the map Mr. Tacket kept nailed to the big-room wall.

Corbin stayed away, his Model-A being no match for Greezy's sled roads that had turned into one giant mud hole after another. Between the grumbling of thunder, the steady downpour and bunching ourselves into taut knots around the fire in the grate, sleep came early.

In the darkness, the rain seemed all the more intense, pouring off the roof like it was loosed from a dam. I lay awake listening to its force, and to the ceaseless drops that plinked and plunked their way into pans and buckets and jars we so carefully placed to catch what the roof couldn't hold back. But it was only a background to Wilma Lee's crying and disturbingly mournful laments about how she just knew the rain was fixing to wash the pillars right out from under us, sending us all toppling to a watery grave.

Somewhere in the midst of it all is when I first heard ol' Bartley cut loose: a high tenor howl, long and scolding. At first, we just listened then hollered out for him to hush up. But when he wouldn't, we became a little less sure, a little less bold with our command. But it wasn't until Mary Olive started hollering from her bed by the stove, that we became a little more keen to the signals ol' Bartley was sending. That's when we first heard the knocking: tentative, but persistent. Then the voice: "Seriann?" coming as a question in between Bartley's condemnations.

"What on earth?" Seriann said. "Boys, get up! Get up, Rubin. Get up Wilson. Somebody's a-knocking."

We scrambled for our britches, but before we could even find them, Wilma Lee had already reached a point of hysteria, groaning and sobbing as if at death's door. "Lord, Mommy," she cried, "somebody's *died*. Lord God! Hurry, Mommy! See who it is. Lord, it's some of the family! I know it's one of the family's died."

"Wilma Lee," Seriann snapped, "if you don't hush, I'm gonna bust 'at hole you call a mouth."

Wilson and I scooted barefoot toward the kitchen, with Seriann holding the lamp and Wilma Lee wailing in the background. Again, the voice through the pounding rain, "SERIANN?"

"WHO IS IT?" bellowed Seriann.

"IT'S ME, IMOGENE!"

"What on earth?" said Seriann, lifting the latch.

At first, it wasn't clear *what* stood before us as Seriann raised the lamp. Three figures, back-dropped by a barrage of rain and lightning, huddled together on our porch. They waited motionless, the rain behind them driving against the ground like water being poured out of a boot.

We came closer, still unsure, straining to get a better look. The mixture of thunder and downpour dampened our sight as much as our hearing. We squinted and inched even closer, staring like they were sideshow freaks. "Lord, honey, come in," Seriann said. "What on earth?" *What on earth* had taken over as the all-out expression of Seriann's shock.

Imogene hesitated, then stepped limp and tentative through the doorway. She was drenched, her wool headscarf and coat soaked through. Our eyes met in the dim light for only a second before she turned away. "Come in," Seriann said, coaxing the other two. They moved through the doorway even slower than Imogene. The first one, the little one, was weighted down, soaked to the bone, her head wrapped in a scarf, and her face buried within its folds. It wasn't until she removed it and tilted her head that the light fell on her face. For a moment Seriann and I stood motionless, forgetting about the door standing wide open and the rain blowing across the kitchen floor. It was Dixie.

"Close 'at door," Mary Olive growled, indignant about Wilson's ignoring the obvious. I stepped in between Seriann and a tall feller who seemed even taller in his wide-brimmed hat, and gave the door a hurried slam. Except for the breaking sounds of thunder and the ferociousness of the rainwater on our tarpaper roof, we just stood there hanging in the silence. All three were withered looking and soaked, hats, scarves, and shoes, as wet as if they had swum across the creek. Was this a dream? Could we all be standing here? What time was it, anyway? *What on earth?*

"Lord, honey," said Seriann, "git them wet things off. You'll take the croup." Seriann was a realist, first and always. Wilson and I helped with their coats, but it was of little consequence. They were soaked clear to the skin. "C'mover here where it's warm," she said, motioning them toward the stove.

"Put on the kettle," said Mary Olive to no one in particular, but before anyone could move, she was up and doing it herself. "What on earth"—*what on earth*—"are you'ens doin' out in this rain?" Seriann demanded. "An' at this time a' night?"

Before they could answer, Wilma Lee came waddling into the kitchen, her eyes swollen and raw looking from crying, looking pasty and more disheveled than Imogene and Dixie put together. "Yew might as well tell me right now," she said, "Who is it that's died?"

"Hush, Wilma Lee," said Seriann. "Take 'eez girls and git 'em sump'm t' put on. They're gonna be the ones who's died if you let 'em stay this way."

"Lawd-a-mercy," cried Wilma Lee, "it's Dixie and Imogene."

"We know who they are, Wilma Lee," said Seriann. "We jus' need you to get 'em into sump'm dry." But then without waiting, Seriann jumped up and led them into the upper room, Wilma Lee following behind, slew-footed and wrapped in a quilt.

The tall feller removed his hat and hooked it on the back of a chair. He looked to be about eighteen, and stood dripping by the stove.

"Ye'r the one they call Aug, ain't chee?" said Mary Olive.

"Yes'm. Augustine. Aug to most."

"Dixie's brother."

"'At's right."

"Figured 'at's who ye was," she said. "Seed ye a time'r two when ye was just a young'n. You growd some."

Aug nodded.

"Wont ye a chair?"

"No thank ye. Reckon I'm well enough without it." Aug was soaked down to his socks, but refused our offer of something dry except an old blanket Mary Olive draped around his shoulders.

Mary Olive busied herself scrounging around in the cupboard while Wilson let ol' Bartley in to huddle by the stove. Aug and I were mindful of each other, but careful not to make eye contact. Neither of us was given to saying anything, but between the rain lashing against the side of the house and the kettle boiling on the stove, there was enough distraction to preclude anything being said.

"Well, we got us boiled water, I reckon," said Mary Olive. "Ain't got nuthin' to put in it 'cept coffee, or a little sassafras root."

"Atta be fine," Aug said. "Coffee, I mean." Aug looked scared and rocked from side to side, his boots squishing each time. A few of the cats appeared out of nowhere to inspect this stranger who was leaking rainwater on their floor and letting it run under their stove. They made eye contact all around as if to ask if anybody intended to do anything about it.

Just then, Seriann came back into the kitchen, followed by the other three. Imogene was uncommonly quiet. Dixie was wane, her skin the color of clay. Mary Olive tended to her, adding scraps of cornbread to some milk and setting it in front of her. She sat at the table and daubed lifelessly at it without looking up. When Mary Olive handed Aug his cup of coffee, he drank as hard and fast as he could without burning his mouth.

"Well now, *childern'*," said Seriann, "where in the world are you'ns headed?" Glances darted back and forth between them, but nobody said anything. Finally, Imogene said "You tell it, Aug."

Our eyes went to Aug. He was trembling from the wet and cold, but just for a moment became still, like he was being stalked. "Well," he said, his dark, deep-set eyes searching us out one at a time and seeming to plead for our understanding, "this is how it is. First off, me an' Dixie got us a sister named Hazel we ain't seed in over nine year 'cause a' her runnin' off when she was but fourteen ... an' that bein' on account a' what Haman done to her ... thangs that ain't right. I know 'cause me an' Joncy, we's talked. Joncy's our brother. He don't live up home since they opened the mines over on Henry Clay. He stays ov 'ar in their camp houses." We waited while he gulped at his coffee, wondering where he was headed with all this. He was shaking so hard we couldn't tell if it was from nerves or from being so wet and cold. Mary Olive took another blanket off her bed and added it to the one already wrapped around his shoulders. "Thank ye," he said, swiping at his lips. "Well, anyway, I got to studyin' 'bout Hazel runnin' off the way she did, and how Haman's awl the time runnin' his mouth about Dixie, touchin' on her an' sayin' how purdy she is. 'At's the reason I was goin' ov 'ar two and three times a week, keepin' lookout." He stopped at this point, his eyes wild and afraid, to see if we were picking up on what he was saying. What he got back was stillness. "Well," he went on, his eyes looking straight down into his cup, "next thang I knowed, Dixie was at my door an' lookin' like she'd been run over by a coal car. I board over on Winston's Creek. Cut timber what time weather's good. Work sawmill in between. But I ain't hit a lick in over a month, 'cause a' lookin' after Dixie. Been borrowin' from ever'body I know to keep us alive. Nigh on six weeks now." His eyes led us to Dixie. "Ain't nuthin' on her that's broke best I can tell, but she's still carryin' some a' the marks Haman left on her. Told me she fought him good the night he come at her, grabbed a butcher knife what time he was knockin' an' jerkin' on her. That put a end to it in a hurry, drunk as he was. He passed out adder that, liquored an' lost. Said she sat up the rest a' the night with his shotgun in her hands. Last time she was ever gonna take a beatin'." Aug paused to sip at his coffee then pulled the blankets tighter around him. Mary Olive filled his cup again while the fire in the stove rumbled against our combined silence.

"I'D A' KILLED HIM RIGHT THEN!" blurted Wilson.

In a three-part chorus and in perfect unison, absolute mayhem broke loose from Seriann, Mary Olive and Wilma Lee: cussing Wilson up one side and down the other, telling him to bite down on that tongue of his and to mind his own business, then demanding to know what the hell that dog was doing in the house, anyway. Finally, when their chiding settled to a light roar, they told him that nobody had asked his opinion in the first place—and furthermore, to get his little briar-hoppin' ass back to bed. None of it made the slightest difference to Wilson. He just curled up even tighter around ol' Bartley and waited for the silence to once again regain its hold. Dixie never looked up, just kept nibbling at the cornbread soaking in her milk. Aug didn't seem to care that Wilson had said what he said. "It's awright," he said. "Jesus knows I come close to it often enough."

The disdain on everybody's face was locked even heavier on my own. I thought about Bobby and what he was liable to do once I told him. He'd already said that since turning fifteen he had to be doing what needed to be done. I didn't know exactly what he intended to do, but his words now eased over me with the same disquieting sound as the rain pounding against the side of the house.

"'At's about awl I can say," Aug said, "'cept I'm needin' to get back to work. Ain't no way I can be with her awl day an' awl night both. Haman knows this too, an' he'll come after her—and with the devil at his side."

I added more wood to the stove while everybody continued to search each other's faces for answers. "But," Aug said after a long pause, "I b'lieve if Dixie was t' stay on with youens, it'd be a blessin'. 'At's how come Imogene brung us here. Ain't no where else she can go, don't b'lieve. But it's fer shore an' certain, she cain't ever go back home. It'd be like openin' the gates a' hell an' pushin' her in."

Aug's words seemed to hang in the air long afterwards, reverberating against the trailing stillness. Dixie had stopped eating, her head bowed over her bowl as if in prayer. Her hair hung in straight sheets on either side of her face like blinders, the way it had in school. It was her own little hiding place when there was nowhere else to go: her own little world, smaller than small inside her tent of hair.

Seriann watched her for a time then rolled her head toward Imogene, as if bidding her to speak. "I didn't know what else to do," Imogene said, her face contorted.

"It's awright, Honey," said Seriann, "You did honorable."

"It wasn't till yesterdy," Imogene said, "that Aug come to me. He was hid up and waitin' for me below Floyd Belcher's. Right there at the bend an' outta sight. It was raining and I was comin' from school when he stepped out in front a' me. 'Bout scared me to death. I thought it was a crazy person, but then it come to me who he was. Said Dixie told him to come to me; said I wasn't scared a' nothin', an' I'd be the one to trust. And that I'd know who could help. That's why we're here. I figured you'd know more'n anybody what to do." Imogene shook her head like it was all too much for her mind, like she was trying to wake herself from a bad dream.

"You did what was best, honey. Now put it outta yer mind." Seriann was mindful of the shame that had found Dixie and brought her to us; alert, as well, to the gauntlet being passed into her hands. "Ain't nothin' or nobody gonna bother this here young'n long as I'm alive," she said, her tone starched, intense; an angel, albeit a vengeful one. "If Haman Flowers was to come around here, I'd shoot what ass he's got plum-off quicker'n a frog fart in pond water." She'd thrown us a curve ball in the middle of anguish. We laughed before we even knew it. "Don't reckon he can shoot faster'n me," she said, "nor run faster neither."

"He damned shore cain't be no meaner'n you are," piped Mary Olive.

Seriann's smile was right away deep, the wrinkles stretched tight around her eyes. It had been laughter at the right time, what Seriann knew we needed in the face of such monstrosity. I chanced a glance at Aug. He looked a little off center. We waited for Seriann to fire off another volley, for more of her irreverence; instead, she seemed to take her cue from Aug and the empty solitude that encircled Dixie. "You'ns don't need to worry no more 'bout it," she said. "S'long's we do what we're gifted with, Dixie'll be as fair as day." Then she paused, a look of puzzlement around her eyes. "What do you reckon Haman's liable to do?"

"Cain't never tell 'bout Haman," Aug said. "Been expectin' him for sometime, but ain't nuthin' 'bout him that's predictable. He's likely scouted us. Knows more'n we think, I'd say. He's waiting. We just don't know for what. But he'll try an' find her. Bring her back if he can. Thang is, cain't nobody ever tell I come here, 'less he try an' kill me. An' if 'at was to happen, Dixie'd be good as dead too."

At that, Seriann eyeballed everyone once around. When she got to Wilson, she stopped and said pleadingly and lovingly, "Don't you ever tell a livin' soul, Little Brother, what you heard here tonight."

"HE BETTER NOT," bellowed Wilma Lee, "OR I'LL TEAR HIS HEAD OFF AND FEED IT TO DILLARD PRATER'S HOGS!"

"Now just HUSH," said Seriann. She was all at once grave, her voice every bit as lethal as the squint in her eyes and the angle at which she'd cocked her head. "Wilson," she said in an exacted tone, "don't you know that I'll pull your soul right up through your throat while you're still breathing, if you was to ever mention this to another living bein'?" It was a question phrased as a statement of fact.

"You needn't be tellin' *me*," said Wilson. "You'd better be tellin' Miss *I love Cobbie Parsons* over there."

"Now you just SHUT YOUR OL' CROOKED MOUTH," said Wilma Lee.

"Now I want both a' you'ns to HUSH!" barked Seriann. For a moment, the rain's relentlessness and the faint rumbling from the stove were the only sounds. "Wilson," said Seriann, her long bony finger pointing right between his eyes, "I'm tellin' you, I'll let Haman Flowers have you if I ever, as long as I breathe, EVER hear a word a' this comin' outta your mouth. Do you hear me?"

"Yeah, I reckon," said Wilson, more than just a little accustomed to Seriann's threats and the spells she cast.

"You hear me or not?" she repeated, wanting something more definitive.

"Yeah, dammit, I said *yeah*."

"Cuss me again an' I'll stop feedin' you." Her eyes were serious and black, and without tolerance. Wilson's only response was to bury his face in ol' Bartley's neck. "Well," she said, "I reckon we can leave it alone then."

The rain had let up some, but still there was thunder rolling far off in the distance. It was hard to tell if it was moving away with the rain, or moving toward us with more. Dixie sat hunched so low over her milk and cornbread that her nose almost touched her bowl. Seriann watched her without so much as a sound, then turned to Wilma Lee and said, "Dixie can crawl in with us." Just like that. The final word. Dixie was ours.

We watched Aug shiver through the last of his coffee. His expression never changed. He just nodded his own brand of thanks, removed the blankets from around his shoulders and walked toward the door. He waited before saying anything. Then, looking down at the wet hat in his hand, said, "I'm thankin' ye, Seriann."

It was hard not to feel Aug's hurt: him staring at the back of Dixie's head, not knowing when he'd see her again and trying to think of something to say. Finally, he said, "Well...bye, Sissy." Dixie never looked up, never saw the struggle there on his face. She just sat there frozen, as if she had been stripped of everything decent, no longer with the strength to even raise her head. I tried to imagine how far away she was at that very minute, how lost she was within herself; tried to lay hold of the depth of her nightmare, but it was all too severe and too far removed for my thinking. There was something in me that was thankful for Aug and his strength to stand in the face of Haman Flowers, knowing that Dixie was infinitely better off with us than anywhere else.

"What on earth," *–what on earth–* "will you do tonight, Sissy?" Seriann asked Imogene.

"I reckon I'll be awright," she said, "if Aug'll get me back to the house."

We waited while Imogene hugged Dixie, who clung to her like she was her mother. Finally I helped Imogene struggle into her old wet coat, then waited again while Seriann found her a dry scarf for her head. She thanked us then gave me a glance that lasted longer than it should have before she stepped onto the porch. Aug nodded a final farewell before he pulled his waterlogged hat down tight over his head and pulled the door shut behind him. Their footsteps were lost in our yard-turned-to-mud, and by the hammering of a renewed downpour.

"I knowd it days ago," said Mary Olive, stretching out a hand like she was fixing to swear an oath, "when them kittens was born without a breath. I knowd sump'm was a-comin'."

"There's too much t' think about and too much to do to get caught up in a state a' hang-dog," Seriann said. In an instant, and with the speed of a black snake after a rat, she had Dixie on her feet, into an old pair of bloomers, and into bed with Wilma Lee. In one big swoosh and without as much as a good night, she had ol' Bartley back on the porch and Wilson and me back under our covers. "Things'll be better come mornin'," was all she said as her witch's shadow danced across the wall behind her, then disappeared with her through the curtain door.

"I knowd it days ago," I heard Mary Olive say, her low-talk rasping from the kitchen. "Knowd it as well as the Lord put green in the grass," her voice scaling upwards with a cadence of a preacher, "that them kittens was a tellin' me sump'm'."

Thirty-Two

Thurston Caseboat's Tombstone

The rain was relentless, its onslaught steady and unchecked until the creek had no where to go but over its banks and into low places like Mary Olive's yard and garden, leaving us floundering in acres of backwater.

We continued to set out pans and buckets and most everything we had to catch what the roof failed to wick away, what drizzled nonstop through its cracked and tired tarpaper. They were odd shaped and many colored: jugs and jars, kettles and tins, their numbers equal to the frequency needed to empty them. After a time, Mary Olive thought it might be best if we just cut a big hole in the floor and let the rain run straight through. Preposterousness suited Mary Olive more than most, but it was her way of lessening whatever burden was at hand: in this case what was monotonous, sodden and sour, things the rain had become.

By the end of the seventh day and with no letup in sight, the splash and overspill around each container collected at such a pace that half-hearted attempts to swirl a mop at them seemed almost unworthy of the effort. By midnight we were dulled, tired, and ready to let Mother Nature have the last say—that is, right up until a sizeable portion of the roof's tarpaper let go, and sent the rain pouring through the loft slats in what could only be described as a waterfall.

"LORD HAVE MERCY!" "LORD GOD IN HEAVEN!" "LORD HAVE MERCY GOD!" Petitions, over and over, imploring and pleading, echoed all around me. I was numb, dumbstruck, stumbling from room to room with Seriann gathering things off the floor and piling them on the beds, all the while listening to her cuss and pray for strength in the same breath. But the upper room was overwhelmed, ceding by the second to a drubbing cascade while the wind continued to tear away and work its way under the remaining tarpaper until an even bigger piece let go, then another. That's when the fire in the grate went to black, when the logs and coals hissed and steamed and gasped a final breath, and when the cats went to crying in sinister tones. But right when it was impossible to imagine how things could get any worse, there was a rumble and a shift. We came to a dead halt waiting for another, waiting without saying, but knowing that the rain had worked beneath the timber footings, and that the house might crumble in on us if they continued to shift or sink deeper in the ever-increasing mud.

Space and time were all a blur, parts of an unknown that shot off in all directions and linked us to a helplessness heretofore unknown. I stood fastened and transfixed by Wilma Lee's fever-pitched death knell for Dear Jesus to have mercy and for Father God in Heaven to send His angels to put us on solid ground. It was unbroken and unrestrained, and the prelude to Mary Olive's divination, bellowing how she knew that this was punishment for Wilson taking a slingshot to old man Thurston Caseboat's tombstone.

With the world seeming to be like it was in the time of Noah: with me and Seriann struggling to move things clear of what now was a tributary from the sky; with Wilma Lee wailing and Mary Olive casting out devils; with the only lamp we had beginning to sputter from the spray and the house threatening to buckle under us; with the only warmth left coming from our shivering; and with Dixie looking at me without life in her eyes, I began edging everybody across the slicker-than-slick floor to the porch. Next thing I knew we were wrapped in sodden blankets and slogging toward Big Will Hollow.

I slept that night on a pallet of quilts next to the Yonts' big potbellied stove, with Ben on one side and Bobby on the other. Gracie had been frightened out of her wits at the sight of us standing on her porch in the middle of the night, in a pouring rain and the glare of lamplight. "Your face looked scary as midnight under that lamp," she said to Seriann. "I was thinkin' maybe you'ns was robbers." Hers was a softening enchantment—not unlike her brother Corbin's, except for being twenty years older and without the benefit of studies. She was quick to shepherd us into dry clothes and warm beds, then stayed awake long afterwards, almost to the point of annoyance, making certain all was well.

Bobby and I sat for a time after the lights were dimmed, while the rain continued to inundate. For once, he seemed to be without a voice, his eyes shifting from me to the floor to the walls. It was a strained expression that held him, like an animal trapped and confused, one teetering with disbelief and trying to understand how he had, in the middle of the night and in a deafening downpour, opened the door and come face to face with Dixie Wainwright; how he had, in the pitch black of night and in the glare of a coal oil lamp, guided her through the black hole of his front door and into his tiny little world.

He made a tired effort of picking at the bark on a piece of kindling before he said, "Where'd she come from, anyway?" ...his voice emptying into the night.

I lay awake listening to the rain, tired from having explained everything that had taken place the night Dixie showed up. Bobby said nothing afterwards, just rolled over and drew the covers around him, leaving me alone with the rain and the stop-and-start of Ben's breathing. The thoughts of Mary Olive's house holding on for dear life, taking on so much water that it was likely to wash away at any minute, bore in on me like cannon fire, then came to me in dreams. I woke throughout the night to the rain and its assault, and to the feeling that I was on the verge of being uprooted yet again, of being without a place to call home. A whole lot like Dixie, I surmised. Each time I woke, Bobby's breathing was as still as the grave: never the steady rhythm that signals sleep. I didn't dare speak, still I wondered about what was rummaging through his mind and keeping him awake long after it should have. I drifted off time and again, the floor's cold hardness penetrating right up through the dream that kept repeating, the one of me and Mary Olive astraddle the peak of her house and drifting in the giant, mud-stained flood waters of the Big Sandy River.

By noon the heavens had dried up, the morning shower having weakened to a drizzle, then to a sprinkle, and then to nothing at all. But the sky, dismal and gray and the color of spoiled meat, seemed to be a thing beyond repairing: its clouds, low and fast running, but without the smell of rain. We wasted no time in getting to Cousin Truman after we weighed in on the damage. On the back of ol' Hank was the only way we could get there, Bobby up front and me behind him. Ol' Hank was surefooted and strong enough to slog through four miles of mud, some of it a good six inches deep, then strong enough to pull a sled crafted from hickory logs all the way back. It took us the better part of a day to load and haul what Truman figured he needed. We slept another four nights at Olin and Gracie's, their passion to feed, bed and care for us as something we were in no position to refuse.

School was closed for over a week because of the roads being washed out, reduced to little more than sluices and without footing. Cousin Truman spent a whole day bracing, leveling and adding supports to a corner timber, then another three days replacing what roofing had blown off with giant pieces of corrugated tin he'd stripped from Greezy's abandoned camp houses. After adding fresh tar to the cracks and seams and holes, the house looked beat up, struggling to hold on. After that, we divided ourselves up amongst family and friends while the house and most everything in it dried out. Dixie and Wilma Lee went to stay with Imogene. Seriann, Little Sherman and Mary Olive went to stay with Cousin Truman and Inez. Ol' Bartley and me stayed with Bobby, and Wilson went to his Cousin Cordell's, whose family was already sleeping four to a bed.

We stayed gone a full ten days waiting for things to dry out then spent the next week salvaging what we could and washing down most everything with lye. And though the rains didn't return, the sky stayed a bleak gray-upon-gray. It was a miracle that the house hadn't shifted anymore than it had; a miracle that it wasn't sent crumbling like a matchbox into the creek, and us along with it. For all it meant to us, and despite Cousin Truman's heroic efforts, it still looked like a thing wanting to be forgotten. But it was all we had and the one thing Mary Olive held nearest to life. Making it livable again was about as galling as it was corporal and took most everybody in the family to put it back together. Cousin Truman even brought brethren from the church to help. Then, after nearly three full weeks of airing, scalding, and bleaching, we finally made our way back in.

Up to that time, I couldn't remember the rain being anything but accommodating, something that helped sustain the life we so desperately clung to; something that quenched and renewed, cooled and cleansed, and helped the Big Sandy flow ebulliently to the Ohio. I learned, though, that its excess had a distinct and uninviting nature. The bad news was that there were now more than just a few who knew the whereabouts of Dixie Wainwright. The good news was that we didn't have to replant the peas.

We spent two full days washing everything that could be beat against a rock. Still, there were some pieces that refused to give up the whiff of mildew, nothing that I was right-away aware of until Seriann went about sniffing what we put on and fixing her mouth like she'd bit into a green apple. When she finally confirmed our suspicions that we were about to have *another* backbreaking day of washing—just to be on the safe side—we were alive with insurrection. Wilson stomped and thrashed about, and Wilma Lee stewed and cussed and proclaimed that nobody in their right mind should have to live with the likes of Seriann and be made to slave day in and day out, and that she was leaving, as God was her witness, as soon as she could find a way to get a bus ticket out of here. I never felt like I had much of a voice when it came to such things, so never bothered to raise an objection beyond a posture of helplessness. Still, our combined protests were not enough to sway Seriann and how right she thought she was. And when Saturday came, so did another round of washing.

Worshday meant that we were up at daylight, building fires: a big one in the yard under the washtub and a stout one in the stove. There were three tubs in the yard: one for boiling clothes, one for scrubbing, and one for rinsing. Three tubs that had to be filled with water—water that was drawn one bucket at a time from the creek when it wasn't muddy, and from the well when it was. It took thirty-five trips—one bucket at a time—first Wilson and then me—and that was just for starters.

The tub used for boiling the clothes sat on a circle of rocks out and away from the house because of the fire beneath it, its water scalding and kept that way throughout the day. It was heaped with lye soap, musty and medicine smelling, what Cousin Truman and Inez made from hog renderings and wood ash. Boiling the clothes was the first step, a way of breaking down sweat and soil and putting an end to things like ticks, fleas, chiggers, and lice, things we were forever on guard against. We stirred the clothes while they boiled, pushing them around with saplings stripped of bark that were long enough to keep us backed away from the fire. After a time, we lifted them out with the same saplings and carried them to the next tub, where Wilma Lee and Seriann—and now Dixie—scoured them against washboards.

There was always the chance of being scalded when transferring clothes from the washtub to the scouring tub, so we did it piece at a time, with deliberate steadiness and everyone standing back out of the way. After being washboarded, the clothes were lifted out and carried to the rinse tub, where we sloshed them and wrung them over and over till we freed up what soap we could, then hung them to dry. In the winter, they hung stiff and frozen till we brought them in the house and laid them across tables and chairs, and across the lines we nailed from one wall to the next. Even then it took days before they were dry enough to sprinkle, roll, and make ready for ironing.

Wilson and I did the stirring, lifting and carrying from one tub to the next. We built the fires and kept them going, replenished the water in the washtub as it boiled away, kept the water in the scouring tub changed-out and warm from big pans we heated on the stove, and time after time added water to the rinse tub to keep it clear and free of soap. From the time we built our fires until we put them out, Wilson and I would fetch and carry upwards of sixty buckets of water, and chop what seemed like a wagonload of wood. We never stopped to eat—only when we were done—which was at the end of the day, when the fires were out and the tubs emptied and hung on ten-penny nails on the side of the hen-house. It was a hell of a path from dirty clothes to clean ones, but we did what we knew how, the only way we knew how, and the way everybody else did.

Thirty-Three

March Winds

When March winds began to kick and bluster and send our washtubs tumbling across the yard, and when big branches on our crabapple tree swayed and scraped against the upper room window, ol' Bartley would get up under the porch and hover with the cats. He was a legendary brave heart, but operated pretty much on the side of spinelessness when up against something as faceless as the wind. Prudence was both his manner and demeanor when it came to the wind, coming out of his hiding place only to eat and do his *business*. At night, though, despite the cats and their shameless ramblings, Bartley was the law. He was, in the strictest sense, the first and last word in securing what was ours. He was our main defense while we slept, and bayed in death-defining tones at whatever was given, besides the cats, to moving about in the dark. He was merciless and unforgiving of passers-by, confronting all things he figured had no business within the perimeters of his post and place. A timeless guardian, ol' Bartley was, as auburn haired as any of our Irish ancestors, and always at the ready to put himself up for our cause—whatever it might be.

For anybody seeking entrance after dark, it was only those with a familiar scent or voice that could be said to have a latchkey, those like Corbin or Bobby. For all others and all else, there was a toll to pay. It was the code ol' Bartley brought with him and what held him to a higher calling.

So the night Haman Flowers came around, even with his quieting footsteps, muffled even further by the rushing sound of the creek, ol' Bartley saw to it that we were awake and waiting when he was still a good fifty yards away.

"*HUSH* Bartley," Seriann scolded, but ol' Bartley's instinct had gone to full alert, the hair on his back like quills on a porcupine. "*HUSH*, I said." For a second, Bartley whined like he'd been struck. Seconds later he changed to a growl so deep and low that I thought it must be coming from the graveyard, from the bowels of the earth. It was enough to move Seriann to the porch, shotgun in hand.

"WHO'S 'AR?" ...Seriann's voice trailing through the blackness like it was conjuring spirits.

"Momma, get in here," begged Wilma Lee, "You'll get us all throat-cut."

"Wilma Lee, I won't yew t' hush. Yew got sump'm to say, say it to Jesus."

Except for ol' Bartley's growl, which had grown even deeper, we waited: frozen, trying to listen for a sound that might come back to us out of the black.

"*Quiet*, Bart!" Seriann shushed. Bartley paid her no more mind than if she were a bush he'd just pissed on. "*Shush*, I said!" But ol' Bartley was having none of it, and in a flash he was off the porch and into the night. From the blackness beyond the yard, we could hear him charging, thundering through the creek and the brush, the sounds of hell tearing from his throat. In an instant, a trial of life and death filled the air: thrashes and kicks, clenched teeth and shunted breaths. Blows, blunt and heavy, massive and ugly, came without stop. Curses, hard and vicious, and aimed at Bartley and the Almighty, exploded between gulps of air. But ol' Bartley was crazed, lost to the single-mindedness of protecting his pack. On and on, his sinewy mass ripping and tearing at what we could only imagine was flesh and bone.

"MOMMY, DO SUMP'M! HURRY, MOMMY! HURRY!" Little Sherman's agony echoed in each of us. "PLEASE, MOMMY! GOD, MOMMY! PLEASE!"

In a flash, Seriann was off the porch and into the great abyss. It was only seconds before we heard the first of it: BOOM, a shotgun blast that filled the night. Bartley, the king of wolves, still pressing. "EAT HIM, BART!" Seriann screaming. Running. "EAT HIM ALIVE!" Her voice shrilled in the grip of the devil. Then BOOM! ... the shotgun a second time. Buckshot filling trees along the creek. My heart skipping beats. Little Sherman trying to break free. Wilson holding him tight. Ol' Bartley shredding the night, devouring. Still, another BOOM! ... a third shot. A scouring shriek and footsteps, ponderous and plodding. Going away. "DIE YOU SON OF A BITCH!" Seriann's curse. Crazed, and my mind the color of blood, I was off the porch and running without seeing ... Wilson and Little Sherman on my heels. Dixie was leveled to stillness and holding the lantern. Wilma Lee's yodeling torment above it all.

Seriann grabbed at us out of the dark, her breathing shunted, then hurried us to where ol' Bartley was rolled onto his side. Whimpered breaths said he was hurt and bad.

"BRANG THE LIGHT! COME QUICK!" Wilson's voice was harsh, demanding. With four sets of hands, we lifted Bartley and carried him to the house, then laid him on a blanket by the stove. It was right then that Bobby and Olin came through the door ... shotguns loaded and ready for whatever.

We paced, frantic and wild, telling what we knew and what we didn't. They'd heard gunshots, Bobby and Olin, but thought it was hunters. But then they heard hollering: Seriann's. That's when they come running, but too late to make a difference.

What happened to us was over about as quick as it began, proof that it didn't have to be long to be ugly. Bobby and Olin stayed just long enough, then left with worried looks and with Bobby unable to lift his eyes from Dixie. They would be back come morning.

Ol' Bartley was battered, blood oozing from his nose and ears, and from the gashes on his head. Still, he checked to see if we were all there, if we were okay. He didn't seem to bother much with the pain, only with his delight in being the law and seeing that his family was intact: that he had preserved his line.

Mary Olive commenced to gather ointments and salves and all what Grandmaw stocked us with when Dixie stepped barefoot between us. She bent down to get a closer look at Bartley, her pained look giving way to one of purpose.

"I need for somebody to heat me a butcher knife," she said, holding me in her gaze. I stared back, not knowing exactly what she intended to do—just stood there waiting for somebody to shed some light on it when she said, "Or maybe you'd rather wait till that buckshot decides to pop out on its own." Bartley's hindquarter was sprayed with shot. Dixie ran her hand against the grain of his hair to show us where they'd gone in, but not come out. From there we were in a fight to heat up Mary Olive's only butcher knife, draw a pan of water, and lay out needle and thread—all what Dixie called for. We had an idea of what she was fixing to do, and stayed back until she was through doing it; till she finished cutting and digging and sewing—like she'd watched Haman do often enough with the gang of hounds he kept; and like he'd made her do the night he come in with a leg blue and puffed and weighted with shot—the consequence of his night thieving. She said she'd never forget how Haman sat without whimpering, just kept a locked look on her cutting and digging, mostly on account of his head being so full of liquor. "I could a' cut it clean off before he knew what was happening," she said, the look in her eyes indicating it was a lost opportunity.

I watched in amazement all during the time she was doctoring, parting ol' Bartley's flesh and probing for the shot that lay buried. She was focused, dutiful; my one recurring thought being that she was Grandmaw all over again.

Six buckshot amidst some bloody pieces of fat is what Dixie finally held up to the light. I didn't have words to put to it, but there was a reverence about her, a gentleness of spirit that I wanted for my very own. Away from what was vile and too often a part of Dixie's existence, there was a kind of victory that attached itself to her, one that said, "*Yes, I am set apart.*" But it was the kind of separateness that crossed over to the beguiling, to the brink of what was extraordinary and amassed in wonder.

Seriann had shot at whoever it was that dared to try us, then stood and listened to him clamor up the creek bank and into the hills. There had been three shots, the last one being hers: the one that put an end to it. It had been the Lord's will, she was certain, seeing as she only had one shell to begin with. But then it may have been some of Seriann's buckshot that found Bartley, too. She couldn't really tell, only that she let go with what she had, then stood halted by footsteps in a dead-heat to get away, and with Bartley unable to chase. We sat for a time studying on what we didn't know: who, exactly, was it that dared test us? Did he escape without a scratch?—or was he out there somewhere bleeding to death?—or maybe dead already? We would know more come morning.

The next morning we found large spots of blood where Bartley stood his ground. We followed the spots along the creek bank and down into its bed, but the blood trail ended in the water. A few feet beyond, though, it picked up again. Large spots, like what we might see from an open artery: a trail that led across the road then up a sharp bank into the hills.

When we made our way back to the house, ol' Bartley was at a decided list on the porch. His battle had been thick, rooted in the only struggle he knew: for life and territory—and nothing but death would have kept him from it. From the hunter-protector-provider pool of his ancestry, he rose to take his place without a thought to the cost. That same spirit had lifted him to a height only few could ever know, and now fostered him back to his place on the porch: a place where he was free to sniff and stretch and scratch, to settle into a loaf and a laze, despite the arrogance and lack of thanks from the cats; a place where he once again took up the mantle of being our gift and what kept us safe from all that stalked the night.

When Bobby and Olin showed up, we showed them the blood trail along the creek bank then inched along retracing where Wilson and I had been earlier. That's when Olin noticed a hat snagged in the brush between the bank and the road. Bobby and I recognized it right off as the one that had always sat cocked but true on the head of Haman Flowers.

It wasn't long before Dixie Wainwright's name was synonymous with our family. She had by acquaintance become connected, locked and sealed to us. Word was out and folks spoke of her in hushed tones as if that somehow lessened the severity of their gossip, shielded them from the fullness of its sin. Nobody knew *why* she was living with us, exactly, but *not knowing* never stopped them from postulating. And from the accounts that came drifting back to us, most were right. Haman Flowers wasn't as opaque as he would have liked.

Mr. Tacket eventually found his way to us: on a Friday and after the schoolhouse had emptied for the weekend, his thick square frame filling our doorway. "I hope my being here's not out of line," he said. "It's just my concern for Dixie ... for all y'all."

"You're always welcome, Mr. Tacket," Seriann said. "Fact is, I been meanin' to come see you what with Dixie being with us now."

"Her being here is pretty much common knowledge," he said. "I know her daddy as well as I want to. I just trust he's smart enough not to come to the schoolhouse, and to know I'd never let harm come to those I've been entrusted with."

"That's the very reason she's here, you know; 'cause a him. We already know what he's got in mind. Already been here oncet. Never know when he'll be back."

"Ain't no fiction to that," Mr. Tacket said. "I've seen what his kind can do. Saw Dixie the day she come in late. It was the first time, but I knew it was only the start. The devil won't ever be denied, Seriann. It might take him a mite longer with some, but he's gonna inflict a torment wherever he can, and it's his disciples, them like Haman, that'll carry it out. The devil needs their help just like the Lord needs ours. Men like Haman Flowers have their time here on earth like the rest of us. It's the master he serves what makes the difference. I suspected what I'd be up against when I went to see him. What I come away knowin' was that he's beyond learnin' a lesson. He's learned all he's goin' to. It ain't but one answer for them that's got the devil for a soul. Ain't but one thing that'll satisfy the balance a' nature, one thing and one thing only that'll make right what's a bane in God's kingdom."

"You meanin' we outta *law* him?"

"Ain't no lawin' a man like Haman Flowers. Don't know that the law'd do much about Dixie's beat places, now that they're gone. I mean, what would they have to go on besides our word? Might say it was just a whoopin'. Besides, the law don't mean nothin' to Haman Flowers. Cain't respect sump'm he don't care nothin' about. But above that, there's no *time* for law; the law's too slow. Hell, he'd have us all butchered an' hangin' in his smoke house what time the law got around to him. I ain't for takin' a chance on him doin' more harm. Next time could be a harm of an undoable kind."

"Well, then, what is it you reckon we outta do?"

The ensuing silence prompted him to invite Seriann onto the porch where they talked in hushed tones.

Mr. Tacket left a short time later without coming back inside, without offering a goodbye to anyone but Seriann. That night, Little Sherman fell asleep without an utterance of the Old Troll. Bobby stayed away for obvious reasons and Corbin was still nowhere to be found. The day had been one so typical of late winter: desolate and bleak and in search of color. It was that way, or so it seemed, inside each of us as. We were together, yet separated by our own darkness. We sat huddled around the grate without as much as a word, searching inward and staring blank-eyed into its fire: muted and nibbling, and reminding us of things frail and impermanent.

Mary Olive snoozed in her rocker while Wilson, with little patience for winter's long life, soured his way off to bed. After a time, Wilma Lee accompanied herself on the dulcimer and sang what verses she knew of "*I Wish My Baby Was Born*" and the bits and pieces she could remember that Corbin taught her of "*Knoxville Girl*." The life Dixie had shown in tending to ol' Bartley had begun to bring her into a new light. She sat with a harmonizing ghost about her, as spellbinding as the firelight on her cheeks, and all the while tied to Wilma Lee's doleful renderings.

I could only wonder about Haman Flowers, and if he could know anything apart from the claw marks that scared his soul. I never knew the likes of him: what was scurrilous and hardened by lack, what was removed from anything not draped in shadows, or without the life for anything beyond his own indulgence. Mary Olive was certain that Haman was devil sent. "See it now," she said, her eyes rolled up high, "crossed this way a-horseback, a dark one in a slow walk across a great divide; in the middle of the night after the moon had sunk below the horizon; past the eyeless and them leanin' against tombstones, into a land set aside and bound by what seeks the grave."

I lay awake watching Seriann move from room to room, her shadow slithering from one wall to the next. She was heavy in thought and long silences as if listening for ol' Bartley and portents of things cloaked in trepidation. She came to me just before she put out the light, her black hair trailing to the small of her back and said: "You'll need to go to the head of Shop Branch sometime soon. It'll be your eyes tellin' me what I need to know."

I had a clear view of the moon that night through the window above my head. It was full.

Thirty-Four

As Dazzling As War Paint

The days Imogene wore her hair pulled back and tied into pigtails made her face appear flushed and her freckles as dazzling as war paint—even made the air around her seem ready to give off steam. Her freckles also had a way of adding to her swagger: all that waited to tie you into a pretzel. Smarter ones knew to be mindful of her on such days.

Hers was a presence run through with grit, daring even the most determined to question it, but one that kept her too often shaped by it, veiled and alone. Dixie was the lone someone allowed to see behind that veil—to the softer side—the side Imogene was so dogged to conceal. But then there was me, almost indiscernibly being allowed a now-and-again glimpse of that secreted realm. But I was never one to rush toward the unknown.

Even at fifteen, Imogene's temperament was legendary, made out of stuff like flint rock and dried cob. But it was about the time Imogene's hips began to take on the shape of things ready for harvest, that her disposition became somewhat more temperate. Not to say she lost venom, only that she managed to harness it more effectively. Growth was erupting in each of us, inside and out, and Imogene was no exception, except for her softer side becoming somewhat more accessible.

Throughout the winter I was aware of how often Imogene took note of me, how her eyes would search me without being rushed. But with the first warm winds, I began to notice how I was given to staring back, to studying her—her eyes, her mouth, her feet—and imagining the sensations that might come were I to ever, say, have contact with them.

Mr. Tackett made much about March twenty-first, the first day of spring. The Vernal Equinox he called it, but all I could remember was how the sunlight trickled through Imogene's hair and turned its brassy hen-red color into endless subtleties of auburn and gold, copper and bronze; and how that same warm sun bathed the back of her neck and held me to its pulse, kept me dazed to her freckles—honeyed and alive. Those were the beginnings: the days when I would push myself up tight against my desk and lean as far forward as I could to lock into the scent of her soap; when the brusqueness of her seemed to peel away and die to bluer skies, and when I began to know my own corruptibleness. They were days full of yearnings and destined to stay that way—even long after we smoked that first cigarette.

Thirty-Five

And a Foot Held Off the Ground

Not that Cobbie Parsons was indifferent to anything Dixie was going through, but, increasingly, I became the go-between for him and Wilma Lee: hand delivering scraps of paper I could only assume were love notes. It was something I was loath to do, but succumbed to only after Cobbie offered to kill my dogs, as need be, for the next twenty years. Even though I knew I'd probably never collect on it, I figured it was as heartfelt an offer as Cobbie could make. And so, against my better judgment, I gave in.

"Looky yander," said Mary Olive, her eyes excited. "Ain't that the purttiest thang?" It was a double-barreled derringer, one barrel on top of the other, a .41 caliber Remington—what Dempsey had forever carried in his pocket—its shiny blue steel and pearl handle flattening into the palm of my hand with a density that spoke to its seriousness. I rolled it over, examining it, aiming it. "If you have to aim it, you're too far away," she said. "Meant to kill the feller next to you ... or across the table. Why they call it a *gambler's pistol.*"

I tried to image where it had been: the tight spots it had seen, the gamblers who'd owned it, handled it, kept it within reach—up a sleeve or in a boot. If only it could talk.

"Where'd you get such a thing?" I asked.

"My Dempsey took it off some feller in a poker game a lifetime ago," she said, "that an' a half box a' shells." Mary Olive was bug-eyed, her grin and gold tooth consuming. "We shot it out there in the yard a time or two, till we got the feel of it. Here, let me show you what else." She took it and wiped off its imaginary dust with her apron. "Breaks in two just like my shotgun, only the other way." She turned it upside down and broke the handle away from the barrels. There was a cartridge in each chamber. "Keep it loaded," she said, grinning. "Least I know they's two bullets where they're supposed to be."

A longhaired tabby stuck its nose under the curtain and meowed, sensing, I supposed, the sudden unevenness in the air. "Ain't you worried about it going off?" I asked.

She laughed. "That's the good part. Have to cock it to shoot it. Cock it once and pull the trigger, and it shoots out the top. Cock and pull the trigger a second time, and it shoots out the bottom."

She knew all about it, pleased with herself and holding it like it was a child. "Dempsey said there wasn't another one like it east a' the Mississippi. Andrew Clemmons offered me fifty dollars cash for it after Dempsey was gone. I said 'What is it I'm supposed to do with fifty dollars, Andrew? Go to town?'" She threw her head back and laughed a good one. "I wudn't take a hundred dollars an' a cold-nose hound for it," she said. "It's what Dempsey give me, an' I can just about feel him next to me when I hold it.

"Ain't many shells left," she said, slow to put it aside. "Have to send to somewhere back east if I want more. "Might as well be to the moon for all the good it does me. I ain't even got the spit for a stamp."

"That's real interestin'," Corbin said from across the room. He was soothing by the fire, his legs stretched and crossed at the ankles, his arms laced across his chest. "Mind if I have a look?" His voice was light, his smile big enough for two.

Mary Olive laid her head to one side, then slowly handed it over like she was surrendering it to authorities. "Don't hurt yaself," she said, winking in my direction.

Corbin rolled it over, held it up to the light, tossed it back and forth from one hand to the other, then dangled it from his little finger. "Sissified, if you ask me," he said. "Pearl handle puts me in mind of somethin' belongin' to a French whore." His smile was now tighter and growing by the second. "Now this is what gets it done," he said, his other hand coming up from his boot like a flash of lightning... "and what every man needs adder dark." What he held was tiny and shimmered in the light. It was a derringer, the identical make and model of Mary Olive's, except that his was silver-plated and with a burl wood handle. "The sister," he said, holding up the one with the pearl handle. "The brother," he said, holding up the other. He laughed deep and chesty at the irony. Mary Olive and I drew in tight, disbelieving and clown-faced, examining them like they were newborn babies.

"'Pon mah honor," Mary Olive said, holding one in each hand, "if this ain't like bein' in love." She laughed and tried a little two-step shuffle, but nearly stumbled into the grate. "Reckon the Annie Oakley's gone plum outta me," she said settling heavily into her rocker. That was right about the time Bobby and Wilson came through the door with their arms full of kindling. "Hush now," cautioned Mary Olive. "Truman and Seriann are the only ones who know anything about it ... and now the two of you, of course." In a second's time, the derringers were secreted back to their rightful places, Mary Olive wrapping hers in the silk handkerchief that was Dempsey's.

Bobby and I went to the head of Shop Branch that first Friday in April, as shiver-damp as it was cold, and under the cover of night. Haman Flowers' place was as quiet and ghostlike as it had been two months earlier when Mr. Tacket came calling, when Bobby and I watched from the time-tested outcrop of rock above his house. The night sky was its fullest black by the time we got there, the mountain behind us even blacker. We were all but invisible. Still, there were footsteps and our brushing against undergrowth that tried giving us away, sounds that carried clear and true in the night. The outcrop of rock was all we were willing to hazard. Any closer and we would have spooked the dogs. Only the faintest outline of the cabin could be detected, a silhouette against the night. To know anything outside the amber glow in its windows was all but impossible. I don't know how long we lay there, breathing through our mouths and chancing only a now-and-again whisper before noticing a sudden flash, a flare. Steadying then dying. A match? It was hard to tell.

It was only seconds later that the front door opened and the amber light from a lamp spilled onto the porch, a jolt to the darkness and a hint of someone off to the side, sitting alone on the porch. It was Emmaline holding the light, she and little Fayella scurrying to the toilet. Last call before bed. There was safety in numbers after dark, even in the head of Shop Branch. We watched in dead silence, Bobby's breathing telling me how still he was, how deadly he was willing to be.

It was only minutes before they returned, their light reaching the far end of the porch where someone was sitting, but trying to stand. Slowly. Awkwardly. Painfully. Emmaline on one side, Franklin and Fayella on the other. Steadying. Guiding. Moving toward the door. Hobbling. Listing. One arm in a sling, a crutch under the other, and a foot held off the ground. It was Haman.

From that very minute, we knew for certain that it had been Haman who had come against ol' Bartley and Seriann. But his being so crippled up caught us by surprise. Was it from dog bites, buckshot, or both?

Seriann seemed to set up a little straighter after we told her what we'd seen. She was silent for the most part, just sat there drumming her fingers on the table, and listening with a hardness about her mouth and eyes. We knew as well as she did that there was only so much time before Haman would be back.

I was sure that the Lord loved Seriann, not just because He'd tested her with one trial after another, but because He'd equipped her with the ferocity and fortitude she needed to overcome them. She was full of conviction, as much at home in her secular world as Cousin Truman was in his spiritual one, though hers was without that certain measure of peace that comes from knowing where you'll spend eternity. But as volatile as she was at times, she was never—as far as I knew—derelict in her duties as mother, protector, provider, or friend; never without the nerve to stand up for the underdog, or take the part of the blameless; and never given to speaking ill of anyone, except those she felt were long overdue for it—those *needing a fresh perspective* as Corbin liked to call it. Knowing Seriann meant becoming attached to her—although for a significant number, the attachment was fixed with fear. Though love, at times, played a part in her relationships, it was selective and tempered, apart from the fierce and loyal sort she reserved for family. But, it was that fierceness that trumpeted her the loudest, that bore claim to her reputation and her attention to those less able to fend for themselves: children and the elderly, the lowly and the downtrodden, even the endless passel of stray cats. The fact that her will was as tough as her hide was reason enough to fear her, but it was a maternal heart and a spirit-to-nurture that added balance to her tenacity, that eventually drew people to her. And though she was capable of things as calculating as the Cherokee warrior that inhabited her soul, she was, in the same breath, possessing of a calm as unrippled as a slick-dark river under a harvest moon. Because of it, she was held with both regard and caution. I suspected in the course of time we would come to know it with greater certainty.

The first time Aug came to see us was late afternoon on a Sunday, nine days after Bobby and I went to spy on Haman. He came hungry looking and straddling a borrowed mule. The darkness on his face said there was more to his being there than just looking in on Dixie.

"Is 'at you, Aug?" Seriann shouted from the porch, knowing full well it was, her voice bouncing off the rock cliff behind him.

"Don't mean to bother ye none, Seriann. Just wonderin' about sissy."

"She's gone to Truman's with Mary Olive an' the childern. Be back sometime tonight. Come sit. Got a fresh pone a' bread."

Aug slid to the ground then waited before he led his mule across the creek.

"I swan, if you ain't a sight," said Seriann, her smile as tight as her tone. "Been wonderin' 'bout you, an' if everthang was awright." Aug's eyes trailed downward, as if Seriann's words had landed at his feet. Dead air hung like a great weight between them. "Let me fix ye a bite a' bread," she finally said.

"Seriann, I come to tell you 'bout Haman." Just like that, Aug's voice was dire and with a bit of tremble.

Seriann said nothing, just heaped spoonfuls of sweet potatoes and pickled corn onto a plate. "There," she said, adding a hunk of pone and motioning for him to sit. "Now, what was it you was sayin'?"

Aug ate like it was his first time in days, not bothering to talk or make eye contact. He finished almost before he got a second wind, and didn't say no when Seriann filled his plate a second time. "Don't reckon there'll be a contention with Haman," he finally said, his face close to his plate. "Not fer a time, no how." He did little chewing, just shoveled in what he could as fast as he could and swallowed hard. "He's bad off," he said. "Come in a while back dragging a broke foot, an' a hand near shot off."

"Don't reckon," said Seriann, her tone as insipid as her expression, her eyes chancing a dart in my direction.

"It was a sight beholdin'," Aug said. "Sorrowful a thang as I ever laid eyes on. Nothin' at the end of his sleeve 'cept hangin' meat and shot bone—nuthin' even fit fer bait." Aug's breathing was heavy around the bread and sweet potatoes in his cheeks. "I'd been ov 'ar since dark checking on Momma an' them litt'lens, Franklin and Fayella, when I heared him bellerin' in the lane—like it was the end a' the world, and him in hellfire. I grabbed the lamp, but he was just about bled out time I got to him. Hand mangled an' mauled, an' hanging like it was bear clawed. He was crazy pained, his eyes wild—like the Devil in him was tryin' to get out. Grabbed me by the throat an' tole me to chop it off—what was left of it. When I wouldn't, he slung me outta the way like I was scrap meat an' staggered off to the wood pile, to the axe. Next thang I knowed..." he stopped short, his eyes fixed with recollecting, "he went down on his knees. Just give out—gone but for what little breath he had left. Just slumped down in the dirt holdin' onto the axe like it was gonna swing itself if he held it long enough. That's when Momma stepped outta the shadders an' into the lamplight like some haint risin' up out of a swamp. Just stood 'ar like she was cut outta stone: not a flinch, not a word, studying on Haman like his wallerin' suited her just fine."

We waited while Aug moved off to the water bucket and drank deep from its dipper. "'Fore I knowed it," he said, "Momma stepped toward him an' took hold a' that ax, her eyes with that empty look. I knowed what she was thinkin', 'cause I was thinkin' it too." He paused just long enough to swipe at the breadcrumbs on his mouth, to give us time to grasp his meaning. "Haman was near gone 'fore she slung his arm 'cross a big log. It wasn't but a heartbeat 'fore 'at ax went up over her head ... 'fore she brought it down like a freight train."

I could hear myself swallow, could feel cold clear into my feet. Seriann sat with her eyes beaded, her breath so shallow I couldn't tell when it was going in or when it was coming out.

"It was a god-awful sound to that ax," Aug said, "...the way it bit into that log like felled timber thumpin' the ground. They was stillness adder that ... quiet-like all around; Haman's mouth shaped to scream, but nuthin' comin' out—just his shakin' like he was hit by lightenin', his eyes rolled back, an' gawpin' like he was plumb outta his head. His hand—what was left of it—layin' there in the dirt, an' Momma just hoverin', fixed on what she'd done, eyes as blank as parchment."

We waited without a word while Aug remembered. "We poured near a pint a liquor down him adder that, fast as he could take it, 'fore I held him down an' Momma put a hot poker to his stump an' burnt it clear to the bone. It's a stench to burnin' flesh, but Momma just kept right on runnin' 'at poker 'round an' 'round till he passed out. We wrapped him up tight adder that, dragged him inside the barn and covered him up. His foot was god-awful broke an' swelled to nearly bustin'. Still that way. Can't hardly hobble 'cept with a crutch I made him. But it ain't nuthin' 'at won't heal, given time."

"Which hand?" Seriann said without looking up, her eyes locked on the floor.

"Which hand?" Aug repeated, then waited. When Seriann didn't say anything, he said "Why, the left one. Does it make a difference?"

"Only if that's the one you shoot with."

Thirty-Six

Ruby Mae McHone

Corbin's house sat on a big piece of flat ground at the north end of Pikeville. Willow trees, draped in eerie sadness, flanked it on both sides and lined the long two-track that connected it to the road. It was red brick with a porch and four huge pillars across its front, and with white trim in a state of need: dappled and peeled and diseased looking. It was double stacked and built stout, but a long time ago, age clinging to it above all else. Except for a faint light through the front windows, it looked abandoned, incapable of warmth in the cold-gray dank of an early Sunday morning.

Five cars lined the two-lane that wound itself in a circle in front of the porch. Bobby and I stood for the longest time sizing the situation and wondering whether it had been a good idea to come here in the first place—but there was the matter of Seriann to consider, and her lingering suspicion that all was not quite right.

The C & O Railroad had been the clear answer to our predicament. Its running along the Big Sandy River from Elkhorn City to Ashland, and all points in between, put us in direct route to Pikeville. Hopping on, even in the black of night, was almost too easy: its cars so loaded with coal so much of the time, and lumbering at the speed of a plow mule at the end of a hard day. Getting off was easier yet: just look for a flat spot, or a grassy one, and hit the ground running.

I almost didn't recognize Corbin when he answered the door. Surprise and bloodshot eyes greeted us along with the pungency of liquor and cigarettes. The strain on his face said he hadn't slept in a while ... maybe more than a while.

"Well, if angels could fly," he said, pushing back hair that didn't want to stay pushed back. "I'm at a loss for words—which is not often the case as you well know." His laughter was infectious, as always. "Come in, come in," he said, and with that, bid us into an empty room with the same hand he used to tuck in the tail of his shirt. "Welcome," he said with a dry mouth and a grand gesture, "to my little piece of the American dream," then looked around as if seeing it for the first time, "...it's humbleness never in question."

There was a pallor to Corbin's face, like he'd lost a measure of blood, and several days of black uneven stubble. Through an open doorway four men sat hunched over a poker table with cigars and whiskey. One of them was noticeably bigger than the others, and sat as if two chairs would have been more comfortable. He looked up, the chew in his lower lip full-to-overflowing, studying us until he was satisfied we posed no threat, then returned to the game. The one with his back to us never bothered looking. The other two glanced our way but only for a second, just long enough to dismiss us with a disinterested nod.

"Well...," Corbin said, closing the door behind us, "What may I say is the honor?—and at such an hour?"

The room we stepped into had the airiness of a fair-sized corncrib and seemed to echo our voices up a long staircase that twisted its way to the second floor. And though its walls were as faded and peeling as the outside trim, it had a feel of timeliness: an elegance and stateliness that seemed to long for days gone by. I felt like I'd walked into a storybook, right down to the white, glass-smooth floor and a ceiling so high it ate into a fair-sized portion of Pikeville sky. The chandelier over our heads was strung with baubles and beads, and connected by endless strings of dust. It hung from what seemed like a mile of long gold chain, and, like most everything else, seemed to gasp for breath: flickering with a murky yellow glow.

"Let me guess," Corbin said when we were too slow to respond. "You were just in the neighborhood."

"Well, truth is," Bobby said, "we been worried about you. Well, not me, but Momma. She's been askin' about you." Lying came so natural to Bobby.

Corbin stood for the longest time in a posture of reflection, mystical-like and provoked by thought, staring but not seeing. "Well then," he said, licking moisture into his lips, "can I offer you something? Coffee? A seat at the poker table?" It was as if he had heard nothing Bobby said.

Before we could answer, a voice, velvety and throaty, trailed down to us from the top of the stairs. "Corbin? Who is it, honey? Do we have comp'ny?"

Corbin's eyes settled on me in a gesture of folding, of being brought to the light of scandal. And though awkward, it was a gaze of composure, one that said *I know what I am and now you know too*; one that proclaimed without pretense the fact that he was, after all, nothing more than a man, mortal, and with as many faults. "Oh well," he whispered, "life is so often an impish mixture of time and place, is it not? ... and when you least expect it."

"Corbin..."

"Yes, darlin'," he said without lifting his eyes from mine, "there is, in fact, comp'ny. My nephew, and a good friend." His eyebrows did a quick lift, as did the corners of his mouth, and there was an ever-so-slight tilt to his head. I took it to mean that he would be all obliged if this could be *our little secret*, just between us men.

"Well, now," came the voice again, this time cooing, "isn't that just like you not to tell me."

He turned and smiled as *the voice* came down the stairs. It belonged to Ruby Mea McHone, an old acquaintance, I would later discover, of some standing. She wore a smile a mile wide, and the air seemed to part as she descended. Her hair was short and wavy, and so fair it was next to colorless—and so tight to her head it looked for a second like she might be bald. She was small and lean and wrapped in something so thin it could have passed for curtains, something that came to a halt in the middle of her buttercream thighs. It was pinkish in color, and matched the tiny satin slip beneath it—and it billowed about her with each delicate and deliberate step, until she stood within arms reach and looking at me through sky-blue eyes. Her face was round; and her lips were full and of the same red that blazed from the cans of Prince Albert tobacco. A beauty mark dotted her left cheek just below her eye. She was doll-pretty.

"I'm Ruby Mae McHone," she said, dangling a hand at the end of her fully extended arm.

"And this here's Rubin Cain," Corbin said in the next breath. "An' this here's my nephew, Bobby Yonts." I shook her hand, red fingernails and all, the same that shone from her toenails, and said that I was pleased to meet her—all the while feeling like I was siding with the enemy. Bobby just nodded, but then was forced to shake her hand when she put it up near his face.

"Pleased to meet you boys," she said. "I must say, you're much bigger and better lookin' than Corbin let on. Honey, whyn't yew tell me they was such *men*?"

"Yes," said Corbin, "imagine me forgetting something like that." He gave a raised eyebrow and a gentle suck to his teeth, then said, "Ruby May here is of the Williamson, West Virginia, McHone's," as if that was supposed to mean something to Bobby and me. "Old family friends," he added. "Been visiting for a spell, haven't you darlin'? ...but regrettably must take her leave for the sake of other interests." She glowed with Corbin's showered attentions.

"Family business," she blushed.

"The McHone empire," Corbin said too loud for the room, its cracked and peeling walls echoing it back to us.

"Corbin, you do go on," she gushed. "But I'm afraid he's right. Business interests make it necessary that I redirect my time an' resources to where they're most needed."

"And unfortunately for us here in Pikeville," Corbin chided, "that would be back in Williamson."

Right then one of the poker players—the big one, as big as Ben—ambled to the door and closed it gentle like, shutting us out. I shot Bobby a look. He was grinning and nodding his head. It was Hooker Hopkins. Corbin just stood there, unruffled and wavering from the lack of sleep and trying to steer around what liquor still ran through him.

"We'll miss her," he said, referring to Ruby Mae, "but there'll be other times."

"May I offer you boys something?" said Ruby Mae in her sweetest voice and baby-doll nightie.

"Breakfast sounds good to me," Bobby said.

"Uh ... actually, I b'lieve we were just fixin' to leave," I said.

"Now, you don't have to run off on *my* account," Ruby Mae drawled.

"There's places we need to be," I said apologetically.

"Things you need to take care of, I reckon," she said admiringly. "But *do* come back—and *do* come by, if you're ever in Williamson."

The early dawn was just the way we left it before we knocked on Corbin's door: cold, gray and dank, a morning where our breath matched the mist rising off the Big Sandy. We slogged along for a good piece without saying much, Bobby rebuking me for running out on what could have been a breakfast we both needed, though I suspected what really occupied his mind was pretty much the same thing running around in mine: Ruby Mae McHone and the *more-than-casual interest* she shared with Corbin Fairchild.

US-23 was all but barren so early in the morning, and its dirt shoulder just short of mud. A handful of cars whizzed by without the slightest regard to our turned-up thumbs, or our being hunched against the cold. "I've heard Momma talk about the McHones'," said Bobby over the crunch of his footsteps. "There's a fair pocket a money there, brother man. Sober gold. Coal mines mostly, and red-liquor smugglin', what time the gov'ment put a halt to whiskey makin'. Own their own bank. God strike me dead if I'm lyin'. Y'ever heard tell a' such a thang? Ownin' yer own *bank*? Now, by God, that's gettin' 'er done. Rob the damned thang whenever you want to, I guess. Just lock the doors, shut out the lights, and take however much you want. Kick back, smoke a big cigar, walk on home an' eat supper. Now that's a life: ownin' yer own bank. An' if I know Corbin, he's got his reasons for gettin' close to Ruby Mae. He plays it right, he might be in for a right smart piece a' the action."

Bobby's banter was like a lullaby, warming me with its argument and irreverence. Being cold came with the briskness of the morning, but his chipping away at what was jaded, jilted, and gilded never failed to get my mind off being broke and hungry. He was like a sunbeam sometimes, what got me up and over what would otherwise hold me down. But it was his not knowing what was around the next bend that suited him best, what kept him wily and tuned in to what he might discover. I couldn't help but think he wanted everything in his way to be tangled just so he could figure a way out.

We were part way to Pikeville's North-end bridge, not knowing what our next move would be, when Corbin's Model-A rolled to a stop alongside us. The bone chill of the morning was cause enough to jump in without being asked. We sat rocking and shivering, trying to rekindle the warmth Mother Nature had taken away overnight. Corbin sat cocked in a half-stupor watching us with amusement. "Got a mule to ride, if you'd rather," he said.

Corbin's eyes followed me in the rearview mirror as he drove. They were bloodshot, but not vacant, searching, I figured, for what might give him an understanding of what I was feeling. A few times our eyes met and became locked, spellbound and unable to turn away. I suppose it was about as close as we got to looking into each others' souls, into the muddiness of our failings and the weaknesses we kept buried inside: things that rail to the heavens as being without excuse, and too indulged to see the need for forgiveness.

We pulled to a stop at the top of Dry Fork Hill. It was still early, gray on gray and with a damp bite already part of the day. There was little movement except for wrens flittering in and out of the rough, and little sound other than roosters far off, their crowing bold and brazen. None of us were especially full of life, the ten miles having passed in great voids of quiet reflection. Sleep tugged hard.

"I just want you to know," Corbin said, looking straight ahead, "that life, in the fullness of its complexity, is, in the strictest sense, forever unfolding—*unearthing* if you will—and bringing to mind that things are not always what they seem. And though there are those things that need to be regarded with suspicion, I am not one of them." A posture of collectedness was interrupted with several sizeable attempts to suction his sinuses. "I know," he said, "there's prob'ly a swill of specifics crashin' 'round in your brain pans, not the least of which brings into question honorableness, mine in particular. But in order to lay aside any misgivings, let me make one thing clear: Miss McHone and I... Well, it's complicated."

We waited while his tongue went in search of moisture. Annoyed that there was not nearly enough, he searched under his seat for what might help. Nothing! "It's like this," he said. "Miss McHone and I, because of a mutual interest in hardcore revenue, have entered into a joint venture—my involvement being altogether less ardent. You see, there's a matter of solvency to be considered. *Mine.*" He paused, giving rise to the word, allowing it time to penetrate. "The lack of which has become an embarrassment of uncomfortable proportions. I say embarrassment because the Fairchild's and McHone's are such longtime political allies, as close as family can be without being blood, and with its bank now in receivership of my holdings. As it turns out, Miss McHone was all obliging, even inviting me to West Virginia for a time, in the interest of our pursuits. It went as I thought it would, leaving me with the need to reciprocate. Which I'd say was quite evident. All of which was testimony to our mutual interests. I must say, however, that my courtesies were as necessary an evil as I'd ever heaped on myself, the lack of which stood to undercut what dignity was left in the family name."

Bobby and I gave each other embattled looks. Finally, Bobby put them to words. "So you're tellin' us that Ruby Mae's got you over a barrel and you'd better kiss everthang she wants kissed—or else she's gonna take everthang you got. Now, is that it or not?"

Corbin gave us a thoughtful, but strained smile. "That's pretty much it," he said.

We sat for a time with the engine running, its manifold heater rattling and warming like a wood stove. "It didn't start out to be much," Corbin said. "At least, I didn't intend it to be. Went there with the notion of borrowing just enough to give me what footing I needed. Poker playin' had left me a mite off track. At first, I thought it was just a dry spell. Nothin' we ain't all been through at one time or another. Surely nothing beyond a minor inconvenience, and surely nothing that would sustain a lingering hardship, or so I thought. So I stayed with it, thinkin' the clouds would lift at any time. I was doublin' down on every bet just *knowin'* that the next card would be the one to bring the sun back into my very dark and private sky. Went on like that for weeks, bettin' 'bout as fast as I could borrow, till Clyde Birchfield said out loud an' right in front of everbody that he was tapped out. Just like that. Said I was already into him for five hundred an' he just didn't feel comfortable lettin' it go any further. I just sat there lookin' at all them faces lookin' back at me. All five of 'em. Humiliatin' thang, to go 'round the table askin' for a handout, but I did. Just had to bet one more hand, one more time. It's a hell of a feelin' to knock on a locked door, one after another, and have nobody answer. That's how it felt when they commenced to say how sorry they were, and how much I *already* owed 'em. It was nearly *four thousand* I was down, an' they weren't havin' anymore. Quiet stretched out in front of us like a long lazy summer afternoon till they just laid their cards down an' walked out, each of 'em gentle-like an' sayin' good night, an' get some rest, an' horseshit like that to smother the discomfiture. It wasn't till they left that I noticed the money: what was in the pot an' what they walked away from. Just left it there on the table. I was never anymore aware of how far I'd sunk."

I sat with a fix on Corbin and the haze of cigarette smoke drifting around his face. He looked wadded and full of thought, his mind so carefully crafted, so finely tuned, yet with a look that said '*What can you possibly think of me now?*'

"I must tell you," he went on, "I was pained by it on account of the sore I'd put on the family name. You have to understand: them with money run in tight circles, an' my reputation was up against it. Wasn't nobody to the point of comin' right out an' askin' me for what was owed, but there was a posture that spoke to their impatience. I was all the time thinkin' I could make good with one big score, but turns out, my luck had soured about like a warm drink a buttermilk. I even run up a sizeable I.O.U. with Henry Claypool, an' the *last* thang you want to do is piss off the grocer. Truth is, I'd just about sucked the life out of everbody I knew, an' borrowed against the home place like it could go on forever. Only thang that kept me out of the poorhouse was U.J. an' Don'l Mac. Shining was still king, but not enough to resurrect what I'd pulled down. That's when I thought of Cecil McHone: richer'n Fort Knox, and an old friend a Daddy's. But little did I know that Cecil had gone off to heaven and left it all—and I do mean *all*—to Ruby Mae.

Thirty-Seven

Grinnin' Like a Mule Eatin' Biscuits

The rain was consistently annoying throughout April, a light but constant drizzle that kept the ground renewed with mud and all of us under such a cloud of mildew that the schoolhouse stoves needed the attentions of a January. Their warmth was the only way we had to bake away the dampness in our clothes, the wool pieces being the worst, their drying by the stove choking out what oxygen there was while leaving an odor like ol' Bartley's bed. And even though the sky was gray and misty most of the time, it prompted the smell of the earth and opened us to the glory of the hills: redbuds and bellwort, crocus and dogbane: all that sought to begin anew.

By month's end, we began to lay aside our shoes and know the earth again with the soles of our feet; when we stopped wrapping ourselves like rag dolls and opened up to the promise of higher and hotter suns. And though our gestures were small, they were of conquering significance: we had outlasted winter ... *once again.*

Something surely must have been in the air that first week in May, something that worked to stir the excitements of spring and move Cobbie Parsons to come calling on Wilma Lee, albeit as drunk as any ten men. It takes nerve to put your heart out there on your sleeve, and Cobbie found it in the ebullience of firewater. And though honorable in the main, he made it only as far as the creek before stumbling face down in the rush and tumble of its churning mud foam. Wilson and I pulled him to his feet, got him inside, and propped him up in a chair alongside Mary Olive's bed. He only lasted a few short seconds before spinning himself out of his seat and against the corner of the stove, his head leading the way. A spray of blood reached clear to the middle of the floor. By the time we got him up and back in his chair, the ugly gash above his right eye had painted his face a brilliant scarlet, in the text of a hobgoblin butchered. Wilson and I worked feverishly to keep the blood from running down his face and into his eyes, finally wrapping his head tight in rags. Half the coffee we gave him spilled down his chin and mingled with the creek water on his shirt; the rest of it slopped onto his pants and the floor. It was questionable whether he knew where he was, or whether it even mattered, but still he managed to smile from deep within his stupor, the warmth and familiarity of his yellow-green teeth as clown-like as the glazed emptiness in his eyes. It was the first time Cobbie had come a-callin' on Wilma Lee. His being bolstered by the courage only liquor could afford, made him a visitor none of us were ready for, least of all Wilma Lee.

"Look at him," Mary Olive said. "Grinnin' like a mule eatin' biscuits. Right now, I b'lieve just one a my thoughts would bust his head wide open."

In the midst of our laughter, Wilma Lee fled to the lower room, struggling to hold back sobs. This was her Cobbie, after all, and his comedic sorryness had been a stab to her heart.

Up to this time Seriann had said nothing, only watched the whole of it unfold with an unchanging look of disgust. After Cobbie's second cup of coffee, however, she leveled about as harsh a warning as I'd ever heard, one guaranteeing that Cobbie's sorry ass would be hit over the head with an ax handle, cut into little pieces, stuffed in a sack, and floated down the river without ever a grave marker or anyone even knowing he was gone, if he were to *ever* show up here again muddy or bloody, or smelling with the likes of whiskey. "You'd just be gone," she told him. "I'd make sure not even bloodhounds could find ye."

Though Cobbie's understanding of what Seriann said was uncertain, he nodded in agreement and left smiling like he'd just found Jesus. He made it back across the creek all right, but then slipped and fell going up the bank on the other side. He lay there in the mud for a time before signaling to us that he was okay. Once on his feet, he was so covered in muck and dirt it was hard to tell his front from his back. But then once he got to stepping, inertia took him the rest of the way, propelling him up the road in the opposite direction of where he lived. Though Seriann's warnings to Cobbie had been dire, we had to believe that they hadn't registered any more than Mr. Tacket's arithmetic lessons.

I don't know that there was a phrase that depicted the passions of apple-blossom time more than *spring fever.* Whatever the phrase, its pull was undeniable, quickening the heart and spilling up and over even onto Corbin Fairchild.

I heard the rattle of his Model-A long before I saw it stop alongside the alder bushes that lined the creek. Seriann was brooming the yard: what lay between the gate and the steps, when she straightened long enough to see Corbin's hand go up in a grand wave.

"Well, looky here," she said leaning on the broom, the smile on her face all telling. "Devil or saint ... don't rightly know which."

Nimbleness from one big rock to another secured Corbin's way across the creek. "Howdy, ma'am," he said stepping into the yard. "A day of unparalleled magnificence we're having, don't you think?"

Seriann stood glued to her smile. "Well, now," she said, "depends if you're ridin' around in a big ol' limousine, lookin' an' smellin' like a fresh bath, or sweeping bird shit outta the yard." They both stood with surprised looks before letting go with high-tenor laughter, the kind so common to airiness and spring.

Corbin was as welcome as a summer rain, even after staying away so long. "Brought you somethin'," he said, his face aglow.

"Well," Seriann said, "should I believe it's in a big ole box too big to carry 'cross the creek, or somethin' you got hid up there behind yer eye teeth?"

"Oh, but madam, I speak of a thing beyond the common, infinitely above the vulgar; a thing surely meant for your Cinderella dreams."

"I'm waitin'," she said.

"Why, I speak of an invitation to a ball," he said. "Mine! The grand premiere of Pikeville's first an' only *gentlemen's* club ... *private* mind you ... owned an' operated by yours truly." He stood transfixed by a shameless grin and waiting for something to come out of Seriann's gaping mouth.

"I might could get excited if I knew what you were talkin' about."

"Brain child of one Ruby Mae McHone," he said without flinching. "Banker and investment speculator who was kind enough to help me out of a rather sizeable financial shitstorm, for—what shall we say ... concessions."

"An' this is what she come up with?"

"Among other things." he said. "But that's another page."

"Who is she, again?" said Seriann, bypassing all other pages.

"Her daddy and mine were old friends. Not family, mind you, but with ties about as deep. Turns out he left everything to Ruby Mae, including a bank."

"What bank?"

"Some bank with the words *national* an' *independent* attached to it. Over there in Williamson, West Virginia. Not all that far, if you'll recall, from where Devil Anse Hatfield raised a family."

Seriann took a deep breath, wrinkled up her brow and said: "Well now, what was it about this invitation?"

"Well, it's like this," Corbin said, "I got to thinkin' 'bout that dress somebody got you for Christmas, and ... well, I'd sorta like to see what it looks like with you in it. Fact is, I'm more than a little curious about what the two of us might look like together: you in that dress, an' me with a black tie and a six-shooter strapped to my hip."

Seriann remained motionless, her eyes locked onto Corbin's. "I'm thinkin'," she finally said, "that them with good sense'll know enough to get out of our way." Their laughter was enough to bring Mary Olive onto the porch in a waddle and wiping her hands on her apron.

"Well now, buddy, if I had to die," exclaimed Mary Olive. "I thought you might a' quit us in favor of all them book-read people in Pikeville."

"Well, I did," he said, "but then I got to thinkin' about yer cornbread, and how I was prob'ly more deserving of it than anybody—on account of havin' such refined taste, an' all. So I thought I'd give you another chance."

Mary Olive shook her head. "Just another one wantin' a handout. Come on in, but mind yerself; I'm already lookin' for an excuse to run you off."

So, Corbin came home in a manner of speaking, back to the banter of those who cared most about him, and showed it with the fullness of circus and a bit of unspoken prayer. He stayed the rest of the day, his presence making us feel as though we were on higher ground. Black-eyed peas, fried potatoes, and cornbread made up our plates that night, kept us filled long afterwards when we crowded together in the upper room, vying for our share of limelight and listening to Corbin tell what all he was fixing to do. "A gentlemen's club is not entirely unlike ownin' yer own bank," he said. "Essentially in the same vein of profitability when you limit the bulkiness of involving Uncle Sam—"

"Corbin," Seriann said, cutting him off. He stopped and gave her a look that said he was listening. "You know, I'll need new shoes."

The night still carried the dew-chill of the mountains, but being next to the window and the wash of the creek was like being lulled to sleep, night sounds coming as clear and crystal as the stars. The same was true of Corbin's and Seriann's voices as they stood airing by the gate.

"Ain't you gonna ask me where I been?" Corbin said.

"Well..." Seriann drawled, "I would if I thought I could get the truth, but I've lived long enough to know *why bother* whenever there's the mention of another woman."

"Meaning Ruby Mae McHone?"

There was a long pause, the spill of the creek flushing and filling the night with a chill of its own. "Look," she said, "I know you got your mind made up with what you want to tell me, but I don't know if I got the heart to watch 'at pretty mouth pretendin' with what I don't wan't to hear."

"I simply wanted to—"

"Save yer offerin's, Corbin. We had us a good ole time here tonight, an' it was a blessin' that you come back around. There was more'n me who missed you, but what on earth could you possibly say that might lay aside your bein' gone so long without a word? 'Less there's a woman in it. I might be dumb, but I ain't *plum* dumb."

"I know that for a fact," he said. "I was just hopin' to explain myself, now that we're alone."

"A body that stays gone, the way you do so often, shouldn't want to be tellin' about it, 'cept to alibi."

I could hear Corbin let go with a big breath.

"I'm hard knocked, Corbin," she said. "You outta know that by now. But you stayin' away was a strife. Unbecomin' to you. Unbeholdin' to me. I don't doubt you've done worse, but it don't play down yer crime. I guess maybe I'm part to blame for expectin' too much, allowin' how I was so keen to yer ways, yer fiddly words. I know we never uttered lastin' thangs to one 'nother, and I ain't got no right to claim you, but it ain't all that hard to know we were more'n just friends. An' then you just up an' run off, like it was all falsehearted. Truth is, I'm more bewildered than harmed by it."

"You need to hear—"

"I ain't needin' to hear nuthin'," she said. "Simple truth is I'm not askin', not now or ever, where you been. I'm just not able to give it the right mind. If I was to stand here an' listen to what you wanted to say, I'd be pretendin' right along with you—an' pretendin' is one thang I ain't ever been all that good at."

"I hope this is not an incrimination. As full of fire as you are, I know you wouldn't judge me without the facts."

"Whose facts? *Yours?*"

"I'm not without principles, Seriann. All I'm wantin' is to tell you what I was up against."

"You mean why it was necessary to stay gone without a word when I wasn't but thirty minutes away?"

"I could a' done better," he said.

"Oh, Corbin," she said. "Corbin, Corbin, Corbin, my angel an' my man." Her words fell in a lullaby near to a cry. "There wasn't an hour that

I didn't think about you. Where you were, what you were doin'. Left me wonderin' if you ever thought how hounded I was not knowin' if you was dead 'r alive, or if you was ever comin' back. You just up an' disappeared like I didn't mean a thang, like *none* of us did. An' that's the hurtin'est kind a leavin' there is. 'Course I suspect you know that. Still, you did it; then didn't do nuthin' to change it."

"Seriann—"

"You need to rethink what you want to say to me 'fore you come around here callin' me pretty names. I don't know what it was that kept you away, Corbin, but I have my suspicions. But if you're hopin' to come around me again, you better trust it's sump'm you've put behind you. I ain't never had much forgiveness for this sort a thang. It's never as satisfyin' as drawin' blood, what I'm used to. I'm just hopin' that time will give you back to me, an' that fraud won't come with it to wear away the good. But I pray for your sake, *an' mine,* that I've heard the name Ruby Mae McHone for the last time."

Corbin was without sound, the creek gushing and indelicate behind him. "One thang fer certain," Seriann said, "you created a divide that I'll need time to get across. There's reason enough to be happy that you come back, I reckon, but I'm careworn with findin' delight in yer arms right now."

I lay as still as I could, chilled by Seriann's words and straining to hear above the creek water coursing and sloshing and filling the hush that lay between them.

"I covet a place for us, Corbin," Seriann said as tenderly as I'd ever heard her. "That shouldn't come as a surprise. My heart's big and desirous, but your walkin' off the way you did was a weight it wasn't made for. I thought about askin' after you," she said. "Thought to send word to U.J. to see if he could tell me somethin'—but then figured you was gone an' stayin' that way for a reason, so I let it be. I reckoned if you wanted me to know anythang a-tall, you'd come back around. And though it's taken you a while, you finally did. I hope it's sump'm you won't be sorry for ... or me either."

The night seemed to close in around Corbin, cloaking him in a stillness that was almost measurable: the dash and din of creek water drowning out all that was so want to resist. "I'm sorry," was his only utterance ... then his footsteps, crunched and careful and going away.

At first, Bobby stayed away after Dixie came, but then began to take more interest with the brighter light and warmer winds. It troubled him that she was with us because of such wrongful deeds. Still, he came around, sitting with her for hours on the porch: in the sun and in the evening, and even a few times in the shadow of the moon. She was far different to Bobby, still quiet and with few words, but softer to his ways. Bobby pressed hard for her high regard and good opinion, sitting without touching and listening even when there was only the stir of wind between them.

To say Bobby was at a loss and that his time with Dixie was rare and unfamiliar would have been near the mark. Bobby always thought large scale, always played hard at being big, but the somberness that sometimes lingered with Dixie left him knowing there were things beyond what he could shape, things that had blemished what he knew to be blameless.

"You know," he said to me, "I could lower the hammer on Haman Flowers quick as I could swat a fly. He'd never know a thing, and nobody else would either. An' far as I know, I'd be doing ever'body a favor." He spoke like he was the voice of reason. Confident. Justified. "Just puttin' an end to a mistake is all it'd be, same's you would a mad dog." He wasn't after feedback, only the steady comfort of his voice: the poetry and vibrato that accompanied the silent slice of his knife spelling out Cornbread Red in the huge silver maple beside his house. "Hell, I'd do it just knowing it was the right thang, then sleep like a baby that very night—just like Hooker Hopkins."

Just before school let out for the summer we got another one of Woodrow's letters. We never ceased to marvel at how the post office was able to decipher them and get them to us. "Looks like he wrote it with his feet," said Mary Olive. Wilson said it looked like he was hangin' upside down in the middle of the night with his hands tied behind his back and the pencil held between his teeth. How those letters ever found their way to us was anybody's guess, though it was certain that both magic and miracle played profound roles. They all came with the same encrypted-abbreviated-encoded-hieroglyphic scrawl and with the same red, white and blue border around the envelope. And though they didn't come but about once a month, Seriann kept them tied together with a ribbon in the top drawer of the bureau in the upper room. Despite the novelty of trying to interpret word after word, his letters never bore anything beyond the lonely and morose, even the macabre. They were letters depicting only the worst and saddest of times: fights and brawls, and their inevitable punishments; the loneliness and weekend drunkenness; the bleakness of the landscape; the monotony of life on an Army base; the inane, Godless banter of those around him; the drudgery of their tasks; and the stark, oppressive faces that he had to look at day in and day out. They were cold shivers delivered in an envelope, so full of dread that it was hard not to want to run around in the sunshine after reading them. "Sounds to me like he's committin' suicide ever time he writes one a' them things," said Mary Olive.

In Woodrow's latest letter, he told us that his best buddy had been stabbed outside a whorehouse somewhere in Columbus. He said he bled to death before he could get the help he needed, and that the fellow who did it had escaped from a lunatic asylum, where he'd been most of his life for cutting up his mommy and daddy into little pieces and using them to bait bear. He went on to say that somebody broke into his locker and stole his only pair of shoes and all his Marvel comic books. He then told us he was being shipped to some place called Wyoming. He didn't know much about it, but was told that there was so much snow that it had to be pushed out of the way two and three times a day just so air could get in. And that it was a place with Indians hiding everywhere, just waiting to cut all the white throats they could. I didn't know how Woodrow made it from one day to the next without scaring himself to death, but reckoned he had sense enough to know when to keep his guard up and when to duck. Seriann walked over to the schoolhouse that evening and had Mr. Tacket show her where Wyoming was on the map. She left thinking Woodrow was just over the hill.

Thirty-Eight

I Am That Friend

May first—Mayday—my birthday; a day when Imogene's copper-wire hair had been pulled back and tied into one long braid, and her face particularly scrubbed and shiny; a day when her wrath had been tempered and humbled enough to be almost nonexistent; and a day when she left me a gift with Seriann—an act not so much done out of shyness, but out of a fear of ridicule should she be discovered. She was certain I wouldn't tell for the same reason. It would be *our* secret. She had, with this simple gesture—whether she intended it or not—established for us something clandestine. I wasn't sure what to do, but knew for certain that I couldn't tell anyone, not even Bobby. Discovery carried the rider of ruin. And even though Imogene's demeanor toward me was a carefully concealed affection, what was most revealing was that I didn't mind. Fact was, I *liked* it, and the little fire it ignited in my belly. But I knew I was no match for the harassment that was sure to come if my feelings were made known, so I kept them, and her gift, a secret.

I thought for a time that Imogene's gift might prove to be more than I was ready for, and debated on giving it back. But giving it back would have increased the chance of her lighting into me and exposing what needed to be kept hid. So I swore Seriann to secrecy, even though she thought I needed a somewhat different bearing: one more open and with a clearer path to the heart.

Imogene's gift was a letter, one that told me how weak her back became whenever she thought of me.

May also came with the certainty that these were the very last of our school days, and that from here on out, they would simply be times remembered. I don't know as any of us had as much as a tinge of regret. Cobbie and Clifford and Preston had failed again, but there was simply no sense in wasting any more time with school. They had what they needed to work the fields and the mines, and there was nothing in books that would ever make them any better at it. They had youth and a sense of humor equal to their rawness and lack of caution; they had brawn and desire and the certainty that they would live forever, and they had the need to put it all to the test. That was as hopeful as it got on Greezy Creek.

Bobby was unclear what path he wanted to take, except that it would *not* be one going anywhere near a coal mine. He never shied away from work when there was a dollar to be made, but he never had the stomach for the abysmal lifestyle of eternal darkness. He was like his daddy in those regards. He could and would work hard, but, by God, it would be above ground: where a person could make the distinction between night and day. He could and would hoe corn right along beside men twice his size for a dollar a day. He was all about hard work and hustling for a dime, making every move count for something. Lately, hiding bottles of moonshine up and down the creek for Corbin had become much more serious and finely tuned. They were lessons that helped Bobby understand the world as a marketplace, a thing full of prospects, provided one had the mind for it—and the daring.

The last day of school in that May of 1937 wasn't much different than the rest, except for helping Mr. Tacket lock everything up for the summer. At the end of the day, he took the time to say how truly glad he was to have been our teacher, and that we ought to make the time, now and again, to come see him before we start having children of our own. I don't think he thought any of us would, but, like most folks, it was just something he was given to saying. A lot like, "Y'all come back, now. Y'hea?" After that, we just mostly wandered off the way we had most every day, as if we'd be back tomorrow.

Imogene handed me a folded piece of paper before she left. "Here," she said. "I wrote you sump'm." I turned it over in my hands and began to unfold it when she stopped me. "Don't read it *now*," she said, staring me dead in the eyes. I stopped cold, eyeballing to make sure nobody had seen me and waiting for further instructions. "You don't have to write me nuthin' back," she said, "unless you want to." I nodded my understanding, and noticed the hope in her eyes that I would.

"OK," I said, and for a very long moment just stood there without the slightest notion of what to say next. Slowly, the schoolyard emptied, final goodbyes echoing to me from across its hard-packed expanse.

"Well, I guess I'll see you sometime," I said. She smiled, and for a second I thought she might do something like cry. To my surprise, she reached out and touched my hand. It was the same kind of touch I remember my momma having: warm and gentle, nothing like I thought could come from Imogene. I welcomed it. And though it was a gesture that had caught me unaware, I was left knowing that I longed for more.

"Bye," she finally said, then turned and headed toward home, down the dusty path toward Lower Fork. I stood for the longest time watching after her and the sun bouncing off her hair, and how, all of a sudden, it seemed as meaningful as her touch. I waited until she had gone beyond the bend in the road before I read what she wrote.

Rubin –
(who is that friend ?)
(Greasy Creek----America----American)
that sees you from sun to sun and knows your name.
well, I'll express my-self this way, to all here at Greasy.

To gain, to make, to win, to be, a friend,
one must first approach one to another friendly.
This have been admissible here toward me from you.

May the blessing of the Lord and Savior Jesus Christ
remain in hearts souls and minds of each and many----
above all YOU----from this day. Who am I at Greasy?

(I am that friend.)
Imogene

Thirty-Nine

Twinges of Compunction

The day after we locked up the schoolhouse, Cousin Truman was at our door hours before daybreak, even before the miners put out to work. The moon sat low in the east, its quarter barely casting a glow, when I heard his Model-T draw to a stop. He'd come for Dixie. He was taking her to Caney Creek, to Grandmaw's, along with Seriann and Wilma Lee, but only Seriann would be coming back. The plan was for Dixie to live with Grandmaw, and since Mary Olive was sure that Haman Flowers didn't know Grandmaw Spicy any more than he knew how to read, she decided that Wilma Lee needed to be there too, so Dixie wouldn't be left without knowing a soul. For the time, anyway, it seemed like the best plan, and one that needed to be carried out in the dark of night without anybody knowing, and before Haman Flowers got back on his feet. With that, we hugged our good-byes.

That same day, Corbin came and took Bobby and me to Pikeville. It was a celebration, his way of showing us how proud he was that we had toughed it out, left a mark impossible to remove. We had outlasted the eighth grade, all the schooling Greezy Creek provided. For most, it meant that they were finished; despite Corbin's protests, it had the same meaning for Bobby.

The top was down on the Model-A and we sat squeezed together on the front seat, and me never feeling more like a king.

Pikeville lay ten miles to the north of Mary Olive's, on US-23. It was a right turn after crossing over the swinging bridge at Shelby Creek, then a left after crossing the concrete bridge that spanned the Big Sandy. I had never been to Pikeville, only to Stringtown on a dark night; then again when Bobby and I hung from the side of a coal car on a night equally as black on the way to Corbin's. I saw it briefly from Highway 23 when Corbin drove past it on an early Sunday morning, but to set foot in it was something I had yet to do.

Bobby had been to Pikeville time and again with his daddy: to the stockyards at the foot of Town Mountain. And he'd been to the wholesale warehouse on the south end with Ol' Man Andrew to load dry goods for the store, but, as often as he pleaded, neither of them ever took him to Main Street. There was simply no time, let alone reason.

Ol' Man Andrew would just flat-out say, "We're here to work, son. Here to get it an' get it back home." Olin was not as abrupt, but just as unyielding. "There'll be plenty a' time for town," was his hiss and boo. "The problem, as I see it, is that you'll like what you find."

Corbin kept us laughing most of the way, nipping on a pint bottle of moonshine—what he called *scat*—and telling us tales about the women he knew, about their finer lines and unmentionables, things Bobby and I listened to with ears as big as saucers. It was what men talked about, I reckoned: what they shared. A social order we were all-too ready to join.

We sweated and bounced along until I was sure we had gone beyond where we would be able to find our way back. But I no sooner thought it than we pulled onto a big iron bridge that took us over the Big Sandy and into Pikeville's upper end.

"Here she is, boys!" Corbin crowed. "Pikeville! County seat. Trial site of the Hatfield's an' McCoy's. Take a good look! There ain't a prettier sight to be seen ... and it was me, by God, who brought you here."

"Gaahhwwd almighty," said Bobby. "Lookit that'n *there*." He was pointing to a girl in front of Goff's Furniture. "And that'n ov 'ar." Bobby was in hot pursuit of everything in a skirt, thoughts of Dixie Wainwright far from his mind.

My head spun this way and that trying to drink it all in. From every direction and angle, brick buildings, three and four stories high, lined the streets, one after another: a courthouse, a bank, a five-and-ten-cent store. Things I'd only heard about swarmed around me in bold reality. Bobby's chatter was non-stop and prolific, about being able to rob the bank and then go to jail just across the street. My mind was bombarded. It was almost too much at once: all of this, all at the same time, all in the same place.

Corbin drove slow enough for us to get an eye full then parked at an angle in front of the Hatcher Hotel. From there, we strolled from one street to the next, Bobby talking a mile a minute and asking non-stop, rapid-fire questions faster than a dozen Corbins could answer. I was slack jawed, not knowing where to look next. Newness of every sort swept over me, filled in around me. Concrete streets and sidewalks; store windows big enough to drive a car through; real live moving picture shows I'd only heard about; a huge park with a drinking fountain; drug stores and cars of every sort; men in suits with gold watch chains, and shoes shiny enough to see your face; women with hats and nylon stockings, and smelling like lilacs; cafes and pool halls; stores with clothes just for men, and others just for women; men hauling blocks of ice; a man astraddle a bicycle; and more girls than I could ever imagine. It was enough to make me want to fall down.

I made mental pictures as fast as the sights passed before me. Bobby was a show unto himself, pointing and motioning to this and that, pulling me here, nudging me there. He seemed to leap from one side of the street to the other, like he'd been loosed and set free. All I wanted to do was stop and stare, take deep breaths and wonder if places like New York and Paris, places Mr. Tacket had told us about, could be any grander than this.

Corbin was good and drunk by this time, and told us he was fixing to take us to a soda fountain and buy us something called a hamburger. He walked between us so we could help steady him, but then made us stop every few minutes so he could sit: first on the courthouse steps, then on one of the chairs in front of Murphy's five-and-dime. We kept this up all the way to the park, where he proceeded to pass out on one of the benches—the hamburgers long forgotten.

Corbin's arms and legs were all over the place, his whole body as limp and lifeless as a feed sack hanging on a nail. Bobby was all for leaving him there while we lighted out on our own, sure that nobody would bother him so long as we made him look like he was just taking a nap. With that, Bobby stripped him of his coat, rolled it up and placed it under his head, then laced his arms across his chest. As a final touch, he crossed his ankles and placed his hat over his face. "There!" he said. "He looks like he's on a back porch swing, enjoying a summer afternoon." Corbin was a picture post card of leisure, and we laughed like it was our last. "Just one more thing," Bobby said, and very gingerly removed Corbin's billfold from his pants pocket. "Now," he said, "let's go get them hamburgers."

For the next hour and a half, we combed nearly every square inch of Pikeville. From the alleyways to the courthouse steps, we became its adopted sons. We not only ate at one soda fountain, but two. Those hamburgers were sent from heaven. A hamburger and a Pepsi: ten cents. The thought of spending Corbin's money while he slept was a tad unnerving for me, but the height of amusement for Bobby.

"Why, he sat up as plain as day and told me to take it. You heard him yourself."

"No," I said, "I didn't."

"Yeah, I'm sure you did," he said with his best clown face. "You just forgot. He said to take it all. Just save him enough to get back home or get outta jail. Hey, we aint' spendin' nothin' 'cept what he set aside for us. We're just savin' him the headache a' walkin' around an' takin' the shine off his shoes. Just knowin' he's ov 'ar restin' is a comfort to me." He stopped long enough to chomp a big bite out of his hamburger. "Makin' these hamburgers slide down like a piece a birthday cake."

It was hard not to ride Bobby's train, despite my twinges of compunction. At my insistence, we checked on Corbin after a time, but just briefly and from a distance, watching to make sure his belly rose and fell in unbroken rhythm before we made another landmark leap: before plopping down fifteen cents apiece and walking into the Weddington Theater. We were going to the moving picture show. It had been a toss up between the Weddington and the Liberty, but the Weddington had a painted poster of a cowboy named Tom Mix that proved to be an irresistible magnet. And, it was a double feature. Despite my hesitation about spending Corbin's money—the thought of it reeking havoc in the margins of my mind—I was, in the same breath, consumed with grandeur. From the smell of freshly popped corn to its cozy solitude, the Weddington, in one fell swoop, had moved me into hallowed ground. I felt consecrated, advanced in rank from country bumpkin to city dandy.

From the moment we pushed aside the thick red curtain separating the lobby from the seats and the big silver screen, we went from brazen and bold to a state of awe. We thought we'd seen it all, only to be shown that we hadn't. We sat in the luster and glare of the screen, our heartbeats pronounced and the grins on our faces paramount to a reach into eternity. "This must be what it feels like when you join the church," Bobby said.

Newsreels, astonishing accounts of a world we only imagined, stark and real accounts of people and places we would never come close to knowing, rolled before us like dreams. Then a funny book, something called a cartoon, came to life right before us: a wisecracking, carrot-eating rabbit getting the best of some dimwit with a double-barrel shotgun, and all the time to jerky-jangle music. I ate popcorn without tasting it and without ever looking away from the screen. By the time Tom Mix appeared, I was collapsed, lost and irretrievable to the world outside. It was the grandest leap we'd ever made.

Four hamburgers, six Pepsis, two popcorns, and six candy bars later, we found Corbin sitting with his elbows on his knees and his head resting in his hands. It had been survival instinct and the appeal to my better self that prompted us to leave before the second feature.

We walked with Corbin to a downstairs pool hall, where he splashed water on his face and tried to smooth the wrinkles out of his suit. Without being asked, Bobby handed him his billfold. "Here," he said with his best church grin, "'Bout forgot I had it."

"Well..." Corbin said, a little taken.

"Figured it was the right thang to do," Bobby said, stifling a laugh, "Cain't never know who might be wanderin' around, lookin' to gain from a feller's circumstances. An' yours wasn't too promising; or defensible either."

Corbin stood braced against the bathroom sink, sizing Bobby up and dangling the billfold. "Now ain't that thoughtful of you, young Bobby Yonts," he said. "Do I need to count it?"

Bobby's blue eyes, measured and wry, did most of the smiling. "It's all there," he said. "I mean, what's left is all there."

A tricky little smile worked its way onto Corbin's lips. "I believe you've mistaken me for a rich uncle, young Bobby. But then I don't reckon you took any more than I owed you. Am I right?"

"As right as it gets!" Bobby said.

Corbin squared himself with the mirror and combed his hair with very deliberate strokes before seating his hat just so. "Well, then," he said, rolling his head in my direction, "young Rubin—my very special friend, my cousin, my partner and very nearly my son—how much do you reckon it cost me to have you and Bobby look after my billfold?"

I paused, not knowing what to say, "I reckon 'bout a dollar an' a quarter in all," I said.

"Well then," he said, opening his billfold, "lets just round it up." And with that, he handed us each a greenback five-dollar bill. The prettiest thing I'd ever laid eyes on, and leaving my fingers numb where I touched it.

"You tellin' me this is mine?" I asked.

"Ever penny of it," Corbin said. "You've done me proud, schoolin' the way you have. Upstarts ain't always tolerant of such, but I'm hopin' you'll come to see this day for what it is: me bein' pleased—an' for what books can do, if you let 'em."

I slept well that night. It was the happiest I'd ever been.

Forty

Stored Up, Laid Up and Squirreled Away

The following Monday, Bobby and I started working fulltime for Old Man Andrew, from seven in the morning till four in the afternoon, six days a week. We hadn't been there more than a few days when Andrew gave Bobby the job of clearing the logjam on the second floor. It was one enormous room where Andrew kept most everything he owned and what he bought in bulk for the store. He called it his warehouse: forty years of what he and his daddy had stored up, laid up, and squirreled away, and by the looks of it—worth more in sentiment than dollars. There was also his refusal to discard even the least of it.

Bobby's job was to clean it up, which meant sorting, arranging, straightening, stacking, wiping it down and sweeping it out. From the beginning, it was a job far greater than Andrew wanted to involve himself with personally. But then after nearly a week, the place looked about like it did the day Bobby started. Short on options, Andrew sent me to help. It was clear he wasn't keen on Bobby and me working side by side and out of his sight, but the enormity of the job was more than Bobby alone could handle. So, with more than a little reluctance, he placed us together.

Our job was to work in the warehouse three hours a day, from eleven to two, until such time as it was clean and orderly and fully inventoried—and he didn't care if it took us until our hair was gray. The only stipulation was to stay clear of the thick oak door with a lock about the size of a dinner bucket. It was the door that walled off the upper end of the warehouse, and held the secrets of Horace's old office. Nothing behind that door was our concern, he told us, his face punctuated with a sternness that, up until that time, we'd seen only on Pearl. By noon on our first day, Bobby had cleared out enough space to squeeze in next to it; and for the next two hours monkeyed with that irresistible lock.

"I'd like to help you boys out," Andrew wheezed, winded from the twenty-three-step climb, "but I hate to leave Pearl alone." His face was puffed to a reddish purple. He took a quick look around, then left holding a handkerchief over his mouth and nose.

The oppressive heat and humidity there on the second floor, along with the dust, dirt, and lack of a breeze, hampered our ability to draw a clean breath and made the smell of rat droppings considerably more noticeable. Neither of us was especially excited about working in such conditions, and looked on it like Andrew was doling out punishment. Considering what we were up against, Bobby concluded that what Andrew was paying us wasn't enough. Our first thought was to quit, but then put that to rest when we thought of the repercussions from Olin and Seriann. Besides, we figured what was behind that big oak door, and our chances of getting to it, was worth the duress. But then knowing that Andrew was liable to slog his way up the stairs at any given minute made us realize we needed a plan, one that provided precise cover and a means of escape. Going against the grain was what I abhorred, but the very thing that Bobby lived for.

Bobby was basically honest, but also a hardcore pragmatist, doing what fit even if it required slight of hand. If there was something he couldn't buy outright or trade for, or something he felt was beyond the reasonable bounds of negotiation, he simply waited for the right time and stole it. It was much cleaner than haggling. He never saw much sense in causing a dispute, or creating hard feelings just because of unreasonable demands by petty and unreasonable people. It simply wasn't worth his time. Besides, he reasoned that if stealing it would help teach the sons-a'-bitches something about fair trade, it would be worthwhile, even instructive. Breaking into Horace Clemmons' old office held the same sway.

The general store was, by every stretch, the hub of the creek: not only the center for everyday commerce, but the main gathering place for news political, personal, and otherwise. It was the place where acquaintances were kept and appearances kept up; a place open enough for the *unspoken-for* to have respectful contact, and a place ingratiated with talk of family and crops, dogs and the weather, and such. The store, or A.C.'s, was the main terminal for most of what was bought and sold, swapped and traded, shook on and sworn to; where checks were cashed and the mail handed out everyday at noon. Being as it also served as the Post Office, it provided the perfect excuse to gather and mingle, and keep track of what your neighbors got through the mail without being obvious. Tales and gossip, what the almanac said about this, and what the preacher said about that, the store was the respite we all held to. And though Greezy had slightly better than a couple hundred families, it was in many ways one big one onto itself: just the right size to keep track of everybody else's business—and picking up the mail every day was one way of making sure it stayed that way.

From the upstairs windows, Bobby and I kept track of most of the activity. There was little that escaped us, even the mundane. By the time June rolled around, we could tell within a span of thirty minutes who was likely to show up and even the nature of his affairs. I began to understand how predictable people could be, how locked-in they were to habit—even Imogene. She came around every day at high noon, announcing her arrival by throwing rocks and green apples, and whatever else was handy through the warehouse's open window in the back. Cobbie and King Charles came around on occasion, but always nearer to quitting time, ready to share the jawbreakers Bobby routinely fingered on his way out the door. But Imogene came for the sheer fun of it, right there at noon when the mail came, her timing as precise as the gold watch Andrew liked to pull from his front pocket and examine with great authority.

At first, Bobby thought we could hide from Imogene, but the rocks and green apples just kept whizzing through the window. She was, as always, too powerful a force to ignore, and always good for the most outrageous tales and the latest gossip, things we were too weak to resist.

After awhile, her visits became our break time, unauthorized as it was. But then Bobby began to grow suspicious, figuring she was coming around for more than just fun and games. He began to suspect that she was stuck on me, something I claimed to have no control over, and making him swear not to mouth a word of it, unless the whole creek turn it into something I'd have to refute with every breath. It had to be that way; even loose-end rumors were too much for the closed network of Greezy.

The second-floor was so big and its clutter so vast that Andrew couldn't tell what we'd done even after we did it, so Bobby and I never strived for much beyond a gentle pace, never seeing the sense in the needless stirring of dust. To Bobby's thinking, it didn't make a hairs difference if we ever finished. Andrew was going to keep us there till he was satisfied, and only God knew what it would take to do that. Besides, it just wasn't healthy to be moving about quick-like in a place so lacking in air. It was logic that defied argument, and one I had no trouble accepting. But the day Imogene's rock come flying through the window and cracked me across the bridge of the nose was the day I began to understand the need to rise above my fate. That locked door loomed as an ever-growing magnet.

Forty-One

Aunt Jesse Parker

Cobbie Parsons, as innocent as he was ham-fisted, and with an ever-growing affinity for Wilma Lee, had it figured right off that Seriann was hiding something. He knew it down deep in his guts, despite our repeated insistence that Wilma Lee had gone to live with a distant aunt over in West Virginia and had taken Dixie with her.

"Hard telling when they'll be back ... if ever," was the way Seriann put it to him. As dogged as Cobbie was, he continued to come around day after day, wanting to know if we'd heard from her. After a time, his persistence grew into annoyance when he refused to believe a single one of our lies.

In between Cobbie coming and going, there were any number of others snooping and inquiring, trying to needle out a single thread. "Where was Wilma Lee, anyway?—an' 'at girl of Emmaline's? What in the world's come of 'em?"

"They's both of 'em over in West Virginia, takin' care a' Aunt Jessie Parker." It was Seriann at her lying best. "She's a aunt to Wilma Lee's natural daddy. Bless her heart; more'n ninety year old, and awl by herself in 'at big ole house." Each time she told it, it became sprinkled with a little more color, and after a while, Aunt Jessie Parker had grown into a bona fide legend. Wilson, Little Sherman and I sat alongside one visitor after another, marveling at all the trials Seriann put poor old Aunt Jesse Parker through.

"It's for their own good," she'd tell us after they left. "If you don't tell 'em what they want to hear, they'll just make sump'm up, an' 'fore you know it, they'll have you guilty of a hangin' crime."

We were forever faithful to the premise that Dixie and Wilma Lee's whereabouts was our secret to keep. We knew there was a trembling balance between what we said and what we didn't. Still, it didn't stop most from trying to squeeze us. We just had to be more resolute in our diversion than they were in their pursuit.

Over the course of weeks, however, Seriann's veil of secrecy began to unravel—as did her tales about Aunt Jessie Parker. There were simply too many people to fool, and too many noticing that she and Cousin Truman motored out of Greezy a couple times a week, and never heading anywhere but up Shelby Creek toward Caney. Before long, rumors began to fester and grow ugly, the most prominent one being that Seriann had sold Wilma Lee and Dixie to some whorehouse up the river. But given the last word, Seriann didn't much care what rumors folks concocted. She was just happy that they finally came up with one satisfying enough to put a halt to all the others. Now they could get back to whatever it was they did.

We were never sure what Seriann was liable to do from one day to the next, but it wasn't long after the whorehouse rumor became lively that she and Cousin Truman came rolling home way up in the night. It was a night with just a sliver of a moon, and we heard them long before we could see them. By the time they rolled to a stop, we stood huddled on the porch without a light. Bartley raised his head long enough to sniff and moan himself back to sleep; the cats darted and slinked out of sight, whining and carrying on like we were on the verge of a storm. That's when we noticed a shadow sitting like a sack of meal on the seat between them. It was Wilma Lee.

Bringing Wilma Lee home was Seriann's way of restoring a sense of quiet; like closing the book on a case that was nobody else's business to begin with. In the end, though, it only created a bigger mystery. Where was Dixie, anyway?

Like clockwork, Cobbie was there at our door the very next evening, stinking of sawmill timber where he'd hired on with Wince Creed. I don't know who had the bigger grin, Cobbie or Wilma Lee—but I do know Seriann wasn't grinning at all, despite Cobbie having brought us each a Baby Ruth.

Bobby kept the big oak door blocked with feed sacks and barrels. He had them stacked and arranged in maze-like fashion to where he could get in and out with only minimum effort, and where they could give him cover.

As usual, Old Man Andrew was unpredictable about checking on us, clomping up the stairs whenever he felt like it and keeping us on constant alert. The stairs creaking and popping under the weight of his 'possom gut was our only warning: what amounted to precisely twenty seconds before his bald head rose up like a big bubble out of the stairwell. It was a game of *on guard* we played what time Bobby probed the secrets of that big lock.

It was about noon on one hot Saturday afternoon in mid June when it happened; when Bobby stepped from behind his stack of boxes and stood still as a statue in the sprinkles of dust and sunlight spilling through the window. He just stood there rooted to the spot and oozing a look that was close to rapture. His smile was cut deep and glowing bright enough to start a fire. That's when he raised his hand the way I imagine Moses did when he parted the Red Sea. It was the lock, and he held it like a polished apple. The sun through the window was pouring over him like a light from heaven, and I was just about to shout when he put a finger to his lips. We stood there wide-eyed and going through the motions of having just discovered gold when one of Imogene's green apples came flying through the window and cracked me up side the head.

Getting rid of Imogene took longer than expected, her account of Ollie Tate being drunk and falling off the footbridge in front of his house being more fun than we expected. After that we opened the big oak door.

The door was thick and heavy and opened with a creak, its hinges high pitched and oil-starved. Behind it, light filtered weak and pale through drawn shades and a sea of boxes stacked chest-high from one side of the room to the other, and from front to back without a space between them.

"Gawwd almighty," said Bobby, his heartbeat in a thud above my own. Spread out before us, case after case of whiskey with writings that told of it being U.S. Bonded, with names like Scotch and Rum and Gin, names we'd never heard of. Where were we anyhow? At the threshold of heaven or the gates of hell? Were we safe, or about to die? We knew only one thing for sure: Pike County was as dry as a thirty-year-old milk cow, and all this whiskey—wherever it came from and however it got here—was enough to put us in leg irons for the rest of our days, should we be found with it.

One thing we hadn't counted on before opening the big oak door was the silence we created. There's something about *quiet*, especially when there isn't supposed to be any, that hastens and quickens the senses. Ours had been like a hand-written invitation. In less time than it takes to aim and shoot, and breathing like he'd been running from the law, Andrew's voice came laboring at us from the other side of Bobby's maze.

"Stay right where you are, boys," he said, his big pear-shaped frame wheezing while he cleared a path. "Well...," he said when he finally squeezed through the last of it, "'peers we got us a *situation*."

For several very long minutes, Andrew towered over us, sucking and blowing and doing what he could to level out his breathing, struggling as much to exhale as inhale. It had been his third trip of the day. We believed his face turning all red and purple twice a day was his limit. We had never been so wrong.

Andrew postured himself, then said, "Can't say I didn't warn ye." His words were husky and bounced around inside my skull like a rubber ball. I expected him, at any minute, to pull out a pistol and kill us both on the spot. Sweat came in giant beads across my scalp and forehead, under my arms and in the small of my back. I regretted ever listening to Bobby. If only God would deliver me from this, I would never listen to Bobby again. I swore it. "But ye just wouldn't listen," he said, "would ye?" The glare in his eyes demanded an answer. After a long moment of silence, our obvious fright was answer enough.

"So now what do we do?" he asked. "What is it that you've forced me to do?" His speech was steady and drawn out, as heavy as his manner. His tiny blue eyes seemed devilish, darting back and forth between us, steeling us. My throat was dry and painful. "I like to think a' m'self as a reasonable man," he said, his eyes searching us to see if we agreed. "But this leaves me feelin' like y'all've put me in a corner." He waited then added, "Betrayed my confidence is what ye've done." He stopped to let his point sink in, then asked, "What is it, you reckon, I oughtta do about it? I ain't got the kind a' time to be wastin' it on a chain gang, so I shore as hell cain't turn ye loose. Couldn't trust that ye'd keep yer mouths shut." He breathed deep, shaking his head in a total quandary. My throat now began to constrict, like I was being choked by sand and barbed-wire. All at once, Andrew began to rock, shifting his weight back and forth, the boards under his feet groaning with the added pressure. He swiped at his face time and again with his big white handkerchief, wheezing as though each breath might be his last. Finally he stopped and looked us square in the eyes. "All this here," he said, directing our gazes with a big sweep of his hand, our eyes following it like it was divinely appointed, "all this whiskey ... all these hundreds a' cases, so many it's a wonder the timbers ain't let go an' killed us all 'fore now. Four hunert cases in all," he said, blowing the attic dust from his nose on the same white handkerchief he used to wipe his brow. "At twelve bottles to the case." His eyes flashed, and for a moment seemed to dance. "'At's forty-eight hundred fifths a' U.S. grade, gov'ment bonded hooch, boys. *Red liquor.*" He paused to let the magnitude of it sink in, then gave us a quiet-eyed stare that seemed to nail our shoes to the floor. "Aannnd," he said in an exaggerated drawl, "yer gonna sell it." He hesitated while his smile crept like a blacksnake into his oversized cheeks. It was a smile that asked, 'Whatta ya think about that?'

Forty-Two

If Only For a Night

The storm cloud above Corbin and Seriann gradually gave way, losing strength in the light of a bejeweled and verdant June. The evening of the gentleman's club celebration only served to augment what they found in each other. We waited, not knowing what to expect, when Corbin came to get her. He came through the door dressed like a purebred millionaire, a bankrolled politician, and undertaker all in one. A black, double-breasted suit with silver pinstripes and black-and-white shoes had us believing he was some kind of riverboat gambler, looking for big-money action.

"Laaaaaw, childern!" Mary Olive howled, "I wan't you'ns to get a *gander*!" She was alive and kicking. "He's done gone plumb uptown on us. Don't reckon 'at's a *diamond* stickin' outta that purple tie."

"Just a litt-len," Corbin said. "Mother's. Part of a ring I paid to have stuck on the head of a pin."

She studied him up and down, turned him 'round and 'round. "If you ain't lookin' as close to a crowned head as I've ever seen," she marveled. "If yew was mine, I'd be braggin' on ye."

"Well, now," howled Wilma Lee, "if you'ns thank 'at's sump'n, just take a gander at *this*!" And with that, Seriann stepped into the kitchen in her red dress, satiny and clinging to her like it was wet. For the first time ever, her scrawniness vanished before my very eyes. In its place stood a princess as regal as the red shoes that adorned her feet. Her raven hair shined like sunlight off a crow's back, and her earrings sparkled and dangled, reminding me of the gold chain on Andrew Clemmons' watch.

In a heartbeat, the slack came out of Corbin, straightening him like he'd backed into a hot stove, his smile equal to the one in his eyes. We whooped and hollered and Seriann let go a dapper little hotfoot clog taking us even further into a fairy tale. It was inconceivable that Greezy had ever seen the likes of this.

They left in a hurry, with all of us following them through the schoolhouse bottom and across the footbridge to the road. It was like they were leading a parade. We stood proud and waving as they pulled away, the sun fading and washing us all in a golden haze.

"There goes two of a kind," said Mary Olive, her voice as soft as evening shadows, "...spirits as old as they are new." She looked at me with a bit of longing, the gentle breeze stirring the feather-tufts of her hair. "Like me and Dempsey once was," she said. "Like they's lost in the wake of moons and slow running rivers."

"I believe you got poetry in you, Mary Olive." I said. Her smile was faint and with a bit of fracture, a bit of regret.

I don't know that I slept that night, visions of the gentlemen's club with its spirited music and laughter, and with its rooms full of women like Ruby Mae McHone and Seriann—all of it filling me to overflowing. And, too, there was Corbin attending to the book-smart and fine-threaded, those with place and influence, and with thoughts of things a long way off from what I knew. All of them: princes and princesses, if only for a night.

Daylight slipped in around us with distant echoes from roosters up and down Gardner fork, their anthems announcing the crows in the garden. Corbin's Model-A was unmistakable, and it rumbled right up till it stopped in front of the footbridge. I watched the two of them step into the pale velvety light rising above Ripley Knob; watched as they pulled at one another, clinched in a perfect fit, kissed, murmured, laughed, then kissed again.

Tiptoeing into the kitchen was not as easy as they had hoped. “Well, now, childern, if this ain’t a sorry sight,” Mary Olive said, offering up a taste of Old Regular Baptist condemnation. “Bonnie and Clyde come to breakfast.”

By this time, Wilma Lee felt put upon for being woken up so early. “I just hope yew ain’t tore ’at dress runnin’ from the law,” she said.

“Yeah,” said Wilson from under his covers, “she’ll need it when her an’ Cobbie Parsons run off to New York City.”

It was a morning of high spirits just as the first ray of sunlight lit the porch. I’d only been half asleep most of the night, waiting for their return—for their accounting. By the looks of them—tattered and still full of Saturday night—I knew I’d have to wait even longer. Corbin crawled up on the bed next to Wilson and Little Sherman; Seriann crumpled next to Wilma Lee. Mary Olive and I ate breakfast alone: corn flitters and ice-cold milk we kept in a bucket near the bottom of the well.

Forty-Three

Ten Cents Apiece

Sun through the store's upstairs window came unchecked the way it had for a week, keeping the floors dried out to where they popped and cracked even without being walked on. The added weight of Andrew on the stairs only inflamed them, sent them snapping like they were being split into kindling. By the time he reached the top step, his tongue was half lulled and his eyes faint and rolled back to where they were mostly white. He stopped to gather breath, then started right in. "Don't care if it takes ye forty year," he said, his nasal tone exaggerated from the climb and his needing a drink of water. "It's high time 'at shit be outta here," he said pointing toward the door and the liquor that lay behind it, "an' I reckon yer quick enough to figure out the *how*." He paused, his big meaty hands in a slow massage across his chest. "Two thangs, though, 'fore I cut ye loose," he said. "One, don't ever ask me where it come from; and two, don't ever tell me who you sold it to. Closest I wanna be to this is you handin' me the money. An' when it's all said an' done, I wanna waller around in a hay stack a' dollar bills so high that if I was to fall off I'd starve to death 'fore I hit the ground. Now are we clear? We've already wasted a week just lookin' at it. Time to git it an' git it gone." He paused in a fight to breathe deep. "One last thang," he said, wiping his baldhead with what looked like a dishtowel, "they ain't no gettin' caught. Gettin' caught means forty year a' hard labor, a cold biscuit and a cup a water a day—if I don't kill you first. Far as I know, ye ain't got nobody to watch out for 'cept Virgil Blair, an' I ain't never liked 'at sneaky sumbitch noway—all the time lettin' on like he's dumber'n Dolly Damern's chickens. Thorny mean is what he is. Eyes in the back of his head makin' up for a cripple hip. Don't ever think he ain't watchin'—an' don't ever think I ain't either." That was the last thing Andrew said before easing down the stairs to the loose mob waiting for their mail, and the stone-serious and wizened face of Pearl.

"'At sumbitch is full-moon crazy," Bobby said, his grin labored. "But he's just cracker meat to me. Cain't pay him no mind, 'less you wanna end up like Pearl. Only thang we need do is tough it out." He was looking hard at the ceiling, his blue eyes searching. After a time he turned and faced me straight on. "Got me a notion, brother," was all he said, his smile sneaky and knowing, his eyes lit like a cat's in firelight.

For nights on end I couldn't sleep for thinking about all that liquor, and what Bobby and I were up against. Andrew knew that success depended on discretion; and what better way to ensure it than to incriminate those who had found him out; make them partners. It meant a risk greater than I wanted to take, but one I was powerless to do anything about.

Andrew wasn't at all conflicted about selling whiskey. He just didn't want to get caught. His standing with the Old Regular Baptists afforded him an almost tangible immunity against anything that might suggest impropriety. But good church standing aside, Andrew was first and foremost a businessman, far too pragmatic for Old Regular Baptist guilt. There were secular needs, after all, and money as the hub around which it revolved—and no one understood it better than Andrew Clemmons.

On the surface, things looked promising. With a recent upturn in outlying coalfields, we had miners with money and red liquor at a dollar a bottle. Bobby saw it as fate having shined its light on our otherwise dark and muddy road. I saw it as hope heaped in wishful thinking, its light pale and flickering.

Andrew laid it out how he was going to pay us ten cents apiece for every bottle we sold. It was easy math, but figures Bobby loved to work day after day. It was a flat rate, non-negotiable. We figured we had little choice considering the circumstances, but had no idea how to go about selling United States Government bonded whiskey without hanging or doing considerable time in some federal penitentiary. But in matters of liquor, whether making it or selling it—and more exact, when doing it outside the law—we soon came to realize there was only one thing we could count on: the inventiveness of Corbin Fairchild.

At Bobby's coaxing, Corbin parked across the road and down the old camp-house lane in front of the pool hall, then walked the fifty yards or so to the back of the store. He was right on time: eleven thirty, a half hour before the mail run, before Imogene, Virgil Blair, and the rush of Greezy's faithful showed up in numbers.

"Awright now," he said, "this better be good." He stood with his hands on his hips, and staring up at us with an expression that said *I ain't got all day*.

Without a word, Bobby held up a fifth of bourbon, it's soft amber color sparkling the sun. Corbin brought up his hands to shade his eyes, then craned his neck and cocked his head to get a better look. "Is 'at what I think it is?" he said.

"Hold out yer hands," Bobby said. And with that he let it drop the full fifteen feet into Corbin's waiting hands. Corbin did a number of takes, left and right and over his shoulders, before giving it a hard look. After a short pause, he sucked at his front teeth, rolled his head to the side and spit, then with a grin the size of a screen door, looked up toward the open window and said, "Y'all got any more a' these?"

I never paid much attention to Virgil Blair before Andrew turned me to bootlegging, never gave him much beyond an occasional nod, something he was always mindful to give back, slow and easy like while peering out from under the dust-colored Stetson he kept pulled low on his long bony face. He came to the store most days and sat on the porch while Andrew passed out the mail, always ready for the latest gossip and a fresh twist of Brown Mule—though his brand of gossip had more to do with listening than talking. The mountainous plugs of Brown Mule he packed between his cheek and molars made him look wildly out-of-balance, like he had an abscess ready to rupture. It seemed near impossible that his cheek could grow so bovine, be so stretched, extended, and distorted, that he could barely put his lips together to spit. And his hip, shot clean through and so frozen, that his walk was an up-and-down, side-to-side rock. The shot had been a mishap of his own doing: practicing fast draws with a Colt .45. I could only think of pain when I looked at Virgil Blair.

What time Virgil wasn't sitting in the shade of the store's big front porch, he was on the back of ol' Jake, meandering from one fork to the other, his pearl handled Colt .45 dangling like a piece of benighted armor from his hip. Virgil was never crippled what time he was on the back of ol' Jake.

Taller and thinner than most, Virgil was, everything about him long and lean: his arms and hands, his ears and nose, the shape of his face—even his eyes drooped and sagged, making them appear longer than they were wide. The pitch and crown of his Stetson added still more height, making him look even longer than he was. Sitting up there straight and tall on the back of ol' Jake seemed to stretch him to the height of poplars.

Despite the obvious pain of mounting and dismounting, Virgil chose horseback as a way of getting around. Said he liked the smell of horse-shit over what comes out the back of a car. Besides, ol' Jake could take him where a car and his cripple hip couldn't get to, places he too often needed to go.

I remember the first time I shook hands with Virgil Blair, his long bony fingers encircling my hand like a net. He was looking down on me from atop ol' Jake. "Do I know yer daddy, son?" he asked, still with a grip on my hand, and with a voice so deep it sounded like it was coming from inside a cave. I remember staring up into his long, sad eyes, and how they waited without blinking.

"Don't reckon I'd know sump'm like 'at," I said. "His name was Adam

Cain."

"WAS?" Virgil asked.

"Yeah," I said to his wise old eyes. "Been gone close to six year now." I was vague. On purpose.

"Heard tell of an Adam Cain," he said, "dyin' from a gun shot 'bout that time. Over on Caney Creek, I b'lieve."

Our eyes locked until mine dropped. He gave my hand a slight pump and said, "Yer a fine young man, son. And I'm awfully glad we met." His eyes blinked slowly, like I imagined a toad would do in the sunlight. He tipped his hat before he rode off, keeping ol' Jake to a slow walk. I was certain he meant no harm—but as he rode away, the image of Daddy came back hard and vivid, as if he was right there with me, as if we were together again without hunger or hurt, or that red trail of blood above his head.

Forty-Four

Half Naked and Throwing Dice

The gentlemen's club was straight up purgatory to hear Mary Olive tell it, devilish with poker tables and the whatknots of society half-naked and throwing dice, even though she'd never been there.

We'd worked hard at finding excuses not to hoe, Wilma Lee and Wilson being the loudest at it, till the weeds got big enough to strangle us. Doing it midafternoon and without a cloud, though, left us sun-dogged and wanting to quit about the time we got started, but then knowing the weeds would outrun us if we did.

"Even got one a' them there *roulette* wheels," Mary Olive clamored above her chopping and hacking at the ground. "Ain't 'at what you told me, Seriann?"

"Yes, Momma," Seriann gasped, straining to say anything at all.

"An' it right there in the house he was raised in," Mary Olive went on, speaking of Corbin. "I bet his Momma an' Daddy'r right now tryin' to claw outta the ground."

The sun was next to torture, raining its own brand of fire. We stood the brunt of it, blistering with sweat and listening to Mary Olive carry on about Corbin and the blot he called the gentlemen's club.

"I wished I hadn't uttered a word of it," Seriann said, her voice soured by the heat.

"Had to be the sorriest sight ever was," Mary Olive said, not content to let it die. "Room full a' heathens politickin' an' runnin' 'round like they was full a' gunpowder."

"Don't reckon Corbin ain't doin' nuthin' but what people want," Seriann said.

"You know," Mary Olive said, "years back, we had our own gentlemen's club right here on the creek." Her cackle was as hard as the sun was hot. "Horace Clemmons an' 'at bunch a snakes he run with. They spent more time up 'ar on the upper floor of his store than they did with their own childern. A 'course nobody I know of ever got invited to join in, so it's hard tellin' what awl went on. Little a' ever'thang I reckon. Thievin'est bunch I ever heard tell of. Steal ye outhouse door if ye didn't lock it behind ye. Couldn't nobody ever prove a thang, though. Mostly 'cause the deputy sheriff was one of 'em. 'Bout the same, I'd say, as 'at bunch Corbin fools with. Ain't no bigger crooks alive than them what's elected, an' them with money. Ain't nuthin' they can't get away with. Just doin' what they want, 'cause they can." Her face was shaded by her big blue bonnet, the chop of her hoe in keeping with my own. "Reckon most a' Pike County was there," she said, "'cept maybe them that was preachin' the next day. Had to be the awfullest lot, puckered up to one 'nother an' carryin' on like a barnyard full a John D. Rockefellers."

It was near evening by the time we finished, just before the sun disappeared altogether. We sat on the porch watching fireflies, and trying to catch what little breeze there was.

"I'm slop heavy," said Wilma Lee.

"Starved to death is what *I* am," said Wilson.

"An' awl of us too tired to cook," said Mary Olive. And that's the way we left it—cornbread crumpled in milk, green onions, and killed lettuce making up our supper. With any luck at all, one more hoeing come the middle of July would be the last of it.

Seriann grew restive in the days that followed: a flight of spirit uncomforted and seeming to cry out for simpler things. The gentlemen's club accounted for most of it, offering up shares of consternation and keeping her stirred; leaving her feeling led away and without a way back.

"That gentlemen's club," she said, "was a night I'll long remember, a thrill an' a gladness, but nuthin' I want to go back to. Ain't nothin' in it far as I can tell but a hard time—an' I had me enough a them."

Most of what Seriann was feeling she kept to herself until Cobbie Parsons started coming around like it was a habit, his lankiness donning our doorstep more and more till we were all but resigned to his intentions: his full-press courtship of Wilma Lee.

"Lord help us," was all Mary Olive would say whenever Cobbie ventured into the yard and onto the porch. "Reckon some just cain't help lookin' hard up."

"Soap an' water'd take a lot a' that away," said Seriann.

"I'm just afraid a' what might be under it," said Mary Olive.

And so it was, day after day, Cobbie and Wilma Lee growing right along with the heat of summer and fighting to stave off desire in light of Seriann's vexation. What time Cobbie was there, Seriann was on the porch and Mary Olive in the kitchen, their intentions clearly to squelch what little privacy he and Wilma Lee so eagerly sought, a tactic meant to protect us all.

"We ain't about to have a litter a' Cobbie Parsons' runnin' 'round here," Seriann said. It was her reasoning, and what we all hoped would be warning enough for Wilma Lee.

Forty-Five

Dollar-A-Bottle Frame of Mind

Of all the vices in the world, the one that seemed to lay hold of a disproportionate number of mountaineers was the craving for *a good drink a' liquor*, a savored and appreciated cultivation of appetites ranking right up there with *a good chew a' baccer.* The fact that Pike County was dry except for beer contributed to the covertness of moonshine making and the covetousness of its taste. The idea that it was forbidden only added greater significance to it's worth. Throw in the risk of selling it, let alone buying it, and it became costlier yet. But for all its twists and turns, its drama and danger, it just never seemed to matter much to Corbin Fairchild. He simply loved the game it provided, and getting rid of Old Man Andrew's stash of red liquor was as simple as dropping a bottle of it into his outstretched hands. It was love at first sight, dollar signs flashing through his smile the way a new dawn lights up the sky. His selling it at the gentlemen's club for twenty-five cents a shot was like found money, a profit nine times over on each and every bottle—something Ruby Mae McHone couldn't say no to. Four hundred cases was not all that extreme when considering the half-dozen other private clubs she bankrolled in the further reaches of Virginia, West Virginia, and Tennessee. It was Corbin's idea to use Ruby Mae's money, and get all Andrew had while he was still in the dollar-a-bottle frame of mind.

We paid Andrew in hundred-dollar bills, forty-eight of them, clean and stacked without a wrinkle inside a cigar box. It was good faith money. Up front. Take it or leave it. At first we thought we'd take our share off the top, but then figured it would be much more satisfying to watch Andrew count it out to us, something sure to cause him pain. Instead, he stood there staring at it like it was septic, baring contagion.

"I don't know what to make a' this," he said, the watery light from his warehouse windows alive with dust and floating in front of his face. The sweat on him was thick and shiny, beaded, and ran and dropped off the end of his nose. "I don't know who in hell you are Bobby Yonts," he said, his voice quavered, "but you're scarin' hell outta me." Giant sweat pockets swelled under his arms. "You just a hillbilly peckerwood, boy, top to bottom, an' you runnin' 'round with forty-eight hunned dollars like it was forty-eight cents. I don't know who you know or who yer dealin' with ... an' I don't care to ... but I'll tell you right now, you scarin' what's left a' me." He took a deep breath and smeared back the sweat on his face with the sleeve of his shirt. "I ain't never seen this kind a' money in my life ... not all at one time, no way. I'm b'lievin' they's an imp an' a haint on it, shor's they's a devil." He swallowed hard and licked his lips. "If I had half a mind, I'd give it back to ye right now." He shook his head, trouble taking the better part of him. "I'm b'lievin' there's a fiery furnace waitin' for the spender." His eyes were on the money while he talked. "I ought to quit this whole thang right here and now," he said. "But I ain't goin' to. Scared as I am, I ain't turnin' back. I been at it a long time—me an' the old woman—both of us draggin' an' tryin' to hold on to nuthin'. I'm tired an' I been tried, an' now I'm tired a tryin'. I figure old man left this liquor here not meanin' to, but now I got it, an' it's on me to decide what to do with it." His voice was stern. "Now I could pour it out or help get it to where it can do what it was made to do; I could listen to the angel on my right shoulder, or the devil on my left. Old Reg'lars would *church me* shore as hell, but I'm a business man 'fore anything else, an' this, by god, far as I can tell, is business; devil or not, angel or not."

We waited in the stifling heat listening to Andrew wheeze, his chest rising and falling, laboring, his words hanging in the air with fear and dread, before a bottle cap came whizzing through the window, ricocheting off one the barrels and landing just inches from where we stood.

Andrew stepped with full authority to the back window. I could hear Imogene high tailing it out of there, dirt and gravel grinding under her feet.

"So now," he said, toweling away the beads of sweat around his mouth, "where are we?" We waited while his breath caught up with him. "I'll tell ye," he said. "Way I see it, the fox is on the run an' we gonna hunt. But there's a quandary. You see, you boys ain't but half done. 'Less you plan on havin' everbody climb up these stairs and do their drankin' right here, you need to get this shit outta here. I'm tired a livin' with Virgil Blair sittin' on my porch ever'day, an' me knowin' I'm just a breath away from the big stony lonesome. Now I'm payin' ten cents a bottle *on delivery*. I ain't payin' out on a job half done. How you do it is yours to deal with. Your money's here," he said, giving the cigar box a little tap, "an' it's waitin' on ye." He left without looking back, the creak of the stairs moaning his departure.

We didn't like being told our cut would have to wait, but Andrew was determined not to leave loose ends; there was too much at stake. It wasn't long before we understood he wasn't all that wrong. But then getting a boxcar of liquor out of his attic and past the ever-suspicious attentions of Virgil Blair bullied us right up till the next day when Imogene came to the back window with the sound of a whippoorwill: soft and low, with its own kind of beckoning. The pieces just sort of fell into place after that.

We told Andrew that the buyer of his liquor wanted twenty-five cases twice a week, every Tuesday and Friday, and wouldn't take delivery from anybody but Bobby.

"Good! The less I'm involved, the better," were the only words out of Andrew's mouth. The only problem, a somewhat elevated dilemma, was that Bobby didn't have a driver's license—much less a car. But then I never knew details like that to matter much to Bobby.

We lowered them with a rope from the upstairs window, case at a time. So simple it bordered on genius: put the liquor, case and all, inside a burlap sack, cinch its top and lower it out the window. About an hours time was all it took to load twenty-five cases into Andrew's Model-T truck he kept parked at the rear of the store.

One o'clock in the afternoon is when we did it, when the store was least busy and when Virgil Blair was sure to be gone. The old camp-house lane behind the store was all but grown-over, its houses ghost-empty and spooked with wind; nothing with breath but what flew and flittered, slithered and crawled. It was almost too easy.

All was going well that first time, right up till I felt a set of eyes staring at the back of my head, strong and keen and sharp enough to turn me around. I waited, dead still except for my eyes in a slow search. It was like I was in the presence of something, like a spirit had settled in the high grass and attending my every move.

"What's the matter?" Bobby whispered down to me.

"Nuthin'" I said. "Just wind, I reckon." I gave one more quick check before turning back around. Nothing. Still I felt it, as real as the sun bearing down and me. Don't know what causes such a feeling, but I was certain it had the mark of things that can't be explained, that lurk beyond what we know. Maybe being on edge with all the stole liquor was cause for jumpiness and what gives rise to imagination. Still, it came thick-like to where I was made to turn again. This time, though, it was in full view and stone still. A vulture. Looming. Sizing. Imogene.

We stood facing one another, squared-off and without a word as if expecting the other to go for a gun. I stepped toward her, slow and steady. She was unflinching, grounded. I stopped within inches of her, but she held fast, as pressed down as a rail tie.

"You up to sump'm, Rubin Cain," she said sucking on a reed and with her eyes squinched to slits.

"Last one," Bobby hushed from up top.

I turned and scurried back to load the last case. When I turned back around Imogene was gone, and without a sound ... as silent as the dust in the road.

I didn't say anything to Bobby about Imogene being an eye-witness to our smuggling, but her showing up unexpectedly had the makings of spoil, something that was sure to push us into an unwanted light with its mere mention. The kiss of death couldn't have been more puckered. We might have stood a better chance being written up in the Pike County News.

It was clear that Imogene and I needed to talk ... and before the day's end. But because of her daddy's dogs, I knew I couldn't get to her after dark without being found out; and I couldn't send word by Wilma Lee on account of Seriann not trusting her away from the house alone—the lure of Cobbie Parsons being too strong a temptation. With options dwindling faster than the sun, I figured my only chance was to *come a-calling.* So I did. In broad daylight. And to the baying of foxhounds straining at their chains.

A white-hair in a rocker was trying to make out who I was stopped out there and lingering in the middle of the road. I hollered my howdy and he stopped rocking long enough to holler something back, spit what was brown and silky over the porch rail and motion me in. Nobody was a stranger in broad daylight. If you weren't known, you soon would be. It just wasn't all that complicated.

"C'mon in," he said, straining to focus. A sizeable pinch of snuff swelled his lower lip, the permanence of its dark brown stain running from the corners of his mouth down across his chin.

"Howdy," I said, easing myself up the steps and onto the porch. He didn't say anything, just scrunched his upper lip and squinted like he was in considerable pain. "Names Rubin Cain," I said, reaching out a hand.

"Please to meetche," he said, giving my hand a simple-but-soft pump without saying who he was. "From here 'bouts are ye?"

"Up the road," I said, "On Gardner Fork. Nephew to Mary Olive Compton."

"Uh huh," he grunted then sent another burst of 'baccer juice sailing over the edge of the porch, the biggest part of it hitting and sticking to the rail, the way thousands of others had by the looks of it: thick and brown and permanent, hanging the way lime deposit does from the tops of caves.

"I was hoping I might have a word with Imogene if she was here 'bouts," I said. He gave me a confused and sufferable stare, eyes and lids working in an all-but impossible attempt to get clearer sight. But before he could gather himself, the screen door swung wide. It was Imogene, barefoot and looking well-nigh to a full-blown woman.

"Well, fancy this," she said, her smile in perfect stride with her welcome.

I stood a little awestruck not knowing exactly what it was I came to say when her mother pushed her way out the door and onto the porch between us. She was tall and handsome in the way of Randolph Scott, and the obvious source of Imogene's thick red hair and freckles. Her name was Ester and she offered me a seat on the big swing at the end of the porch, then confirmed herself by plopping down right next to me, walling me away from Imogene.

"Did you meet my daddy?" Imogene asked.

"No," I said. "Only person I spoke to was your grandpaw," motioning to the white-hair in the rocker on the opposite end of the porch.

"That's my daddy," she said, smiling demurely. "Gillum. He married late."

About that time Gillum leaned into it, raised up out of his seat and let loose a rain of amber-colored spit, half of it spurting down the front of his shirt, the other half splattering, yet again, onto the porch rail. He hacked deep, spit out what snuff was used up onto the laurel growing alongside the house, then settled himself and made a project out of replacing it with fresh.

Before I knew it, Ester cleared her throat and brought my attention back to our end of the porch. "Well, now," she said, "help me figure out who you're kin to, Rubin. It was Rubin, right? Rubin Cain?"

"Yes'm." I said, and from there, and to my amazement, she rambled through generations of Hopkins' and Cain's and Riley's, and finally leaving me with the feeling that we were somehow related. Imogene all the while dallied with strands of her hair, twirling them into ringlets from one finger to the next. She watched me from over Ester's shoulder, feigning interest and rocking just enough to keep me focused on her bare feet and the tilt of her head; on the pull of her eyes and smile—all of it toying. She bit her tongue, licked her lips, stretched in the most inviting way;

mocked Ester behind her back, and never missed the chance to unseat me.

We rocked for sometime in the spell of dusk, Ester and I savoring our discoveries and fumbling for small talk. At last, and seeing that my chance of being alone with Imogene bordered on impossible, I said I needed to be moseying. Ester was quick to say that it had been nice to meet me, but said nothing in the way of welcoming me back. Imogene walked me to the edge of the yard, while Ester watched us from the porch swing. I told her in a faint whisper that we needed to talk, and asked if there was any chance she might sneak away.

She just beamed at me and batted her eyes. "Bye," she said, turning and giving me a swooned toss of the head. I tried covering my look of desperation before giving Ester and Gillum a goodbye wave. I didn't know how much Imogene knew, if anything, about what Bobby and I were doing, but I knew she suspected us of the worst. What I hoped for was that she wouldn't give us up to the world, or go blabbering about what she didn't know, before I had a chance to bait her. My suspicions told me she was not above bribery: chocolate bars, I figured, being my best bet.

It wasn't uncommon for young'ns to come to the store with orders written out for Pearl. What they couldn't carry home would be Andrew's to deliver, which he did as often as twice a day until Bobby made him believe that it wasn't all that good for his heart—him being as big as he was and with the added strain of lifting and toting—something Andrew recognized as being true enough. All in all, it was a shameless process of manipulation, but one that allowed Bobby the chance to demonstrate how circumspect a driver he could be.

Wrangling every occasion possible to get behind the wheel of his daddy's car was something Bobby had done ever since being big enough to see over the steering wheel ... even sitting on Olin's lap before that. *Lap driving* is what Virgil Blair called it: Bobby doing the steering while Olin did the shifting; up and down the creek till he was seasoned and as familiar with the ruts in Greezy's roads as the mules and sleds that shaped them. By the time he was twelve, he was handling it all. His not having a license never made a difference to Olin—a detail he just laughed at. Driving was just something Bobby seemed born to; inbred with instincts suited for steering and gearing—things that just came together when he was behind the wheel. It wasn't long before Andrew saw what he had in Bobby, and all the more reason to send him bumping into Pikeville with stolen liquor twice a week, driver's license or not. Two hundred cases a month was credential enough for Andrew.

Olin had no argument with Andrew handing Bobby the keys, seeing as how Andrew was offering Bobby another nickel an hour. But the onus was then on Olin to convince Virgil Blair that he needed to turn a blind eye. After all, Bobby was simply making deliveries. Nothing complicated beyond what Virgil wanted it to be. They sealed it with a handshake, a bond as formidable as signing in blood. It was as easy as Sunday morning after that. The irony, though, was that neither of them knew the contents or the limits of what Bobby would be delivering.

Bobby had a knack for making things worse, oftentimes just for the sheer sake of it. In particular, the way he laid on the horn and threw up a big waving hand each time he passed Virgil Blair. Bobby's driving without a license was something that bore in on Virgil like an itch he couldn't get at. But being duty bound to honor his agreement with Olin, he let it slide, knowing that the law was not always immune from politics, or the profits of acquaintances.

The first time I rode with stolen liquor in the truck was late afternoon on a Friday, just after Andrew locked up for the night. We got as far as the top of Dry Fork Hill, where Virgil sat hunched over the horn on his saddle, right there in the middle of the road. He just sat there, blocking any chance of us going around him, his tongue daubing at the cud in his jaw, and with his long droopy eyes beaded down on us.

"Hey, Virgil!" Bobby said, his head halfway out the driver's window. Virgil spit without lifting his eyes. "What's the holdup?" Bobby's smile ate up what space there was between them. Virgil said nothing, just sat there staring until my heart went to pumping pints at a time. I saw Bobby shift in his seat what time ol' Jake slugged his way over to the driver's door, just like he knew where Virgil wanted him to go. He snorted and curled his lips, his spit thick and foaming around his bit. Bobby tried looking around his big head, but ol' Jake was too close and blowing too much grassy breath for Bobby to see much of anything.

"Wherr ye headed there Bobby Yonts?" Virgil asked, his deep baritone heavying the air.

"Tryin' to get over to Shelby Creek an' back 'fore dark," Bobby said.

Virgil leaned in close, looking like he was trying to get a whiff of something. He saw me and nodded, the look on his face sorrowful, a look I imagined was intended solely for me. "What awl you carryin back 'ar?" he drawled, his eyes in a hard study.

"Twenty-five cases a' red liquor," Bobby said without a second's hesitation. "Finest in the county. Wantche one?"

Virgil sat for the longest time staring and shaking his head, knowing full well he could never get a straight answer out of Bobby. "I still can't figure Andrew givin' you the reigns to his truck, Bobby Yonts. My guess is he's got a might more faith than he does good sense."

Bobby chuckled and said as far as he knew Andrew was as right as he ever was, and letting him drive was living proof of it. Ol' Jake was nearly in Bobby's face and working his tongue like he was trying to dislodge something from the back of his throat. Virgil just sat there, holding Jake's big head to where he could slobber on the door and down Bobby's arm. "C'mon," he finally said to Jake, pulling him up and away. "Say howdy to yer daddy fer me," was the last thing he said to Bobby before spraying the road with what Brown Mule had collected in his cheek.

We moved out in a slow roll, and with Bobby yelling out to Virgil that he'd be glad to bring him a case of that red liquor anytime he wanted it, the smell of ol' Jake's sweat and the scrape of his teeth against his bit trailing after us.

Bobby watched after Virgil in the rearview mirror, then laughed and slapped at the steering wheel. "He likes muscling me so I won't ferget he's top dog. His way a sayin' he's got an eye on me, I reckon." He looked over at me with a wide grin. "Might do us good if I was to act scairt."

We pulled off the highway onto Corbin's long winding two-track, back to where his house sat in stately quietude, and where big oaks spread thick and hushed what rumbled from the road. There had been changes since I was last there, but to my thinking, none that could have been more majestic, its decay now replaced by splendor, brought to life I was sure by the pluck of Ruby Mae McHone.

I stood marveling at the new paint, the borders of white encasing the windows and enhancing the brick. Bright and fresh and all around: the porch, the pillars, the door. It spoke of life, elegance and taste, and of a time worth remembering.

I stood in the same place I'd been just two months earlier: in the room just inside the door with nothing but a staircase winding upwards toward the loft and a hanging bauble of lights. Only now, it greeted me with sparkle—the way first light shimmers on dew—and I stood there feeling lost and small within it.

Bobby led me down a long hallway to a large room at the back of the house, an old food pantry where cases of stacked whiskey from his previous trips lined the walls. Corbin opened each case as we brought them in, making sure he was getting what he paid for.

"Well, now," Corbin said, pleased-to-swelling with the inventory: all accounted for, nothing broken, and as bonded as Andrew Clemmons' word. "I b'lieve today's goods and services have been summarily satisfied," he said, his smile trailing after his words.

"For lighter moments," he said, handing us each a dollar bill. He nodded, proud, "The revelation of dividends," he declared.

To hear Corbin tell it, the gentlemen's club was as political as it was private; as protected as it was well attended. "It's like a who's-who of city council members," he said, "businessmen and most of the chamber of commerce, all of the sheriff's department, professionals of all kinds, and anybody with an affiliation who feels lucky enough to lay his money down." He spoke with a wide eye and a grin to match, then opened the big double doors to the main room, *the casino*, like he was leading us out of the wilderness and into the promised land. He stood there marveling as we stepped around him into the smell and feel of what was well-heeled. "Behold, gentlemen," he said with a giant sweep of his arm, "the dream and the language it speaks. Laudable. Don't you think?"

The gentlemen's club stood awash in the umber of an Appalachian sunset. It unfolded before us with a reach as wide as it was high, with a collection of liquor and the prospects of fortune, and with no limits on either. For those political, elected and selected, it opened up a whole new breadth of fantasy: a craps table, a roulette wheel, padded chairs and green felt table tops where poker and blackjack came together like fatback and cornpone, giving a layered and hazy loftiness to the stuff of favor. It was artful with picture paintings, gilded and frilled and rich with light. A bright red carpet from wall to wall made the floor look like a lake of fire; and there was a bar that ran the length of the room, black and shiny and with the word *Invictus* inscribed in big gold letters across its front. A mirror, almost as long as the bar, hung on the wall behind it, and made the room look almost twice its size. Add to it a medley of red liquors, and one had the notion he was far from Kentucky's back roads, dripping in that privileged and protected cigar smell of success.

"Invictus," said Corbin as if addressing a large audience. The looks on our faces were blanked in question, chasing after its meaning. "It's Latin," he said. "It means *in victory*. The name I've chosen for the club, an' a symbol, I b'lieve, for what best represents a sigh of relief and respite from a prickly road."

Forty-Six

Hard Evidence

"It was awl the right people, an' righteous amounts a dollar bills," Seriann said, loosening up somewhat about the gentlemen's club: about Invictus. I knew she would come unglued if I was to come clean about being in cahoots with Corbin and Old Man Andrew, so I choked it back for the sake of preserving what we had. Still, there was a part of me that wanted to tell; that wanted the relief that comes from unburdening my mind. But it was Corbin's rule to never leave a trail, nothing that could be traced—particularly the things we said. It was a cardinal rule if one intended to stay ahead of the game, to say nothing of the law. Even then, there were no guarantees. There was nothing so damning as hard evidence, and nothing as unforgiving as one man's word against another's. There were rules for everything, evidently—even villainy.

Forty-Seven

Windfalls of Sport

We were overnight successes, Bobby and me. *Red Liquor Barrons!* How we did it and got away with it was a stone-cold mystery to Andrew, and something he was all too content to let stay that way. He was good about not asking questions. What he didn't know, he figured, couldn't be held against him, ignorance being the thing least likely to incriminate him. He may have been right; we just never had occasion to put it to the test. I suppose the bigger part of our coming out on top was luck. That, and our being dumb enough to keep going despite the ever-present scare of being found out. But after a time, the steady flow of dollar bills and never having to explain ourselves had the windfalls of sport, something that made bending the law seem like our own invention.

Andrew made good on his part, paying us after each delivery. Thirty dollars twice a week, money we split fifty-fifty. I kept mine hid in a mason jar up under the floor in the hen house, along with the pocket watch Imogene gave me for Christmas. Bobby never hid any of his but what he couldn't get ahold of in a minute's time. He was a straight-up honkytonk man with appetites too outsized for anything but the free flow of *getting*, and it was hands-on money that made it happen.

In just one week we made more money than what could be worked out at the store in three months. We never breathed a word of it—only what was laughed out loud when we were alone. At the end of the day, it was our understanding of Corbin's cardinal rule—*the less said the better*—that made our campaign so effectual.

Imogene took the bait: chocolate, day after day, along with my pleas not to tell what she had seen, or even thought she'd seen. It was easy for her to oblige me in light of Hershey bars. But then there were the promises I felt compelled to make: assurances of picture shows and hamburgers once we could figure out the how and when. They were promises never to be forgotten, redeemable when the moon and stars were right—all for her confidence and accord.

Forty-Eight

The Loam and Long Shadows

Cousin Truman was as good a man as God ever gave breath. Despite his constant admonishments to abide by the Holy Ghost, Bobby and I never grew tired of his council and spiritual discernment. He had a way about him that made us want to listen; a light that emanated from his pale, silver-blue eyes that kept us glued when he talked about things of the spirit, about Abraham, Isaac and Jacob, and about how we were all seeds and heirs to God's kingdom through faith. It was all very confusing, but spellbinding: the way he talked without hesitation, moving through the scriptures with the ease of creek water over moss-covered rocks. From the foundation of the world to the book of Revelation, he was as tireless as he was convicted. And even after dumbfounding us time and again with both wonder and weariness, he left us desirous of the hope declared for all who would believe. That's why it was doubly troublesome when we stole his horse.

It was on a Sunday morning, right when roosters were hitting high notes and the mix of sun and dew parlayed into a haze as thick as soup, that Aug stood halted at our gate, the soreness of ol' Bartley and the scattering of cats as his welcoming.

Mary Olive was already up, her hands in flour and with a fire in the stove, when he first called out. "Hello the house," he said, his voice a low bawl. I had my britches on before Mary Olive opened the door.

"Lord, honey, what on God's earth'r you doin' out here 'fore the chickens quit layin'?"

"Don't mean to problem ye none, Mary Olive," Aug said easing his way through the gate.

"Don't reckon they's much chance a' that," she said, motioning for him to come ahead and shushing ol' Bartley back to his pallet. "C'mon in here by the stove an' tell me what in God's name's got you on the road this time a' mornin'."

Before he could answer, I stepped through the curtain into the kitchen, barefoot and shivering, half asleep and fighting to pull my shirt over my head. I gave him a shuddering nod before grabbing the water bucket and heading for the well, and before running headlong into Seriann coming through the door—her feet carrying what was wet and muddy from the dew, and her hair sprouting like straw: a witch without a broom, I thought, or the light of moon.

"*Childern,*" she said, "if this don't beat all ... an' it but six o'clock in the mornin'." Her dryness sheared through the fog, mingled with the steam whistling from the kettle. "Aug, honey," she said, "what on earth?"

Shame seemed to blanch Aug, hang him lifeless inside his shirt. "I'm just under a burden fer sissy," he said. "Dreams comin' on me of a night." Each of his words seemed heavier than the one before it. "...of a day, too. Spells. Piney thangs: her reachin' t' me an' me tryin' t' reach back. I'll give a day's work if you'ns'll take me to 'er."

By the time I got to Bobby and he got the bridle on ol' Hank, Olin and Gracie were easing their way out of the holler on their way to Little Hattie, the Old Regular Baptist church at Rock House. By the time we walked to Cousin Truman's at the head of Greezy, and knowing we had four miles to go to get to Grandmaw's, Seriann decided we'd be better off if we didn't have to switch riders so often. She was staring up at ol' Gert grazing on the side of the hill.

Cousin Truman and Inez were already cleared out, motoring to Dorton, to the Old Primitive Baptists for four hours of urging The Holy Ghost.

"You sayin' we ort take 'at mare?" Bobby asked.

"I'm declarin' it an act a' mercy," she said, sounding a whole lot like she was *born again*, her voice a proclamation. "What little meat I got left on my ass is 'bout gone. If they's gonna be more walkin', it's gonna be me on my way back to the house." In the next instant Bobby was drawing ol' Gert in with a bucket of oats he carried from the barn.

Taking ol' Gert didn't seem right, and Aug and I argued that we'd just as soon walk, but Seriann was quick to remind us that it wasn't just getting there, we had to walk back too: eight miles through mountains full of copperheads and rattlers, and without a way in or out except by wit and what a horse could tramp while there was still daylight.

Despite the intolerance Virgil Blair had for horse thieving, Seriann felt little in light of what punishment might befall her, and nothing in the way of compunction or whatever hindered her will.

"Put it on me," she said. "Truman'll just have to whoop me if he's of a mind to." I could see the sparkle in her eyes and that bad-behaved smirk at the corners of her mouth: the look that said there wasn't a chance that Truman would ever harm a hair on her head. But then there was no need to bother about it one way or the other, because it was pretty much all her rock-hard, wire of a body had to say about it, except that there was more at stake here than a borrowed horse.

In one sure motion, Bobby had the bridle over Gert's head and the bit between her teeth. Sanctioned crime wasn't something that came along everyday, and it suited Bobby like glory defined, as pleasing as red-liquor money.

Took Gert. Gone to Grandmaw's. It was a simple message I scratched out with a lump of coal across a plank and left leaning against the screen door. Minutes later it was Seriann and me on the back of ol' Gert, Bobby and Aug on ol' Hank.

The morning's light seemed to fall full and flush on Seriann, glistening the blue-black of her hair. She was like a renegade washed in things celestial, lustered and kissed by the sun. "Let's rob us a bank," she hollered. And just like that we were off, the guilt of helping ourselves to what wasn't ours left in the dirt under Gert's hoofs. There was more at stake here than a borrowed horse.

The air was heavy, like we were breathing water. The high altitude and dark shade of the mountains did little to lessen the sputter that foamed in heaps around the bits of ol' Hank and Gert. The climb was steady and toiled away at their haunches, layered them in blankets of sweat. We stopped often, where rises and gaps between crests allowed unchecked streams of air and where water oozed clear and cool from springs. We followed the ridgeline that stretched between Hopkins Fork and Poor Bottom, and the rugged slopes and grades that rose and fell between Little Fork and Bowling, until we had climbed to nearly three thousand feet, to the Flatwoods and the trail that led down to the head of Pine Fork. From there we could see the smoke rising gently from Grandmaw's cabin.

July had a way of adding its own breath of fire at one in the afternoon, baking the ground and reflecting the sun's rays in waves like fevered dreams. Even shade seemed to shimmer in the light of day, prickle the sweat that sopped us and left us raw. Time seemed to stand still there in the head of Pine Fork, in its thickets, dense and interwoven and without the slightest movement. The clomp of hooves and our cry of "*Hello the cabin*" brought them to the porch: Grandmaw under a shawl, in long sleeves and a skirt that ran to the tops of her shoes; Dixie in her bare feet and a feed-sack dress no doubt made by Lorali. They stood wiping their hands on dishtowels and staring back from under a canopy of vines that twined through a fusion of lattice. It was right then that our coming became the work of angels.

"*Lawd-a-mercy*," warbled and lifted, carried on the wind and rolled across the face of the mountain. It was the loudest I'd ever heard Grandmaw, her tiny whoops welling and rolling, all but her feet in a dance. The surprise of horseback riders coming out of nowhere had been almost too much to fathom. Seriann was quick to quit ol' Gert and gather Grandmaw and Dixie in her fast, bony arms. The three of them pressed together, each a tiny sparrow, petitioning what lay locked up in family and the hardscrabble of belonging to each other, despite the divergence of roads.

There was a mad scramble for center stage: so much to say and so little time to say it. But then I came to realize how time could be beat back if everybody talked at once, which is what we did, our screeched-and-heralded laughter choking out everything around us. I saw it as a convergence of souls. It was affection ripened by difficulty that washed over us, collected and more or less swept us out to sea. While Grandmaw pinched our cheeks and checked under our eyelids, as she was so wont to do, Dixie stood speechless, her hand over her heart and her smile like a prayer. "If I had to die," was pretty much the summation of what she had to say.

From first sight, Dixie was not the crushed little bird that had come here months ago, not flinching or turning away our offers of touch, but standing straight and glad, her smile now her voice. Though still thin, she was no longer frail; and her eyes, no longer downcast and avoiding, but full of inquiry, welcoming and pulsing with a sense of belonging.

There is a keenness that comes from faith, that makes us malleable and ready, that armor-plates us and brings us full circle to the common good. It is devotion exclusive of no one who's ripe for its inheritance, and the one thing that had joined Aug and Bobby to us from the beginning. The same was true of Dixie; no longer decreased by circumstance or place, but one who now waited with a new heart.

"You like a angel, baby girl." Aug's voice was quiet, his turn familiar and unaired, giving rein to the life he felt.

"I knew you wouldn't forget me," Dixie said, her smile full, older, more of a mother than a child, her eyes soft and deep into the moment. While Grandmaw and Seriann set about to find enough plates for the table, she put her hand on Aug's shoulder. He seemed weak to her touch.

"I reckon yer awright," he said, his eyes soft as rain.

"Good as I've ever been," she said, "short a' missin' you'ns." It was enough for Aug, and he headed back to the horses, to their tending.

Dixie watched after him, her face pink, a canvas for July's swelter, before turning to Bobby and all that begged to be said. They were like wax figures caught in uncertainty: Bobby gripped in secret, Dixie searching for what was beyond the blue there in his eyes. Bobby searched for solid ground, for a foothold, then watched as she turned and moved off toward the little room at the back of the cabin, leaving him quieted and accepting of her spell. A minute later she returned with his horsehair bracelet tied to her wrist.

We stayed to early evening, enjoying the fullness of Grandmaw's poke salad, sauerkraut, and boiled potatoes, and telling what we knew about family and friends ... and about Haman Flowers.

"He'll be pert' near right 'fore long," said Aug, speaking of Haman. "Though it's a fever 'at's been at him of late: his mind devilin' about *the nuthin'* where his hand ort to be. Throbs at him night an' day ... him a-starin' off to nowhere ... his eyes on thangs cain't nobody else see, like he's holed up with the devil." He paused, giving air to his account, his eyes darting between us, sensing our need to know. "Gets around on his foot right smart like," he said, "but I cain't tell nuthin' about him; never know what he's apt to do till he does it."

We left in time to make Truman's before nightfall, and to take what was coming for taking ol' Gert. Grandmaw was the tiniest speck in my arms and clung to me long after the others said good-bye, her tiny heart and face—tender and mending—holding to the innermost part of me, my spirit withering in the light of all she was. "Oh, Lord" was all she mumbled before letting go.

"Bye ... and come back," was all that Dixie said, her voice with a twinge of forbearing.

Aug's account of Haman lingered with us long after we left, hushing us—all except for Bobby, of course—through the loam and long shadows of the Flatlands. It was dark when we left ol' Hank in the pasture with Gert, darker still by the time Truman drove us back to the house, our transgression forgiven and forgotten in the same breath. We'd get ol' Hank come daylight, but tonight it was the face of Grandmaw and Dixie that fueled our night. But then, too, there was the knotted vision of

Haman Flowers and the threat of all that was barbed and uneven.

"He mumbles yer name, Seriann." Aug was hesitant, unsure. "I've heerd him of a night. 'Bout you takin' sump'm away from him an' him aimin' to settle the score." It was the last thing Aug left us with before ambling off in the dark. We stood on the porch, in the dot of fireflies, listening after him, his footsteps intruding on the night then giving way to the creek and the music of its water.

"Lord, young'ns," Seriann said, her voice angling with spirits, "hit's a stiff road to Shop Branch: a black heart an' a perdition."

Forty-Nine

Old Regular Baptist Traditions Notwithstanding

Corbin came often in the days that followed, those early days of August seeming to fix him with a star, one that brought to life sourwoods and doghobble blossoming in angel wings of pink and soft lavender high on the bluffs. The heat also came, August's expression of hellfire we were unable to affect except with porch shade and begrudging wafts of air. Like the heat, Cobbie Parsons seemed an equal difficulty, his steady presence like the exasperation of a second hoeing. Then there was Lorali coming unannounced to stay the week—or the month, or the summer, we just never knew—but with scissors and needles poised to cut and shape and splice what was forever needing it: shirts and britches, curtains and dresses, all that could be fashioned from feed sacks and the better part of hand-me-downs. And of course there was the constant invasion of Bobby and the transient interruptions of family and neighbors coming and going, always with the idea of advancing the limits of common sense and opinion. It was a point in time, a substantive track to a higher place and what we thought to be our cross-to-bear, meted out for our good. But then there were those pale lights of dawn that released us from Haman Flowers and his infiltration of our dreams. It was little wonder Mary Olive went to talking in tongues when we least expected it, and throwing dried dog bones like they were dice: looking for a sign, an open window to the unknown.

August's dusty heat was as snagged as it was snarled. Bobby, however, even with the added tension of transporting stole liquor, seem to blossom. His partnership with Andrew Clemmons had lifted him to new heights, to where he wanted to be now that he was out from under the confines of school and free from all those hours wasting away in books.

"This is where I belong," he said, taking in all that was around him. "Out here with things fast and deadly and full of fire."

I never once doubted Bobby's sincerity, never failed to believe that it was things fast and deadly and full of fire that called loudest to him, that kept him vigilant to find them. It was a notion that proved me right time and again, but I couldn't exclude myself. I was, after all, half of the equation. Though a great deal more ordinary, I was still part of the mix that made us a team. The idea of fast and deadly and full of fire, however, held notions a bit more severe than I wanted to cuddle up to. I could never understand why a body would sidle up to things that most tried to avoid. Then again, I had to think that none of us were ever really all that far from such things, considering the darker sides of our natures.

It was right after we'd squirreled away a hundred dollars apiece that things began to grow more ambitious. With our pockets lined, Pikeville loomed large: drawing us like a magnet and gradually counting us as its own.

I don't know what it was that eased the grip on my being so tied to home; maybe it was Mary Olive and Seriann sensing a want in me beyond a collection of back roads and the taste of beans. But little by little they allowed me the slack of freedom, at least in part, sensing in me where my spirit longed to go. I imagined it was their way of letting me ease into the inevitable, what awaited, good and bad. I suspected it was the same with Olin and Gracie: their reins on Bobby stretched-to-breaking and that his time at home was going to be less and less whether they agreed with it or not.

Unrest was the hot coal within Bobby, something that fanned the need to *get on with it*; what pushed him to things fast and deadly and full of fire; what kept him knowing that being on the edge was where he felt most at home. There was only so much Gracie could do with a stick of stove wood across his back, and just so often she could use it before it became a wall between them. The reliance on love and their prayers seemed most always to make the biggest difference, what got us through nights when hope ran thin, when there was no way of knowing if we would make it home in one piece, or make it back at all. I think it was this same reliance that Mary Olive and Seriann held to, the same, I was certain, that sustained Olin and Gracie, Old Regular Baptist traditions notwithstanding.

Right out of the gate, Bobby and I were lost to the idea of meek, sneaking off to Pikeville even when it was less than opportune, and staying gone way beyond the rule of good sense; but want and impulse pulled at us indefensibly, and in no time Pikeville became about as familiar as Greezy. From the train tracks to the river, from Fronto's café to Short's soda fountain, from the Freemont Hotel to the long staircase that led down to its shadowy basement pool hall, we were part and parcel of its rhythm: as common to its maze of sidewalks as Olin Yonts was to its stockyard. It was, in every light, a place where we could stroll without concern and pretend to be kings. Saturday nights had become altogether new.

On our very first shopping spree, Bobby bought a pair of white patent leather shoes, crimson-red pants, and a blue and white striped shirt. To him it was the look of affluence, and he strolled down the street like he was some movie star in search of an adoring audience. He insisted on outfitting me as well, and put me in a pair of black and white wing-tipped shoes, black pants, and black shirt. People pretended not to notice when we walked by. The boys in the pool hall, though, were not so delicate. Their catcalls were strained and full out: Bobby looked like the American Flag, they said, and me like some harmonica player in a blues band from New Orleans—the perfect get-ups, they insisted, for hoeing corn. But Bobby was as unmoved as he was unshaken. To his way of thinking, we had captured the look of prosperity, and with a flash of a dollar bill, bought Pepsi's all around. That was good enough for everybody. We were flush, by god, and there was no having it any other way but to show it.

Dollar for dollar, the picture show reigned as the number one attraction. From cartoons to newsreels, from Buck Rogers to Gabby Hayes, we were undaunted devotees to the silver screen. Regardless of what was playing, we saw it, and most often twice. But where I was content to be an appreciative observer, Bobby was altogether interactive, pretending to be the star in every scene: one day acting and talking tough like James Cagney, the next running around trying to save the universe like Buster Crab. He went from one cowboy hero to another: from Johnnie Mack Brown to Tom Mix to Bob Steele, from Tim Holt to Roy Rogers to the Cisco Kid. One minute Tarzan, the next Errol Flynn. There were days when he wore his old hat with its brim pinned up in front like one of the Bowery Boys, and days when he'd smoke cigarettes after the likes of Humphrey Bogart and Clark Gable: like they were some sort of fashionable candy. From lover to fighter, from comic to gangster, Bobby was all things the silver screen portrayed and everything that helped him shed the coal dust and black dirt bottoms of Greezy Creek.

Wildroot Cream Oil in our hair and spit and polish on our shoes was the custom, and we treated each with the veneration of things greater than ourselves. It was part of our motive and ceremony, our quest to reel in Pikeville's steady stream of daughters—their variety and number as endless as they were seamless. "Artful" is what Bobby called them, which made our pursuit all the more graceless and outside the scope of traditions except our own. What we didn't know about engaging the fairer sex was stark and evident, constituted by a lack of foresight and anything sustainable beyond the first hello. But we were eager, our bliss and ignorance somehow clouded in the wake of Bobby's confidence, his bequeathed heart and affections for Dixie only minor interferences, nothing that would dampen his curiosity to sample what else might be available.

"I'm young and confused," was all Bobby would say when the memory of Dixie came too close, and as far as I knew, the extent of his discomfort. And though out of sight, he spoke of her often in quieter moments, grappling with his spirit and leaving me knowing she was never far from where his heart was, where he allowed her to be.

The money in our pockets chased after us as sure as we chased after Pikeville. What we saw as good fortune became a thing all too natural, and after a time something we embraced as a consequence of our cunning. And though it was a shared sentiment, the money oftentimes left me feeling as if I was under the weight of something unclean.

Bobby worked hard at taking Old Man Andrew's money for granted, believing that it would be there forever, whenever he wanted it. After a time, he was better known in Pikeville than he wanted to be. The girls, the picture shows, the poker games in back of the pool hall and shooting nine-ball for a dollar a game had all become his stock in trade, though rarely a profitable one. It wasn't long before he was as well known for covering bets as he was for loud clothes. It was just another wrinkle, as indelible as his handle, the one he threw around like an outlaw, like it had been written across the sky in a hail of bullets: Cornbread Red. It was Pikeville, full of innocence, but only for a while.

Fifty

Haney's

The steady flow of Hershey bars stood Imogene in my debt, kept her hushed up for what she only pretended to know. It had been the whispering, she told me, that back and forth between Bobby and me that made her know something wasn't right. She just couldn't figure out what, even after that last burlap sack was loaded.

She came clean only after I pressed her, baited her with "*Tell me what you know and I'll tell you the rest.*" It was a charade that finally fragmented right in front of me, proving it was no match for my chocolates and sonnet-filled promises. I didn't have to stand good on what I'd promised, she said, didn't have to hold up my end of the deal. It had been her pretense, after all, her misgivings, that caused me to weigh her with chocolates and vows in the first place. I stood silenced in the air of her admission, her failed attempt to outride the truth; she stood waiting for absolution. To me, the Hershey bars were of little consequence beyond the significance of them being shared, but not so my promises: expressions finite and binding, professing all I intended. And, for the first time, more than I wanted to take back.

Pikeville's pull was greater than the will we had to stay away. Bit by bit, we began to reveal its many layers, each one carting us a little further off the beaten path, back, I was certain, to where things survived without blessing: cattle rustling and dog fighting, high-stakes poker and women who made a living at providing pleasure ... plenty that was out-of-bounds, if you had the interest and asked the right questions. But then, it wasn't anything I ever sought. Ever. The consequences loomed too large, as if there was a noose just waiting to be slipped around my neck. But that was never the case with Bobby. The fast and deadly and full of fire drew him in like a divining rod to water, left him wild to probe its secrets and possibilities: a game he was both determined and destined to play. And that left me following in his wake, pulled along by that unexplainable magnet that lay deep within him.

The money put Bobby where he wanted to be, opened doors to side streets and back alleys, but then it was a constant dodge to keep ahead of those trying to take it away. After a time, there were just too many standoffs; too many times on the dark side of the tracks. A few times it came down to hiding out. And though hiding went against Bobby's grain, it often proved the better part of survival ... and what eventually led us to Haney's.

Haney's was a juke joint about a quarter mile north of town, tucked in alongside the river and out of view of all but those daring a reach into things nameless and unforeseen. It was like so many other juke joints that lined the banks up and down the Big Sandy, Russell's Fork, and Shelby Creek. Haney's had a jukebox, booths along the wall and a few wood tables in the middle of the floor, pushed aside when the need arose for dancing. Its owner, Lucian Haney, was about as rangy looking as a coyote that hadn't eaten for about a week, and who never once balked at serving us beer. He sold potato chips and peanuts, cigarettes, and anything with alcohol he could get his hands on. He could also make a hamburger served on light bread, if pressed into it.

The walls were painted red, inside and out. Except for the purple haze that filtered from the jukebox, and the neon signs above the bar making us feel smart about drinking Schlitz and Budweiser, there was nothing to light the way beyond the yellow glare of a single light bulb dangling from the end of a black chord directly over the dance floor. It was a place one might expect to walk into and never be heard from again. For me, it had the makings of something that had died but never been buried. Bobby said it reminded him of something that was supposed to be dead, but just refused to take a final breath. Whatever it was, it wormed its way under our skin the very first time we crossed its threshold and its smell of mildew, tobacco smoke, and grease.

The women at Haney's laughed and talked loud, smoked store-bought cigarettes (Chesterfields, Camels, and Lucky Strikes), and drank bootleg whiskey, which Haney served in chipped and cracked teacups. They wore bright, shiny dresses and nylon stockings with black seams running up the back, pearls and earrings, high-heeled shoes with open toes, and with toenails painted as red as autumn apples—the same red that lit up their fingernails and glowed from the fullness of their lips.

The men were mostly scary, laughing and talking like whoever did it loudest was cock of the walk: the one to be feared, the one who ran the herd. They were cut more from burlap than silk: bulls and dandies, they were, emitting with aromas of turnip greens and whiskey, and with their minds full of want and what comes from shooting out the lights.

It was after two in the morning when we walked into Haney's that first time, when hiding out at the pool hall became too much like work and after we lost everything but a dollar playing three-card rummy with Whetsel Rowe. Whetsel owned his own taxicab, but spent most of his time in the pool hall hustling strangers at nine-ball. Tonight it was rummy. He was always decent enough after taking your money, even apologetic, and would even run us home for a pint of liquor. Bobby could always come up with a pint of liquor.

When we walked into Haney's that first time, we did it not knowing if we would walk out alive, all eyes following us to a corner booth and lingering what time Roy Acuff lit up the jukebox with "*Wabash Cannonball.*" But Bobby was beyond caring, and any attempt to sway him otherwise. We ordered up beer and Haney served us without as much as a twitch. We were drunk pretty much after the second one, but managed to sneak out just as somebody got knocked halfway across the dance floor and into the jukebox, just as the sparks went flying and the lights and music all went out at the same time. We hid in the tall weeds down over the riverbank, listening to the ugliness of glass shattering and those wanting to bring on doom. Finally, a chilling and deafening blast from a shotgun we figured was Haney's sent everybody clamoring and scattering, staggering, and stumbling their way into cars and into the night until all was silent except for the strains of somebody mumbling from inside. We waited a long time before breaking cover, visions of blood and somebody sprawled dead in the middle of the floor following us back to town. An aftermath of silence seemed to engulf us and settle in the grunt of bullfrogs along the river. Despite the cluster of stars, smoked and festered images pushed in around me and rose in a haze of neon against the blacker than black sky. Haney's was hardtack, even for the coarsest cob; new to us, but old in the ways of the hills, like a forgotten branch to a broke-back road; slippery-elm slick and out-of-bounds deadly.

The last coal train had come and gone, leaving Bobby and me but two choices: walk the ten miles back to Greezy or sleep out the night in Whetsel Rowe's taxicab. Hitching a ride to town was easy enough once we crossed the bridge at Shelby. Getting home was another story, our never leaving Pikeville until the wee hours of the morning being the main reason, the scarcity of freight trains and their too often going in the wrong direction being another. Walking was always a likely consequence, but tonight, half drunk and in a state of give-up, we opted for Whetsel's cab. He could drive us home come morning—for a pint of liquor of course.

We got as far as Olson's market before we saw a bread truck parked out front with its motor running. That was the last coherent memory I had before Bobby jumped behind the wheel. He said something about God helping those who helped themselves and in the next instant I was wedged in beside him, holding on while he jammed gears and raced us through streets shadowed and deserted but for the drunks in the streetlights of Sunday morning. Looking over our shoulders and in the rearview mirror was all at once far more germane than worrying about what was out in front of us. It was a reach for the stars and it left me in a blur, but Bobby drove that bread truck clear to the top of Buggerman Mountain, then just got out and left it there on the side of the road. We walked the rest of the way, five long miles without a moon.

Of all the uncertainties we lived with, Sunday mornings were, by far, the least of them. To my best recollection, they never bore anything but consummate peace. Except for footsteps and voices, and familiar rattlings from the kitchen, life seemed laid over with elements of calm, as if every living thing had taken time to breathe a little deeper, linger a little longer in thought and dream. The most notable exception was when I walked in near the bloom of daylight, at the end of that five miles and to the anthem of roosters, to find Seriann and Mary Olive sipping coffee just like they were waiting to hear all about that bread truck.

"Well, looky yander," said Mary Olive, "if it ain't that little Cain boy."

I tried mouthing something, but nothing came, my eyes desperate for the refuge behind their lids.

"An' him up an' already dressed fer church," said Seriann.

"An' purdy enough fer baptizin'," said Mary Olive, "though I 'spect he ought do sump'm 'bout that liquor on his breath."

Their eyes stood me upright, livened the throb in my head. "I'm just gonna lay down," I said, aiming myself at the curtain in the doorway. Its coarseness against my face and me crumbling in a heap on top of Wilson was the last bit of reality before the strains of "*Shall We Gather at the River*" came at me camp-meeting strong: Mary Olive, Wilma Lee and Seriann joined together in three-part harmony, their soulfulness sending the cats caterwauling and scratching for places beyond the door.

I lay in a stupor, the fermentation of beer and moonshine churning at my innards, its wretchedness fouling my mouth. There was nothing I could do to stop their song's lament, and nowhere I could go to ease my own. The pounding behind my eyes increased with each new verse, brain spikes shunting through me: the price for my transgression.

In one swift motion, Mary Olive swept aside the curtain to the lower room, her tiny frame haunting the doorway. "You need preachin'," she said in a voice that meant *now*.

The Primitive Baptist Church sat alone in the upper-end of the big bottom near the mouth of Main Fork, and in the shade of a lone, giant-sized cottonwood. Its one room was on the scale of a single room at the schoolhouse, but its sagging floor and weathered coats of whitewash left it looking whipped and empty-eyed. Thick wooden shutters covered its windows and were opened for light when they weren't used to block a balling sun. The only ventilation was its open door at the back and what windows could be jarred loose and pried upward in aging and swollen frames. Rows of wooden benches without backs were lined one behind the other on both sides of the room, leaving only a center aisle for coming and going. A platform just one-step high, and running all the way across the front, distinguished the altar. A small cast iron stove with a vent pipe running straight up through the roof sat halfway up the aisle. It was simple and austere, in the manner and tradition of Godliness. And though the church was only a quarter-mile away, it only opened its doors once a month. Even then, Mary Olive attended only when the spirit moved her.

The church had a shared congregation spread over four different locales. One week, meetings were held in Wolf Pit, the next week in Rock House, the third in Dorton, and the fourth in Greezy Creek. It was part of the old rider circuit, a round-robin affair that rotated each week for the convenience of its members, travel being the major hurdle. Knowing that getting from place to place for most rested somewhere between an obstacle and a hardship, the church came to them. This week was Greezy's turn, and the spirit had moved upon Mary Olive—a prompting, I was sure, brought on more by my recurrent nights of indiscretion than any visions she may have had of the end times.

The churchyard was, in and of itself, a comfort zone: a favorite stop for those too drunk to make it home from a Saturday night, its grassy knoll resembling a field hospital for the wounded. Young and old alike lay amid the dirt and rocks; some with miner's caps and coal dust still on their faces, some with shoes and some without, a few with the aftermath of spit-up on their shirts, and those bruised and bloody. Here, in the

Primitive Baptist Churchyard, these sons of Greezy Creek, reduced to the lowest common denominator by the clear, silver-sheen of moonshine, slept without regard to the elements or the worries of rattlers and copperheads. Cousin Truman, forever the sentinel of good will and preservation, made a point of arriving early to nudge these beleaguered souls into wakefulness and point them toward home before being discovered by a fiercely intolerant congregation. His was an act of selflessness, charity and grace, one that protected church members and drunks alike.

By the time we maneuvered Mary Olive the quarter mile to the church house steps, I had sweated clean through. Big drops oozed down my brow and into my eyes, and there was heat near to combustion under my arms. Cousin Truman welcomed us, but Mary Olive went around him like a milk cow sidestepping a blacksnake and led us directly to the front row.

I sat next to her—she made sure of that—swabbing the remnants of alcohol seeping from my pores just as Cousin Truman stepped to the lectern. Heat poured in around me, drowning me with indifference. On my other side, Seriann and Wilma Lee sat too buoyed, too fragrant, their faces too painted. Lorali sat on the other side of Mary Olive, smiling and fanning, doing little but suffocating me with more hot air. Little Sherman and Wilson moved out of the sun pouring in on the front row to the shade in the back. I attempted to move with them when Mary Olive grabbed hold of my arm. I was in no position to protest.

I knuckled under, trying to ready myself for what Cousin Truman was about to say. Without warning, my head, suddenly too heavy for my neck, began rolling from side to side until Mary Olive went to elbowing me. My hands and feet were swollen to the point of bursting, and, for the first time, breathing became an effort. With each heartbeat—drumbeat—my blood gasped for air, begged to be cleansed from the waste and dregs of what still sloshed through its veins.

After ten minutes or so, the sun drifted just enough to lay shadow across the altar. About that time Cousin Truman cranked 'er up, bellowing toward the loft and spitting in the corner about every third word. They were petitions full of volume and tempo, interspersed with moans and groans and the likes of hog calling. The sustainment of *amen* could be heard around the room—low and prophetic at first, then fervent and gratified. The next thing I knew, Seriann rose and stood with her arms above her head, swaying to some imaginary rhythm; her eyes lost but to their whites, and chattering and chanting in what surely must have been Cherokee. My neck suddenly found the strength to hold my head upright and I was locked squarely on Seriann's quivering lips and chin, on her eyes rolled up and back—vanished somewhere in the hollow of their sockets. Right about then, Wilma Lee jumped to her feet with a "whoop" and commenced to babble "Jesus, Jesus, Jesus ... Jesus, Jesus, Jesus" while bouncing up and down in a frantic—up and down, up and down, up and down. More Cherokee, I was certain: a tribal dance, something that preceded going into battle or throwing a virgin off a cliff. Every fiber in me was suddenly come to life. No tiredness, no sleepiness, just adrenaline crashing through the gateways in my brain. Then all at once, Mary Olive came off her seat like a bull busting through a barnyard fence and went to jiggling across the floor, babbling in time with Truman's power and exultation. She had a little finger stuck in her right ear and with her other hand cupped around the left one. I was afraid to move, but still looked behind me just in time to see Wilson and Little Sherman scooting out the door. But then in a blinding flash Lorali was on her feet, jerking and jabbering like she'd been dropped on her head. I can't remember how long it went on, but the next thing I knew, Cousin Truman let up, went back to low and mournful, breathing like a bloodhound after an all-night hunt. As he quieted, so did everybody else. But it was only when he went to wiping his mouth with a huge white handkerchief that we knew he was done.

When Cousin Truman stepped off the altar, John Lee Saunders, a preacher from Rock House and the second of four to preach that day, rose to take over and put us through our paces yet again. But by then Mary Olive was too spent to even sit up. I helped her to the shade of the cottonwood just outside the door, fanned her, and cooled her with water from a spring at the foot of the hill. We left just as John Lee began to kick into overdrive, his voice in high lonesome tones and with what seemed like enough wind to tear the locks off the doors.

* * *

Come Monday morning, Virgil Blair looked down at Bobby and me from atop ol' Jake just as we were about to go into the store. He just sat there studying us for telltale signs that might convict us on the spot, the same look he gave us most mornings.

"You boys in town Saturday night?" The red flag went to waving high and mighty whenever Virgil went to being sociable. It was best not to lie seeing as Virgil never asked a question he didn't know the answer to.

"Shore 'nuff," said Bobby, "Rode in with Cletus Blackburn." Bobby knew Virgil had done his homework and gladly fed him what he already knew.

"Stay long?" asked Virgil.

"Long enough, I reckon," said Bobby. "Why?"

"Playing a little three-card rummy, I'd say." Virgil winced around a pained grin.

"Yeahp, an' shootin' a little nine-ball. Same ol' stuff." Bobby was careful to give Virgil only what he was sure of. It was a game the two of them played often enough.

"I'd say it's hard catchin' a ride in the middle a' the night," Virgil said, fighting to add more chew to the already distended cavity twixt his cheek and gum.

"Couldn't get one," said Bobby. "Had to walk it. Ten mile, an' it pitch black. Four in the mornin' 'fore we got here."

Virgil made a big deal out of tobacco spit and took his time about sluicing off what was about to overflow from his lower lip, letting it spill on the ground next to us. "Well, ah'm just glad you boys'r awright," he mumbled. "No tellin' what a feller's liable t' run into in the dark."

"I know whache mean," Bobby said. "Like 'at bread truck we damned near run into top a Buggerman." Bobby knew he knew, and took it to him, wrestled it right out there in the open. "Damnedest thang I ever seen. Sittin' right there alongside the road. Figure it must a quit on whoever was drivin' it. Crazy."

Virgil stared at Bobby for the longest time, as if searching for a crack in his armor. He had no way to prove it, but we knew he knew; and for the longest time, the three of us waited for the other to say the next word. Finally, Virgil tipped his hat before turning ol' Jake toward the narrow dustiness of Lower Fork. "Tell yer daddy howdy fer me," he said, the same thing he always said when going away from Bobby. It was his way of saying it was over, and we had Olin to thank for it. I guess he figured it was every lawman's fate to have somebody like Bobby Yonts as a tormenter.

It took us two full months to get all the liquor out of Andrew's attic and into Corbin's hands. I don't know that I ever got over being scared about it, not until Bobby drove off with that last load at the end of August. But by the time the whiskey was gone, so was most of the money. Our return to paucity carried a sizable bite; much bigger than if we'd never risen above it in the first place. King of the hill one minute and feeding from the hog trough the next had a way of rubbing out the stars we imagined alongside our names. What it came to was independence denied, an end to the fantasy of self-absorption and a freedom that once rushed at us full gallop. After that, things just sort of went off-minded, all except for me continuing to work for Old Man Andrew—but only on Saturdays because of going off to school with Imogene, all the way to Pikeville.

Imogene and I rode with Olin right about daybreak, picking up miners and hauling them to the coalfield at Esco, then again in the evening when he brought them back. He made four dollars a day: fifty cents a man, a quarter each way. He hauled eight, though he could have hauled ten if it weren't for me and Imogene taking up two seats in the cab.

Olin let us off at the upper end of town, right where the big iron bridge stretched across the Big Sandy. He went on to the stockyard after that. Though it was locked tight and without the sound of auctioneers except on Saturdays, it was an everyday event for those who made their living from buying and selling. The big field alongside its pens stayed logged jammed for the biggest part with the oddities of pickup trucks and the endless assortment of things warm blooded and otherwise; things with beaks and bills and snouts, things hoofed and winged and bred for farming. Livestock trade was as essential to Olin as moonshining was to Corbin—as fortunate a thing as Imogene and I could ever invite—and he never asked us for a dime. Outside of that and all that plied us with ethic and fortitude, things just seemed to crawl up out of the ground about that time, out of shape and tied forever to consequences.

Up to the time I went off to school, I never ventured off the creek without Bobby, never had the want to do otherwise. But even at the height of our waywardness, there were times when I grew weary of it, when I was worn-out and spent-out both; times when Bobby was left to his own devices. It wasn't often that he left without me, but it happened enough for me to know that his restlessness was both host and harbinger to the recklessness that took up more than a sufferable share of him. He just wasn't going to stay home so long as he had the breath and means to do otherwise. The means, however, slowly thinned till it was gone, having poured through his hands like summer rain.

The summer had been all we expected: full of whiskey and paying customers, and never a doubt about tomorrow being more of the same until tomorrow became today. Nearly three months after Andrew paid us for the first time, the countless excursions into Pikeville, the hamburgers and picture shows, the innumerable times in the pool hall, and the regrettable times we sat staring at bad poker hands, the thankless times we bankrolled our buddies, and the times we left it all at Haney's, played out in the way of an epitaph. We had amassed a fortune, or so it seemed, then spent it in a headlong romp like it would last forever. Maw Ramsey's and Noah Branham's, honkytonks at the mouth of Rocky Gap and at the big bend in the road on Shelby Creek, played their own hands and took every dime we willfully laid down. Beer and music and the sweet smell of women, high stakes poker out in the open, and all that tempted the silver from our pockets, moved on us—ruinous and without revival.

I never told Bobby, but I was glad when the money ran out: relieved that I was at last out from under its hold, its means to the imperfect.

From the beginning it had extracted pieces of me, even worked to discard the touch of those who cared most about me. I wanted what money could give, its newness and sense of strength, but never stopped aching for that sense of peace I had without it. For all that it promised, I still wanted what came without cost: the breezes that rolled down the hill and the blessings they brought to a hard day, the new hand of morning and the permanence attached to Grandmaw and Cousin Truman. I still wanted what was most simple: the distant cluck of Mary Olive and the feel of the earth, the smell of sweat that rolled off of Ben, and the comfort from Seriann and ol' Bartley being next to me on the porch. I wanted all I was born to, what all was allotted to things deep and primal: what all was carved and hewn out of the mountains. The money wanted a voice and the bigger part of who I was. In many ways, it was the final word, what twisted me into a knot and left me clamoring for the quiet that lay secreted away on the tops of mountains, and in the deep earthen pull of its hollows.

Despite the grand schemes surrounding it, money was never backward about reinforcing the false sense of who I was: self-importance exacting its own price. In the end, the money wanted more than I wanted to give, to take in unlike ways and leave me owing. It was like a spike that needed to be continually driven, a work and a labor, and filled only with the want for more, a thing that left me out of kilter and unrepentant, so often out and away from what gives courage to be the gift we are.

I couldn't help but think of myself as anything short of pitiful, having squandered so much in so short a time—and with so many up and down the creek struggling just to keep families fed. Time and again Cousin Truman tried reeling us in, tried talking straight man-to-man with his face squinted like he was under a burden. He was well-intentioned and used terms like *gluttony of the flesh* and *carnal nature*, and how we needed to be mindful of what he called *intemperance*, and how we ought not let our wants move ahead of our needs, or place them before our own common good. He said we had let one foot take us into a fantasy world and had forgotten to anchor the other one in reality. Balance, he said, was the saving grace to wellbeing and that we needed to keep in mind that the further we drifted from the certainties of life on the creek, the harder we needed to hold onto the lessons it taught. For our part, though, and a thing most ill, was that we listened with the offshoot respect of fifteen year-olds; our thoughts never toward prudence or tomorrow, never aimed at anything higher than our own heedless desires. I knew down deep that every word Cousin Truman said was the truth, but that hint of knavery that lived eternally in Bobby—and that trace of burlesque in his eyes—mocked any feelings I had of remorse. It was like he had a power all his own, every bit as guiling as Truman's—even in the midst of Truman's redress. It was that same roguish playfulness that peered from beneath his auburn-colored brows with each and every penny he let slip through his fingers. I suspected things would never change with Bobby. Whether or not he thought of himself as wasteful, the twinkle in his eyes was the point of my remembering every decadent moment we shared. And despite my feelings of self-loathing for all I'd squandered, it was Bobby's eyes and their reach into my soul that made me know I'd do it all over again.

Fifty-One

Just Before We Went to Making Apple Butter

Dog days came bad-mannered and testing, the hillsides filled with the rasp of jar flies vibrating the air and leaving our mouths parched from the mere listening. The heat seemed to still everything around us, defying us even to speak. Each in his own way tried to hole up, shade and as few clothes as possible as our only expressions of relief. Even the slightest noise seemed to rankle, voices in particular: Wilma Lee's above all. For some time, Wilma Lee had been graveling, adding to the heat and the impossible notion that there was no relief in sight. They were disturbances of the first order, aimed mainly at Seriann for not letting her and Cobbie ever have a minute to themselves. They were groaned complaints, withering tones so unnerving that Mary Olive likened them to giving birth. But then after days of it, Seriann gave a conditioned approval, the nub of it being swift and sustainable pain should they disregard *the sacred.*

"I will put you both to *sleep,*" she said, every syllable passing through her lips like they were being chewed from a big block of wood, "chop yer heads off and leave 'em to bake out there in the road if yuins dare to mock my trust." It was a vow sealed in the alum of mortality, as only Seriann could do.

"You mean yer gonna let that long drank a' piss come 'round here lookin' to slobber awl over her?" Wilson said.

"You'd better shut it up," said Wilma Lee, "or I'm gonna break my fist off on that one jaw tooth you got left!"

And so it was in the messiness of loud voices that Seriann pointed a crooked finger at them both. It was settled. Cobbie could come a-calling and he and Wilma Lee would be allowed uninterrupted time alone—so long as they didn't get off the porch. Mary Olive just rolled her eyes toward heaven and said, "Lookin' to me like it's clabberin' up for rain."

All went well for the first week, until the steamy business of hormones weighed in with a trump hand, and Seriann ran Cobbie off with a shotgun, this time for good. According to Wilson the porch hadn't been big enough to hold them and all that bubbled up inside them. It only took a matter of days before they slipped off to the hen house. Wilson was right there when Seriann kicked in the door, but then he was in such a fit of laughter telling me about it that I was having trouble understanding everything he was saying. What I came away with was Seriann suspected something when Cobbie offered to help Wilma Lee gather apples on a Sunday afternoon. But after they'd been gone just a *little too long*, Seriann grabbed the shotgun.

"She took off like a army sergeant," Wilson said. "Went di-reckly to the hen house, jes' like she *knew* they's in 'ar." He said when she kicked the door in, Cobbie had his pants down around his ankles and had Wilma Lee sitting on a twenty-gallon lard bucket with her legs up over her head. He said next thing he knew, Seriann let go a blast that tore a hole in the loft right above Cobbie's head. He said Cobbie and Wilma Lee both screamed like they'd been hit. Then, with one motion, Cobbie let go of Wilma Lee, grabbed hold of his britches and ducked past Seriann while she went to reloading.

"He was like a greased pig getting through 'at door," said Wilson.

Anyway, I guess this sent the lard bucket shooting across the floor and Wilma Lee landing on her back with her legs thrown open to the world. Wilson stopped here to clap his hands and catch his breath, then went on to say that Cobbie was just about halfway across the yard when Seriann let go another round that tore a hole in the side of the house next to his head. All the while, Wilma Lee lay there hollering for Jesus Lord God to put a stop to Seriann. By the time Seriann reloaded again, Cobbie was across the creek and doing his level best to shimmy up the other side, his pants only half-way up and his shiny white ass glistening like a fruit jar in the sun.

"If 'at wasn't bad enough," Wilson said, "Mary Olive sicced ol' Bartley on him as he went by. But ol' Bartley knew this wasn't his fight, an' just slinked off under the porch. By the time Cobbie made his way up the bank, Seriann was draggin' Wilma Lee through the hen house door by the hair of her head, and her screaming like she was being readied for butcherin'."

That was in the middle of September—just before we went to making apple butter—and right when Woodrow came strolling through the door, all the way from Wyoming. "Lord childern!" cried Mary Olive. "It's Woodrow, an' he's come a-soldierin'."

Almost overnight, I again became Wilma Lee's currier of letters, her barer of love to Cobbie. Helping to keep the fire lit was next to treason, I figured, but somehow, in the aftermath of running whiskey and patent disregard for the selfless, I had the notion of being immune to its politics. In the end it was Wilma Lee's heart and longing that I felt the most, things that made me know I could make a difference for her sake. Besides, I was the only one she had: her only hope for what I figured was destined to be, anyway.

Woodrow looked *filled-out* this time around, like he'd been getting all he wanted to eat whenever he wanted it, and he talked a mile a minute: not like the old Woodrow, all slumped and lazy and drawn up into himself. It didn't seem to matter what we wanted to know, he just started talking about what he thought we needed to hear, and chewing around every word. It was a marvel the way he used his fork like a shovel, heaping mounds of collard greens and cornbread into his cheeks without seeming to take in air. I thought things might change once Bobby walked in, but no: he just kept on talking and shoveling, without giving Bobby the time of day. After Cousin Truman strolled through the door, he slowed down just enough to nod, but then started back up like he only had a day to visit and six months of tales to unload. We were all happy to see Woodrow, thrilled even, but after wading through half a cooker of beans, a whole pan of bread, and what seemed like an endless account of his soldiering. Well ... there was only so much a body could take.

I stayed with Bobby what time Woodrow was home so it wouldn't be so crowded at bedtime and around the table. As it turned out, it hadn't made much difference because of Woodrow being drunk and gone most of the time. From one day to the next, nobody ever knew where he was, who he was with or whether he was dead or alive, only that he managed to stagger through the door most mornings about daylight, only to repeat it again come dark. A week later, after what seemed like a hard-fought journey, we were all standing in the middle of the road saying our good-byes once again.

Corbin came to drive him to the bus depot yet again, where he could catch a "Greydog" back to Wyoming. Woodrow had been talking non-stop all morning and was beginning to catch a second wind when Bobby interrupted him just long enough to ask what Wyoming was like. Woodrow said it was like living on an Indian reservation, but with a whole lot more to eat. We all laughed even though we never understood what he meant. When we asked him when he was coming back, he said he was thinking about taking some leave time in Mexico: that he'd always wanted to go overseas, and believed that Mexico was as good a place as any to start. The whole family just stood around with blank expressions while Bobby laughed out loud and called him names like Poncho and Zorro and The Cisco Kid. That made Woodrow madder'n a wet hen, and when he got in the car with Corbin, he pointed a finger at Bobby and said, "Ah'm goin' get you when I come back." Bobby said, "Whyn't you get me right now?" But in the next instant, Corbin pulled away. We all watched and waved, and with Seriann pleading out loud for him to write more often until he and Corbin disappeared beyond the big bend in the road. We stood there in silence listening to the Model-A slowly fade away, and feeling a whole lot like Woodrow's time with us had been just a figment of our imaginations.

Fifty-Two

Up, Mule

Haman Flowers' mule was short, thick, and red—and with the eyes of one possessed. He called him *Mule.* It was mid-afternoon and hot enough to bake bread on a flat rock when I looked up from the porch and saw Mule standing in the middle of the road, covered in the dust that filtered fine as powder in the heat, and in the ratcheted whir of katydids. Haman sat hunched and holding onto Mule's rope bridle, shifting his chaw from one side of his mouth to the other, his leg cocked side-saddlish and staring at Seriann from the shadow of a bowler hat. The quietness between them stretched to breaking. His shotgun rested in the crook of his arm—the one without a hand. Seriann stood and leaned against the porch post, her arms folded across her chest, steadied and without a word. It was like a step into eternity where an underpinning of evil trumps even the direst kind of hatred. In short order, Haman pulled his arm out from under his gun and held it up so Seriann could have a look ... just held it there, its stub like a copperhead asleep in the grass. "Up, Mule" was all he said before easing off in a slow walk, his eyes and their trail of sin never lifting from Seriann. We listened for the longest time, until Mule's hoofsteps faded to nothing behind the thickets that lined the creek. The look on Haman's face told us we'd see him again. We had no idea what he was liable to do, only that it was sure to be something everlasting.

Fifty-Three

It Came Like a Bolt

"I *Have No One to Love Me*" played through Wilma Lee with the softness of a night wind, a ballad she coaxed up and out, the strings of her dulcimer as intricate as angels. Ushering in the evening was not always without its lament; if not our own, then whatever Wilma Lee conjured from her difficulty with hormones and heartbreak, moods that left us feeling like we'd been yanked through a knot hole. Tonight was much the same, the porch girded but sagging with our weight, the settling dew and speckles of fireflies in place of the day's swelter.

"*Farewell to friends and relations*," she sorrowed, "*this is the last you'll see of me.*" One could not hear and disbelieve. "*I'm gonna end my troubles by drownin' in the deep blue sea.*" On and on, empty but for the pain and desolation, pouring out what remained of Cobbie's memory. We sat joined to her wretchedness, not bothering with tourniquets of pardon, giving her nothing but our consoling presence. Misery was its own sentence.

"So, you're sayin' it was Haman Flowers what come around that night?" The night had cooled and Corbin framed his questions barrister-like and in the gluttony of stars. "And it was that hat of his caught in the brush that made you know it?"

"'At's right," I said, certain of what I knew.

"An' yer tellin' me it was that same hat you saw hoverin' above the barrels of a twelve-gauge when you was just a boy?" I nodded, eerie with wonder and not knowing where he was headed. Corbin pondered for a time, sucking on his teeth and looking down and away like he was trying to bring his thoughts into focus. He seemed bothered, and held out his hand as a way of hushing us when we tried to interject this or that. He was fixed, ruminating: agitated in a way that scrunched his face and kept the porch in quiet. We waited, lingering while he tried to close the gap. At last he turned, his face a dark study.

"An' when was it," he asked, his eyes dead on me, "you last had hold a' your grandmaw's .22?"

"That very day," I said. "Just run off an' left it when I was told to *git*."

Corbin sat still as a cat, his eyes in a dead stare; the faint trace of a smile caught on his lips, his glare penetrating my very core. He cocked his head, raised his eyebrows and waited for the connection to hit home. It came like a bolt.

Moonlight spilled in through the curtains Lorali had made from her passel of feed sacks. Outside, the creek was hushed, its water tottering from rock to rock. I lay awake, my mind racing full out and not wanting to accept what amounted to the truth: that it was Haman Flowers who had had my gun all the time; who had sited me down a double-barrel and sent me in a run years ago ... and with Grandmaw's .22 laying at his feet. And if it was him who carted it off, then it couldn't have been anybody but him who brought it back. Who else knew who it belonged to?

It had been Corbin's simple reasoning that added light to the mystery, one I somehow regretted knowing. Haman Flowers had packed me out of the mountain and propped me up alongside the outhouse; no doubt saved my life—a truth I would have sooner left alone—then later left my gun in the very place he left me. The hardness of it was wakeful and left me tossed and turned, listening to the tranquil breathing around me and wondering if simple reasoning would tell me why.

* * *

Fewer things strike the heart like a dose of not knowing, and it was the uncertainty surrounding Haman Flowers that clouded me with a sobering measure of it. Corbin, on the other hand, wasn't as doubtful about who Haman was or what kept him shrouded in darkness. "There's things about Haman Flowers," he said, "that need tearin' down, things that've been allowed to go on far too long." His tone came with a share of finality, as ominous as Cousin Truman lamenting about the tribulations awaiting those on the last day.

The night had chilled, the frosts and moons of October already scented with hickory fires. Corbin sat pokerfaced, held in thought by the sizzle of embers. He liked knowing things that nobody else knew, and he liked keeping it that way.

Just then Bobby came through the door, red-faced and winded, his eyes going directly to Corbin. "It's Haman Flowers," he said, his words coarse and ill-omened, blanketing our silence.

"What about him?" Seriann said, her voice rising, grave.

"*About* him or somebody *like* him," Corbin interrupted, his tone heavy with being one step ahead, already in the know, "bringing hell down on me last night." Eyes widened in the dim light, except for Seriann's narrowing to slits. "Severely halting the flow of goods and services, namely mine, to them with a thirst for what's bona fide." The same hush that slowed Mary Olive's rocking to a dead crawl brought an irksomeness from the back of Wilma Lee's throat, like a cat coughing up a hairball. "Made waste of what I *built*," Corbin said. "Took a shotgun to all that was copper and put together for gain. Settlin' a score, maybe. Cain't be sure: I ain't ever'body's friend, you know. Then maybe it was just for sport ... or just evil for evil's sake."

"I knowed they was sump'm a-comin'," moaned Mary Olive, "soon's I seen 'at rooster in my dream, an' it standin' on top a' the outhouse with a black snake in its mouth."

"What all'd you hear, Bobby?" Corbin was eager to sift fact from rumor.

"Just that Haman Flowers lost ever'thang he had last night playin' poker at Verlin Honeacres. Had 'em a barn full. Two games goin' on.

Both of 'em big, an' ever'body purdy well drunk. It was U.J. what walked away with ever'thang." Bobby was on edge. "Won big—but then on the way home, he said somebody come out a' nowhere and stuck a barrel in the small of his back, an' said '*Just drop what ye got on the ground and move on, 'fore I blow yer backbone through yer belly.*'" U.J. said he knowed it was Haman Flowers, mostly 'cause he could smell him. Said it was like mule sweat."

Corbin could be as mysterious as cat's eyes. Waiting for him to speak often meant listening to your heartbeat until he got ready. When he finally did speak, it was like he'd spent the time formulating what he needed to say in as few words as possible. "Saturday night's the only time U.J. and Don'l Mac ain't working the still," Corbin said. "Ever'thang he'd worked out an' ever'thang he won is gone, I reckon." He thought long and hard after that, his divining mixing with the fires light. "Best I can figure is sometimes you *get*, and sometimes you *get got*. Reckon this time around, me and U.J. found it out the hard way." We waited, heightened. "Must be," he went on, trance-like, "desperate men do desperate things. All I know is Haman Flowers ain't got a whole lot these days, 'cept a shotgun and the mind to use it. He's been used to havin', by whatever means. He'll take till somebody takes him. Guaranteed. But then, I s'pect last night had more to do with you," he said, his eyes rolling toward Seriann, "than anything else." He leaned forward, gouged at the logs in the grate, the poker like a sword in his hand. "He's just using *me* to get at *you*." More quiet befell us after that, the echo of Corbin's words as scorched as the ashes that dropped from the logs.

"What else?" he said to Bobby. Bobby shook his head.

"Nothin' 'bout U. J.'s mule?"

"No. Why?"

"'Cause U. J. was just part of it," Corbin said. "Seems like somebody had it in for ol' Jenks, too. Cut his throat. Just imagine! It's only something a creature unfit apart from the bowels of hell could a' done. No way a' tellin' for sure whose name's on it. But then sometimes a body just knows."

Corbin's words silenced us in the same way the scattering of leaves silenced the earth outside our door. Sunday night wasn't usually filled with such onerousness, and we passed looks between us—ones rounded with a fear of the unknown and that this was not the end of it. There would be a reckoning: the gravity of Haman Flowers' actions and the burden of consequences Corbin was made to assume demanded it. It was part of the law that made Appalachia so unforgiving. Forgiveness, only in the rarest circumstances, was ever meted for resolution—and only after long-suffering even entertained. Pride and reputation, hallmarks of the high-mountain creed, were more often the cornerstones from which we fostered our hate and plotted our revenge. Pride and reputation, reinforced through ages and generations, were the things that caused us to risk the ravages of an-eye-for-an-eye and maneuver around the moral indices of the Bible. Pride and reputation took the highest precedent when honoring family names, even if it meant a time-and-again reach beyond the rock-footing civility of loving thy neighbor. Pride and reputation were traits we cherished most, strived hardest to protect, even what we sought to preserve on our tombstones. It was what we understood best in a landscape that gave far less than it demanded.

We huddled around the fire feeling a sense of danger, yet a bond of family. It was a feeling born of the certainty that said *not all the Haman Flowers' in the world could do this to us and get away with it*. I allowed myself to feel Corbin's sense of injustice. I couldn't help but feel that it was something in full compliance with survival, with right winning out over wrong. For reasons I couldn't explain, I was made bigger by it: noble even, despite what harm might come. The worry, though, was that it wouldn't come to Haman Flowers' alone.

For four long days, Corbin and Hooker Hopkins worked alongside U.J. and Don'l Mac trying to restore the remnants of a still torn apart by twelve-gauge buckshot. Then for several days after, drove the roads looking for Haman Flowers. I don't know that it ever crossed Virgil Blair's mind to wonder why they were meandering from one fork to another at all hours, but then it was never easy knowing what Virgil knew. For

Corbin, though, it didn't much matter. He was going to finish what was in him, regardless of what Virgil knew. The mystery, though, unexplainable as it was, was that Haman seemed all-too aware of being hunted.

"Ain't no way a' findin' him if he don't want findin'," Bobby said. "He knows they ain't but few breaths left in him, if Corbin has his way. He's holed up, reckoning it out. Hard tellin' what he's apt to do, but I'd say it'll be sump'm ain't nobody's ready for."

Fifty-Four

Chary and Without Contrition

Sitting next to Imogene on the front seat of Olin's truck five days a week, and with her leg pressed next to mine, never ceased to fill me with stirrings altogether familiar with my fifteen years. It was what prompted me, day after day, to walk with her after Olin dropped us off, even carrying her books as far as the footbridge in front of her house—the place where Ester waited, as might a mother hen in fear of hawks. But the litheness that hung between us, fragrant-like and aired in the dryness of autumn, kept me undeterred, roused but for the front-porch hacking of Gilliam and his permanent reminders of snuff. Little did I know the thin shadows of October would be the last of it; when Imogene would go off to Louisville to live with more affluent kin, Ellis and Sophie Wingate; invited, actually, to come keep house and tend to Jerry Jeff, their one and only child. Room and board and a weekly stipend being the carrot on a stick, all it took to lure her from the grind of Greezy and all that was so slow to change.

"She's a schoolteacher and he's a banker," she said, her smile tentative in the way of white lies, her eyes searching mine for some sense of gladness or approval, neither of which ever came. Theirs was a "Big ol' house," she said, and helped herself to words like portico and vestibule, loggia and veranda, words I'd never heard before; words, I was certain, that had, in recent days, been inked into letters from Ellis and Sophie Wingate. She went on in feigned excitement, holding us both to a reality that sought to undo more than console. The vision of her already there, kept by the leverage of privilege and society, weighed me right along with the leaves withering and waiting for winter. "There's even a hothouse," she said, "an' runnin' water." I took it to be a place time-honored and on the scale of Corbin's in its day.

We rode together right up to November, paid attention to each other when we could, walked and talked and said our final goodbyes while Ester watched with ever-mounting suspicion. The mile between her house and mine was walked with steps not wanting to be made. Time and seasons had left me knowing with all-consuming certainty where my heart lay.

Notes from Cobbie came almost nonstop, day after day. He left them at the store with Bobby, who, in turn, read them, though he swore he wouldn't, then passed them along to me so I could sneak them to Wilma Lee. But her infrequency in answering became more the rule than the exception. I couldn't be sure that her fires were past being out, only that they were past being their brightest.

Mary Olive was, in a straight line, our right of entry to life's bale of blood and butchery, hell's fire, and what roamed about after the sun went down. She had the lead roll to what we could only know as the impenetrable, and the stirring force, *always*, to Lorali's visions—exciting her to where her eyes seemed to disengage like she'd been visited by the Holy Ghost, and with warbling sounds bouncing off the roof of her mouth: grave warnings from the beyond.

Always, there was that intangibleness about her, what we knew as *other worldly*—a certain wooliness that latched her to things beyond the pale of our senses, things conjured only by visions. Throw Lorali into the mix, and things just sort of ... well ... offered up their own prophecy. It was like they had their very own ghosts limping in and out at will, thickening shadows and rummaging in the spaces where we lived. Seriann, too, was never far from it, adding her own take to what creaked and moaned when nothing was there. It was simply living with the likes of what moved about from one world to another, joining this one to the next, and what sent icy drafts snaking up our backs: things chary and without contrition. The cats felt it most and went about circling and yowling like they'd lost their way, like there was nothing left but to hurl themselves into an endless abyss. "It's a death rattle I'm hearin' of a night," Mary Olive whispered. "Swearrrrr," she said, "a thumpin' comin' up an' outta the garden, settin' the roosters to crowin' long 'fore daylight. They's a slight a-comin', a sin an' a scorn, shore's they's a world."

Corbin being marauded by Haman didn't help matters, and prompted Mary Olive with even greater visions of the end times. For days on end they rang from her as bold and clear as if straight out of Mr. Tacket's big brass bell: famines, hills struck with fire, starving dogs eating one another, and creeks running with blood; visions fraught with crows pecking out our eyes and great two-headed beasts with fangs, claws, and tails rising up out of smoke and fire, devouring trees and rocks and babies. And there was pestilence and eyeless riders on dark horses coming through cracks in the walls, the ground opening up and swallowing us whole. She brought poor Lorali near to tears on more than one occasion, and left the rest of us wondering if somebody had poisoned the well. It came to a head one afternoon when she had a vision of Corbin in the yard studying his own shadow, his back to the sun. "It's Satan a-comin'," she whispered, her cheeks hollowed, her mouth an open hole and as rounded as her eyes.

After a time, looking for Haman Flowers took on a vain character. Corbin's sense of being wronged, however, was without letup, its severity edging upwards to where he sent Hooker Hopkins straight to the head of Shop Branch to wait Haman out. Bobby was the one who showed Hooker where to hide, where he could see without being seen. After a day and a night without the first sight of him, Hooker killed his dogs, all eight of them; shot them close up and left them sprawled in the mud in front of the cabin. That very next Saturday, Haman came to sit on the front porch of the store.

He sat off to the side, clear to the lower end, making work out of fitting twists of King Bee into his cheeks. He was quiet for the most part, but restless, sending long spikes of 'baccer spit over the steps and into the dirt. Like most Saturdays, the store was caught up with coming and going; people crowding in to swap tales, knives, and the what-have-yous of life on the creek. Haman offered nothing to anyone, just kept pace with his eyes and waited, I suspected, for disorder and the likes of human contrivances.

Without as much as a word, I kept edging closer to him, pretending not to pay him any mind, all the while sweeping away the road dust and feeling myself in the corners of his eyes. When I finally came too close, he settled on me with a hard stare: a darkness in the full light of sun. He sat lopsided in one of the chairs that lined the porch, one knee crossed over the other, his bowler hat resting just above his brows. He menaced without moving, snuffing and stirring the air, the stubble of a beard and the brown-black of 'baccer juice in the corners of his mouth, his one good eye going between me and all that moved.

I swept clear to the end of the porch, past where he was sitting, then stopped. He raised his head just enough to catch me in full light, then waited like expecting me to say something. "Reckon I ain't never had no trouble with you," he said, looking off in the direction of the cottonwoods across the road. "Don't reckon we ought start." He waited, silence falling on us both before rolling his head back in my direction.

"Why'd you pack me outta the mountain?" I asked. It was like a shot fired in the night.

He rested in the hush, his eye in a blank stare beyond the cottonwoods. "Reckon you was hurt bad 'nuff," he finally said. "No need to add dyin' to it." He rolled his head back around to me, the air heavy around him, watching me for signs that would tell him something beyond what he already knew. I stood staring back, my eyes unable to unfasten from the contradiction, beguiling as it was, that scorned him, that lay over him in an almost tangible disregard.

Unnerving silence seemed to find its place in the backsplash of movement and voices caught in the effort of trade. I wanted to be gone from all that eked from him, yet couldn't bring myself to move. "Yer daddy was a good man," he said out of the blue. "Helped me some with shinin', back when you was needin' fed. Knowed who you was all along." Sound seemed to evaporate, giving way to the tide of blood pounding through my brain. I was without words as he stood up to leave, "Reckon it was maybe yer daddy," he said in the direction of the road, "that packed you outta there."

Folks say Haman Flowers came and sat in the same place for nearly a week, waiting on who we now know was Corbin. His being there hardly raised an eyebrow, outside of his all-of-a-sudden being without a hand—something whispered about to no end, but nothing anybody bothered to talk about—not out loud anyway—fearing, I supposed, the worst kind of evil just by the inquiry. He just sat there, out of the way and at the annoyance of Andrew, keeping time with the shadows and the passing of the sun. Virgil sat at the upper end, his usual place what time he rested ol' Jake. For hours, he and Haman sat staring off and never speaking, both with their jawbones full of chaw and spitting as if to keep the dust down in the road.

Bobby came and went same as always, wrestling groceries and hauling supplies, doing all what Pearl and Andrew insisted on for profit. He was good at anything, Bobby was, particularly at staying gone once he got behind the wheel of the delivery truck, something he considered a compensation all its own. Bobby was never one to set policy, but when Haman began camping out day after day, he tried convincing Andrew how Haman's menacing-assed nastiness was beginning to scare the hell out of customers, and how they ought for the sake of business help him to another side of town. It was a suggestion Andrew just waved off, but one that Bobby felt compelled to bring up every time he had to look Haman's way. It was a silent confrontation between them, bound mostly by stone-cold stares and a hidden promise of *I'll kill you if you as much as take a step in my direction.*

Why Haman was there ceased to be a mystery once Aug came to see us. "He's wantin' to get at you," Aug said, his eyes difficult and on Seriann. "He's sayin' it was you who took from him, and it's him that's gonna take from you. Said it'll be in a way you won't ferget, like it is ever' time he's made to do without a hand."

We sat with whispered voices what time Aug was there, quiet nearly descending into reverence. He stayed with us right up till the sun was all but gone and the mountains descended into blue, the strain of his nightmare contrary to hope.

"It's a evil in him we cain't get to," Aug said before he turned to leave. "Not on this side a' the grave, anyway."

Wilma Lee walked him to the gate, lingered with him while talking in muffled tones, then held the light while he crossed the creek—then lifted it high over her head as if it might somehow light his way, even long after he was swallowed up by the night.

What gives a man reason to do what he does, or to chance beyond what he's able, isn't always clear; what causes him to choose one path over another, or dream about what he expects to find once he gets there, is just part of what molds us into great unknowns. Mary Olive says men *do* simply by a residing presence, the thing that homes itself to his spirit. There was little guessing about what homed itself to Haman. Still, it was hard to tell what he had in mind when he went to sit on Andrew's porch beyond flushing Corbin into the open, him being his own bait.

"*Never play another man's game*" was a hardened rule for Corbin. "*There'll always be a hole card you can't see, one little something you can't know till it's too late.*" I had no doubt that it was what kept him away from the store what time Haman was there, unwilling to play to a stacked deck. After a time, Haman seemed to get the message—enough to send him on his way, I was certain, in search of something even darker.

Fifty-Five

There Is No End

Dry Fork can be a forsaken place in the dead of night, its miles of long twisty road and acres upon acres of bottomland, its smattering of houses and barns and all of it under the endless void of darkness can make for a haunt, even with a sizeable moon. According to Virgil Blair, it was there, in one of its long stretches without a cabin, that Corbin stopped his Model-A and dragged a big tree limb out of the road. The last thing he ever did.

It was Hawk Bilbry who found him, right at daylight and on the way to his hog lot. Saw him curled up in the road alongside his Model-A and with its motor still running. Said he jumped the creek to get to him, but knew he was gone soon as he got close: a bloody hole, shredded and about the size of a cabbage head, square in his chest. He sent one of his young'ns running to Virgil Blair after that. By the time Virgil got there, there was a small nest of neighbors all swearing they thought they heard something up in the night, but none of them believing it was more than just hunters or something they dreamed. That was right before we got there, Olin and me, right when Virgil rolled us to a stop.

The early morning sky was murky and with every intention of staying that way. Between the chill, the mud-sodden road, and the frosty breaths, we stood huddled and lost to disbelief, horror staring back at us in the new light. I was wobbled, on the brink of blacking out, listening and watching Virgil point to this and that, directing his mind to what might have been. I don't know how long I stood there before easing my way to the back of Olin's truck and letting go what little breakfast I had in me. After a time, and under Virgil's direction, the neighbors moved Corbin and the Model-A to the side of the road. I rode with Olin to drop off the miners and then to Pikeville, where we got hold of High Sheriff Garland Sawyers.

By the time we made it back to the creek, Andrew's big delivery truck was parked off to the side and Bobby was on his knees in the mud, holding Corbin in his arms. Word traveled fast on Greezy. Bobby's heaving sobs and the echo he sent deep into the mountains were the last things I remembered before breaking into a thousand pieces.

The speed at which word traveled at such times was hard to fathom, its reach as cruel as it was consuming and laying Seriann to waste. The pitch of her wail came to us as soon as we rounded the bend, its tone of raw nerves raking across the valley like the shattering of glass: insanity, reaching up and out and releasing to the world what was beyond measure.

Bartley was nowhere to be found, his place on the porch abandoned to the dirge that ravaged the air. We made it as far as the doorway, Olin and me, Seriann seeing but not seeing and awake to a rage known only by the deepest loathing. All that was closed to good spilled in and out of her like a river racing toward places without end.

"Oh, little brother," she moaned, clutching at me with all the strength she had left. "Only God knows how much I loved him." A chorus, over and again, rending what remained of memory. "Oh, Lord Jesus," she chanted, chanted, chanted, frothed and fell, her hair a mass of tangle weed and her eyes in a place where only spirits know and groan on our behalf. "Lord God," she begged in endless petition and in a voice next to madness, "take me with him."

For days, the air was thick with what was run asunder. Long suffering had crippled us, the want of Corbin and the lessening will to live without him dragging Seriann to her knees. Wilma Lee and Lorali, no less stricken, managed to slip into their own house of horrors, regret sealing off what was left of reason, what was shaped by obsession. Mary Olive was less disposed, going about mumbling to herself, staving off the death knells and recanting what lingered unfinished and what degraded us with second thoughts. "We're a-mourned," she said. "Long on tears an' memory both." She made a duty out of filling the spaces that closed lifeless around us. "It's a here an' now that'll lay on us all our days," she said, her gaze narrowing, searching for what needed to be found. "He was a good young'n," she said, offering what she could to Corbin's name, to the emptiness that swirled nonstop within us. "He'll be with us always," she said, her reckoning assured. "There is no end."

Hollowed stillness had a way of settling in around Mary Olive when she was near to passing through the veil, when she was given over to *seeing*. From gospel singing and the sweet smell of whiskey on her breath to the clover pastures of her mind, she was the richest part of life's cracklings. "It's come to me many a-time," she said, bringing her rocking to a halt and slanting her eyes toward mine, "that they's more to our bein' here than what's parceled out." I waited, not sure of what she wanted me to know. "Our being here is just a *part* of it," she said, "an' Corbin's being gone ain't nuthin more'n him going to what's next." She stayed that way, fixed with knowing, until I nodded my understanding. "There's *forever* written on our souls, Rubin. Ain't no gettin' 'way from it." It was the extent of her take, reckoned to a refinement of dreams and what she knew to be believed. "Heaven's hand's on it all."

Garland Sawyers had been quick with his assessment, going over the obvious and leaving the rest to Virgil. "Weren't much to go on," said Virgil, his drawl gathered in empathy, allowing for our loss, his deep resonance raining down from atop ol' Jake and blending with autumn's soft prattle of leaves. "Weren't nobody saw nuthin', just them that heard a shot up in the night. No spent shells, no footprints; nuthin' 'cept it bein' a twelve gauge what killed him ... an' Lord knows they's enough a' them here 'bouts to arm a regiment." We listened without a sound, right down to Little Sherman, right down to Bartley marshaled in the dirt. "There was a big tree limb dragged off to the side," Virgil said. "Sump'm, I s'pect, somebody laid in the middle a' the road, knowin' he'd have to get out an' move it." They were words ungovernable, blotted and halted, jolting us into seeing. "Weren't no robb'ry to it," he said. "Just killin'."

We stood on the edge of the creek bank blanketed by Virgil's long sad eyes and the effort of his words, the gentle tumble of the creek adding to what was in the wind. He studied us for a time, sorrow wrangled in the creases of his face. Our eyes said most of it after that—his too—things too tattered for the heart and its indulgence. "I'm sorry," he said, his tone gripped with remains. It was his tender bid at good-bye.

Fifty-Six

In Ways Profound

It rained the day we buried Corbin, in a drizzle that held to us like frost. Seriann rode up front with Truman and Inez. I rode in the back with Wilma Lee and Lorali. Mary Olive stayed back with Wilson and Little Sherman; said she no longer had the will to put up with final goodbyes, their sacrament and ceremony. "I've seen enough of it," she said. "The dyin' an' buryin' both. Can't give myself to it no more. I'll be lucky to get through my own."

Though Seriann swore she couldn't go, she did—at the last minute—then rode without uttering a word. She walked braced between Cousin Truman and me all the way to the casket, then fainted dead away at first glimpse. Cold cloths and water and too many hands trying to help made confusion out of what was inelegant for us all. After several insufferable minutes, we helped her to the back of the room, where she sat trembling in the cold draft coming under the door. But it was afterwards, her holding onto the coffin and not allowing the lid to be closed, that we ever so gently urged her away, the look on her face routed and trounced and begging for understanding.

The long walk up the hill, slipping in the mud and straining with all our might to keep the casket from tipping, left us lathered and even colder still. Ben and Hooker Hopkins on opposite sides took the brunt of it, holding fast through all the times footing was lost. It was a long climb from the road to the graveyard, but one not wanting in mourners: black hatted and hooded, and standing in a drizzle that was determined to be all day. The preacher was brief for all our sakes, the first shovels of dirt commencing with his quick amen.

We waited in the sopping rain while everyone left, waited to pull Seriann up off her knees and out of the mud. It took the strength of Ben to get her down off the mountain, her isolation in harmony with what was lost and gone.

Lorali went home with Truman and Inez, leaving us feeling all the more alone, the paleness of her eyes trailing long afterwards with the promise to return.

Seriann stayed to her bed in the days that followed, long stretches of inward dwelling, weak and solitary, and with the pall of night. She came to me some days later, ran her tiny hard hands through my hair; the softening light of Indian summer eased into her smile.

"I ain't been much count these days, have I, Rubin?" Her voice was tender, worn out from pain. She stood staring out over the hills, taking in their ragged splendor. I said nothing, just waited for her daring or her love, whichever was most ready.

"Oh, Rubin," she said with a weakened breath. "I believe I've come to know my soul these last days ... in ways profound." There was a song at work. "Come to understand what it needs to continue, what it desires for completion." She seemed suspended, a butterfly aloft. "And it's this day that I've come to raise my hand before God Almighty Hisself, right here on the splintered planks a' this porch, and declare by all the angels in heaven that I will, if it be my eternal damnation, devour the sin that's come upon us: cut out the heart of the devil that dared to try us." Her eyes were tighter now, prayer like. "This day," she said, "and at this hour, humbled by God's love and made strong by His favor, I swear it."

She was as black as her hair, but with the faintest smile, seamless but for the stir of her oath, and knowing what it was that her soul desired. It froze my blood.

"I want," she said, her voice with the telltale signs of the spirits that possessed her, "my face to be the last thing Haman Flowers ever sees." She paused, her manner in agreement with all of creation. "And," she said, "the image he'll take with him on his way to hell."

Fifty-Seven

Needin' to Kick a Hole in Sump'm

For days we went about in a fog, in a wake of scarcity and a lack of direction. There was a tilted scale attached to Corbin being gone, something uneven and out of step. And though death had leveraged us to the point of our undoing, his memory, in an odd way, was like birth, coming to life with each new day.

In the end, Corbin's killing went unanswered, left to simmer along with countless others: victims of pride or vengeance or rage, or whatever else the mountains could summon. With no evidence of any kind to arrest, let alone convict, we were simply left to our own devices. But then, hard evidence isn't always the only thing to go on; sometimes a body just knows.

Bobby stayed away at first, just sort of withdrew into a cave of his own making, but then came around after a few days, not to talk, but just to be within reach. Even then he was absent. It was dark when he first showed up, and still we sat on the porch, at his choosing, in the damp chill of November and huddled under coarse layers of wool; the cold helping us feel a little more alive. We stayed that way, filling the night with breath and hedged against what might come in place of peace, until the moon came full over Wolfpit, bathing us in ghostly light.

"I'm needin' to kick a hole in sump'm," he said, his voice an interruption to the creek's icy trickle. It was a familiar tone, unsettling, chancy. And just like that, he was off the porch and across the creek. I waited before going inside, until his footsteps were long gone.

For more days than we cared to confess, things just seemed to roll over on us, lose shape and the look of familiarity. It wasn't until the short cold days of December that fragments of commonness rejoined us. Ruby Mae McHone closed the deal on Corbin's house and land almost overnight, offering an uncontested amount and freeing the family from all the usual haggling, leaving Invictus' doors set to reopen at her command.

Corbin's Model-A ended up at Olin's, in the mud out behind the barn; and U.J. and Don'l Mac ... well ... they just sort of walked away, Corbin's killing tracking too close to home. It stayed that way for just a short time, until they struck a deal with Ruby Mae: one that left them willing, once again, to hazard the risk of running shine. By the middle of December, supply was back in full swing—demand never having subsided.

What little money Bobby and I made working for Old Man Andrew now went toward the family. With the bootlegging dried up, we were left with little to nothing between us. After weighing our options on the first Saturday night we felt like being a part of in a long time, Bobby decided our best shot was to try Homer Lawson.

"You gonna fight Homer Lawson?" I said.

"Way I see it," Bobby said, "we can't lose. I just need to keep movin'. That's all there is to it. Keep sticking and jabbing. Keep bobbing and weaving and dancing. Hell, it's only for five minutes. He'll never touch me." His eyes shone like they were suns. "He can't hurt me if he can't hit me. Hell, I'm fast as a black snake. You know that." And with that he commenced to skipping and dancing and throwing one shadowy punch after another. I knew he was beyond the point of no return when he starting feeling sorry for Homer. "Why, poor old Homer ain't got a chance against Bobby 'Cornbread Red' Yonts, the Greezy Creek Kid." He fainted, dodged, then threw an upper cut through the thin night air. "He's too big. Too slow. Can't handle the likes of this red-headed lightening bolt." He bobbed up and down like he had springs on his feet then let go a series of left jabs and then a hard right ... silent except for the crowd noise in his head and the bullfrogs in the creek.

"Yeah," he said, "it's time for big dog to move on out, cause little dog's moving in." He thumbed his nose and danced even closer, back pedalled, then landed a couple make-believe body shots. "Hell," he said, "I don't know why I didn't think of this sooner. Don't hardly seem fair to Homer, but hell, he's the one asking for it." It didn't seem to matter to Bobby that Homer outweighed him by fifty pounds. "It's just five minutes," he said. "You don't have to be big to win. You just have to be the quickest ... and that's me!"

He went to quiet after that, just stood there in the lamplight filtering from the kitchen window. He raised his head to take in the stars, all but consumed by the jolt of Corbin's memory. "Ain't nuthin' quite right no more," he said, his eyes strained and just short of calling out. And there was no laughter, not even the attempt.

"Maybe we ought to wait for another night," I said.

He rolled his head in my direction and brought his hand to rest on my shoulder. "Comes a time," he said, "when waitin's a coward." His chest was swelled, heaving, and his hand like a rock. There would be no waiting.

We walked in dead earnest, the memory of Corbin ever present, though we spoke nothing of it—suppression as our solace. By the time we got to Homer's, Bobby was good and riled, like he'd already fought, maybe even twice. When he laid his quarter down, I laid mine on top of it. Homer looked up, then around, puzzled. "Who you betting on, son?"

"Me!"

"YOU?"

"ME!"

"Well, hell," Homer said with a full-size grin. And with that, a barn full of hobnailed-Saturday-nighters commenced to bellow and stomp and fog the air, a spectacle full of nerve and mockery. But when Bobby stripped to the waist, their noise went to thunder. It was no ruse, and betting became furious: would Bobby last the five minutes?—would Homer knock him off his feet?—would Bobby land more punches, outscore Homer?—on and on. Then, as was customary, Homer and Bobby met in the middle of the floor.

"Now, I don't mean to hurt you, son," Homer said. "It's just what I do." After that, he took him a big pull from a pint bottle of clear corn liquor, packed his cheek with a plug of Brown Mule, then plunged his fists into a bucket of cold water. About that time, the barn door opened wide, and in its cold blast stood Hooker Hopkins. For a moment, the whole lot seemed to inhale, draw back. I reckoned it was respect (or was it fear?) for such an injurious piece of work, one severe with stature and reputation both. He hesitated just long enough to size up what was about to happen, the clamor, little by little, edging its way back to full throttle. He eyeballed Bobby, then me, then stepped through the noise and placed a five-dollar bill on top of our quarters. "On Red to win," he said. The noise rose to riotous, such commotion that Homer stood there breathing hard before reaching into his pocket and coming out with a ten, held it up for all to see then laid it ginger-like on top of Hooker's five. The noise was deafening and for a long moment Hooker stood staring with a dead-pan smile, surveying the crowd and its wildness. In one smooth motion, he reached for the tight little wad he kept tucked inside his long, black coat and peeled off another five. The pot was right and the noise swelled to crescendo. "Will there be any others?" Homer hollered around a grin as tight as a barbed wire fence. It was done.

"Well, awright then," Hooker said turning to face Bobby, "Let's have us a go."

Like all the other matches, it was a "no-hold," "no-hitting-below-the-belt," "one-knock-down-ends-it-all" match. If they both stayed on their feet for the entire five minutes, the winner was determined by who scored the most clean hits. By and large, it was pretty easy to tell the winner, although it was Luck Hanner who had the final say. Luck never bet, so he had nothing personal to gain. Luck just liked being there, and the brutality of it all. It was his idea of a perfect Saturday night. If it was too close to call, the money was divided equally. Luck's word was final. That's just the way it was, and just the way everybody liked it.

It was right after Homer plunged his fists for the second time into the bucket of cold water that Luck rang the bell, and about ten seconds after that that Homer bloodied Bobby's nose. Wham! Right out of the schute. Bobby looked like a hobgoblin with all that blood pouring out his nose and down across his chin, but it just seemed to wake him up, even make him madder. That's when he went to dancing, skirting and scooting, all the while spitting the blood that wouldn't stop. Spitting and jabbing and dancing, and staying the hell out of Homer's way. Then he struck like a snake. Wham! Caught ol' Homer square on the chin. Then again and again, his big square hands and thick arms bouncing off Homer like a rubber ball. But it was points, and he kept dancing and spitting and trying to separate himself from all the blood running into his mouth. Homer was like a stalking giant, constantly moving in and keeping Bobby back pedalling. "DANCE" I heard myself scream, but my cries were drowned amongst all the others. Still, Bobby seemed to rally from the screaming, sliding this way and that, each time barely ducking under and away from Homer's thunderous blows. Hooker stood straight and stone-faced, looking like he was trying with all his might to conjure for Bobby all the power from all the spirits from all the ages. Out of nowhere, Bobby landed a right square on Homer's nose, as if Homer had stood still and let him do it; but there was no blood. It rocked Homer for a second, long enough for him to clear his head, and just long enough for Bobby to come back with a left uppercut square under his chin. Homer reeled and spun, but held on—how, nobody knows; it was a star maker, but then in a flash he came at Bobby like a she bear covering her cubs. Wild blows, forceful and deadly, beyond anything I'd ever seen Homer throw, one after another, cracking against Bobby's arms and glancing off his head. I swore I could hear his fists slicing the air, but Bobby found a way, and jabbed again and again, each time blistering Homer's jawbone and nose. But there was no quit in Homer, or nothing in Bobby that would say I've had enough. But then, just as Bobby went right, Homer went left. In a flash, a left hook sent Bobby's feet out from under him like he'd stepped on ice. It was over. In a breath, Homer grabbed Bobby and pulled him to his feet, set him on a milk stool, and cooled his face with a wet towel.

The din and pitch of the crowd gradually eased into chatter. I was wet under my arms and clean to my drawers. When I turned, Hooker was standing square shouldered and looking as calm and unbothered as a bull in a field of clover. He gave me a wink and a smile, smooth and rascally. For the first time in many days it left me feeling like there was still some solid ground.

"GAAAWD...DAMN!" exclaimed Homer. "I ain't never been fought like 'at in awl my life by no fifteen year old."

"Sixteen," said Bobby.

"Well, sixteen then," Homer said. "But I'll be damned if ye didn't 'bout wipe my ass fer me." He lowered the towel from Bobby's face and said, "Didn't mean to hurt you none, son." Homer was as good hearted as he was a fighter. "Just quiet yeself. You'll be awright in a minute." He poured what was left in the water bucket over his head and said, "That nose is puffed up like a powder milk biscuit, but I kin tell it ain't broke. I know they're broke soon as I hit 'em. Yourn held good." He stopped, took a deep breath, then said, "By God, if you ain't as tough a sumbitch as I ever fought." He looked around and made it so everybody could hear him. "Man needs to be *wary* a' them with red hair," he said. Homer always kept everybody laughing. "Damned if they ain't like a hot wire. Ain't seen one *yet* that wouldn't fight a buzz saw. Ain't never been whupped so bad in awl my life as when I come up against some wiry little sumbitch from over in Haysi, Virginia. Redheaded, he was. Wore me plum *out!* Fists like a adder's tongue an' runnin' me in circles. Stuck me so many times I got to boilin' over. It was all downhill adder that. But hell, I wadn't the only one. He fit one adder the other 'at night. Had all kinds of wind. *Still* been fightin', if we hadn't run outta money." Homer's chest and arms were shiny with sweat, as intoxicating as his huge grin and sordid tales. The whooping and hollering and the big coal stove off to the side added to his cordiality, covered us like a blanket against the night's reach. "Don't reckon I'll ever ferget it," he said, "but I reckon rememberin' makes me better for it. Jest have to watch out fer them redhaired."

Homer was as genuine as the coal seam in the cliff out behind his house. I couldn't help but like him, despite the licks and lessons he laid on Bobby. Just as we were leaving, we turned to see him standing in the middle of the floor talking to a tall, lanky, sandy-haired feller who was being egged on by his buddies. "Now, I don't mean to hurt you, son," he said. "It's just what I do." After that, he took a big swallow from what looked like some of Corbin's finest—even offered it to his challenger—freshened his cheek with a plug of Brown Mule, then plunged his fists into a bucket of cold water. That was just before Luck rang the bell.

Outside, the stars were as cold as the night as we stood listening to the insurrection coming from the barn. Hooker pulled a pint bottle of crystal-clear shine from inside his coat and held it out to Bobby. It was just what the doctor ordered.

"It'll be the last time you'll need to fight for a quarter," Hooker said, "'less you want to."

"I just needed to kick a hole in sump'm," Bobby said.

"You reckon you've done it?"

"For the time."

Hooker laughed and offered up the bottle again. "Things change, boys," he said, taking on a sober tone, "an' we cain't always be ready for it. But we're fixin' to be awright. Startin' *now*." He took the bottle, turned it up, and swallowed hard. "Corbin was my friend an' my brother," he said, his breath frosty. "An' his bein' stripped from us the way he was mocks us." He waited, his huge chest swelling and re-swelling, moon shadows filling the deep creases in his face. "*Undignified* is the way I see it," he went on, "sump'm made to haunt us if we was to walk away an' leave it. An' I ain't about to be haunted."

We rode with Hooker into town, then to Corbin's. He shut off the engine and we sat in the long dark drive leading up to the house, passing the bottle back and forth till it was gone.

"Me and Ruby Mae, we got us a deal," Hooker said. "Thangs'r fixin' to change ... and real soon." Bobby and I sat without talking, the moonshine rifling through us. "First off, though," he said, his eyes lost in the black hole of night, "'fore anything else, thangs need to be put right."

I pretended to understand what he was talking about, yet all the while believing it was something I was better off not knowing. Bobby only nodded, his head light from the whiskey. For a time, we waited in silence before Hooker geared us back on to the blacktop. Bobby's face had swollen, his nose and under his eyes; the steady chatter of Hooker's Model-T offering only a thinned distraction, only a veiled comfort, by the time we got to Dry Fork's long twisty road. I tried imagining the night Corbin got out of his car to move that big tree limb out of the way, blackness all around, swallowed up in a void as deep as it was wide except for the spray of his headlights and the reality of the ground he walked on, of the hills just out of reach.

Hooker was silent, his huge frame hunched, too big for the Model-T, all the time drawing nearer to where Hawk Bilbry found Corbin. The night lay tossed, its persuasion deep. I huddled against its seeming infinity, its facelessness ... and that's when I saw him. Just a glance. Out the side window. In the faint mist of the headlights. It was Ben. And he was running. Break-neck and thunderous through a harvested cane field that bordered the road. His massiveness contorted. Monsterous. A shotgun, both shield and spear, in his hands.

Shivers sheared through me like cracking ice. I fought to say something—anything—but nothing came—only an open mouth and the need for breath. What in the name of God was he doing? And so far from home... What was he after? Or what was after him? I could almost feel him lunging, trampling the earth, splintering what dared to get in his way. And why the gun?—in the pitch black of night?—bounding like a runaway?

The light from Angus Walker's pool hall filtered yellow-brown through the dust on its windows. It was well onto one o'clock by the time Hooker rolled us to a stop.

"I'm gonna drop ye here," Hooker said. "I got sump'm I need to tend to." He stared after us hard and long—as black and cold as a coalmine—before turning and heading back up Dry Fork Hill. Bobby and I walked in the road's ruts, furrowed and gripped in a deep freeze, the moon having disappeared long before. I was still dumbstruck, and wondering where Ben was at this very minute—if he might all of sudden come galloping out of nowhere and shooting the guts out of whatever moved. I couldn't help but search the shadows, listening for what might be out of time, for what the night might render. I fought to bring what I'd seen out of my mouth, but the words were determined to stay deep and without voice. It was at the fork in the road, where Gardner Fork separated from Main Fork, before we saw another light: pale slivers between the planks of the church house, at the far end of the bottom.

A wood stove and only a latch on the door made the church house the perfect place for poker on wintry Saturday nights: a safe haven and a ward against the cold. Bobby and I stood shivering and with our breaths rasping, knowing that Haman Flowers was in there with his one hand and hard mix of rotgut shine, with the smirk of poker on his face and his shotgun within arm's reach.

"I don't b'lieve I'm through yet," Bobby said.

"With what?" I asked.

"The *hole*." His voice was iced.

I waited for a short time, both of us rooted in thought, before peeling away. The liquor had tagged Bobby, left him clouded and wanting more. I could only think in terms of less, the night having been too round with what I couldn't forget. When I walked away, I said I'd see him tomorrow, but he said nothing in return—just stood there, black on black with the night and the single mindedness of kicking what remained of the hole.

Fifty-Eight

Ben an' Bobby Got a Secret

Word of Haman Flowers came fast and full out. Wince Creed was the first to reach us, limping across the creek and onto the porch right about daylight and at the warnings of ol' Bartley. Others followed after him, some coming as close as the gate. Others hollered out from the edge of the road, each with his own account, but with the same ending. Haman Flowers had been killed. Shot to death on the Old Primitive Baptist church house steps. His chest had been blown clean away—at close range—same as Corbin Fairchild. The only difference being a bullet hole below Haman's left eye. I lay half awake, cold and disbelieving, listening, the smell of Mary Olive's pipe and the sound of her rocking drifting on the same air as Wince Creed's bloody tale. I edged out of bed and into the kitchen.

"Brutal," Wince said, shaking his head like it had been one of his own children. "Bloodiest damned mess ever was."

Mary Olive hacked and leaned over to spit in the coal bucket. "Shame," she said, "but tell me again 'bout 'at bullet hole in his head."

"In his cheek," Wince said. "Below his left eye."

"You want a cup a' coffee, Wince?" Seriann said, butting in.

"Another time," he said. "Right now, I reckon I ought take word to Haman's old woman, Emmaline." He nodded, sure of what needed doing. But dread seemed to weigh in on him, hold him in place. "You know," he said, his voice coming like an interruption, "It ain't on me to talk ill a' the dead, but I don't reckon they's all that many carin' all that much ... if you know what I mean?"

Mary Olive pushed her tongue into her cheek and pretended to cough, then recommenced to rock and send smoke rings up near the ceiling. Seriann continued to knead flour and water into flat little cakes, and dropping them into a skillet of hot grease. Wince craned his neck to take a closer look.

"Hoecakes," she said. "Just the thing with molasses."

I left right on the heels of Wince, and sprinted the quarter mile to where Virgil Blair and a sizeable team of on-lookers milled about, pie-eyed and taking up what space there was between the church house and the road. Haman lay sprawled across the steps like something that had been buried, then dug up by dogs. A brown hole called out from his chest like it had been opened with dynamite. And there was that speck ... that dot ... below his eye. A bullet hole, they said: powder burns to prove it. The sight of it put me in mind of vermin snuffed out and left to rot. I slunk my way to the back of the church, leaned against its sanctity, its sagging timbers and the frost that clung like paint. It was a place without eyes where I could, if only for a minute, take some deep breaths. The sight of Haman with his mouth agape and his flesh withered in the rime—his time on earth over and done except for the stench—had been more than I was ready for. The wintry air, new and clean, helped keep me upright.

Thoughts of Saturday night turned over in my head like one of those newsreels at the Weddington. Did I know more than I wanted to? What was there, anyway, besides bits and pieces of this and that? Certainly nothing beyond things circumstantial, things gummed up for the most part, meager against what prowled the heart and mind. Still, there were things ...

Virgil lingered over it all, easing here then there, between this and that, listening, watching, waiting for High Sheriff Garland Sawyers to come zipper everything up. *Who, what,* and *why* lay etched in Virgil's face. We locked stares at one point, but only for a moment. Still, there was something in his eyes that said *I know more'n you think I do.* It was a look that left me sweating despite the cold. I tried easing away without him noticing, but I knew him better than that. Still, I hugged the hill all the way to the back of the schoolhouse, then headed for Bobby's.

I had a feeling Virgil was dug in, certain of his oath to uphold the law, which was, too often, a curse—and, too often, as lethal as it was binding. Postured and anchored to the rudiments of duty, he was, wherever it led him, even when it came to the good riddance of Haman Flowers. Then again, he may have been like the rest of us when lights were out and thoughts came unbridled and without solution: alone and trying to get to a safer place, numbed and not caring all that much.

Bobby was sitting on an overturned bucket holding his head in his hands. The barn was freezing cold and Ben was sitting behind him in the corner of a stall, his knees drawn to his chest, rocking and mumbling. "Ben and Bobby got a secret. We got a secret, don't we Bobby? Ben and Bobby's secret. Right, Bobby? Ben and Bobby. Our very own secret." Again and again. Rocking. Rocking. His eyes flat and fixed, and full of what he chanted.

I moved closer to Bobby, touched him on the shoulder. "You awake?" This only made him slump a little further, but only for a second. He rolled his head, then examined his hands like they were apparitions.

"Ben and Bobby got a secret. Right Bobby? Ben and Bobby's Secret ..."

"You still look puffed," I said, my eyes working between him and Ben, "where Homer worked you over."

He looked up as if seeing me for the first time, words seeming to lay dead on his tongue. The cows moved about, lowing, their sacks full.

"You need me to help you?" I said.

He stood and straightened himself, then held tight to the wall. "Me an' Ben..." he said, trying to think through the tear in his mind. He rolled his eyes from me to Ben, then squeezed them shut, still holding tight to the wall. "Me an' Ben..." he said again, holding his hand up to keep me from speaking. "We..." And that's where he stopped. I waited, knowing not to press. Just waited, me and the cows, their eyes wide, their sacks stretched and veined. "You need to go home," he said, his voice rough as husk.

"I come to tell you 'bout Haman Flowers," I said. "He's dead. Found shot to dea–" He waved me off, stopped me in mid sentence.

"Go on home," he said. "Just go on home."

The very next day Aug dug a grave deep in some empty holler clear the other side of Griffie Knob. It was a day's work: the going and coming, the digging and the burying. "Back country" is what Aug called it, where the head of Snake Branch connected with the head of Winston's creek; where it collected and opened to a flat shadowed in pitch pine and black gum; where it lay undercut with chinaberry and winter creeper, wild hydrangea and green briar, all the things that whispered day into night, and lay undisturbed but for hawks and the wind. It was right handed from the head of shop Branch, up the ridge and out of sight of human kind, out and away from that lone arch of rocks stacked and left by the Cherokee for us to wonder about (some say more than a hundred years ago on their way to the Cumberlands, to Tennessee and the Carolinas). It was the place where Aug took Haman–wrapped in burlap sacks and laid across the back of Mule.

"I went an' got him soon as Wince Creed come with the news," Aug said. "I wadn't there no time when Garland Sawyers told me I could take him. They was plenty still millin' about; took four of us to heft him across Mule's back. I walked him outta there same time that Garland and the coroner drove away. I kept watching over my shoulder at Virgil scratchin' around, looking for what he could find."

We sat around the table with little to no eye contact listening to Aug's account, guilty with pleasure at Haman being gone. We were quiet and attentive for the most part–Wilma Lee a little more than the rest of us–and allied but for Little Sherman wanting to know who Aug had buried.

"His dog," said Mary Olive.

"What kind was it?"

"Mongrel."

"You put him in a coffin?" Somehow, they were all the right questions.

"Weren't no coffin," Aug said. "Nor no marker, either. Just dropped him in the way he was. Covered him in dirt and come on home. Already forgot the way back." Aug stayed on till after dark.

It wouldn't be his last time.

Fifty-Nine

A Thousand Times a Thousand

Winter was full upon us, dustings of snow sweeping back and forth across the yard and our fallow-gray garden, its wind howling across the porch and under the door. The draft around the windows reduced the curtains to hurtful little dances, and whistled past the pieces of cardboard wedged where we thought they would do the greatest good—the lot of us layered and staved against what kept us reaching for life around the stove.

"Seriann?" I said with an uplift to my voice, questioning.

She said nothing, just lifted her eyes, pausing for a moment from some patchwork sewing. "Remember," my voice tuned to the stove's low rumble, "what you said about wanting your face to be the last thing Haman Flowers saw before he went off to hell?"

Her eyes were all-seeing, feral. She laid her sewing down and swept her mane back off her face. It was late and we were alone except for Mary Olive asleep on the half-bed by the stove, her jagged breathing as assaulting as the camphor she kept rubbed on her chest. I waited, gave way to the light drum of her fingers on the table. Testing Seriann was risky business, even in the best of times. Yet here I was, over the line and with no way out but the way I came in. She cocked her head and raised her eyebrows. A gesture that said, '*What about it?*'

"I was just wondering," I said, my tenor soft and aimed downward, "if you meant it?"

She watched me for a time then went to stand by the stove, the silence between us slipping in and around all the places we chose to hide. "There's not a day," she said, her gaze hard on the newspapered walls, "that Corbin don't come to me; not a night he don't make his way to my dreams; not a time I can't feel the knife of his bein' gone twist its way into me." She stopped, caught by her thoughts. "It ain't sump'm I'd wish on another livin' bein'," she said. "An' it's with all my heart and all my mind—my body and my soul—that I meant it a thousand times over. A thousand *times* a thousand." She gathered deeper into her wool sweater, into her own arms. "Haman Flowers cain't never be dead enough for me," she said, "or gone long enough, either."

That was how she left it before easing off toward the upper room, her shadow leading the way, dark into darkness. I stayed up just long enough to bank the fires and put out the light, to get lost in what she said. I don't know that her words brought me any closer to knowing what part she played in Haman's demise, if any, only that I was certain of no longer wanting to know.

The wind continued to rattle the windows long after my attempts at sleep. I could feel its lift, even there under the quilts, like a pulse in the walls. I lay with my back pressed against Wilson's, part of me praying that the cabin's frail bones would hold through the night, that it wouldn't splinter and pull apart. The other part of me was tormenting with visions of Seriann, Bobby, and Hooker, and wondering where they were when Haman was shot. It was never a question that Haman deserved what he got—not in my mind anyway—but the troubling idea of someone close to me pulling the trigger kept me tossing way into the night. Had Seriann gotten up before daylight, then slipped out and back while we slept? What had seized hold of Bobby? What had he and Ben seen? *Done?* What secret did they share? And what about Hooker "*having sump'm he needed to tend to*" in the middle of the night?

My mind felt chased, the air in me sucked out. The glow of the grate flickering against the loft came as the lone comfort, its milky umber helping to melt away what was left of me. It was easy to see that my world now was not the same: changed forever, along with those I loved. The longer the wind pushed and added its trial to the cabin's brittleness, the more I understood that any one of them could have—and *would* have—pulled the trigger if they'd had the chance. But then, like most everything else, it was all a matter of how I wanted to believe.

Snow fell in great clumps the day Dixie came home, flakes the size of buttercups weighing pine boughs clear to the ground. There was whiteness to it like I'd never seen; spotless and adrift in its own light; heavy and silent and full of Christmas. Grandmaw came, too, her clothes tied in a bundle, her cures in a kit bag. Wellness was never any more at work, crystalline and new and settling on us inches thick, like the snow.

Tearful was the way we started, the way we always did, gladness being at the heart of it, Dixie's return adding its own high tide. Still, the snow was no less forgiving, ever-thickening despite our celebration. But it was Truman and his urgency to get Dixie into Shop Branch before the snow rendered the roads impassable that brought it all to a halt, so quick to leave that hellos seemed to ride on the same breath with goodbyes. We ran after them, Wilson and me, the slip and slide of the snow holding us to half speed, our snowballs aimed at the Model-T's windows, though clear of their mark time after time.

The snow that day was like a bridge to all things, and we ran through it like it was our first time: scooped it, rolled in it, left prints of angels to catch the light of stars and guide the way of kings. It was lustrous in the early evening, encompassing yet set apart, as free of impurities as the embers at the bottom of the grate. I stood alone in its fresh breath long after Wilson went to sit by the fire, its wash reminiscent of brighter days, its cover sanctifying, despite what lay beneath it. Such fragileness—without error, infinite and tied to remembering—and for the briefest moment, allowing me to know that we were, one to another, enough.

Christmas came with the crush of Corbin's memories, the wrench of his image all-too familiar. It was a weight bullying us without letup, all the more condensed by the season. Woodrow took Christmas in Wyoming, right there at Fort Frances E. Warren, his leave-time exhausted. Still, he managed to send a ten-dollar money order, the same as he did most months, along with his letter of despair—only this time with the promise of marrying an Indian maiden, a Blackfoot he'd met in Cheyenne.

Lorali came Christmas Eve, joining us with an odd assortment of bags and grips, all with earnest intentions of permanence.

Bobby remained quieter than usual, the season failing to lift him above the hollow plane left by Corbin, even with the advent of Dixie.

There was a letter from Imogene waiting for me at the store, full of happy thoughts and bright tomorrows: all the things wished for, yet somehow bent on worsening what remained unsaid.

Cobbie Parsons came around about noon on Christmas day, giving our door a knock like he was suddenly amended with manners. He stood stretched out when the door opened, a tiny red box at the end of a long boney arm, and staring into the face of Seriann. Silence was never so loud, even after Wilma Lee moussed up behind Seriann. Then it was the three of them. Just standing. Blinking. Not saying a word. Cobbie running his hands through his cold wet hair and swiping at his nose with his coat sleeve, Wilma Lee ready to bite a hole in her lip, and Seriann standing still as backwater and with her arms folded across her chest. About the time I started feeling sorry for Cobbie, Wilma Lee, steered by some Christmas ghost, reached around Seriann and lifted the little red box as if not to disturb the life she imagined it held. Seriann never lifted her eyes, never shifted, just reached and closed the door. Slow. Methodical. Cobbie just stood there, frozen, his hand still outstretched, disappearing.

Grandmaw stayed on right up to the New Year, till Truman came to take her back to Pine Fork. She halted just before walking out the door, and turned to us all with the idea that Lorali would be better off if she was to come to Pine Fork and live with her—permanent like—now and forevermore. A little strangled sound trickled out of Lorali, a sound that caught and choked, her blue eyes giving way to red and what was becoming fogged and thickened with tears. A gift of gold couldn't have meant more. They left in a gentle rain, full of *what seemed right* and holding to what Mary Olive conceded was born of providence. For days, the rain filled in behind them, soft and clement, and dissolving what remained of the snow.

Except for the rudiments of survival and the time spent working for Old Man Andrew, winter painted us with its brutish skies, its impossible wait for color and life and all that rousted hope. But with the first signs of spring, Bobby was once again beginning to show signs of life, coming and going in a blur more than usual, stirring fires for nothing more than to put them out. He never talked about the night Haman Flowers was killed, never mentioned anything about what he'd said in the barn or what kept Ben cowed whenever I came around. Even when I asked, which was only once—months later—he looked at me like he was all of sudden without a compass, then dismissed it as unworried as shooing a fly, like I'd never said a word, smiling it into oblivion. But then I never told him what I knew about Ben, what I'd seen that night from the backseat of Hooker's car. After a time, not telling only deepened the reason why I shouldn't.

Bobby courting Dixie began in earnest about the time the redbuds gifted the hillsides with their lighter shades of garnet. It was their bouquet that framed him, what he brought Dixie that first time. Aug had moved back in and met us at the door, invited us in with a nod then disappeared into another room even before we sat down. We took it as his approval. Almost at once, quiet crept in around us; thick burlap curtains and the turbulent eye of Emmaline hushing even a low burning fire in the grate. We smiled and thought of nothing to say, the dim light and pungent smell of ashes as starved as the places to sit. Fayella, pale even in the shadows, eyeballed us without utterance, combing and smoothing, combing and smoothing, the long gray strands of Emmaline's hair. With each breath, time seemed to move toward a darker hole. I was about an inch from heading out the door when Dixie finally came through the curtain. Her faint halo in the cabin's muted light was the last thing I remember before taking my leave. I had only Bobby's accounts after that, his talk of Dixie and what he had in mind for the two of them ... and for his taking over the world, of course.

What came to Bobby and Dixie in those first months of knowing they were put here for no other reason but to glory in each other, was tantamount to love, though most of it by fire. From one day to the next, each proved as passionate as the other about what made a difference, things often worlds apart. And though Dixie was a bedrock of ethics and morality, Bobby, in his growing context of Cornbread Red, was more a devotee of profit and all but dismissive of the laws that precluded it. For Dixie, life meant nurturing what God was so generous to give. Bobby's mental picture was somewhat narrower and never with the intention of nurturing anything without the likelihood of a return; *gain* being what lent itself to stability and authority, what readied him for life's inevitabilities. Though similar, they walked divergent paths; and though committed to the idea of '*to have and to hold,*' rivaled in the way it was done. Still, the greater gift—what they brought to one another—continued in an upward spiral. And though there were times of thunder and rain—to where it threatened to wash the ground out from under them—and when there were devils and lightening in the wind—and nights as dark and long as hell's fire was consuming—they never gave in—to the storm or to its eye. They were Bobby and Dixie ... and they never shrunk from it, never turned from its adoration and what was burned into creation from the beginning. It was just that way: the way, they were certain, it was meant to be.

We went back working fulltime for Old Man Andrew that summer, Bobby and me. Letters from Imogene continued steadfast, as dependable as the sun coming up; some coming back-to-back and before I could even answer the first. They were full of high notes, things spiked with interest and bearing reasons for her staying gone, opportunity topping the list. They came in all manner and variety: perfumed and with petals of roses; some inked on the fairest stationery; some penciled on notebook paper; some with snapshots of Ellis, Sophie, and little Jerry Jeff: and one with a sketch of the rope swing outside her window. They were easy for the most part, eager for another: fragments of the heart, as best I could understand. And while I was glad she was caring enough to write so often and with such expectation, I was, in the end, left to sort what came from her goodbyes.

Sixty

Skip-Step Music

It was nearly midnight and dungeon black when we pushed Corbin's Model-A from behind the barn and into the lane. It took Ben to get it out of the mud, the juice from a quart jar of pickles as his price—that and the promise of us taking him along. Once in the road, and with the clutch in, Bobby kept us in a quiet roll all the way to Mary Olive's, and out of Olin and Gracie's earshot. After a dozen or so cranks, and to the already drunken laughter of Clifford, Preston, King Charles, and Cobbie, we were in a dead heat to Pikeville.

Both sides of the long driveway leading up to *Invictus*, were lined with cars of every ilk, bumper to bumper and spilling three and four deep into the grass. We parked out by the road and crept close, talking in low tones and hunkering in the shadows. Suits and ties came and went, pushed their way into the light with a range of sparkle and on the high notes of laughter and skip-step music.

"What the hell is this?" Clifford asked.

"I reckon if you was Old Regular Baptist, you might think it was hell." Bobby said.

"Looks more like heaven to me," quipped King Charles, his breath syrupy with 'shine.

We huddled like baby coons, eyes glazed and blinking: wilding. "*Opportunity* is what it is," whispered Bobby, looking us each in the eye, his smile wide enough to fly. It was always *opportunity* with Bobby.

Hooker Hopkins stood out like a riverboat in a hay field: obvious and Invictus' stamp of welcome, the one who tended the door and bid good evening to those coming and going. His being nearer to seven foot than to six, and with enough material in his suit to cover a milk cow, made his giant sway as intimidating as it was calming. He was deliberate, but cordial, an overseer and enforcer sporting the genteel. I could only imagine his new image was Ruby May's doing, and more for her sake than for Hooker's.

"We goin' in or we just gonna sit here?" Preston was full up on nerve.

"Go ahead," said Bobby. "Just tell 'at little sumbitch at the door to get outta the way. Tell him who you are an' where yer from. That oughtta straighten his tie."

"I know who he is," Preston said. "Ain't many who don't. An' I know you'ns is tight. That ort get us in."

"They's a might more to it than that," Bobby said, his grin devilish in the faint light. "An' none of it includes broke and hungry."

Right then light spilled into the yard, past Hooker's silhouette in the doorway. He was saying goodnight to an older gentleman, and good evening to a couple coming in. It was then that Ben stood up with his arms raised, like a bear standing on its hind legs, like he was wanting a hug. Hooker paused, stepped in our direction, then stood staring, disbelieving. They looked like father and son: oak trees come to life, bonded by a one-time carrying of a coffin. In the midst of their connection, Bobby scrambled us back into the night.

"RUN RASCALS!" Hooker yelled, his laughter rolling up our backsides, "'FORE I TURN THE HOUNDS LOSE!" Within seconds, we were squeezed and jammed together once again in the Model-A, fighting for air and a place to be loud. We found it at Haney's.

The swish of taffeta and clouds of perfume descended on Ben like gentle rain once we walked through the door. Arms draped him lightly, heavenly, laid feather-like across his shoulders. And there was the print of lipstick on his cheeks, the tease and the play—all for Ben. Mountainous was a curious draw and Ben swelled in the light of it, seemed to grow even thicker because of it. Revelry was the name of the game, and it overtook us, became us, entwined us with the jukebox and the blaring sounds of bluegrass and honky tonk, its music fueling the room with rank heartedness and the want to devil. But then there was the bewilderment on Ben's face, giddy but profound, and not seeming to matter except to Bobby. He watched Ben like a mother watches her young, as if he knew things better off forgotten.

Bottles of ice-cold Schlitz repeated time and again on the strength of Cobbie's sawmill dollars, but then came to a sudden halt when the state police rolled up close to the front door. Duck and dodge and every man for himself beat a track out the back, toward the cover of darkness and the rushes along the river. Ben ran with us without knowing why—and with one of the girls under his arm, his prize. It was a pleading, scolding Bobby that finally set her free. After that, river fog settled in behind us, covering us until the lights in Haney's went to dark and the crunch of patrol cars on Haney's gravel road wound slowly away. Minutes later, Pikeville crept into view, its dim lights reflecting off the Big Sandy, then fading like love gone wrong in our rearview mirror.

Except for Angus Walker's pool hall, Greezy lay forlorn at three in the morning. It was right when we turned up Main Fork and passed in front of the church house that Ben's voice broke through the cussing and tough talk like a bullhorn. "BEN AND BOBBY GOT A SECRET. DON'T WE, BOBBY?"

Bobby swerved and reached to put his hand over Ben's mouth, his face a ghost. It was only a second: a brake, a skid, the front end clipping a fence post in front of Judge Lewis' and coming hard against a rock. It was like a log ride over a waterfall. We all piled out, cussing and laughing, then stood around wondering what to do about a busted tire and no jack. One by one, Preston and Clifford, Cobbie and King Charles peeled away and stumbled toward home, leaving Bobby, Ben, and me shivering in the early morning cold with nothing but a lug wrench and the light of stars. That's when Bobby got the idea to remove the lug nuts and see if Ben could pick up the front-end just long enough to switch out the tire: off with the flat, on with the spare. Preposterous until Ben squatted over the front fender, until the whole right front-end seized in a groan and came off the ground like it was under a black magic spell. Ben stood there, human granite that he was, locked and braced, the front-end of the Model-A caught in his hands like a tin wagon, defying gravity, and Bobby twirling the lug nuts like we had all night.

We drove till we got past Mary Olive's, then shut it off and pushed it the rest of the way: *up* the road, *up* the lane, and back into the mud behind the barn. It was four in the morning and we stood halted by a darker-than-dark, pre-dawn sky. Bobby disappeared just long enough to come up with another quart of his mother's pickles. In one huge upturn, Ben swallowed the whole of its juice. It was easy relishing in Ben's delight, and the way it left us smiling clear into our socks. I don't know that I ever felt so good, or as alive.

I strolled on home after that, the brilliance of morning stars cold and crystalline and frosted as thought. I couldn't sleep after crawling in beside Little Sherman, and lay awake in the craw and crow of roosters, watching the shadows from the mountains roll away. There was a song to the mountains that morning I couldn't quite understand, only the impression they left; one that reached into the part of me where things lay ancient and undisturbed, making me know I was as tied to them as to the faces Almighty God sent to steer me. We were one, the mountains and me, inclined toward loneliness and all that would be free. It wasn't until Mary Olive drew back the curtains and allowed the softness of dawn inside, that sleep had its way. That was the last Saturday night, for years to come, that Bobby and I spent together.

Sixty-One

Dangerously Full of Wonder

After Ruby Mae and Hooker came to an understanding with Pikeville's elected, after everybody understood his piece of the puzzle, a sense of teamwork seemed to surface and fill the void left by Corbin. But it was Bobby not being a part of it, even after continued petitions, that set him to another course. Hooker and Ruby May cared for Bobby in much the same way Corbin had, but refused to involve him in the operation. His being big enough and tough enough was never a question; it was simply a case of *too soon*. They weren't about to put him in harm's way just yet, in big part due to Corbin's memory. But then there was also Olin Yonts to deal with if something were to go wrong—which, in their line of business, was all too frequent.

At the gut level, Olin Yonts knew everybody who was anybody in Pikeville: judges, magistrates, constables, bankers, lawyers, council members, sheriff, and jailer—all the good ol' boys who made up its political backbone: the very ones Olin campaigned for and knew like kin.

From the stock market to the courthouse steps, Olin Yonts was a gentleman farmer of the highest order, and the go-to person come election time. It was a station he commanded from an unofficial position of power. Without him elections could veer wildly off course, something those running for office were acutely aware of, and all too willing to make good on by granting him the rights and privileges of their very own. In the overall scheme, Olin Yonts was nothing short of collateral for Pikeville's cadre of political elite; someone who could and would get out the vote, and someone they loved to protect; his influence with voters being the sort of thing that forged friendships and futures in the same handshake ... and if Olin made a dollar or two in the process, well, that was just fine too. It was worth every penny. What were friends for, anyway?

Two dollars, a half pint of liquor, and a ride to the polls was what it took to seal a vote, to eliminate fate from the equation and give surety to the destiny of Pike County. The voters enlisted with Olin because Olin said it was the right thing to do. Simple. Such influence. And of course the two dollars and the liquor didn't hurt. All in all, it was a political process in the mold of one good ol' boy looking out for another.

Beyond the incalculable two-dollar transactions, a little something for his gasoline and time (and the liquor of course), Olin never asked for much, but when he did, it was little effort for friends in high places to make sure he got it. Clean, quiet, and under the table, things got done the way Olin wanted with no one ever the wiser—and for the most part, no one too terribly disadvantaged. Theirs was an all-around mutual respect, as deep as their all-around mutual fear.

So when Hooker and Ruby May decided that Bobby was not quite ready for what they had in mind, they were, in the long view, guarding against the reach of Olin Yonts' retribution in light of what might veer off course. It was highstakes, with highstakes risk. So, at least for the time, it was a solid No to Bobby.

Olin knew all there was to know about the gentlemen's club, about Invictus, and although he stayed away, he knew those who made it a habit. It was what came to those highly trusted. Still, he was never averse to realizing an additional dollar where one could be made. So, when Hooker and Ruby May set about to ready Invictus for bigger game, it was Olin they turned to, because it was Olin who got things done, who mustered Pikeville's influential to the lights of Invictus. As far as Greezy Creek's Old Regular Baptists were concerned, Olin's wheeling and dealing was *just business.* They not only saw him as a source of strength and power, but a bonus to have him on their roles ... and that, in the long and short of it, was good enough.

After Ruby May put all the pieces in place, she went back to West Virginia. Hooker continued doing what he always did, but now with the added concentration of Invictus. He had, by default, taken over the biggest part of the moonshine trade for miles in either direction; and though a portion of the profits was divvied up as a gratuity against *uninterrupted operations,* there never seemed to be anything but plenty for all—a fact that never got away from Bobby. But after nearly two months of trying Hooker's patience, Bobby finally gave up and joined the Army. He was tired, even at sixteen; had reached his limits with farming and working for Old Man Andrew, of waking up to the same old sun. The Army was the perfect out, and he left with only a simple goodbye. He just wanted to be gone.

A month later Bobby was back. An official letter from Judge Lon Paul Aldridge saying that Bobby was only sixteen, and with school records to prove it, was all it took. Olin had prevailed once again. A week later, Bobby up and joined the three-C's, the Civilian Conservation Corps: an arm of Franklin Roosevelt's New Deal that put thousands to work clearing timber, building roads, and helping reforest public lands. In the wake of all the mines closing, it became the answer to Appalachian joblessness, connecting hundreds of miles of public roads and opening us up to outsiders. Overnight, it became Bobby's perfect escape—and this time with his daddy's approval. He just wasn't going to stay home any longer.

Bobby never ceased being at war with himself, with his struggle to pull free from *not having.* Nothing, it seemed, could ever come too soon or in big enough chunks. He thought big and played big, his drumbeat filling him with the want to suck the life out of everything every minute. What couldn't be latched onto and reeled in on the spot, was road-mapped for a later time. But seeing as how life was too arresting for timid portions, it only stood to reason that Bobby would grab what he could while he could, and that I'd be pulled along in his wake. But this time was different. Despite our being partnered thick as blood, I went back to school while he went off to the three-C's.

Before he left, I made one last trip with him to the top of Ripley Knob, a goodbye we shared with the cows. We climbed indifferent to the slopes and sloppy with remembrances of Saturday nights. We stopped close to the big oak tree where he kept his lard bucket buried, moved the flat rock out of the way, and lifted the lid the way we'd done dozens of times before. We stood there in a clouded stillness looking into a cavern as hollow as the wind stirring through the pines. "You know what that is?" he asked around a hardened grin. I looked at him dead-on and waited. "It's all that's left of our Saturday nights."

I never knew Bobby when he wasn't aiming to walk on water, or test the limits of what tried to confine him. To him, it was a matter of staying close to the pulse of things, to what linked him to hope. For the most part, I was timid to Bobby's ways, a left foot down to his right—but not enough to turn me around. Over time, it proved a gleaning: trimming and laying wide what needed to be opened up. But it helped me to see the connection: the pipeline that ran between us, intricate as it was. And though it fed me from sources calloused to what set my mind at ease, I still held fast to what it gave, afraid to let go in the midst of the ride. Loyalty seemed to be what emerged, what bolstered me with a sense of belonging. From there, fear took a backseat, became less of what I was. I knew fear well enough, the self-induced constraint that tried keeping me from going to places I knew I was meant to go if life was to be lived, if there was to be any life at all. Bobby was that leg up, that push that took me to the next rung; his odds-and-ends brand of chance that hammered away at the steps I needed to take. Still, there was that part of me that wanted less jeopardy, that wanted to cling to the familiar, to the more solid tracts of ground. I'd come to accept that side of me: the fragment that remained anchored and shaped around things common and better known. But I'd also come to accept Bobby for the abandon so fastened to him; that oversized part of him that lived for risk and always at the expense of peace. And though I was far-flung from such risk and the price it exacts, it was never far from me. I saw it often enough, muscling its fair share from the part of Bobby insisting on being Cornbread Red.

"Yer a dandy on a mission, Bobby Yonts," is what Mary Olive said to him as he was fixing to leave for the three-C's. "And," she added with a fresh pipe, "dangerously full of wonder."

Sixty-Two

Absent of Anything Common

After Bobby left for the three-C's, life seemed to take on the unremarkable, laid-by like an autumn field, seedless and without variance. In and around us, life droned and dwelt with an off kind of regret, a laxness against the thornier rudiments of our everyday climb. Even our nights of theater were all but gone, even at the trying. The loss of Corbin was still too new, his memory a weight far too severe for much beyond melancholy, Seriann being the proof of it. Just the mention of his name was avoided for the sake of accord. There was only one time that I came close to it, and then only indirectly: when Seriann sat closed-gated, the smoke from her cigarette rising and disappearing, the fire in the grate next to going out and she not caring one way or the other.

"Hey," I said with more whisper than voice, trying feebly for a connection. She rolled her head then lowered it, a weight all at once too onerous for effort.

"Don't know what it'll take to smother my hate," was all she said. The night stretched before us, muted, infinite. She added a bit more wood and coal, her frame bent and tender. We went silent after that, both of us in the soft glow of firelight, the thought of Corbin pushing down. It was as close to mentioning his name as I cared to get.

Snows came and went, as did suns and moons, as did hillsides ripe with color and then blank of it, over and again, from one season to the next. Bobby dotted our presence when whim and leave time allowed, but even then, devoting most of it to Dixie. He had cut a decided path for himself on the road to Shop Branch, a gate that swung wide to his coming. And though he was fastened to Dixie hip and thigh, it was the three-C's that allowed him the cleanness of independence. He swore he'd never leave it without a plan that would lift him above the cow paths of Ripley Knob. There was never a hint of anything that suggested otherwise.

I continued to ride to-and-fro with Olin every day, all the while with an increased understanding of his influence: that not everything was the way it seemed, only that it had the potential so long as Olin Yonts had a say in it. Alignment with Olin's star carried dividends well into this life.

Imogene's letters continued, but shallow-breathed and without timbre; only missives of what was longed for, and, like mine, refusing to die. It was nearly two years before they took a final gasp, fading like so many dreams at first light and giving way to her contentment at being gone. I knew I had no rights to Imogene, no right to even claim that I did. Still, lessening my grip on her memory was like denying something natural. So I did what I thought was the next best thing: I let the line out as far as it would go without turning it loose. It was the thinnest of hope; still I allowed it for the sake of all else. The crude reality of her slowly becoming nothing more than a part of the past danced in and out of my mind, ragged-edged and exacting its own toll. I was weak to loss, fearful of its pain, careworn to avoid the more of it—even the least of it. I liked the idea of Imogene and me, the tension that clung to our letters, the complicity I imagined to be there. I wanted nothing to do with parting so I held tight to the line, to the last thread between me and what I saw as her growing rejection, the worst kind of loss. There was nothing preventing me from letting go except what waited in the way of longing; nothing that time wouldn't reconcile given enough resolve. But it was that push at the gut level, that insurrection of the spirit—low and way down—that I lacked, that kept me tied to what Imogene and I had become: worn and without luster. Yet it was the unknown beneath it all that moved to dispose me, to disquiet even my more harmonized parts.

In much the same fashion, Seriann took to her own ceremonies: pressing, in tried and tired ways, for what would become anew. And though we were in so many ways lost even to ourselves, we were not alone. There were always the tangibles: cats still came and went, as did gardens and crows and the clang of school bells, as did the amble of the creek and ramble of the road, as did the shadows and the sun on the mountains. We were born to it all, bent by its caprice—and for the stoutness it apportioned, made better.

Somewhere in the midst of it all, Wilma Lee hit her stride. She took to going to the store and making sure she was there when the mail ran each day, not so much for the letters she never received, but for the implications: her socialization, her coming out. It was time. And though Seriann was forever leery, it proved to be short lived; only a matter of days, in fact, before Wilma Lee came bounding through the door and with deafening clarity, announcing that she was "*gettin' married*."

With all that was predictable of accusation and outrage, plummeting even to the lower levels of her personal hell, Seriann erupted onto a stage as bloody as hog-killing time in November. Wakefulness was never any more indelicate or brutally brought to bear, and Cobbie Parsons was never any more verbally scourged and bared to the bone. She-devil executioner that she was, Seriann tongue-lashed Wilma Lee into a fiery pit. Charges of betrayal railed up and down the mountains and across the valley floor. "Behind my back!" "A disgrace!" "How *could* you?" Around and around and back again. In the end, it was exhaustion, plowed under and soaked through, that seesawed its way between them. For days there was no talk, no eye contact, only the deep, dense, simmering of minds waiting to let go.

Days later, when words finally worked their way up and out of Wilma Lee, we learned that it wasn't Cobbie Parsons after all that she intended to marry. "Well, who, then, in the name a' Jesus, is it?" Seriann's scorn was powdered and packed, but there was no answer, just a smile, broad and tortuous. Wilma Lee had scored a direct hit.

Two weeks into it, and with Seriann every bit a seething cauldron, Wilma Lee finally came out with it. "It's Aug," she said, her head low, her nose just above the gravy in her plate. "It's Aug an' me what's wantin' cobbled."

After a few days, the shock of Wilma Lee's announcement paled, then lost color altogether. Mary Olive's simple reminders that Aug was as good a young'n as the mountains ever made worked to thaw some of the chill that came off Seriann. In the end it was Aug over Cobbie, a trade-off Seriann came to embrace as an increase. Still, it was weeks before Aug got up the nerve to come around, then did it in the only way he knew how: with his head bowed and his words falling on the floor. His gentleness and having a heart for the right things were ingredients enough for Seriann. And so it was in the spring of 1940, on the first Saturday in May, and with the hillsides bedazzled with sweet clover, bluets and fire pinks—and all of them a part of Wilma Lee's bouquet—that we had us a wedding.

Wilma Lee never looked so dirt-free, her hair twisted high up off her neck and tied with a garland of rockcress, winking touches of teaberry and wood poppy, and wearing a white linen dress that lay softly off her shoulders and draped clear to the tops of her bare feet—all of it bringing her nigh to angels, and all of it Lorali's doing. Lorali stood taller than most, triumphant in what she'd put together a stitch at a time: the sweep of fabric, aired and billowy, and the embroidered crocuses and mayapple, elaborate and intertwining, and encircling Wilma Lee's waist in a brocade absent of anything common.

The yard was full by the time Wilma Lee stepped onto the porch. The running children, the roughnecks, and the loud talk stumbled to a hush the minute she came into view. There was quiet—like the laying on of hands—reaching clear into the road, recognition for what was radiance come to life. Except for quick breaths and a smile chiseled into her cheeks, Wilma Lee was the blown-up bride, and combed to advantage. Hats were removed and heads bobbed in agreement to her life-sized ascent. Mr. Tacket met her at the bottom step, offered his arm proud as a peacock and walked her with mincing steps through the gallery of neighbors and their snappish scents of rose water and pomade; past the daggered glare of cats lining the underside of the house, and Hillard

McPeet's mournful fiddling of "*Here Comes The Bride.*" Approval was round about and gaining: a flower here, a hand stretched forth there ... a sigh, a salutation, a wish. Sanction. Some were straight spined and stalwart, some softened and made to believe, each one taken by it in his own way, forgetful of all but the here and now. Young and old, men and women, neighbors and kin—a meadow of humankind, wildflowers all, pressed and painted—were living testaments to the throb of what was most certain to be love.

The yard had been swept clean and made ready with a mismatch of benches and chairs, most of them from the church house, and arranged to allow Wilma Lee a brief but furtive walk to an arbor loaded with sarvis blossoms. The early evening was mild, with a warming sun lingering in a sky as cloudless as it was blue. Cousin Truman and Aug waited under the arbor with the smell of fried chicken wafting from the kitchen stronger than it needed to be and mingling with the tobacco smoke from Mary Olive's pipe. From the beginning, and for the sake of abundance and long life, Mary Olive insisted that the ceremony be during the waxing—the *increase*—of the moon, and that the vows be made on the half-hour, on the rising of the clock's hands.

From start to finish, Cousin Truman was focused wholly on the sacred, his Bible opened to passages admonishing and encouraging, stirring us without excuse to God's law and what was required of man. I sat fidgeting between Mary Olive and King Charles, the smoke from Mary Olive's pipe coming at me from the left and the whiskey and onions on King Charles' breath coming at me from the right. A gentle breeze wafted but failed to cool, even seemed to make Aug all the more jumpy. Perhaps it was the hot breath of scripture or maybe it was more in line with what Preston and Clifford held to: the anticipation of the prize, the benefit and consummation of two melding into one.

About half of the guests were about half-drunk by the time Cousin Truman pronounced them man and wife, the final words not entirely out of his mouth before Hillard McPeet's fiddle tore into high gear, drowning out the sweetest of all proclamations. "*Ole Dan Tucker*" pelted us as fitful as the kernels of corn thrown in a steady rain. Alongside

Hillard, Eck Farley clawed his banjo into life; and next to him it was Wilson in a dead-dog run, hammering and tearing at the strings of his old flattop. Cousin Truman being drowned out seemed to make little difference. The ballyhooing and jousting, the scrambling after the chicken and what all was brought to pass, the fiddling and the nipping what was clear and full of fire, echoed from cliff to outhouse. Wilma Lee and Aug (our very own prince and princess, sealed for all time) paraded about in a sweat, hugging and shaking hands, until Ben, at Bobby's goading, caught hold of them. He lifted them both—Wilma Lee on one shoulder, Aug on the other—and walked them around the yard, Hillard's hair-raising fiddling of "*Turkey in the Straw*" clamoring the air.

Ben left right after setting them down, long strides marking his way home; chicken legs between each finger and his hands cupped over his ears, the least of it proving to be too much. Cousin Truman and his family left with Grandmaw and Lorali just before dark, along with the handful of Old Regular Baptists needing to ready-up for Sunday's cleansing. Olin and Gracie left a short time later, their girls in tow, before the whooping and hollering and clogging reached a point of no turning back, before the intake of *muleshine* turned the yard into a pure mud floor. Except for Rowland Yates's horse getting loose and tearing through the garden, and Darryl Sinners and Harlen Causey knocking the snot out of one another—rolling across the yard and into the creek, blood and mud flying ever-which-way, and Seriann finally stepping in to spray buckshot near to the top of their heads—things stayed pretty much within the bounds of biddable, if one was to overlook the intoxication, bountiful as it was.

Mary Olive made it to about midnight before I carried her off to bed with the help of Turner Phelps, but not before we interrupted Evelyn May and Cainy Billiter in the ultimate expression of pleasure right there on top of the quilt Lorali spent months putting together. It was only minutes later that Franklin and Fayella curled up beside Grandmaw, and only minutes after that that Dixie wedged out a spot right next to them. All the while, fiddlers and pickers spelled one another in endless rotation; Wilma Lee stepping up time and again to join her half drunk, red face to their jangle and clang: sometimes singing, sometimes flat footing, the mud oozing between her toes and blackening her wedding dress clear to the knees. Aug tried more than once to keep up, as did others—but except for stunted spurts from Seriann, Wilma Lee was unmatched. Her raw stamina and nips from the bottles of those all-too-ready to make the night a memory, made the difference, adding fire in ways common to those at long last free of shackles.

Seriann slipped in and out of the shadows most of the night, like a watchman to the crowd that refused to give up on a good time. But they finally conceded when first light made a silhouette of Ripley Knob. Aug and Wilma Lee sat on the porch, propped up only by the night's memory, staring off into the great void of mountains and hollows where they would carve out a life together. There wasn't much left to any of us by the time they slumped off to Shop Branch. Seriann watched after them, her eyes recounting, I imagined, what could have been with Corbin: what all was lost without him.

Here and there across the yard, one after another lay crumpled and liquored to the point of lifelessness, unmindful of the dew and chiggers and the rising screech of roosters. They would find their way soon enough.

After a time, Cobbie got to his feet—as drunk as any man could be and still be upright—just long enough to cry and slobber and say how happy he was for Wilma Lee. He finished by giving us a little goodbye salute, then staggered off with Preston, Clifford, and King Charles, each leaning on the other, a sober breath nowhere among them.

Bobby stayed without reason except what might come from Dixie, his solitude equaling that of the porch. Beyond the faint ripple and spill of the creek, he sat drunk and swollen and staring out across the road, the smell of whiskey and sweat clinging to him like yellow does to corn, yet with the early morning sky seeming to darken him.

"I can't tolerate but one drunk at a time," he said through a heavy breath, "and today, by hell, I'm it." That was the last of it before he staggered to his feet and got himself across the creek and onto the road. He looked like a stranger going away, detached even from himself. I wondered, as I often did, about his peace, if he would ever find it, and if he would ever know it when he did.

Within a month, Wilma Lee was back—bags and all—paradise not being all that easy to come by in the head of Shop Branch.

"It was 'em eyes," she said. "Emmaline's an' 'at litt'lin, Fayella. It bein' so dark up in 'ar an' them a-starin' at me outta the shadders. Creepin' 'round like they's cats; stalkin' me like I was sump'm to eat. Them comin' up behind me without even me a-knowin', like they's 'bout to snatch off a piece a' my hide. Never did hear a one of 'em utter a word. Just stare, mornin' to night. Look a hole right through ye. Make ever' hair ye got stand up twice. I got to where I was 'bout ready to grab me a butcher knife. Aug's gonna have to find him another, 'cause this'n ain't a-goin' back. Not in this lifetime."

Took nearly two weeks for Wilma Lee to give it another try, Aug's pleading and Seriann's hardened tongue finally getting the best of her. Two weeks after that, she was back again. This time it was Haman. "I could hear him of a night," she said, "scratchin' out by 'at log where Emmaline cut his hand off; him a diggin' 'round fer it I reckon. An' many a night I could hear him a-walkin' 'cross the porch, see his shadder in the window. You think I'm a-lyin', don't ye?" Our eyes jerked from one to another: looks of puzzlement and bewilderment and pain. We hunkered closer. "An' there wadn't nobody told me 'bout his well, an' it bein' lined with tombstones. I know you'ns think I'm crazy." We pursed our lips, rested with deep wrinkles in our brow ... and waited. "An' 'em *goats*," she said. We leaned in. "'Em goats is what's carryin' his ghost ... what ate his hand. It was Franklin what told me. An' I don't b'lieve it'd take much fer 'em to start eatin' on *us*. It's his name in their mouths. Haaaaaamon. Haaaaaamon."

I don't know if it was fate, or chance, or some quirk of nature, but within a week of Wilma Lee being back with us, Emmaline was gone. "*Heart just give out*" is the way Aug explained it. He found her in the early morning, sitting with her mouth and eyes wide open, and with Fayella combing and smoothing, combing and smoothing, her long gray hair. Days later, after Emmaline went in the ground, a man and woman, official looking, with papers and a state trooper by their side, came and took Fayella away. It was for the best, they said; she'd be in a place that could care for her in a way she needed, even help her get better. We all knew it was the crazy house.

With Emmaline and Fayella now gone, and with Aug's promise to get rid of the goats for a milk cow, Wilma Lee agreed to give Shop Branch one last try. And though Mary Olive's thought was that the people from the crazy house ought to have taken Wilma Lee along with them, she later thought how lucky they were to have left her where she was. "Lord knows, they'd more'n likely end up just like her if they's to be around her very long." Still, Wilma Lee kept the road hot with her to-and-fro, though over time became less and less intrusive and more and more pregnant.

In the four years I ginwhacked for Old Man Andrew, Virgil and I never got much beyond simple hellos and half salutes, all that either of us wanted to bother with. It wasn't anything disrespectful, just a social disconnect that never seemed to narrow, yet nothing that either of us let make a difference. Fact was, there was an ease that came from not having to grouse around for something to say, though I was sure he was as capable as any, should the occasion arise. Things stayed that way right up till the time Ester Riley came around, beaming with news of Imogene being engaged to some well-to-do from Lexington. I was sweeping the porch at the time and don't remember much of anything except trying to smile, which I was sure looked like anything but. I watched and waited while she carried on, while her words went out to one after another. It was news that touched me with a cold hand, reviving, yet again, the darker side of remembering.

I waited until Ester and her news left for home before giving in to the sting of it. She walked off not bothering with goodbye, contentment pointing her way. I don't know how long I stood there with the hot afternoon sun beating down on me before I heard Virgil. "Didn't marry till I was forty-year-old," he said, his voice out of the blue and with that from-the-bottom-of-a-well timbre. He didn't look up, just kept whittling a hickory stick to a point. I slumped down on the top step, heavy with the weight of Ester's news and with the broom still in my hand waiting for why Virgil offered up what he did. But then after a time, it was evident he'd said all he intended. I sat leaning against one of the porch posts and watching the whittled shavings pile up between his feet. Virgil's words had been a reach in my direction, a door opened just a crack and for reasons I couldn't explain, only that there was something agreeable to it.

"I get eight dollars a head for ever'one I jail," Virgil said, peeling back the bark on a sourwood stick. Virgil and I had come to where we talked most every day. Mostly it was him talking and me listening, him understanding the void that mulled inside of me. "Don't know that to be a rank point, though," he said, "'cause, fact an' truth is, I'm yet to do it a first time." He smiled real big, squeezed juice from his apple-size cud, and sputtered it careful-like into the Prince Albert can he used for a spit cup. "Cain't see the good in it," he said. "Me gettin' eight for puttin' 'em in and them havin' to come up with fifteen to get out. 'Sides, I ain't got no wheres to put 'em. Have to stand guard over 'em long enough for Garland Sawyers to get here, an' 'at's apt to take nigh on a week, dependin'." He let go with a deep haw, just one, then spit again. "Far as I can tell, just bein' on hand is plenty enough to keep most in line. But then, they's always 'at one or two." His eyes did a quick dart in my direction. "When's 'at Bobby Yonts comin' back around, anyway?" he asked, his knife blade against the sourwood as whispered as the wind.

Dixie was no less a surprise in the seasons that followed, spending disparaging amounts of time with Grandmaw and Lorali—Wilma Lee and her growing brood squeezing the life out of tolerance there in the head of Shop Branch. And then there was the imbalance of her waiting for Bobby, an annoyance even for the most stalwart of hearts. But then it was the need to be more, beyond what waiting could give, that brought her out of Shop Branch for the last time. It was at her asking that I spoke to Olin, asking if he could find her work similar to Imogene's: housekeeping and tending to children; what needs be. It was like Olin had it in his pocket all the while, just waiting to be asked. Without much beyond packing a bag, he had Dixie moved into the Haywood Pritchett House on the far lower end of Pikeville, a lush heap of a place with a lawn that rolled all the way down the bank to the river. Olin was a genie in a bottle.

Haywood Pritchett was one of Pikeville's more prominent attorneys, and not at all shy about his holdings. He was from money, and given to it even more by his profession. Although not always available to his wife, Avondale, and their three daughters, he was sympathetic to their seemingly endless and ongoing needs—thus, the addition of Dixie. Haywood was also an usher at the Methodist church, and an uncommon and most recurring regular at Invictus.

Keeping house and learning the Pritchett's ways came easy enough for Dixie, but then it was Avondale heartening that she continue with school—the high school being within blocks, and Avondale heading up the board of education—that edged her toward its reality. And so it was in the spring of 1941, and at the end of an arduous four years I hardly remember as anything remarkable, that I lay claim to a high school diploma, and Dixie took a first step toward betterment and self-rule. It was also the time when the last of Imogene's letters arrived with a picture of her in a cap and gown, straight-spined and blameless, with starch in her collar and a strand of pearls.

Resolute and unswerving seemed to say as much for Mary Olive as the granite peaks that filled the skies above us; her gristle and cure-all magic of moonshine (her *quivered lightenin'*) keeping her full-front to the wind. But then there was the will and the sharp edge of long-suffering that punctuated her soul: what was tailed to a storm. She was a root, deep and tangled, and reconstituted daily to all that was unwilling to go quietly. It was in and around her that life repeated in fragrance and touch and surprise; that Cousin Truman and Grandmaw, Lorali and the sustainable lines of family flowed in and out in faithful streams; that Little Sherman continued to warm us even after going off to school; that Wilson, in inexhaustible ways, persisted in trying our souls; that Seriann worked against the long dark of nights to wrench free from the loathing that saddled her; and that I allowed indifference a place too long filled with regret.

I went back working full-time for Old Man Andrew that summer, the way I had for the past four years. Only now there was nothing to mark the end of those days except the coming of fall, the store now an endless cycle without much in the way of alternatives beyond sawmills and coal mines ... neither of which came with the components of permanence. For the time, anyway, I was Andrew's. But then I came to realize that time was what I needed most. Necessary if the blinders were to be lifted and I could finally see what was meant to be seen: Imogene moving away from me at the speed of light.

The dry rake of autumn came almost before we were ready, its colors in a grand hoorah and readying our reserves for the long gray push of winter. Pearl took to bed about halfway through November, water-weak, but with a cough I could hear clear to the last camp house, coming and going; jags that left her bug-eyed and blue each time she started in, her breath never any more conflicted. Andrew was all-in attentive, but what with the ordering, the back-and-forth to the wholesale house, keeping the books and waiting on the timeless in-and-out of customers, inventorying the shelves, sorting the mail, and running to Pearl whenever it sounded like she was down to her last gasp, days lagged without spirit; the heaviness of it all helping itself to what was left of willpower. By the end of the second week, Andrew said he didn't know if there was enough left in him to even drop dead. "I b'lieve with all mah heart that Pearl's about done," he said, weightiness slumping his shoulders, pulling down on the lines around his mouth. I said nothing, just tried avoiding his eyes, not wanting him to see how right I thought he was. "We'll be needin' us some help real soon," he said, his tone done-in, confessional.

He closed his eyes and leaned up against one of the porch posts, the lack of sleep bending him in the way of a willow. "Church in the morning," he said, his voice faltering with the light. We stood braced by the chill, just the two of us in the gray of evening, in the haze that was soon to be Saturday night, allowing our minds to cool before we finally called it a day. I waited till he locked the door behind himself, then listened to the floor creak under his footsteps as he edged toward their little rooms and Pearl's relentless croup.

Sixty-Three

You Won't Be Out Much

Andrew had come early morning, stepping onto the porch and pecking on the screen door without Bartley as much as whimpering—uncommon for a dog aging and edgy as he was—like he knew Andrew—like Andrew had been there before. Even so, it had been Andrew's posture: humped in a knot and with his hat in his hand, offering to bring Seriann on at the store, that invited the firebrand in Mary Olive.

"If yer fixin' on payin' her what she's worth, you won't be out much," Mary Olive said, laughing out loud.

"I b'lieve we can work things out to where it's suitable," Andrew said, hope playing in his eyes. It was a wilted plea, not at all like a businessman in the habit of getting whatever he went after. For reasons I couldn't explain, Seriann was more intent on silence, leaving Andrew looking like his underdrawers had worked their way up too high. "I'd need you to start a-Monday," he sniffled in the direction of the floor. "Though Tuesday'll work just as well if it suits you better."

Not talking can oftentimes come across louder than its intended, the absence of anything to say carrying the sound of a ten-pound hammer on a steel rail. The passing minutes seemed to stand still in the light of sweat beads and body heat, and all that wants to be scratched. It's hard to tell what prompts such silence, or what sustains it once it comes, but there was something lingering in the air that was thick enough to cut; something that bade me to stand down. It wasn't until Andrew finally flopped his hat against his pant leg and turned to go that Seriann said, "Awright then."

Andrew stood for a moment letting her words take hold, but still without a full-on glance in her direction. "Would that be a-Monday or a-Tuesday," he asked, his eyes aligned with the stovepipe. When Seriann said nothing in return, he said, "I reckon either will be just fine." He excused himself with a nod and a slow turn out the door.

Andrew's coming by had been a full-on surprise, his proposal even more so; his unease topping it all. Mary Olive waited till the engine in his old truck turned over before she pushed her tongue into her cheek and sent me a darting look. "Well, now," she said, rolling her eyes toward the loft and drawing on her pipe, "I found that to be most innerestin'." Seriann busied herself with rolling a cigarette while Mary Olive continued to muse aloud, "What in the world," she said, her eyes still upward toward heaven, "would cause 'at man to come 'round here an' ask you, of all people, to come tend store?" Seriann flicked a stove match against the bottom of her chair and watched it burn close to her fingers before touching it to her cigarette. "I wonder," Mary Olive went on, "why is it—"

"'Cause there ain't another woman on this whole damned creek," Seriann interrupted, "without a passel a' young'ns to nurse an' a man to pick up after." She was her own indictment, aching with truth. "'Cause Rubin's showed him he's worth ever' dime he's worked out, and he's got it figured I'll be the same." She paused to drag squinty-eyed on her cigarette, not bothering to wave away the smoke. A minute later she stepped to the window, taking her thoughts with her. Outside, an icy wind whistled against the door, set the rockers on the porch to creaking and rattling what few jelly jars we kept on a shelf by the stove. Mary Olive contended herself with looks in my direction, passing me glances that said *there's more going on here than what decent folks are wantin' to confess.* I stayed right still till Seriann spoke out the window, toward the water bucket clanging against the well. "You reckon they's a chance a' me showin' my face at the store without people talkin'?"

"Not with them holes in your sweater the size of pie pans," Mary Olive said.

Seriann tugged at her sweater, gathering it tighter, wringing it for its morsels of heat. "I know how people talk about me," she said, "'bout what I've done; 'bout the men I've had an' the young'ns I got. But I can't give it no mind if I'm gonna have peace. What they think about me ain't none of my business, no way." She let go a tired sigh, as if the answer might be in the breath she blew against the window.

The stove baked full out, although its heat seemed to be in short supply against the coolness of what went unsaid.

Ol' Jake stood shuddering amongst a buildup of folks outside the store, his breath chafing the winter air what time Andrew passed out the mail. Virgil sat hunched in his saddle, resigned and ready for a bone-chilled Tuesday and the "*go-on*" of gossip. That was just before Olin Yonts eased his pickup to a stop smack dab in line with the middle of the porch. Life seemed to take a big sucking breath when Seriann opened the door and stepped out, her smile charging the frost that had overnight dragged us headlong into winter.

"Reckon you'll do just fine," Olin said, offering up encouragement in a voice louder than usual and marked with the say-so of a last word. Olin stood a head taller than most, his hat making him ever taller, his smile making him ever broader. He was expeditious, Olin was, holding court and rendering a verdict within a matter of seconds, his remarks weighing in with the strength of scripture. "Don't b'lieve it'll take her long to catch on," he said to the open air, like he was addressing a town meeting. "She's a good'n an' I s'pect Andrew'll be better off with her." Olin's declarations cracked on the icy air, seeped with unwavering certainty into the understanding of those already purple from the cold. All eyes turned to Andrew, his pear shape sweating under the arms like it was a dog-day afternoon. "Let me know if you need anything else," Olin said to him before tipping his hat all *refined-like* and easing his way back behind the wheel.

All afternoon, one after another filed into the store to see for themselves: Seriann in an apron and standing behind the counter like a fresh and pliant Pearl. After a time, Virgil Blair came and stood by the stove, warming and waiting his turn at ordering up a pack of Beechnut chewing gum.

"Never suspected there was enough room in that mouth for chewin' gum an' chewin' tobacco both," Seriann said.

"Ain't," said Virgil. "It's for you." And with that, he reached out with thick, weathered fingers, all knobs and knuckles and twisted with fifty-odd years of arthritis, and placed it like a bird new from its nest in her hand. "Yer gonna do just fine," he said, the gentlest smile illuminating the brownest teeth.

And so, at least for the time, Seriann was the new reality, slotted into a most visible place and as true as the jarring spasms that horsed within Pearl's chest.

Sixty-Four

Scorched With The Scent of Death

Static was pretty much all we could get on the radio, morning to night, coming through the speaker a lot like a milk cow chewing on meal. Even with a fresh battery, static got the biggest play. We were never ones to rely on the radio for much beyond what we could pick up on Saturday nights from places like Renfro Valley, and shows like the Grand Ol' Opry: shows that kept us glued to the fatherly intonations of Red Foley and the unpredictable jubilance that screeched and howled from the likes of Roy Acuff and Minnie Pearl. And though its place there on the bureau was silent for the most part, it elevated us during those times when words and songs could actually be understood; allowed us, even long afterwards, the taunt of worlds beyond our own. It had been a gift from Bobby, one of the many things he'd salvaged of Corbin's before his house was sold to Ruby Mae. Something he thought Seriann would treasure. And though reminders of Corbin seem to live there in its oak grain, we gathered round it like we did the fire, hunkered and still as mice, as if waiting for second-coming revelations, but then so often having to settle for the likes of pork prices and what we could expect to pay for feed, –twaddle that scratched and clawed the air like fingernails on a blackboard.

Radio signals were at steady odds with the mountains and its deep-veined hollows that worked round the clock to blunt even the strongest of waves. But that first Sunday in December, the mountains seemed to melt away, to lay low to news that trumpeted from the blackest fissures of our knowing: news that emptied into our cabin unhindered but for its trepidation.

Olin Yonts was the first one to us, then Cousin Truman, then one after another up and down the creek, their talk of wreck and ruin and what came scorched with the scent of death: Pearl Harbor and its reality filling us with its blotch and stain.

Sixty-Five

A Blister and a Boil to Angels

Christmas came and went with the weight of time. Its vague idea of goodwill was little more than a reminder of the hours before I joined ranks, before I marched off to places opening up to armies. News of war blurred our every thought, interrupting what we said and how we went about our days, its urgency made even bigger by the unknown. Fear and anger—even rage—harkened nonstop, belying what remained of good tidings. Newsreels down at the Weddington and Liberty brought its devastation within arms reach, shaped our intolerance and girded us for what was to come—its message an open sore, a blister and a boil to angels, despite our observance and inky jots of heralding.

Cousin Truman came by every day after I enlisted, spent time just talking, offering his heart and making sure I was anchored to the portals of scripture—those portions ripe for my understanding, anyway. Friends and family poured in 'round the clock, their goodbyes heavy-hearted and propped up with things like wildcat liquor and rhubarb pie. Come evening, we sat camped around the grate without much passing between us, mindful of the days till I was gone. Seriann smoked more than usual, and cried when I wished she wouldn't. Little Sherman went about like he was stuck to me: at night he slept in the middle even when it wasn't his turn, bareing the depth of his alliance. Wilson was excited that I was going off to whup the snot out of everything connected to the other side, and fuming mad at Seriann for not allowing his fifteen-year-old, unshaved face to enlist. Wilma Lee, as predictable as April rain, went about crying nonstop from the time she walked through the door to the time she left, day after day, making a scandal out of calling on the Almighty to bury alive all those who brought this on in the first place. Mary Olive was quiet beyond quiet, what I imagined was turmoil turned inward. When she spoke, it was of the devil and the weight he was to the world. I knew it as truth: her divining coalesced as spirits.

The night before I left, Truman brought Grandmaw and Lorali to help weigh-in against the imminent. We sat bunched in spirit, yet somehow unable to sound the depths of what was innermost: what begged to be said. Mary Olive was on edge from the start, and after a time eased off to the lower room. Then, before we wondered much about it, she eased back with a pint jar full to the rim with what she called '*a taste a' kick*.' Eyes were never any more open or accepting of light. A kind of thankfulness just seemed to swell up around us. After a time, and for reasons I couldn't explain, it served as a bridge to the bits and pieces of ourselves that we were incapable of uncovering: the uncertainty, and how it was hinged to all that sought to tear us apart. We sipped at Mary Olive's liquid corn, beholden to its razored bite and its thinning out what was left of reticence. From there we roiled into what fates we were certain awaited, all of which hardened the claim of our kinship. It was our inheritance to be resilient—even defiant should the need arise. Tonight was a bit of both, the bond of blood and the strength of no-tax liquor melding us into one.

"They's a darkness 'pon me," said Mary Olive, interrupting a lull. "Sump'm 'at's come against me this quarter, even before that Pearl Harbor war even got started."

"Cain't say we're geared up for yer third eye tonight, Mary Olive." Grandmaw was casual, stabbing at the fire like it was going to jump out at her, the poker nearly as round as her wrist.

"It's just sump'm 'at's been gived to me," Mary Olive said. "Been that way awl my life: seein' things plain folks ain't got no business knowin'."

"You reckon you might be a witch, sister?" Grandmaw raised her eyebrows in my direction.

"Ain't no way a-tellin', far as I know," Mary Olive said. "Alls I know is sometimes there's a whiteness to it, sometimes a blackness, an' all of it so plain to see that it scares me when other people cain't."

"You have any idea what other people say about you, Mary Olive?"

"I bet it ain't nuthin' I wanna hear. Am I wrong?"

"Well ... just that you dance with angels and sleep with the devil."

"I'd say 'at's about right. But how's 'at any diff'ernt from the Old Reg'lars?" It was here that Lorali clapped and rocked and caught her breath, muted laughter and the twist of liquor lifting her near out of her chair. How knit together we were in the mix of firelight and the distance of stars, how aligned and enlarged even in the thought of leaving. Still, the rumble of voices contended for what excuses there were for taking me off to places indifferent to Appalachian suns. But for this time and this place, and with the warmth of family and the frost of departing clashing for the upper hand, I had little doubt about what awaited me. Bartley seemed to know the truth of it and lay where he could see my eyes, watched me in a way mothers check children for breath in the middle of the night. It was a bruised reality, raw and a bit ragged despite the courses of liquor, and all of it vying for contentment. And though it was a time full of unknowing, it was the clarity of heart that lifted us in invisible ways, that kept us shaped to who we were, to our roots and raisings, to what was rolled in umbrage, and what waited with the promise of Saturday nights.

"I cain't help you none with the Ol' Reg'lars, Mary Olive." Grandmaw was pat, thankful for what light there was in good sense. "But seems to me they're likely to get past St. Peter without a hand from you."

"You reckon my *seein'* the way I do is liable to hold me back?"

Grandmaw laughed. "Law, honey, they's a lot more to it than that. You ain't exactly been a breath a mornin', you know. I s'pect your pearly gates to be more like iron bars."

"I ain't denyin' I done my share a' livin'," Mary Olive said. "Might've even gone overboard a time or two. Tryin' to get the most out of never bein' more'n twenty mile from where I was born an' raised, I reckon." She paused, telltale signs of recollecting consorting with the liquor. "A body's gonna peck around till it finds a home. May not always be worth a damn, but I ain't seen one yet that wouldn't trump a grave. But then bein' barefoot an' hungry never helped none; just made a home that much harder to find." She waited while she rocked, her steely silence gathered to what she kept salted away. "Mine's been a natty road," she said. "But I'm glad I walked it. But that ain't sayin' I wouldn't take some of it back."

"Wouldn't do you no good if you tried," Grandmaw said. "Lord already knows what all went on behind ever closed door you ever had. It's certain to be lightnin' when you're made to own up. How you come about that gold tooth alone might be enough to bring a mountain down on you. My guess is the Lord'll have to find a special place to put you." She smiled all sparkly-eyed and poked gently at the fire. "But I'll say one thing: I wouldn't mind havin' one or two of your memories."

Mary Olive chuckled, her smile broadening the room. "That's all there is, anymore," she said. "Memories. I just hope I don't lose my mind before I die."

"I b'lieve you may be well on your way," Grandmaw said. "I just hope you got enough sense to beg the Lord to forget, 'fore it gets too late. That way you won't have to ask Him to forgive. Ain't likely He would, anyway. I b'lieve it'd be askin' too much."

"Forget or not, forgive or not, they's still a darkness on me that ain't none a my doin'."

Grandmaw stood, straightened herself, smacked her lips like she wasn't quite finished with the last taste of *kick*, then added another log to the fire. "You been havin' these darknessess long as I can remember, Mary Olive. Besides you seein' things like snakes in the bed, what makes this time any different?"

"It's more like a feelin' this time than anything else. One minute hot, the next one cold."

"Well, what in God's name would you have us b'lieve it is?"

"The devil."

Right then, squat little choking sounds began gurgling up and out of Lorali, corn whiskey and Mary Olive being full of midnight taking her to a dissolving humor. "Now, Lorali, they ain't no sense in carryin' on," Mary Olive said, her tone condensed and avowed. "You're actin' like the devil's gonna waltz in here an' lift yer dress up over yer head."

"Might do us some good if he did," said Grandmaw. "'Course you know him a lot better'n I do."

"Just the same, it's for all our good to know it's his hand, inky black, that's on what's come ... an' what's yet to be."

"Well, it ain't the first time we been face-to-face with the devil."

"I'd say of late, though, he's got where he wants to make a habit of it."

"How is it, Mary Olive, that the devil's all the time rattlin' around outside your door?"

"His way a' strikin' up a friendship, I reckon," Mary Olive said, sipping and not bothering to pass what little was left in the jar.

"I b'lieve it's got more to do with you leavin' a light on for him."

"Now that just shows how much *you* know," Mary Olive said, her gold tooth flashing like sunshine on a raindrop. "*Light* is the very thing he don't *need*. It's darkness that he brings, an' what he leaves when he's gone."

"It ain't no mystery they's a darkness," Grandmaw said. "We're already in it. Pearl Harbor an' places we never heard of, armies a-marchin' an' comin' 'gainst one another. It's a darkness sure, an' it'll be draggin' us by the hair of the head 'fore it's done."

"What about the whiteness?" I asked, my voice like a wet towel slapped against a rock. "You said sometimes there's a whiteness to it." Stillness followed like it was practiced.

"That's the prized part," Truman said. "That's the Lord's hand coverin' it all. What commenced in blackness will die to whiteness." His voice was full of declaration and guarantee. "Bible teaches we ought not listen to them with a third eye, but sometimes it's the *Lord* allowin' us to see. Cain't all the time be evil. Just look at Isaiah an' all the prophets. *They* were allowed to see. We just now beginnin' to see, if we open our eyes wide enough. It's a darkness proper right now, but it's plum fulla kingdom-come on the other end."

I sat across the table from Seriann, drinking coffee as black as her eyes and listening to the soft rumble of fire in the stove. We sat this way often enough, quiet winding in around us to where words became intrusions.

It was solitude of our own making, a kind of dwelling with things less provoking. Tonight was its high point, the idea of lives interrupted eking onto the only plain we knew, and blanching in the dimmest lamplight what we tried hardest to disguise: the fear that was most on our minds. But it was her steely silence that held us to what we kept locked away: those things that looked back at us when we closed our eyes.

Mary Olive lay heaped under a mound of quilts, her ragged breaths coming to grips with dreams. The in-and-out of her darkness was a trip we made more often than we wanted. Its vividness was at the heart of things out of hand, like it was with the righteous and intolerant in a world gone mad. The whole of it—the tangle and turmoil of war—left me feeling like part of an endless line, one of an untold count crossing the old troll's bridge, and knowing all the while he was down there with teeth quick and severe. I was certain that nothing could remain as it was, unchanged or untouched, save for those girded in hallowed traditions: those unwavering spirits inclined toward what all was wrought in Jesus. But over time I saw her darkness as the most visible light, despite it hovering and pointing toward the end of times.

We had spoken of war in the calm, attentive to keeping its fullness at arm's length. It was, in our estimation, the blunt end of things random and full of chance, of blurred dawns and the thing farthest from our Eden. What could we know of it, beyond its shamelessness to make us over? It was the farthest thing from change any of us ever wanted. The only hope was the whiteness to Mary Olive's reverie, and that it be all Cousin Truman claimed it to be.

I don't know how long Seriann and I sat gripped in stillness before I drifted off, before sleep slumped me forward on the table, my head pillowed in the crook of my arm. Roosters brought me back, sat me upright to a reality as frayed and faded as the tablecloth's pattern of tiny bluebells worn near to white. Seriann sat watching me, the way I was certain, she had all night: with eyes fitful for sleep. I don't remember Truman ever leaving, only his coming through the door with Inez, their figures barely a silhouette against daybreak. Then, one after another, we filled in around the table and sat like a tribal council, our talk low and in-between sips of coffee, thoughtful and full of solemn breaths. Cold biscuits (yesterday's) and apple butter sat ignored in the middle of the table, the idea of eating as weak as the dawn. Dread seemed to hang with each beam of light that peeked over Ripley Knob, a sun ball that came way too fast—as did Olin and Bobby. Olin didn't bother sounding his horn, just waited with the motor running, and, I reckoned, with the same knot in his belly as the rest of us.

It was all so disjointed, those last few minutes, so run over and without the least connection to things lasting: bothered and dithered and without sense, a concentration of halts and faints and things lost to color. We said our goodbyes on the bank of the creek, in silence and with arms that refused to let go. "The Lord's hand's on it all," Grandmaw said, her voice murmured and bird like, her doily of a handkerchief pressed to her lips and their tremor. I said nothing, only watched out the back window as we pulled away; burned my memory with their bewilderment—huddled and as fragile as morning mist. I watched long after they were out of sight, until there was nothing left but the traces of snow across the mountains and a mud road that fell away behind me, one that wanted only to bring me back.

Part II

Sixty-Six

Emptied of Simple

Pikeville's Greyhound Bus Station looked like an Armed Forces Center when I arrived—the same, I imagined, as every other train and bus station in the country. We poured in from every corner of the world: soldiers of every kind, with families there to grab us and fall to pieces in our arms. We had come home from the South Pacific, Europe, even Japan. Japan was my last assignment, shipped there from the Philippines just three weeks after Nagasaki's collapse, just a short time after Japan said they'd had enough. As an M.P., I was part of Japan's occupation, part of the peace-keeping—radiation from the atom bombs being the last thing on anybody's mind. For months we'd heard how things were already over and done with in Europe. I guess they were just waiting on us, so the whole thing could be put to rest. Things were pretty much a blur after that, except for discharge papers pouring in like heavy rain. And just like that, my time was up: my duty rolled up behind me. I remember being handed my papers and feeling numbed to the core, the aftermath coming in a howl as exultant as anything I'd ever unleashed, in part to stave off tears. But then joy came in a multitude of packages, tears being one—drunk being another.

It took the Army three and half months to get me out of Japan, and then another seventeen days to float me across the Pacific to Seattle, Washington. They served us Christmas dinner twice on that boat ride: once before we crossed the date line, and once after. It was Christmas Day both times, and both times complete with all the trimmings. Seattle wasn't much to remember except for the rain and its sky being without a sun most of the two months I was there. Processing out was about as infinite as it was complex. Sending me straight home would have been far simpler than sending me on to Ft. Knox, Kentucky, but simple wasn't the Army's way. I could have walked home from Ft. Knox, and gladly would have, but the military's time-honored intricacy of bidding farewell, declaring us free from the diseases of war, took time. Three weeks later, they bought me a bus ticket to Pikeville.

Stepping off that Greyhound bus was like stepping into a sea of hallelujahs. There was only a handful of us that day, but the joy in the voices and on the faces of those who greeted us washed over me like a wave. I was gobbled up by pure strangers, hugged and passed from one to the next. It was rejoicing, resounding, and emptying into the streets stretched with red, white and blue banners. Pikeville had not forgotten its sons and daughters.

No one from the family met me because no one knew I was coming, but out of nowhere Whetsel Rowe grabbed me, picked me up and slung me around like a dancehall floozy. Almost before I knew it, he had me in his cab, riding me through town and blowing his horn. He had him a real live soldier boy, and the throng of onlookers said they were glad of it.

By the time Whetsel rolled me home—free of charge—I was so racked with nerves and with my chest so swelled I thought I'd have to take off my shirt. But then it all happened so fast: ol' Bartley jumped to his feet as soon as I stepped out of the cab, smelling me long before he saw me; then in a tenor known only to a fox-on-the-run, came across the creek with more feet in the air than on the ground. Right behind him came everybody else. They knew. It was a rain of all that ever lived in gladness.

In no time, the Yonts' flooded in, swarmed me, as did Old Man Andrew and a mess from up and down the road. Whetsel's taxicab had sent a signal loud and wide. From kin to neighbors, from the top of Wolfpit to Joe Bonner Hollow, they came one after another. It was a scene of jubilation, everything but fiddle playing.

Bobby was in route, according to Olin, had been for months, coming from the south of France. "Prob'ly through New York, wouldn't you say?"

And there were others: Preston and Clifford; King Charles and Jarred Stump; Vardy Keene and Vester Blige ... all alive and coming home. There were a number who hadn't gone: Aug being one, something about a bad heartbeat; Cobbie being another, the sawmill taking the first few fingers on his right hand. "No need to worry 'bout me," Cobbie said to us just days before we left, "I'll be makin' a home for myself right here in 'B' Company. I'll 'B' here when you leave, and I'll 'B' here when you get back."

For days, friends and relatives stormed over us, asking too many questions and wearing me thin. Woodrow sent letters, one after another, letting us know the war was over. He had stayed stateside throughout its entirety, never getting much further than Wyoming, as best we could tell. The reasons were nothing short of spectacular: his being on special assignment with military intelligence being one, in charge of watching out for enemy invasions that might come through Wyoming being another. The least barmy had him somewhere off in the desert standing guard over munitions dumps. To hear him tell it, the hardest part lay ahead: trying to put things back in order, now that all the part-time soldiers had gone home. He and his Blackfoot wife were expecting their third.

Week after week more and more found their way home. Then, nearly a full month later, right when apple blossoms raced through the orchards in a glory of sight and scent, Bobby Yonts flew by us in a dust squall. Whetsel had waited, looked for him day after day. It was only a matter of time. Finally, he brought him home near drunk and leaning out the window. "TIE UP YOUR WOMEN!" he screeched as he went by,

"CORNBREAD RED'S BACK IN TOWN."

Except for Mary Olive, it was a footrace to the Yonts'.

Little by little, things peeled away. What had been a life interrupted slowly began to reseat itself. Still, the past four years came to me around and again, in thought and dream alike, their memories clutching me with a tight fist, so much a part of me that I was unsteady about letting them go despite their torment. Sorting what I wanted from what I didn't wasn't something I could do overnight. Things I wanted to forget I couldn't, and things I wanted to remember came with things begging to be left alone. There was an exacting price to it all, something that left my heart and mind splintering in directions emptied of simple.

Time and again, I returned to the mountains, back to where Cousin Truman said you could hear the voice of God, if you were still long enough, and cared enough to listen; back to where things like the easiest breath restored what was broken. I found wholeness there, sanctuary, gardens in which I allowed myself the sanctity of peace: a refuge from what sought to keep me in the twist and twine of jungles halfway around the world.

When I finally laid eyes on Bobby after better than four long years, it was like that first breath out after a wanting-swallow of Corbin Fairchild's demon rum—like earth and fire in a scorched burst—and both of us damned near lifting one another off the ground. But then, emotions as hot as a coke oven gripped the whole family, a dozen of us clattering and bringing to an end what we had, for four long years, dreamed about and prayed for.

"You look like you've been through a war," he said, his grin biting into each word. Bobby was still a rocket and a high beam. Nothing had changed, as far as I could tell, except for a new leanness: a sturdiness that came rolling right up through his jaw bone and into his smile; straight and tall as a poplar and the sparkle-blue in his eyes even lighter—if that was possible.

For days, Bobby and I went from one end of the creek to the other, inviting ourselves here then there, reliving. We had seen so much, and felt even more: me in the South Pacific (New Guinea and the Philippines, and then Japan); Bobby throughout North Africa, Italy and France. There were stories on both sides that we fought off telling, but with so much still alive within us—the days and nights of four long years, and with life so delicate a consequence—here then gone for so many—warped and drudged for the rest (its images never to be undone)—left little wonder that stories eventually found their way up and into the light. Mostly it was in the liquored-haze of daybreak, in the afterglow of the din and light of juke joints, that we remembered the blood and noise of places that refused to die.

I was given more to remembering than I wanted, prone to dark stretches even in the brightest day. Nothing could have been further from the truth for Bobby. The claw that dug into Bobby the deepest was his need to make up for lost time. The mad rush to bring Corbin's Model-A back to life, and to throw-in with Ruby Mae and Hooker took on a life of its own. Where he was headed was all-too predictable. What Dixie had waited for would have to go on waiting, despite Bobby's professed love. She was still the object of his affections, but not the sole object of his desires. Bobby came on his own terms, something that would never change. I now understood how those four long years had made a difference, how our lives could never be the same as before, or as simple.

What with so many returning home and with an escalating demand for goods at an all-time high, more and more mines began to reopen. Road Creek and Red Clay were working full out, hiring just about anybody who had the will. This meant paychecks—nothing beyond what would provide bare necessities and what could be traded for at the company store, but paychecks nonetheless. It meant better times, and even more significant, it meant more cars and pick-ups. Almost by the day, they began to align themselves against the backdrop of pigpens and chicken coops, more and more becoming the tools of necessity. Even where there were children running around half-naked in yards so barren and hard packed that chickens fought one another for fragments of gravel and glass, there was a car—in one dilapidated state or another—jacked up, and more often than not, with a hillbilly hard at its underbelly.

So much had happened while I was gone, not the least of which was Olin Yonts' rapt fascination with logging and sawmilling. "*Leaping to higher ground*," was the way Mary Olive put it, adding another layer to his influence. But it was necessary, given that Bobby had gone off to fight, and three of the girls had married and left home. Beyond the necessities of a garden and a milk-cow, the old ways simply lacked the hands it needed. The sawmill meant revenue, and its first year was solid, even ascendant.

The mill took up nearly an acre, halfway up into Big Will Hollow. A saw blade bigger 'round than a wagon wheel whirred with the sound of a thousand locusts each time it hogged its way through a log, its spray of sawdust, by degrees, raising and softening the ground around it. Puffs of blue exhaust belched non-stop from an old stack pipe at the conveyor's upper end, and combined with the sour-ripeness of fresh-cut timber to stink the air. It was everything suggestive of no-frills and raw-boned determination. And it was Aug and Wilson and Ben as its linchpins.

Olin took Wilson on when he turned seventeen, a year before he could legally join the Army. By the time he was eighteen, Olin had talked him out of it. Wilson was better off with Olin, seeing as it kept him out of the mines—a profession all but guaranteed for mountain boys coming of age. So it was Aug, Wilson, and Ben, despite Ben's onset of monstrous and crippling headaches, who turned trees into planks and helped supply lumber companies up and down the Big Sandy. And though we were proud of Wilson, we had to hand it to Aug, working the way he did, and all the while keeping up with Wilma Lee—them already with four and another one on the way. "Way I got it figured," said Mary Olive, "she'll have fourteen by the time she's forty."

... And then there were the new roads: widened and grated and resembling bona fide networks of transportation; real roads and a new swinging bridge across the Big Sandy, joining Lower Fork with the black top highway. And there were poles and power lines for electricity running along the river and beside the railroad tracks, and making their way into Greezy at Sutton.

... And there was Dixie: finished with high school and, if word was to be believed, already with one foot in Pikeville College—all with the backing of Haywood and Avondale Pritchett. It seemed as if she understood that life could be far richer if she wasn't bound by somebody else's dreams, Bobby's in particular, or waiting for what amounted to more of the same. I saw her preparing for an earnest resolution to what Bobby brought in the way of chance, or what came without alternatives except his own.

... And, of course, there was Seriann, still without an ounce of fat, and flat-out having taken up with Mr. Tacket. "She ain't got near the book sense for somebody like Arlan Tackett," Mary Olive said. Mary Olive was forever undiluted, but way past caring. "Got the whole creek talkin' nineteen to the dozen," she said. "But I b'lieve she's good fer him ... an' I b'lieve he knows it."

... And then there was Grandmaw nearly taking to flight when I ran up on her porch; tried catching her breath through her groans and tears, despite the weakness in her knees. I guess I came near to killing her just by showing up. "Ain't never seen you lookin' so long-legged," she said, her eyes in a song, "like a angel come back from the beyond." I stayed with her for three days (her and Lorali), never letting my eyes drift from her for very long, afraid somehow that I'd blink and she'd be gone. I'd been away too long, still yearned for what I held most sacred, even though it was right in front of me. I'd never known Grandmaw to sit for such long spells, or reach to touch me so often. She wanted nothing more than to listen to me talk, hear the sound of my voice. I thought of its irony, and how she used to send me into the hills so she could have a minute's peace. She was still determined as ever, just not so able.

"It's because a' Lorali," Mary Olive said, "that she's still able to sworp around. Lorali goin' to live with her was as good a thing as you comin' here with me."

... And there was Little Sherman in the fourth grade, but doing the work of those in the sixth—and with a benefactor, unknown to anybody but Seriann, who made sure he was outfitted and without need. "It's his daddy," Mary Olive said in a low tone. "We ain't supposed to know who he is, an' Seriann'll never tell." She cackled, hacked and spit into the yard. "But the bigger 'at boy gets, I b'lieve I'm beginning to know who it is. 'At's sump'm you can't hide ferever. Looks too much like him. Acts like him too." We eyeballed each other for a few seconds before she leaned in close. "You know who he is," she whispered before laughing big.

"I do?"

"Uh huh," she said. "You'll figure it out."

... And there was Mary Olive, still feeling the power, as big and wide as opinion.

It was a full two months before I lagged to a slow roll, before I could realize the fullness of my own presence. I lay awake most nights trying to make sense of all I'd been a part of and the crimes I'd seen, trying for peace and wondering what was next. I had no idea where I was headed, only that there were any number of roads crooked to improbable that beckoned. Many had hired on at the mines, but I couldn't bring myself to that kind of reality without feeling like I'd reenlisted, the thought of its confinement pushing me further away from its possibility. The coalmines were a lifeline for many, oftentimes a choice that rested solely on there being no others. For me, it was not knowing, from minute to minute, if the top was going to let go and bury me alive, or if the tiniest bit of methane from the tiniest crack might find its way to a carbide light and blow the mountain down on us all. There were a hundred different ways of not making it out once you went in: mishaps with coal cars and conveyors, dynamite and falling timbers; the results all pretty much the same: dead. Just another good ol' boy gone. But then gone was gone, and that oftentimes meant rolling him off to the side and taking him out at the end of the shift. Coal mining was a choice, one I'd renounced even without ever once giving it a try.

Many were headed north to Detroit, where it was told a feller could hire on with Ford Motor Company one day then walk across the street and hire on with Chevrolet the next. Jobs were begging for bodies to tend the assembly lines, and the hillbillies of southern Appalachia were burning up US Highway 23 to get to them. Carload after carload left out of Pike County, knowing that jobs and money were only five hundred miles away and theirs just for getting there. Shared flats and sleeping rooms, three and four to a bed, were common to every rooming house in the city, all for the chance at a life apart from coal seams and deep-dark hollows. Wives and children would come later, after the groundwork was laid. Stories came nonstop about how up-landers had taken root, and how Detroit was becoming dotted with hillbilly bars and hillbilly music, and how it was all wrapped in the rawness of mountains. So many stories, and all coming from the very mouths of those who lived them, men who made their way back *down home* after their shift ended on Friday, then all the way back come Sunday evening—just in time for their shifts on Monday morning.

I'd had my fill of being gone, of being reduced to nothing but remembering. For now, familiar ground and the stuff of unknowns held me in place, kept me from looking past what was all around me, even quieted the fear that it might somehow up and disappear the way it had some four years ago. What mattered most with leaving was what was missed, and I'd done my share of missing. And while visible means of support eluded me, hope did not. The provision of what might come was good enough, at least for the time.

Sixty-Seven

Broke-To-Brittle

Cousin Truman had taken to working on me with the Bible, with the heft of its endurance and what all was penned in assurances. Mary Olive wasn't so sure about the long of it, only about Jesus. "I like preachin' as well as the next," she said, "but ain't got no patience for church, them high minded and runnin' round with their innards in a knot, tryin' to live by a buncha rules they made up for theirselves. Unnatural, if you ask me. S'long's a body can stick to what Jesus is, don't none of the rest of it matter." She thought for a long moment. "Just can't let church get in the way a' the truth," she said, her gold tooth sparkling the sun. "We *all* imperfect," she said. "We can't hep it. All 'ceptin' Jesus, that is. Ain't nuthin' or nobody can do it any better. He lived it. An' if you don't live it, you don't believe it. 'At's Jesus. An' 'at's all there is." Smoke rings rose up and around her head like a celestial cloud. "Wouldn't hurt Seriann to cleave to a right good dose of it—or that heathen, Wilson, either."

I had long thought about where I stood in the eyes of the Almighty, how I might be perceived in His earthly garden. I invoked his name often enough what time I was gone, petitioned his protection; comforted myself with the belief that I was somehow worthy of his favor. Still, there were times I couldn't bring myself to believe, even when hellfire lit up the sky. Yet, it's the aftermath that's left me broke-to-brittle, wanting a taste of something more: something to add strength to the shell that carries my name.

I was as alone as I'd ever been, even after being reunited with all I loved. A blank page couldn't have been more unattended, more robbed of place. Cousin Truman saw it right off and took me aside, began cutting away what lay festering, and wanting to tear free. But the last four years was not put down so easily, erupting over and again, encrypted in some way to last a lifetime. But then there was 'The Word,' Cousin Truman said, 'Jesus, the life within life, the manna for our spirits, our first and last resort.'

By the time corn was knee high, Bobby had thrown in with Hooker and Ruby Mae like it had been ordained. There was never a question about which way he was headed, only an adjustment of sites to put him dead center of where he wanted to be, his nerve every bit as equal to his daddy's influence. With business at an all-time high, jobs and the price of coal on the upswing, it was only a matter of time before Cornbread Red was a name known up and down the river as Hooker Hopkins' right arm.

Talk of me joining him was never-ending, and always with the promise of things bigger and better. I said No so many times, it seems he would have tired just from asking—but then that would have been somebody else, not Bobby Yonts. For all my objections, he never let up, just kept moving toward what was fast and deadly and full of fire, even after four years of having played at the world's deadliest game. But then it wasn't *his* game, or even his world ... until now.

It was closer to sooner than later before Bobby moved into Corbin's house—actually Ruby Mae's house—in the rooms apart from Invictus. From that time on, it was like Corbin had come back to life—with the exception of Ruby Mae, of course. She showed up only once a month to give the books an accounting. Even then, she was never misgiving about her tender side, as she called it, and what it took to make her all the more content. I don't know if Bobby ever moved in that direction, only that I asked not to know if he ever did.

Always a day ahead was in Bobby's every stride, measured and quickstepped from porch stoop to running board, daylight to dark. I was maybe closer to his dealings than I should have been, going along just for the ride on occasion, the way I always had, still part of what made us a team, just not part of his payroll. Spontaneity and unpredictability served Bobby the way it always had, only now with an even greater foothold in light of the advantages Olin gave, what with so many willing to look the other way.

Scooting along US 23 and route 460, looping back and forth between Pikeville and Elk Horn City, in and out of the innumerable branches and hollows in a foray of unconcern, I marveled at how some things never changed. For so many, it was a taste for the old ways, for the familiar, for the hardpan flavor of doggedness that made change a bitter pill. Oddly, there was something self-righteous about it, something tied to suffering, something that embraced putting up with disparity as being noble. Yet it was that very thing (the old ways) that kept Bobby in the game, that kept alive the demand for goods free from things like taxes. Nobody taught it any better than Corbin, and nobody understood it any better than Bobby: trusting in what wanted most to be left unchanged.

"Ain't heard you mention Imogene Riley's name," Mary Olive said, her eyes lofty on the rock cliff across the road. I could almost hear the hiss of acid in the pit of my stomach.

"Now, Momma, he don't need to be hearin' what all you think you know," Seriann said, jumping in ahead of me. "Imogene Riley's like another lifetime." Her head raised just a mite from the beans she was stringing, her eyes narrowing in on Mary Olive.

"Well, I know they was writin' right smart at one time."

"Well, one time is one time," Seriann said. "It ain't now. An' that's all there is to it. Rubin, you wan't you some a' that cobbler I put together? Blackberry! I know you love blackberries."

"I b'lieve I'll have a little bit a' that," said Mary Olive.

"Well, you can get some for all of us then," Seriann said, her eyes in a cold bead.

Mary Olive was about halfway out of her rocker when I said, "I heard from her, you know," tremor lining my voice. Mary Olive eased back down. "Just one letter, in all them years." Seriann didn't look up, just slid another bean over the needle and down its thread, slow like, then laid her hands in her lap. "It was early on," I said, "just months into it, but I saved it. Look at it every great while, just to make sure I didn't miss something. Turns out it's always the same." There was easiness to the creak in Mary Olive's rocking, something that kept our eyes turned inward and off of one another. "It was quite a while before I could get my mind around what all she said, but then time has a way of softening things. Still..."

Quiet filled in around us, lingered limp and lifeless even in the fresh rush of the creek. "Dixie's good about comin' to see us now and again," Seriann said, her tone confiding, her hands back to working on the beans. "Spent the night with us a few times. I reckon her an' Imogene still write to this day."

The door had been opened. What I wanted to know was mine for the asking, if I dared. "It's been better'n three years," I said, "since her letter." Seriann stopped to take in a long breath, then looked off toward the garden to let it out. When she turned back around, her eyes were leveled on mine. "It was full," I said, "of what she thought I needed to know ... or what she needed to say. One or the other."

Neither of them said anything. I took it as their permission to go on, if I wanted. I waited, the words of her letter resurrecting. "Her being married was at the heart of it," I said. "Somebody she'd met there in Lexington. Went on about what a good person he was, about his family having their own business, and how much they all thought of her." I'm sure they knew all of this from Dixie, but then there was my side, my wound. "Said she never thought it would actually come to marrying, but then fate just laid it out that way. She feared it was bad manners telling me in a letter, but then thought it would be worse not telling me at all. She went on and on—eight pages worth—remembering little things we'd done or shared, and how she'd never forget them, or me—something I didn't need to hear. But she never once mentioned that she was happy."

"'At's 'cause she ain't," Mary Olive blurted.

Seriann pursed her lips and made a face like she needed to spit. "Now, how in God's name do you know that?" she asked Mary Olive.

"You live as long as I have," Mary Olive said, "an' you know a-plenty." It was a point not to be argued, short and stout, both a preamble and an addendum to all she acquainted with knowing.

"Uh huh," was Seriann's only rejoinder. "Go ahead on, Rubin," she said.

"'Bout it," I said. "But then it was after I'd read it for the umpteenth time that I realized she never said she loved him."

"'At's 'cause she don't," Mary Olive said, not bothering to look up. Seriann rolled her eyes, something Mary Olive let pass while she knocked the ashes from her pipe. After a stilled moment, Mary Olive rolled her head toward me. "'At's 'cause she don't," she said again. And that was that.

The blackberry cobbler left us hushed but for the clack of spoons and our minds racing with what wanted to be said. After a time, Mary Olive took her a big breath, then disappeared inside the house. A minute later, she was back. "Here," she said, stretching out her hand. "Figured you'd be wantin' it sooner or later. Truman 'bout went crosseyed tryin' to fix it. I swear, 'at young'n can fix 'bout anything he sets his mind to." It was the pocketwatch Imogene had given me nearly nine years ago, the one she pilfered from poor old Gillum, the one I left with Truman before I went off to the war. He'd made it like new, its secondhand silent except for when I held it to my ear. Like the heartbeat of a gnat, it was. He'd even shined it.

"Been keepin' it put back," Mary Olive said, "waitin' for a time you'd be ready for it." She sniffed at the air then settled back in her rocker.

I took my time with it, running my fingers over its face, tracing the scrollwork along its back, its mix of gold and silver—warm and worn and as smooth as moss—coming to life right there in my hands. "Don't seem right," I said. "About Imogene, I mean. How the pieces just don't seem to fit. So much a feller can't understand, I reckon: things about the heart, what it's liable to do." Despite the blackberries and their sweet bursts of heaven, chewing was mechanical, each morsel growing bigger with each bite. "I never wrote her back," I said. "Tried, but just didn't have the mind for it." I could still feel what went on inside me the day her letter came, how excited I was just to sit there with it in my hands. But then after reading it, I felt like I'd been drained, emptied of soul. Still, there was an understanding between us, though it was never mouthed: that the times we did share were those of gain, times that left us knowing what we were to one another. My having done nothing about it, ever, was its own sentence; it balled up and rolled through my guts like a spool of barbed wire. "The simple truth is," I said, "there's more to *forgetting* than I got the power for."

"Maybe you ain't meant to," Seriann said. "Could be you're in line to *forgive*. Not just for her peace, but for yours, too. There's more to a wrong step than what meets the eye, Rubin. There always is. Sometimes it's a right foot out front when a left one woulda been better, but we cain't always know it till we've stepped it off."

"Lord knows you'd know that better'n anybody," Mary Olive said.

"But it ain't nuthin'," Seriann said, "that ought to torment a body for time and duration. She wrote that letter for all the right reasons. You just need to see it."

"Maybe I'm blind, but all I can see is her pairing up with someone she didn't love. How she could push aside what little hope there is to begin with hazes my understanding."

Stillness carried the rub of my words. Both of them shifted in their chairs, held me with their eyes: looks that said I knew the *why* behind it all, if I were to think about it hard enough. It was slow in coming, but come it did, and as even as a summer wind. "A baby," I said, my voice barely above a whisper, the brush of air through the poplars and the creek's gentle cascade the only other sounds. "She was going to have a baby."

Spirits attend us at the oddest times, and so often in the most sparing ways: offering balm and even catching us in the lurch of falling. I don't know what spirit it was that wrested me so completely, only that it did; left me with a feeling of flight, of shedding what was aimed at my imagined hurt. In its place, and for the first time, I saw Imogene in some far-away light: off and out of reach, apart and alone with her one wrong step, helpless but for the words she scratched one-by-one in a letter meant only for me.

Sixty-Eight

Because I Was Afraid to Say Otherwise

Come the middle of August, Preston, Clifford, King Charles, and Cobbie pooled what money they had and bought a 1939 Ford Coupe, filled its trunk with boxes of saltine crackers and cans of Vienna Sausage, and headed north to Detroit without a spare tire. We were still laughing about it when they showed up two weeks later, their pockets lined with money and hell bent on not keeping any of it. It was something they made look easy until late Sunday, when they headed back to Detroit half drunk and pushed to make Monday morning's shift. A week later they were back again, and the week after that—so recurring it was almost like they'd never left in the first place. After about the tenth trip I became a part of it, standing up to the dare that kept me mired between afraid and undecided. Overnight I became part of their third-floor, cold-water flat, with a bathroom down the hall we shared with five others. I also became part of Chrysler's Dodge Main Assembly Plant on Detroit's east side; part of the greasy spoons and sour smelling bars that dotted most every corner; sleeping all day and working graveyard, from eleven at night till seven in the morning, take it or leave it. I took it since the rooming house was only two blocks from the plant's front gate, six minutes even in a hard rain. I worked the assembly line, helping to hang solid steel bumpers on the back end of Dodges until its suffocating rhythm dwarfed even the tightest held reasons for a paycheck. It was on a Friday—four weeks after I started—that I finally said the hell with it, before I squeezed into the Coupe's backseat between Cobbie and King Charles and headed back to Greezy, this time for good. The drive took ten hours—the Kentucky part of it on a narrow, switchback, two-lane—before we rolled to a stop at the foot of Dry Fork Hill, at the mouth of the lane leading to Angus Walker's. Poster Haggard and a score of familiar faces stood bunched and milling in what light seeped from the pool hall's dirt-caked window. Poster was drunk enough for two, and tottered in our direction once he caught sight of who we were. He was deliberate and blank-eyed, but managed to lean in close without falling over. "It's Virgil Blair," he said, the whiskey on his breath reaching clear into the backseat. "A hole shot in his side the size of a fist."

A practical joke is what started it: Jordy Crow jumping on the back of ol' Jake and riding off like he was leading a battle charge, while Virgil was in the pool hall knocking back the day's dust with a cold RC. "Rode him all the way home," Poster said, "even put him in the barn." Wadn't no stealin' to it, just Jordy thinkin' he was funny." He stopped to snort and cough and grapple at blowing his nose. "But it set a fire under ol' Virgil, buddy. Left him to walk it, him cripple an' it bein' adder dark, an' it better'n a mile. Hard on him, I'd say. Left him raw, an' 'at hip a' his tender. Wadn't no time 'fore he was back, him an' ol' Jake both sweated like they'd plowed half a Greezy. Come up 'em stairs like he was a young'n, wavin' 'at gun in the air an' darin' sight an' sound alike. 'At's when Jordy broke and run. Out the door and down 'em steps four at a time, and poor ol' Virgil right after him in a limp an' a hobble—them ol' legs a' his lettin' go at the wrong time. Went down 'em steps face first an' sideways, on his belly an' on his back both. Sounded like a punkin bustin' wide open time he hit bottom. 'At's when his gun went off, up under his ribs at point-blank range. They loaded him in Angus' old car. Blood ever'where, an' Jordy holding on to him like it was his daddy. Took off outta here with 'at motor screamin', gettin' him to the hospital." Poster steadied himself against the front fender, long enough to pull a pint bottle from under his shirt and hold it out, offering. First time I could remember everybody waving off a drink, not wanting even a taste, but then it wasn't everyday that Virgil Blair took a .45 caliber slug up under his ribs. "Pure craziness," Poster said. "All of it."

It was near to one in the morning by the time I rode ol' Jake back to his barn. Liddy was waiting up, the lamplight weak and warm in the window. Liddy was all Virgil had, barren as she was for forty years. I was the last person she expected to see on her porch in the middle of the night, and a far cry from the solace we sought, but I did what I could with what she was loathe to hear. It had taken some time for the news to reach Olin, but within an hour's time the three of us stood looking down on Virgil, feverish and ghost-gray, half in and half out of knowing. The bullet was still inside him and too near the heart, lodged there after bouncing around, tearing up the patch and passing through a lung, lost to all efforts of retrieval. Liddy said nothing, just eased the sheet back like she was uncovering a guarded secret. Blood oozed and glistened, helping itself to the bandage tied tight around Virgil's middle.

Garland Sawyers found us soon enough, his face winced and full of questions; pawing, scratching, and pacing till I thought he'd wear a hole in what fight we had left—till Olin led him away—till daylight marked their way back.

One after another filled in around us as the morning wore on, waiting for better news or a last glimpse, it was hard to tell. With each wave of doctors, and each with an expression as helpless as the last, we knew Virgil was beyond the limits of medicine. But then it was just like Virgil not to go along with quitting, cob that he was.

It was near to noon when Olin pulled me aside, saying it was time he spoke with me. He meant in private. Without seeming obvious, we walked a short distance out the hospital's entrance and along a tree-lined lane, where we looked out over Pikeville. The Methodist Hospital sat high above the town, on a hill with a wide vista: the perfect place for discourse of a private nature. What Olin said was short and to the point. Virgil was a short time here, that much was certain, and Garland Sawyers needed a deputy sheriff for Greezy. He said he'd spoken with Garland and convinced him that I was his man: war veteran, MP, smart, fit, level-headed, fair-minded. Since deputy sheriffs were appointed, it was a lock; he just needed the nod from me. But there was more. This is where he became confidential, looking over his shoulder and talking in low tones. Garland was no spring chicken, he said, and long past wanting to hang it up. Deputy sheriff was the perfect stepping stone for somebody with designs on being high sheriff, and election time was coming up in little over a year. He now talked in richer tones, steady, firm, assured. And I would have his backing, start to finish, if I was of the mind. It was the hammer down on the final nail. All he needed was my Yes. He pressed me with his eyes, his hand on my shoulder. "Think of the possibilities," he said, his smile—the one that had altered politics and politicians alike, and for as long as anyone could remember—stretching into worlds I knew nothing about. I gave it to him—my Yes—partly because it was what he expected, but in larger part because I was afraid to say otherwise. It was Olin Yonts, after all.

I did what I could to answer the endless streams of questions from concerned and curious alike what time Virgil lay dying. The sundry questions that came at me demanded it. But after the second day, fever took him head on: left him mumbling about ol' Jake and Haman Flowers, and needing to put decorations on his mother's grave. Friends took turns sitting with Liddy night and day. She was determined not to leave his side, every minute or so wiping him with cool rags and forcing water between his parched lips. Doctors came at regular intervals to change his dressing and swab out the hole in his stomach with alcohol, sulfur, and god knows what all. For all the good it did, I wondered if Grandmaw's doctoring wouldn't have been more suitable. Virgil's fever never broke; by the end of the third day his eyes pooled dream-like, leading me to believe he was seeing things the rest of us couldn't. If he saw me at all, I was certain he didn't know me—not until a smile trailed weak and tired across his lips and stayed long after he closed his eyes. I stayed at his bedside that night, watching and listening to him struggle with breath. Breath-in, breath-out; breath-in, breath-out, louder and more pronounced in the room's dimness and scent trail of alcohol, in the frail silence of Liddy slumped and half-asleep in the dry October air wafting feather-light through the window. I stayed that night as if I knew to stay, as if I had been sent for that very reason, and until there was that fallen silence that said there would never be another breath-in.

Garland Sawyers drove all the way from Pikeville to swear me in the day we laid Virgil down, before I allowed trouble of the purest kind. Most of Greezy remembered me as a boy, and for that reason didn't see me as much beyond someone playing a more mature game of cops and robbers. Still, I did what I could to ease their minds. Mostly, I gave them hope enough to believe that we'd all live to see better days. It was as much as anybody could offer, plus it had a vague reference to scripture—something far more likely to help me than hurt me.

Deputy sheriff was never a question of qualifications, just one of those jobs for somebody with a need beyond coal mining. The pay wasn't enough to live on, coupled with that one little niggling detail about the likelihood of being shot at any given moment, for any given reason. With the thought of Virgil still on everybody's mind, his dying with a gaping hole in his stomach and burning up with fever, it was a niggling little detail with ever-widening implications. Knowing that most on Greezy learned to shoot long before they started school, meant that most could kill you without half trying, if they took a notion. And given the infinite number of reasons for pulling down on a lawman, it made taking the job seem foolhardy: as if one just up and put aside any hope of long life and contentment. It was the general consensus that anyone wanting such a job in the first place was not all together favored with good sense, and therefore the least desirable to defend against wrongdoing. I never thought of it in quite that way until after I was sworn in.

The process was quick and unceremonious, and leaving me overcome with dread. It settled murderously within me, so deep that it seemed to add weight and even slow my steps. Second-guessing myself was not part of my custom, yet I did that day, when I began to understand the fullness of my charge. It's a severe reckoning when one is brought to the point of asking himself, "What have I done?"

Knowing that I was now the law—the lone ranger to some twenty miles of mud roads and its hundreds of cutting, kicking, shooting mountaineers—had all the trappings of hardship and loneliness, all of which came with a fifteen-dollar-a-week paycheck. I was alone now, the only one to call the shots: to decide, to reason, to act. It was a revelation prompting feelings that I ought to be lamented more than revered.

The whole family was busted-out prideful and filtered in like I'd come back from another war, offering up pieces of advice like they were slices of blackbird pie. Mary Olive was all-in, her gab full of what we intended to do now that *we* were the law.

Cousin Truman held out that with the right teachings we might one day beat our swords into plowshares, and not have to exclude the tenants of forgiveness when dealing with each other. In the meantime, he was resigned to such occupations as mine, same as he was with soldiering: goodness holding back the tide of offense in accordance with the rules of engagement, and, for the love of God, aligned with His will and purpose. Grandmaw was just sorry that there had to be such evil to make *lawing* so needed. "Wouldn't it be better if we could all just get along?" she said. "We're here for such a short time anyway." And then Seriann, quiet with satisfaction—the way she had been ever since I'd come home—with her newness with Mr. Tacket and running the store ever since Pearl became a quiver of bones, seeming to add a new heartbeat. "We ain't never had lawin' in the family," she said. "Don't know how I can live it down, after bein' on the other side for so long." She thought nothing of belly laughing now, clapping her hands and coming into the open like she had when Corbin was still with us. She'd been such a part of the darkness, but now such a part of the dawn.

For the most part, we avoided the obvious: what might become of Bobby and me, and our divergent paths. My only hope was that it would, somehow, someway, take care of itself.

* * *

"Hey, buddy! I hear tell they's bootleggin' goin' on up in here." Bobby was leaned part way out the window of his Model-A and rolling his eyes, deadpanned.

The store was near to closing and the front porch empty but for some little toe-head lingering with a peppermint stick. It was unseasonably warm for early November and though I'd only been peacekeeping better than a week, I'd already gotten into the habit of making Andrew's front porch my place of choice, same as Virgil had for forty years. I brought my chair down to all fours and stepped off in Bobby's direction. "You know," I said, leaning on his door, "you ain't all that bad lookin' for somebody too sorry to work."

"It's all that good breedin'," he said, his smile razor thin, his eyes tipped to laughing.

"You know where a feller can get a good drink a' liquor?" I said.

"Might, but it'd take hard-earned dollars."

"How 'bout credit?"

"How 'bout me datin' yer sweetheart?"

It was a contest, always, a ball kept in the air; a back and forth that demanded a straight face until one or the other went to laughing or boxing.

"Don't reckon you'll ever change," I said.

"Don't reckon I want to."

"They's plenty a' reasons why you should, you know."

"I know. That's why I don't."

Bobby was heaven and hell all rolled into one, brake and accelerator both. I was happy some things never changed. Just being within arms reach of him was like a bridge to all the things we ever did, things that just opened up with the sound of his voice; things that refused to be put away without at least a thought. I suppose it was a kind of brotherhood that kept me feeling that way; nothing you could put words to, kind of like those bolts of ice blue in his eyes.

"You know you can always come work with me," he said. "Guarantee I'll turn 'at fifteen dollars a week into twenty dollars a day."

"Yeah, but then there's that thing about having to live with myself."

Bobby loved laughing big. "You really are sump'm else," he said. "'Course I know you got plans." He gave me one of those big twitchy winks. "Could be we'll be workin' closer'n you think 'fore it's all over."

"You just never know," I said. We'd figured out long ago that many times things passed between us without ever being said. A raised eyebrow or a tilted head sometimes said more than all of our words put together. It was that way when he sat there smiling up at me, like he was proud of the way I turned out; when he shifted into low gear and crawled away with that see-you-later look etched on his face. It was all that needed saying, though he did give me a lazy, half-hearted wave as he disappeared up Dry Fork. I didn't wave back. I didn't have to. He knew.

Sixty-Nine

A Right Introduction

From the start, it was Olin who saw to it that I had what I needed: a right introduction and a clear picture of what he called *standing*: where lines had been drawn long before I was ever thought about, some soft-to-bending, and others never to be crossed. There wasn't much that wasn't on one side or the other, and Olin was more familiar than most with their divides—any number of them being his doing. He wasted little time in raising my name to registered voters, expending fair amounts of effort even with the most secluded. After a day or two, I realized how penetrating his reach really was, and how I benefitted with each handshake and each mile we logged peeling back the layers of who I was. You couldn't be effective without being personable, was Olin's take, and I was brought to know that the time we spent working people into friends made for dividends of another day, and of a finer kind. The whole of it, though, left me to wonder who needed fearing most: men like Haman Flowers, or men like Olin Yonts?

A few days after we started, the dirt on Virgil's grave not yet settled, and the oaks and maples still shocking the hillsides with glories of red and gold, Olin stopped for a copperhead stretched out in the middle of the road. He just eased the truck off to the side and reached under his seat for the .38 revolver he kept wrapped in a towel. He never said a word, just stepped to where that copperhead could look him in the eyes—then shot him nine times. That's what he said to me when he came back to the truck, "I shot him nine times." They were words that filled every empty space in the universe, hung there for every living thing to take note while he reloaded. Half done was nowhere to be found in Olin Yonts.

By the end of the week, we'd covered what was known of Greezy, its sled roads and hollows, glad handing and getting an idea of who was who. That was my preamble, my sendoff and leg up from Olin Yonts. From then on it was mine to deal with, only with the name of Olin Yonts inscribed as the sway to all ends.

I'd made several inquiries into a sidearm, but as it turned out, I didn't have to. Olin saw to that as well. Just left it there on the front seat of my Chevrolet, under an oily rag. I wasn't under any illusions about its necessity, only about the shotgun he left alongside it: a twelve gauge—sawed off so that it looked like a long-barreled pistol with a stock, and what he thought ought to be my calling card.

"Get yourself a holster for that thirty-eight," he told me. "It'll do for the most part. But that shotgun out in the open will do a sight more in the way of talkin' than you ever could. Speaks for itself in a way that won't ever be misunderstood." He gave me a wink and a little nod, signs that his word was without the confusions of bureaucracy. "Liable to be hateful to some," he said, "them disagreeable few, but it'll be a comfort to most. It's a serious kind a business your're in, Rubin. Stern, but laudable. But then laudable ain't above needin' a little help from time to time. Feller needs the right tools." The air seemed to quiet when Olin spoke, like it was laid over in reverence.

"Violence," he continued, "is blind to most everything that runs contrary to it. It's a smilin' face one minute, a rattler strike the next. One-sided, except for them quick enough to feel it comin'. Knowin' it can mean the difference between breathing an' not. Havin' the right tools can mean livin' to tell about it. You the law now, son. The peacemaker. An' these here thangs? Just tools. For peace."

I didn't know much about cars, but I knew what a Cadillac was, and how a sighting of one in Pike County could raise a stir. It was like that—a stir—when Bobby pulled his new wine-colored LaSalle convertible, about as long as a hot summer's day, alongside my ten-year-old Chevrolet Coupe, black as coal dust on a Bible. Bobby knew when the mail ran, when the store was ripe with humankind, and he sat behind the wheel of his LaSalle smiling like a cat with a bird in its mouth, basking in the grandeur of attention.

"Y'know, I been lookin' for sump'm 'bout like this to get my hogs to market," said Cotton Childers.

Laughter was ripe and rowdy, and rifled from one to the next. Bobby knew the game well, its exchange of insults, and gave it back as fast as it came, before he pulled up a chair next to me on the porch. We gave each other a sizable eyeballing before saying anything. Finally, and in the direction of his Cadillac, I said, "I'll give you fifty dollars and a hundred-pound sack a' taters for it—just the way it sits. 'Course you'll have to come dig the taters."

"You ought not be so generous," Bobby said. "Somebody's liable to take advantage."

"Where'd you steal that thing, anyway?" I said.

"I can get you one just like it in a day's time."

"I bet you can, at that," I said, "but it's the price I'm worried about, an' I ain't talkin' about dollars."

He sat there with a cheeky smile, watching me like a clock about to chime. "You know," he said, "if you ain't careful, this deputy thing's liable to make you plum sober."

I tried not to laugh, but old times and old haunts came calling out to me from the creases of his grin. He was rocked back in his chair, jack-legged and caught up in his own snickering. Laughter just seemed to find its own cause whenever he came around, followed him like he was the breath it needed.

"It's my new face," I said.

"Deputy face," he said. "Strong. Solemn. Like 'em wanted posters, but all the time light and happy on the inside."

"Like a Bugs Bunny cartoon."

"You know, 'at's about enough to scare a feller."

"Got me a big ol' gun, too. Loaded up tight with powder an' ball."

"What in God's name for?"

"Yankees and bootleggers mostly ... and them crazy enough to think I ain't mean enough."

"Yer exactly the kind a' feller I'm lookin' for."

"I got me enough trouble already," I said.

He brought his chair down hard. "We never did get around to Wanda and Maxine," he said. "What say I come get you 'bout midnight? We'll make some memories."

"I'll think about it," I said, my grin as deep as his.

Finally, he stood and leaned against one of the porch posts, his mind all at once far off. "Snow'll be here soon," he said looking off toward the tops of the trees. I could hear the restlessness low down. Before I could say anything, he stepped off toward his car and the commotion still milling around it.

"Where you headed?" I said.

He paused and turned his collar up against the chill. "Hot date," he said.

"Anybody I know?"

He gave me one of his all-knowing smiles and kept on walking. Not saying anything was like having the last laugh. It was vintage Bobby Yonts. Without a backward glance he was gone, this time in a long slow wheel toward Gardner Fork. But then it was only minutes before he was back, roaring past me and the throng still milling about the store, his horn blaring and with so much dust kicking up behind him it looked like he was being chased by a storm—and on the seat beside him sat Mary Olive, her eyes enormous, her face a heave of wonder and go.

Winter was nettlesome that year: its snows sloppy-wet, its days bare-boned and with a gray that was never ending. The time I spent sheriffing was self-appointed for the most part: driving the roads at odd times and staying close to the gossip whenever the mail ran. None of it in the way of anything new until spring, until the rains quickened the creeks and livened the hillsides in assorted shades of emerald; until the mountains and their rich-on-rich earth opened with the quietness of crocuses and bluebells, mayapple and rhododendron, and until the deep mud ruts in front of Andrew's gave way to the face of Imogene.

Few things had made a difference since my coming home, nothing that rested me above the hard scrabble of effort and what I choked back in dreams most nights. Not until Imogene came picking her way through the mud, that is. By now, I was more than used to surprise, what with all the noise that came from giving out the law: all the clamor that lingered in thanklessness and opposition, all that lay twisted in foolery and hate alike. Surprise was the forerunner of all that came my way, but none of it with the air and jolt of seeing Imogene with the misty backdrop of mountains through her auburn hair.

She plowed straight ahead, keen and eager, sloshing through mud the way I imagined Wilma Lee did on her way to the hog lot each day, there in the head of Shop Branch. I brought my chair down about the time she mounted the steps, then rose to my feet what time she kicked the mud off her boots. I guess it may have been my stare, or maybe my shadow, or even the spirit that accompanied me—it was hard to tell—only that she stopped short, halted for no clear reason for four to five good heartbeats, then turned to find me, frozen and pale as a ghost.

Every word I ever knew was somehow suddenly scrambled, locked sideways and crossways somewhere the other side of my windpipe. How Imogene had come out of nowhere was spell-like, but she had, and for those first few moments I stood imprecise, as if without legs. My mind jumped out ahead of itself, teetering in a cascade of eight mislaid years, and all the while with my heart about to beat through my shirt. I don't know what broke first, my chance at a voice or her reach to steady herself against the post. I could make out light and blotches of color, but no sound. It was just the two of us, within arms length, mindless and clouded and without the requisites of footing, only disbelief, and eyes combing for the threads that still remained, trying to stem the tide of time and circumstance.

"Look at us," she said daubing at her eyes, a half-laugh invading the uncertainty that lay between us.

"Ain't we a sight," I said out loud and to the attention of onlookers. It was the kind of attention I preferred not to have, but at that moment I was about as far from caring as I'd ever been. Seeing her was like a feeling of being unlocked, of being tighter than a jailhouse door and finally having it swing free. Still, I was far away, alone with the green there in her eyes, with the years and the thoughts of what might have been.

"I'm happy to see you, Rubin." They were words she managed through watery eyes. I fought the urge to grab hold of her, pull her to me, breathe her into me; resisted the primal instinct to fall on my knees and bury my face in the thickness of her skirt, and tell her I'd never felt so above the clouds. She searched my eyes, the way she had many times before. They were looks I remembered still, looks that recognized two lives in concert, the precision of their connection and their place in the world. I drank her in: her hair, her lips, the slant of her neck. There weren't words...

"I don't want you gettin' the big head about this," I said all of a sudden. "And if you ever tell it, I'll swear I never said it—but I don't reckon I've ever been so happy to see anybody in all my life." She smiled real pretty, but real sad.

"Ain't nobody needs to know that but me," she said, "but I'll remind you of it if I ever get the chance." Her smile lingered, yet with a well of tears.

"Oh Lord," I said, "You ain't makin' this easy." For some reason, it started her half-laughing again.

We stayed that way for a time longer, she never quite getting a bridle on the laughing/crying thing, and me never able to spit out more than a handful of words. It was awkward and I was out of my depth, but then I wouldn't have traded places for all the salt in the sea. She touched my arm before turning to leave, then left it there for all the world to see before she finally whispered, "Bye." She walked off without ever going into the store. I watched her walk away, my insides screaming for her to turn around ... to come back ... to stay.

* * *

I never gave much mind to Gillum Riley, he being fifty-odd years older than me and never, as far as I knew, with the need to venture much further than his porch; his plot of ground and the iron will of Ester making up his safe place. Time's feeble grip is often the deciding hand for folks like Gillum, leaving them with little use for what's beyond their front gate. Still, there was his downhill slide bumping up against coffered prayers and Old Regular Baptist attempts to pull him back from the rim of his abyss. Despite the dire nature of it all, and given that I was the new deputy and looking for ways to enlarge myself, I figured paying respects to a dying man couldn't be the worst thing. Then, of course, there was the matter—if not the full-blown, even shameful aim—of allowing myself another encounter with Imogene.

I had no idea how long Gillum would last, only that he was already being talked about in the past tense. When I arrived, Ester pretended surprise but then welcomed me as only she could: with a stature straight and a handshake strong, things she brought commandingly to the world.

Gillum was on the porch when I got there, laid out on a cot and draped in a white sheet like the next move would be the morgue. It was Ester's idea, something about it being a blessing if he could see the hillsides leafing out. As far as I could tell, Gillum wasn't seeing much of anything; his jaw dropped open, and his eyes wide and disallowed of anything certain. The Old Regulars were gathered around him in a circle, laying on hands and chanting prayers long and forlorn.

I stood back out of the way, the Old Regular's incantations ringing to celestial levels, while Ester pardoned herself without a word and disappeared behind the porch's screen door. I craned my neck for signs of Imogene, but she was nowhere to be seen: content, I supposed, to allow the Old Regulars their invoking without any help from her. I stayed for a time in the enchantment of their prayers, and long enough to know what the Old Regulars already knew: that Gillum was not about to recover from whatever beset him. It was only minutes later that I caught a glimpse of Ester leaning out her kitchen window and whispering to Johnny Kendrick. In the next instant, and from behind the Old Regular's huddled wall, that I saw her slip Johnny a pint bottle in exchange for a greenback dollar. I got the distinct impression it wasn't preserves she was selling when Imogene came out of nowhere, scolding and pointing to what all was taking place on the porch. "What's wrong with you?" she chided, her disdain just loud enough. "Daddy's out there a-dyin' an' with the whole nation a' Old Regulars praying him up, an' you're in here bootlegging." I slunk down behind the Old Regular's wall of supplication, then off the porch, across the creek, and finally onto the road—all the while with Johnny Kendrick slinking off through the bottom behind the house. I glanced over my shoulder just in time to see Imogene coming through the screen door. She saw me about the same time, the pulse of our stares long and unashamed.

Bobby Yonts' inroads had become as tangled as they were varied, and soaked to the bone with prosperity. Those looking to share in the good times had only to toss their hat into Bobby's ring; Ester Riley being one of the first, her penchant for bootlegging neither too shy nor too above what Bobby required.

I was at odds with how to handle Bobby's moonshine trade. Turning a blind eye, it seemed, had worked to my detriment: made me out to be less than I wanted to be, less than some folks expected—but worse still, what most expected all along. Virgil had been able to keep a lid on bootlegging for the most part, keep it off the roads and out of the public eye, but things changed with Bobby. Bobby had, shy of flat-out opening up a liquor store, filled his ranks with folks raring for riches, Ester Riley seeing the advantages early on.

Bobby was a new hand in an old game, but a game he was hell-bent on playing. From Ford's Branch and Island Creek to Millard, Pompie, and Cloy, Bobby's inroads continued to advance without as much as a side-step. Never needing to go more than a quarter mile to distribution points figured to be the kind of service folks took to. It only made sense, and saved Bobby from having to hide it under roots and rocks, and then always needing to go dig it out. What he established were supply lines, vital links for those with a dollar. Those who threw in with him—those like Ester

Riley—saw it as a hedge against hard times, and a supplement to good ones. It was back-pocket money, the folding kind, and out of reach of Uncle Sam. Life was good with Bobby Yonts.

I moved out of Mary Olive's and into a cabin owned by Rayford Kinney (Rafe) about the time violets and larkspur purpled the ground. Rafe's cabin was just a bit of a thing, made of mud and logs, and leaning just-ever-so. It was on Main Fork, about a mile from where it forked away from Gardner, just below the old Hopkins cemetery and alongside the road at the mouth of Joe Bonner Hollow. Rafe let me have it for ten dollars a month and promised to shore up the outhouse and fix the holes in the roof if I'd help him pull two of his wife's back teeth, which I did, and which he did. Still, I went to see Mary Olive everyday, a habit I clung to for the sake of family. But it was my moving out that opened the door for *her* bootlegging. She said she'd bootlegged most of her life before I got there, and how else did I think she stayed alive with no man, and nobody but Truman and Lorali drifting in and out just now and again to muscle things around? It started a long time ago, she said, back when that blackheart, Lawyer Bearsox, shot and killed her Dempsey for no good reason.

"Tried takin' in warshin' for a time," she said, "but that was too much for one. Took in mendin' and sewin' till I was about to go blind. Wadn't enough in it to keep a kitten alive, no way. Then Horace Clemmons come around, like he always did when his wife wasn't lookin', all the time with liquor on his breath and more'n just a little to say." She shook her head and chuckled to herself. "Law, honey, he was a mess; had the guts of a gov'ment mule, but there was always sump'm 'bout him I liked. He didn't much care that he was married, but I did. But that never stopped him from tryin'. I think it was because he couldn't ever close the deal (she smiled), that he liked me so much; that kept him comin' back. When he first mentioned bootleggin', I thought he was just talkin' to hear hisself—but it didn't take long 'fore I caught on that runnin' the store wadn't all he did. Shouldn't have surprised me none. He was always so full a' the devil." She stopped and smoothed back a few strands of hair that had stirred loose, then fastened them with a bobby pin she separated with her teeth. "He was always partial to me," she said, her trail of a smile saying there was much more to the story than she was likely to tell. "An' he liked my gold tooth. Said it reminded him of a madam he met oncet up in Cincinnati." She stopped to laugh and kick out her leg. "He had plenty a sense, just never liked to use it—'cept to stir things up. Said whatever was on his mind, an' without ever a thought to what would come of it. Awfullest things ever was, but they kept me laughin' to where I'd wanna pee myself. I never once gave bootleggin' a thought till he promised me a nickel for ever' bottle I sold. Why, I made more in my first two days than I did all week darning socks. Still, I took in mending just to keep the family from knowin'. Don't reckon Seriann ever knew till she got old enough not to care." She stopped and looked me square on. "What I'm doin' now ain't got nuthin' to do with you, little brother. It's just me doin' what little I can to have a bit extra. 'Sides, I always had me a crush on Bobby Yonts." She laughed real big and cleaned out her pipe with the handle of a spoon. "An' I'll tell you this," she said, "he's a might more generous than Horace Clemmons ever thought a' being. We all comin' out ahead on this, Rubin: them a-buyin', an' me a-sellin'."

She laid her pipe aside and went to move the cornbread off the stove to where it could cool. "Seriann's tryin' to make a life for herself there at the store," she said, "but she ain't able to put nuthin' back. Spends most of what she makes on that young'n, an' he's gonna be needin' more as time goes on. Me, I'm just doin' what I need to while I can. No tellin' what's liable to come of it. Alls I know is the here an' now, an' it ain't none of it all that promisin'. They's just one way to make hay, Rubin, an' that's to put seed in the ground." She stood with her elbows out and her hands on her hips, her lips pursed and her eyes questioning—waiting, I supposed, to see if any of it registered. "C'mon," she finally said, "let's get us a bite a' these butterbeans 'fore I cook'em to death."

Gillum took his last breath just a few days after I moved into Rafe Kinney's cabin, and, as far as I know, without ever seeing the hillsides sprout. He was laid out right there at home for three whole days and nights. I went to pay respects on the second night, along with friends and neighbors and Old Regulars bunched shoulder to shoulder, talking and smoking and offering up love. The casket sat against the far wall, and with Gillum looking like he never quite let go of his pain. I stood looking down on him when a hand on my arm caught me by surprise. Imogene moved in close, smiling; her face within a whisper, the scent of rosewater in her hair. "There's somebody I'd like you to meet," she said, looking down at a child, freckled and red-haired, and leaning against her leg. "This is Callie," she said, her eyes unhurried and inclined to mine. Nothing could have been more obvious as to who Callie belonged to.

I bent slightly and offered my hand, "Awfully nice to meet you, Callie," I said. She waited to be coaxed, then took my hand so very briefly, little more than a touch. Imogene watched me with a mother's care. "She's beautiful," I said, meaning it. Imogene reached down and smoothed Callie's hair, her eyes quiet, absorbed. "I'm glad you came, Rubin," she said before turning Callie and inching her back through the cluster. Her subtle manner trailed after her, as did her quick glance over her shoulder, her eyes unable to contradict what lay locked and out of the way.

I stayed away the day of the funeral, but then thought better of the wake, opportunity being the bigger part of motivation. I found Imogene right off, huddled with Dixie and Seriann, and said something about being sorry for her loss, but then got interrupted right in the middle of it by a tall, pushy feller with black sweaty hair, asking her how long this thing was going to last.

Without standing, Imogene said, "Rubin, I'd like you to meet my husband, Colin Ward." Colin gave me a held-breath, down-the-nose read, and shook my hand only after I offered—all of it without saying a word, the flush of bile on his lips. The next instant he was back facing Imogene, postured and wanting to know if he couldn't, for God's sake, just slip out the backdoor and head on home. The melancholic pall was *utterly annoying*, he said, and, if Imogene bothered to recall, there was the more-than-little matter of his having a *job* ... and if she would just make his excuses, he would be back for her and Callie at the end of the week. Without waiting for her reply, he turned and angled his way through the wealth of those who thought to mourn. Straight off, Imogene rejoined her eyes to mine. And though we never heard Colin open or close the backdoor, we rested in the confidence that he had ... and then in the thankfulness for it.

Bobby had a way of owning his reputation without the first thought of apology, and came squeezing through the Old Regulars like it was an everyday thing. It had been nine years since he last saw Imogene, and he stormed right into the middle of us to gather her up—their memories, expectedly, beset with the tenderness of so much time. I could almost hear Mr. Tacket's big brass bell.

Just days after the power company finished putting electric lines all the way up Main Fork, Olin dropped in on me to make sure I had what I needed, and that the cabin was fit to stand a good rain without washing off. He wasn't all that talkative; Ben's headaches growing worse and coming more often had him dogged, laboring just to get his words up and out. I never thought to feel sorry for Olin, but then I never expected to see him so done-in. We talked in between long pauses and him fighting to push back thoughts determined to have their way. He stood leaning against the doorjamb and looking out across the road, wiping at the sweatband in his hat and squinting up at a glaring sun. Finally he just shook his head and stepped off toward his truck without remembering a goodbye. About midway of the yard, he pulled up and came back. "'Bout forgot," he said, taking an envelope from inside his shirt. "This here's for you." He held it up like he was serving a summons, then laid it on top of the barrel I used for a table. He tapped it with his fingers and said, "This is just between you and me. Ain't no crime to it, just a little off-the-books something to help out. If they's any crime at all, it's what the county's payin' you. More exact, what they ain't." He nodded then walked off.

"You're same as family now, Rubin," he said when he reached his truck. "It's watchin' out for one another that's the main thing." This time it was me doing the nodding, not so big as it was slow and accepting. A smile cut across Olin's face for the first time. He put his finger to the brim of his hat and gave me a tight little salute before he drove off in a smudge of road dust thick enough to taste.

A twenty-dollar bill made for a thin envelope. I didn't have to think long about where it came from. It had long been a tradition between Corbin and Virgil Blair: a monthly token of appreciation Corbin was all too happy to pay, a little something to help avoid interference and what might interrupt the flow of his corn squeezings. Bobby knew the drill, and so did I. I stuck the twenty in a Bible Truman had given me, in First Timothy, right on top of the passage about those coveting after money and piercing themselves through with many sorrows.

I can't say what the reason was for Colin coming back sooner than he said, but it was just two days from the time he left that his big green Packard sat like an open sore in front of Ester's. It was still early morning when I eased by, a faint trail of chimney smoke the only sign of life. I stopped a little ways down the road, just out of sight, the morning-mist deep with quiet, and adding to what comes from being alone. I sat there with the motor running, my mind clouded with the thought of Imogene soon to be gone and bathing in the shimmer of city lights. It left me feeling like I'd staggered into one of Luck Hanner's haymakers, one aimed up under my ribs. There was a calm that tried to get at me, but there was also something beneath it that refused to be still, pulling me back to memories I never wanted to forget. It wasn't long before I eased back on the road, tired of waiting for that hidden something to come and raise me above what I couldn't understand; to prop up what I knew was at an end.

The morning lagged thick and humid the day Olin came with news about Ben, how his headaches had beat him down and turned him into a nameless thing twisted in seizures. His words were mumbled and hard to follow. He sat stoop-shouldered on the edge of my bed, rolling his hat like he was looking for ticks on a dog. "He's still at the hospital," he said. "Mother's there with him. Bobby, too."

The day was still breaking, and a few of the feistier roosters still in a state to remind us. I moved to the shelf above the wash pan and pulled down a pint bottle Bobby had given me some time back, unscrewed the lid and held it out to Olin like it was something meant for situations exactly like this. He stared at it long and hard, then took it down like life's elixir. I joined him.

"Took him in yesterday evenin' when it got bad," he said. "That's where it happened; right there in the hospital. Awfullest sight I'd ever seen. Him thrashing about like he was crazy, an' them taking six or better to hold him." His eyes seemed pleading, more to be understood than pitied. "It was like I knew to take him when I did," he said. "Be gone for sure if I hadn't. Weren't nothin' but the Lord's hand on him, I reckon."

The sun peeked in and out through the wisp of early morning clouds, changing the light on his face but never the paleness. We stepped outside and stood in the dirt and sprigs of grass Rafe dared call a yard, till he doffed his hat and climbed back into his truck. He was worn thin, and mopped at the sweat around his eyes.

"Ain't none of this gonna hold us back none," he said, willfulness clawing its way back. "Election's gonna help us all." He said it like it was a fact. "You at the heart of it now, Rubin. We'll get'r in high gear soon's we file."

May was the deadline for filing, and I signed my name with a trembling hand. With the stroke of a pen, I was on the public record, my hat formally in the ring as a candidate for Pike County Sheriff. Olin was all smiles, and went about holding me up to those whose business it was to know. I had no delusions about destiny. The fate exacted by Olin Yonts was difficult enough.

With typical piety, spring greened in around us, warm and quiet, heralding our soon to be summer. Splashes of mountain laurel rolled from crest to knob, connected and filled the slopes with a regal fairness, all of it in harmony, except for the letter Old Man Andrew held in his meaty hand—the one addressed to me—the one without a return address. Before handing it over, he looked at it with narrowed eyes then held it up to the light, straining to make out who it was from. Several others nearby added their own squints, then soured of it after a time.

"I'd like to have that whenever you get finished with it," I said, my sarcasm not unnoticed. Andrew handed it over with a suspicious eye. I stuffed it in my shirt pocket and walked off, but not before he said something about the inconsiderate nature of someone excluding a return address on U.S Gov'ment mail. From the postmark, I had a hunch who it was from.

Rubin (what wanders only to come again ... what calls and is so denied), I am thanking you over and again for your respects. Daddy would have attested to your character...as I do now. Right now words can't be found for all I want to say. Time, though, will unravel them; this you must believe. It is then that I will write again (my hardened promise).

Imogene

Seventy

For All That Rejoices

It was odd seeing my face on so many signs, bright red ones with PIKE COUNTY SHERIFF in a half moon above my picture, and ELECT RUBIN CAIN—VETERAN FOR CHANGE! printed below it. Olin had so many signs made they were damned near a blight. He plastered them all over town: in storefronts and yards, on lamp posts and every inch of highway in and out of Pike County's four mountain districts. His heavy-handed assault swooped over the county without regard except to its outcome; and certainly without concern for my tongue-tied inabilities to state my case, the most damaging of which was in front of the courthouse with my opponent, Cordell Yokum, spouting with deafening clarity about my utter lack of experience.

"He's not but twenty-four year old," shouted Cordell through some cone shaped contrivance held up to his mouth, "and not a shred of lawin' know-how on the municipal stage!" Cordell was about an inch high, but silk-tongued and without the least bit of civility when it came to running me down. Olin thought he was priceless, and laughed hard enough to be an all-out distraction, even after Cordell pointed a crooked finger at my being new and untried. Showmanship came natural to Cordell, stomping and shouting and clapping his hands. But it was his zingers landing square on the mark that kept the back of my neck itchy and sweated, him hollering loud enough for the whole county to hear; taking me down the river about being lost when it came to Pike County's judicial system (or any other for that matter), and about my little-known, but overly-cozy relationship with individuals known for their illegal trafficking of liquor. In ten minutes time, he had me whittled to a peg and feeling like he'd set the cap of lost-cause square on my head. But then there was Olin, still laughing and glad-handing everybody within reach.

A week later, Olin wrangled a five-minute spot for me on WLSI, Pikeville's own radio station, where I was asked about each of Cordell's bickering points, the first three of which dealt with my lack of experience—points that had, ironically, left me in a position to offer fresh perspectives. It was youth, I told them, and lack of experience that made me less encumbered with what smacked of worn-out ways, what kept so many balled-and-chained and afraid to take a step forward; people without vision relying instead on frontier tactics and what their grandpaws used to do. As to the fourth point, I took exception to the words *overly cozy*. It was true, I knew the names associated with the liquor trade, and I certainly wasn't blind to the fact that moonshining ran deep in our part of Appalachia, but hadn't witnessed it since my being discharged as a military police officer in the United States Army (careful here to add emphasis to both). "I have no control over who I know," I said. "My whole life has had people coming and going like the seasons, at every juncture and for all kinds of reasons. And I believe I'm richer for it, better able to understand what cultivates and what contradicts a man's spirit. You have to live it to know it so intimately, and what I lived through as a boy, and what I was brought to know in the war, makes me twice the age I am."

They were flowery words, and what Olin and I had worked on right up to the time I blew my breath into that microphone, but it proved to be the defining moment. After that, I felt like the election was ours for the taking. Still, we pressed it from sunup to suppertime, up and down the numerous creeks, forks and forges; in and out of cafes, pool halls, and general stores; schools and businesses and shacks along the river. Every town and easement to it, every hollow with a road and everywhere a warm body stood, sat, or squatted, I stopped to shake howdy, give my best toothy grin and promises of law and order only a man with my moral outrage and military training could bequeath—and with Olin trumpeting my every word. But then none of it seemed to make a difference to Cordell, except to make him bear down that much harder. He'd sunk his teeth into something plump and juicy, and wasn't about to turn loose just because of me and Olin Yonts. "I'm a duration man," he told us in front of the lunchtime crowd at Fronto's Café, "start to finish. Just like an ol' hound. Don't know when to quit." He was quick to wink and laugh, like he had enough tricks up his sleeve to change the course of rivers, but was just waiting for the right time. "I'll see you boys around," he said through strong teeth and a need to edge away; with a tone that dismissed and with a wink that seemed to ricochet off coffee cups and slices of pecan pie.

Soon as he was out of sight, Olin went to snickering and hitting his hat against his leg. "Hooo-Weee," he hooted, "if 'at ain't the silliest sumbitch that ever ate breakfast."

A month into it and ol' Cordell was still winking and waving, still enjoying his unofficial tally of leading by a mile. By the middle of September, though, Olin upped the ante; his timing marked by the big envelope he fanned in front of his face. "Ruby Mae sends her love," he said, his grin widening, "and support." He dropped the envelope into my hands, then helped me shuffle through its contents: six hundred dollars, all in twenties. "It's for those little unforeseen expenses," he said, grinning for all he was worth. "For disclosure and surprise. It's time, Rubin, you get used to that feller in the mirror being sheriff."

The following week came with a barrage of newspaper ads and radio spots, endorsements from the chamber of commerce, the board of education, and outgoing High Sheriff Garland Sawyers himself. For all its suddenness, notoriety had descended, its roller coaster ride like a June bug tied to the end of a string. Olin had run up the score on ol' Cordell, and it was money and whiskey in the right places and in the right hands that added to our sum. Such recognition coming so sudden—the bulk of it with an IOU, I was certain—was disquieting, if I let myself think about it. The conditions it exacted was a toll I wasn't sure I could pay—but then I had Olin.

* * *

To my advantage, Bobby kept a reverential distance in the months leading up to election, his trips in and out of Greezy checking on his stores more in keeping with the moon and stars. September's dog day's, though, its parched creek beds and drone of jar flies touching on every nerve, came with a single exception. I saw his wine-colored LaSalle coming from far off, shimmering in the sun like some ancient apparition rising up out of the swelter. It was on a long flat stretch of Dry Fork oddly close to where Corbin was found shot to death that we slowed, then eased alongside each other, my door within inches of his.

"I hear tell the law up in here's lookin' for me," he said, his tone dry and grinned.

"Was," I said in an edifying manner, "but I believe I got'em bought off."

"Reckon I owe you anything?" His eyes started with their dance, bright and blue and with its own errant beat.

"Could be," I said, "...dependin'."

He locked me into one of his I-know-something-you-don't-know looks, then went to sniffing at a letter he pulled out of nowhere. "I b'lieve this here damned thing's got perfume spilled all over it." His lip was curled. "Here, see what you think." He dangled it at the end of his red-haired, square-fisted, Popeye forearm, then waited, looking witless, till I saw who it was from: ... Imogene.

"Yer a sorry piece a' hillbilly," he said. "You ain't never said word one to me 'bout any a' this: 'bout you and her." I sat with a blank look, feeling a tad like I'd betrayed a trust. "But we *are* gonna talk about it," he said, his contention as airy as the day was hot. "But it ain't no rush 'cause I already know all there is—at least up till now." Glee had a way of finding a nesting place at Bobby's center. "Dixie an' Imogene's tighter'n dried rawhide," he said. "There ain't three days go by they don't write." He smiled like he knew all there was to know. "Dixie don't keep nothin' from me. You oughtta know that by now." He pointed to the letter. "Imogene figured it'd be safer coming through me than Old Man Andrew. She needs to be careful—bein' married an' all. I'd say she's right. Thought about reading it, then figured I'd just wait an' let you tell me all about it." His whole head seemed to light up as he rolled away. He watched me out his window, his eyes still in a dance.

Rubin (for all that rejoices),

I am finally with words ... and finally with enough nerve to tell you how heartening it was to see you after so long, to know that you are well and safe and finally back—Lord have mercy God—from that devil war. You standing there on Andrew's porch was like having four years of prayers come to life, prayers I'd offered up by the minute, it seemed. What a mess I was seeing you so tall and filled out and every inch a man. I kept wondering what happened to the boy I knew so long ago. It was everything I could do not to run my hands over you, to make sure you were real. But the whole lot of it (you and me and time, what used to be and what's come to pass, what's locked away in memory and out of reach) left me about as turned around and upside down as I wanted to be, stumbling after what to say and how to say it. Don't know that I knew my name what time we stood there. You had to know it was all I could do to keep my head—to feel you so near and not be able to feel you at all. It was like being denied something rightfully mine. But then I don't know how touching and locking onto one another would have been possible without paying a price (me being married and all). There's so much to tell, Rubin, so much in my heart that wants to be righted, but letters seem so off the mark. There's already been more than enough time between us, and I'm just about crazy wanting to know what stars you now wish on ... if any at all. I don't know how or when or even if we'll ever see each other again, but just know that it won't be from my lack of trying. Thank you again for being at Daddy's funeral, and for being all you are to me—whether you intend it or not.

My heart,
Imogene

I rolled her letter over and over in my hands, trying to wrench the last bit of life out of each word. But it was between the lines that disquiet rippled with aching familiarity, the way it always did. What was I to make of it, after so long? There were worse disturbances, I was certain—but for the life of me, none that came to mind, and none more consuming than the feeling of not knowing what was next. The looks that had passed between us, and the feelings they conjured, were somehow even more pronounced now that she was gone, their images lingering with a certain fire. I felt divided, scarce, flat and gray, and wanting to jab something with a sharp stick.

I spent two whole days in the cabin not giving a damned if the sun went up or down when I determined it'd be a hell of a sight easier feeling sorry for myself if I was to wash and shave. A burning sun pushed me toward it, and though it helped, I was still a far cry from dignified. But it was right when I took to throwing my wash water into the yard that I thought I saw movement through the sunflowers growing tall alongside the road. I waited in the doorway, naked from the waist up and with the wash pan still in my hands, when I heard whistling. Seconds later, Imogene came marching into the yard like a strong wind.

"Didn't figure you'd be standin' here half naked," she said without breaking stride; her eyes electric and aimed straight into mine. The next thing I knew, she grabbed hold of the wash pan, pushed me back inside, and closed the door behind us. My world was changed forever.

Seventy-One

The Wings and Winnings of Victory

Imogene's life with Colin Ward had reached a point of breaking. Their marrying in the first place had come with the strings of necessity, an obligation long-since satisfied in both their minds. Hanging on only underscored their regrets and the need to be out from under it all. My all-of-a-sudden dropping out of the sky was like a new morning (her words), a sign that maybe there was a higher order at work: something that mitigated the mire that lapped up around her and Colin. The fate of her unhappiness and the brittle ground she and I found ourselves on was far from ideal, yet I knew the condition of her heart. Moreover, I knew what confirmed it: the promise of *us* and what might come.

Cordell's short little legs looked like they were bicycling most of the time, running him here and there. Olin's no-let-up tactics had left him a little off kilter, winking less and looking like he was about nine pounds short of ten. How Cordell looked didn't mean a tinker's damn to Olin; his thrashing around like a fish on dry land only added to the fun. By the day, Olin managed to tighten the noose on him by gaining one endorsement after another, from one civic group to the next—even from the Daughters of the Confederacy. A week into October, Cordell looked as dry and brown as last-felled leaves.

With the election just two weeks away, Olin insisted we make one last sweep to let people know that a vote for Rubin Cain was a vote for uprightness and all the things that endeared. It was a gentle sweep where I smiled a lot, and where Olin busied himself with whispered man-talk, gentle laughs, and half-pint bottles of liquor dealt slight-of-hand. It was more than enough. I carried all four districts.

The day was sunny but with a discernible chill when we finally emerged from the courthouse; Olin and Garland Sawyers on my flanks—all three of us being applauded by a cadre of supporters, all the while with me scared half to death and thinking about what was to come, the realities of which were still unknowns. It was later, on the drive back to Greezy, that I thanked Olin for all he'd done, for what seemed like dreams and months of magic all rolled together. He just laughed and said, "Son, you were sheriff six months 'fore the polls ever opened." It was a moment of truth, the way I'd come to know it with Olin Yonts, as gripping as the chills he caused in my spine. "Reckon you might want to thank Ruby Mae one of these days," he said, "and Bobby too ... for their *generosity*." His tone was level, confiding, his eyes never drifting from the road, just staring straight ahead, going home.

Mary Olive called me "Big Law," a name as teeming as her platter of pork chops—courtesy of Truman's newly butchered hog—her fried greens, yellow corn, and fresh-churned buttermilk: the wings and winnings of victory. Family came and went like the sun coming up and going down, their good wishes etched forever on a man I barely knew and a boy I tried hard to remember.

I stayed the night, as did Grandmaw and Lorali, giving in to Mary Olive's pleadings. It was just as well, seeing as how Grandmaw wanted to talk. We sat at the kitchen table, just the two of us, out of earshot and with the lamp dimmed to a glow despite the electric bulb dangling from a chord I distrusted and refused to use. Grandmaw talked just above a whisper: her nature, more often than not, when it was just the two of us. Just being still and listening to her soft musings took me back; in an instant, I was that boy once again, the where and how and why of him a twisted lot. It was time, Grandmaw told me, that I know the whole of it. It was about my daddy, she said ... long before I was even a thought.

Seventy-Two

Equal Portions of Propriety and Bloodshed

Lester Trout was lucky if he stood five and a half feet, even with his boots on, but was about as thick and muscled as a railroad car. Even his face carried the density of stone.

"Square, is what he is," Seriann said from behind the counter, "but in a purdy way, don't you think?" I knew better than to dispute anything Seriann had to say, but there wasn't any way in hell I was going to admit to Lester Trout being *pretty*.

"Stout looking," is all I said.

Lester was Greezy Creek's new deputy sheriff, someone keen and steadfast, and knowing he had skin in the game. It was mid-morning, and just a handful hunkered around Andrew's stove when Garland Sawyers swore him in. It was over and done with in a minute's time. When Garland offered up his hand in congratulations, Lester grabbed hold of it like a pump handle on a well and sent nerve-pain shooting all the way into Garland's neck. Garland did his best not to show it while the rest of us slapped Lester on the back and taunted him about finally making it to the big time. Lester pinned the badge to his shirt right then and there, then pulled out a long-barrel .38 revolver he'd wedged between his belt and his backbone, and moved it around to the front where everybody could see it. From that day forward, that's where it stayed: jammed inside his britches, its handle in plain view just above his belt buckle.

"Now, how you reckon 'at young'n's gonna sheriff and sell liquor at the same time?" Mary Olive was best with the truth, laughing and slapping her knee. It was well known that Lester had bootlegged for Bobby ever since Bobby threw in with Hooker and Ruby Mae.

"One way of not havin' to worry about the law," chuckled Seriann.

"Could be he's smarter'n all of us put together," cackled Mary Olive.

"Be crazy not to buy from ol' Lester," said Wilson. "Silvermoonshine served up with a free get-outta-jail card." This was enough to get everybody to hooting and stomping, and sending the windows to rattling.

"DRUNK WITH A *GUARANTEE*!" howled Seriann.

"SHERIFF WHISKEY!" shrieked Mary Olive, the fun near to rocking the foundation out from under us.

I spent considerable time with Garland Sawyers leading up to my swearing-in, getting to know who all was under the sheriff's command—his posse and cadre of loyalists—and listening to his take on budgets and regulatory directives, politics, religion, and anything having to do with attitudes, viewpoints, ways of life and moral edicts. He was about the talkingest damned feller I'd ever met, and many a time waited for him to take a breath before I could get a word in edgewise. But then there were times when he kept right on talking, even on the inhale. We even got around to discussing Haman Flowers' killing and the lack of evidence to warrant much more than a cursory investigation. Nothing to go on, he told me, except his chest being opened up with a twelve gauge—and an odd little slug that Virgil Blair found, along with a shard of Haman's skull, after everybody had cleared out. "Brought it to me in a little jelly jar," he said. "He wasn't sure it'd amount to anything, but felt that he could rest better knowing I was aware of it. Didn't take no time a-tall 'fore Joncy Applegate—our firearms specialist, and best there is in my 'pinion—to recognize what it was. Knew it right off. Didn't even need to scope it. Forty-one caliber, he said. Derringer. I gave it back to

Virgil next time I saw him ... jelly jar an' all. Told him I couldn't see as how it had any bearing. And that's the way we left it. I'd already written my report, and just didn't want to fool around opening it back up. I was just glad to be done with it all." Garland's revelation had been immediate, had jolted my breathing. Keeping a poker face was never any more vital. It was the sort of evidence I wanted left exactly like Garland left it: *buried.* There were only two .41 caliber derringers I knew of, and both of them too close to home.

At Garland's urging, I moved out of Rafe Kinney's cabin and into the Hatcher Hotel just before Christmas; bought my first suit of clothes, then a week later did it again—custom and expectation being the driving force, what seemed to be in keeping with the almost-new Chevrolet sedan with *Pike County Sheriff* inscribed boldly on its doors. Hooker Hopkins dusted me off when I walked into Invictus for the first time, my suit as slick as my hair, my celebrity as thick as the noise of a full house. Bobby said the suit made me look like a bigger crook than all of Pikeville's lawyers put together. It was the sort of compliment that sassed its way across his tongue, that kept him at arms length from the likes of moderation and all that wanted to be plain. The gradation of patrons was across the board at Invictus, from the schools of small fish to the bigger ones that fed on them, and Bobby moved me from one to the other without missing a name. Despite my rising star, he was still my biggest heckler, but then always my most ardent backer. Being at Invictus was one of the first times I'd stepped out on my own since the election, the first time many had seen me without Olin Yonts or Garland Sawyers in tow. The very idea had a timbre all its own, roiled in the pitch of things high and commanding.

My swearing in was presided over by Judge Aldridge and attended by a handful of well-wishers, a pesky little reporter from the *Pike County News,* and Olin Yonts wearing a hog-sized grin. I was picture-snapped a half-dozen times and with as many people, then escorted up to my office right there in the courthouse, with my name already inscribed on the door. The issuance of a snub-nosed .38 Special—and a badge, of course—lost most of its ceremony in the barrage of questions from the *Pike County News* reporter: questions I knew little to nothing about, but was somehow able to fend off with carefully framed answers and promises I had every intention of keeping. The transition of power was immediate, but Judge Aldridge suggested that Garland stay on for a short time, till I was dug in: till I could tell the good guys from the bad. Though I was outwardly confident, I was secretly glad he'd suggested it.

Celebration was low key: coffee and pie at Fronto's Café, then a chicken dinner later that night at the Pinson Hotel, all of it on the county's dime, and where I was left knowing that I was now part and parcel of a continuation crafted with equal portions of propriety and bloodshed—the guts of it with the sour mash breath of good ol' boys doing for one another—like it was the world over I suspected.

My new address at the Hatcher Hotel allowed Imogene's letters to come unabated, the desk clerk never bothering to care one way or the other, despite their scented bouquets. My wanting to look over my shoulder each time they were handed to me, however, was something I would need to unlearn. Our situation seemed less arbitrary the day she came calling at Rafe's cabin, fantasy and reverie taking up the better part of commonsense. Even in its purest form, our action was not without umbrage, though nothing that would prompt amends, even now, even in the least. What we were ready to rally around and share with the rest of the world couldn't be helped; we were simply the culminations of what began in wonder, unmarred except by indulgence. Heaven's gate was never more open, its light never more pronounced—as eager, in fact, as the fire that sought to shape us, that woke us to what lay sleeping and forbidden. Patience, though of the essence, became a thing removed; it's absence wiping out what was left of caution and making our blend and bond no longer an option, but a necessity. For all its complexity, we were something far more exact than our crime, as definitive as our casting aside of Colin. The thought that we might somehow be as one was its own source of strength, as clear-cut as the lie that had defined her marriage, as finite as the fever we were becoming.

Seventy-Three

Ready for Thirteen

Ol' Bartley was old by dog years, his will making him longer-lasting than I ever thought possible. It was Olin who came to tell me, to give me the news of him being gone; the shine on my new sheriff shoes just two days old. We buried him right alongside ol' Red, the hillside as wet and cold as I could ever remember, as uninviting as death itself, the gray mud beneath the snow defying us shovel after shovel. Little Sherman wrapped him in a flowered feedsack, then spelled me with the digging, his twelve years proving he was ready for thirteen. He teared-up when we finally lowered ol' Bartley down, his hands knotted around the end of that feedsack like it was almost a sin to let go. We piled up rocks as a marker, said how much we'd miss him, how there'd never be another one like him—then pitched our way down the slope, knowing one day how we'd say goodbye to one another in just the same way.

Part III

Seventy-Four

Randle Cain

John F. Kennedy was in his second year of presidency when Fayella Flowers made her final move back to Greezy Creek. She wasn't much bigger than she was at fourteen when she was put away in what we used to call the crazy house. Fayella was twenty-one when the state turned her loose, when it was decided she no longer presented a threat to herself or to others. But then her sister, Dixie, was never quite so sure. Dixie was still more of a mother to Fayella than a sister, and kept her within arms reach even after her release. All Fayella really wanted was to come home, make some sort of life in the head of Shop Branch—even after Randle Cain, a man twice her age, began to lay claim to her. Randle was not to Dixie's liking, but there was only so much she could affect. Her being so far away—living with Avondale and Haywood Pritchett on the far lower end of Pikeville—effectively left the door wide open for Randle. Almost overnight Randle had Fayella's head filled with hopes far exceeding the bare warrants of Greezy, and what all might come of her returning to

Shop Branch. In just a matter of weeks he had her standing before the justice of the peace, and only days after that that he had her moved off to Keen Mountain, Virginia. It was a full fifteen years before she made her way back to Greezy, Randle and six children in tow.

Randle Cain lived alone for the better part of his life, and for good reason: no one would have him. No one until Fayella Flowers, that is, and who was to say she knew the difference, even after he routinely knocked her around and locked her out of the house for days at a time, to teach her lessons only he and the devil could understand. Randle was a drunk and a thief of the lowest order, and only a coalminer when it suited him: when credit ran dry or money for liquor became as scarce as the food he failed to provide. As a rule, what he stole was *life*—as sure as if he'd made a deal with Satan himself. He robbed Fayella and the children in ways measured only by desolation, left them sallow and unfinished, dull and sunken and half-starved, and without even the dignity of a raised head, as if he'd ransomed their souls. Correctness and self-worth were not his to pass along, nothing that separated him from thievery, drunkenness and mistreatment. But it was the child abuse that set him apart, the littlest one—Clayman Ray—always catching the worst of it. Randle's relentless accusations that Clayman Ray was not his kept him riled to where he would, on drunken sprees—which were more often than not—lock little Clayman in the pen where he kept his dogs. The rest, Fayella included, he ran out of the house with a shotgun, leaving them to the night and to what all ambled about in the dark. It was under the porch—in the dirt with the rats and snakes—where they huddled together and fended for themselves. Come morning, he'd call to them, ask if they intended to stay out there forever, or if they were just too stupid to know any better. But little Clayman Ray he would leave out with the dogs until somebody got brave enough to go get him. Church charity, neighbors with an eye toward the truth, and Dixie (always Dixie), supplemented Randle's take from the welfare rolls and helped fill the cavity of his making. Randle was senior to Fayella by some twenty-five years. He was also the only son of L. Tom Cain, the man who raised my daddy. Randle and my daddy grew up in the same house at the same time, but there was nothing—thank God in heaven—that connected them by blood.

"Back before you was even thought about," was the way Grandmaw had started-in. From there it was a stop-and-start process, all the while stilling me with her eyes, languid and blue and as soft as the quiet in her hands, making sure I was ready for each word and each one thereafter.

My mother's people were really the only family I had, she said. My daddy, Adam, was taken in by L. Tom Cain when he was just two years old. L. Tom had been a good friend and neighbor to my granddaddy and had honored his deathbed wishes to raise his boy, Adam, after he was gone.

Rantz and Sarah Wright, my grandparents, Adam's momma and daddy, died within two days of one another after the wagon they were driving rolled off a cliff near the top of Town Mountain. The road they were on was more of a pass, hacked into a steep slope and forced around giant boulders. It was given more to walking and the sure-footedness of mules than the wagon they were in. The pass was crowned and pitched in the wrong direction, toward the cliff, but it was the quickest way to get to John's Creek and Sarah's dying sister.

According to L. Tom, the horse my granddaddy was driving was all but give-out after the long climb up the mountain. Granddaddy had rested him on and off, but near the top, he stood straining to hold the wagon from sliding backward. He was a strong horse, but it was raining hard, and when the wagon started slipping, granddaddy put the whip to him, but there wasn't much left in him; the harder he pulled, the more rock and mud gave way under his feet. Finally, he reared up from the sting of the whip, and that was when the weight of the wagon commenced to get the better of him. Grandpaw whipped him even harder, but when he reared up for the second time, the angle of the road and the mud under his feet proved too much. They all went over the cliff in flashes of lightening and a pouring rain, the horse lurching for all he was worth and sounding for the world like he was screaming.

Miners on the road at the time said the rain was coming down in sheets, and it was hard to tell what happened, exactly. It had all happened so fast, they said: "The horse an' wagon flippin' clean over back'ards, quicker'n they knew what to do." Grandmaw Sarah was already dead by the time the miners got to her at the bottom of the cliff. They said there was so much blood it was hard to tell which was hers and which was the horse's. Granddaddy's fall was broken somewhat by scrub pines perched on a small outcrop about twenty feet down. He held on spitting blood for nearly a day before he took his last breath. "*His insides was all busted,*" was the way L. Tom told it. But he hung on long enough to get L. Tom's word that he'd take little Adam and raise him like his own.

Adam Wright was my daddy's real name, but L. Tom raised him as Adam Cain. It was the only name my daddy ever knew, and the name he passed on to me. I think back sometimes on how Momma and Daddy had both been raised by someone other than their real mother and father, and how the same had happened to me. The only difference was that I was older when it happened. Still, it seems like we were marked: like there was a hand somewhere trying to stop our line, a hand that just missed each time.

Grandmaw's tiny face had winced upwards by the time she finished telling me. She sat staring for the longest time, hunched and as still as the dark that crept in around her eyes. "Now you know the truth of it," she said.

On oft occasions, Bobby could be talked into tagging along with Dixie and her whatnots of canned goods, bags of flour and beans, rings of bologna and a few crumpled-up dollar bills—all for Fayella and the children.

"Never a time she didn't need it," Bobby said. "Like it was with doctors; never a time she didn't need one. An' all on account a' Randle." I'd been called often enough to similar sites, even rolled into Fayella's a time or two after she got back to Greezy. Each time it was the same: the pale brittle bones and blank stares of her and her children not really understanding the why of their harm, the pain an integral part of their helplessness.

Franklin and Fayella had been Dixie's to raise ever since they quit diapers. And now, these many years later—and on the heels of being granted a professorship at Pikeville College—she was still at it, at least with Fayella. Franklin, though, was longtime gone: just up and run off with the carnival that came through Pikeville during the war years. In actual fact, he left with the snake oil salesman by the name of Heaven Tidewater: a man partial to black leotards, red silk capes, and a tiny handlebar mustache. It was no secret that Franklin favored the airier side of being, away from the goings of dirt and sweat and such. He was only fifteen when he left—Aug bringing Wilma Lee to Shop Branch being reason enough—but then he never came back, even to collect his clothes, things bright and hand-sewn—his *lighter things* as Wilma Lee called them—down to their last weave and stitch. It was Wilson who saw him last, in front of the cotton-candy stand wearing white cowboy boots, wisp of a thing that he was, and smoking from the end of a long cigarette holder. Aug went to fetch him after two days and found him postured on a scaffold alongside Heaven Tidewater himself. He was handing out bottles of colored water, winking and agreeing with what was hawked as an ancient Indian remedy, what fatted and made well. When Aug told him he needed to come down from there that very goddamn minute and get his bony ass home, Franklin stepped to the edge of the scaffold, stretched his cigarette holder out over Aug and gave it a tiny tap. The ash and its intent sent Aug back to Shop Branch with the last image he ever had of his little brother.

Randle Cain drifted to Greezy sometime after the war, when he'd drunk up what money his daddy had left him. Lower Fork was where he lived, near the head of Gillespi Hollow in a shack not fit for much but holding back a little wind and rain, and sometimes not even that. He was forty-six when he first caught sight of Fayella at the post office. Marrying was the farthest thing from Fayella's mind, figuring nobody would have her after being locked away for seven years in a *state house*. Pretty much that way for Randle, too, being last on a long list of least-sought-afters. But it was Randle's strange and sudden interest that seemed to soften the hold on Fayella's loneliness, his steady press and visions of a better life adding a glimmer of hope to the black hole of her existence. Tying the knot just seemed so natural. But then going off to Keen Mountain, Virginia, was like following the trail of a fool: like mining in Virginia was any easier than it was in Kentucky, like believing there were diamonds there in Keen Mountain's coal. Coming back to Greezy fifteen years later seemed the smart choice, given there was more to be got for doing less: more family and neighbors to take up Randle's habitual slack. But then there were the marks he left on Fayella, which never seemed to go away, and the mind-scars etched eternally in his children. Randle was L. Tom's only natural son, just a year older than my daddy. And though they were raised up together, they never counted one another as brothers. About the only thing my daddy ever said of Randle was that he was born to this earth for no other reason than to blight his family's name. As far as I know, Randle never proved him wrong. And the day I was called to Greezy's Primitive Baptist Church House was the last time the family would ever have to worry about it.

Seventy Five

Iced in Uncompromising Certainty

After seventeen years of sheriffing, one might think that surprise was hard to come by; that lawing would have been honed to where things were less unfamiliar; that I would have this thing figured out to where cause and effect made perfect sense, and where I could attend to even the worst of it simply over morning coffee. It was the sort of notion I tucked away during unguarded moments, before the truth of it came storming back, as it always did, iced in uncompromising certainty. Surprise was manifest if nothing else, wakeful and around every bend, even when I expected it. It was understood I didn't like my Sundays interrupted, particularly on mornings when I'd been out most of the night; but then it was Lester Trout figuring I'd want to know. "*Brutish,*" he'd said over the phone. Nothing that could wait. Something I needed to see for myself, his descriptions cussed around words like *hardhearted* and *coldblooded*.

"Plime blank the way Tate Embry found him," Lester said, "...him and his dogs adder runnin' fox all night." Lester talked out the side of his mouth: the side stretched with chaw, even at seven a.m. "Come got me right off," he said. "It barely daybust."

It was mid December, the morning sky thick with gray and the beginnings of frost out over the ground. I stood looking down on Randle Cain the way I looked down on Haman Flowers some twenty-six years ago, stiff and spread out like the five points on a star, a cavern for a chest and a bullet hole in the middle of his cheek—the left one. Quiet squeezed in around me despite Lester's going on. A heavy build up of clouds and a steady patter of rain only added to it. I shut my eyes against the recollections of Haman, time inviting chinks of memory. Randle was beyond anything I could help with, already hours into the abyss of what I imagined Satan had in store for him. His corpse sprawled across the church steps was the mirror image of Haman Flowers: his face angled toward heaven, his eyes and mouth wide with horror. Buzzard bait.

Lester kept up the banter to one after another gathering by the minute, spitting 'baccer juice and finding ways to add to his office. I watched with the interest of someone absorbed in his duties, involved, back and forth between a squad of state police and a closing crowd, my words few to none. The spectacle of death was always fodder for a gathering, for the run-on of speculation. The sight of Randle Cain, and what was intended for his humiliation, being the perfect case in point, his cold, colorless, twisted frame feeding on the minds of those who remembered Haman Flowers twenty-six years ago, and on these very same church house steps. It had been a picture too vivid to forget, a gargoyle held up to a people not easy to forgive—like now when they looked at Randle.

Lester was his own attraction: surmising, deducing, construing ... sorting through the overflow of guesswork and conjecture. He was, stride for stride, a clearinghouse for what lay in wait, for what churned in exhibition. Without looking his way, I listened to his parrying and buffering what was ramped in fascination. Lester was the only one I knew to ever knock Homer Lawson off his feet—a thing people respected in a place like Greezy. He was just a year and some months older than me, but seasoned by the likes of farming and coal mining, and what all came from determination. There was no training for deputy sheriff. Just knowing the difference between right and wrong was about all anybody could ask, that, and being ready for what's liable to sour at the drop of a hat. I never gave a damn about how Lester went between bootlegging for Bobby and keeping the peace. Life was hard enough just sorting through the slag of humankind.

All around me, the state police milled ill at ease, snapping pictures and roping off the site; easing over the ground looking for what might give a clue. The coroner was the last to arrive, and other than me and the staunchest hangers-on, the last one to leave, driving off behind the ambulance carrying Randle's remains. I don't know how long I stood there riveted by Randle's blood dissolving in the rain; alone with the morning despite the numbers rivaling for my attention. I didn't know what I hoped to see. So often what we see is what we *want* to see, what we hope will bear the secret to the peace we so desperately seek. Other than the notion of good riddance, there was nothing about Randle that moved me toward any sort of personal armistice. To say otherwise would have been a lie. I was calloused enough to know that about myself. What others saw in me was hard to tell: if they recognized me out of respect, or if I was just something to be tolerated, spoken to out of some sense of obligation or even fear. Either way, it made for real inquiry given the circumstances, and what lay ahead—what dared to be uncovered.

Word reached Mary Olive long before I got there, though her complaining about me not coming around often enough registered even before I had my coat off. And then there were the children, and me not bringing them around as often as I should: offenses that far outweighed what had happened to Randle Cain. Seriann and Lorali were a tad more forgiving, but only by a jot, pardoning my excuses—my "big law busyness"—even more in the wake of the morning's event.

Truman had *gassed* the house, Mary Olive said, beaming that he'd been able to tie her new stove and heater into the gas line that now ran the length of Greezy. We sat drinking coffee made over a gas flame, muddling with what we knew of Randle, his stock and kind, even his demised resemblance to Haman Flowers. Seriann sat stiff and with the air seeming not to move about her, the mention of Haman still cold and unwanted.

"Same everything," I said, "the place, the how. Every detail an exact imitation ... even the day." There was only so much I chose to tell them, despite a bout of questions, grisliness keeping me in check.

Mary Olive had just turned ninety-two and was still every bit a believer of what goes around comes around. “Could be my ’magination,” she said, “but I b’lieve the air gets better ever’time somebody like Randle Cain gets carted off.”

I could almost make out Grandmaw’s tiny face peeking out at me from the headscarf she kept tied up under her chin, her toothless grin the complete response to Mary Olive’s unfettered presumptions. I couldn’t help but see her at every turn, imagine her still in the trail of dogwoods and the scent of teaberry, foraging through the spring mix of ginseng and cohash, bloodroot and wild yams. Eight months of being without her, and still somehow too harsh an entity, too jagged a cut. To say I missed her would be too polite, absent the incursions on my heart. It was emptiness that ambled me off to mountaintops in search for even a remnant of her angel. I found her there as often as I knew I would: in the quietest footfalls and the screech of eagles; in the heavy scents of earth, and all that rushed to life—even today, down here in the valley floor, in the disruption caused by Randle Cain and his ravened goodbye.

“Lester got to Fayella a little bit ago,” I said. “Said she just looked at him for the longest time, then told him she wouldn’t be needing Randle’s corpse unless the county wanted her to burn it. Wasn’t a dime-one for burying. Said government cheese and powered milk was all that stood between her and her young’ns starving to death. Besides that, she said none of them had the strength, much less a shovel, to dig him deep enough for their liking. ‘A dog shit him and the sun hatched him,’ she said, ‘and it’d be best the world over to see him floated down the river tied to a shit house door. Let the coyotes have what the buzzards can’t get at.’”

I sat with one eye on Seriann, waiting for her to add her own disgust, to draw from what she kept hid away. Even after all these years my suspicions still fumbled for a clearer picture of who it was that decided we’d had enough of Haman Flowers. I didn’t much care from a lawman’s angle; to me, justice had been done. Same with Randle. The problem now, though, high sheriff that I was, was not being able to turn my back on it. Then there were the state police and their way of crowding in, making it uncomfortable for jurisdictions that were slow to cooperate. I'd been dragged in before, collaborating, tag-teaming, and didn't look for this time to be any different. The pinch was it being a Greezy Creek killing and the state police expecting more out of me than usual given it was my home turf and me knowing just about everybody who lived here.

Times had changed since Haman Flowers; killings were not so easy to put aside anymore. Randle's killing being so much like Haman's had implications I hadn't thought about, allegations I wasn't ready for. It was unnerving to think that after twenty-six years Haman could reach out from the grave, that his ghost, for so long a rot to the dirt it lay in, could bully us. Where Randle's killing might take us carried its own unrest. But it wasn't too difficult to imagine it leading us right back to Haman Flowers, before all was said and done. Like a sling blade, justice was: back and forth, dissecting layer at a time, and now, because of some romantic notion of like-punishment for like-kind, it had been set into motion once again. Whodunit? The possibility alone bore the strike of a rattler.

More and more poured into Mary Olive's as the morning slipped away, all wanting to be heard, their hard talk and opinion grating on me like a yapping dog. I eased up and away after a time, begging off on red-eyed gravy and powder-milk biscuits, and promising to return sooner than later—a vow hedged on conditions random at best.

I drove the length of Lower Fork not bothering with left or right, just the road ahead, a niggling quiet threatening what remained of peace, even sense. How had I come to be here, anyway? Me, the son of a coalminer, handed from one to another and graveling for what little life was so tightfisted to let go of ... and now leading the parade? How had all the loose ends come together anyway? It was a persistent taunt, what I studied on most nights while everybody else slept; the sound of their rhythmic breathing in contrast to my mix of angst, my wide-eyed disquiet in concert with the mantle clock, its pendulum swing and hour-by-hour reminders of unrecoverable sleep. The whole of such uneasiness stalked me without quit, that and a ready dose of unpredictability keeping the ground soft under my feet, even in the light of seventeen years, even with me thinking that each one would be my last. But there were times when the string of my subsistence drew nigh to breaking, through no fault of my own, as I saw it: just what comes from continuing in the light and darkness of the law.

I stopped at Sutton and waited for the lineup of cars to take their turn across the swinging bridge. A thin mist rose up off the river, soft and silvery above what meandered green and gray. The bridge came and went in the thick of it, its far end only implied, vanquishing in the thickness of river-fog and what was left of the rain. The bridge was a WPA effort sometime during the war, barely wide enough for coal trucks, and never more than one at time. It was more than just a one-laner; its giant swing and sway made it a one-at-a-timer, coming and going, walking or driving—first one then another. About halfway across is when it went to bobbing and bouncing like a clothesline in a windstorm, where I stopped to wait for it to settle and stop bucking before going the rest of the way. The grades and curves of the highway beyond lay blinded by the same silver mist curling up and over the river's banks. I edged through its turns at little more than a crawl before cutting away and taking the road through Cloe, its gentle twist and roll tempering the squelch of my radio and the reminder of who I was, what I was sworn to uphold, and what all lay bruised in grievance.

There was a distance to me at times, a coldness I couldn't ignore, one that said all was right with the world even after I looked down on Randle Cain all shot to hell. Maybe it was all the time and all the mud I'd tracked through getting to the sorryness so prevalent where I least expected it, its only aim to wreck and pull down. It was hard to say for certain, just that it was becoming an imposition to always stay inside the lines when justice was sometimes better served when I didn't. And I was all about justice.

Haman's homicide had been the perfect crime because of so many willing to accept it as God's wrath—swift and indefensible; the same sentiment that was rising up around Randle, one that didn't favor my combing the county looking for a name to pin it on.

My first thought was to step back. The state police had the lead in cases of homicide anyway: muscle rights. My fading into the background would be easy enough, like letting go of what didn't belong to me in the first place. But then my presence was to make a difference—or in Randle's case, trying in the very least to care. But then time had a way of cooling aspirations, those lofty and otherwise; mine were no exception. It was a marshland, this killing of Randle Cain, and as sheriff I was in it deep enough to where I could taste it clear to the back of my throat. The whole thing spoke to what was so out-of-hand, so innately Greezy ... what was so innately me, if truth be known.

Given the right set of circumstances, or enough pain, I never discounted the fact that we were all capable of acts cold and bloody. In Randle's case, wrong being on him like a stain, I understood it even more. It was a killing deserved, to my way of thinking, though nothing I'd ever let be known. Personal feelings were too suspect, too near the margins of offense to be trusted aloud. Discretion was the only safeguard, given what I knew. And what I knew most was that sooner or later there would be a name accountable.

The first and only piece of real evidence came just a day later, when the county's medical examiner dug the slug out of Randle's brain: a .41 caliber, as rare as the pistol that fired it. It was the lead the state police needed, or so they said. The rest was just formality: find the gun, find the killer. Be home by Christmas.

For weeks afterwards, the state police went damned near house-to-house trying to sniff out a lead on that .41 caliber pistol—a derringer they concluded. Questioning was particularly focused on the poker players who'd been with Randle the night he was killed. They'd been at the church house and Randle had been the last to leave, according to Grady Struthers. So dead-broke pitiful, Randle was, that Grady let him have the last few swallows from a half pint of moon.

"Left him sittin' in the middle a' the floor about as drunk as he wanted to be, and with the fire going out in the stove. Four in the morning, best I remember." Grady was a crippled drunk, thin and wobbly and about as tall as a twelve-year-old. He drank while we talked—big swallows—and offering it up to me after each time. "State police already been up in here twice," he said, his gaze on the barren poplars lining his hollow, the cold wind edging him about. "Reckon they think I did it," he said, the bright blue in his eyes straining through the bloodshot and blur. "I ain't but seventy," he said, winking, "and a hunnert-pounds strong. Hunnert an' ten if you count my billfold." He chuckled, his bones near to rattling. "They ain't gonna find nuthin'," Grady said, his smile thin and wide. "I been growed up in these hills all my life, and I know one thang: I can get in an' out of 'em without a soul ever knowin'. It's Indian, second nature, coverin' tracts an' never leavin' a mark. They weren't nuthin' left 'round 'at church house, Rubin, 'cept a cold wind a-blowin'. Troopers in an' out lookin' for signs, but they ain't one to be found 'cause they wadn't one left. An' awl that rain? Heh! I'm surprised they found *me*." There was a comfort to Grady, his laughter, his years, his lack of worry. "Now they tell me they're looking for a derringer." He shook his head and scratched the back of his neck. "Hell," he chuckled, "they might as well be lookin' for the old woman who lived in a shoe."

I saw Grady's words play out in the days that followed, in the state police effort to uncover that mysterious pistol, even coming down on poor Fayella like she was some sort of Moll Flanders. The .41 caliber slug was the only hard evidence they had, nothing more; not an empty shell casing, a footprint, a hair, a thread; nothing in Randle's hands or under his fingernails. Nothing. The rain hadn't helped, its steady patter most of the morning ridding what might have had a bearing. Beyond simple, devouring hate, the motive seemed to confound the state police. Although those of us who knew Randle firsthand, saw his undoing as anything but complicated. After a time, what few troopers remained came to understand Randle like the rest of us: in a highly charged light. Even in the loosest sense, Randle weighed in as bad-tempered, brutal, and broke the biggest part of his life; none of them a crime in its self, but selling government cheese and peanut butter—the only things Fayella and the children had between them and starvation—in order to satisfy his want for liquor, was, even in the eyes of those who'd never seen the inside of a church, a crime worthy of Old Testament retribution.

By the day, Grady's words worked their way onto my plane of acceptance: that scorched place of beliefs and assessments where I wallowed in points of view. The deeper they went, the more obvious they became. There were no clues forthcoming, nothing except for what was most evident: that Randle's killing had been as necessary as Haman's twenty-six years ago. But the link between them was nothing the state police seemed interested in. Trying to tie them together was a stretch, given the absence of any real records outside of some hen-scratching left by Sheriff Garland Sawyers, now dead fifteen years.

Haman Flowers of Greasy Creek, Ky. Found dead early Sunday morning, December 13, 1936, on the steps of Greasy Creek's Primitive Baptist Church. Shot twict. Shot-gunned in the chest at close range and a bullet hole below his left eye. No suspects or any evidence that might lead to one.

That was it: all Garland saw fit to write. It served as a bit of a lark, macabre as it was, but left the state police less than enthusiastic about the name Haman Flowers. Trying to connect him to Randle Cain had the dispatch of a wild goose chase, something they wanted no part of. They weren't here for Haman Flowers, anyway. They were here on account of Randle Cain. Haman Flowers, or whatever the hell his name was, would have to rot on his own.

With the New Year only a day away, the state police begrudgingly closed their books. Still, they insisted that the sheriff's department keep at it, as did the D.A., assuring us that they were only a call away should anything come up. The message was clear: Randle deserved what he got, the glut of testimonies serving to harden the ugliness of his everyday life. Whoever did it was more of an avenging angel, they said, only with a shotgun and a .41 caliber derringer.

Except for our insider's understanding of Randle and the polluted things that possessed him, the sheriff's department added little to what was already known, and nothing that seemed to make any difference. Our conclusion, after another month of posturing, fell pretty much in line with what the state police left us with: the whole of Pike County was better off without Randle taking up anymore of its time or space. My allowing an ongoing investigation with evidence equivalent to a bare landscape would be nothing short of throwing good money after bad. And so, without the resources or even the concentration for a continuance, we pulled our own plug. For the time, anyway, it was a closed file: a mystery we were content to relegate to those who might someday give a damn.

The state police were done—had been for over a month—and for the record, so was I. But then there was Coalter Hatfield.

Seventy-Six

Coalter Hatfield

Coalter Hatfield, ragged and sore looking as he was, just wasn't quite convinced that we'd done all we could to resolve the case of Randle Cain. The minor detail of a killer still out there offering up murder as an aid to what ails was a scenario too rich for a loner like Coalter to ignore; too absorbing for an aficionado of crime novels—G. K. Chesterton, Raymond Chandler, Mickey Spillane, books collected in great heaps on the backseat of his 1948 Ford Coupe—to just sweep Randle Cain aside.

Coalter Hatfield was long past retiring, but figured that working crime scenes for the state police was far more likely to keep him alive than if he were left to his own devices. A fabled, but peculiar type, Coalter was: an inspector with an uncanny sense of which way the wind blew, exacting and by the book when he needed to be, outside the lines when no one was watching—just whatever worked. Expeditious carriages of justice, after all, often had a blind eye. The only rub of any consequence was the ever-present stank of liquor on his breath, the same that leached from his pores and attended him fore and aft.

He was waiting for me on the courthouse steps a full three months after the file on Randle Cain had been designated as a *Cold Case*. We eyed each other with sweet contempt, like we'd both reached for the last pork chop at precisely the same time.

"This is about Randle Cain, isn't it?" My radar was up and keen, and I wanted no part of small talk. I knew I was right before he opened his mouth. It wasn't easy hiding my distaste, but then I was never much good at it in the first place.

"Good to see you, too, Rubin," he said, his voice gravelly and punishing from a long night of crime novels, bourbon, and cigarettes ... but mostly bourbon. I hadn't seen him in a while: three years, anyway. He didn't come around except in cases of homicide, and only then when he felt like it. I knew enough to keep my distance; Coalter's steady barrage and grandiose goings-on about being a direct descendant of William Anderson "Devil Anse" Hatfield had a way of filling the air with willful pomposity, something that left me reaching for what might settle my stomach each time he brought it up, which was first, last, and always.

Part of Pikeville's proud tradition was having been the seat of the Hatfield/McCoy trials back in the 1800's (the feud itself beginning sometime in 1865 and lasting clear to 1888). It's the very court that sentenced and hanged Ellison "Cottontop" Mounts, a member of the Hatfield clan, for the murder of Alifair McCoy. The plaque outside the courthouse and its account of the trials is a component of Pikeville's historical landscape. Coalter knew every fact there was to the Hatfield/McCoy feud: what triggered it in the first place and what kept it alive; what preceded each episode of violence; who the names were—on both sides—and what part each of them played. He was a living fact sheet of Hatfield/McCoy tribal warfare and curator of its lore, from the first offence to the last one buried. It took more than a dozen killings and just as many wounded before state militias on both sides (West Virginia and Kentucky) were called to restore order. And though it was the hanging of Ellis Mounts that marked the end to the paralyzing string of violence, trials continued as late as 1901 before all was done, before peace finally returned to the Tug Fork Basin: to the Hatfields of Mingo County, West Virginia, and the McCoys of Pike County, Kentucky.

The one mitigating factor that Coalter felt so right to profess was that the McCoys fought on the side of the Union, and no doubt had a hand in killing what may have been some of their own neighbors ... even kin. The first real violence and first casualty was the murder of returning Union soldier Asa Harmon McCoy by ex-confederates Homeguard led by Jim Vance, a member of the Hatfield clan. Asa's murder, as Coalter was so want to proclaim, simply fell into the category of justified and even necessary: the same proclamation I hoped he'd ultimately profess for Randle Cain.

Coalter stood quivering from the cold, barely able to hold his cigarette and smelling of whiskey at seven in the morning. "I'm bettin' there's a cup a' coffee somewhere up in there," he said motioning with his head toward the courthouse's catacomb of offices, but meaning mine. He looked frayed, yet hardened, his face swollen and without color, his eyes red and rheumy. How he stayed alive was anybody's guess. "Thought I'd lend a hand," he said after I said nothing. "See what I can do." He gave me one of his possum-in-a-turnip-patch smiles. "So much left dangling and all," he said. "Disturbing."

"I've seen my share a' killings," Coalter said, rifling through the pictures of Randle Cain sprawled out dead on the church house steps, "but this one's ripe." He stopped and dropped the stub of his cigarette in the mud. "We're talkin' about focus here," he said. "A killer with just one thing in mind: make Randle as dead as dead can get, and make damn sure he stays that way. It's Haman Flowers all over again." Coalter never forgot anything: dates, times, and places in particular, the hallmarks of his life as a gumshoe. He chuckled and rubbed his hand across his gray stubble. "Taste?" He offered a tiny flask, one he picked from the inside of his coat pocket like a pack of cigarettes. I shook him off, but it mattered little to none. He helped himself the way I get after Kool-aid in the middle of July, draining it to the last drop. We were back at the crime scene, just standing with a March wind tearing at our pant legs and figuring what the hell to do next. Without thinking I'd object, or without ever caring, he decided we needed to partner up. The rest, for me at any rate, was a race to get to the inevitable: his leaving.

"Twenty-six years is a considerable time," Coalter noted. "But I'm thinkin' there might be something tying these killings together." Beyond the gnaw and fever of bourbon, there was nothing Coalter liked better than conspiracy. “If I’m right, we could be in for a real toasty time. Could be a real mean sumbitch back there in some holler not liking what we’re up to. It being twenty-six years an’ all, an’ him thinking it’s a thing over and done with. Damn! Just the thought a’ him sweatin’ damned near makes this fun.”

I went back to the car and waited with the heater turned on high while Coalter walked around the churchyard, his raincoat too long for his legs and too wispy for the bite in March’s wind. His moving about sniffing and staring—at what I couldn’t imagine—his head leaning this way, then that, like he was listening to something in the dirt and rocks—maybe trying to connect with Randle’s ghost, or maybe Haman’s. Finally, he just stood there—the tail of his coat whipping and snapping, his wolf-like hair, thick and collected (a cap of its own)—deep in thought and airing what clouded his mind.

He was chaffed and chattering by the time he got back to the car, his hands stiff and his breath fresh and raw with liquor. I waited while he rocked and shivered in front of the heat vent. It was some time before he spoke. “Could be we got one killer for both,” he said. “Maybe finding a name for one is all we need.”

“Two for one?”

“Sump’m like ’at.” He finished rubbing his arms and hands then fished around in his long coat for a spanking new pint of bourbon, no flask this time, just a bright shiny bottle like it was right off the shelf: U.S. bonded, Kentucky stilled and bottled. He cracked the seal and offered it up like a cup of coffee.

“I need for the sun to be down ’fore that even starts to look good to me,” I said.

“Suit yourself,” he said upending it, his throat a sluice gate, wide and welcoming. I waited, not acknowledging his one long lingering pant and the hotness it added to the air, while he replaced the lid and tucked it back inside his coat.

“I’d appreciate it if that was the last time you did that in my company or in my car,” I said. A controlled seethe crept over his face, contemptible but owing to my station, then waited for some give in my expression, but one never came. "We the law," I said, "but we ain't above it." And that was the end of it, though we both sat in the wind-rushed sound of March for sometime before speaking.

"So you're thinking there's something to it? Clues to Randle, I mean, being locked up in Haman?" I was back to business. "Or maybe the clues to Haman are locked up in Randle?"

"Little a' both would be my guess," he said, trying for dignity, although already pink-eyed and it barely ten o'clock. "Funny how time can counsel in the quietest ways," he said, the sting gone from his tone. "Mostly, in cases like this, you'll find what you're lookin' for in good ol' boys' whisperings, them having figured out who and what and how; putting together pieces one at a time; mixing and matching and finding their way to the truth." He stared off into the morning, the wind buffeting the life out of an already desolate looking Monday morning. "Ours is a rare talent, Rubin," he said. "Mainly finding the right questions for the right people, though a backward reach of twenty-six years is a stretch, given we ain't got but one single piece of evidence. What other option do we have but to question? It's fundamental to what we do." For once, Coalter didn't seem so full of himself. Begin at the beginning, the simplest of all adages, was pretty much what he was saying, what made most sense. But then there was my piece of the puzzle, and what awaited on the other side of its revelation.

Seventy-Seven

There Would Be Signs

The sky was near black by the time I pulled up in front of Liddy's, the ground already soft and waiting for another downpour. Two days of rain had left the creeks up, loud and hurried and in a hell's rush to get to the Big Sandy. Coalter was slumped against the passenger door, suffused in the afterglow of a whiskey breakfast. He slept on even after I slammed my door.

"Lawww, if you ain't a sight," Liddy said, one hand on her breast bone, the other motioning me in toward the little space heater she kept in the middle of the room. "Thought my heart might stop when I saw 'at sheriff's car pull up," she said. "Took me a minute 'fore I realized it was you under that big white hat." She laughed then offered to make us coffee. It had been a full seventeen years since I last saw Liddy. She looked old, but then I had to remind myself she looked old seventeen years ago. "You know I'm eighty year old now," she said from the kitchen, her voice lit up like she was proud, like it was a little impossible to believe.

"You look the same to me, Liddy," I said, trying for an inside track. "It's like you ain't aged a day since I last saw you." We talked in short bursts, memories taking up most of it, doing what they could to reconnect us. She waved me to the kitchen table and served me coffee in a cup and saucer (one chipped, one cracked), then set me out a slice of custard pie before helping herself.

"I was real sorry to hear about your grandmaw," she said. "If there was ever an angel..."

I tried swallowing around the knot at the mention of her name. "She was a blessing," I said, the words not reaching the depth I wanted.

We left it there, Grandmaw's image paired to my inner sanctum, when Liddy sat up with a start. "Heaven on earth!" she said, looking over my shoulder out the window.

Coalter was hunkered and squinting, trying to peer through Liddy's curtains. "He's with me," I said just before throwing the door open. "How 'bout a cup a' coffee," I growled. He bolted upright like he'd backed into a sharp stick, embarrassed but glad to see me. He took a step closer, cautious and doing his best to peer past me into the living room, ambush never to be dismissed.

He pushed past me, reeking and tremulous, too much liquor or not enough was hard to tell, although Liddy's steady flow of coffee seemed to swathe and even throttle the bite of its whiff. Getting the cup to his mouth and then back to the saucer, however, was proving to be a task. "I might be better off with a straw," he said. "Or maybe one of you could hold my mouth and the other just pour it in me." It was a side of Coalter I'd never seen: self-effacing, even endearing, and stirring Liddy to laughter.

Small talk, the kind that lent itself to trust, slowly gave way to our being there. "Figured somebody'd come around sooner or later," Liddy said, her eyes fixed on her coffee and the soft breath of air she sent across its top.

"I've meant to come around before now, Liddy. But anymore, it seems like I'm in a race with time. Just ain't never enough of it."

"Don't matter. I'm just glad you finally made it ... an' I'm glad you brought Mr. Hatfield." She smiled her biggest and broadest. "Pie, Mr. Hatfield?"

Coalter waved her off as if food of any kind would surely be the end of him. "Thought about you," she said to me, "when I heared what happened to Randle Cain. Terrible thang. Put me in mind a' Haman Flowers. Though I don't guess I'm the only one."

"Ahhh ...," Coalter cleared his throat. "Excuse me if I sound a little diagnostic, or even a little prying—but with your permission, I'd like to wade in here." He gave her a nervous smile and swabbed at his forehead with a wadded handkerchief he struggled to dig out of his coat pocket.

"Just wade right ahead," Liddy said.

"Well, then," he said, "at the risk of impertinence, I'd appreciate clarification on one finite, but critical detail." Coalter was solicitous, even submissive. Liddy leaned in, her eyes attentive. "Now I'm of the understanding—and correct me if I'm wrong—that it was your husband, Virgil Blair, that was deputy sheriff at the time Haman Flowers was killed."

"That's right," Liddy said. "And it was Virgil what found him!"

Coalter sat up straight, his eyes wide. "Well now, he said, "that's quite a picture."

"It was hard on Virgil," Liddy said, her eyes narrowing. "Not just that night, but ever'day after. Hard on both of us, is more like it. 'Bout as tough a time as I ever knowed."

"Why is that, you reckon?—if you don't mind me asking?" Coalter's tone was considerate, sincere. I sipped my coffee, waited.

"'Cause a' what he knew," Liddy said, "and what he wasn't allowed to say. Left him feelin' like he was breakin' the law." She sat back in her chair, crossed one knee over the other, and raked her fork through what was left of her custard pie.

"Now that's an oddity, if you don't mind me saying." Coalter now empathy defined. "Bein' hushed, I mean: a crime in itself if you ask me." He stopped, his cup shaking mercilessly to and from his lips. "That had to have been a great strain." Coalter's eyes were set in a soft stare.

"More like a condemnation," Liddy said. "Kept him up nights walkin' the floor, talkin' to hisself."

"Ever say anything to you about it?—what he wasn't supposed to tell?"

She hesitated, licked her lips. "Virgil wasn't ever one to talk," she said, "even to me. He'd set out there on the porch or hunker up by the fire many a night without word one. But Haman Flowers' killin' left him balled up like a pine knot. He never slept half the time anyway. Up all hours, creepin' around, scarin' me half to death, shushin' me like he was listenin' for lord-knows-what, drinkin' in night sounds an' actin' like he was on the verge of hearin' somethin' from the beyond. It ain't nuthin' I'd ever want you to talk about, but I swan if he wouldn't just about talk to ghosts; nights he'd be mumblin' an' carryin' on like there was a cabin full, an' there not being a soul or a thing on earth with him but his shadow. Next thang I'd know, he'd be headin' out, an' it bein' the middle a' the night. Saddle ol' Jake an' clop off down the road an' it black as a coalmine. It was that way the night he found Haman. Took off outta here like sump'm was a-callin' him. I spent the night with the covers up over my head, prayin' Almighty God was out ahead of him, in between him an' whatever it was he tormented with. He was one of a kind, Virgil was; took being deputy to heart. County paid him next to nuthin', but there were other thangs that made up for it. People were grateful for all he did. We never went hungry a day in our lives."

She stopped and looked across the table like she was seeing Coalter for the first time. His smile was kindly, though there were beads of sweat on his upper lip, his hand on the flask in his coat pocket. "But did he ever share anything with you?" he asked, licking his lips, "—about that night?—about Haman?—about what he saw once he got there?"

She studied him for a moment, a light seeming to rise up behind her. "Just once," she said, letting out a big breath. "Just one time that he ever mentioned it."

"Is it anything you can share with us?" Coalter was courting.

She thought about it, then ran her finger around the rim of her cup. "It was after months of it fussin' with him, an' purt-near gettin' the best of him, is when he come out with it. Said he needed to clear his mind about sump'm, keep it from eatin' at him any more than it already had." She sipped at her coffee, her eyes in a search for what lay hidden. "Garland Sawyers was clear about not wantin' any part of it," she said. "Mostly 'cause a' Olin Yonts wantin' it buried and forgot about. 'Course we can't never know for sure. It's just what Garland told Virgil." She was looking somewhere off in the distance, trancelike.

"What was it," Coalter asked as gently as he could, "that this Olin Yonts wanted buried?" I shifted in my seat, the clack of my cup and saucer like thunderclap in the stillness.

"The truth." She smiled, her lips stretched to quivering.

"Which was ... ?" Coalter was near to snapping, sweat now beading in the edges of his hair.

"Reckon I might be the onliest one he ever told," she said, her eyes aimed at the kitchen window, the yard beyond, the sky darkening by the minute.

I could see Coalter's hand tighten on the bottle in his pocket, his posture just short of begging. "Told what, Liddy?"

She looked down and away and picked lint off the sleeve of her sweater, summoning courage I assumed.

"That it was Bobby," she said lifting her eyes to Coalter, then to me. "That it was Bobby and Ben Yonts."

We said goodbye to Liddy about the time the sky let go, then sat in the car for the longest time studying the slug she gave us sealed in a jelly jar, its lid screwed down tight. It was the very slug she said Virgil found on the church house steps, right in with a piece of Haman's skull. "*Kept it in 'at little jelly jar,*" she'd said. "*Didn't want to chance losing it. Never did do nuthin' with it; just kept thinkin' he might.*"

Coalter kept glancing at the bourbon bottle inside his coat pocket and listening to the rain, the smoke from his cigarette reaching into every corner of the car. "I have to wonder about what Liddy said," he mused. "How much was her own and how much remained of what Virgil actually told her? It's been twenty-six years, don't forget; time enough to fill in missing pieces with thoughts and dreams and the constructs of imaginings." Coalter sounded like he was inside one of his crime novels, maybe all of them at once: deducing, scaling castle walls, preserving what was on the side of right.

"From what you tell me," Coalter said, "there were plenty of reasons to hate Haman Flowers, as many reasons as there were people who knew him. The same with Randle Cain. But it takes a special kind of hate to bear down on somebody with a shotgun: to blunt an existence, to watch a body split apart, its life and all its forces empty into nothingness. Damn." He shook his head, pulled the bottle out of his coat pocket and rolled it from one hand to the other. "You might better take me back to the motel," he said.

"I don't know if I believe her at all," I said. "Bobby Yonts was just sixteen, and even as wounded and angry as he was over Haman killing his uncle Corbin, I can't fathom the heinousness of that crime being a part of who he was, or is. If it were true, I would have picked up on it over time, knowing him like I do—like a brother. There would have been signs. It ain't the sort of thing that can be glossed over, become resistant to conscience."

"I know he's your friend," Coalter said. "Still, we'll have to talk to him." Coalter's tone was serious, his eyes on his bottle. "It's just business," he said. "Just talk. See where it takes us. That's all."

Part of me wishes we hadn't gone to see Liddy, but then Coalter would have pushed until we had. Beginning at the beginning meant just that, and Liddy was as close to the beginning as we could get.

"*Virgil didn't exactly see the killing,*" Liddy said, "*just two bodies running away, through the bottom behind the church house and around the side of the hill.*" Her eyes had been uneasy, darting between each word, fighting to find balance. "*Virgil wasn't able to make out much,*" she said, "*just that there were two of them, one the size of a mountain, and him carrying a shotgun.*" She'd been careful about what she said and how she said it, asking the Almighty time and again to forgive her for speaking ill of the dead, which I never thought she did. "*Virgil knew right off who they were.*" She'd been clear on that. "*He had eyes like a cat when it came to the dark, an' there wasn't many in this part of the country as big as Ben Yonts.*" Her words had lingered, hung in the air long after I wanted them to. No one ever knew Ben to go off on his own, only with his daddy or Bobby. It was easy to surmise that Bobby had been the one by his side. "*Virgil didn't know if they'd heard him when he came down the road,*" she'd said, "*only that they ran like it.*"

We'd said No to more coffee, then waited while Liddy went to stand by the stove, warming her arthritis over its flames. We didn't ask for details, just waited for her recollections. "*I ain't sayin' it's true,*" she'd said, her eyes almost apologetic, "'*cause Lord knows I cain't tell about such, but I b'lieve it might a' been the start a' that boy's ruin. Ben, I mean. Them headaches takin' him so bad. I heared all about it.*" Her words were soft, letting us know what a shame she thought it was. "'*Ever time he comes to mind,*" she'd said, "*it leaves me thinking about what he might a' done ... or seen. Either one would a' been a torment.*"

It was true: Ben had lived with it till he couldn't any more, till the pain in his head sent him over the edge. It was Olin who finally took him to the state hospital in Lexington, where they fixed wires to his head and filled him with electricity—seven times over fourteen days—and near the end with seizures so bad that it broke bones in his neck. He never came home, just went from the hospital to Justice's funeral parlor to Anne Young's Cemetery. His was a rare instance, the hospital said, one in ten thousand, but those who oppose such treatment put it much higher ... but then who could ever know for sure? Close to ten years now and I still see him as the giant he was: eye level with a draft mule, me on one shoulder and Bobby on the other. I never knew about his night with Bobby and Haman Flowers, what he saw or what part he might have played, but I wondered, like Liddy, if it had triggered his troubles, set him on a path without hope or pardon. Haman Flowers, and whatever devils possessed him, seemed as formidable as when he was alive, even reaching out and grabbing hold of Ben years after going in the dirt.

"You're right about signs," Coalter said. "There's always signs: a hesitation, a slip of the tongue, eyes that never quite rest; things that betray the ordinary, the everyday, if only for an instant." He thumbed one of his novels while he talked. "Corral enough suspects and you're bound to get one fated with betrayal, one with the signs that say *it's me*. At that point it's just a race to the finish: you and the killer; him trying to duck around the very signs that gave him away, and you upholding what you were sworn to do: upbraid injustice."

"Upbraiding injustice for the likes of Haman Flowers and Randle Cain don't sit as well as I'd like it to. I would a' pulled the trigger on either one of 'em."

"You ought'n say that too loud, Sheriff Cain. Liable to prejudice you when you least expect it. A 'course I never heard nothing." Coalter smiled, licked his finger and turned a page. "But the way I see it, is you got yourself a real dilemma." His smile was part devil, part dog. "Could be your best friend is a killer." He snickered, turned a page. "Even if it ain't him, it'll more'n likely be somebody you know, maybe even somebody in the family. Now, that's a dilemma I'd want no part of, justice be served or not." He eyed his bottle. "You gonna run me back to the motel or what?"

Coalter was staying at the Colley Motel about five miles south of town, a place far enough out of the way that he wouldn't have to deal with anybody ... and with a liquor store about fifty feet from its front door. It was the ideal setup, exactly the way Coalter would have designed it had he been given a say.

This whole damned sheriffing thing was fitful, if I was honest about it: a lot like trying to stay upright in the midst of what was trying to kick my legs out from under me. A sense of endlessness seemed attached to my days—days as long as they were mean, and with the bad ones always trying to outdo the good ones. It was a story as rough as hickory bark, but I never gave up thinking I could make a difference, bring fairness and order by my own good will. Coalter's presence, however, wore on me like itching powder. Mainly, his incessant butting-in where he didn't belong, and on things I would just as soon leave alone.

From one year to the next, the strains of high sheriff continued unchanged except for there being more of it—the constant unknowns making it downright scary. Yet I kept on, never minding the guts I brought to it time and again, the unnerving nights and its slate of unease. It all had a way of mounting up, yet I was steeled to its cause despite the negative light so many were willing to shine, and the reprehensible acts done out of spite to the office itself. Why I stayed was a mystery, given all the clabber as to how I needed to rule; all the midnight runs in the name of sanctuary; all the times I quietly compromised my station for the sake of politics; all the stepping over lines never meant to be crossed. Some of those who'd retired did so under the guise of seasoned hardness, others with a wavering spirit ... but none ever with the notion of returning.

Celebrity, for good or bad, kept my comings and goings all too visible when all I wanted—so often—was a place to hide. Bobby was every bit the same, his renown all too tied to his whiskey running; his brand of corn liquor making inroads as far away as California, its perfumed bite preferred over what was taxed and legitimately distilled; its packing and shipping constituting a round-the-clock operation, and stills that never quit. We decided years back for the sake of appearances that it was best not to keep open company, even limiting it to simple nods when we passed on the street. High stakes demanded discretion, and given that our professions were about as far apart as east was from west, and public opinion being what it was, we eased off, sidestepping what might come by way of perception, ardent that none of it come into play should the dam ever spring a leak. The effects of our association were best left alone, lessening the chance of it being brought into question, or having to defend it against what might be seen as currying favor. Outcomes depended on what was cautionary and above board, what was so often perceived. Prosperity demanded it, and so did keeping our relationship away from the eye of public scrutiny. The gentlemen's club, however, was common ground, a safe harbor for political elects from the whole of Pike County: judges, mayors, councilmen, prosecutors, public defenders, magistrates, the endless horizon of commissioners, the sheriff and his appointees, the police force, uniformed and otherwise, and all of their wives and closest friends—and all under the protective cover of Invictus' hush-hush confidentiality. We were never far apart, Bobby and me, but then we never expected to be, even with margins so well defined and tightly drawn. But now with evidence—circumstantial as it was—casting new light on his already dubious reputation, I figured being more circumspect might not be the worst thing I could do, given Coalter's nose for willfulness.

"The sooner the better," Coalter said, looking up from his book. I gave him a quizzical look. "Gettin' me back to the motel," he said, the hauteur of his bourbon still vinegary.

We drove away from Liddy's in a steady downpour, the sky as dark as her tale, the hardness of the rain graying what was left of winter. Coalter looked up for a brief second as we passed the church house, then returned to his reading and the unending chain of cigarettes.

I couldn't get Bobby out of my mind. What would I do if Coalter were to, all of a sudden, come up flush: uncover indisputable evidence that it was Bobby who killed Haman Flowers? Where in hell would that leave me? In spite of all I knocked up against, Bobby was one who never shied away, who never counted me as anything but a priest and a king. He put it out there, Bobby did, his heart and mind, and what he had left of a soul; never wavering, ever, in his holding me up as a brother, even when it wasn't convenient, even when political constraints ran high to the moon. Bobby was a lot of things short of Old Regular Baptist ideology, and he'd be the first to confess it—but the idea that he might somehow be the shooter of Haman Flowers was in the quietest recesses of my mind, a gathering storm.

Lester Trout was on Andrew's porch, reared back in an old cane chair and looking out at the rain as we went by. I gave him a honk and a wave. He didn't budge, in body or expression, just raised his little finger. What a comfort it was that some things never changed.

Seventy-Eight

Wadn't Man What Killed Haman Flowers

Magpies lined the fencerow between the yard and the creek, their chatter splintering the solemnness of spring: the still air, the soft sun, the gentle run of the creek. Forsythia filled in behind them, yellow as the sky was blue. Mary Olive sat rocking, her face all but lost in the shadow of her bonnet.

"Come on," she said motioning to me. I stood in the road beating back the memories, her house sagging and listing and filling me with years lost and gone. "Reckon you need help gettin' 'cross the creek?" she cracked, her gold tooth agitating the porch shade.

"You might want to give me a hand if it wouldn't be too much trouble," I said easing down the bank then picking my way from one flat rock to another. I stepped into the yard a little more winded than I wanted to be.

"You might wanna think about losing a pound or two 'fore you try that again," she said, her smile set against the dalliance of April's sun and the sweet ripening of tobacco tailing from her pipe. "Come on up here an' set down 'fore you lose what little breath you got left."

The porch shade was as still as the air. She hugged me real good and for a long time without getting up. She was the spit image of Grandmaw. So frail now. "You look to me like you're fixin' to go another ninety-two year," I said.

"Don't know that I would if I could," she said, grinning, confident of where she was headed if she didn't wake up tomorrow. "What on earth are you doin' out here so early on a Sunday morning?"

"Come to take you to town," I said. "Been so long it'd be like your first time."

She chuckled, dug a stove match out of her apron pocket and added fresh fire to her pipe. "Got me all the rememberin' I need a' town," she said, "though they's a whole lot to be said about first times." She puffed her tobacco to a red glow, then shook out her match and tossed it in the yard. "I 'member the first time my daddy took me," she said. "We lived so far back in the hills, weren't nary a road 'cept for the creek, nor a path neither 'cept the one 'tween the backdoor an' the outhouse. An' no store to speak of 'cept the one on the river, the one Daddy hiked to ever' spring an' just before winter. For flour and salt mostly, and sugar. Took me with him onct. Thirteen or better I was, barefoot an' hair tied up in a ribbon. Year adder that, we took an old log barge clear to Pikeville. First time for both of us. Lord, I'd never seen such a place. Stores ever'where ... and the likes a humankind I ain't never seed: them fine-stitched and barefoot both. Fine hats an' dresses, shined shoes that clicked and tapped with ever' step; gentlemen types in suits an' vests an' postures that said how high up they was. 'Don't ever look'm in the eye,' Daddy said. 'It won't do for a lady.' It wadn't till years later that I knew what he was talkin' 'bout. But I was young an' barefoot an' all of a sudden wantin' what I didn't have. So I smiled back when Daddy wadn't lookin', thinkin' I could somehow come away with whatever it was the Lord blessed them with. When I got home, I told ever'body how loud and busy it was an' how glad I was I didn't have to live there. Down deep I couldn't forget how full a wonder it was an' how I longed to be a part of it. I thought many a time to go back when I filled out, but that was right about the time I met an' married Hollister McEuen. I finally made it back when Hollister up and walked off. That's when I met Dempsey Compton. I knew from the very minute I laid eyes on him, he'd be the ruin of me. I was right, but it ain't nuthin' I'd ever change. Been back a few times since, just to stand in the spot where he drew his last breath. Sometimes when the sun's just right an' the breeze comes up off the river, I can almost hear him, how he spoke my name ... what some say was the last word he ever uttered."

She sat for a time lost in memory, her eyes lulled, pleasuring, it seemed, in the tall grass and the jungle of weeds where the garden used to be; where butterflies and hummingbirds mystified with their flight; where a ragbag assortment of cats, silent as smoke, added to the texture and color of a soon-to-be summer. "I got all I need to remember about town," she finally said.

I was just about to tell her how built-up it was since the flood, how after nine years things were once again taking shape and being put back together better than ever, and how Invictus had become damned near a palace, when Lorali came through the door with glasses of cold lemonade. She hugged me, gave me a nervous little curtsy then went back to her sewing. "Bless her heart," Mary Olive whispered. "Don't know what she'll do onct I'm gone."

"You going somewhere?" I said.

"Sooner or later..." She looked at me with a shuttering gentleness; her thin smile as hopeful as her submission to the truest of truths. "You know," she said, "the month my daddy died, was the onliest time I ever seed a red bird an' a white owl at the same time." Her voice was soft, obedient to the silence that gripped us. "Not together, mind you, but one over thisaway an' one over yander." She pointed with her pipe. "Fifty-odd year ago," she said, remembering. "An' it weren't till early this mornin' that I saw it a second time." She rocked, looking off to the yard. "Seems to me," she said, "that their showin' up together is between two thangs: what wants buryin' an' what wants to be birthed. See it plain as day it bein' a choosin': holdin' on to what's over and done with, or bravin' the newness that's come to take its place. It's a dread and a hope both, but it takes shedding one to get to the other. We're all leavin', Rubin: a little at a time, then all at once. I've lived longer'n most, but I've come to know that no matter how long we're here, we'll always be wantin' one more day."

I said nothing, just tried to imagine just for a minute what it would be like without her. What on God's earth was all this living about, anyway?—all its goodbyes?

"You know," she said, "I've seen enough dying to know it don't have to be a torment. But there comes a time when you just get tired ... when friends and lovers are gone, an' the world's no longer the one you once knew ... when you just want to melt away into the promise of peace." She looked up at me, her eyes in a twinkle and seeming to take on a quick breath. "You know, it ain't the dyin' that bothers me," she said. "I wudn't care a bit about it if I just didn't have to lay on my back for so long." Our laughter met head-on. We relished in it and sipped at our lemonade, the morning, warm and yellow and washing us in a pale glow.

"Well," she finally said, "you gonna tell me why you're really here, or you gonna make me guess?"

I scratched and pawed, gulped the last of my lemonade, then went to sit on the edge of the porch. She waited without a word. I pained in the telling, starting and stopping time and again with Liddy's account, from what she knew about the killing of Haman Flowers and the name she put to it, careful never to mention the one piece of hard evidence: the .41 caliber slug. Sweat beaded by the time I finished.

"Memory can be a vexing thang," she said, "full of ugly and lovely both. So much in there when you get to be Liddy's age. So many faces and voices, times and places. Hard sometimes to keep 'em straight." She rocked gently and puffed on her pipe ... her piece of heaven. "I'll tell you what Truman told me the day they found Haman Flowers." She stopped to lick her lips, remembering. "Said it wadn't man what killed Haman Flowers as much as it was the Almighty. Said the way we live has a whole lot to do with the way we die. Haman Flowers bein' perfect proof. But you'll need to ask him about it. I just can't recollect all what he *did* say. But he thinks the world a' you, an' I b'lieve you ought to go around an' talk to him."

We sat for a time without a word passing between us before Wilma Lee and Aug's oldest boy, Hunter, pulled up behind my car and came jumping across the creek. He held both arms over his head and made out like being under arrest, then gave me a big hug. All six of their children were pretty much like him: good-natured and without that *beside-yourself* trait of Wilma Lee's. He called Mary Olive Great Mam, gave her a gentle squeeze, and went off to the cold biscuits on the stove.

"He's a good boy," she said. "Hard workin'. The whole lot of 'ems the same way. Don't know how in the world they all turned out to be so much like Aug: best turned young'ns the Lord ever made. I b'lieve Wilma Lee might've got the best a' the deal when she married Aug. 'Course you can't tell her I said it. You might want to hire Aug on one a' these days, now that I think about it. They ain't a finer feller livin'."

"Don't know that I'd do that to him," I said, laughing. "I think too much of him."

The sun was high-powered by the time I stepped off the porch and into the yard. "Reckon I'll head on out," I said. "Ol' lady's liable to think I got me a girlfriend, if I stay much longer."

She stopped her rocking and looked down on me from the porch. "I don't know what in the world you intend to do 'bout this mess, Rubin, but if I was you, I wouldn't tell another soul. They's too much that people'll add to it. I know you'll talk to Bobby one day, but I wouldn't be in any hurry about it. I can tell you're awful bothered, an' I b'lieve you need to get it straight in your own mind 'fore you do anything else." Her pipe smoke drifted close, eased my senses.

"Go around an' talk to Truman some," she urged, "him now a full-on preacher an' all. Won't do for none of us anymore but to talk to Truman with what we got, don't matter what it is." She studied me for a long moment, then knocked her pipe against the arm of her rocker. "It was a long time ago, Rubin," she said. "Some things you just need to let go of. Life is short anyway. Ask me, I know. Why make it a hell for yourself or for somebody else, if you can help it?"

I closed my eyes to the sun, its warmth working to ease the stiffness in my neck. I didn't want to leave: her old home place was insulating, a haven like no other. What ethical responsibility was I dealing with, anyway?—what moral boundary, now that there was incriminating evidence, circumstantial or not? I felt like I was in a box, and with Coalter watching me bounce from one wall to another. But then Coalter had gone off to wherever the hell he goes, and with the slug Liddy gave him. He'd said little, just that he'd be back. That was four days ago.

I turned around about halfway through the gate and looked up at the sun.

"What is it, little brother?" she asked.

"I was just wondering whatever happened to that little derringer you had?"

"Still in there in the bureau drawer far as I know. Been so long I 'bout forgot it was there till them state police come cattin' an' moussin'. Told'em I didn't even know what a derringer was. Didn't feel a bit bad lying about it, bein' there's a chance a' them takin' it. Sooner give 'em Wilson." She laughed. "Why you ask, anyway?"

"No reason. Just wondering. Just thinking you might give it to me one day."

"Honey, you just go right on in there and get it. It's yours if you want it."

It was right where she said it was, right where I knew it'd be, right where it always was, wrapped in its silk handkerchief and with both barrels loaded: the way I'd left it. I rolled it over in my hands the way I'd done so many times, marveling at its composition and configuration, how it fit my hand like I'd been the model for whoever made it. And now it was mine if I wanted it. I smiled for the longest time, then tucked it inside my boot the way Corbin always did. It felt right, like it was where it needed to be: like it was home. But then I put it back. There was confusion enough.

"I'll get it another time," I said on my way out the door, bending down one last time to gather her in my arms, before making my way across the creek and up the bank, my smile trailing after me.

Seventy-Nine

It Ain't Good

Five days, and not a word from Coalter. He'd just up and left without so much as a *so long* or *see you later,* nothing that might leave him open to questions like *Where you going?* or *When'r you coming back?* It was tedious (what Mary Olive called teedjus) trying to work with someone like Coalter: the consummate loner, unavailable except when it suited him. It was wishful thinking that he might have lost interest, that he wouldn't be back. But I knew better, just like I knew his disappearance was the mark of his weakness, one that only a week-long binge could satisfy.

I could never be sure of Coalter's motives, much less his whereabouts half the time. His last words had been something about having the slugs from Haman Flowers and Randle Cain analyzed. If I could believe him, it was sure to be the start of something bigger than either of us was ready for. The upside to his being gone was that I could now noodle around without his interference.

I could make out the Big Sandy from Bobby's back porch through the bright green buds on the willows and water oaks along its banks. Its current was faster than usual from the rains, churning up molasses-colored mud off the bottom. Hooker poured coffee, hot and black, its aroma helping to beat back the morning chill, its bite helping to ease the bleakness of a gray, fast-moving sky. We talked with our collars turned up and our hands wrapped around our cups; like old friends, like old-timers gathered on the courthouse steps—the ones in straw hats and suspenders.

"You know, it's pure comfort to sit out here and think about what all we got, where we come from and what it took to get here." Hooker was his usual reflective self, grateful even for hard times. He lived downstairs, in a little room off the kitchen. *Caretaker* is what he called himself, a dispassionate translation for bodyguard, doorman, and bouncer what time Invictus was open for business. He also kept the honkytonks out across Pike County shelved with Bobby's special blend of kick, even helped tend bar when trade was high and Invictus's own Graham Bentley, bona fide bartender and Englishman, was in a snit an' a sweat. Hooker wore a number of hats, but that was the way he liked it and what kept him close to the business, the only family he knew.

"You ever regret not marrying?" I asked.

"Think about it from time to time," he said, "but I just ain't the husband type." His hulking frame seemed to mock what was so obviously susceptible. "Known plenty a' wives in my time, but ain't never met one 'at's quite *quiet* enough for me." He smiled wide, his eyes shot through with pleasant nature. "'Sides all that, intrigue's got a claw in me I just can't pull out. Me an' the dark side a' the street just seem to get along. I ain't nuthin' a wife would want. Then there's 'at housekeeper we got; cookin' an' cleanin' the way she does. She's plenty wife fer me."

Bobby sat without a word until Hooker gulped the last of his coffee and made his excuses, knowing that I was there for a reason: business with Bobby.

"Well," Bobby said, examining what was left in his cup, "what is it that's got you so worked up at eight o'clock in the mornin'?"

"Is this a bad time?"

"The law bein' here at eight o'clock in the morning makes it one."

"Didn't mean to drag you outta bed."

"You didn't. I ain't been in it yet." He rolled his head in my direction.

"I just need a little help with something," I said, "that's been keeping me up nights."

He watched me with interest and a hint of suspicion. I took in a big breath and puffed out my cheeks. "It's this thing with Randle Cain, and his killer still being on the loose. I'm gettin' knocked around by higher-ups to come up with a name. Like this whole thing is on me." I paused, hoping he might grasp a little of what I was up against. He said nothing, just sipped at his coffee and watched me with unblinking eyes "I know you and Hooker are out amongst every expression of mankind Pike County has to offer, and I just thought you might a' heard something."

"Zat it? That's your eight-o'clock-in-the-morning dilemma?"

"Well, there is one other thing." He squinted like he was taking a bead on me. "Randle's killin' was so much like Haman Flowers', this bloodhound from the state police name a' Coalter Hatfield done decided it's worth looking into. Been beatin' the bushes under my feet here lately, like he's glory bound to put his name in lights." Bobby ran his tongue across his teeth, retasting his coffee, his expression as lulled as the morning. "Noses around with homicide," I said. "One a' them Sherlock Holmes types. Shows up just whenever he feels like it, mostly when ever'body's give up, thrown in the towel. Drunk biggest part a' the time and with his nose in a book, not caring that he ain't welcome, an' claimin' to be kin to Devil Anse Hatfield. Just asking to be shot, if you ask me." Bobby said nothing, just waited, the way he often did ... to see where I was headed. "The whole thing's crazy," I said. "Haman being gone twenty-six years an' all, but I don't quite know how to turn Coalter's faucet off. But then, and so help me if this ain't the God's truth..." I scratched my head and pawed at my neck. Bobby was all of a sudden without the need for sleep. "You remember Liddy Blair? Virgil's wife?" I waited till he gave me the go-ahead look. "Well, Coalter dragged me out there to see her, and damned if she didn't tell the awfullest tale I ever heard. Got to going on about that morning Virgil found Haman all buckshot. Talked us into believing near every word she said, then gave us something Virgil kept hid all these years, something he found after Aug hauled Haman away."

Bobby rocked forward and tossed what was left of his coffee into the yard. "What was it?" he said, his voice grainy.

I slid to the front of my chair and leaned in his direction, "A piece of evidence," I said. "Nothin' I can divulge, what time Coalter's still scratching around. I hope you understand." The silence that fell between us was like what hazarded sunless chasms. “But that’s just part of it. The other part is what Liddy told us about that night, about what Virgil saw.” Bobby shifted in his chair, lifted his eyes from mine to the river. “It’s just circumstantial: what all she said and what all she remembers. But if she’s right,” I waited before going on, the morning chill suddenly a welcome, “it all but puts you and Ben right there that very night. Now, don’t get me wrong, I ain’t saying you had a part. Lord knows, my crystal ball just ain’t that sophisticated. But sooner or later, Coalter Hatfield’s liable to turn this evidence he’s got into something bigger’n we’re ready for.” I watched him for the longest time, his eyes never lifting from the long slope of grass and its gradual descent to the Big Sandy. “It was a long time ago,” I said, “and Liddy’s mind ain’t what it used to be. That’s all I got. If you wanna talk, let me know. It’ll be just between us. You know that.”

I got to my feet feeling like I’d been manhandled by Hooker and several more like him. Bobby stayed put, his eyes in a straight line on all-and-nothing. “Bobby,” I said as I turned to leave, my voice as sodden as the threat of rain, “this evidence that Coalter’s got?” He rolled his eyes just enough to take me in. “It ain’t good.”

Seven whole days, a full damned week, since Coalter up and disappeared. No calls. No messages. Had he dropped dead?—drunk himself into next month? Who the hell knew? Beyond simple curiosity, I couldn’t even begin to care. But then there he was: same shirt and suit of clothes he had on when left, like some slobbering dog crawled out from under a log, smelling like piss and lice.

“Well, well, look who’s here,” I said. His eyes weren’t open—not all the way, anyway—but he seemed to understand. “Where the hell you been?” I said.

He waffled about, sniffing the air and trying to see me through squinted lids. He searched his pockets for a cigarette without luck, then ran his raw-looking fingers through his matted hair. “Business,” he finally said, then followed me upstairs to where he knew there was coffee. Evidently, he was back on the case.

Taped to my door was a note from the nightshift dispatcher that NeviJo Yonts had called. NeviJo was Bobby's oldest sister, the one who never married and by default stayed-on to care for Olin and Gracie. The note said *Please call. Urgent. NeviJo.* I called first thing, knowing NeviJo wouldn't be inconvenienced at seven a.m., and found out the urgent part was Olin wanting to talk with me—and soon. "It's about Haman Flowers," she whispered, then hung up without a goodbye.

I got to Olin's about mid-morning, right when Coalter was finishing his fourth, maybe fifth, cup of coffee: double cream, double sugar. Olin was waiting out on his porch, a shawl spread over his legs, his every part in a quaver—Parkinson's ordering what days he had left. "You're lookin' a whole lot like Wyatt Earp these days," he teased, his voice fighting for steadiness.

"But not nearly as bold, I'd say."

He smiled, but his eyes went straightaway to Coalter. "This here's Coalter Hatfield," I said, "of the state police." They nodded, not bothering with handshakes.

"Coffee?" Olin asked.

I was just about to say 'I'm full up,' when Coalter said, "That'd be fine. Heavy cream, heavy sugar—if it's not too much trouble."

Olin looked me over: my badge, my eyes. He was pleased. "I knew I was right about you from the start," he said, "all them years ago. You've shore done us proud, son. Any regrets?"

"None I'm ashamed of."

"Said like a real lawman," he laughed. Coalter sat on the edge of the porch and dug rather openly at his scalp, a strained, even severe look on his face, collecting and examining what his long yellowish fingernails dislodged. NeviJo came through the door with his coffee and for the time, he stop scratching long enough to smile.

"NeviJo said you wanted to talk," I said, anxious to get to it, her whispered warnings fresh in my head.

He studied Coalter for a moment before he spoke. "Bobby come by," he said, careful not to say too much. I nodded, not saying anything before I knew where he was headed. "We talked ... 'bout younger days, back when Ben was with us ... Corbin ... all the rest." Olin licked his lips, smiled and gave Coalter a burrowed look. "How you likin' 'at coffee Mr. Hatfield?" Coalter was locked into the beat of the sun, his hair's wooly tendrils warming as it went higher. Still, he gave Olin an appreciative and fanciful smile. Life was good.

Olin, crippled as he was, was still a force to be reckoned with, even feared. Still, he waited like he was unclear how to begin, then just came out with it. "Reckon you might as well hear this as Rubin here, Mr. Hatfield. It was *me* what killed Haman Flowers," he said, his voice unafraid. Just like that: right at us, poker-faced and without dithering. "Went to play poker," he said. "Knew where they was playin', in the church house. Where they always played when snow come on the ground. Got there too late, though. Weren't a soul there but Haman Flowers, an' him standin' there with a shotgun. I knew right off what had happened. Robbed 'em is what he'd done; robbed 'em an' run 'em off, what he did whenever he could. He was stagger-drunk, an' I just stepped into him an' tore 'at shotgun right outta his hand—he just had the one, you know. But then he pulled down on me with a knife quicker'n a rattler, an' made to come at me. That's when I let him have it. Tore a hole in him big enough to jump through. Right there on the church house steps. I had my .38 inside my belt—always pack it when I play poker—so I just squeezed one off, right at his head, just for good measure. Hated that sumbitch anyway. That's all there was to it. I come on home adder that. Ain't lost a minutes sleep over it in nearly twenty-seven year."

I sat right still, staring out across the road and listening to Avery Coleman's dogs bawling and clamoring to get out of their pen. I turned to him and said: "I thank you for this information, Olin." His eyes were red, bagged and sagged, and full of loss.

"I'm eighty year old now," he said, his voice aimed somewhere over the porch rail, "but ready to take what's comin' to me. I've already talked it out with Gracie." Gracie and NeviJo sat in the swing at the far end of the porch, listening. "NeviJo's still with us you know. Her and Gracie'll be fine. You just go on and do what you have to."

I sat with my head down and my eyes closed, agreeing with the tiny breeze coming off the hill, thinking how not a damned thing he'd said added up. For one thing, Haman's shotgun had never been fired, its chambers still full when they found it. For another, it wasn't a .38 caliber slug that entered and exited Haman's skull, but a .41 caliber: from a derringer.

I sat for a while longer, waiting, knowing full well what Olin was up to—and knowing full well that Coalter knew it too, something that was sure to implicate Bobby even further in Coalter's eyes. A full-on confession from Bobby's daddy, a man at death's door, trying to put an end to a twenty-six-year-old mystery was just too convenient. But given Olin's influence, it had been worth a try; his confession certainly enough to call off the hunt and send Coalter Hatfield back to where he came from. But then Olin had mishandled the details. Bobby's fault or his own was irrelevant. What mattered was what Coalter heard, and what he'd be quick to jump on: Olin's deceit and the attempted obstruction of justice.

Finally, I stood and walked to the edge of the porch. "All these years," I said, "and I never reckoned it was you." Olin nodded. A faint smile crept across Coalter's lips. "I'm 'bout as ready as I can be to put this whole thing to bed," I said, "but if it's all the same to you, I'd like to keep this just between you and me—and Coalter here, of course—just for the time being." Coalter gulped the last of his coffee, a right smart size of it overflowing his unshaved chin and onto his coat. "Ain't that right, Coalter?" I said.

"However justice can best be served best serves me," he said, his brown coffee smile suddenly giving way to a GERD insurrection. He coughed big and long, and holding his hand up in a gesture to say he was okay, that he would need no help. Finally he said, "Let me ask you one thing." He was still unsteady, wheezing and holding onto the stair rail. "Do you by any chance own a derringer?"

"No sir, I don't," Olin said emphatically, smiling, happy to be of such service. "But I'll tell you what I never bothered tellin' the rest of 'em, them that were in here catin'-an'-mousin' some months back."

Coalter raised an eyebrow—then two—as if somehow that might help him hear better. "And what is that?" he asked in a grin too wide.

"That I used to," Olin said before I could stop him. "Belonged to my wife's brother, Corbin, 'fore he was killed. He didn't have no family but us. Just natural that we gathered up what all belonged to him. Brought it all here: clothes, car, everything personal."

"And you say a derringer was part of it?"

"Yessir. Purdiest little thang you ever seen. Silver-plated. Burl wood handle."

"Sounds like one-of-a-kind," Coalter said, scratching again. "But then you said '*Used to.*' Does that mean you no longer have it?"

"Had it about a minute," Olin said, "but Bobby took it for his very own 'bout as soon I brought it through the door. But what's a derringer got the law so charged up about?"

"You reckon he might still have it?" Coalter asked in his most befriending fashion, ignoring Olin's question altogether. "I mean, as far as you know?"

Olin laughed. "Don't reckon you could ever get it away from him, it being Corbin's an all. Carries it in his boot, just the way Corbin did. I don't blame him, you know, what with the kind a business he's in. I always liked a thirty-eight, myself. Never without one my whole life. Even now." And with that he reached under the blanket laying across his legs and pulled it out, its long barrel jerking in his hands to where Coalter and I went to ducking and pleading with him to put it down.

"Ain't I sump'm?" he laughed, then put it back under his blanket. "Liable to shoot my dick off, if I ain't careful ... what's left of it anyway."

Coalter laughed and stepped forward to shake his hand. "Ain't many like you left," he said.

"You boys remember what I said now, 'bout Haman Flowers. I'm ready to take what's comin' to me."

"We'll remember," I said. "But you can't forget we have to keep it quiet, at least for now." I gave him my best assurance and nodded until he started nodding back. We had us an understanding.

"Yeah," he said, his hands cradling mine, his body in a judder. "At least for now."

I knew about Bobby having Corbin's derringer all along; knew it the very day he brought it home; knew that he likely had it with him the night he fought Luck Hanner—the night the light in Haman Flowers went out.

Still, given what I knew (me and only me), none of it was adding up.

Coalter hung around for the next couple days, not saying much of anything beyond our needing to confront Bobby. "You needn't be waitin' on me," he said, "'cause I've been ready for some time. I'm just waitin' on you." Which I took to mean *why the hell was I stalling?* "Ain't no use denying it," he droned, like a tire with a slow leak. It was his way of getting my attention whenever he thought his message might have eluded me, which it never did. "Both slugs from the same gun," he said. "*The same damned gun.*" It was the evidence he'd brought back from the state police lab, undeniable as it was. The slug from Haman Flowers and the one from Randle Cain were fired from the same gun.

Coalter's whole premise rested on one bare-faced fact, enough for him to insist on a showdown with Bobby. "He ain't goin' nowhere 'cept to *the big stoney lonesome* by the time I'm finished with him. Where he belongs. Don't matter if Haman Flowers needed killin' or not, it wasn't his to decide." He talked into his book, his eyes never lifting from its pages. "Unfortunately for him, and for you, we got us a job to do." He licked a finger and turned a page. "And parliamentary proceedings, of which I had nuthin' to do with," he said with a depth of gravity, "gives the commonwealth of Kentucky, and its assigned deputies, license to pursue and prosecute killers of every stripe." He stopped long enough to fondle a cigarette from its pack, his long, tobacco-stained nails as thick and curved as talons. "It's ours to carry out Kentucky law, Rubin, with its no statute of limitations on the order of murder—something I'm sure you're fully aware of, like it or not." He lit his cigarette, and with the first inhalation, doubled over in a jagged convulsion, nearly hitting his head on the dashboard and lasting until he was able to get the lid off his whiskey. He bubbled a mouthful, defying my order, then sat for a time, flushed and the color of sunburn, then took another run at his cigarette, inhaling a deep lung full—even deeper than the first time—then sat with his eyes closed, relaxed in the arms of nirvana. He took several long drags before opening his eyes and realizing the flask was still in his hand. "Sorry," he said. "Force a' habit. Like a reflex, anymore." I said nothing, just watched and waited while he replaced the lid and tucked it back inside his coat.

"Who would a' figured it?" he said, picking up right where he left off, as if nothing had happened. "Shame, though, you two bein' so close an' all." His digs about me and Bobby had the lingerings of soured milk, the smoke from his cigarette the choke of rotted meat. He slumped back in his seat and began reading his book, leafing through it page by page, each rustle an even greater irritation.

By the third day, Coalter began reading aloud, swatches of this and that, as if I might actually give a damn about what he found worthy, to where the air between us took on serious density. Even though he didn't chance another nip from his flask, I took his continuing to read aloud—after I specifically asked him not to—as an outright taunt to my authority. When I finally asked him how he'd like it if I was to pull his rickety ass out of the car and knock it over the side of the mountain, he reverted to silence, interrupting it only to voice his theories about what all Liddy Blair had said: what Bobby had to answer to. My pleasure was mercilessly finding fault with his incessant examination: what all he tried to piece together against Bobby, which served only to hurl us into an even deeper abyss. By the end of the week, I was *done* with partnering up, and braked hard in front of the Colley Motel and told him to "Get out!" He gave me a lingering look, then told me in a slow, drawn-out smile that my crippled defense of Bobby Yonts wasn't likely to play well in a court of law. He liked waiting between thoughts, smiling while their messages took hold. I didn't, and took off without waiting, and with him still holding on to the door. I watched him in the rearview mirror as he stepped off into the night and imagined the crunch of gravel under his feet, its sound defiant of the law he worked so hard to uphold.

I don't know that Coalter ever got anyone to care about his assessment: about it being the same person who killed Haman Flowers and Randle Cain. But it was Liddy Blair's account of what she remembered from that infamous night twenty-six years ago that kept him dug in. There was substance to her tale, he was certain, enough that it left him wanting to know what really happened. Left us both wanting to know, if truth be known. It wasn't just because I hated Haman Flowers; I secretly believed in righteous killings (that who lived by the sword, ought to die by it), and

I wanted to know with all that was in me who else thought the same way; who it was that had the spit and cuss and conviction to say "*Enough is enough.*" I wanted to know who it was that was so much like me. Unlike Coalter, I didn't much care who it was. What was done was done, and for the better as far as I was concerned. My continuing to dig for answers was not for Coalter, or for justice for that matter. It was for me.

Eighty

To Every Thing There is a Season

Don't do a right smart a' heavy liftin' these days, Rubin," Truman chuckled, pleased at it being Monday morning and that folks were back to *doing*. "Most a' what I did my whole life was young-man's work," he said. "Don't know much else, but it ain't much help now that I'm seventy-nine goin' on eighty. Got me way more tools than I got effort. Still cut hair, but most a them's quit me since I went over to the Old Reg'lars."

"How long's it been now? Ten year? Hell, I'm still trying to get over it. The Old Regulars always seemed a little odd to me."

"I know, but we like it that way," he said, laughing big like he couldn't help it. "But, Buddy, let me tell ye, just 'tween you an' me, they ain't all that much difference 'tween none of'em: just enough to start 'em to hair pullin' if you's to get 'em in the same room." He shook with laughter, most of it from his belly. He loved to laugh, Truman did, always honed toward the lighter side, what kept him near to the heart. "Don't know exactly why I crossed over," he said. "It's sump'm ever' man has to decide fer hisself. But fer me, I b'lieve the Ol Reg'lars have a little more hope than what I grew up with ... an' at seventy nine, I need all the hope I can get." He whittled while he talked, whittling just to whittle. "Still get 'em comin' 'round to get their shoes soled an' saws sharpened; 'bout the only things I do for pay anymore. Old Reg'lar preachin' don't pay nuthin' ... same as the Primitives. But then I don't want nuthin'. What I have is a callin', gived to me by the Holy Spirit. Been with me long as I can remember. 'Course you already know that—I'm just goin' on. Got me a gov'ment check comin' ever' month, but tell you the truth we don't need all that much what with a good milk cow, hens that lay, an' a killed hog ever' winter. That an' our garden ... why me an' Inez got it good. How 'bout you, son? You doin' all right?"

We talked about the world as we knew it, our corner of it, and how we'd like to fix it until things grew quiet. "Ain't heered the name Haman Flowers in over twenty-six year," he said, rolling his eyes up from his whittling. He knew why I was here. "Mary Olive told me you might be around ... and why." His voice was full of caution, his whittling uninterrupted. "No need in worrying 'bout me sayin' nuthin'," he said. "Ain't my nature to rumor. Wouldn't even whisper it to Inez. Might as well put it up on the screen down at the Liberty as to tell Inez." He smiled, then stopped his whittling. "Been thinkin' long and hard 'bout what all Mary Olive told me," he said. "About Bobby Yonts and what Liddy Blair come out with after all these years." His tone changed in mid-sentence, first sympathetic then sarcastic. He sniffed and rocked his chair back on its hind legs.

"It's been a spur to my peace," I said. "Figured we could talk it out some."

He was mindful of my conflict, what lay rooted in the lines of my face. Finally he brought his chair back down to all fours,

"You know," he said, "the way we live has a whole lot to do with the way we die. Haman Flowers 'bout the best example I know of." The light breeze across the porch was suddenly more pointed. "But it works the other way too, for them holdin' to what's right. The Almighty's behind it all, Rubin: the good and the bad both. But what we have to remember is that He's spirit: takes care a' things spiritual, what's Holy Ghost. Made us to do the physical part, what's down here on earth. And to my way a thinkin', killin' sump'm 'at needs killin' is helpin' Him gain right order. It's a partnership. He needs us just like we need Him: Him doin' the spiritual and we doin' the physical, the sweatin' part. The heart knows what it knows, little brother. And when we take time to listen to it, we'll know when it's time for what He intends." He rolled his head, smiled, then turned back to the yard. "*To every thing there is a season*," he quoted with a long breath, *"and a time to every purpose under heaven. A time to be born and a time to die; a time to plant and a time to pluck up; a time to heal and a time to kill.* It's Old Testament, and as plain as anything you'll ever read." He waited, his evoking of scripture adding to his countenance. "I know what Haman Flowers was, son, an' I cain't see a wrong in puttin' him where he belonged." His eyes were soft and fixed on mine, a posture that seemed to ask if I followed his drift. I wasn't sure that I did, but I waited, hoping he would add another layer of meaning.

"Reckon the one who kilt Haman was just doin' what the Lord wanted him to," he said. "Restoring order; doing the physical part." He nodded his own affirmation. "To every thing there is a season," he repeated, his voice low and spoken to the yard.

He was comfortable with the quiet, Truman was, its soft air fitting him far better than Inez's incessant going-on. He made a concerted task out of stropping his knife blade against the sole of his shoe, then slicing off the top layer of a wart budding out on the side of his thumb. "I b'lieve I'm more than just called of God, Rubin. I b'lieve I'm sanctioned. I b'lieve I know when He speaks—when He speaks to me, anyhow. It's of the heart, son. Nothing anybody outside the Holy Ghost can understand. An' I can tell you without doubt-one that it was Haman Flowers' season." The assurance between us fell away into uncommon quiet, as kept as thought.

"That's a right mouthful," I said. "You and the Lord, I mean—hearing from Him the way you do and being so bent on doing His work, the physical part. You almost make it sound like it was you who pulled the trigger."

"Is that a question?"

It was a second or two before his sharpness took hold. "Didn't intend it to be," I said, "but what if it was?"

He pulled in a deep breath and fondled the stubble on his chin, then shifted in his chair where he could look me straight on. "I had enough cause, you know: the everlasting torment he put on the family, what with Corbin and the blackness he hung on us all—the eternal scars he left us with. And the unspeakable acts he done, what most don't have the stomach to utter, things a man ought to be skinned alive for—things he done to them girls a' Emmaline's, the one that run away 'cause she had to, and the strife he put on little Dixie to where we had to hide her. There was pure scare bred in that man, fixed right to him, comin' an' goin'. There was just a brokenness to him that left many a life in pieces. Our fight, those of us who declare God's kingdom, is against what Satan brings. An' I can tell you, Haman Flowers was one of those things." His gaze gave no ground. "You just need to know one thang, Rubin Cain: if the Lord's in it, I'm in it. Ain't no such thang as coincidence, son, only divine order. It was time for killin'."

I sat for the longest time just staring out across the yard, my eyes level with the smokehouse and the door hanging loose on its hinges. His answer was carefully crafted, carefully vague, haunting and with just the right amount of suspicion—yet absent of any real claim. Truman had the makings, all right, particularly if he thought it was the will of Almighty God. But then even if it was him, it'd never be anything he'd admit to, nothing he'd ever trust to man's understanding. It was the sort of thing only somebody like Truman had the mind for, something meant only for those trained up in the ways of the Lord.

"You ever own a derringer?" I asked off-handedly.

"'At's the same thang 'em troopers asked me," he said. "when they were in here bothering around. Mary Olive's got the only one I know of, though I never said nuthin' about it. Easy enough to get a hold of, if any of us was to need it."

I settled a little deeper in my chair and waited while the rush of blood slowed and eased its way back to where it belonged. Where was the truth?

"I'm glad we had this little talk," I said, feeling the need to get away, to clear my head. We said goodbye with a hard handshake and a bear-of-a hug.

Coalter's car was still at the Colley Motel. It was still early when I went by. He was likely still smarting and working himself into a day off, the liquor store being just a few steps away.

"Lord, honey! Look at you, all dressed up under that hat. I b'lieve yer purdy enough to show off. Seriann was her unqualified self: unreserved, convivial to the point of breaking open. "Set yeself an' let me get you some a' this banana puddin'. Just right then put it together." She scurried and gathered up coffee cups and plates, trying to make up for the three months since we last saw each other. "Here," she said, setting a quart jar of something I didn't recognize square in front of me. "Get you some a' these pickled eggs me an' Arlan put up." But before I could even reach for them, she had the lid off and was spooning them into a bowl. In an instant I was surrounded by coffee, pudding and pickled eggs, and her wanting to know if she could fry me some bologna. She was a template of time and motion even at sixty-three, and still working every day at the store.

"Arlan's gone to church," she said. "I still won't go. It's just so much about it that feathers my gizzard. You reckon I'll ever get over it?" She laughed and smoothed back her silver hair, not really caring about an answer. "Ain't seen you in so long, little brother, I'm 'bout 'fraid to ask what brought you all the way out here. Lick Creek ain't fit for much, 'cept hidin' stole horses." We laughed hard—the way we always did—the way we liked to.

"I know," she said, pouring herself coffee, "you ain't come all the way here for nuthin'. And I know it ain't no social call, or you'd a brought them young'ns."

"Them young'ns are so big they don't want to fool with me no more," I said. "I think it's because I won't hand over dollar bills like their momma."

"I don't know how on earth you've survived with four girls—an' ever'one of 'em a redhead. Law, what a mess."

"Five, counting their mother."

Her laughter rolled up and over the both of us. "Like a lifetime sentence," she said. "You and Truman both: punishing for a former life, I reckon. If I'd had three more like Wilma Lee, there wouldn't have been a crazy house big enough to hold me."

Mercy God, how she filled a room. Being alone with her was a stark reminder of the word *unique* and how it was pressed so lastingly into what she knew as love, what she wielded as the ultimate good. Even now we sat in its light, its certainty.

"Well, truth is," I said, clearing my throat, "I'm here 'cause a' Randle

Cain. Not so much of him being killed, but because of it being so much like Haman Flowers."

"An' why would that have anything to do with me? Unless, of course, you think I had something to do with it." Her smile was mocking.

"Don't know what I think anymore. Don't even know what I'm after. Already got two confessions. Well, more like one an' a half." I smiled, my cheeks full of pickled eggs.

"You been at this ... what? ... four or five months now? I'm just wonderin' why yer even botherin'? Ain't like either one of 'ems worth the ground they're put in."

"Well, truth is, I closed the book on Randle months back. Now all of a sudden, this old timer the state police keeps around shows up on my doorstep 'bout a month back—feller by the name a' Coalter Hatfield—wantin' to know how we're measuring up: if we've come any closer to puttin' a name to it. You'd think he was hoboing, to look at him—clothes looking like he slept in 'em, an' him smellin' like a bull's ass. But he's been around long enough to be a legend, a super sleuth of some kind. Anyway, he just dropped in outta the sky one morning, slummed around for a day or two, then headed out with some evidence he wanted forensics to look at. Last I saw of him for a week. Him disappearing that way ain't all that big a surprise, drunk that he is. Falling off the map for days at a time. He's holed up right now, but he'll be back; just don't know when. Meantime, I'm just fiddling with loose ends, going places I don't much care to go, asking questions I don't want to ask. But I'd rather do it without him than with him."

We sat with the silence pushing in on us before she said, "I know you've been up against it, Rubin, tryin' to make sense of pure craziness, but you have to know that I don't usually allow the mention a' that name in my house." She spoke of Haman Flowers. "It's like openin' the door to a deep dark hole. Just hearin' it triggers sump'm black inside me."

I nodded my apology. "I should've knowed better."

"It's awright. You'd think I'd be over it by now. It's only been twenty-six year." Her smile was sweet. "But they's sump'm 'bout wrongdoin'

I just can't cotton, even to this day. Just hangs on, like kin waitin' to be fed." She paused. Thinking. "'At man—if I can call him a man—was *wrong* the minute breath came into him. He was ours to punish with, no mistake about it. The Lord was clear on that, but then He made me. Put a hate in me for wrongdoin', and made me mean enough to deal with it ... with him." Her eyes were soft, and off on what lay deep inside.

"Do you remember what you told me," I asked, "that night when it was just the two of us?—after Aug put Haman in the ground?"

"Yes," she said. There was quietness to her voice.

"So do I," I said, remembering all too well the diseased look in her eyes.

She looked away then back, ran her fingers through her hair. "You wanna hear me say it?" She waited, calm as the minutes that ticked away on her kitchen clock. "Well, I'll tell you. I did it. I killed Haman Flowers. Killed him part way that night he come around. Killed the rest of him ever' night since. For twenty-six years now, I've been killin' him. Ever' time he's come to mind. Ten thousand times, and ten thousand on top a' that. Ain't a day goes by that I don't kill him a dozen times. I just wished to God I knew where his grave was so I could build me an outhouse over top of him. I just want to detest him ever' way I can 'fore I die."

I sat dumbfounded, as I often did, not knowing what was real and what wasn't; what was confession and what was insinuation; what was professed and what was contrived; feigned and firsthand. What I did know was the maze I was in and the game I was ill-equipped to play.

She sat with her eyes flat and even. After a time, we smiled, adding a sense of peace to the sunbeams, white and satiny, through her kitchen window. There were already close to a dozen who'd come forward, who'd confessed to killing Haman Flowers, who wanted the recognition, even the praise; one after another to where I dismissed them with a wave of the hand. But that didn't negate the fact that Haman's real killer was still out there. Was it Seriann? Not in a million years. Truth be told, she was still angry that somebody beat her to it.

The puffs of air through her screen door teased the hairs on the back of my neck. I'd been out-maneuvered, but then I was dealing with Seriann. I chuckled to myself, at her artistry. She sat without moving, her smile a painting.

"Tell me about Sherman," I said.

Eighty-One

Now That You Don't Give a Damn

Did you kill Haman Flowers?" I was finished with tactics. April was gone, and with it thirty sleepless nights. If there was to be redemption, I wanted it as soon as earthly possible. No frills. No small talk. Something Hooker was positioned to handle.

"Well, it's good to see you too, little brother." His laugh was as dense and loud as he was thick. "Set down here 'fore you give us both a heart attack. What the hell's got you so wound up, anyway? Ol' lady been holdin' out?" He rolled with a deep chuckle and swiped his forehead with a dishtowel. "You plum scary today."

I was all at once feeling like a jackass. "Sorry," I said, sounding like I'd been whipped without a fight. "I was just trying to make some sense out of something that happened a long time ago, and how it might have something to do with Randle Cain."

"Randle Cain," he said, searching his mind. "That sumbitch over on Greezy? The one 'at whupped up on his wife an' childern 'bout twice a day?"

"That's the one."

"Heard about him. Big talk here at the club for a while, back when the state police was crawlin' all over the place. They strolled in here one day fulla badges and guns, an' wantin' to know what we knew about Dixie Wainwright an' her relationship with Bobby. Come to find out it was her sister 'at sumbitch was whuppin' up on. What little I knew came from

Bobby. Told me him an' Dixie went traipsin' over to Greezy ever' whipstitch carryin' food an' money, tryin' to keep life in 'at woman an' her children. Said her eyes were beat shut 'bout half the time, childern down to skin an' bone. Them troopers was pretty hopped up, but never got nowhere. I know they was thinkin' Bobby an' his woman had sump'm to do with 'at sumbitch's lights goin' out, but Bobby was way ahead of 'em. Had witnesses from here to Ashland, sayin' he was right here all night long." He chuckled. "Bobby always says the only things that count when yer up against the law is a fool-proof plan an' a air-tight alibi." He looked at me and smiled. "Now, what was it you're wantin' to know?"

I was suddenly numb and without an ounce of caring. "Just something about an old case," I said.

"Haman Flowers, you said."

"Yeah. Just a bunch of nuthin' really."

He watched me from the shadows of his eyes. "Killed the only friend I had in this world," he said, his voice graveled over. He sat hunched with his elbows on his knees and shaking his head like trying to rid it of the memory. "Why in the world would you be wantin' to know 'bout *that* devil? It bein' near to thirty year ago?" His eyes held me, fixed me to my chair like I was powerless to get up and leave.

"Ain't me," I said. "State police are back, looking under rocks and tiptoeing through graveyards. Feller name a' Coalter Hatfield mostly, thinkin' whoever killed Haman Flowers come back an' did the same thing to Randle Cain."

He sat without blinking, his face a stone. "And why would he even care?"

"'Cause he didn't know 'em like we did," I said. "Didn't know 'em enough to where he could feel good about walking away; say '*I don't give a damn*' and mean it ... like me. But now I'm drawn back into it, trying to stay ahead of him, making sure he don't accidentally uncover something that'll bring hell down on us all. It's a burden when you have to relive it, be reminded of its squander." We sat nodding, agreeing.

"Feller ought not live with a burden," Hooker said. "Reckon that's why I like it here so much, doin' what I was born to do. Same's true for Bobby. Makes for a longer life, I believe: doing what you want. Something you ought to consider, Rubin. Guarantee we'll find you a place here with us, an' at twice what you're worth." He laughed and slapped me on the back.

Brotherliness seemed to overtake us, to prevail. We sat in silence for a long minute before I stood up to leave. "Reckon I'll head on out," I said.

"It was me, you know."

"Beg pardon?"

"Me what killed Haman Flowers all them years ago, that cold night in December right adder I dropped you an' Bobby off in front a' Angus Walker's pool hall. It was 'at night Bobby fought Luck Hanner, when the three of us drove out to the club an' talked about the changes comin' ... about makin' things right." He sat with the dishtowel around his neck, holding onto both ends and with his eyes in a hard glare, like he was daring me to defy him. After a drawn-out silence, he cocked his head and said, "That's all. Just wanted to put yer mind at rest, now that you don't give a damn. I never did. Still don't."

I studied him before pushing my chair back under the table. I didn't ask him about Randle Cain, just gave a little squeeze to his shoulder, then turned and left without looking back.

I drove clear to the top of Grapevine Mountain, skidding and sliding on a narrow piece of road till I couldn't go any further. I set the brake and walked to where the road stopped altogether, then emptied my revolver as fast as I could pull the trigger, its report clearing away the stink that was somehow in lockstep with my every move. Bobby knew what Coalter was up to; my visit had made it clear. The rest was pure Bobby Yonts: get any number confessing to the same crime, or at the very least give them enough information to confound what was suspected. Then, before you know it, you got a real circus on your hands: a hung jury before it even goes to trial. But then it left me wondering why he thought it was even necessary to go to the trouble?

Emptying my gun had helped, quieted even the tiniest voice long enough for a needed reach into my soul. Still, there was a stirring, a wanting to know, once and for all—for my own sake—who killed Haman Flowers; wanting it just long enough to lay aside the idea of not giving a damn, just long enough to feed the lawman in me.

After five days of Coalter's holing-up, I called the Colley Motel and spoke with Juanita Henry. After exchanging the expected niceties, I ask if she'd seen Coalter Hatfield in the last couple days. I told her that I was concerned about his health and thought, God forbid, that he might have keeled over in his room: drowned in his own vomit, or some such thing. Juanita just laughed and said she didn't suspect that was the case, because she saw him most every day going-to or coming-from the liquor store, and some days twice. I suspected she said something to him because two days later he came limping up the courthouse steps just as I was leaving for the day. Dog meat couldn't have looked worse.

"Let's go talk to Bobby Yonts," he said, the smell coming off him strong enough to water my eyes.

"Not now," I said. "It's Saturday night, and for the time I'm as done as I can be with the shadowy side of humanity. Find me Monday." And I meant it.

Eighty-Two

To Enlighten or Bewilder

I wasn't ready for Monday or the innumerable surprises I knew awaited me from the weekend; least of all I wasn't ready for Coalter Hatfield. So I went to where I go when things teetered toward desperation: to the mountains, the way I always did. I went to shed what was so ready to weaken and undermine, back to their deepest parts, their sun-dappled hollows and secreted meadows. But mostly I went to their peaks where I could lie in pine needles inches thick and give way to their treaty.

Elevation seemed to matter. The higher the peak, the quieter it was, their summits preserved in solitude, reserved only for the quietest thoughts, and where my temperaments, so often ready to fragment, could be laid aside. There was a sense of spirits there, in the rocks and wisps of wind. I thought of those peaks as places haunted, without movement or sound except for what stirred through the hardwoods: cherry and maple, chestnut and yellow birch; up there where cloud banks were close enough to touch and pine scents thick enough to taste, all of it reminding me of the aloneness that lived there, and how tied to it I was.

I never stopped believing the mountains could heal, even after Corbin was gone and the heart was torn out of Seriann; even after Imogene and Bobby decided that Greezy Creek no longer had what it took to hold them; even after Grandmaw was gone, after the light from the sun seemed dimmed to an eternal haze. My believing in their healing powers was just something that evolved over time. They never failed to open me to their shapes and colors, things aboriginal to Kentucky highlands: rhododendron and azalea, stonecrop and pinesap, columbine and bleeding heart, wood rush, viburnum, sage and sorrel—all high and hearty, and away from eyes that would adore save for the ruminations of hawks and eagles, bobcats and bear. There was favor there on those mountains, what came to rest me, grateful for my homage.

But no matter how high I chose to go or how long I chose to stay, Bobby was there with me—even in my hiding—even in the wind, soughed and with a voice that assailed; his name in the calls of wren and ruffled grouse, in the rush and vague shadows of light, in what rustled and rattled when all else was collected in quiet. But what do I do with him now, here in this sanctum, this Eden, with his light on the brink of going out?

I knew Bobby was there that dreadful night of Haman Flowers. Liddy had been careful, precise for Virgil's sake, his honor—of that I was certain—as was Coalter. I also knew Coalter's patience was growing thin, despite the enjoyment he received from circling his prey, inching ever closer by the day. Sooner or later he'd get to the heart of it, with or without me. Face-to-face is the way he wanted it, in the same space with Bobby, looking for signs: the bridge to Liddy's claims, to the truth. What Bobby chose to tell, whether it be to hearten us with one voice or defame us with deceit—to enlighten or bewilder—would determine the field we played on.

When I finally showed my face about midafternoon, Coalter was waiting for me on the courthouse steps looking like something pistol whipped, his coffee—or what he would have me believe was coffee—in a paper cup, and his raincoat thrown over his shoulder even though the day was sun-drenched and well above seventy degrees. The plan, he said, was to visit Bobby Yonts with or without me. It was my choice. And with that he went off to the park with a dog-eared book to wait me out. At six that evening, he was leaning against my car with what looked like the same paper cup, and looking tarnished by what lay in its bottom. He was ready for Bobby Yonts, for a one-on-one, or so he thought, and left me little choice but to join him. We stood there looking at one another, neither of us caring much about what we saw. Finally I said, "Follow me."

It may not have been the best time. Monday was a time when Invictus and Cornbread Red were anything but open for business, but I suspected that would become evident soon enough.

I knew we were in for a dogfight as soon as Coalter flashed his state police ID and Bobby asked him where he stole it. Nobody laughed.

"This don't have to be ugly," Coalter said, rubbing the back of his neck like he was needing something to hold onto. He shot a glance in my direction as if to ask *Ain't that right?*, then made some licking sounds behind an almost sheepish smile. He had that smell, humid and raw: the kind that ferments in the pores after so many years in the sodden hold of bourbon. Bobby said nothing, just seemed to swell even bigger than he was, waiting for the right excuse, I imagined, to put an end to Coalter once and for all, ridding the world of his muddling despair.

"What is it you're needing from me, Mr. Hatfield?" Bobby asked, his voice griddle flat.

Coalter's eyes darted this way and that, as if looking for something out of range, then offered Bobby a cigarette from a crushed pack of Lucky Strikes. "I'd just as soon get on with it, if you don't mind," Bobby said, agitated at Coalter's bumbling. Coalter patted his pocket for a light, but came up empty. When neither of us offered, he shrugged and said: "Well, suppose we begin at the beginning." He smiled, traces of sweat beginning to show across his upper lip. "As in your whereabouts on the night Randle Cain was found shot to death."

"Suppose you tell me why I should go through all this bullshit again, when I've already gone over it with your people and it's already part of the record? Now, you either don't know how to read, or you're indicating that what I've said is a lie. Which is it?"

The silence returned, as frozen as the bones of Haman Flowers in his lost and forgotten grave, sealing all three of us in a kind of wooliness—just what Bobby intended, I'm sure, and just before a smile, dark and menacing, crept onto his face. Coalter's eyes did a quick dart in my direction, more than just a hint of fluster in his cheeks. He needed to be careful, Coalter did. Frustration had a way of watering one's hand, the last thing anybody wanted when dealing with Bobby Yonts.

Coalter nodded then let his chest fill with air. "I'm not ... ahh ... here to accuse or ... ahh ..." He held his breath, searched for impossible words. "I'm just wantin' to talk."

"I bet you do," Bobby mused, the toothpick in his mouth going from one corner to the other. "Drink?" He stood with the door open to Invictus motioning to us with a wry eye—*the spider and the fly*.

"That might not be a bad place to start," Coalter said with a quivering smile.

It was 25-year-old, single-malt Scotch that Bobby sat on the bar, its sweet whiff finding Coalter the second the lid was removed.

"Is that all you got?" I said. Coalter turned to look at me, silent objection screaming from his eyes.

Bobby stopped, waited, his hand resting on the bottle and Coalter looking like he was about to drown, then returned it to its rightful place: on the top shelf behind the bar, alongside the glut of even more exceptional choices. The tiniest smirk accompanied his reach under the bar. What he brought out was his bread and butter, what made him rich and kept him that way. It was silky-looking and see-through, as transparent as air itself. "Fire on The Hill," he said, holding it up like a prized pig.

"Kentucky Thunder!" I echoed.

"Mule Train!" he exclaimed.

"Scalded Dog!" I countered.

Our laughter was crowed and hyena-like, indulged by the moment and divorced from all else—how easy it was. Coalter watched with envy, from a perch unfamiliar. "You're still just crazy enough," Bobby said, his eyes pooled in that same endless blue, that Irish light as ill-behaved as it was remarkable. Memories, every shape and size, came in a torrent, despite Coalter's intrusion.

Bobby held his liquor up to the light—water from a high mountain spring couldn't have been clearer—then gave a thump to the bottom of the bottle. It bubbled big, its bead large and lasting. Purity—Corbin Fairchild's hallmark—now Bobby's—the way only U. J. Slough could make it.

"Two fingers," he said, "the way of gentlemen." He poured with a light touch and a smile as warm as May.

"To gentlemen," I said, raising my glass.

"To old friends," he said, touching his glass to mine. We turned briefly to Coalter, but said nothing. The burn was immediate and halting. I could feel my eyes swell then tear. Coalter held his eyes shut, chewed its aftertaste, then smiled as if he might light up the room—the idea of tax-free, bootleg liquor not getting in the way of his need.

"Another?" Bobby's voice as inviting as the bottle he tilted toward our glasses.

"Another time," I said. "We're on the clock. Right?" I said looking at Coalter. Coalter said nothing, only gave me a look like I was taking food out of his mouth.

Bobby left the lid off, slid the bottle up close to Coalter and leaned forward, elbows on the bar. "I know why you're here," he said deep into Coalter's eyes.

I couldn't help but sit in awe of him, the way I had most of my life: at his brigand, his *Bobby ways,* even with the cloud of doubt so ready to dismantle his world. "I don't mean to spoil a good time," Coalter said, his temper hushed some by the whiskey, "but there's still some hunt in this thing with Randle Cain an' him *checking out* the way he did. So much like Haman Flowers. Mystifyin'. So much left blowin' in the wind, like takin' a whuppin' for a lawman such as myself." He gave Bobby a brooding look.

"But of course. A lawman ... such as yourself." Bobby mocked, taking Coalter off his mark.

"But," Coalter said, sure of his ground, "this new evidence we got ahold of ... well ... take your breath away."

"I hear it'll do that if you're not real careful," Bobby said. "'Bout like good whiskey." He added a trickle to his glass. Sipped. Coalter watched with a dry mouth, the tip of his tongue coming and going, as dry as a cat's.

Bobby pulled a lighter from his pocket, flicked it and held it up, a gesture that sent Coalter fumbling for his Lucky Strikes. Bobby looked at me out of the corner or his eyes while Coalter leaned far over the bar, straining to get at the flame. Monkey on a string.

"Maybe we could dispense with the formalities," Coalter offered, inhaling deeply, "weed through the hearsay, get us an understanding." Bobby sipped again, then weighed the taste on his tongue before swallowing. The picture of composure.

"The image of Randle sprawled across them steps," Coalter went on, "that hole in his chest big enough for a coal truck an' with that bullet hole in the middle of his face..." He shook his head; such a shame. "Pure chance I thought. You know, twist a fate: him bein' *dressed out* like Haman an all. But then the particulars started rollin' in, addin' up." He stopped, bewilderment beating him about the eyes. Coalter was not a stranger to the game. "After that, hell, a blind man could see the likeness. No fluke to it, near it or about it. Who killed Haman, killed Randle." Bobby was unreadable, poker-faced. "From what Virgil Blair knew," Coalter said, "... or I guess it's more accurate to say *from what Liddy Blair told us*, it's hard to figure how Virgil never come up with Haman's killer."

"Don't reckon he ever wanted to," Bobby said.

"Maybe," Coalter said. "Or it might a' been he was scared off: afraid a' what he might find, who it might be. Then, again, you may be right: it might a' been he knew and just let it go. Lot easier that way, handing out justice like you would moon pies. Some here, some there. Never enough to hurt nobody, but just enough to keep things sweet, to keep folks from losing faith. Now, me? I'm plime-blank contrary—just happy to *get after it*, like a dog on a bone. Surprisin' what comes of it, like how I got this evidence I don't know what to do with. Went back twenty-six years. And now, twenty-six years into it, we're gettin' the oddest assortment wantin' to be Haman's killer: them that *didn't* wishing they *had*, I reckon. Craziest damned world ever was."

He said nothing after that, just let it go flat, allowing quiet its place. Quiet always had a way of rearranging, freshening, freeing us to take another run at it.

"Ain't that what most of us do anyway?" Bobby said. "Hand out our own kind a' justice? Help who we want an' hurt who we have to? Ignore who we can an' try to fool the rest?"

He was a moving target, Bobby was: forever marking territories, changing boundaries, never content but to be one step ahead. He was my protector back when there were no lines on his face and the limelight of Saturday nights intoxicated. They still pulled at me, those times, and with unforgiving clarity; just opened up whenever Bobby walked into the room. Like now. "Two fingers?" he asked, his simplicity teetering on sophistication.

The whiskey was still hot and dry on my tongue, inciting, insisting. I could only imagine it was the same for Coalter, only more so. I stared at the bottle, then back at the steel in Bobby's eyes, still not able to pry myself from all the years. He seemed so secure, Bobby did: safe in his own skin, surrounded by attainment, his deportment proclaiming mastery over all that was his.

"What the hell," I said. "A *gentlemanly* two fingers."

"What we consider cordial," Bobby said, pouring as if it were a craft.

Coalter lit up like a candle, a drooling look, worshiping. We all lifted our glasses, gave each other a curt nod, and knocked back two fingers without so much as a breath. The fire raged.

Bobby set his glass gently on the bar, then stood staring at it as if answers lay in the bottom. "Are we off the record?" he asked.

"Off the grid entirely, if that's the way you want it." Coalter made tiny sucking sounds, getting all he could from his tongue.

"What is it you expect to get outta this, Mr. Hatfield? From all this twaddle about Randle Cain an' Haman Flowers, when there ain't a minute on God's earth worth wastin' on either one of 'em?"

"I'm just wantin' a little piece a' the truth, Mr. Yonts. Just enough for some peace a' mind. Besides that, you gotta know there's more than just a little problem with somebody runnin' 'round thinkin' its all right to kill whoever he thinks needs it. Don't get me wrong, it's not that I disagree with the killing of Haman. From all I've heard it was justified, in my opinion. But I can't have that kind of casual pursuit going on in my backyard. Kind a' flies in my face, if you know what I mean. Just ain't the sort a thing that delights a lawman *such as myself.* You see, vigilantes have a tendency to scare hell out a' people and keep me up nights. It has a way of tarnishing my image, everbody thinkin' this killer's smarter'n I am, an' him thinkin' he can't be caught. It ain't the kind of world I intend to live in, so long's I have the means to do something about it. Now, besides all that, there's this other little tiresome point about it being my *job* to look into things like *murder.*"

A hint of amusement seeped in around the corners of Bobby's mouth, high-minded, feral. "There's a killin' 'round here 'bout ever' fifteen-twenty minutes. It's a wonder the county can bury 'em fast enough, but that don't mean *vigilante.*"

"Maybe vigilante ain't the right word," Coalter said. "Maybe it's just your everyday Billy-the-Kid needin' to take it up a notch. Either way, there's some real scary evidence I'm havin' a hard time walkin' away from."

Bobby let his head roll slow-like to one side, his eyes a little beaded, the kind of posture that asked *What kind of evidence?*

Coalter let him hang while he tried to work some moisture back into his mouth, then said, "Same exact month and day. Same time a' night. Same exact way and on the same exact site. And the bullet hole? Same exact spot: under the left eye, midway down." He stopped, his smile round, his eyes big with surprise. "If nothing else," he said, "I'd at least like to talk with this person. First to thank him—off the record of course—and then to tell him how he just can't do that no more."

I thought it strange that Bobby would chuckle, but I chuckled right along with him, together in that lofty place of memories and light hearts. Without asking, he poured us two more fingers.

Coalter swallowed fast and hard and without looking left or right, almost before Bobby finished pouring. I ran my finger around the rim of the glass a number of times before holding it up to the light, before closing my eyes and taking in its vapors, before letting it eat its way down my craw. I allowed its fire a slow escape. Bobby seemed to watch from afar, the furrows in his forehead deepening just ever-so slightly before quick-tossing his in the same fashion as Coalter, like it was something dutiful, to be done without delay. The swirl began up high, behind my eyes, light as fairies in the twilight. I bathed in its eddy, its churn, sensing its halo beginning to rise above my head.

"It just seemed to make sense," Coalter said, the whiskey loosening his tongue to the point of daring. "To go back to the beginning, I mean. Back to Haman Flowers, the two cases being so similar. I had to believe the full story was still out there just waiting to be told. There's always a part, in my experience, that just somehow never makes it to the light of day. Not enough persistence with investigation is what it boils down to: everybody too quick to get home to supper. Takes a bloodhound to turn it ... what I am." He laughed, feeling good about himself, and not shy with self-congratulation, for thinking himself so clever. "It ain't arrogance, the way I see it: just plain old paying attention." He went on and on, his nasal monotone drifting clear into Invictus' high ceilings. Coalter was alone, the way he was so often, basking in his obsession. It was his game, the one he played at everybody's expense, the one where he saw himself as the all-time champion of the law and its enforcement. "It's why I am who I am," he said.

Bobby tilted his head and motioned for two more fingers. Coalter's smile was radiant and appreciative, his glass raised in salute then coming down hard on the bar, its whiskey gone in a flash. "I know you were there, Bobby," Coalter said, surprisingly calm, "...the night Haman Flowers was killed. You an' your brother, God rest him. I'm just hopin' you won't insult me by denying it."

Bobby was steady, his manner unchanged. "Now how'd you come by somethin' crazy as that?" he asked, almost with a happy face.

"Witness," Coalter said. "Somebody who eyed you and Ben both. That very night. That very place. That very time. There's always somethin' we never count on, isn't there?"

Bobby gave a thoughtful pucker and said, "An' what else? I mean as long as we're *off the record*. You know, *just talkin'*."

The glasses between us sat eagerly waiting while the ground under us slowly softened, threatening like some trapdoor eager to empty us into nothingness. "I got the slug that come outta Haman," Coalter said. "...I mean as long as we're *just talkin'*." He locked eyes with Bobby, neither of them unable to back off or let go. "Had it put under a microscope and up against what come out a' Randle. My own doin', by the way: paid for outta pocket. I got my own way a doin' things. Don't like bein' interfered with." Bobby's attention quickened, connected with the quiet that suddenly lay over us like a grave blanket. Coalter leaned forward, his weight against the bar, the ash on his cigarette way too long. "Two slugs," he said. "Twenty-six years apart, and both of 'em forty-one caliber. Derringer!" We all waited without word, without sound or time or the gears of life. "An' get this," Coalter said in a low tone, "from the same gun. The...same...damn...gun."

Bobby pulled out an ashtray from under the bar and held it under Coalter's cigarette; then gave the back of Coalter's hand a gentle tap. The ash fell away, silently and to Coalter's amusement. Bobby waited then leaked a long steady breath. "Well, now," he said, reaching for the bottle and trickling a measured two fingers into our glasses, then adding what was closer to three. "'Pears you got yerself a mystery." He raised his glass. We raised ours, nodded our complicity and swallowed hard. Three fingers off to the region of demons and devils, and fanned by the heat of the moment.

"As much as I *wanted to*," Bobby said, wiping his lips with the back of his hand, "and as much as I *intended to*," his words were drawn out, deliberate; his eyes dimmed, watery, half scarlet, "you can't, from the deepest part of what tells you better, think it was me." He leaned hard on the bar, smirked. "Or can you?" He was the master, Bobby was; affect and control his greatest lines of defense. I knew he was on his way to drunk, maybe even well past it—but then so were we. Still, I knew enough not to wander too close to the minefield he was laying.

"I don't want to," Coalter said.

"But?"

"There's this pesky little thing we in the profession call *evidence*. What am I supposed to do with it?"

"Id like to think you'd walk away, knowin' it was the right thing to do."

"An' barring that?"

"I'd hope you'd put it with some common sense to get you past it—help you see it for what it truly is."

"And what might that be, *exactly?*"

The air around us was heavy enough to carry, the space between us all at once fuzzy, unfamiliar. "That we're all better off," Bobby said. "That things happened the way they did because of good ... not the other way around." Bobby's wiry eyebrows drew closer together, making a show of thinking. "You may be right," he said. "Maybe I am guilty ... partly, anyway. I craved for both of them to draw a last breath often enough. But anymore, I'm like that ol' river out there: spillin' along, not really giving a damn, just happy to be part of the long slow meander now that Haman an' Randle's gone back to dirt." Bobby studied his empty glass, a thoughtful grimace accompanying him. "Could be Cousin Truman's more right than anybody."

"Cousin Truman?"

"A friend," said Bobby, "Ol' Reg'lar Baptist preacher, same as family to me. Heard him tell my daddy, years back, that Haman's killin' looked to him like the work a The Almighty: Him sending us somebody—maybe more than *one* somebody—with guts enough to do what was needed. But then I have to wonder: who sent you, Coalter?—a man with an idea tryin' to undo the whole thing." Bobby's eyes shone with disdain: that cornflower blue now turned to blue ice. "What that is, *exactly*, Mr. Hatfield, is prob'ly the closest thing to the truth you're ever liable to get."

Coalter gave a noisy breath and pawed at his stubble. The air was heady, liquored, the trap door near ready to spring. "A forty-one caliber derringer is a rare find," he said. "Don't reckon they's more'n one in all a' Kentucky, much less Pike County. But I'm guessin' you'd know more about that than me." Coalter's long yellow teeth looked ready to gnaw. "Only thing the state police have is the slug they took outta Randle; somehow it bucked and bounced around, then came to rest in what little brain he had. That's about it. Now, Me? I got a much bigger picture, as you can see. Ever'thang, in fact, but a name ... and that's beginning to narrow considerably." His smile stretched, sinister.

I sat in silence, sizing the flush in Coalter's face. The slugs being from the same gun was bothersome. Was it possible?—or could the state's forensic lab have made a mistake? It was an irony Coalter was blind to, but given my very own unique and elite piece of the puzzle, an irony fraught with possibilities, the biggest of which would serve only to prove one thing: that Bobby was innocent. *Or was he?*

Coalter drew his chin in tight, his clumsy hands currying his tangled mane. "You know, it ain't easy bein' me," he said, twirling his glass, signaling Bobby that it was empty. Bobby didn't move, just held Coalter in a hard stare. Coalter smacked his lips and went on. "Always the one to get to the bottom of it ... that's me." Once again Coalter was lost in his own reverie, grinding it out in a self-proclaiming posture. On and on in an aching soliloquy about his persistence and how it paid off, got us to where we were.

It was a hard reach to pat himself on the back, for being the super sleuth he thought he was, but he managed—each and every syllable its own arrogance, and all the while believing he had the trump card. Still, I let him ramble on, deducing, surmising, putting all the pieces together for our benefit—his way of moving in for the kill—each utterance a tortuous annoyance; his air equal parts arsenic and obnoxiousness.

He let it play out as long as he could, as long as Bobby and I would listen. Solving the mystery of Haman Flowers and Randle Cain had been just so easy, a point he was unwilling to turn loose, impertinence and condescension aimed at the infirmity of others to unearth even a shred of evidence—his main target being me, I was sure.

He finally stopped, dull and trite, and said he knew Bobby had a derringer, and would he be so kind as to let him see it. "I know it'd be real easy," he said, "to tell me you sold it years back or some whore down in New Orleans got away with it; that you lost it in a poker game or swapped it for a milk cow; that it's more'n likely changed hands a dozen times in the last twenty-six year. And I might even be inclined to believe you, but I got a nose that tells me it just ain't so. That pistol is too much a part a' you; your uncle Corbin's, I believe. You'd never part with it or leave without it. It's fixed to you like a knot on a tree. Just wouldn't be a party without it. The slug from Haman Flowers will be its own testimony. The one taken from Randle, too, I surmise."

Bobby smiled then gave a thoughtful rub to the deep wrinkles in his brow. "You know, you got yourself a real mean streak, Coalter. 'Course I guess you know that." Bobby was locked and loaded, the sight in his mind aimed for a kill shot, everything shy of pulling the trigger. "Somethin' in you," Bobby went on, "that pleasures in the game, deadly as it is." He paused, undid the lid to his whiskey and drank straight from the bottle, then poured Coalter two fingers without wiping where his mouth had been. Coalter watched with a sour look, but didn't refuse. "Something in you," Bobby went on, "that revels in the complexity of pain ... so long's it's not your own." Coalter watched after the liquor in his glass as if somebody might come along and snatch it away. "But from my side a' the street," Bobby said, "you just a hot-ass mess a' conjecture, best I can tell. Self importance out ahead of it all, and the thing that keeps you from even imagining that there could be another side but your own." Bobby leaned in, both hands on the bar, his face too close to Coalter's. "You think it's real clever comin' in here an' drinkin' my liquor, talkin' like you actually have sump'm to say. Truth is, you got just enough to make yerself believe you're something. What it is, is spit. The sad part is the mean streak keeps you from knowing it, all the time relying on it as a means of defense, and something that keeps you from being slammed to the ground. Never mind what resemblance you might have to a mule's ass, or what begs for charity. *Evidence* you call it. Slanted handlin' of details is closer to the heart of it: what you configure and what you think might influence a jury, truth never mattering all that much."

Bobby's affront had little-to-no effect. Coalter sat smiling, the liquor an insulation to insult when given his assurance of the upper hand. To Coalter, what was implied was a far less troublesome horse to ride than having to deal with the burden of evidence and witnesses and endless testimony. Full-on proof was for Coalter little less than courtroom drama, far too removed from the swiftness of frontier justice: what he knew as most satisfying. Corner 'em an' corral 'em, rope 'em, tie 'em an' hang 'em. It really didn't need to be any more complicated than that.

"You know," Coalter said, "it'd be plum vulgar a' me to pat you down right here in the middle a' yer own gin joint." They both smiled, all knowing, all in, closer and closer to the root of it. "If I was a bettin' man, I'd say somebody in your line a' work was liable to have a derringer up his sleeve and another one in his boot ... be a fool not to, actually." He raised his glass a tad, the tremor in his hand causing the whiskey to nearly slosh over the top, then brought it shiveringly to his lips, the craving mindless of what defiled him. "AHHH," he thundered, the torch of whiskey having its way at his interior, the fire and the sugar reaching all the way to his need. "Am I right?" he asked, his words professed, slurred, his long yellow teeth hankering for raw meat.

"You know," Bobby said, "it's always been to my advantage to know who's in my camp. I'm thinkin' you ought to know the same thing. Might help take the sting outta the unexpected." And with that, he raised his arms. "Nuthin' up my sleeves," he said, his smile reaching clear into the next room. But then he reached toward his boot, and faster than a cat might pluck a bird out of the air, came up with the prettiest derringer ever made: Corbin's, nickel plated with a burl wood handle. There was only one.

Coalter never flinched, just sat there with a smile widening like the mouth of a river ready to breach. "Well, now," he said, "ain't that a surprise," his sarcasm as thick as his tongue, his eyes as heavy as the cloud of smoke from his Lucky Strike.

Bobby never said a word, just laid it on the bar, then offered up another taste of whiskey; just unscrewed the lid and tilted it's open mouth toward Coalter's glass. "Well, now," Coalter said, pinching his nose, his tongue loud after moisture, a heaviness and quietness easing into him as easy as air, "don't mind if I do. No reason for bodies to be uncivilized." He weaved even though he was sitting, and with a smile glued to his face like it couldn't be removed with a crowbar. "The law," he said, "is ever'body's friend, no matter how we chose to see it. Been my friend my whole life. Why I am who I am." He tried laughing, but it came without salt or substance. "Yessiree," he slurred, "a balanced scale, and with men like me to keep it that way ... as unfortunate as it may be for some."

Bobby filled Coalter's shot glass to overflowing, letting the whiskey overrun its sides and down onto the bar. "Well, now, that's quite generous," Coalter said, his words fighting their way through clenched teeth, "but you've left me with a real trick, I'm afraid: getting it where it needs to be without making a plum fool a' myself." But making a fool of himself vanished about as quick as it came to mind. He lowered his head and slurped without lifting the glass, like a horse slurping from a trough. Then with even his eyes seeming to sway, pinched it between his thumb and middle finger and tossed it back with more than a hint of desperation. He swiped his mouth with the sleeve of his coat and sat there reeling ever more gently, each second easing him closer and closer to where he longed to be. Silence trailed across the bar like a soft-pillowed dream. Coalter closed his eyes and began chewing, though there was nothing there but his tongue.

"Another?" Bobby asked, then poured achingly slow and without waiting for Coalter's answer. Coalter sat weaving, weighed down with fault and flaw, until his head toppled forward, hard, his chin bouncing against his chest. I caught him just before he slid off the stool.

"Well," said Bobby, "that was rude."

"His way of saying goodnight, I reckon."

"What is it we're supposed to do with him, now?" Bobby wanted to know.

"Carry him back to the motel and wait for him to die, would be my guess." We smiled the smile of old friends, the devil still at work somewhere deep within us.

Eighty-Three

Sometimes You Just Need a Place to Hide

It was near nightfall the next day when Coalter got himself undrunk enough to call me. I'd gotten him back to the Colley Motel and laid him across his bed, fully dressed, coat and all—the way I suspect he slept a good deal of the time. He sounded like hell, sore of soul and wanting. I told him my day was over, and whatever he wanted to do with Bobby Yonts would have to wait till tomorrow. That had been the last word before his receiver clacked and rattled and finally nested its way to silence.

It was after five o'clock the next evening before he called again, carrying on about how the onus was on us to get back to Invictus and bring this whole thing to a head. There was no getting around it, so I went to get him; his car was still at Invictus, where we'd left it two nights ago. It was a muddled affair, one where Bobby refused to relent possession of his derringer and where Coalter went to waving his arms and going on about withholding evidence and obstruction of justice, whereby Bobby hauled off and shot a hole in the door frame next to Coalter's head. For the longest moment, a hush as frightful as the naked torso of Hooker Hopkins lunging down the hall toward us, shaving cream heaped on his face, froze us where we stood. Hooker stopped just shy of knocking into us, breathing hard and looking for smatterings of blood. Bobby stood with an unnerved expression and blowing into the barrel of his derringer.

"Do I need to be here?" Hooker asked.

"Sorry," Bobby said. "Fly on the wall. I hate them damn things." Hooker looked Coalter over real good before turning and lumbering back down the hall.

Coalter and I just stood there waiting to see what Bobby might do next, knowing full well he had another round in the chamber and was as likely as not to use it. But then he quick-dropped it back in his boot and came out with a knife about the size of a Jim Bowie. In less than a minute, he had that slug dug out of the doorjamb. "There," he said, handing it to Coalter. "That's all you need. The derringer stays with me."

Coalter just stood there with the slug in the palm of his hand, eyeing Bobby and wishing with every fiber in him that he had the strength and the guts to rip his throat out and eat him right there on the spot, hair and all. He finally dropped the slug into his shirt pocket and tapped it several times, feeling it next to his heart. For a very chancy minute afterwards, the report of Bobby's derringer still rang through the halls. It made little difference to Coalter, ruffling his shirt pocket like it contained a gold nugget, satisfied that Bobby's days were numbered.

"I'm just one man," Coalter finally said, not knowing when to shut up and risking being torn apart, "but if I can be honest with you, there's times when I know I'm more'n anybody wants to deal with, something along the lines of an *equalizer:* the extraordinary redeeming the indiscretions of those less than exemplary." I never knew anybody who enjoyed being hated as much as Coalter, who actually liked being the *sonofabitch.* It was the horse he rode, the one juried in black and spurred unsparingly by a kind of self-loathing, if truth be known. He limped off without another word. That was the last we saw of him for ten days.

I waited a few days before I got up the nerve to stop by Bobby's. I went there without a clear notion of what I wanted to say, more to clear the air than anything. I stayed longer than I intended, and, against my better judgment, allowed myself a few rounds, or maybe it was more than a few, of Bobby's private stock. But somewhere in the middle of it, Bobby finally got around to asking me where I stood with it all, his expression unflinching as if for once in his life unclear about what I might say. I tried laughing, but with little consequence. Instead, I felt myself growing hot—whiskey hot—and rubbing the back of my neck. After a lengthy pause, I said, "It's a mite more complicated for me. I'd like to think I stand with the law, however it plays out; do what I can and hope I can somehow make a difference, whatever that might be."

His smile came quick, muscle tight. "Well, I'll be damned," he said, enjoying his disbelief. "Sheriff Cain. Making a difference, whatever that might be." Laughter came easy to Bobby. He used it like a stabilizer: diffusing or energizing, just whatever was needed to control the moment. The more dire the situation, the more radiance it seemed to have.

The whole idea of Bobby being Haman's killer hadn't done much but keep me up nights thinking how best I could rid myself of its thought, but mostly how best I could rid myself of Coalter. My being with Coalter when he presented himself to Bobby had been solely for the sake of posturing, what would best reflect my cooperation in any report he might write. Irrespective of Coalter's backwoods investigation, it was a long shot that Bobby was Haman's killer. It was a supposition that had more flaws than probabilities, but was not entirely impossible.

In an easy motion, Bobby held one of his bottles up to the light, examined its clarity then plunked it down in front of me. "Pour us another one," he said.

I poured, unsteady and unfocused, as close to two fingers as I could manage. Bobby stared at his glass for the longest time, sniffed a bit then let his eyes come to rest dead on mine. His smile was wide. "I don't think you wanna hear me say I killed Haman Flowers, do you?"

"I don't want to hear nuthin' close to it," I said, "but I ain't gonna run from it if I do." It was true: the last thing I wanted to hear was a murder confession from Bobby Yonts. But then it was the one thing I'd imagined time and again, what racked me and sent me to the tops of mountains more times than I cared to count.

I was whiskey-warm from my eyes to my knees, and shored only with some obscure notion of justice and how it should be administered. "It's a real barrel a' snakes, this business I'm in, Bobby. Sometimes you just need a place to hide; other times you just have to stand an' fight, hoping justice won't be all that blind."

"Whoa," he said, his head hanging just above his glass. "*Justice?*" His smile crept like an evening shadow. "What kind a' justice we talking about? What them lawyers in Pikeville connive over? This for one, that for another? *Courthouse cowboys* ... you got the money, you got the way? *That* kind a' justice?—or something a little less backroom: something with the makings of '*cross my heart and hope to die,*' ''*pon my honor and swear to God?*'" His eyes were glazed, rocked and unblinking, his smile now gone. "If it's really justice you're so concerned with, what about all the people them devil-bred bastards, Haman and Randle, stole from?—people with nuthin' to begin with who sweated from daylight to dark with a borrowed mule just to feed their young'ns? How 'bout them?—or the wives they battered blue?—or the childern they half starved to death, abused and *messed with?*" His eyes and words fell to stone cold. "An' for them like Corbin?—them they *killed?*" I couldn't remember when I'd been so lost for words, so taken in by such quarrel, my own dissonance and the whiskey widening the divide. "Who gives a damn, Rubin, who killed either one a' them ill-birthed sons a' bitches? It's an offense to anyone who knew 'em that Coalter's even spendin' time with it. I'll tell you one damn thang," he said, "an' you can live with it or take it to hell with you when you go: you can know it wasn't me what killed either one of 'em, 'cause I'd a shot 'em till there wasn't nuthin' left to shoot."

I sat limber legged, feeling the swell of whiskey and the curse of being dead-center to a muddy and forbidding crossroad. Coalter said it was only natural that Bobby would deny it. It's what the guilty do; even more so with the flap of murder so intricate, so compounded. I'd heard it a thousand times myself: the disowning, the pleas of innocence, the conferring of oaths on the heads of those most loved. I stopped being surprised after the very first one, seventeen years ago. Now, it's jadedness I try my best to fight off, its bane contrary to the devotion that once ran with the likes of ol' Jess and Bartley.

The minutes ticked by, calling into account and condemning our minds, fighting off the reality of our lives. With the quiet squeezing down on what life there was between us, I said in my most practiced sheriff's voice, "Even if it was true, you'd never have to worry about it. It'd be something never spoken by me."

He waited, hell dug into his face and ready to snatch me into a thousand pieces. It had been the wrong thing to say—as calloused as it was unthinking—and even worse, impossible to withdraw. Just the idea that I still had room for doubt, after all this time, cut him deep.

With the world seeming to crumble between us, he gulped the last of his whiskey and slammed his glass to the bar. Then, in a tone that rejected all we were to each other, said: "Reckon you'd better be gettin' to your supper."

He left me sitting alone at the bar, the cavernous of Invictus and the dusty breath of moonshine never more mocking.

Eighty-Four

Bring Coalter

Chloe Bligh, my secretary for seventeen years and clearly a lover of fried cooking, stuck her head inside my door to tell me that I had a call, and would I like a cinnamon bun. Before I could answer, she said it was someone who refused to give his name, just said something about it being *personal*—and that she'd made the cinnamon buns herself. Mondays were never free from the weight of weekend insurrection: mutineers and drunks and all those convinced that their time on earth was to make sure the rest of us had a right good taste of hell. The off-chance of it being without incident was something I gave up on years ago, mysterious phone calls not excluded.

"Sheriff Cain," I said, trying for authority at seven a.m. while Chloe waddled in and plopped a cinnamon bun about the size of a cabbage head in the middle of my desk. There was no answer on the other end, though it was obvious there was someone there. I gave it a minute, waited while Chloe pretended to tidy up here and there; who was on the other end mattered to Chloe Bligh. But then my all-dismissive look put an arch in Chloe's back and helped her to make a show of leaving: drawing in her chin and rolling her eyes like it was going to be *one of those days*. The other end of the line finally stirred with a tired breath while Chloe eased her way out without ever once lifting her eyes from mine, even while she *slowly* closed the door behind her. I had a stronger than usual premonition that it was Bobby on the line, so I took a chance at putting things right. "You're up early," I said.

"Ain't missed a sunup in twenty year," he said. "Like an old rooster: 'fraid it might not come up without my urging."

"One of the extras of workin' hoot owl," I joked.

"That an' a desperate conscience."

We laughed. Lighthearted. Understanding the situation Coalter had put us in. "I know things," Bobby finally said, his tone soft, distant. "Things about things."

I knew what he was referring to, and he knew I knew. "Then why don't you help yourself, if it's gonna make a difference?" My words seemed to float away in the short silence that followed, before he took a slow breath and put the phone back in its cradle.

"GET IN!" was the sum total of Bobby's greeting, clipped and ardent and as sassy as his new coral-colored Lincoln. He was parked in front of the courthouse right there on Main Street, the passenger door wide open, and him not caring if voters liked what they saw or not: the two of us cavorting. I was a bit more cautious.

"Why don't we just go inside?" I suggested.

His stare said he was giving me to the count a' three.

"Damn, boy! Why so feisty?"

He said nothing, just drove us around the block to the pool hall and parked on the shady side of the street. I gave him a wrinkled look: a mix of vanguard confusion and tottered surprise.

"Reckon we need to talk some," he said, his eyes catching shards of light even in the shadows: blue half-moons warming, warning. I nodded, complicit, the sting of confrontation softened by nearly a week of avoidance. Still, there were insinuations lingering in the back of my mind, and all that remained to be said.

"I 'spect you know about Woodrow comin' in," he said on a light note.

I followed right in behind him, soft tact and all. "First time in twenty-four year."

"Remember that time me and him was about to fight right out there in the middle a' the road?" We laughed, the picture of it still vivid, even more comedic with the telling.

"I remember 'bout everything we ever did," I said. "'Cause I want to, I reckon."

He looked away, took a long sniff of air and shook a smile on his face. "It was all good, wasn't it? You and me, I mean. All what we got into, what we couldn't stay away from."

"In an' out of everything wrong and advised against."

"Lord what a mess: two young'ns loosed outta Greezy Creek. Now that's a book."

"Wasn't nuthin' in the world like what we lived, what all we dealt with ... good an' evil both."

"How you reckon we're still alive to talk about it?"

My head swarmed with places and faces, remembering what all we'd embraced, feared, and fought off, all that lifted us out of ourselves, and all that tried to hold us back. "Nobody'll ever know what we took to them nights," I said. "Or what we brought back."

"Put a hand on the Bible and still nobody'd believe it."

"Best part's how we made due all the times we didn't have a dollar between us. Somehow it didn't matter. We never missed a beat." It was a chord sweet and holding of truth; what sent us to snickering.

"Yeah," I said, turning to face him, "it was all good. *Was* and *is* both."

We sat for a time, kept by the hastening of summer, the trek of jasmine making its way from the surrounding slopes and the clack of billiard balls making their way upward out of the cellar. It was like old times, away from home when the long shadows minced with the closing of blinds and the turning of locks, the shop keepers and their end-of-the day melodies.

"I just right then come from Greezy 'fore I corralled you," he said, his tone thoughtful, leveled out. He gave a quick rub to his lips and said something about needing a drink, then dismissed it almost in the same thought. I got the feeling he was warming up to something, what he wanted to say in the first place, but couldn't quite turn the corner. "Don't know why, exactly, but I drove up to the top a' Wolfpit an' just sat there starin' off into nothin', just me an' the wind high up, it sweepin' the pines the way it does. Like I was in a dream an' it clear as a bell: you, me, them cows comin' outta the holler, lookin' down on Haman Flowers' cabin. Funny how a time can relive itself—what we don't want to turn loose of, what we can't."

"Don't know that any of it's easy to forget. Even when we want to."

"Whaddaya reckon comes over a feller at a time like that, Rubin? When he wants to go back?—do it all again?"

"Maybe it's realizing he didn't pay enough attention to it the first time."

"Give about anything for the chance to be back there grubbin' through the rocks an' briars, fists full a' green onions an' cornbread, dreamin' big ... even if it was just for a day. B'lieve I mighta been a bigger part a' creation back then, Rubin; all of it so full a wonder, without fences. I never had much time for *used to be*; always too busy with *right now*. But just like outta nowhere, them days came an' found me, clung to me like moss on a stump. Wadn't nuthin' I could fight off, or even wanted to; just stayed with it long as I could before drivin' off, before my mind folded in on me altogether. Crazy as hell, I know, but it was the first time I ever felt so drawn back, yearning for the way it was. Don't know what got ahold of me, really, just something that bit down hard, kept me remembering, kept me wanting to. Next thing I know, I'm turning up Main Fork like I didn't have a choice. Went all the way to Rock House, relivin' every bend in the road. Wasn't a single place without a memory."

He stopped. Waited. Reflecting in his own way. "Come by Andrew's on the way out," he said, his recall now upward, fastened with a grin. "He was out there sweeping the porch—'bout all he does anymore since he let Sherman take over—his gut hangin' down to his knees and listenin' to Lester rattle on like he'd just been elected governor. Stopped to see if he was feelin' generous, maybe buy me a Dr. Pepper. Just sump'm I do outta meanness, knowin' that sumbitch wouldn't let go of a nickel if he knew there was dollar about to take its place." He chuckled, the vision of Andrew's penny pinching hard to obscure.

"Sherman's just like him," I said. "Runs 'at store like a church on Sunday. Precision tuned, that boy is; cash register savvy, to hear Seriann tell it ... first copper penny to last."

"I have to laugh when I think about all them rumors all them years about him bein' Andrew's."

"It was like a rumor come to life after he got grown," I said. "Why, he's more like Andrew than Andrew ever thought about being. Talks like him, even walks like him: flatfooted. Like he's ready to head-up on his face about every other step."

"Even turned like him. Swear. He used to be so sweet, all the time wanting to crawl up in my lap and tell about that old troll. Now he's busy figuring out ways to get that nickel outta everbody's pocket."

"Seriann says he'll mark it down whenever she gets a cracker outta the barrel. Has to hide herself a bottle a' pop or he'd take it outta her pay—an' that his own mother. About once a month he'll sneak her a penny piece a candy: slips it in her apron pocket like he's committin' grand larceny." It was good to cut loose, clear our minds, laugh like we were jacked on shine.

"Sherman was taking inventory when I walked in," Bobby said. "Looked up just long enough to see who I was an' give me a little nod. I could tell he was right in the middle of numbers and wasn't about to take a chance on missin' count, bein' off on a can a corn or a moon pie. That'd be a dime he'd never get back."

We coughed and hawed just short of slapping each other on the back. The thought of Seriann and Andrew, though, was nowhere within the framework of my belief system—even after all these years. But then it was nearly thirty-five years ago, when times were lean and the rules of engagement and survival what they needed to be.

"Anyway," Bobby said, as if suddenly remembering, "Woodrow's coming in, an' Seriann's wantin' to make it a big deal."

"Sunday, I'm told. At Mary Olive's." Seriann had called me earlier in the week, excited that I be there.

"Corn pone, killed lettuce, and onions. Soup beans, boiled potatoes an' fried greens. Inez's pork chops and Seriann's chicken. You'll want to be there."

Nothing was better than laughing with Bobby. Nothing. His thickset: jaw, hands, and chest emanating the kick of a mule.

"So why was it, anyway, that you gobbled me up in front of the courthouse? To tell me about Woodrow?"

He jutted his chin and went to tapping his fingers on the steering wheel, a look somewhere between compliant and serious. "First off, I wanted everybody to know we were brothers. That we get drunk an' go places together. And that it ain't no crime." His words were exact, aimed at lifting the scab on our charade, the insufferable game we'd played for too many years: pretending alien status for the sake of our Baptist society and votes, disallowing ourselves even the fringe elements of acquaintance, all for the sake of a life dependent on public opinion.

"That's full a' guts," I said.

He smiled, comfortable, not needing to be reminded who he was. "Let me ask you sump'm, Rubin." His tone was collapsed, without haut. "I wanna know outright if you got doubts about me, an' about the things Coalter Hatfield's layin' down." He sat still as ice.

I shifted in my seat and tried massaging some feeling into my eyes. I knew what I said would have meaning long after I said it. The truth was I *did* have doubts, the evidence—incriminating on the surface—being what it was. But there was another factor that no one knew but me—not Coalter or any branch of the law, not family or another living soul. It was possible, I knew, for Bobby to have killed Haman; that there was a way. Even though the likelihood was minimal, it was not out of the question. After several deep breaths and with the air seeming to thin all around me, and with each of us staring off in our own direction, Bobby opened his door and stepped out.

"Come on," he said, brushing it all back, "let's go shoot some nine ball 'fore we forget how."

I got out and just for a minute wondered what it would be like if we did: if we walked down those steps again, just the two of us, like it used to be and with Whetsel Rowe there to take our money?

"I gotta be gettin' back," I said, sliding my hand along the length of his Lincoln's highly polished fender. "Nice ride."

"See you Sunday?" he asked.

"Count on it."

We stood in an awkward silence, groping for words that weren't there, before I finally turned and walked off. I didn't get far before he yelled: "Oh, one last thing."

I turned, wondering. "What's that?" I said.

"Bring Coalter."

I stood with a look of bewilderment, not knowing if I'd heard him right, when he added, "Haman Flowers: I aim to have an end to it."

Eighty-Five

Like Flies Around a Butter Churn

Coalter had been low-key for days on end, not showing his face and not leaving his motel room except for short trips to Jerry's Restaurant—and those injurious walks to the liquor store. Holed up, he was, for ten days running. Strange, considering how he now had what he wanted: the slug from Bobby's .41 caliber derringer. But his not having done anything with it was puzzling. When I went to invite him to Mary Olive's, he looked nearly on a par with roadkill. He said *No* a number of times, his temperament tawdry and guarded. But after several days of making promises I never intended to keep, he gave in. That was just before he went to mumbling around the liquor on his breath about it being a complicated time, how the state police wanted to rein him in, permanent like. "*Already past retirement*," they told him. "*Time to turn the page.*" It had been a short burst of bullet points: manpower, tighter budgets ... all that lent itself to thinning the herd. The one consolation was their willingness to let Coalter finish his investigation into the murder of Randle Cain, although they were quick to add that the sooner he could put a lid on it the better.

"I'm gonna see this Randle Cain thing through," he said. "Don't give a damn how long it takes. Their budget can go to hell. It's my last ride, an', by God, I'm gonna do what needs doin', even though there's a sizeable piece of the puzzle still missing." I took it to mean what was still unresolved regarding Bobby's involvement, the uncertainty of it keeping him all the more drunk. He sat with his head nearly touching his knees, a quart sized bottle of Wild Turkey on the nightstand next to him. "Retirement," he uttered. "I don't even know what that means." He lit a new cigarette with the old. "I told 'em I'd be in touch," he wheezed then commenced to cough himself nearly purple before getting a monster-size swallow of bourbon past his Adam's apple. "Ahh" was his only sound, the fire in his breath reaching me across the room. "I'm a short-timer now, Rubin; wind in my sails all but gone." He gave it a hard thought then swiped at his nose. "But I mean to do the right thing," he said, his eyes hard on the Wild Turkey. "You can count on it."

My mind stayed busy with what Bobby had in store, what manner of gunfight he'd be bringing to Mary Olive's. I was leery about what I might be walking into, and even more so, what affect it might have on the family. Coalter wasn't exactly what you might call a *desirable* guest, or even a decent one, and Bobby was never one to hold back. The combination made for volatility. Even Chloe Bligh noticed my troubled state.

"Here," Chloe said, pulling a rhubarb pie from out of nowhere and landing it square in front of me. "You been lookin' a little drag-mouthed lately. Thought this might tighten you up a bit."

I eyed her for a long minute. She eyed me right back. "You expecting me to eat this whole thing?" I said.

"If you wanna do yerself a favor. Look at it this way," she said, "half of it for dinner, the other half for dessert." She smiled warm and wide, her cheeks like cream puffs, and handed me a fork. About the time I took my first bite, she said, "Now, tell me what's got you bothered."

"Thank you for the pie, Chloe," I said between one big bite after another, my chewing finally getting the best of her. After a time, she took the hint and left with her usual huff, but not before saying that she'd be right outside if I needed to talk.

I picked up the phone several times to call Bobby, to ask what my bringing Coalter was all about—but each time knew it would be no use. He had a plan, and that was all he intended me to know.

By the time Coalter and I arrived, the whole family was milling about like flies around a butter churn. I was surprised by how well Coalter had cleaned up, and how he'd seen fit, somehow, to somehow minimize the trace of liquor on his breath.

"Everybody, this here is Coalter Hatfield," I said, "one a them leftovers from the state police we been having to deal with." One after another offered up his own brand of howdy, Coalter seeming to bask in the attention. Bobby just nodded from across the room. We stayed on the porch, we men, waiting while the women worked at a fevered pitch to get it all on the table. They only had to call us once.

As was the custom, the men ate first: Woodrow, Cousin Truman, Wilson, Sherman, Aug, Mr. Tackett, Coalter, Bobby, me and a handful of neighbors. The women flew around us in a sweat, their dutifulness pushing them at every turn to make sure we had all we needed: full bowls, warm bread, cold water, more of everything while sidestepping and keeping out of each others' way, even swooshing away the flies ... all that was expected and due our rightful place.

The women and children ate only after we were finished, making do with what was left, and for the most part, after much of it was cold. It was simply the way it was: the hill way, what we all grew up understanding as right and proper. Only after things were cleared, cleaned, and put away, did the women join us and add to our talk. Today, though, we gathered to say goodbye to Woodrow right out there in the middle of the road, the last time being some twenty-four years ago.

Woodrow had only been here a day, but made it all too obvious that he was anxious to get back on the road. Without saying, it was the same sentiment the rest of us shared. Big around as a rain barrel and with his hair greased back in a ponytail—a tribute, he insisted, to his wife and the Blackfoot way—there just didn't seem to be much about him that we clung to anymore. Twenty-eight years in the military and a government pension kept them in sugar and lard, and with a ready access to the PX. That and welfare commodities—and a move back to the Blackfoot Nation—made life reasonably tolerable.

All those years of Woodrow being away left us scrambling for ways to reconnect, but then his having to guess who Wilma Lee and Wilson were only added shame to embarrassment. But then when Sherman had to be introduced... Well, twenty-four years of *not bothering* played like the parched harmonies of a cigar-box fiddle, its chords of concordance lost to minor keys, if they could be found at all. Woodrow's inner man, though, what I remembered most, remained intact, churned with the same self-indulgence. When he talked, which was his most given compulsion, it was, each time and every time, too loud and too fast, and with himself as the topic of choice. Only now he talked without showing his teeth, though I could tell they needed more work than they were worth ... and there was little he could do to hide the liquor on his breath, even with the help of pickled beets, buttermilk, and onions so generous on Mary Olive's table. He sweated more than I remembered, shaved less, seemed to take no notice of his talon-like fingernails, or the haggard mop of his eyebrows—now thick as a hen's nest and rough as rope. Time had a way of dealing with us all, some more roundly than others.

Woodrow's letters, mercifully, had come to a stop long ago. Now it was only cards at Christmas and phone calls on Seriann's birthday that kept him linked. But it was because of the cards and phone calls (always of the same ilk, *broke and needing)* that preserved his place as a fading flower.

Seriann packed him out with boxes of canned goods, what ready cash she had, and enough chicken to last him till he was back home in Wyoming: a three-day trek with overnights in the backseat of his car. More a stranger than family now, none of us gave much thought to ever seeing him again, or to his wife and children we only imagined from his pictures. It was hard to figure what kind of emotion his departing triggered. Mostly, we just stood there looking like we were lost until he went out of sight, and his car's soft trail of dust chased us back inside for another round of Wilma Lee's chocolate pie.

"How long you reckon you'll be with us, Mr. Hatfield?" Mary Olive asked, her feet stretched out in front of her and resting on a twenty-pound lard bucket, her thick hose rolled down to her ankles.

"Cain't rightly say," Coalter said, his pose thoughtful, careful. "Ain't got a real clear picture of what I'm after. Close, though. Be outta here in due time."

"I'm understandin' yer more interested in Haman Flowers—an' him in the ground near twenty-six year—than you are Randle Cain, an' him so freshly kilt that the worms'r more'n likely still diggin' their way to him. Though I 'spect they'll turn around an' leave once they get there, once they get a taste."

"It's a complicated set of circumstances I'm dealin' with," Coalter said, "one havin' a bearin' on the other."

"I'll just say this," said Mary Olive. "They's bad history 'tached to both. Two dark marks, one black as the next."

"I'm gettin' that from most," Coalter said, picking at his teeth with the flap of a matchbook, his eyes darting, vigilant.

"Don't reckon you'd know of anything for my feet, would you Mr. Hatfield?" Mary Olive asked. "Killin' me here lately: swole up like puffer snakes, them big ol' veins thumpin' me of a night, hollerin' at me of a mornin'. It's a punishment, but I'd soon have it as to have either one a' them hog-callin' sonsabitches—Haman an' Randle I'm talkin' 'bout—walkin' the same ground as me an' mine. I'm just glad it's a contention we don't have to deal with anymore. I know I speak for the biggest part a' Pike County. It's a blessin' they're gone, my 'pinion. 'Course, I guess you've heard that too."

"Heard plenty along the same lines," Coalter said, weariness seeming to settle in around his eyes.

"It'd do me good to be able to tell you I did it," Mary Olive said, "knowin' I's the one who sent 'em back to outer darkness, where they come from. But other than good riddance, there ain't much I can brag about in the way a' their goodbyes. But I'll say this: Haman Flowers wasn't nuthin' but evil hard at it, an' Randle cut from the same cloth." Her tone was now inner-directed, her blue calico dress reaching past us into spring. "The devil's in their souls so deep there weren't no gettin' him out. I knew it the day I first laid eyes on 'em, jacklegs that they were. Minds the size of a bat, bringin' hell to life. Them bein' gone is just a little less Satan we have to deal with. I just wonder how they're enjoying their time in the fires? Coffee, Mr Hatfield?" Coalter sat nodding, and with his forehead wrinkled up like a washboard.

"What'll ever come of it, Mr. Hatfield?" asked Cousin Truman. "Randle's killin', I mean." Truman's eyes were narrowed, effusive, wanting to know.

"State police was done with it a month after it happened," Wilson blurted, not waiting for Coalter to respond, and all too happy to bring what he knew to the table. "Lost interest after they found out what he was. Ain't 'at right, Rubin?"

"'Bout as right as I've known you to be, Wilson," I said. "They didn't want to fool with it no more'n anybody else, I reckon." The air was calm, casual: the family reared back, occupied with the coffee, the pie, their full bellies. "For them, it boiled down to being short on evidence," I said, catching Bobby from the corner of my eye. He was busy being still, but hanging on every word. "But that wouldn't do for Coalter here. Right, Coalter?"

It pleased Coalter that all eyes went directly to him. His mentioning that Randle's killing had ties to Haman Flowers had opened the door for what he routinely sought to be: the center of attention. Before getting to the root of it, he proceeded to fill us with overgenerous ideas of what a legend he was, all of it as tedious as the sun coming up and going down. After the longest twenty minutes on record, and with heads starting to bob, I had to wonder if he'd ever get to the question itself.

"Had a whole bunch thinkin' I was crazy comin' here to Greezy," he said. "'*Tryin' to make sump'm outta nuthin'*,' they said. Laughing at me behind my back an' to my face both for trying to tie two killings together, them being twenty-six years apart." He smiled, his foot tapping out time on the linoleum, knowing his tenure was short, breathing life into what little time he had left. "But like I told Rubin here, you gotta stick with what you know, and to me that meant turning over all the rocks: going back to the beginning, if you ever expect to pick up a trail. What I found, though, was a trail gone cold; not just cold, mind you, but no trail a-tall." Coalter was odd, but no fool by any means, and that only made him more intriguing, since one just never knew what rabbit he was liable to pull out of his hat.

"But I suspected," he went on, "that there was still a number a' witnesses around, them with memories long enough to recall Haman Flowers an' what he looked like all juked-up across them church house steps." He paused and smiled, his flight of daring almost too much, even for himself. "Knowin' Greezy the way I do," he said, "its people hard-pecked, I figured there was a trace of the story still simmerin', a last part still waitin' to be flushed out." He stopped here, smiled wider. "Seems I was right."

Except for Mary Olive hacking and spitting about every third word Coalter came out with, we sat mostly in silence, wondering when in the world he'd be finished. "But I stayed with it," Coalter said, his eyes snake-like, drifting just-so from one to another, "fittin' one little piece after another into a puzzle ever'body else quit on. '*Lost cause*,' they said. For them, maybe, but not me. I don't make a habit a' quittin'."

"I b'lieve I have to use the toilet," Mary Olive barked, interrupting Coalter's nauseous tide. It was enough to stand us up, even consider another piece of pie. Some made their excuses, Sherman being the first, the store's books suddenly needing attention. But then after a quick exit, he returned a few minutes later, trudging under a box of store goods and saying it was for Fayella and her children. "'Bout kills me," he said, "when they come in the store, knowin' they ain't got a nickel between 'em." He set the box down in front of Aug and said, "Don't want no thanks, and don't want her knowin' who it come from. Gotta go." That was it. In the next breath Sherman was out the door and across the yard. We sat there a little bewildered, seeing as how he was least known for generosity.

"Who's that for again?" Coalter asked, his curiosity molten.

"Fayella Flowers," I said, "or rather, Fayella Cain. Randle's wife ... and her children."

"Mighty generous," Coalter said.

"It's hard on a woman here in the mountains, Mr. Hatfield," Mary Olive was quick to point out. "Harder still with a gang a' young'ns."

"Harder still with one like Randle up in yer face," Seriann chided.

"The Randle part is nothing she has to worry about now," I said.

"Although," Bobby said, "Mr. Hatfield seems to be keeping him alive with his *ongoing investigation.*"

I turned to bring Bobby into full view. His eyes bored a hole, his fingers drummed. "But," I said, "the DA's now thinking there's been enough time and money spent on it. Figures the state police had it right all along. Just need to bring the whole thing to a halt and move on."

Truman's head was bobbing, his expression a study in concentration. "What's your take on it, Mr. Hatfield?" he asked in his best defense attorney voice.

"Well, sir, Randle's killin' bein' so violent, I figure it deserves a mite more attention than it originally got. I know he was a despised lowlife, much like Haman Flowers—but I figure if I come up with a name, it's gonna help restore confidence in the public eye. Then too, if I could come up with a name for one, it might invite a name for the other."

"What's your take, Rubin?" Bobby's voice came like a thrown knife.

Everyone's eyes did a quick fix on me, as if I had the final word. "Thought about it long an' hard," I said, my voice trying for persuasion, "and, truth is, I've always taken Randle's killing real personal, what with Greezy being the crime scene an' all. Been a huckleberry on my name for months now, something I'd like to be shed of. I feel like the whole county's markin' time, waiting to see what I'm gonna come up with—voters wantin' their money's worth. But here lately, I'm 'bout as close to not givin' a damn as I can be."

"If I was you, I wouldn't worry about not givin' a damn," Wilson said. "Could-a been you were the only one to begin with."

Everybody laughed but Coalter.

"Inez, why don't you sit down there and finish that pie," Mary Olive said, the roundabout of Randle's killing having long lost her interest.

In the next instant, Inez shoved in beside me on the kitchen table's long bench. It was the last piece of pie, one I'd eyed for the better part of an hour. I was getting ready to ask if anybody minded, but then, Inez, before I could protest, had the first bite halfway to her mouth. That's when the talk became loud and commonplace, reaching levels to where the name Randle Cain no longer registered or even mattered.

"Here's 'at little derringer," Mary Olive said, coming through the upper-room curtain, all the while unwrapping it from its silk handkerchief. I came partway off the bench, grabbed it, but too late to make a difference.

"What in the world we got there?" Coalter said with a long breath, his eyes big as full moons.

"What I aim to give Rubin," Mary Olive said, proud that she'd remembered. "What he's been wantin' for some time. What he asked me for a while back."

I looked at Bobby. He crossed his arms and leaned in against the table. My field of vision seemed to constrict, the ruckus all around me drowning my power to think, reason.

I looked down at the derringer, then at Coalter. He sat motionless, his head cocked in confusion—first this way, then that: at Bobby, then me, then the derringer.

"You reckon it'll still shoot?" Mary Olive laughed above the din.

Coalter's eyes were fixed on the derringer. Nobody moved. But then he reached out a hand, slow and petitioning. I offered it up like I was handling a robin's egg. He eyed it for the longest time, rolled it over in his hands, broke it open. I could feel my pulse clear into my feet.

"Keep her loaded, I see," Coalter said to Mary Olive, his eyes doing a quick dart in Bobby's direction.

"No sense in keepin' a empty gun," Mary Olive said. "When you need a gun, you need it loaded ... generally speaking. Law, if I had to look around for shells at a time I ought to be shootin'—tryin' to remember where I put 'em, an' then getting 'em to where they'd do some good—the fightin' would likely be over with, an' I'd more'n likely not be there to see it. On Greezy, you're either loadin' or shootin'. Guaranteed you cain't do both when them shootin' back's already decided you need to be in a graveyard."

For the first time in as many days as I could remember, I felt fettered, body and soul. Right there with Inez's big bottom squeezed in tight along-side mine on the bench, I realized the root of my conscience had been shredded and lifted out to dry. I knew why Haman and Randle were no longer with us, why the uncomplicated understanding of right and wrong had dealt them so deadly a hand. The acts of murder had done us all a favor, and for all the right reasons: for the peace we sought, and for the burdens we wanted only to be gone. Yet there was still the unknown: the killer was still at large, the reminder now resting in Coalter's hand. I knew from the deepest and darkest place that occupied my soul that my prior knowledge of Mary Olive's derringer could only work against me. "*Withholding evidence: Obstruction of justice.*" I could hear Coalter now. "*And what else was I hiding, anyway?*" He'd want to know. Yet, there was a part of me that was all-too willing to look the other way, the way Virgil Blair had been; the part that dared not probe too deep for fear of a face too close to home.

"What's the matter, Rubin?" Cousin Truman asked, alerted to my musing.

"Wha-?"

"You look a little peaked. You awright?"

It was right about then that a few of the neighbors began packing up, covering dishes and offering up lavish affections. Goodbyes were agonizingly long at Mary Olive's, everybody holding on to each other and promising not to be such strangers—all for the sake of not feeling so guilty for being just that. Things quieted after that, after Inez propped her feet up and began fanning away the day's sweat.

"Swearrr, if it ain't a thunder," said Mary Olive. "So many heads a-tawkin' an' gaumin' up the air. Had toothaches I'd rather spend a day with."

The cats finally dared to stir, peering through the screen door and signaling that they were ready for whatever scraps were left. The creek could now be heard again, full bodied and running with spring rain. We sat as if breathing our last, the evening soft and without a wind, sealing up crocuses and morning glories in its long stretch of shadows.

"What are you studyin' on, Rubin?" Mary Olive asked, her voice as light as the curl of smoke rings above her head.

Coalter still hadn't said a word—just sat there limp-shouldered and with the derringer now on the table in front of him.

"How sorry I am," I said, "that I've forgotten how to unload the burden I've put myself under, and how restful life can be if I just allow it." My words came unhindered, certain, braving the solitude now attached to the day. "I'm just tired," I said, "of *sheriffing,* of chasin' one sorry sumbitch after another. Don't know how this road I'm on got so twisted—don't even know that it matters—all I *do* know is I'm sure as hell ready to get off. Need to get back to sleeping nights and not being in so foul a' mood—something my girls let me know about often enough. Figure the devil's lost two of his main players when he lost Haman and Randle, and I'm believin' that'll be enough to give me a little peace ... at least for the time."

True stillness is one of those unexplainables that hovers just out of reach and ties us to the unknown when we least expect it. We sat for the longest time in its spell, like what rests there on the tops of mountains, its impenetrable silence connecting us to a kind of loaming. Only a single voice brought us from it, soft and abiding and as lasting as time.

"I was just sixteen when I first fought Luck Hanner," Bobby said. "It was just before Christmas an' colder'n a river bottom ... me an' Rubin figuring we could make a dollar. But it wasn't the real reason. Not for me, anyhow. I was just wantin' to knock life outta sump'm. Needin' it as bad as I was wantin' it. Corbin being gone hangin' on me like a loadstone, clawin' at me night an' day ... like he was tryin' to come back. It was a hurt I couldn't put down. So strong at times it made me feel like I wanted to be with him, even like I ought to be. That night at Luck's—all I could think about was wantin' to maul. Didn't matter what. Didn't have to be Luck, it just was. Wasn't nuthin' that could a' stopped me. I was wantin' to rid myself of so much. Luck whupped me, but it didn't matter. It even felt good gettin' the hell beat out of me. I wanted it as much as I wanted to give it." He stopped, his eyes lost, searching his mind for the rest. "Hooker come in just before we threw down," he said, "then took me an' Rubin to Corbin's when it was over. We just sat there in his car sippin' shine an' talkin' 'bout how things needed to be put right. It was way up in the mornin' time Hooker dropped us off right there in front of Angus Walker's. We'd run out of places to go, so just headed on home—ruts in the road froze over an' us half drunk. We got as far as the schoolhouse, then just stopped, there not bein' a sound 'cept for the creek, nor a light one 'cept what was comin' from the church house—them playin' poker—way it's always been on Saturday nights what time it's cold. I didn't care nuthin' about the cold—just stood there after Rubin went on to the house, still wantin' to kick a hole in sump'm. I was never good about goin' home, so I eased back down the road. Got to where it forked and here come Brother Ben, sweated like a hog and carrying a shotgun." He stopped again, a surprised look on his face, like it was the first time he'd heard himself tell it. "I knew where he'd been," he said. "Knew the mountain he'd crossed over and why. He was lookin' for Corbin's killer. That way night after night: him headin' out adder dark an' never a shell one in his gun. Never could talk him outta going. Never could convince him the killer wouldn't be there. But Ben was Ben." He stopped, anguished. "How he nightmared over Corbin: dreams chasin' him of a night, even catching him a time or two." He waited. Remembering. "I told him where we could find Corbin's killer, if he wanted to come with me. He listened to me like he did Daddy. Followed me like a pup. Wasn't but a minute later when we got there—to the church house—light seepin' through the planks, voices clouded, drunk. We hunkered down over the bank, next to the creek. Wasn't long adder that 'fore they started comin' out. Staggering. Cussing. First one, then another. Some goin' up the road, some down." He stopped, his eyes fixed, frightful. "Then right there—right at the end of it—come the devil hisself. Bowler hat cocked to one side, shotgun slung over his arm, light filling in behind him. A goblin an' a fiend, just standing there still as a stick, listenin' to the night. Then the light went out, and here come the last one. Couldn't tell who he was, just that he had a shotgun in one hand and pulled the door shut with the other. Two of 'em just stood there for the longest time, talkin'. Muffled, though nuthin' I could make out. But then it all changed so fast. Like a death angel with a bolt a lightnin', that last man was. His shotgun like a sword of fire. Just took him one step back and let it go, like it was one motion. Quicker'n a rattler strike. Lightenin' and thunder all at the same time. Haman never knew what hit him. Hellfire buckshot full in the chest is what he got. Knocked him down like a sledgehammer. Over 'fore he had a thought—even of dyin'. One second breathin', the next not. That quick." A haunt seemed to cloud his memory, but nothing he could erase. "But that was just the half of it," he said, "'fore at man took a pistol out of his pocket, stepped to where he could look down on Haman—an' him already gone—then shot him again." Bobby looked wrung out, and ran his hands through his hair. Nobody moved. Nobody made a sound. The stillness as quiet as the paper on the walls.

"It was then that Ben went to whimpering," he said. "Scared him near to death. Did me, too. That's when he heard us and started edging our way, shotgun in one hand, pistol in the other. He didn't take more'n a few steps before I saw who he was ... 'fore I come up outta the creek an' said his name. That's when he stopped. Answered me. Whispered my name. We just stood there in the middle a' the road, it comin' daybust, not knowing which way to go. That's when I saw the pistol up close. It was a derringer." He stopped, licked his lips. "That one right there," he said, directing our gazes to where it rested directly in front of Coalter. "That very one."

It's deceptive how the mind remembers: recalling what it wants, clouding what it doesn't. But that's the thing about reaching back. You never know what you'll get from one time to the next, your mind separating what wants to be kicked to the side of the road and what wants to be mentioned in the same breath with Jesus. Sometimes the mind just needs to be unlocked and swept clean, flushed and opened to the bitter scents of yesterdays. Bobby had done just that: opened the door on Haman Flowers' ghost, abled himself, after twenty-six years, to move beyond the shit of it all.

Coalter was a study in sobriety, blanked and waiting for what was next.

"We all know what Haman was." Aug's voice came out of nowhere, weakened with the mere mention of Haman's name. Aug was not accustomed to a lot of talk, speaking for the most part only out of necessity. He sat with his head low, his elbows on his knees and a cigarette burning between his fingers. "And we know all the things he did," he said. "How he ruined a sister I ain't seen in thirty year. How he did Dixie. How he poisoned the very air around him. How he took from so many—too often what was precious and matchless—and how he *delighted* in it. How he lorded over us, an' how he hated with such fullness. How ever' part of him, from his hair to his soul, was brackish." He stopped, clenched his teeth. "I knew he was at the church house that night," he said. "Sellin' liquor an' playin' poker. He knew I was comin'. It was my idea to meet up an' rob Judge Lewis' store soon as the poker playing was done, adder er'body cleared out. He was all keyed up about it, like I'd come over to his side. He was steady an' all natural-like when I walked in. They was two games going on. He sat in one, I sat in the other. Just leaned my gun in the corner and laid my money down. It was hours 'fore we broke up. Haman knew to hang back, knew what we planned to do. I was the last one to leave. Haman waited outside till I shut ever'thang up. We stood there together for a time, him on edge the way he always was, never trustin', never at rest: all the time shushin' an' listenin' for what was out there in the dark, his one hawk eye jerking this way then that, scared a' what might reach out and grab him, I reckon. I stood there listenin' to him profane, knowin' it'd be his last time. Funny, but I felt the strangest calm. Like I could think as clear as melted snow. Like I could know beyond the dust and dirt of earth—like angels had me wrapped in the warmth and light of heaven. There weren't no thinkin' to it. Just the doin'. Just steppin' back and pullin' the trigger. Simple, for all the good it did. Never even crossed my mind it might be wrong." Aug took a long pull from his cigarette, but never looked up. "Ever'thang was so still adder that. Quiet as underwater, as right as the cool breath a' night." The missing pieces rolled in nonstop once Aug gave them voice, veils lifting on one thing after another, light filling the darkest spaces.

"I meant the derringer to be the last word," he said, "...what carried Seriann's name." Eyes and heads rolled ever so slowly toward Seriann. She sat motionless, the smoke from her cigarette rising in a smooth white swirl. She was as she always was: decided, unbound; how she went to stand by the kitchen window, how she added her tobacco to the faint breeze of evening. Aug raised his head for the first time, waited till Seriann gave him a motherly smile. "The derringer was somethin' we talked out," he said, his eyes in a straight line with Seriann's. "Somethin' she wanted as a way of addin' her name to it. I knew that very night it was no turning back when she slipped it outta the bureau drawer and into my pocket." He lowered his eyes and then his head, sunk back into the sanctity of truth. "It was just one last thing to do, seein' him sprawled across them steps like he was. So I did it." He nodded at the derringer on the table in front of Coalter. "'*Goodbye from Seriann*' is what I told him, right before I pulled the trigger. Middle of his cheek is where I hit him: a hole on the left to match that sinning scar on the right—the way I sent him back to the devil."

Aug sat back in his chair and smoked without lifting his eyes. We had, each in our own way, retreated, sought the comfort of times less burdened with truth. Bobby and Aug's accounts, hard-fisted as they were, wore like a wool shirt on a dog-day afternoon. The mystery of Haman's killing was now gone, its wakefulness taking hold of me with a cold, meat-hook of a hand, the way Haman did when he crawled out of his grave and into my dreams: hunched on the back of Mule and in the light of the moon, his eyes piercing and the color of embers under the shadow of his hat.

"Must a' been pretty much the same with Randle Cain," Coalter said, his voice shocking the air, rude and interrupting, like shattering glass.

Aug looked up, confusion around his eyes. "Randle Cain?" he said, his voice rising in question. "I didn't have nuthin' to do with Randle Cain."

Eighty-Six

The Truth

Coalter's eyes were far off, not connecting; alone in some place I was sure I'd never know. I knew what I wanted to say—what needed to be said—but didn't quite know how. At last I just come out with it. "Funny how things can get all shot to hell if we're not real careful about our aim." I turned just enough to look Coalter straight on, "... how we can sometimes misinterpret things even with the best intentions, even when all signs tell us we're right."

"Somebody wanna tell me what he's talkin' about?" Mary Olive said.

"Truth," Coalter said, his eyes unblinking, his manner weighted. "He's talking about truth, and how we cain't ever know it till we stop warring against what deserves a voice."

Coalter fished the slug from Bobby's derringer out of his breast pocket and held it up to the light stuttering from the street lamp in front of the Colley Motel, like he was studying it for signs of life, then dropped in into my hand. "Been an enlightenin' day," he said.

"If you're thinking about bringing charges against Aug," I said, "there's a whole room full a' people who'll swear he never said a thing, *including me.*"

He watched after me for a brief moment, his smile wide. "I know," he said, his voice gentle, even kindly. "I don't look at it like I been beat, you know. Believe it or not, I still believe in the system. So long as justice leaves a mark, I'm good with it.

"Then whatta you suggest we do about this derringer?" I said, holding it just to where it caught the light.

He eyed it like a precious stone, his smile wily, wolflike. "It's not anything I'd ever want to get rid of," he said, "knowin' where it's been, who it's served. Part a Greezy's legend now. If it was mine, it'd be in my boot of a day, an' under my pillow of a night."

"You reckon the state police has any use for it?"

"They don't deserve it," he said. "They'd just see it as more work, sump'm they ain't got the time for—patience either. They washed their hands of Haman Flowers decades ago, Rubin," his voice dropping off to near nothing, "... an' now me." His look was out the window, on the darkness beyond the sputtering street lamp. "There's satisfaction in seein' efforts come to a worthy end," he said. "An' I believe in this case they have. Aug's not deservin' of anything but to be left alone, my 'pinion. That's pretty much how *I've* always wanted it: to be left alone. Now I'm afraid of it, of what ain't there." He turned to face me. "It's pretty thin comp'ny," he said, "just me an' what memories I can't forget. Not a whole lot to count on."

I watched him as if seeing him for the first time, or the last, his silhouette wilted in the half-light. "Come back anytime, Coalter," I said.

"I'll consider it if you'll do sump'm with that slice a' heartburn, Mary Olive. Leave you feelin' picked clean, that one." He smiled, big and toothy. "Y'all'r full a' surprises."

"It's a family thing," I said.

"A thing I know very little about, actually." He gave a heavy shrug, opened the door and stepped into the night. He closed the door behind him with a sense of reluctance, then reached back through the window to shake my hand. "Maybe we'll work together again someday," he said, "if ever I turn *private eye*." His hand felt like a dry knot, but warm.

"There's still Randle Cain," I said, not believing I actually spoke it aloud.

"Still Greezy's unsolved mystery," he said in a chesty laugh. "I'm just afraid it'll take another twenty-six years." I'd never noticed the fun in his eyes until now. "You boys'll just have to go on without me," he said. "But I don't envy you none. Actually, I'm afraid a' what you'll find. Somebody close, I'm betting ... family, I'd say. You're as good a lawman as I know, Rubin. A little soft, maybe, but upholding. We see a lot, you and me, doing what we do. An' I'm believin' you'll know what to do if a name's ever put to Randle. As for me, I'm as done with Greezy as it is with me. Your D.A.'s ready to run me off and the state police'r ready to turn me out. Tell you the truth, it's a good time for leavin'."

I just nodded, wished him well, then eased the car back onto the blacktop. I could see him watching after me in the rearview, in the fading light and under the slip of a moon.

An unsettling air followed me all the way to Monday morning, Chloe Bligh being at the office before me and falling all over herself with a butterscotch cake she made for my birthday.

I picked up the phone after it rang several times, and after Chloe gave me one of her *do-you-mind-answering-that* looks while she made a Main Street production out of cutting the cake.

"Which end do I speak in?" It was Mary Olive, the first time ever I knew of her talking on a telephone, and obviously asking for help in how to use the damn thing. "Now wait. Now what? Hold it like this?" Lord knows where she was calling from, or how she got to it. "What all do I say? Just hello? Well then. HELLO!?"

"If the Lord hisself was to tell me it was Mary Olive on the other end of this line I'd still not know whether to believe it or not."

"Right here?" I heard her ask someone. "Right into this thing? Well then. HELLO!?"

"Honey, you've already said that twice. Now I'm saying hello back."

"Rubin, honey, is that you? Lordamercygod," I heard her cackle. "I can hear you plain as I can myself."

"You'll have to excuse me if I say I'm confused. Where on earth are you?"

"I'm at Olin and Gracie's. Bobby come got me early this morning, 'fore he went to bed I'd say, then brought me up here to where I could wish you happy birthday."

"Well now, ain't you the miracle of the day."

"Well it's more to it than that," she went on, but by then Chloe was leaning, leaning, to the point of tilting, trying to pick up the tiniest fragment of who and what.

"Hang on a minute," I said.

"That'll be fine," I said to Chloe, my tone waving her off. "Go ahead an' set the rest of it out for whoever wants a piece." She gave me a deep breath, a slow exhale and a *whatever* wave with the cake knife. "And close the door," I said. I might as well have shoved a twelve-penny nail through the bottom of her foot.

"Well now, tell me what else you want me to know." I said.

"Cain't be talked about over this here 'lectric wire. You'll need to come here, and you'll need to tell me when."

"Well, how about tomorrow?"

"Make it when you get outta work. It's liable to take a while."

"All right then. Tomorrow. Six o'clock."

"Make it seven."

"Well then. Seven."

"Happy birthday," she screeched. "Now what am I supposed to do?" I heard her ask somebody, presumably Bobby. "Just put it back down on this thing here? Here, you take it." And that was it, before it went silent.

I arrived a few minutes before seven, selfishly hoping for a taste of cornbread and a plate of beans. What I found was Aug sitting on the porch, smoking, his back up against a post.

"Don't get up," I said, not bothering to hold back a grin. He laughed and shook my hand, offered me a spot on the porch where a couple of wirehairs and a Main coon lay twined, asleep in the balm of evening. I was able to scoot the wirehairs—limp and lazy as they were—but the old embattled Maine coon with a gray muzzle, arthritic bones, and hair missing from a long streak in his tail, was having none of it. Still, I managed to nudge him just enough. He made no attempt to hide his annoyance, waited till I was settled, then pushed his back expertly against my thigh—the price for infringement, and with the burden on me not to move.

Aug and I did a big-grin stare down, took in some deep breaths and spit like mule drivers. I craned my neck trying to spy through the screen door, but detected no movement of any kind. Finally, I caved in, the quiet and secrecy stretching me to my limit. "Where's Mary Olive and Lorali?"

"Gone to Millard with Wilma Lee an' the girls." He smiled wide and easy. "Ice cream cones. Ever' Tuesday."

"I'm just plum outta the loop anymore," I said.

He laughed and flicked the ash off the end of his cigarette with the tip of his little finger, then opened his mouth without any kind of an exhale, just let the smoke find its own way out. There was artistry to Aug.

"Reckon she forgot about me coming?" I asked.

"No, she didn't forget. Cornbread an' beans on the stove; stewed tomatoes and greens. Just go on an' get it."

"Hell, I may get it twice," I said. "Why'd they leave you behind, anyway?"

"Buddy, they ain't enough ice cream cones in Pike County to get me in a car with five women all the way to Millard an' back."

I laughed outright, knowing the full effect of five women and what it meant to be outnumbered. Aug finished his cigarette and flicked it high over the gate and into the creek, then sat upright, letting his legs dangle off the porch.

"You finally get Coalter Hatfield run off?" he asked.

"Yeah, but I don't believe he cared anything about wanting to go. I believe he got to where he liked us.

We both chuckled and settled in, the laid-back rhythm of the cats reaching to our core. The air was as still as fog, and we lingered for a time just being thankful for it. Aug's voice was heavy when it finally broke. "Why is it you reckon I ain't remorsed," he asked, "over what I did to

Haman Flowers?" I didn't know if he was truly after an answer or just thinking out loud. I said nothing, but couldn't ignore the sudden feeling that there was something stirring. "Not a pang nor regret-one," he said, "nuthin' that ever backed me away from a mirror." His eyes were trained on the gravel and grass Mary Olive called a yard. "It's a hell of a thing to confess, but I swear I had a lighter step after I put him down—a bigger one, too. Feller ortn't feel that way, don't b'lieve. Ain't natural. Liable to be harder on me later on, come reckonin': when it's time to own up, answer for what I done." He studied on what he said and its unavoidable downside. He rolled his head slightly to bring me into view, his long black hair falling across his eyes, glistening in the last of the sun. "All them years, Rubin, and me never feelin' a need to repent, even after Cousin Truman got me to join the church, even after Dewey Childers held me down under that *baptism* water longer'n he needed to." He smiled: part reverent, part cheeky. "Should a seen me," he said. "I come up outta that water damned near blue, coughin' an' spittin' and thinkin' that was the best sign I could a' had for it not being what I needed in the first place. Dewey standin' there with his hands over his head and shoutin' hallelu-iah—all the time grinning like he finally got me back for whuppin' his ass when we's just boys, right out there in the schoolhouse bottom." He nod-ded toward the school. "Front a' ever'body. It was a whuppin' he needed; sump'm we both knew. Tickles me, though, that he'd still smart about it, an' it thirty year ago." His smile was turned with fun, but then seconds later looked gray and serious.

"Might call it wrong-headed," he said, "me not being ashamed." Still, I said nothing, hoping that what he needed was just to air what he'd kept bottled up for twenty-six years. "Up till the other day," he said, "they was just four people on earth who knew what I'd done: Bobby, poor ol Ben, Seriann, an' Wilma Lee. I told Wilma Lee just before we married. Sooner have her jump an' run *then* as later, but she never. Swore an oath that she wouldn't ever—long as she lived, and on the lives of the childern we'd have—tell another livin' soul. I don't know that she ever did. Now that they's a few more knowin', it won't be long 'fore they's more on top a them."

The Maine coon all of a sudden pushed against some mysterious nothing and moved in tighter and hotter against my thigh. It was an act of determination not to push him away, my need to air and scratch my leg mounting like a storm. It was his aging backbone, arthritic and barely able anymore, needing, or so my conscience would have me believe, the one bank of heat worthy of relief. I let him sleep on.

"Maybe it's the way it played out," Aug said, "...so grisly an' all... that's got me to thinking how people are liable to see me like a monster.

"You need to put your mind to rest, Aug. It was a long time ago. Anybody old enough to remember knew who and what Haman was, and what kind of end he deserved. I'm sure they're all thinking he got exactly what was coming to him. Besides, it'll never be nothing more than rumor. People'll always put what spin they want on it, but it'll stay a mystery. There's simply no proof of any kind, let alone enough to convict anybody."

"But I already confessed it."

"You and a half dozen more."

He looked up and smiled. "I know all about what Bobby did," he said, his smile tender. "Steerin' you and Coalter 'round to er'body but me. It was Bobby that told his daddy 'bout what he'd seen. Had to on account a' Ben bein' so thrown off by it. That's all it took: just one word from Olin for Virgil to let it die. It was enough, the way Olin's word always was."

Truth had an iciness once it got a taste of fresh air; once it began to work its way, bit by bit, into the light, siphoning the secrets we kept buried ... often without intention on anyone's part.

"Truth be told, Aug, folks would more'n likely name a day after you if they knew the truth; might even memorialize you with a statue. Not every day a canker's cut out." I tried for the lighter side, but Aug was in another place.

"Truth's a funny thing, Rubin; double-edged from what I know about it. So many times hurtin' and healin' at the same time, its benefit not all the time possible without its difficulty. One thing about it, though, it sure as hell trumps a lie—and there's always one, isn't there? The one we keep hid, the one that suffocates who we make every effort to be."

The tone in Aug's voice had taken on an eerie familiarity, as if it were my very own: steely, even accusing. I had a deep understanding of what Aug was talking about, perhaps more than he realized, the secret part of me holding onto unmentionables, most often out of fear. I reckoned it was what most men did with what they wanted to keep hid, so often even from themselves.

"I don't think there are any monsters, Aug, aside from what we create for ourselves." I just left it there, plain and without the need of explanation.

Aug sat nodding, almost rocking. "I know about monsters more'n you think, Rubin. Lived with one most a' my life, him feedin' and breathin' too near to things that mattered; forever reminding us he was part a' the dark. Odious and contrary—pure monster—and I knew him as well as any man could. Even came to know how they's a thread of monster in ever' one of us—and how it can unravel, given the right circumstances. We all capable of heinousness, Rubin, depending on the situation." He paused, confident of its truth. "Might say I reached that point with Haman, 'fore I shot him open. I told myself it wasn't really me: just the circumstances, nuthin' anybody else wouldn't have done in my shoes." His voice was raspy, shallow, his eyes glazed.

"I ain't got the makeup of guilt, Rubin," he said. "Not when it comes to fixin' what needs fixin'. He paused, searching the lines in my face. "I b'lieve you're the same way." I suddenly felt warmer than I should have, and was quite certain it had nothing to do with the cat. "I mean wrong's wrong and too many times the law's just too high-hatted to grub it out, leaving the fullness of right rotting on the vine." My reason for being here seemed to elevate by the minute. I just needed to be still.

"They's just too many sides to a courthouse to suit me," he went on. "Too many tryin' to find ways to twist and warp and turn a wrong into something less than it is. Wadn't nuthin' the law could a done with Haman or Randle either, hard evidence being what it is: mainly, *not enough of it*. But we all know what they done, unspeakable and otherwise. Wrong like that don't deserve a trial. It just needs fixin'; continued wrong, permanent fixin'." He stopped dead-stone still and rolled his head in my direction. "I b'lieve you know what I mean."

His voice seemed to drop right into my lap, its message frosted over and clear as Bobby's best corn hooch: any of us could make an errant step given the right circumstances; when haste and passion get the upper hand; when temper blinds us to consequences. But what happened to Haman and Randle was a far cry from something impulsive, nothing that might be thought of as accidents. Fact is they were quite the opposite. They were acts of the heart, plotted and mapped out. How different it is when we acknowledge them for what they are, own up to them. How different it is when we're moved to touch fire to powder and ball. These were no chance happenings—these killings of Haman and Randle—nothing that could be written off as fate or mishap. These were embraced meditations, conceived and carried through to a decided end by those having had *enough.*

"Why are we talking about this, Aug?"

"Just hopin' you might help me get my mind straight, get a hold on what's crashin' around inside my brain pan. Damnedest thing: regret never playing a part in what I done. Still, they's somethin' that won't turn me loose; somethin' I cain't explain, houndin' me like it does when I'm all by myself. No matter if it's daylight or dark, there's that *something* that demons me, that comes a whisperin' to me like dyin' breath. Somethin', Rubin, that keeps drawin' me back—for twenty-six year now—to that same church house, early-early on that same Sunday mornin' in December. Like clockwork. Every single year—never failin'—like there's a toll I have to pay; year after year pullin' me back to that very spot ... just like it did this last time ... this past December." He paused, letting his eyes settle on mine.

I didn't know quite where Aug was taking me, but I had an indelicate feeling it wasn't a place I wanted to go. I tried clearing my head, but my senses were too keyed, too keen, too aware of what he might be harboring.

"I might be wrong here, Aug, but it sounds to me like you know more'n you're saying." My words were steady, careful. Aug said nothing, just gave me a long meaningful stare, one that left me feeling I needed to *tread softly.*

"Let me try to understand," I said, my voice calving and without the breath it needed. "Are you saying—?"

"Yeah," he interrupted, his voice dropping an octave, "I was there."

I felt like a piece of live art; Aug's eyes studying me with sober intensity, waiting for my next move.

"*There?*" I said, my mind racing, trying to separate what I knew from what I didn't. "I'm not sure I follow you."

"Oh, I believe you do."

"You mean *there!* At the *church house!*"

"I was afraid the first few times," he said, his words hard fought, "those first couple years, waitin' off to the side till them playing poker cleared out, till I was made to be alone with what I did. Never did get much better—all them years—but I learned the hardness of it, what makes each of us accountable to ourselves. But this last time, seeing somebody take Randle down to dog meat, I knew I was lookin' at the same monster that took hold a' me. I recognized him right off, the ice in his eyes, the devil's hand on him the way it had been on me. Dewey Childers says the devil ain't got no power over us so long's we been washed in the blood, so long's we go down in the water an' come back up. But then he don't know the devil like I do.

We sat for the longest time with the encroaching shadows, the early bats, the crickets, the taste of distant dew, and what was left of loneliness and whippoorwills reckoning us to our roots: our mountains, our home.

"So you saw—"

"The whole thing," he said thinly.

There was no movement except for what the wind stirred: the rags on the clothesline, the high grass along the fence, and the willows bent low in the creek. The Maine coon seemed to sense that the hairs on my neck were a little on end. He rolled his head, making sure I could see his irritation. I let my hands wander over him, his warm frail bones providing the germ of warmth I was so suddenly needing. For several long minutes, we sat without talking, against the kind of stillness that lingered after Grandmaw closed her eyes for the final time: a long silk of quiet as finite as the slow steady march of her memory.

I hadn't had any delusions about killing Randle Cain. It was just something I'd come to—or it to me—up there on the tops of the mountains—just me and the notions of *what ought to be*. I never wavered, even in the beginning, right up to the time I pulled the trigger. Randle's heinous deeds demanded no less, deeds I'd been called to witness too many times. But there were never any witnesses strong enough to stand against him, Fayella and the children too bruised in body and soul to risk the cost. But after repeated accounts and the firsthand reports from Dixie and Bobby, it became all too clear that it was time for Randle to go—the same thinking, I was certain, that ran through those who'd ever witnessed the effects of his crimes. It was only a matter of time before somebody besides me paid Randle a final visit. But I couldn't wait for that to happen, not in good conscience, anyway; couldn't free my mind of what might take place in the meantime: how much more he might unleash on those who did nothing more than carry his name. Time was not on my side. Brutality tolerated was no longer an option.

I'd gone to the mountains just weeks before, after the trees had dropped their leaves and before snow of any kind. It was unlike what I was used to; its winds stiff and harsh, its welcoming stark and barren, all that gave rise to my discontent.

I suppose it was the time of year—Christmas, and what it meant for Fayella and those so robbed of hope—that made me think of Randle Cain and all those so expert at stripping away even the barest rudiments of joy. I couldn't think of a more exact way to bring closure to Randle's road than to join it with Haman Flowers' in the exact same way: same Sunday morning in December, same place, same crater in his chest, along with a similar hole in the middle of his cheek—just below his left eye, from a .41 caliber derringer.

My car easing along the roads of Greezy was not an uncommon sight, never anything to be overly concerned about, even at the odd hours before dawn. I liked folks thinking the law never slept, which in my case was more truth than not. Fact was, I was in and out of Greezy often enough looking in on Mary Olive and Lorali, but then there were times I used it as a way of breaking away from the grind—the heaviness of keeping the law needing its own escape. That early Sunday morning with Randle was no different. I'd waited down the road from where Main Fork veered away from Gardner Fork, where Randle would have to pass on his way home. I knew he'd be the last to leave the church house. There was simply nothing to go home to: nothing he cared about, anyway. He went home only when there was no place else to go. We saw each other about the same time. He knew my car, as did most everybody else, and staggered in close while I rolled my window down to the cold and his breath reeking of whiskey.

"Always meant to ask you," he said without a hello of any kind, "are we kin or not?" His eyes were wild, his lips loose and dewy.

"I'm just fine, Randle. How 'bout you?"

"Yer out kinda late, ain't ye?"

"Protecting," I said. "Makin' sure I get a paycheck at the end of the week. Y'ever think about wearin' a coat?"

"Aim to steal me one fer Christmas. You sure we ain't kin?"

"Close enough for a ride," I said. "C'mon. Hop in."

The stink of humankind was on him thick, like turnip bins and winter mold. He snuffed and hacked and pushed his hair back off his face, its unruliness falling like long black whips down over his collar. I sat with the engine running, staring at the hardness in his eyes, the hungriness in his cheeks, his nerve.

"What'r we waitin' for?" he said.

"If you ain't in no hurry, I want to run by the church house real quick," I said, easing my way into Main Fork's mud lanes. "Make sure it's shut up proper," I gave him a sideways glance, "what with so many so quick to use it on Saturday nights." I smiled. "I'd say you prob'ly know some of 'em." We shared a laugh. A minute later, we pulled into the churchyard.

I shut the motor off and pretended to listen for sounds and watch for movement in the shadows. With the silent shush of my finger, I reached for the sawed-off shotgun under my seat, the gift from Olin Yonts some seventeen years ago, illegal as it was. Before opening my door, I leaned in close to Randle and whispered, "I'm deputizing you. Now go 'round to the other side and wait for my signal."

He sat back a little stiff, his face startled. I put my finger to his lips letting him know that silence was the code. After a second or two, he slid out and walked with surprising stealth to the far side of the church, unsure of what he was looking for. I made a number of sheriff-type moves, sliding here and there through the shadows. Finally, with enough charade, I called out to him in a low voice. Those were the last words he ever heard. I dropped him as soon as he got even with the church steps, blew him into the farthest reaches of hell—the only place that would have him, I was certain. I positioned him like I remembered Haman, then stood there looking down on him, half expecting him to come to life just long enough to cut me in two with his bone-handled Barlow. But there was nothing but a kicking wind and the smell of a cold rain coming, the only signs of life before I pulled out the derringer I snuck from Mary Olive's bureau drawer. I pulled the trigger without ever thinking why I shouldn't, without a worry about the consequences in this life or the one to come, hoping only that it might get him that much closer to hell's fire.

I drove slow and quiet out of Greezy. Lights were still out everywhere, even at Angus Walker's, and with daybreak not even an hour away. I went straight home and waited for Lester Trout's call. It came shortly after first light.

I felt drained, watery, uncertain of where to go from here. "So what do you intend to do, Aug?" I asked, my voice now leaden, mired in the certainty of being found out.

"Same thing you did when you heard about me," he said, shifting his gaze upward, toward the beginnings of star shine. "It ain't for me to do," he said. "This whole account was for your sake; to help you once the demons start."

I sat naked to the truth, to the feelings so unlike any other, waiting for what might dare lift me up and bring me back to the way it was before; set me in a green pasture on top of a mountain, away from what now sought to undo me. I don't know where it was coming from, but I was, all at once, wanting to be chastened, made to endure my wrongdoing, my transgression, my sin: what I'd deliberately chosen to do.

"I know what carryin' a secret's like, Rubin," Aug said, his tone calming, attentive. "It's somethin' you're never done with, or it with you. It's somethin' that eats on you mornin', noon, and night, under every sun and moon, in dreams and out. Get to where you'll be lookin' over your shoulder 'fore long, careful a' what you say an' who you say it to, 'cause you'll never quite know who might put two and two together, who might pick up on a slip or be good at reading between the lines. It's like havin' yer own ball an' chain. But it don't have to be. A secret gets a lot easier when you have somebody who'll help you carry it, knowin' you got somebody to talk to."

I never knew Aug to be so lyrical, so willing with his senses, his speech so void of economy. "Who else, Aug?" I asked. "Who else knows?"

"Not another livin' soul, as I know of." He waited, the chisel of his manner turned inward, wanting, it seemed, to offer words running toward forgiveness. "Let's just leave it at that," he said. "Less said the better, for both of us. But you can know there'll never be another word mentioned, 'less it comes from you. My hand on it."

I sat there with the only image I had of Haman and Randle: their slithering out from under a rock and taking one step too many in the wrong direction—what left them foundering, decidedly and forever. It was a collapsing picture, but forthright. One, I prayed that would, with the hand of time, allow the stanchions of rest to return, permit what memory I had of them to turn to powder and blow away.

"You see it now, Rubin?" Aug said.

I was far off, my mind only half lit, turned under by my own indulgence. I lifted my head in his direction, not sure that I followed or even heard him right.

"The monster," he said. "You see it now?"

Eighty-Seven

There is This One Little Thing

I left Mary Olive's without a taste of her cornbread, and sworn to a truth I would take to my grave. Aug was unbothered for the most part, but unburdened: cleansed, save for what he was unable to forgive in himself. It couldn't have been easy for him, holding onto a secret as big as the sky, and finally bringing it to light—first his, then mine. Odd, how we came to walk the same path, as if we were the same person, separated only by time and circumstance. Mary Olive's account of Aug's rightness, his being a fair-fit for wearing a badge, was something I came to favor after his disclosures, his evenhandedness and not being quick to judgment coming in apt supply. He was a package worth having and one I'd have no trouble selling, even to Chloe Bligh. But thanks to Bobby, Aug was already entrenched with the C & O Railroad. From switchman to engineer in just a year's time was no coincidence; Bobby's sway had picked up where his daddy's had left off. In quieter moments, I envied Aug his job, for never having to worry about things like who might be coming up behind you. He was miles ahead of most, Aug was, with a clear conscience and a better-than-average chance of it staying that way.

Early Sunday morning, and Bobby was sitting in the backyard without a shirt, rocked back in an old cane chair and not caring about a burning sun. He squinted just enough to make out who I was, gave me a ripe grin, and said if I was looking for the Old Reg'lars, I'd have to come back next Sunday; they'd already come and gone. I plopped down on the porch steps and mumbled how pitifully misguided I thought he was, and where was the coffee anyway? Before he could answer, Hooker came through the screen door with three large mugs, hot and steamy and black as slate. We sprawled out like stray toms, and with smiles tight as Andrew Clemmons' grip on a dollar bill. It had been two weeks since I last saw him, since Woodrow's farewell dinner and Aug putting an end to the twenty-six-year mystery surrounding Haman Flowers.

The morning unfolded like a down tic, as soft as the opening of morning glories that once secreted Grandmaw's porch. My showing up unannounced was nothing new, and greeted in the way it always was: with an unspoken melody of *where you been so long, anyway*? Even with our first words, we talked as if we'd been together all night: conversation that was generous and familiar, of life and lives, what was, and what was to come. It was like the most glorious church, but without tenets or expectations—just a journey of thoughts looped and entwined and free as air. It was only after the cleaning crew came rattling with mops and buckets that Hooker got up to oversee and account for the night's exchange. Bobby and I sat without moving any more than necessary, sipping at our coffee, our minds lost in the swell of the Big Sandy silently working its way toward oceans we were glad to forget.

"Whatta you hear from Coalter Hatfield?" I asked, purposefully hurling a dart through the sanctity of his morning.

Bobby raised an eyebrow just enough to allow a sliver of light. "Calls 'bout ever'day," he said, the dryness in his posture matching the one in his eyes. "Thinkin' real hard about movin' here an' settlin' down, making Pikeville his home. Wantin' to be close to you, I 'spect. He sends his love, by the way."

Bobby was more than content to make poor Coalter the butt of his gibes now that Coalter was out of the picture. It was evident he'd picked up where he left off before Coalter came to town: reasserting himself to the laws of randomness and the gauzy lights of outlaws and poets and what remained of river towns everywhere.

"Been expecting you, Rubin," he said lazily, his eyes still closed, his face toward the sun.

"Expected you might."

"Unfinished business. I'd say."

"Right again."

"Unfinished business 'tween friends never sits well."

"Makes for an atmosphere right foul when there's cards still left on the table," I said. "Didn't want it to come down to the two of us wallerin' around in the dirt and each others' blood, fightin' for the right to be right."

"I'm just hopin' we're beyond such," Bobby mused. "I have a feelin' it'd make me a little less than I already am."

There was no *rush* to Bobby today, to either of us, really, only tired wits and breaths taking in the scent of Sweet Vernal spiked and flowering along the back of the house.

"Do I know everything about you, Bobby?" I asked offhandedly, "now that the secret to Haman Flowers is laid to rest?"

"Not likely," he said, languishing in his candor.

"An' why is that?"

"I believe it might have something to do with the shame that'd come with the tellin'. But, then again, I'm a very private person."

I laughed despite wanting to be serious, then gave way to June's early warmth, the gentle stir of honeybees as abiding as the Big Sandy and its slow heavy tide.

"Why don't you just come out and ask me what you wanna know?" Bobby said, wordiness aside.

"Well, all right, then. Why didn't you level with me in the beginning?"

"I take it you're talkin' about what went down between Aug and Haman Flowers," he said, indulgent, hospitable in the old way.

"About why you chose to keep it to yourself," I said.

"It was on account of Aug," he said, his tone without the sluggishness of Saturday night. "'Cause Aug had my undying thanks for doing what the rest of us didn't have the nerve for. He did what a whole bunch of us did a thousand times in thought and dreams alike, but never had the heart and guts and mind to get it done. My keeping quiet was just my way a' savin' him from a bunch a sanctimonious sonsabitches always needin' to pass judgment; makin' sure he didn't get treated like somethin' dug out from under a log." His eyes were now wide and staring off toward the river. "Then there was you, Rubin." I gave him a quizzical look, unsure of what he meant or what boundaries he intended to cross. "The only two reasons I ever had," he said, "Aug and you."

"And why, again, was I a reason?"

"Cause we grew up together. Good as brothers. And scared as I was, I just couldn't put that on you. Hell, Rubin, we was just boys, but I knew enough not to mistake what I'd seen. I knew it was a crime's crime, but I knew, too, the look on Aug's face when we stood there in the road just inches away and with the clop of a horse coming at us. It was a look that begged me to have mercy. He never said a word. Didn't have to. I knew the look. I just nodded to him and said '*Run*.' What passed between us in that split second was a bond he'd never have to worry about. Seein' it like I did, so full on, was a nightmare I couldn't've imagined, and I didn't know which way to go, or who to go *to*. From then on, it was just me tryin' to figure it out. Wouldn't dare trust nothin' or nobody. Hell, Aug would a' been good as gone if talk ever got started. I couldn't chance it. Then there was Ben, me tryin' to keep a lid on him, an' him near crazy as it was. I was even afraid to lay down of a night, afraid I might say somethin' in my sleep. I don't know how I did it, but I did. Part a' the reason I went to the three C's. Just needed to get as far from Greezy as I could. I thought about tellin' you before the war took us, but then the thought of maybe never coming home again was about all the hell I could handle at the time; 'bout all *any* of us could manage, I reckon. I just couldn't put another nightmare on you, brother. You didn't need something like that to take with you. Our heads were already full a dyin'. Time we got back, it was the one thing I never wanted to think about again. I carried enough war around with me as it was. What Aug did was deservin' of my hush—else he would've hung, sure as they's a world. Lettin' dead dogs lie was the safest for ever'body."

I sat there in the warm June sun, softened by his words. "So what changed? What made telling it so important after twenty-six years?"

"Wasn't my decision," he said. "Aug lived with it long as he could, I reckon, till he was *washed in the blood*." He rolled his head, eyed me with stark cynicism. "Comin' clean is part of what's expected, is the way it's told to me: standin' before Almighty God an' all a' man with a new heart, declarin' you been made right an' confessin' what all's kept you down. His lettin' it fly at Mary Olive's was just what he an' Almighty God worked out, best I can tell. Knowin' that Coalter was just a step away from walkin' me to the gallows might have helped him decide. Havin' ever'body together for Woodrow couldn't a' been a more fittin' time to get it out—to be done with it, once and for all."

For just a second, he studied my lack of expression, then said, "I'd like to say I was unmoved by what I saw that night, twenty-six years ago, but it'd be a lie. Watching a murder is enough to change a man, like seein' hell come up right outta the ground. I just kept tellin' myself that Haman wasn't nuthin' but tainted meat, and that *nobody* gave a peep or a pine when he was gone. Nobody. And now I'm just like you: done with losin' my last night's sleep over it. I don't intend to spend another minute thinkin' about what happened twenty-six years ago—or, mind you, what the long arm a' the law's liable to do about it. I got enough to watch out for as it is—most of it over my shoulder—to be caretaker of somebody else's deeds."

I lazed in Bobby's aftermath, in the lyrical chime of his rant, the endless blue of an Appalachian sky filling in along the narrows of my mind, and imagined what my account of Randle Cain might sound like in the aftermath of Aug's revelation. "It took a lot of nerve," I said, "for Aug to say what he did, an' in front of ever'body. I know you two had it worked out. But what I can't figure is how you knew Coalter would walk away from it."

"Didn't," he said. "But it was Aug's call. He knew Coalter was out to hang me, to finger me for Haman, and just desperate enough to manipulate the evidence, if it came down to it. Aug wasn't gonna let that happen. He had this notion that the Almighty's hand was on him an' would guide him. '*Just do the right thing and leave the rest to Jesus,*' is how he said it to me. It was a chance that he took—a chance he took for *me*—for keeping his secret all them years, I reckon. Then again, I knew Coalter'd never get beyond Pike County if he decided to do something with it. Hooker would've made certain a' that. I'm not sayin' Hooker would a' caused Coalter *harm*, necessarily, but Hooker does have his persuasive side: convincing, however unconventional. So, in that sense, it was fool proof—enough so that I gave him my go-ahead. '*Be cleansed*,' I told him. In the end, it was worth it just to see the look on Coalter's face: like a dog caught sucking eggs. All said and done, I don't know as anybody there cared a damn beyond being surprised." He gave me an approving smile then added, "It turned out just like we hoped it would. It's good being right sometimes, Rubin."

I waited awhile before saying anything, knowing that Randle's killer was branded with the same hot poker that had defiled Aug, and even Bobby to a lesser degree. Yes, how good it was to be right—or rather, to guess right. In my case, though, there was no guesswork involved. There was only a chance to set the record straight, to come clean with the one person I thought of as a brother, despite not having been *born again*, or privy to a plan devised of God. There was a story to be told and the only one to tell it was me, if the truth was worth anything at all. I had to wonder whether or not it stood to make enemies of us. But then, how could Randle's killer stand the test of time and bear up under the weight of its rot, except by the truth?

"How about you, Rubin?" Bobby asked after a time, tossing the last of his coffee into the yard. "Do I know ever'thing about you?"

"*Ever*'thing," I said.

"Riiiight," he said, his tone light, riding on the wind.

"And if there was something I *didn't* intend for you to know, it would only be to protect you." He laughed outright. "Just like you did for me. I mean, the less you know, the less you have to lie about. Right?"

"Now you've got it," he said, nodding like a big oak tree in a summer breeze.

"Yeah," I said, feeling low to the ground, close to my lie. "But there is this one little thing."

Eighty-Eight

A Bigger World to Live in; a Bigger Pond to Drown in

Admittedly, Coalter had been more malleable than I first thought, even somewhat circumspect. But the biggest surprise was his being so sympathetic to the victims of Haman and Randle. But then after hearing all the first-hand accounts, their combined depravity would have been enough to persuade even the most ardent. I wondered about what impact I might have had, had I come clean?—fell in line right after Aug? I couldn't help but feel that things would have gone south, and fast, had I spoken up. So many eyes on me, and each of them, I was convinced, hard pressed to see anything beyond the monster Aug was so given to see. And then there was Coalter, hamstrung with duty and its pressure to make sense of a second confession. It would have made it near impossible to look them in the eyes ever again without them remembering what I'd done, and what I might do next.

The Big Sandy's slow march was hypnotic, its soundless push seeming to seal us off from the uneasiness of what I'd grieved us with, what I'd needed to air.

"Things change, Rubin." Bobby's voice was quiet, simple, its slow cadence thoughtful. "I always thought I could change with them, rise and fall with the tide. But I can see now I cain't. I'm just who I am: punched out the way Almighty God saw fit. The one I look at in the mirror is still the same one I been looking at ever since I was frog high. Now there's times when I don't care much for who I see, but I suspect that's true of just about anybody who's done what I have. Just so much more to think about these days. Questions coming faster than answers. A bigger world to live in, a bigger pond to drown in. I still ain't wanting to repent for any of it; it's just now, on account a' Dixie mostly—her being such a part of the college, and so highly thought of around town—that I care about what others might be seeing when they pass me on the street. I suspect that's where *you* are right about now: lookin' in that mirror an' seein' what you ain't never seen before, an' hopin' nobody else sees it. Takes a lot to get a man to where you were with Randle, and I'm just wantin' you to know—make no mistake—there *is* a difference between you an' that sumbitch you sent to hell."

We studied the mountains for a time, their greens: olives and emeralds and limes ripening with summer. "Remember it if you have to," a voice said from inside the screen door. Hooker had heard just enough. "But never speak of it again. It's not worth the price ... or the breath. This is from someone who knows." He waited for his bolt from the blue to take hold, leeching through the screen door to the heart of what mattered. "The words have been written on Randle Cain," he said, "the pages turned. And there'll never be an end to the good you did. Know it for what it was: a right conscience in the right place an' time. The only one who can tell you diff'ernt is you." And just like that, he turned and walked back into the depths of the house, into its long quiet hallways cooled in shadows. Bobby and I sat crossways and contrary—reaching, in our own distinct way, for what we wished was simpler.

Until today, it was only Aug and me who knew what I'd done—and now Bobby and Hooker. Even so, it was the same as no one, knowing that each would take it to his grave. As for me, it was simply something I'd have to deal with on my own. I suspected that would be punishment enough: what I'd have to lie down with each night; what I'd need to deal with each and every time the sun stirred me to life; what I'd be made to see each time I walked through the courthouse doors; and what I'd henceforth know as the dark underbelly of justice ... and me as the perpetrator.

Coalter coming in here an' setiin' up camp," I said, "started the acid drip in my stomach. It was a tightrope I walked all the time he was here, keeping him close so I could know what he was up to next. 'Course him being drunk most of the time helped considerable. But there reached a point when his focus became too near to wanting a name he could fault, unable to see anything but the 'lectric chair and you strapped to it. It was a deadly game he played, and I have to admit there were times when he filled my head with doubts. But then there was the one glaring irony that escaped ever'body but me: the thought that *you* and *I* were the killers. No different. Just the two of us tied to the same righteous indignation, and too scared to even tell each other. But then, whatta you know: you weren't part of it at all. Just me: Rubin Cain, High Sheriff, keeper of the peace despite what it took. And I was right there under Coalter's nose the whole time. ...Imagine that."

The lines on Bobby's face were drawn, his eyes searching mine for what only he could find. He stayed that way for some time, affected, silenced, before shifting in his chair, and with a noticeable voice, saying, "Poetry."

Bobby had always fancied himself a poet; thought anything worthwhile was in some form or another seasoned by its significance—like what I'd done to Randle Cain. "*Poetic justice* is what Corbin would have called it," he said. "Them finally getting what they'd spent their whole lives dishing out."

"What is it with you and this whole thing about poetry?" I said. "I've never pretended to understand it."

"It ain't so much as me having an interest in poetry as much as it is poetry having an interest in me," he said. "It just seems to find me. Like it does you, if you'd take the time to see it. It ain't nothin' I can put to words—just somethin' that latches on, sprinklin' me with this and that, things that tend to elevate me, make me a little more than I am ... and clearly worth remembering." His grin bit tight, his poetry as salacious as the .41 caliber derringer in his boot. "So what else don't I know, Rubin?"

"Just that it was easy. It being Randle made it that way. Just a mongrel at the end of a barrel. Here one minute, gone the next." Tardiness weighed in around us, the sky stretching and lingering, azure and eternal. "But then, with all of it fitting together the way it did—with Randle a corpse, and Fayella and them children never having to worry about another beating, or another day without a bite a bread, their minds free to rest, to breathe without a fear of it being their last—well, it's just about as close to justice as I could ask for."

"Now that, my friend," he said, his eyes in a comprehending gaze, taciturn, seemly, but determined to stay on point, "... *that's* poetry."

Eighty-Nine

The Smile Remained

Mary Olive's first stroke came in the middle of July, right when lotus blossoms began flowering the creek banks and wood asters began spiking their way up through the meadow lilies and mugwort in the dry patch that was once our garden. The second one came just weeks later, sometime in the early morning. And though it was Lorali's custom to check on her throughout the night, it was impossible to be at her side each passing minute. Damaging was the only thing that could be said about it, leaving her wide-eyed, but not seeing, open-mouthed, but not speaking. I went to her most every day, to smooth back her hair and rub her arms and hands; to talk in quiet ways and help us both remember what all we'd lived through, how the Almighty had put us together and what all He'd allowed in our lives.

The third time was well into September, right there in the middle of the day, when the sun was at its highest, and when NeviJo called to say that I needed to come right away. Truman and Inez, Seriann and Wilma Lee, Sherman and Wilson were all there before me, their downtrodden looks telling me all I needed to know. Lorali paced and wrung her hands in anguished silence, her countenance brittle and broken and heaped with what we knew was the inevitable.

Mary Olive lay gathered in quilts despite the tendrils of dog days, the upper room being closed off to light; the air cut with the wretchedness of grief. I knelt beside her and brought my face in close. Her breaths were labored and raspy, weakened from ninety-two years of tested living and decades of pipe smoke. She mumbled something that I knew was my name, something that told me she knew it was me beside her. It was a struggle, but she finally managed to get her hands up to my face, the tips of her fingers like velvet on my cheeks. I took them, frail and gnarled as they were, and pressed them to my lips, choking back what I felt was the hurt of the world. Nobody said much of anything, just the come togetherings of sorrow in between long silences and Cousin Truman's murmured prayers. Her sparrow breast rising and falling only added to the stillness. But then there was a great gulp of air, and just for a moment her eyes became as wide as heaven's gate—seeming to lock on something far away, beyond us all. The tiniest smile toyed at the corners of her mouth, a chink of gold tooth barely visible. "Ohhhhh," she said, her eyes glossed and filmy, her head to one side, listening, or so it seemed. She stayed that way, transfixed, for the longest time, then slowly, slowly, closed her eyes, but not the smile. The smile remained. "Yes," we heard her whisper, her head in the tenderest nod—and that was the last of her.

Softness settled in around us, a hush broken only by sobs. I sat there for many long minutes with her hand still in mine, feeling the rush of spirits and angels and all that attend us, things Cousin Truman contended were for our keeping. '*There is no end*,' she once told me, as if she were privileged to know the divine plan. Maybe it was true; maybe there was no end. Maybe we were just what Cousin Truman said we were: spirit beings sent here for a brief time to experience the physical, like Jesus, and that our time here was nothing more than a test of faith, the determinator of where we would spend eternity. I didn't know about such things, what all came to Truman in the way of interpretation. But then I didn't have to, he said. Just believing them when I heard them was enough, a portent of our faith.

I wasn't sure *what* I believed anymore: sanctity and scarcity feeding from the same trough, favor to the undeserving, injury and difficulty on the backs of the godly. I knew only what slugged its way, what clawed and kicked, what came with sweat and begrudging hope. Beyond that, I knew only of goodbyes and the green blush of mountains, of the clear, primal taste of corn liquor, and of hearts that made us into brothers. The rest was chance, that convergence of risk and certainty, and that long, slow, sweep of Greezy—distant and disjointed, pitted and weeded over—that worked its way into each of us, and what we unwittingly took with us from first breath to last ... from one mountain top to the next.

Part IV

Ninety

What Had It All Been For Anyway?

I suspect Burl will be coming with the mail soon, armed with all the wrong questions and ill-prepared for the answers I was likely to give. Still, his coming had the element of distraction I needed, especially since the days here lately were so given to thoughts of Bobby—like they had been for the last month—since his funeral—and what with the letter from Calvin bringing to mind all that he and I had lived through.

There was little, if anything, that got by Calvin. If it happened within Pike county, he'd know about it with the next edition of the Pike County News, a subscription he'd never quit even after marching off to Cincinnati nearly twenty years ago. News of Bobby's passing made front page—as well it should have, given what all he'd done later in life for Appalachia's poor and needy. It would have been impossible for Calvin to miss it. I doubted his letter was intended to strike a nerve, but fact was, it had opened the door on things I'd laid aside years ago. But then I had to wonder if those times and places could ever be fully dismissed?—ever be so far removed as to make me not want another chance to do them over?—make them less insulating, less likely to leave us with the need to say I'm sorry? Or, at the very least, take the necessary steps for forgiveness.

Bobby wanted to be buried up high, he said: in the old Robinson Cemetery where he could look down on his old home place; where he could see the top of Ripley Knob and the soft scroll of Gardner Fork climbing gently to the southeast, toward Shop Branch where his world began and ended with Dixie. "Put me next to Corbin was one of the last things he told me; that, and "I'll be waitin' for you."

Bobby just wore out, in big part from the way he lived. "Too many long nights and smoky old barrooms," was the way he put it, his voice mumbled through an oxygen mask, but somehow pushing out a smile behind it. It was painful to watch him: his hair white, his arms and neck so thin, his back and shoulders bunched and rounded, every part so weak it was sheer labor just for him to breathe. It had been a confusing time, and scary: the exhaustion, the swelling, the pain ... everything dreaded when we think of lymphoma, one of those medical terms that never failed to shiver me. A year and two months from the first diagnosis before the fight left him altogether. He knew he was leaving, said it to me outright more than once to let me know he was ready—and how he thought it would be a fitting tribute, once he was gone, if I was to wail and beat my chest and throw myself on his casket. He never stopped being Bobby, that streak of devil wiliness too pronounced to ever keep down, right up till he winked at me that final time—till his fingers closed around mine, then fell limp forever.

I stayed at the cemetery that whole day after he was put down, never feeling more adrift. Grandmaw and Mary Olive, Seriann and Lorali, Cousin Truman and Inez, Corbin and now Bobby, all there amongst the weeds, quiet but for their voices in my head. I promised myself I'd come more often, clean off the graves and add what flowers I could, especially on Decoration Day. I didn't know how many more chances I'd have, but I knew it was a promise I wouldn't break.

Dixie stayed on with me long after the procession of preachers and mourners had made their way down the mountain, and long after the diggers had shoveled the last of the dirt. We sat, Dixie and me, without ten words passing between us, staring off into nothingness, with only silence and emptiness to tend us. Don't know how long we sat there before she finally come to herself—come undone, actually—before she commenced to catching her breath and heaving with sobs, squeezing out years of frustration, I imagined—enough for the both of us. When I finally dug deep enough to utter the tiniest word, she groaned, shut her eyes and asked me what had it all been for, anyway? Lives so meant to be together and yet so interrupted, so random. I never did give her an answer; didn't have one to give. I just reached over and put a hand on her shoulder. There were just too many memories, and all of them coming at once—for both of us.

She quieted after a time, her breaths shunting and finally evening out. Surprising how peaceful it was after that: her talking, even smiling at the thought of how different she and Bobby were, the years they'd spent going in opposite directions, yet how tender and inseparable their love remained. Her talk had no starting point, no middle, no end ... just talk. "When he finally got around to asking me to marry him," she said, "I turned him down." She laughed through tears. "Not just once, mind you, but over and again ... preferring my *highly regarded* reputation as professor over the wife of a gambling, bootlegging, nightclubber." She paused, blew her nose, pushed at her eyes with the heels of her hands. "It took a while, but I finally gave in ... knowing I could never love anybody else, and neither of us wanting anybody else. Ever. Remember how small it was? The ceremony? Just the few of us? Just the way we wanted it. It just made it that much more special, I believe. Tender as starlight off the Big Sandy. I always thought we had plenty of time, but I was wrong. As studied as I was, I was wrong. I never thought about him taking sick. Just always thought he'd outlive us all. But then it was on him so *quick*. After that, it didn't take him no time, thank God in heaven, to get rid of that *club*, and everything that was attached to it. Maybe it was just me, but I'd never seen him so happy. It was like a burden had been lifted. Like there was nothing in his eyes anymore but me." She stopped, the tears renewing, quickening. "To think," she said, "what we had, and how we could have had it all them years earlier, if I hadn't been so affected, so self-conscious about what others might have thought." She took her time, gathered herself, then looked out across the valley we knew so well: the schoolhouse bottom; the falling-down remains of the old Primitive Baptist church house, and what we remembered of Haman Flowers and Randle Cain; Mary Olive's little piece of ground, now graded and leveled, and where Wilson had a trailer sitting high up on concrete blocks; Big Will Hollow and the Yonts' big white house with its long stretch of bottom; and the slivered meander of the creek that somehow connected it all—what we knew as home. Dixie said nothing for the longest time after that, just sat numbed it seemed, her face as beat looking as the rags we once scrubbed across washboards. "I think I might just die without him," she said at last, her whole person wanting to topple, the hem of her dress stirring on a waft of air. "I just might stay right here till I dry up and blow away."

We talked on and off throughout the day—just bits and pieces of memory wanting to be aired for the most part—till the sun began to dip behind the crest of the mountain. "I'm gone," I said. She never looked up, just nodded and went back to being alone. I looked back a last time before disappearing over the rise and saw her kneeling in the dirt with her head pressed against his headstone.

What Dixie would return to was anybody's guess, but one thing she could count on were friends like Imogene and me: two friends she would always have.

Before Bobby passed, Dixie was good about coming around now and again to sit and swap tales about this and that, then leave like there was a fire to put out. The same was true of Wilson and Wilma Lee, though their leaving generally took up the bigger part of the day. I hardly ever heard from Sherman, only what people said of him: that he worked seven days a week and had the first nickel he ever made; that he never got much further than the store itself and those few little rooms in the back. Not that any of it mattered that much anymore.

Ninety-One

Quenching Wells

The day was like so many others given the temper of Appalachia in July: the sun venomous in a bluebonnet sky and the air so humid it could be weighed. Kentucky's highlands not only had a way of holding the heat, but keeping it pressed down. It was an innate sense of preservation that prompted us to stillness on such days, and throughout the flush of summer. We learned early on to limit our time in the sun after it had come full view—although more times than not, necessity dictated otherwise. So oppressive it was today that even the ducks and peacocks lazed together in quietude under the lone giant beech tree next to the barn. Even early morning still carried a hint of what was to come, the dew adding its own steam to the mix.

My sitting here on the porch, catching a breath of morning, was a routine as familiar as rising at cock crow—something I was never able to avoid as a boy, and something I never wanted to miss now that I had the choice to do otherwise. The smell of horsemint rested me most mornings, came at me from the patch we grew alongside the house: part of the herb garden I insisted on having in memory of Grandmaw. Off to my right, a huge barn I used for most everything outside of what it was intended for, sat red and weathered and haunted looking at first light. It was where ol' Clive stayed. Clive was my mule, red and skinny and fit for nothing, too old to sell and too much like myself to throw away. He stayed there with Jackaran, the whitest, wiriest and most comical looking Billy goat the county fair ever hung a blue ribbon on—but that was years ago. I don't rightly know why I was so attached to them, only that they added a sense of belonging, as familiar as anything I'd ever known. They governed themselves for the most part, stayed in the barn at night, or whenever there come a rain. Other times, they were in the big open pen south of the barn, or in the huge pasture beyond it. The thing most common, though, was they were always together: in each other's pocket, as I liked to say; as connected as the tide was to the moon; as connected as I had been to Bobby ... and as he had been to me. Outside of that, chickens—Road Island Reds mostly, but some Plymouth Rocks and Dominiques, and even a few Leghorns—wandered aimlessly and openly, pecking and scratching between the rocks and gravel for morsels visible only to them. And despite our taking them regularly for the table, they never hesitated to come when called, when I scattered corn. Beyond that and the cabin I'd built with my own hands, the mountains, raw and rugged and as dense as they were green, rose like a fortress all around me. They were my home, as they'd always been, as much a way of life as they were a place of refuge, as integral to my thinking as they were to my spirit, as much a part of me as the creak in the porch's screen door or the wind through the cottonwoods. Except for the time I spent in the big war, I was never far from them, in my heart or in my mind. It's the early mornings out here alone when I feel most protected by them, most at rest; when whatever joins me does so in light of the peace they provide ... like Imogene, quietly pawing through the herbs alongside the house, looking for what is ready, what will enhance or enliven, the shade dappling her silvering hair just enough. She is vibrant, unaware of how I admire the way she gently combs each plant, each one in its own way speaking to her inner reaches. She looks up at me occasionally, peeks when she thinks I'm not looking; blushes (even after all these years) when she finds that I am watching with the same devotion I've had from the day she put that broken pocket watch in my hand ... magic little moments when her eyes rest on me for just a second, maybe two, the way mine do so often on her: the way they have for fifty-odd years. To me, they are just some of the reminders of heaven, if we but take the time for it. Stars have a way of finding us, of guiding us home if we never give up on the idea of rainbows and what all sifts us in the mix of family and love ... and what fills us to overflowing from the bottom of our own quenching wells.

Acknowledgments

Certainly, everybody I ever knew deserves to be mentioned here. But that straightaway leans toward the "painfully trite," so I will offer what I can in the way of a condensed list and for the sake of brevity. First, to those who hardly knew me: to every stranger who ever passed me on the street, who ever had eye contact with me or came within the sphere of either my aura or aroma, I thank you. To everyone who even once gave attention to who I was or why I was here; to those with conviction enough to share a word, kind or otherwise; to those who embraced me and to those who shunned me, I thank you. To the aloof and the unsure, and to those who fed me and those who didn't, I thank you. For it is the collective "you" who taught me and gave me what I needed to tell my story.

More specifically, I would like to thank those who believed in me and believe in me still. Notably, to my sons, Rob and Eric, I love you more than life itself. Thank you for all you bring to me: for the courage of your hearts and the exactitude of your minds, and for always living up to doing the right thing.

To Johnny Dean Kendrick, a true man of the mountains and the last of a dying breed. From creek beds to sled roads, from bald mounts to the deepest darkest hollows, he taught me more than I ever thought possible about the sweep and swell of Appalachia. Thank you, Johnny.

To Neal and Dianne Keane for their gracious and never-ending generosity, for providing me with my own apartment during my many weeks of research and exploration. Your kindness will forever be remembered.

To Jim and Barbara Rowe who availed me to the respite of their hideaway in the hills of eastern Tennessee. It was there, spirited away in the quiet splendor of the Cumberland mountains, that *Greezy Creek* blossomed into its full potential. Thank you, Jim and Barbara, for always being there and forever feeding me like I was a growing boy.

To John Hribljan who gave me a new compass setting; who eased back my blinders just enough to allow a clearer vision and for insisting that I *think* – something in the overall scheme that proved to be instrumental. Imagine that. To you, John, you have my eternal thanks.

To my fiercely loving friends and dedicated reader-editors, who, through subtle but gentle coaxing, kept me forefront to the wind and believed in me when I needed it most. And so, it is to Jerry and Jay Gilroy, Sue Anne Gilroy, Steve and Patti Brinegar, Leigh Bangs and Alice Shooter, and David and Mary Ann Cain that I offer up my deepest gratitude. Your encouragements remain with me still.

To Peggy, my wife, mentor, and number-one fan, thank you for your insights into the heart, and for bringing them to bear on the souls of my characters.

To Mom and Dad (though now gone) for the endless accounts of your life and times. Mom, thank you for believing so deeply and so forthrightly. The strength of your faith is what I wish for everyone. Dad, thank you for believing in never giving up. I bow to your tenacity. You gave me all the things that matter. There will never be another you.

To my brother Randy (now gone) and my sister J.J., I love you, and I thank you for the strength that comes from knowing you love me back.

To Janie C. Jessee, publisher extraordinaire, for your expertise and your caring ways; for believing in *Greezy Creek*, for your patience, integrity, and flawless professionalism; for knowing so soundly the work and wonder of Appalachia, and for recognizing my voice as an integral part of its story. I thank the heavens for you. Could there be anyone better?

To Shanna Light, and her acumen for the finer facets of syntax. As editor, she never missed a thing (from the first page to last; from the slightest miscue to the most overt). I offer you my deepest thanks.

To Tara Sizemore for her expertise as a graphic designer, and for helping to bring *Greezy Creek* to life—from its cover to its interior layout—and for being so patient and understanding with my steady stream of revisions. To this end, Tara, I offer my deepest thanks.

To my kinfolk who, by my best account, number well into the hundreds (far too many to mention by name, yet all with the same Appalachian roots) and who remain as the backbone to this story. I love you all.

To Tammy Standifer for her unselfish acts of research on my behalf during her tenure with the Pike County Sheriff's Department. So much about the intricacies of Pike County law enforcement during the thirties and forties came to life with her reporting. To this end, Tammy, I remain indebted.

To Cleo Fields, native Appalachian, and educator extraordinaire, who provided a gainful and rewarding female perspective to *Greezy Creek's* life and times. Thank you, Cleo, for your insight, industry, and inspiration.

And so, from the very unconstrained cockles of my soul to the almost certain flappable shackles of my mind (and certainly from the innermost chambers of my heart), I thank you all for what you are to me, and for having waited with the patience of Job for this story to be coaxed onto the page...and then for the ink to dry.

Appalachian Ballads and Folk Songs

Throughout the book, Wilma Lee and her dulcimer give heavenly treatment to the songs germane to Appalachia. Following are their titles and their origins.

	Chapter
"Knoxville Girl" is an Appalachian murder ballad. Earliest recording 1924 by Riley Puckett and Gid Tanner.	18
"Pretty Polly" is a murder ballad and English folk song made popular in the mid-1920's by banjo picker John Hammond; similar versions by B.F. Shelton and Dock Boggs, also of the mid-1920's.	22
"Wayfaring Stranger" like most traditional folk songs, is of an unknown and oft-disputed origin. Depending on who you ask, the song's origin is either Appalachian Folk or Old Irish, with some even theorizing that its origin rests in the Negro Spirituals (in the slave fields of the old South).	22

Chapter

"I Am a Man of Constant Sorrow" is a traditional American Folk Song published by Dick Burnett, a partially blind fiddler from Kentucky, in 1913. An early version was recorded by Emry Arthur in 1928. 22

"Amazing Grace" is a Christian Hymn written and published by English poet and Anglican clergyman, John Newton. It first appeared in print in 1779. 27

"Down in the Valley" (originally known as "The Birmingham Jail") is an American Folk Song written by guitarist Jimmie Tarlton in 1925 while he was serving time in the Birmingham jail for moonshining. Its first recording was by Tarlton in 1927. 27

27

"Sweet Betsy From Pike" is an American Ballad about the trials of a pioneer woman named Betsy and her lover, Ike, who migrated from Pike County (Colorado?) to California during the gold rush era of mid 1800's.

"Great Speckled Bird" is a Southern hymn from the late 1920's written by the Reverend Guy Smith, and based on Jeremiah 12:9, "Mine heritage is unto me as a speckled bird … " 27

"Black is the Color of my True Love's Hair" is a traditional folk song of the Appalachian Mountains, but originating in Scotland. The song has become part of the traditional repertory of Celtic and Appalachian musicians. It was collected by Cecil Sharp and Maude Karpeles in 1916, and appears in Sharp's 1932 collection of English folk songs from the Southern Appalachians. 27

	Chapter
"Am I Born to Die" is a ballad written by Charles Wesley, a leader in the Methodist movement in mid 1700's England. Like so many English/Irish ballads, "Am I Born to Die" has been preserved through the generations and remains a beloved Appalachian tradition.	27
"Down in the Willow Garden," also known as "Rose Connelly" is a traditional Appalachian murder ballad, its origin dating back to nineteenth century Ireland. First recorded in 1927.	27
"Barbara Allen," a traditional Scottish ballad from the 17th century, is the most widely collected song in the English language. Earliest recording was 1907 by Joseph Taylor, collected on wax cylinder and later recorded by Royal Dadmun in 1927.	27
"Come All You Fair and Tender Ladies," also known as "I wish I Were a Little Sparrow" is a folk song popular with southern Appalachians. It's author is unknown; its lyrics and melody handed down by tradition dating back to 1840's Ireland.	27
"Coo-Coo Bird" is a traditional English folk song. Earliest publication was somewhere between 1780 and 1812. At least one collected version was published in the Folk Songs of the Kentucky Mountains in 1917. An early notable recording was performed by Appalachian folk musician, Clarence "Tom" Ashley in the mid 1920's.	27
"Roving Gambler" is an American bluegrass classic first recorded in 1925 by Kelly Herrel.	27
"Sally Goodin" an old-time fiddle tune by Eck Robertson, 1922.	27

Chapter

"Cripple Creek" is an old-time Appalachian folk song. No one knows exactly where Cripple Creek is. Some say it is Cripple Creek, Virginia, while others say it is Cripple Creek, Colorado, written during the gold rush era of the mid 1800's. It is a standard among bluegrass musicians and is often one of the first songs a banjo picker learns. It was frequently recorded by a variety of musicians in the 1920's. 27

"I Wish My Baby Was Born" (also known as "A Brisk Young Sailor," "The Alehouse," and "Died For Love") is a traditional folk ballad originating in England in the early 1600's. 33

"Washbash Cannonball" is a country music song written by William Kindt in 1904 and made popular by Roy Acuff and The Smokey Mountain Boys in 1938. 50

"Shall We Gather at the River" is a Christian hymn. Words and music written by Robert Lowry 1864. 50

"I Have No One to Love Me" is an American folk ballad first recorded by The Carter Family in 1928. 53

"Here Comes the Bride" is a romantic opera written by German composer, Richard Wagner, and first performed in 1850. The most popular and recognizable part of the opera is the Bridal Chorus, better known as "Here Comes the Bride," often played as a processional at weddings. 62

Chapter

"Ole Dan Tucker" is an American song whose origins remain largely obscure. The tune itself was passed down through oral tradition, and the words credited to Daniel Emmett (1815–1904). It grew in popularity and entered the folk vernacular during the antebellum period, and today remains a country and bluegrass standard. 62

"Turkey in the Straw" is a well-known American folk song dating from the early 1800's. Originally a tune for fiddle players, it was popularized during the 1820's and 30's when a myriad of verses were added, each of them rollicking and raucous. 62

About the Author

George Justice holds a B.A. in English Literature from the University of Detroit. He was one of fifteen honored from a field of 400 to participate in a semester-long workshop offered by then writer-in-residence, John Gardner. Justice has been published three times for short stories, twice for poetry. He was the movie critic for Oakland County's *Daily Tribune* (1978–79). As a U.S. Army veteran, he wrote numerous articles (from human interest to military) for *Stars and Stripes*. He is the father of two, the grandfather of two, and with an extended family of over 200 in the hills of Kentucky who serve as the cornerstones to this story. He and his wife reside in Ferndale, Michigan. *Greezy Creek* is his first novel.

Readers can keep themselves apprised of *what's next* for George Justice by visiting his website www.georgerobjustice.com.

Coming Soon: *Edenfield*

The year is 1962 and young Weldon Thatcher, caught between two worlds (boyhood and manhood, cartoons and raging hormones), is coerced by his mother and the local preacher into attending Edenfield College, a Protestant icon and a place straightaway paranoid about influences from the outside world.

Though Weldon is fashioned from a childhood of perfect Sunday school attendance, he brings to Edenfield a curious level of mischievousness and an inclination to know what lies beyond the boundaries of God's moral code and the stuff of religion. It is here, in the grip of an ultraconservative fundamentalist order, that Weldon's secular piety cuts across Edenfield's centuries-old chasm of religious dogma; here that Weldon, in the wake of carnal malfeasance, is given to loss and disillusionment, humiliation and irreparable separation from those he has come to love. The upside is that Weldon never loses his passion for wanting to understand the enigma surrounding man's relationship to God. The downside is the pained imprint left on him by the straight face of religion.

Printed in the USA
CPSIA information can be obtained
at www.ICGtesting.com
LVHW042106100424
777017LV00006B/16